# The Story of King Arthur and His Knights

Howard Pyle

Illustrated by
Roland Wheelwright and Howard Pyle

SMITHMARK

*The Story of King Arthur and His Knights*
First published 1903

*The Merry Adventures of Robin Hood*
First published 1883



This edition published in 1996 by
SMITHMARK Publishers,
a division of U.S. Media Holdings, Inc.,
16 East 32nd Street
New York, NY 10016.

SMITHMARK books are available for bulk purchase for sales promotion and premium use. For details write or call the manager of special sales, SMITHMARK Publishers Inc. 16 East 32nd Street New York, NY 10016 (212) 532-6600

ISBN 0 7651 9983 1

Produced by
Anness Publishing Limited
1 Boundary Row
London SE1 8HP

Publisher: Joanna Lorenz
Project Editor: Fiona Eaton
Picture Researcher: Vanessa Fletcher

10 9 8 7 6 5 4 3 2 1

# Contents

Book 2: The Book of Three Worthies

# COLOUR ILLUSTRATIONS

# The Book of King Arthur

# Prologue

In ancient days there lived a very noble King, named Uther-Pendragon, and he became Overlord of all of Britain. This King was very greatly aided unto the achievement of the Pendragonship of the realm by the help of two men, who rendered him great assistance in all that he did. The one of these men was a certain very powerful enchanter and sometime prophet known to men as Merlin the Wise; and he gave very good counsel unto Uther-Pendragon. The other man was an excellent noble and renowned knight, hight Ulfius (who was thought by many to be the greatest leader in war of any man then alive); and he gave Uther-Pendragon aid and advice in battle. So, with the help of Merlin and Sir Ulfius, Uther-Pendragon was able to overcome all of his enemies and to become King of the entire realm.

After Uther-Pendragon had ruled his kingdom for a number of years he took to wife a certain beautiful and gentle lady, hight Igraine. This noble dame was the widow of Gerlois, the Duke of Tintegal; by which prince she had two daughters – one of whom was named Margaise and the other Morgana le Fay. And Morgana le Fay was a famous sorceress. These daughters the Queen brought with her to the Court of Uther-Pendragon after she had married that puissant King, and there Margaise was wedded to King Urien of Gore, and Morgana le Fay was wedded to King Lot of Orkney.

Now after awhile Uther-Pendragon and Queen Igraine had a son born unto them, and he was very beautiful and of great size and strength of bone. And whilst the child still lay wrapped in his swaddling clothes and lying in a cradle of gold and ultramarine, Merlin came to Uther-Pendragon with a spirit of prophecy strong upon him (for such was often the case with him), and, speaking in that spirit of prophecy, he said, "Lord, it is given unto me to foresee that thou shalt shortly fall sick of a fever and that thou shalt maybe die of a violent sweat that will follow thereon. Now, should such a dolorous thing befall us all, this young child (who is, certes, the hope of all this realm) will be in very great danger of his life; for many enemies will assuredly rise up with design to seize upon him for the sake of his inheritance, and either he will be slain or else he will be held in captivity from which he shall hardly hope to escape. Wherefore, I do beseech thee, Lord, that thou wilt permit Sir Ulfius and myself to presently convey the child away unto some place of safe refuge, where he may be hidden in secret until he groweth to manhood and is able to guard himself from such dangers as may threaten him."

When Merlin had made an end of speaking thus, Uther-Pendragon made reply with a very steadfast countenance in this wise: "Merlin, so far as my death is concerned – when my time cometh to die I believe God will give me grace to meet my end with entire cheerfulness; for, certes, my lot is in that wise no different from that of any other man who hath been born of woman. But touching the matter of this young child, if thy prophecy be true, then his danger is very great, and it would be well that he should be conveyed hence to some place of safe harborage as thou dost advise. Wherefore, I pray thee to perform thy will in this affair, bearing in thy heart the consideration that the child is the most precious inheritance which I shall leave unto this land."

All this, as was said, Uther-Pendragon spake with great calmness and equanimity of spirit. And Merlin did as he had advised, and he and Sir Ulfius conveyed the child away by night, and no one but they wist whither the babe had been taken. And shortly afterward Uther-Pendragon was seized with the sickness as Merlin had foretold, and he died exactly as Merlin had feared that he would die; wherefore it was very well that the child had been taken to a place of safety.

And after Uther-Pendragon had departed from this life, it was likewise as Merlin had feared, for all the realm fell into great disorder. For each lesser knight contended against his fellow for overlordship, and wicked knights and barons harried the highways as they listed and there levied toll with great cruelty upon helpless wayfarers. For some such travellers they took prisoners and held for ransom, whiles others they slew because they had no ransom to pay. So it was a very common sight to see a dead man lying by the roadside, if you should venture to make a journey upon some business or other. Thus it befell that, after awhile, all that dolorous land groaned with the trouble that lay upon it.

Thus there passed nearly eighteen years in such great affliction, and then one day the Archbishop of Canterbury summoned Merlin to him and bespake him in this wise: "Merlin, men say that thou art the wisest man in all the world. Canst thou not find some means to heal the distractions of this woeful realm? Bend thou thy wisdom to this matter and choose thou a king who shall be a fit overlord for us, so that we may enjoy happiness of life once more as we did in the days of Uther-Pendragon."

Then Merlin lifted up his countenance upon the Archbishop, and spake in this wise: "My lord, the spirit of prophecy that lieth upon me sometimes moveth me now to say that I do perceive that this country is soon to have a king who shall be wiser and greater and more worthy of praise than was even Uther-Pendragon. And he shall bring order and peace where is now disorder and war. Moreover, I may tell you that this King shall be Uther-Pendragon's own full blood-royal."

To this the Archbishop said: "What thou tellest me, Merlin, is a wonderfully strange thing. But in this spirit of prophecy canst thou not foretell when this King is to come? And canst thou tell how we shall know him when he appeareth amongst us? For many lesser kings there are who would fain be overlord of this land, and many such there are who deem themselves fit to rule over all the others. How then shall we know the real King from those who may proclaim themselves to be the rightful king?"

"My lord Archbishop," quoth Merlin, "if I have thy leave for to exert my magic I shall set an adventure which, if any man achieve it, all the world shall straightway know that he is the rightful King and overlord of this realm." And to this the Archbishop said, "Merlin, I bid thee do whatsoever may seem to thee to be right in this affair." And Merlin said, "I will do so."

So Merlin caused by magic that a huge marble stone, four square, should suddenly appear in an open place before the cathedral door. And upon this block of marble he caused it to be that there should stand an anvil and into the anvil he caused it that there should be thrust a great naked sword midway deep of the blade. And this sword was the most wonderful that any man had ever seen, for the blade was of blue steel and extraordinarily bright and glistering. And the hilt was of gold, chased and carved with marvellous cunning, and inlaid with a great number of precious stones, so that it shone with wonderful brightness in the sunlight. And about the sword were written these words in letters of gold:-

Whoso Pulleth Out this Sword from the Anvil

That same is Rightwise King-Born of England.

So a great many people came and gazed upon that sword and marvelled at it exceedingly, for its like had never before been beheld upon the earth.

Then, when Merlin had accomplished this miracle, he bade the Archbishop to call together all the chief people of that land upon Christmastide; and he bade the Archbishop to command that every man should make assay to draw out the sword, for that he who should succeed in drawing it forth out of the anvil should be rightwise King of Britain.

So the Archbishop did according as Merlin said; and this was the marvel of the marble stone and the anvil, of which same anyone may easily read for himself in that book written a very long while ago by Robert de Boron, which is called Le Roman de Merlin.

Now when the mandate of the Lord Archbishop went forth, summoning all the chief people of the land to the assay of that miracle (for, indeed, it was a miracle to draw forth a sword-blade out of an anvil of solid iron), all the realm became immediately cast into a great ferment, so that each man asked his fellow, "Who shall draw forth that sword, and who shall be our King?" Some thought it would be King Lot and others thought it would be King Urien of Gore (these being the sons-in-law unto Uther-Pendragon); some thought that it would be King Leodegrance of Camiliard, and others that it would be King Ryence of North Wales; some thought it would be this king and others that it would be that king; for all the world was divided into different parties who thought according to their liking.

Then, as Christmastide drew nigh, it presently appeared as though the entire world was wending its way to London Town, for the highways and the by-ways became filled with wayfarers – kings and lords and knights and ladies and esquires and pages and men-at-arms – all betaking their way whither the assay was to be made of that adventure of the sword and the anvil. Every inn and castle was filled so full of travellers that it was a marvel how so many folk could be contained within their compass, and everywhere were tents and pavilions pitched along the wayside for the accommodation of those who could not find shelter within doors.

But when the Archbishop beheld the multitudes that were assembling, he said to Merlin, "Indeed, Merlin, it would be a very singular thing if among all these great kings and noble, honorable lords we should not find some one worthy of being the King of this realm."

Unto which the Merlin smiled and said, "Marvel not, my lord, if among all those who appear to be so extraordinarily worthy there shall not be found one who is worthy; and marvel not if, among all those who are unknown, there shall arise one who shall approve himself to be entirely worthy."

And the Archbishop pondered Merlin's words, and so beginneth this story.

PART I

# THE WINNING OF KINGHOOD

*Here beginneth the story of the sword, the anvil, and the marble stone, and of how that sword was first achieved by an unknown youth, until then of no renown, whether in arms or of estate.*

*So hearken unto that which I have hereinafter written.*

## Chapter First

# How Sir Kay did Combat in a Great Tournament

It happened that among those worthies who were summoned unto London Town by the mandate of the Archbishop as above recounted, there was a certain knight, very honorable and of high estate, by name Sir Ector of Bonmaison – surnamed the Trustworthy Knight, because of the fidelity with which he kept the counsel of those who confided in him, and because he always performed unto all men, whether of high or low degree, that which he promised to undertake, without defalcation as to the same. So this noble and excellent knight was held in high regard by all those who knew him; for not only was he thus honorable in conduct but he was, besides, of very high estate, being possessed of seven castles in Wales and in the adjoining country north thereof, and likewise of certain fruitful tracts of land with villages appertaining thereunto, and also of sundry forests of great extent, both in the north country and the west. This very noble knight had two sons; the elder of these was Sir Kay, a young knight of great valor and promise, and already well renowned in the Courts of Chivalry because of several very honorable deeds of worthy achievement in arms which he had performed; the other was a young lad of eighteen years of age, by name Arthur, who at that time was serving with good repute as Sir Kay's esquire-at-arms.

Now when Sir Ector of Bonmaison received by messenger the mandate of the

Archbishop, he immediately summoned these two sons unto him and bade them to prepare straightway for to go with him to London Town, and they did so. And in the same manner he bade a great number of retainers and esquires and pages for to make them ready, and they likewise did so. Thus, with a very considerable array at arms and with great show of circumstance, Sir Ector of Bonmaison betook his way unto London Town in obedience to the commands of the Archbishop.

So, when he had come thither he took up his inn in a certain field where many other noble knights and puissant lords had already established themselves, and there he set up a very fair pavilion of green silk, and erected his banner emblazoned with the device of his house; to wit, a gryphon, black, upon a field of green.

And upon this field were a great multitude of other pavilions of many different colors, and over above each pavilion was the pennant and the banner of that puissant lord to whom the pavilion belonged. Wherefore, because of the multitude of these pennants and banners the sky was at places well-nigh hidden with the gaudy colors of the fluttering flags.

Among the great lords who had come thither in pursuance to the Archbishop's summons were many very famous kings and queens and noblemen of high degree. For there was King Lot of Orkney, who had taken to wife a step-daughter of Uther-Pendragon, and there was King Uriens of Gore, who had taken to wife another step-daughter of that great king, and there was King Ban, and King Bors, and King Ryence, and King Leodegrance and many others of like degree, for there were no less than twelve kings and seven dukes, so that, what with their court of lords and ladies and esquires and pages in attendance, the town of London had hardly ever seen the like before that day.

Now the Archbishop of Canterbury, having in mind the extraordinary state of the occasion that had brought so many kings and dukes and high lords unto that adventure of the sword and the anvil, had commanded that there should be a very stately and noble tournament proclaimed. Like wise he commanded that this contest at arms should be held in a certain field nigh to the great cathedral, three days before that assay should be made of the sword and the anvil (which same was to be undertaken, as aforesaid, upon Christmas day). To this tournament were bidden all knights who were of sufficient birth, condition, and quality for to fit them to take part therein. Accordingly, very many exalted knights made application for admission, and that in such numbers that three heralds were kept very busy looking into their pretensions unto the right of battle. For these heralds examined the escutcheons and the rolls of lineage of all applicants with great care and circumspection.

Now when Sir Kay received news of this tournament he went to where his father was, and when he stood before his face he spake in this wise: "Sire, being thy son and of such very high condition both as to birth and estate as I have inherited from thee, I find that I have an extraordinary desire to imperil my body in this tourney. Accordingly, if so be I may approve my quality as to knighthood before this college of heralds, it will maybe be to thy great honor and credit, and to the honor and credit of our house if I should undertake this adventure. Wherefore I do crave thy leave to do as I have a mind."

Unto these Sir Ector made reply: "My son, thou hast my leave for to enter this honorable contest, and I do hope that God will give thee a great deal of strength,and likewise such grace of spirit that thou mayst achieve honor to thyself and credit to us who are of thy blood."

So Sir Kay departed with very great joy and immediately went to that congress of heralds and submitted his pretensions unto them. And, after they had duly examined into his claims to knighthood, they entered his name as a knight-contestant according to his desire; and at this Sir Kay was filled with great content and joy of heart.

So, when his name had been enrolled upon the list of combatants, Sir Kay chose his young brother Arthur for to be his esquire-at-arms and to carry his spear and pennant before him into the field of battle, and Arthur was also made exceedingly glad because of the honor that had befallen him and his brother.

Now, the day having arrived when this tourney was to be held, a very huge concourse of people gathered together to witness that noble and courtly assault at arms. For at that time London was, as aforesaid, extraordinarily full of nobility and knighthood, wherefore it was reckoned that not less than twenty thousand lords and ladies (besides those twelve kings and their courts and seven dukes and their courts) were assembled in the lists circumadjacent to the field of battle for to witness the performance of those chosen knights. And those noble people sat so close together, and so filled the seats and benches assigned to them, that it appeared as though an entirely solid wall of human souls surrounded that meadow where the battle was to be fought. And, indeed, any knight might well be moved to do his uttermost upon such a great occasion with the eyes of so many beautiful dames and noble lords gazing upon his performances. Wherefore the hearts of all the knights attendant were greatly expanded with emulation to overturn their enemies into the dust.

In the centre of this wonderful court of lords and ladies there was erected the stall and the throne of the lord Archbishop himself. Above the throne was a canopy of purple cloth emblazoned with silver lilies, and the throne itself was hung all about with purple cloth of velvet, embroidered, alternately, with the figure of St. George in gold, and with silver crosses of St. George surrounded by golden halos. Here the lord Archbishop himself sat in great estate and pomp, being surrounded by a very exalted court of clerks of high degree and also of knights of honorable estate, so that all that centre of the field glistered with the splendor of gold and silver embroidery, and was made beautiful by various colors of rich apparel and bright with fine armor of excellent workmanship. And, indeed, such was the stateliness of all these circumstances that very few who were there had ever seen so noble a preparation for battle as that which they then beheld.

Now, when all that great assembly were in their places and everything had been prepared in due wise, an herald came and stood forth before the enstalled throne of the Archbishop and blew a very strong, loud blast upon a trumpet. At that signal the turnpikes of the lists were immediately opened and two parties of knights-contestant entered therein – the one party at the northern extremity of the meadow of battle and the other party at the southern extremity thereof. Then immediately all that lone field was a-glitter with the bright-shining splendor of the sunlight upon polished armor and accoutrements. So these two parties took up their station, each at such a place as had been assigned unto them – the one to the north and the other to the south.

Now the party with which Sir Kay had cast his lot was at the north of the field, and that company was fourscore and thirteen in number; and the other party stood at the south end of the field, and that company was fourscore and sixteen in number. But though the party with whom Sir Kay had attached himself numbered less by three than the other party, yet was it the stronger by some degree because that there were a number of knights of great strength and renown in that company. Indeed it may be here mentioned that two of those knights afterward became companions in very good credit of the round table – to wit: Sir Mador de la Porte, and Sir Bedevere – which latter was the last who saw King Arthur alive upon this earth.

So, when all was prepared according to the ordination of the tournament, and when those knights-contestant had made themselves ready in all ways that were necessary, and when they had dressed their spears and their shields in such a manner as befitted knights about to enter serious battle, the herald set his trumpet to his lips a second time and blew upon it with might and main. Then, having sounded this blast, he waited for a while and then he blew upon the trumpet again.

And, upon that blast, each of those parties of knights quitted its station and rushed forth in great tumult against the other party, and that with such noise and fury that the whole earth groaned beneath the feet of the war-horses, and trembled and shook as with an earthquake.

So those two companies met, the one against the other, in the midst of the field, and the roar of breaking lances was so terrible that those who heard it were astonished and appalled at the sound. For several fair dames swooned away with terror of the noise, and others shrieked aloud; for not only was there that great uproar, but the air was altogether filled with the splinters of ash wood that flew about.

In that famous assault threescore and ten very noble and honorable knights were overthrown, many of them being trampled beneath the hoofs of the horses; wherefore, when the two companies withdrew in retreat each to his station the ground was beheld to be covered all over with broken fragments of lances and with cantels of armor, and many knights were seen to be wofully lying in the midst of all that wreck. And some of these champions strove to arise and could not, while others lay altogether quiet as though in death. To these ran divers esquires and pages in great numbers, and lifted up the fallen men and bare them away to places of safe harborage. And likewise attendants ran and gathered up the cantels of armor and the broken spears, and bare them away to the barriers, so that, by and by, the field was altogether cleared once more.

Then all those who gazed down upon that meadow gave loud acclaim with great joyousness of heart, for such a noble and glorious contest at arms in friendly assay had hardly ever been beheld in all that realm before.

Now we turn unto Sir Kay; for in this assault he had conducted himself with such credit that no knight who was there had done better than he, and maybe no one had done so well as he. For, though two opponents at once had directed their spears against him, yet he had successfully resisted their assault. And one of those two he smote so violently in the midst of his defences that he had lifted that assailant entirely over the crupper of the horse which he rode, and had flung him down to the distance of half a spear's length behind his steed, so that the fallen knight had rolled thrice over in the dust ere he ceased to fall.

And when those of Sir Kay's party who were nigh to him beheld what he did, they gave him loud and vehement acclaim, and that in such measure that Sir Kay was wonderfully well satisfied and pleased at heart.

And, indeed, it is to be said that at that time there was hardly any knight in all the world who was so excellent in deeds of arms as Sir Kay. And though there afterward came knights of much greater renown and of more glorious achievement (as shall be hereinafter recorded in good season), yet at that time Sir Kay was reckoned by many to be one of the most wonderfully puissant knights (whether errant or in battle) in all of that realm.

So was that course of the combat run to the great pleasure and satisfaction of all who beheld it, and more especially of Sir Kay and his friends. And after it had been completed the two parties in array returned each to its assigned station once more.

And when they had come there, each knight delivered up his spear unto his esquire. For the assault which was next to be made was to be undertaken with swords, wherefore all lances and other weapons were to be put away; such being the order of that courteous and gentle bout at arms.

Accordingly, when the herald again blew his trumpet, each knight drew his weapon with such readiness for battle that there was a great splendor of blades all flashing in the air at once. And when the herald blew a second time each party pushed forward to the contest with great nobleness of heart and eagerness of spirit, every knight being moved with intent to engage his oppugnant with all the might and main that lay in him.

Then immediately began so fierce a battle that if those knights had been very enemies of long standing instead of friendly contestants, the blows which they delivered the one upon the other could not have been more vehement as to strength or more astonishing to gaze upon.

And in this affair likewise Sir Kay approved himself to be so extraordinary a champion that his like was nowhere to be seen in all that field; for he violently smote down five knights, the one after the other, ere he was stayed in his advance.

Wherefore, beholding him to be doing work of such a sort, several of the knights of the other party endeavored to come at him with intent to meet him in his advance.

Amongst these was a certain knight, hight Sir Balamorgineas, who was so huge of frame that he rode head and shoulders above any other knight. And he was possessed of such extraordinary strength that it was believed that he could successfully withstand the assault of three ordinary knights at one time. Wherefore when this knight beheld the work that Sir Kay did, he cried out to him, "Ho! ho! Sir Knight of the black gryphon, turn thou hitherward and do a battle with me!"

Now when Sir Kay beheld Sir Balamorgineas to be minded to come against him in that wise – very threateningly and minded to do him battle – he turned him toward his enemy with great cheerfulness of spirit. For at that time Sir Kay was very full of youthful fire and reckoned nothing of assaulting any enemy who might demand battle of him.

(So it was at that time. But it after befell, when he became Seneschal, and when other and mightier knights appeared at the court of the King, that he would sometimes avoid an encounter with such a knight as Sir Launcelot, or Sir Pellias, or Sir Marhaus, or Sir Gawaine, if he might do so with credit to his honor.)

So, being very full of the spirit of youth, he turned him with great lustiness of heart, altogether inflamed with the eagerness and fury of battle. And he cried out in a great voice, "Very well, I will do battle with thee, and I will cast thee down like thy fellows!" And therewith he smote with wonderful fierceness at Sir Balamorgineas, and that with all his might. And Sir Balamorgineas received the stroke upon his helmet and was altogether bewildered by the fury thereof, for he had never felt its like before that time. Wherefore his brain swam so light that it was necessary for him to hold to the horn of his saddle to save himself from falling.

But it was a great pity for Sir Kay that, with the fierceness of the blow, his sword-blade snapped short at the haft, flying so high in the air that it appeared to overtop the turrets of the cathedral in its flight. Yet so it happened, and thus it befell that Sir Kay was left without any weapon. Yet it was thought that, because of that stroke, he had Sir Balamorgineas entirely at his mercy, and that if he could have struck another blow with his sword he might easily have overcome him.

But as it was, Sir Balamorgineas presently so far recovered himself that he perceived his enemy to be altogether at his mercy; wherefore, being filled beyond measure with rage because of the blow he had received, he pushed against Sir Kay with intent to smite him down in a violent assault.

In this pass it would maybe have gone very ill with Sir Kay but that three of his companions in arms, perceiving the extreme peril in which he lay, thrust in betwixt him and Sir Balamorgineas with intent to take upon themselves the assault of that knight and so to save Sir Kay from overthrow. This they did with such success that Sir Kay was able to push out from the press and to escape to the barriers without suffering any further harm at the hands of his enemies.

Now when he reached the barrier, his esquire, young Arthur, came running to him with a goblet of spiced wine. And Sir Kay opened the umbril of his helmet for to drink, for he was athirst beyond measure. And, lo! his face was all covered over with blood and sweat, and he was so a-drought with battle that his tongue clave to the roof of his mouth and he could not speak. But when he had drunk of the draught that Arthur gave him, his tongue was loosened and he cried out to the young man in a loud and violent voice: "Ho! ho! Brother, get me another sword for to do battle, for I am assuredly winning for our house much glory this day!" And Arthur said, "Where shall I get thee a sword?" And Kay said, "Make haste unto our father's pavilion and fetch me thence another sword, for this which I have is broken." And Arthur said, "I will do so with all speed," and thereupon he set hand to the barrier and leaped over it into the alleyway beyond. And he ran down the alleyway with all the speed that he was able with intent to fulfil that task which his brother had bidden him to undertake; and with like speed he ran to that pavilion that his father had set up in the meadows.

But when he came to the pavilion of Sir Ector he found no one there, for all the attendants had betaken themselves unto the tournament. And neither could he find any sword fit for his brother's handling, wherefore he was put to a great pass to know what to do in that matter.

In this extremity he bethought him of that sword that stood thrust into the anvil before the cathedral, and it appeared to him that such a sword as that would suit his brother's purposes very well. Wherefore he said to himself, "I will go thither and get that sword if I am able to do so, for it will assuredly do very well for my brother for to finish his battle withal." Whereupon he ran with all speed to the cathedral. And when he had come there he discovered that no one was there upon guard at the block of marble, as had heretofore been the case, for all who had been upon guard had betaken themselves unto the contest of arms that was toward. And the anvil and the sword stood where he could reach them. So, there being no one to stay young Arthur, he leaped up upon the block of marble and laid his hands unto the hilt of the sword. And he bent his body and drew upon the sword very strongly, and, lo! it came forth from the anvil with wonderful smoothness and ease, and he held the sword in his hand, and it was his.

And when he had got the sword in that way, he wrapped it in his cloak so that no one might see it (for it shone with an exceeding brightness and splendor) and he leaped down from the block of marble stone and hastened with it unto the field of battle.

Now when Arthur had entered into that meadow once more, he found Sir Kay awaiting his coming with great impatience of spirit. And when Sir Kay saw him he cried out, very vehemently, "Has thou got a sword?" And Arthur said, "Yea, I have one here." Thereupon he opened his cloak and showed Sir Kay what sword it was he had brought.

Now when Sir Kay beheld the sword he immediately knew it, and he wist not what to think or what to say, wherefore he stood for a while, like one turned to stone, looking upon that sword. Then in awhile he said, in a very strange voice "Where got ye that sword?" And Arthur looked upon his brother and he beheld that his countenance was greatly disturbed, and that his face was altogether as white as wax. And he said, "Brother, what ails thee that thou lookest so strangely. I will tell the entire truth. I could find no sword in our father's pavilion, wherefore I bethought me of that sword that stood in the anvil upon the marble cube before the cathedral. So I went thither and made assay for to draw it forth, and it came forth with wonderful ease. So, when I had drawn it out, I wrapped it in my cloak and brought it hither unto thee as thou beholdest."

Then Sir Kay turned his thoughts inward aud communed with himself in this wise, "Lo! my brother Arthur is as yet hardly more than a child. And he is, moreover, exceedingly innocent. Therefore he knoweth not what he hath done in this nor what the doing thereof signifieth. Now, since he hath achieved this weapon, why should I not myself lay claim to that achievement, and so obtain the glory which it signifieth." Whereupon he presently aroused himself, and he said to Arthur, "Give the sword and the cloak to me," and Arthur did as his brother commanded. And when he had done so Sir Kay said to him, "Tell no man of this but keep it privy in thine own heart. Meantime go thou to our father where he sits at the lists and bid him come straightway unto the pavilion where we have taken up our inn."

And Arthur did as Sir Kay commanded him, greatly possessed with wonder that his brother should be so disturbed in spirit as he had appeared to be. For he wist not know what he had done in drawing out that sword from the anvil, nor did he know of what great things should arise from that little thing, for so it is in this world that a man sometimes approves himself to be worthy of such a great trust as that, and yet, in lowliness of spirit, he is yet altogether unaware that he is worthy thereof. And so it was with young Arthur at that time.

CHAPTER SECOND

# HOW ARTHUR TWICE PERFORMED THE MIRACLE OF THE SWORD BEFORE SIR ECTOR

So Arthur made haste to that part of the lists where Sir Ector sat with the people of his household. And he stood before his father and said, "Sire, my brother Kay hath sent me hitherward for to bid thee come straightway unto the pavilion where we have taken up our inn. And, truly, I think something very extraordinary hath befallen, for my brother Kay hath such a countenance as I never saw him wear."

Then Sir Ector marvelled very greatly what it was that should cause Sir Kay to quit that battle and to summon him at such a time, wherefore he arose from where he sat and went with Arthur. And they went to the pavilion, and when he had come there, behold! Sir Kay was standing in the midst of the pavilion. And Sir Ector saw that his face was as white as ashes of wood and that his eyes shone with a wonderful brightness. And Sir Ector said, "My son, what ails thee?" whereunto Sir Kay made reply, "Sire, here is a very wonderful matter." Therewith he took his father by the hand and brought him to the table that stood in the pavilion. And upon the table there lay a cloak and there was something within the cloak. Then Sir Kay opened the cloak and, lo! there lay the sword of the anvil, and the hilt thereof and the blade thereof glistered with exceeding splendor.

And Sir Ector immediately knew that sword and whence it came. Wherefore he was filled with such astonishment that he wist not what to do. And for a while his tongue refused to speak, and after a while he found speech and cried out aloud in a great voice, "What is this that mine eyes behold!"

To this Sir Kay made reply, "Sire. I have that sword which stood a while since embedded in the anvil that stands upon the cube of marble stone before the great cathedral. Wherefore I demand that thou tellest me what this may foretend?"

Then Sir Ector said, "How came you by that sword?"

And for a while Sir Kay was silent, but after a while he said, "Sire, I brake my sword in that battle which of late I fought, whereupon I found me this sword in its stead."

Then Sir Ector was altogether bemazed and knew not whether to believe what his ears heard. And after awhile he said, "If so be that thou didst draw forth this sword from the anvil, then it must also be that thou art rightwise King of Britain, for so the saying of the sword proclaimeth. But if thou didst indeed draw it forth from the anvil, then it will be that thou shalt as easily be able for to thrust it back again into that place from whence thou didst take it."

At this a great trouble of spirit fell upon Sir Kay, and he cried out in a very loud voice, "Who may do such a thing as that, and who could perform so great a miracle as to thrust a sword into solid iron." Whereunto Sir Ector made reply, "Such a miracle is no greater than the miracle that thou hast performed in drawing it out from its embedment. For who ever heard that a man could draw forth a sword from a place and yet would not thrust it back whence he drew it?"

Then Sir Kay wist not what to say to his father, and he greatly feared that he should not be able to perform that miracle. But nevertheless, he took what comfort to himself he was able, saying, "If my young brother Arthur was able to perform this miracle why should I not do a miracle of a like sort, for, assuredly, I am not less worthy than he. Wherefore if he drew the sword forth with such ease, it may be that I with equal ease shall be able to thrust it back into its place again." Accordingly he took such comfort to himself in these thoughts as he was able.

So he wrapped the sword in the cloak again, and when he had done so he and Sir Ector went forth from the pavilion and betook their way unto where was the marble stone and the anvil before the cathedral. And when they had come to that place where the sword had been, Sir Kay mounted upon the cube of marble stone and beheld the face of the anvil. And lo! the face of the anvil was altogether smooth and without a scratch or scar of any sort. And Sir Kay said to himself, "What is this my father would have me do! What man is there in life who could thrust a sword-blade into a solid anvil of iron?" But, ne'theless, he could not withdraw from that impossible undertaking, but was constrained to assay that miracle, wherefore he set the point of the sword to the iron and bore upon it with all his strength. But it was impossible for him to accomplish that thing, and though he endeavored with all his might with the sword against the face of the anvil, yet did he not pierce the iron even to the breadth of a hair.

So, after he had thus assayed for a great while, he at last ceased what he did and came down from where he stood. And he said to his father, "Sire, no man in life may perform that miracle."

Unto this Sir Ector made reply, "How is it possible then that thou couldst have drawn out that sword as thou sayst and yet cannot put it back again?"

Then young Arthur lifted up his voice and said, "My father, have I thy leave to speak?" And Sir Ector said, "Speak, my son." And Arthur said, "I would that I might assay to handle that sword?" Whereunto Sir Ector replied, "By what authority wouldst thou handle that sword?" And Arthur said, "Because it was I who drew that sword forth from the anvil for my brother. Wherefore, as thou sayest, to draw it forth is not more difficult than to thrust it back again. So I believe that I shall be able to set it back into the iron whence I drew it."

Then Sir Ector gazed upon young Arthur in such a strange manner that Arthur wist not why he looked at him in that wise. Wherefore he cried out, "Sire, why dost thou gaze so strangely upon me? Has thou anger against me?" Whereunto Sir Ector made reply, "In the sight of God, my son, I have no anger against thee." Then he said, "If thou hast a desire to handle the sword, thou mayst assuredly make assay of that miracle."

So Arthur took the sword from his brother Kay and he leaped up upon the marble stone. And he set the point of the sword upon the anvil and bare very strongly upon it and lo! the sword penetrated very smoothly into the center of the anvil until it stood midway deep therein, and there it stood fast. And after he had performed that miracle he drew the sword forth again very swiftly and easily, and then thrust it back again once more as he had done before.

But when Sir Ector beheld what Arthur did, he cried out in a voice of exceeding loudness, "Lord! Lord! what is the miracle mine eyes behold!" And when Arthur came down from the cube of marble stone, Sir Ector kneeled down before him and set his hands together, palm to palm.

But when Arthur beheld what his father did, he cried out aloud like one in a great measure of pain; and he said, "My father! my father! why dost thou kneel down to me?"

To him Sir Ector made reply, "I am not thy father, and now it is made manifest that thou art assuredly of very exalted race and that the blood of kings flows in thy veins, else thou couldst not have handled that sword as thou hast done."

Then Arthur fell a-weeping beyond all measure and he cried out as with great agony of spirit, "Father! father! what is this thou sayst? I beseech thee to arise and not to kneel unto me."

So Sir Ector arose from his knees and stood before the face of Arthur, and he said, "Arthur, why dost thou weep?" And Arthur said, "Because I am afeard."

Now all this while Sir Kay had stood near by and he could neither move nor speak, but stood like one entranced, and he said to himself, "What is this? Is my brother a King?"

Then Sir Ector spake, saying, "Arthur, the time hath come for thee to know thyself, for the true circumstances of thy life have, heretofore, been altogether hidden from thee.

"Now I do confess everything to thee in this wise: that eighteen year ago there came to me a certain man very wise and high in favor with Uther-Pendragon and that man was the Enchanter Merlin. And Merlin showed me the signet ring of Uther-Pendragon and he commanded me by virtue of that ring that I should be at a certain assigned place at a particular time which he nominated; and the place which he assigned was the postern gate of Uther-Pendragon's castle; and the time which he named was midnight of that very day.

"And he bade me tell no man aught concerning those things which he communicated to me, and so I kept his counsel as he desired me to do.

"So I went to that postern gate at midnight as Merlin had commanded, and at that place there came unto me Merlin and another man, and the other man was Sir Ulfius, who was the chief knight of Uther-Pendragon's household. And I tell thee that these two worthies stood nigher unto Uther-Pendragon than any other men in all of the world.

"Now when those two came unto me, I perceived that Merlin bare in his arms a certain thing wrapped in a scarlet mantle of fine texture. And he opened the folds of the mantle and, lo! I beheld a child not long born and wrapped in swaddling clothes. And I saw the child in the light of a lanthorn which Sir Ulfius bare, and I perceived that he was very fair of face and large of bone – and thou wert that child.

"Then Merlin commanded me in this wise: that I was to take that child and that I should rear him as mine own; and he said that the child was to be called by the name of Arthur; and he said that no one in all the world was to know otherwise than that the child was mine own. And I told Merlin that I would do as he would have me, whereupon I took the child and bare it away with me. And I proclaimed that the child was mine own, and all over the world believed my words, wherefore no one ever knew otherwise than that thou wert mine own son. And that lady who was my wife, when she died she took that secret with her unto Paradise, and since then until now no one in all the world knew aught of this matter but I and those two aforementioned worthies.

"Nor have I until now ever known aught of who was thy father; but now I do suspect who he was and that thou hast in thy veins very high and kingly blood. And I do have in mind that perhaps thy father was Uther-Pendragon himself. For who but the son of Uther-Pendragon could have drawn forth that sword from out of the anvil as thou hast done?"

Then, when Arthur heard that saying of his father's, he cried out in a very loud and vehement voice, "Woe! Woe! Woe!" – saying that word three times. And Sir Ector said, "Arthur, why art thou woful?" And Arthur said, "Because I have lost my father, for I would rather have my father than be a King!"

Now as these things passed, there came unto that place two men, very tall and of a wonderfully noble and haughty appearance. And when these two men had come nigh to where they were, Arthur and Sir Ector and Sir Kay perceived that one of them was the Enchanter Merlin and that the other was Sir Ulfius – for those two men were very famous and well known unto all the world. And when those two had come to where were the three, Merlin spake, saying, "What cheer?" And Sir Ector made answer, "Here is cheer of a very wonderful sort; for, behold, Merlin! this is that child that thou didst bring unto me eighteen years ago, and, lo! thou seest he hath grown unto manhood."

Then Merlin said, "Sir Ector, I know very well who is this youth, for I have kept diligent watch over him for all this time. And I know that in him lieth the hope of Britain. Moreover, I tell thee that even to-day within the surface of an enchanted looking-glass I have beheld all that he hath done since the morning; and I know how he drew forth the sword from the anvil, and how he thrust it back again; and I know how he drew it forth and thrust it back a second time. And I know all that thou hast been saying unto him this while; wherefore I also do now avouch that thou hast told him the very truth. And, lo! the spirit of prophecy is upon me and I do foresee into the future that thou, Arthur, shall become the greatest and most famous King that ever lived in Britain; and I do foresee that many knights of extraordinary excellence shall gather about thee and that men shall tell of their marvellous deeds as long as this land shall continue, and I do foresee that through these knights thy reign shall be full of splendor and glory; and I do foresee that the most marvellous adventure of the Holy Grail shall be achieved by three of the knights of thy Court, and that to thy lasting renown, who shall be the King under whose reign the holy cup shall be achieved. All these things I foresee; and, lo! the time is now at hand when the glory of thy House shall again be made manifest unto the world, and all the people of this land shall rejoice in thee and thy kinghood. Wherefore, Sir Ector, for these three days to come, I do charge it upon thee that thou do guard this young man as the apple of thine eye, for in him doth lie the hope and salvation of all this realm."

Then Sir Ector lifted up his voice and cried unto Arthur, "A boon! a boon!" And Arthur said, "Alas! how is this? Dost thou, my father, ask a boon of me who may have all in the world that is mine to give? Ask what thou wilt and it is thine!" Then Sir Ector said, "I do beseech this of thee: that when thou art King thy brother Kay may be Seneschal of all this realm." And Arthur said, "It shall be as thou dost ask." And he said, "As for thee, it shall be still better with thee, for thou shalt be my father unto the end!" Whereupon so saying, he took Sir Ector's head into his hands and he kissed Sir Ector upon the forehead and upon the cheeks, and so sealed his plighted word.

But all this while Sir Kay had stood like unto one struck by thunder, and he wist not whether to be uplifted unto the skies or to be cast down into the depths, that his younger brother should thus have been passed by him and exalted unto that extraordinary altitude of fortune. Wherefore he stood like to one bereft of life and motion.

And let it here be said that Arthur fulfilled all that he had thus promised to his father – for, in after times, he made Sir Kay his Seneschal, and Sir Ector was to him a father until the day of his death, which same befell five years from that time.

Thus I have told you how the royalty of Arthur was first discovered. And now, if you will listen, ye shall hear how it was confirmed before all the world.

## Chapter Third

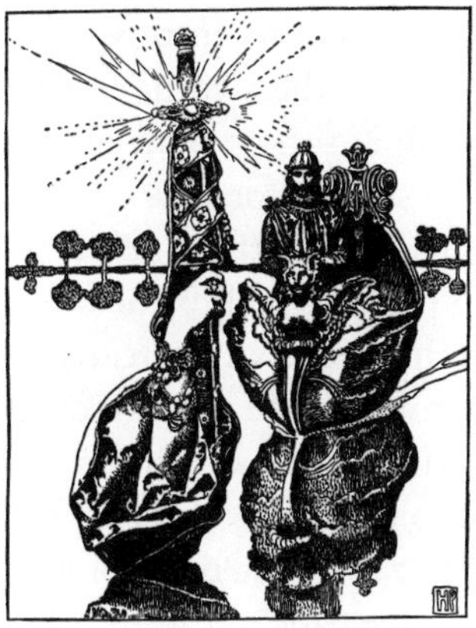

# How Several Kings and High Dukes Assayed to Draw the Sword

So when the morning of Christmas day had come, many thousands of folk of all qualities, both gentle and simple, gathered together in front of the cathedral for to behold the assay of that sword.

Now there had been a canopy of embroidered cloth of divers colors spread above the sword and the anvil, and a platform had been built around the cube of marble stone. And nigh unto that place there had been a throne for the Archbishop established; for the Archbishop was to overlook that assay and to see that every circumstance was fulfilled with due equity and circumspection.

So, when the morning was half gone by, the Archbishop himself came with great pomp of estate and took his seat upon the high throne that had been placed for him, and all his court of clerks and knights gathered about him, so that he presented a very proud and excellent appearance of courtliness.

Now unto that assay there had gathered nineteen kings and sixteen dukes, and each of these was of such noble and exalted estate that he entertained high hopes that he would that day be approved before the world to be the right king and overlord of all Britain. Wherefore after the Archbishop had established himself upon his throne, there came several of these and made demand that he should straightway put that matter to the test. So the Archbishop commanded his herald for to sound a trumpet, and to bid all who had the right to make assay of the sword to come unto that adventure, and the herald did according as the Archbishop ordered.

And when the herald had sounded his trumpet there immediately appeared the first of those kings to make trial of the sword, and he who came was King Lot of Orkney and the Isles. With King Lot there came eleven knights and five esquires, so that he appeared in very noble estate before the eyes of all. And when King Lot had arrived at that place, he mounted the platform. And first he saluted the Archbishop, and then he laid his hands to the pommel of the sword in the sight of all. And he bent his body and drew upon the sword with great strength, but he could not move the blade in the anvil even so much as the breadth of a hair, for it stood as fast as the iron in which it was planted. And after that first assay he tried three times more, but still he was altogether unable to move the blade in the iron. Then, after that he had thus four times made assay, he ceased his endeavor and came down from that place. And he was filled with great anger and indignation that he had not succeeded in his endeavor.

And after King Lot there came his brother-in-law, King Urien of Gore, and he also made assay in the same wise as King Lot had done. But neither did he succeed any better than that other king. And after King Urien there came King Fion of Scotland, and after King Fion there came King Mark of Cornwall, and after King Mark there came King Ryence of North Wales, and after King Ryence there came King Leodegrance of Cameliard, and after him came all those other kings and dukes before numerated, and not one of all these was able to move the blade. And some of these high and mighty lords were filled with anger and indignation that they had not succeeded, and others were ashamed that they had failed in that undertaking before the eyes of all those who looked upon them. But whether they were angry or whether they were ashamed it in no wise helped their case.

Now when all the kings and dukes had thus failed in that adventure, the people who were there were very much astonished, and they said to one another, "How is this? If all those kings and dukes of very exalted estate have failed to achieve that adventure, who then may hope to succeed? For here have been all those who were most worthy of that high honor, and all have tried to draw that sword and all have failed. Who then is there now to come after these who may hope to succeed?"

And, likewise, those kings and dukes spoke together in the same manner. And by and by there came six of the most worthy – to wit, King Lot, King Urien, King Pellinore, King Ban, King Ryence, and Duke Clarence of Northumberland – and these stood before the throne of the Archbishop and spake to him in this wise: "Sir, here have all the kings and dukes of this realm striven before you for to draw forth that sword, and lo! not one of all those who have undertaken that thing hath succeeded in his undertaking. What, then, may we understand but that the enchanter Merlin hath set this adventure for to bring shame and discredit upon all of us who are here, and upon you, who are the head of the church in this realm? For who in all the world may hope to draw forth a sword-blade out from a bed of solid iron? Behold! it is beyond the power of any man. Is it not then plain to be seen that Merlin hath made a mock of us all? Now, therefore, lest all this great congregation should have been called here in vain, we do beseech you of your wisdom that you presently choose the one from among the kings here gathered, who may be best fitted to be overlord of this realm. And when ye shall have chosen him, we will promise to obey him in all things whatsoever he may ordain. Verily, such a choice as that will be better worth while than to spend time in this foolish task of striving to draw forth a sword out of an anvil which no man in all the world may draw forth."

Then was the Archbishop much troubled in spirit, for he said to himself, "Can it be sooth that Merlin hath deceived me, and hath made a mock of me and of all these kings and lordly folk? Surely this cannot be. For Merlin is passing wise, and he would not make a mock of all the realm for the sake of so sorry a jest as this would be. Certes he hath some intent in this of which we know naught, being of less wisdom than he – wherefore I will be patient for a while longer." Accordingly, having communed thus within himself, he spake aloud in this wise to those seven high lords: "Messires," he said, "I have yet faith that Merlin hath not deceived us, wherefore I pray your patience for one little while longer. For if, in the time a man may count five hundred twice over, no one cometh forward to perform this task, then will I, at your behest, proceed to choose one from amongst you and will proclaim him King and Overlord of all." For the Archbishop had faith that Merlin was about to immediately declare a king before them all.

Now leave we these and turn we unto Arthur and his father and brother.

For Merlin had bidden those three to abide in their pavilion until such time as he thought would be fit for them to come out thence. And that time being now come, Merlin and Sir Ulfius went to the pavilion of Sir Ector, and Merlin said, "Arthur, arise and come forth, for now the hour is come for thee to assay before the whole world that miracle which thou didst of late execute in privacy." So Arthur did as Merlin bade him to do, and he came forth from the pavilion with his father and his brother, and, lo! he was like one who walked in a dream.

So they five went down from thence toward the cathedral and unto that place of assay. And when they had come to the congregation there assembled, the people made way for them, greatly marvelling and saying to one another, "Who are these with the Enchanter Merlin and Sir Ulfius, and whence come they? For all the world knew Merlin and Sir Ulfius, and they wist that here was something very extraordinary about to happen. And Arthur was clad all in flame-colored raiment embroidered with threads of silver so that others of the people said, "Certes, that youth is very fair for to look upon; now who may he be?"

But Merlin said no word to any man, but he brought Arthur through the press unto that place where the Archbishop sat; and the press made way for him so that he was not stayed in his going. And when the Archbishop beheld Merlin come thus with those others, he arose and said, "Merlin, who are these whom thou bringest unto us, and what is their business here?" And Merlin said, "Lord, here is one come to make the assay of yonder sword." And the Archbishop said, "Which one is he?" and Merlin said, "This is he," and he laid his hand upon Arthur.

Then the Archbishop looked upon Arthur and he beheld that the youth was very comely of face, wherefore his heart went out unto Arthur and he loved him a very great deal. And the Archbishop said, "Merlin, by what right doth this young man come hither?" And Merlin made reply, "Lord, he cometh hither by the best right that there is in the world; for he who standeth before thee clad in red is the true son of Uther-Pendragon and of his lawful wife, Queen Igraine."

Then the Archbishop cried out aloud in great amazement and those who stood nigh and who heard what Merlin said were so astonished that they wist not what to think. And the Archbishop said, "Merlin, what is this that thou tellest me? For who, until now, in all the world hath ever heard that Uther-Pendragon had a son?"

Unto this Merlin made reply: "No one hath ever known of such a thing until now, only a very few. For it was in this wise: When this child was born the spirit of prophecy lay upon me and I foresaw that Uther-Pendragon would die before a very great while. Wherefore I feared that the enemies of the King would lay violent hands upon the young child for the sake of his inheritance. So, at the King's behest, I and another took the young child from his mother and gave him unto a third, and that man received the kingly child and maintained him ever since as his own son. And as to the truth of these things there are others here who may attest the verity of them – for he who was with me when the young child was taken from his mother was Sir Ulfius, and he to whom he was entrusted was Sir Ector of Bonmaison – and those two witnesses, who are without any reproach, will avouch to the verity of that which I have asserted, for here they stand before thee to certify unto what I have said."

And Sir Ulfius and Sir Ector said, "All that Merlin hath spoken is true, and thereunto we do pledge our most faithful and sacred word of honor."

Then the Archbishop said, "Who is there may doubt the word of such honorable witnesses?" And he looked upon Arthur and smiled upon him.

Then Arthur said, "Have I then thy leave, Lord, to handle yonder sword?" And the Archbishop said, "Thou hast my leave, and may have the grace of God go with thee to do thy endeavor."

Thereupon Arthur went to the cube of marble stone and he laid his hands upon the haft of the sword that was thrust into the anvil. And he bent his body and drew very strongly and, lo! the sword came forth with great ease and very smoothly. And when he had got the sword into his hands, he swung it about his head so that it flashed like lightning. And after he had swung it thus thrice about his head, he set the point thereof against the face of the anvil and bore upon it very strongly, and, behold! the sword slid very smoothly back again into that place where it had aforetime stood; and when it was there, midway deep, it stood fast where it was. And thus did Arthur successfully accomplish that marvellous miracle of the sword in the eyes of all the world.

Now when the people who were congregated at that place beheld this miracle performed before their faces, they lifted up their voices all together, and shouted so vehemently and with so huge a tumult of outcry that it was as though the whole earth rocked and trembled with the sound of their shouting.

And whiles they so shouted Arthur took hold of the sword again and drew it forth and swung it again, and again drave it back into the anvil. And when he had done that he drew it forth a third time and did the same thing as before. Thus it was that all those who were there beheld that miracle performed three times over.

And all the kings and dukes who were there were filled with great amazement, and they wist not what to think or to say when they beheld one who was little more than a boy perform that undertaking in which the best of them had failed. And some of them, seeing that miracle, were willing to acknowledge Arthur because of it, but others would not acknowledge him. These withdrew themselves and stood aloof; and as they stood thus apart, they said among themselves: "What is this and who can accredit such a thing that a beardless boy should be set before us all and should be made King and overlord of this great realm for to govern us. Nay! nay! we will have none of him for our King." And others said, "Is it not apparent that Merlin and Sir Ulfius are thus exalting this unknown boy so that they may elevate themselves along with him?" Thus these discontented kings spake among themselves, and of all of them the most bitter were King Lot and King Urien, who were brothers by marriage with Arthur.

Now when the Archbishop perceived the discontent of these kings and dukes, he said to them, "How now, Messires! Are ye not satisfied?" And they said, "We are not satisfied." And the Archbishop said, "What would ye have?" And they said, "We would have another sort of king for Britain than a beardless boy of whom no one knoweth and of whose birthright there are only three men to attest." And the Archbishop said, "What of that? Hath he not performed the miracle that ye yourselves assayed and failed to perform?"

But these high and mighty lords would not be satisfied, but with angry and averted faces they went away from that place, filled with wrath and indignation.

But others of these kings and dukes came and saluted Arthur and paid him court, giving him joy of that which he had achieved; and the chiefest of those who came thus unto him in friendliness was King Leodegrance of Cameliard. And all the multitude acknowledged him and crowded around that place shouting so that it sounded like to the noise of thunder.

Now all this while Sir Ector and Sir Kay had stood upon one side. And they were greatly weighed down by sorrow; for it appeared to them that Arthur had, of a sudden, been uplifted so far from their estate that they might never hope to approach him more. For now he was of kingly consequence and they but common knights. And, after awhile, Arthur beheld them where they stood with downcast looks, whereupon he straightway went to them and took first one and then the other by the hand and kissed each upon the cheek. Thereupon they were again very glad at being thus uplifted unto him.

And when Arthur departed from that place, great crowds of people followed after him so that the streets were altogether filled with the press of people. And the multitude continually gave him loud acclaim as the chosen King of England, and those who were nearest to him sought to touch the hem of his garments; wherefore the heart of Arthur was exceedingly uplifted with great joy and gladness, so that his soul took wing and flew like a bird into the sky.

Thus Arthur achieved the adventure of the sword that day and entered into his birthright of royalty. Wherefore, may God grant His Grace unto you all that ye too may likewise succeed in your undertakings. For any man may be a king in that life in which he is placed if so be he may draw forth the sword of success from out of the iron of circumstance. Wherefore when your time of assay cometh, I do hope it may be with you as it was with Arthur that day, and that ye too may achieve success with entire satisfaction unto yourself and to your great glory and perfect happiness. Amen.

*"Neither will I yield until either thou or I have altogether conquered the other." (First Book, Part II, Chapter Second)*

*"Ha! my lord King... that sword is no easy thing to achieve."*
*(First Book, Part II, Chapter Third)*

# Conclusion

Now after these things had happened there was much talk among men and great confusion and tumult. For while some of the kings and nearly all the multitude said, "Lo! here is a king come to us, as it were, from out of Heaven for to bring peace unto our distracted land," yet other kings (and they were of great number) said, "Who is this beardless boy who cometh with a claim to be High King of Britain? Who ever heard of him before? We will have none of him except upon further trial and upon greater avouchment." So, for the sake of peace, the Archbishop ordained that another assay of the sword should be made at Candlemas; and here again all those who endeavored to draw forth the sword failed thereat, but Arthur drew it forth several times, very easily, in the sight of all. And after that a third trial was made at Easter and after that a fourth trial was made at Pentecost. And at all these trials Arthur repeatedly drew out the sword from the anvil, and no one but he could draw it forth.

And, after that fourth trial, sundry of the kings and many of the lesser barons and knights and all of the commons cried out that these were trials enough, and that Arthur had assuredly approved himself to be rightwise King; wherefore they demanded that he should be made King indeed so that he might rule over them. For it had come to pass that whithersoever Arthur went great crowds followed after him hailing him as the true son of Uther-Pendragon, and rightwise overlord of Britain. Wherefore, the Archbishop (seeing how the people loved Arthur and how greatly they desired him for their King) ordained that he should be anointed and crowned unto royal estate; and so it was done at the great Cathedral. And some say that that Cathedral was St. Paul's and some say that it was not.

But when Arthur had thus been crowned, all those who were opposed unto his Kingship withdrew themselves in great anger, and immediately set about to prepare war against him. But the people were with Arthur and joined with him, and so also did several Kings and many of the lesser barons and knights. And, with the advice of Merlin, Arthur made friends and allies of sundry other kings and they and he fought two great wars with his enemies and won both of these wars. And in the second war was fought a very famous battle nigh to the Forest of Bedegraine (wherefore it was called the Battle of Bedegraine), and in that battle Arthur overthrew his enemies so entirely that it was not possible for them ever to hope to unite in war against him again.

And of King Lot, his brother-in-law, King Arthur brought two of his sons to Court for to dwell there and to serve as hostages of peace thereafter. And these two were Gawaine and Geharris and they became, after awhile, very famous and accomplished knights. And of King Urien, his other brother-in-law, Arthur brought unto Court his one son, Ewaine, for to hold as an hostage of peace; and he also became in time a very famous and accomplished knight. And because of these hostages there was peace thereafter betwixt those three kingly brothers for all time. And a certain very famous king and knight hight King Pellinore (who was one of his enemies) Arthur drove out of his possessions and away from the habitations of men and into the forest. And King Ryence (who was another of his enemies) he drave into the mountains of North Wales. And other kings who were his enemies he subjugated to his will, so that all the land was at such peace that it had not enjoyed the like since the days of Uther-Pendragon.

And King Arthur made Sir Kay his Seneschal as he had promised to do; and he made Sir Ulfius his Chamberlain; and Merlin he made his Counsellor; and Sir Bodwain of Britain he made his Constable. And these men were all of such a sort as greatly enhanced the glory and renown of his reign and established him upon his throne with entire security.

Now when the reign of King Arthur became thus entirely established, and when the renown of his greatness began to be known in the world, many men of noble souls and of large spirit and of high knightly prowess – knights who desired above all things to achieve glory at arms in Courts of Chivalry – perceived that great credit and exaltation of estate were likely to be won under such a king. So it fell out that, from all parts, by little and little, there began to gather together such a Court of noble, honorable knights about King Arthur as men never beheld before that time, and shall haply never behold again.

For even to this day the history of these good knights is known to the greater part of mankind. Yea; the names of many kings and emperors have passed away and have been forgotten, but the names of Sir Galahad, and of Sir Launcelot of the Lake, and of Sir Tristram of Lyonesse, and of Sir Percival of Gales, and of Sir Gawaine, and of Sir Ewaine, and of Sir Bors de Ganis, and of many others of that noble household of worthy brotherhood, is still remembered by men. Wherefore, I think that it is very likely that so long as words shall be written, the performances of these worthies shall be remembered.

So in this history yet to be written, I have set it for my task to inform him who reads this book of many of these adventures, telling him, besides, such several circumstances as I do not believe are known unto everybody. And by and by, when I shall tell of the establishment of the Round Table, I shall set forth a tabulated list of a number of those worthies who at this time assembled at the Court of Arthur as men chosen to found that order of the Round Table, and who, for that reason, were entitled "The Ancient and Honorable Companions of the Round Table."

For though this entire history chiefly concerneth King Arthur, yet the glory of these great honorable knights was his glory, and his glory was their glory, wherefore one cannot tell of the glory of King Arthur without also telling of the glory of those noble gentlemen aforesaid.

P A R T  I I

# The Winning of a Sword

*Here beginneth the story of certain adventures of Arthur after that he had become King, wherein it is told how, with great knightly courage and prowess, he fought a very fierce and bloodly battle with a certain Sable Knight. Likewise, it is told how he achieved, in consequence of that battle, a certain Sword so famous and glorious that its renown shall last as long as our speech shall be spoken. For the like of that sword was never seen in all the world before that time, and it hath never been beheld since then; and its name was Excalibur.*

*So, if it please you to read this story, I believe it will afford you excellent entertainment, and will, without doubt, greatly exalt your spirit because of the remarkable courage which those two famous and worthy knights displayed when they fought together that famous battle. Likewise you shall find great cheer in reading therein of the wonderful marvellousness of a certain land of Faerie into which King Arthur wandered, and where he found a Lake of Enchantment and held converse with a mild and beautiful lady of that land who directed him how to obtain that renowned sword aforementioned.*

*For it hath given me such pleasure to write these things that my heart would, at times, be diluted as with a pure joy, wherefore, I entertain great hopes that you also may find much pleasure in them as I have already done. So I pray you to listen unto what follows.*

CHAPTER FIRST

# How There Came a Certain Wounded Knight Unto the Court of King Arthur

Now it fell upon a certain pleasant time in the Springtide season that King Arthur and his Court were making a royal progression through that part of Britain which lieth close to the Forests of the Usk. At that time the weather was exceedingly warm, and so the King and Court made pause within the forest under the trees in the cool and pleasant shade that the place afforded, and there the King rested for a while upon a couch of rushes spread with scarlet cloth.

And the knights then present at that Court were, Sir Gawaine, and Sir Ewaine, and Sir Kay, and Sir Pellias, and Sir Bedevere, and Sir Caradoc, and Sir Geraint, and Sir Bodwin of Britain and Sir Constantine of Cornwall, and Sir Brandiles and Sir Mador de la Porte, and there was not to be found anywhere in the world a company of such noble and exalted knights as these.

Now as the King lay drowsing and as these worthies sat holding cheerful converse together at that place, there came, of a sudden, a considerable bustle and stir upon the outskirts of the Court, and presently there appeared a very sad and woful sight. For there came thitherward a knight, sore wounded, and upheld upon his horse by a golden-haired page, clad in an apparel of white and azure. And, likewise, the knight's apparel and the trappings of his horse were of white and azure, and upon his shield he bore the emblazonment of a single lily flower of silver upon a ground of pure azure.

But the knight was in a very woful plight. For his face was as pale as wax and hung down upon his breast. And his eyes were glazed and saw naught that passed around him, and his fair apparel of white and blue was all red with the blood of life that ran from a great wound in his side. And, as they came upon their way, the young page lamented in such wise that it wrung the heart for to hear him.

Now, as these approached, King Arthur aroused cried out, "Alas! what doleful spectacle is that which I behold? Now hasten, ye my lords, and bring succor to yonder knight; and do thou, Sir Kay, go quickly and bring that fair young page hither that we may presently hear from his lips what mishap hath befallen his lord."

So certain of those knights hastened at the King's bidding and gave all succor to the wounded knight, and conveyed him to King Arthur's own pavilion, which had been pitched at a little distance. And when he had come there the King's chirurgeon presently attended upon him – albeit his wounds were of such a sort he might not hope to live for a very long while.

Meantime, Sir Kay brought the fair young page before the King, where he sat, and the King thought that he had hardly ever seen a more beautiful countenance. And the King said, "I prithee tell me, Sir Page, who is thy master, and how came he in such a sad and pitiable condition as that which we have just now beheld."

"That will I so, Lord," said the youth. "Know that my master is entitled Sir Myles of the White Fountain, and that he cometh from the country north of where we are and at a considerable distance from this. In that country he is the Lord of seven castles and several noble estates, wherefore, as thou mayst see, he is of considerable consequence. A fortnight ago (being doubtless moved thereunto by the lustiness of the Springtime), he set forth with only me for his esquire, for he had a mind to seek adventure in such manner as beseemed a good knight who would be errant. And we had several adventures, and in all of them my lord was entirely successful; for he overcame six knights at various places and sent them all to his castle for to attest his valor unto his lady.

"At last, this morning, coming to a certain place situated at a considerable distance from this, we came upon a fair castle of the forest, which stood in a valley surrounded by open spaces of level lawn, bedight with many flowers of divers sort. There we beheld three fair damsels who tossed a golden ball from one to another, and the damsels were clad all in flame-colored satin, and their hair was of the color of gold. And as we drew nigh to them they stinted their play, and she who was the chief of those damsel called out to my lord, demanding of him whither he went and what was his errand.

"To her my lord made answer that he was errant and in search of adventure, and upon this, the three damsels laughed, and she who had first spoken said, 'An thou art in search of adventure, Sir Knight, happily I may be able to help thee to one that shall satisfy thee to thy heart's content.'

"Unto this my master made reply 'I prithee, fair damsel, tell me what that adventure may be so that I may presently assay it.'

"Thereupon this lady bade my master to take a certain path, and to follow the same for the distance of a league or a little more, and that he would then come to a bridge of stone that crossed a violent stream, and she assured him that there he might find adventure enough for to satisfy any man.

"So my master and I wended thitherward as that damoiselle had directed, and, by and by, we came unto the bridge whereof she had spoken. And, lo! beyond the bridge was a lonesome castle with a tall straight tower, and before the castle was a wide and level lawn of well-trimmed grass. And immediately beyond the bridge was an apple-tree hung over with a multitude of shields. And midway upon the bridge was a single shield, entirely of black; and beside it hung a hammer of brass; and beneath the shield was written these words in letters of red:

Whoso Smiteth This Shield
Doeth So At his Peril.

"Now, my master, Sir Myles, when he read those words went straightway to that shield and, seizing the hammer that hung beside it, he smote upon it a blow so that it rang like thunder.

"Thereupon, as in answer, the portcullis of the castle was let fall, and there immediately came forth a knight, clad all from head to foot in sable armor. And his apparel and the trappings of his horse and all the appointments thereof were likewise entirely of sable.

"Now when that Sable Knight perceived my master he came riding swiftly across the meadow and so to the other end of the bridge. And when he had come there he drew rein and saluted my master and cried out, 'Sir Knight, I demand of thee why thou didst smite that shield. Now let me tell thee, because of thy boldness, I shall take away from thee thine own shield, and shall hang it upon yonder apple-tree, where thou beholdest all those other shields to be hanging.' Unto this my master made reply. 'That thou shalt not do unless thou mayst overcome me, as knight to knight.' And thereupon, immediately, he dressed his shield and put himself into array for an assault at arms.

"So my master and this Sable Knight, having made themselves ready for that encounter, presently drave together with might and main. And they met in the middle of the course, where my master's spear burst into splinters. But the spear of the Sable Knight held and it pierced through Sir Myles, his shield, and it penetrated his side, so that both he and his horse were overthrown violently into the dust; he being wounded so grievously that he could not arise again from the ground whereon he lay.

"Then the Sable Knight took my master's shield and hung it up in the branches of the apple-tree where the other shields were hanging, and, thereupon, without paying further heed to my master, or inquiring as to his hurt, he rode away into his castle again, whereof the portcullis was immediately closed behind him.

"So, after that he had gone, I got my master to his horse with great labor, and straightway took him thence, not knowing where I might find harborage for him, until I came to this place. And that, my lord King, is the true story of how my master came by that mortal hurt which he hath suffered."

"Ha! By the glory of Paradise!" cried King Arthur, "I do consider it great shame that in my Kingdom and so near to my Court strangers should be so discourteously treated as Sir Myles hath been served. For it is certainly a discourtesy for to leave a fallen knight upon the ground, without tarrying to inquire as to his hurt how grievous it may be. And still more discourteous is it for to take away the shield of a fallen knight who hath done good battle."

And so did all the knights of the King's Court exclaim against the discourtesy of that Sable Knight.

Then there came forth a certain esquire attendant upon the King's person, by name Griflet, who was much beloved by his Royal Master, and he kneeled before the King and cried out in a loud voice: "I crave a boon of thee, my lord King! and do beseech thee that thou wilt grant it unto me!"

Then King Arthur uplifted his countenance upon the youth as he knelt before him and he said, "Ask, Griflet, and thy boon shall be granted unto thee."

Thereupon Griflet said, "It is this that I would ask – I crave that thou wilt make me straightway knight, and that thou wilt let me go forth and endeavor to punish this unkindly knight, by overthrowing him, and so redeeming those shields which he hath hung upon that apple-tree."

Then was King Arthur much troubled in his spirit, for Griflet was as yet only an esquire and altogether untried in arms. So he said, "Behold, thou art yet too young to have to do with so potent a knight as this sable champion must be, who has thus overthrown so many knights without himself suffering any mishap. I prithee, dear Griflet, consider and ask some other boon."

But young Griflet only cried the more, "A boon! A boon! and thou hast granted it unto me."

Thereupon King Arthur said, "Thou shalt have thy boon, though my heart much misgiveth me that thou wilt suffer great ill and misfortune from this adventure."

So that night Griflet kept watch upon his armor in a chapel of the forest, and, in the morning, having received the Sacrament, he was created a knight by the hand of King Arthur – and it was not possible for any knight to have greater honor than that. Then King Arthur fastened the golden spurs to Sir Griflet's heels with his own hand.

So Griflet was made a knight, and having mounted his charger, he rode straightway upon his adventure, much rejoicing and singing for pure pleasure.

And it was at this time that Sir Myles died of his hurt, for it is often so that death and misfortune befall some, whiles others laugh and sing for hope and joy, as though such grievous things as sorrow and death could never happen in the world wherein they live.

Now that afternoon King Arthur sat waiting with great anxiety for word of that young knight, but there was no word until toward evening, when there came hurrying to him certain of his attendants, proclaiming that Sir Griflet was returning, but without his shield, and in such guise that it seemed as though a great misfortune had befallen him. And straightway thereafter came Sir Griflet himself, sustained upon his horse on the one hand by Sir Constantine and upon the other by Sir Brandiles. And, lo! Sir Griflet's head hung down upon his breast, and his fair new armor was all broken and stained with blood and dust. And so woful was he of appearance that King Arthur's heart was contracted with sorrow to behold that young knight in so pitiable a condition.

So, at King Arthur's bidding, they conducted Sir Griflet to the Royal Pavilion, and there they laid him down upon a soft couch. Then the King's chirurgeon searched his wounds and found that the head of a spear and a part of the shaft thereof were still piercing Sir Griflet's side, so that he was in most woful and grievous pain.

And when King Arthur beheld in what a parlous state Sir Griflet lay he cried out, "Alas! my dear young knight, what hath happened thee to bring thee unto such a woful condition as this which I behold?"

Then Sir Griflet, speaking in a very weak voice, told King Arthur how he had fared. And he said that he had proceeded through the forest, until he had discovered the three beautiful damsels whereof the page of Sir Myles had spoken. And he said that he had found the bridge whereon hung the shield and the brazen mall, and that he had there beheld the apple-tree hung full of shields; and he said that he smote the shield of the Sable Knight with the brazen mall, and that the Sable Knight had thereupon come riding out against him. And he said that this knight did not appear of a mind to fight with him; instead he cried out to him with a great deal of nobleness that he was too young and too untried in arms to have to do with a seasoned knight; wherefore he advised Sir Griflet to withdraw him from that adventure ere it was too late. But, notwithstanding this advice, Sir Griflet would not withdraw but declared that he would certainly have to do with that other knight in sable. Now at the very first onset Sir Griflet's spear had burst into pieces, but the spear of the Sable Knight had held and had pierced through Sir Griflet's shield and into his side, causing him this grievous wound whereof he suffered. And Sir Griflet said that the Sable Knight had then, most courteously, uplifted him upon his horse again (albeit he had kept Sir Griflet's shield and had hung it upon the tree with those others that hung there) and had then directed him upon his way, so that he had made shift to ride thither, though with great pain and dole.

Then was King Arthur very wode and greatly disturbed in his mind, for indeed he loved Sir Griflet exceedingly well. Wherefore he declared that he himself would now go forth for to punish that Sable Knight, and for to humble him with his own hand. And, though the knights of his Court strove to dissuade him from that adventure, yet he declared that he with his own hand would accomplish that proud knight's humiliation, and that he would undertake the adventure, with God His Grace, upon the very next day.

And so disturbed was he that he could scarce eat his food that evening for vexation, nor would he go to his couch to sleep, but, having inquired very narrowly of Sir Griflet where he might find that valley of flowers and those three damsels, he spent the night in walking up and down his pavilion, awaiting for the dawning of the day.

Now, as soon as the birds first began to chirp and the east to brighten with the coming of the daylight, King Arthur summoned his two esquires and, having with their aid donned his armor and mounted a milk-white war-horse, he presently took his departure upon that adventure which he had determined upon.

And, indeed it is a very pleasant thing for to ride forth in the dawning of a Springtime day. For then the little birds do sing their sweetest song, all joining in one joyous medley, whereof one may scarce tell one note from another, so multitudinous is that pretty roundelay; then do the growing things of the earth smell the sweetest in the freshness of the early daytime – the fair flowers, the shrubs, and all blossoms upon the trees; then doth the dew bespangle all the sward as with an incredible multitude of jewels of various colors; then is all the world sweet and clean and new, as though it had been fresh created for him who came to roam abroad so early in the morning.

So King Arthur's heart expanded with great joy, and he chanted a quaint song as he rode through the forest upon the quest of that knightly adventure.

So, about noon-tide, he came to that part of the forest lands whereof he had heard those several times before. For of a sudden, he discovered before him a wide and gently sloping valley, a-down which ran a stream as bright as silver. And, lo! the valley was strewn all over with an infinite multitude of fair and fragrant flowers of divers sorts. And in the midst of the valley there stood a comely castle, with tall red roofs and many bright windows, so that it seemed to King Arthur that it was a very fine castle indeed. And upon a smooth green lawn he perceived those three damoiselles clad in flame-colored satin of whom the page of Sir Myles and Sir Griflet had spoken. And they played at ball with a golden ball, and the hair of each was of the hue of gold, and it seemed to King Arthur, as he drew nigh, that they were the most beautiful damoiselles that he had ever beheld in all of his life.

Now as King Arthur came unto them the three ceased tossing the ball, and she who was the fairest of all damoiselles demanded of him whither he went and upon what errand he was bound.

Then King Arthur made reply: "Ha! fair lady! whither should a belted knight ride upon such a day as this, and upon what business, other than the search of adventure such as beseemeth a knight of a proper strength of heart and frame who would be errant?"

Then the three damoiselles smiled upon the King, for he was exceedingly comely of face and they liked him very well. "Alas, Sir Knight!" said she who had before spoken, "I prithee be in no such haste to undertake a dangerous adventure, but rather tarry with us for a day or two or three, for to feast and make merry with us. For surely good cheer doth greatly enlarge the heart, and we would fain enjoy the company of so gallant a knight as thou appearest to be. Yonder castle is ours and all this gay valley is ours, and those who have visited it are pleased, because of its joyousness, to call it the Valley of Delight. So tarry with us for a little and be not in such haste to go forward."

"Nay," said King Arthur, "I may not tarry with ye, fair ladies, for I am bent upon an adventure of which ye may wot right well, when I tell ye that I seek that Sable Knight, who hath overcome so many other knights and hath taken away their shields. So I do pray ye of your grace for to tell me where I may find him."

"Grace of Heaven!" cried she who spake for the others, "this is certainly a sorry adventure which ye seek, Sir Knight! For already, in these two days, have two knights assayed with that knight, and both have fallen into great pain and disregard. Ne'theless, an thou wilt undertake this peril, yet shalt thou not go until thou hast eaten and refreshed thyself." So saying, she lifted a little ivory whistle that hung from her neck by a chain of gold, and blew upon it very shrilly.

In answer to this summons there came forth from that castle three fair young pages, clad all in flame-colored raiment, bearing among them a silver table covered with a white napkin. And after them came five other pages of the same appearance, bearing flagons of white wine and red, dried fruits and comfits and manchets of white fair bread.

Then King Arthur descended from his war-horse with great gladness, for he was both hungry and athirst, and, seating himself at the table with the damsels beside him, he ate with great enjoyment, discoursing pleasantly the while with those fair ladies, who listened to him with great cheerfulness of spirit. Yet he told them not who he was, though they greatly marvelled who might be the noble warrior who had come thus into that place.

So, having satisfied his hunger and his thirst, King Arthur mounted his steed again, and the three damsels conducted him across the valley a little way – he riding upon his horse and they walking beside him. So, by and by, he perceived where was a dark pathway that led into the farther side of the forest land; and when he had come thither the lady who had addressed him before said to him, "Yonder is the way that thou must take an thou wouldst enter upon this adventure. So fare thee well, and may good hap go with thee, for, certes, thou art the Knight most pleasant of address who hath come hitherward for this long time.

Thereupon King Arthur, having saluted those ladies right courteously, rode away with very great joy of that pleasant adventure through which he had thus passed.

Now when King Arthur had gone some ways he came, by and by, to a certain place where charcoal burners plied their trade. For here were many mounds of earth, all a-smoke with the smouldering logs within, whilst the air was filled with the smell of the dampened fires.

As the King approached this spot, he presently beheld that something was toward that was sadly amiss. For, in the open clearing, he beheld three sooty fellows with long knives in their hands, who pursued one old man, whose beard was as white as snow. And he beheld that the reverend old man, who was clad richly in black, and whose horse stood at a little distance, was running hither and thither, as though to escape from those wicked men, and he appeared to be very hard pressed and in great danger of his life.

"Pardon!" quoth the young King to himself, "here, certes, is one in sore need of succor." Whereupon he cried out in a great voice, "Hold, villains! What would you be at!" and therewith set spurs to his horse and dropped his spear into rest and drove down upon them with a noise like to thunder for loudness.

But when the three wicked fellows beheld the armed Knight thus thundering down upon them, they straightway dropped their knives and, with loud outcries of fear, ran away hither and thither until they had escaped into the thickets of the forest, where one upon a horse might not hope to pursue them.

Whereupon, having driven away those wicked fellows, King Arthur rode up to him whom he had succored, thinking to offer him condolence. And behold! when he had come nigh to him, he perceived that the old man was the Enchanter Merlin. Yet whence he had so suddenly come, who had only a little while before been at the King's Court at Carleon, and what he did in that place, the King could in no wise understand. Wherefore he bespoke the Enchanter in this wise, "Ha! Merlin, it seemeth to me that I have saved thy life. For, surely, thou hadst not escaped from the hands of those wicked men had I not happened to come hitherward at this time."

"Dost thou think so, Lord?" said Merlin. "Now let me tell thee that I did maybe appear to be in danger, yet I might have saved myself very easily had I been of a mind to do so. But, as thou sawest me in this seeming peril, so may thou know that a real peril, far greater than this, lieth before thee, and there will be no errant knight to succor thee from it. Wherefore, I pray thee, Lord, for to take me with thee upon this adventure that thou art set upon, for I do tell thee that thou shalt certainly suffer great dole and pain therein."

"Merlin," said King Arthur, "even an I were to face my death, yet would I not turn back from this adventure. But touching the advice thou givest me, meseems it will be very well to take thee with me if such peril lieth before me as thou sayest."

And Merlin said, "Yea, it would be very well for thee to do so."

So Merlin mounted upon his palfrey, and King Arthur and he betook their way from that place in pursuit of that adventure which the King had undertaken to perform.

CHAPTER SECOND

# HOW KING ARTHUR FOUGHT WITH THE SABLE KNIGHT

So King Arthur and Merlin rode together through the forest for a considerable while, until they perceived that they must be approaching nigh to the place where dwelt the Sable Knight whom the King sought so diligently. For the forest, which had till then been altogether a wilderness, very deep and mossy, began to show an aspect more thin and open, as though a dwelling-place of mankind was close at hand.

And, after a little, they beheld before them a violent stream of water, that rushed through a dark and dismal glen. And, likewise, they perceived that across this stream of water there was a bridge of stone, and that upon the other side of the bridge there was a smooth and level lawn of green grass, whereon Knights-contestants might joust very well. And beyond this lawn they beheld a tall and forbidding castle, with smooth walls and a straight tower; and this castle was built upon the rocks so that it appeared to be altogether a part of the stone. So they wist that this must be the castle whereof the page and Sir Griflet had spoken.

For, midway upon the bridge, they beheld that there hung a sable shield and a brass mall exactly as the page and Sir Griflet had said; and that upon the farther side of the stream was an apple-tree, amid the leaves of which hung a very great many shields of various devices, exactly as those two had reported: and they beheld that some of those shields were clean and fair, and that some were foul and stained with blood, and that some were smooth and unbroken, and that some were cleft as though by battle of knight with knight. And all those shields were the shields of different knights whom the Sable Knight, who dwelt within the castle, had overthrown in combat with his own hand.

"Splendor of Paradise!" quoth King Arthur, "that must, indeed, be a right valiant knight who, with his own single strength, hath overthrown and cast down so many other knights. For, indeed, Merlin, there must be an hundred shields hanging in yonder tree!"

Unto this Merlin made reply, "And thou, Lord, mayst be very happy an thy shield, too, hangeth not there ere the sun goeth down this even-tide."

"That," said King Arthur, with a very steadfast countenance, "shall be as God willeth. For, certes, I have a greater mind than ever for to try my power against yonder knight. For, consider, what especial honor would fall to me should I overcome so valiant a warrior as this same Sable Champion appeareth to be, seeing that he hath been victorious over so many other good knights."

Thereupon, having so spoken his mind, King Arthur immediately pushed forward his horse and so, coming upon the bridge, he clearly read that challenge writ in letters of red beneath the shield:

Whoso Smiteth This Shield
Doeth So At his Peril.

Upon reading these words, the King seized the brazen mall, and smote that shield so violent a blow that the sound thereof echoed back from the smooth walls of the castle, and from the rocks whereon it stood, and from the skirts of the forest around about, as though twelve other shields had been struck in those several places.

And in answer to that sound, the portcullis of the castle was immediately let fall, and there issued forth a knight, very huge of frame, and clad all in sable armor. And, likewise, all of his apparel and all the trappings of his horse were entirely of sable, so that he presented a most grim and forbidding aspect. And this Sable Knight came across that level meadow of smooth grass with a very stately and honorable gait; for neither did he ride in haste, nor did he ride slowly, but with great pride and haughtiness of mien, as becoming a champion who, haply, had never yet been overcome in battle. So, reaching the bridge-head, he drew rein and saluted King Arthur with great dignity, and also right haughtily. "Ha! Sir Knight!" quoth he, "why didst thou, having read those words yonder inscribed, smite upon my shield? Now I do tell thee that, for thy discourtesy, I shall presently take thy shield away from thee, and shall hang it up upon yonder apple-tree where thou beholdest all those other shields to be hanging. Wherefore, either deliver thou thy shield unto me without more ado or else prepare for to defend it with thy person – in the which event thou shalt certainly suffer great pain and discomfort to thy body."

"Gramercy for the choice thou grantest me," said King Arthur. "But as for taking away my shield – I do believe that that shall be as Heaven willeth, and not as thou willest. Know, thou unkind knight, that I have come hither for no other purpose than to do battle with thee and so to endeavor for to redeem with my person all those shields that hang yonder upon that apple-tree. So make thou ready straightway that I may have to do with thee, maybe to thy great disadvantage."

"That will I so," replied the Sable Knight. And thereupon he turned his horse's head and, riding back a certain distance across the level lawn, he took stand in such place as appeared to him to be convenient. And so did King Arthur ride forth also upon that lawn, and take his station as seemed to him to be convenient.

Then each knight dressed his spear and his shield for the encounter, and, having thus made ready for the assault, each shouted to his war-horse and drave his spurs deep into its flank.

Then those two noble steeds rushed forth like lightning, coursing across the ground with such violent speed that the earth trembled and shook beneath them, an it were by cause of an earthquake. So those two knights met fairly in the midst of the center of the field, crashing together like a thunderbolt. And so violently did they smite the one against the other that the spears burst into splinters, even unto the guard and the truncheon thereof,and the horses of the riders staggered back from the onset, so that only because of the extraordinary address of the knights-rider did they recover from falling before that shock of meeting.

But, with great spirit, these two knights uplifted each his horse with his own spirit, and so completed his course in safety.

And indeed King Arthur was very much amazed that he had not overthrown his opponent, for, at that time, as aforesaid, he was considered to be the very best knight and the one best approved in deeds of arms that lived in all of Britain. Wherefore he marvelled at the power and the address of that knight against whom he had driven, that he had not been overthrown by the greatness of the blow that had been delivered against his defences. So, when they met again in the midst of the field, King Arthur gave that knight greeting, and bespoke him with great courtesy, addressing him in this wise: "Sir Knight, I know not who thou art, but I do pledge my knightly word that thou art the most potent knight that ever I have met in all of my life. Now I do bid thee get down straightway from thy horse, and let us two fight this battle with sword and upon foot, for it were pity to let it end in this way."

"Not so," quoth the Sable Knight – "not so, nor until one of us twain be overthrown will I so contest this battle upon foot." And upon this he shouted, "Ho! Ho!" in a very loud voice, and straightway thereupon the gateway of the castle opened and there came running forth two tall esquires clad all in black, pied with crimson. And each of these esquires bare in his hand a great spear of ash-wood, new and well-seasoned, and never yet strained in battle.

So King Arthur chose one of these spears and the Sable Knight took the other, and thereupon each returned to that station wherefrom he had before essayed the encounter.

Then once again each knight rushed his steed to the assault, and once again did each smite so fairly in the midst of the defence of the other that the spears were splintered, so that only the guard and the truncheon thereof remained in the grasp of the knight who held it.

Then, as before, King Arthur would have fought the battle out with swords and upon foot, but again the Sable Knight would not have it so, but called aloud upon those within the castle, whereupon there immediately came forth two other esquires with fresh, new spears of ash-wood. So each knight again took him a spear, and having armed himself therewith, chose each his station upon that fair, level lawn of grass.

And now, for the third time, having thus prepared themselves thereof assault, those two excellent knights hurled themselves together in furious assault. And now, as twice before, did King Arthur strike the Sable Knight so fairly in the centre of his defence that the spear which he held was burst into splinters. But this time, the spear of the Sable Knight did not so break in that manner, but held; and so violent was the blow that he delivered upon King Arthur's shield that he pierced through the center of it. Then the girths of the King's saddle burst apart by that great, powerful blow, and both he and his steed were cast violently backward. So King Arthur might have been overcast, had he not voided his saddle with extraordinary skill and knightly address, wherefore, though his horse was overthrown, he himself still held his footing and did not fall into the dust. Ne'theless, so violent was the blow that he received that, for a little space, he was altogether bereft of his senses so that everything whirled around before his eyes.

But when his sight returned to him he was filled with an anger so vehement that it appeared to him as though all the blood in his heart rushed into his brains so that he saw naught but red, as of blood, before his eyes. And when this also had passed he perceived the Sable Knight that he sat his horse at no great distance. Then immediately King Arthur ran to him and catching the bridle-rein of his horse, he cried out aloud unto that Sable Knight with great violence: "Come down, thou black knight! and fight me upon foot and with thy sword."

"That will I not do," said the Sable Knight, "for, lo! I have overthrown thee. Wherefore deliver thou to me thy shield, that I may hang it upon yonder apple'tree, and go thy way as others have done before thee."

"That will I not!" cried King Arthur, with exceeding passion, "neither will I yield myself nor go hence until either thou or I have altogether conquered the other." Thereupon he thrust the horse of the Sable Knight backward by the bridle-rein so vehemently, that the other was constrained to void his saddle to save himself from being overthrown upon the ground.

And now each knight was as entirely furious as the other, wherefore, each drew his sword and dressed his shield, and thereupon rushed together like two wild bulls in battle. They foined, they smote, they traced, they parried, they struck again and again, and the sound of their blows, crashing and clashing the one upon the other, filled the entire surrounding space with an extraordinary uproar. Nor may any man altogether conceive of the entire fury of that encounter, for, because of the violence of the blows which the one delivered upon the other, whole cantels of armor were hewn from their bodies and many deep and grievous wounds were given and received, so that the armor of each was altogether stained with red because of the blood that flowed down upon it.

At last King Arthur, waxing, as it were, entirely mad, struck so fierce a blow that no armor could have withstood that stroke had it fallen fairly upon it. But it befell with that stroke that his sword broke at the hilt and the blade thereof flew into three several pieces into the air. Yet was the stroke so wonderfully fierce that the Sable Knight groaned, and staggered, and ran about in a circle as though he had gone blind and knew not whither to direct his steps.

But presently he recovered himself again, and perceiving King Arthur standing near by, and not knowing that his enemy had now no sword for to defend himself withal, he cast aside his shield and took his own sword into both hands, and therewith smote so dolorous a stroke that he clave through King Arthur's shield and through his helmet and even to the bone of his brain-pan.

Then King Arthur thought that he had received his death-wound, for his brains swam like water, his thighs trembled exceedingly, and he sank down to his knees, whilst the blood and sweat, commingled together in the darkness of his helmet, flowed down into his eyes in a lather and blinded him. Thereupon, seeing him thus grievously hurt, the Sable Knight called upon him with great vehemence for to yield himself and to surrender his shield, because he was now too sorely wounded for to fight any more.

But King Arthur would not yield himself, but catching the other by the sword-belt, he lifted himself to his feet. Then, being in a manner recovered from his amazement, he embraced the other with both arms, and placing his knee behind the thigh of the Sable Knight, he cast him backward down upon the ground so violently that the sound of the fall was astounding to hear. And with that fall the Sable Knight was, awhile, entirely bereft of consciousness. Then King Arthur straightway unlaced the helm of the Sable Knight and so beheld his face, and he knew him in spite of the blood that still ran down his own countenance in great quantities, and he knew that knight was King Pellinore, aforenamed in this history, who had twice warred against King Arthur. (It hath already been said how King Arthur had driven that other king from the habitations of men and into the forests, so that now he dwelt in this poor gloomy castle whence he waged war against all the knights who came unto that place.)

Now when King Arthur beheld whom it was against whom he had done battle, he cried out aloud, "Ha! Pellinore, is it then thou? Now yield thee to me, for thou art entirely at my mercy." And upon this he drew his misericordia and set the point thereof at King Pellinore's throat.

But by now King Pellinore had greatly recovered from his fall, and perceiving that the blood was flowing down in great measure from out his enemy's helmet, he wist that that other must have been very sorely wounded by the blow which he had just now received. Wherefore he catched King Arthur's wrist in his hand and directed the point of the dagger away from his own throat so that no great danger threatened therefrom.

And, indeed, what with his sore wound and with the loss of blood, King Arthur was now fallen exceedingly sick and faint, so that it appeared to him that he was nigh to death. Accordingly, it was with no very great ado that King Pellinore suddenly heaved himself up from the ground and so overthrew his enemy that King Arthur was now underneath his knees.

And by this King Pellinore was exceedingly mad with the fury of the sore battle he had fought. For he was so enraged that his eyes were all beshot with blood like those of a wild boar, and a froth, like the champings of a wild boar, stood in the beard about his lips. Wherefore he wrenched the dagger out of his enemy's hand, and immediately began to unlace his helm, with intent to slay him where he lay. But at this moment Merlin came in great haste, crying out, "Stay! stay! Sir Pellinore; what would you be at? Stay your sacrilegious hand! For he who lieth beneath you is none other than Arthur, King of all this realm!"

At this King Pellinore was astonished beyond measure. And for a little he was silent, and then after a while he cried out in a very loud voice, "Say you so, old man? Then verily your words have doomed this man unto death. For no one in all this world hath ever suffered such ill and such wrongs as I have suffered at his hands. For, lo! he hath taken from me power, and kingship, and honors, and estates, and hath left me only this gloomy, dismal castle of the forest as an abiding-place. Wherefore, seeing that he is thus in my power, he shall now presently die; if for no other reason than because if I now let him go free, he will certainly revenge himself when he shall have recovered from all the ill he hath suffered at my hands."

Then Merlin said, "Not so! He shall not die at thy hands, for I, myself, shall save him." Whereupon he uplifted his staff and smote King Pellinore across the shoulders. Then immediately King Pellinore fell down and lay upon the ground on his face like one who had suddenly gone dead.

Upon this, King Arthur uplifted himself upon his elbow and beheld his enemy lying there as though dead, and he cried out, "Ha! Merlin! what is this that thou hast done? I am very sorry, for I do perceive that thou, by thy arts of magic, hath slain one of the best knights in all the world."

"Not so, my lord King!" said Merlin; "for, in sooth, I tell thee that thou art far nigher to thy death than he. For he is but in sleep and will soon awaken; but thou art in such a case that it would take only a very little for to cause thee to die."

And indeed King Arthur was exceeding sick, even to the heart, with the sore wound he had received, so that it was only with much ado that Merlin could help him up upon his horse. Having done the which and having hung the King's shield upon the horn of his saddle Merlin straightway conveyed the wounded man thence across the bridge, and, leading the horse by the bridle, so took him away into the forest.

Now I must tell you that there was in that part of the forest a certain hermit so holy that the wild birds of the woodland would come and rest upon his hand whiles he read his breviary; and so sanctified was he in gentleness that the wild does would come even to the door of his hermitage, and there stand whilst he milked them for his refreshment. And this hermit dwelt in that part of the forest so remote from the habitations of man that when he rang the bell for matins or for vespers, there was hardly ever anyone to hear the sound thereof excepting the wild creatures that dwelt thereabout. Yet, ne'theless, to this remote and lonely place royal folk and others of high degree would sometimes come, as though on a pilgrimage, because of the hermit's exceeding saintliness.

So Merlin conveyed King Arthur unto this sanctuary, and, having reached that place, he and the hermit lifted the wounded man down from his saddle – the hermit giving many words of pity and sorrow – and together they conveyed him into the holy man's cell. There they laid him upon a couch of moss and unlaced his armor and searched his wounds and bathed them with pure water and dressed his hurts, for that hermit was a very skilful leech. So for all that day and part of the next, King Arthur lay upon the hermit's pallet like one about to die; for he beheld all things about him as though through thin water, and the breath hung upon his lips and fluttered, and he could not even lift his head from the pallet because of the weakness that lay upon him.

Now upon the afternoon of the second day there fell a great noise and tumult in that part of the forest. For it happened that the Lady Guinevere of Cameliard, together with her Court, both of ladies and of knights, had come upon a pilgrimage to that holy man, the fame of whose saintliness had reached even unto the place where she dwelt. For that lady had a favorite page who was very sick of a fever, and she trusted that the holy man might give her some charm or amulet by the virtue of which he might haply be cured. Wherefore she had come to that place with her entire Court so that all that part of the forest was made gay with fine raiment and the silence thereof was made merry with the sound of talk and laughter and the singing of songs and the chattering of many voices and the neighing of horses. And the Lady Guinevere rode in the midst of her damsels and her Court, and her beauty outshone the beauty of her damsels as the splendor of the morning star outshines that of all the lesser stars that surround it. For then and afterwards she was held by all the Courts of Chivalry to be the most beautiful lady in the world.

Now when the Lady Guinevere had come to that place, she perceived the milk-white war-horse of King Arthur where it stood cropping the green grass of the open glade nigh to the hermitage. And likewise she perceived Merlin, where he stood beside the door of the cell. So of him she demanded whose was that noble war-horse that stood browsing upon the grass at that lonely place, and who was it that lay within that cell. And unto her Merlin made answer, "Lady, he who lieth within is a knight, very sorely wounded, so that he is sick nigh unto death!"

"Pity of Heaven!" cried the Lady Guinevere. "What a sad thing is this that thou tellest me! Now I do beseech thee to lead me presently unto that knight that I may behold him. For I have in my Court a very skilful leech, who is well used to the cure of hurts such as knights receive in battle."

So Merlin brought the lady into the cell, and there she beheld King Arthur where he lay stretched upon the pallet. And she wist not who he was. Yet it appeared to her that in all her life she had not beheld so noble appearing a knight as he who lay sorely wounded in that lonely place. And King Arthur cast his looks upward to where she stood beside his bed of pain, surrounded by her maidens, and in the great weakness that lay upon him he wist not whether she whom he beheld was a mortal lady or whether she was not rather some tall straight angel who had descended from one of the Lordly Courts of Paradise for to visit him in his pain and distresses. And the Lady Guinevere was filled with a great pity at beholding King Arthur's sorrowful estate. Wherefore she called to her that skilful leech who was with her Court. And she bade him bring a certain alabaster box of exceedingly precious balsam. And she commanded him for to search that knight's wounds and to anoint them with the balsam, so that he might be healed of his hurts with all despatch.

So that wise and skilful leech did according to the Lady Guinevere's commands, and immediately King Arthur felt entire ease of all his aches and great content of spirit. And when the Lady and her Court had departed, he found himself much uplifted in heart, and three days thereafter he was entirely healed and was as well and strong and lusty as ever he had been in all of his life.

And this was the first time that King Arthur ever beheld that beautiful lady, the Lady Guinevere of Cameliard, and from that time forth he never forgot her, but she was almost always present in his thoughts. Wherefore, when he was recovered he said thus to himself: "I will forget that I am a king and I will cherish the thought of this lady and will serve her faithfully as a good knight may serve his chosen dame."

And so he did, as ye shall hear later in this book.

## Chapter Third

# How King Arthur Found a Noble Sword

Now, as soon as King Arthur had, by means of that extraordinary balsam, been thus healed of those grievous wounds which he had received in his battle with King Pellinore, he found himself to be moved by a most vehement desire to meet his enemy again for to try issue of battle with him once more, and so recover the credit which he had lost in that combat. Now, upon the morning of the fourth day, being entirely cured, and having broken his fast, he walked for refreshment beside the skirts of the forest, listening the while to the cheerful sound of the wood-birds singing their matins, all with might and main. And Merlin walked beside him, and King Arthur spake his mind to Merlin concerning his intent to engage once more in knightly contest with King Pellinore. And he said, "Merlin, it doth vex me very sorely for me to have come off so ill in my late encounter with King Pellinore. Certes, he is the very best knight in all the world whom I have ever yet encountered. Ne'theless, it might have fared differently with me had I not broken my sword, and so left myself altogether defenceless in that respect. Howsoever that may be, I am of a mind for to assay this adventure once more, and so will I do as immediately as may be."

Thereunto Merlin made reply, "Thou art, assuredly, a very brave man to have so much appetite for battle, seeing how nigh thou camest unto thy death not even four days ago. Yet how mayst thou hope to undertake this adventure without due preparation? For, lo! thou hast no sword, nor hast thou a spear, nor hast thou even thy misericordia for to do battle withal. How then mayst thou hope for to assay this adventure?"

And King Arthur said, "That I know not, nevertheless I will presently seek for some weapon as soon as may be. For, even an I have no better weapon than an oaken cudgel, yet would I assay this battle again with so poor a tool as that."

"Ha! Lord," said Merlin, "I do perceive that thou art altogether fixed in thy purpose for to renew this quarrel. Wherefore, I will not seek to stay thee therefrom, but will do all that in me lies for to aid thee in thy desires. Now to this end I must tell thee that in one part of this forest (which is, indeed, a very strange place) there is a certain woodland sometimes called Arroy, and other times called the Forest of Adventure. For no knight ever entereth therein but some adventure befalleth him. And close to Arroy is a land of enchantment which has several times been seen. And that is a very wonderful land, for there is in it a wide and considerable lake, which is also of enchantment. And in the center of that lake there hath for some time been seen the appearance of a woman's arm – exceedingly beautiful and clad in white samite, and the hand of this arm holdeth a sword of such exceeding excellence and beauty that no eye hath ever beheld its like. And the name of this sword is Excalibur – it being so named by those who have beheld it because of its marvellous brightness and beauty. For it hath come to pass that several knights have already seen that sword and have endeavored to obtain it for their own, but, heretofore, no one hath been able to touch it, and many have lost their lives in that adventure. For when any man draweth near unto it, either he sinks into the lake, or else the arm disappeareth entirely, or else it is withdrawn beneath the lake; wherefore no man hath ever been able to obtain the possession of that sword. Now I am able to conduct thee unto that Lake of Enchantment, and there thou mayst see Excalibur with thine own eyes. Then when thou has seen him thou mayst, haply, have the desire to obtain him; which, an thou art able to do, thou wilt have a sword very fitted for to do battle with."

"Merlin," quoth the King, "this is a very strange thing which thou tellest me. Now I am desirous beyond measure for to attempt to obtain this sword for mine own, wherefore I do beseech thee to lead me with all despatch to this enchanted lake whereof thou tellest me." And Merlin said, "I will do so."

So that morning King Arthur and Merlin took leave of that holy hermit (the King having kneeled in the grass to receive his benediction), and so, departing from that place, they entered the deeper forest once more, betaking their way to that part which was known as Arroy.

And after awhile they came to Arroy, and it was about noon-tide. And when they had entered into those woodlands they came to a certain little open place, and in that place they beheld a white doe with a golden collar about its neck. And King Arthur said, "Look, Merlin, yonder is a wonderful sight." And Merlin said, "Let us follow that doe." And upon this the doe turned and they followed it. And by and by in following it they came to an opening in the trees where was a little lawn of sweet soft grass. Here they beheld a bower and before the bower was a table spread with a fair snow-white cloth, and set with refreshments of white bread, wine, and meats of several sorts. And at the door of this bower there stood a page, clad all in green, and his hair was as black as ebony, and his eyes as black as jet and exceeding bright. And when this page beheld King Arthur and Merlin, he gave them greeting, and welcomed the King very pleasantly saying, "Ha! King Arthur, thou art welcome to this place. Now I prithee dismount and refresh thyself before going farther."

Then was King Arthur a-doubt as to whether there might not be some enchantment in this for to work him an ill, for he was astonished that that page in the deep forest should know him so well. But Merlin bade him have good cheer, and he said, "Indeed, Lord, thou mayst freely partake of that refreshment which, I may tell thee, was prepared especially for thee. Moreover in this thou mayst foretell a very happy issue unto this adventure."

So King Arthur sat down to the table with great comfort of heart (for he was an hungered) and that page and another like unto him ministered unto his needs, serving him all the food upon silver plates, and all the wine in golden goblets as he was used to being served in his own court – only that those things were much more cunningly wrought and fashioned, and were more beautiful than the table furniture of the King's court.

Then, after he had eaten his fill and had washed his hands from a silver basin which the first page offered to him, and had wiped his hands upon a fine linen napkin which the other page brought unto him, and after Merlin had also refreshed himself, they went their way, greatly rejoicing at this pleasant adventure, which, it seemed to the King, could not but betoken a very good issue to his undertaking.

Now about the middle of the afternoon King Arthur and Merlin came, of a sudden, out from the forest and upon a fair and level plain, bedight all over with such a number of flowers that no man could conceive of their quantity nor of the beauty thereof.

And this was a very wonderful land, for, lo! all the air appeared as it were to be as of gold – so bright was it and so singularly radiant. And here and there upon that plain were sundry trees all in blossom; and the fragrance of the blossoms was so sweet that the King had never smelt any fragrance like to it. And in the branches of those trees were a multitude of birds of many colors, and the melody of their singing ravished the heart of the hearer. And midway in the plain was a lake of water as bright as silver, and all around the borders of the lake were incredible numbers of lilies and of daffodils. Yet, although this place was so exceedingly fair, there was, nevertheless, nowhere about it a single sign of human life of any sort, but it appeared altogether as lonely as the hollow sky upon a day of summer. So, because of all the marvellous beauty of this place, and because of its strangeness and its entire solitude, King Arthur perceived that he must have come into a land of powerful enchantment where, happily, dwelt a fairy of very exalted quality; wherefore his spirit was enwrapped in a manner of fear, as he pushed his great milk-white war-horse through that long fair grass, all bedight with flowers, and he wist not what strange things were about to befall him.

So when he had come unto the margin of the lake he beheld there the miracle that Merlin had told him of aforetime. For, lo! in the midst of the expanse of water there was the appearance of a fair and beautiful arm, as of a woman, clad all in white samite. And the arm was encircled with several bracelets of wrought gold; and the hand held a sword of marvellous workmanship aloft in the air above the surface of the water; and neither the arm nor the sword moved so much as a hair's-breadth, but were motionless like to a carven image upon the surface of the lake. And, behold! the sun of that strange land shone down upon the hilt of the sword, and it was of pure gold beset with jewels of several sorts, so that the hilt of the sword and the bracelets that encircled the arm glistered in the midst of the lake like to some singular star of exceeding splendor. And King Arthur sat upon his war-horse and gazed from a distance at the arm and the sword, and he greatly marvelled thereat; yet he wist not how he might come at that sword, for the lake was wonderfully wide and deep, wherefore he knew not how he might come thereunto for to make it his own. And as he sat pondering this thing within himself, he was suddenly aware of a strange lady, who approached him through those tall flowers that bloomed along the margin of the lake. And when he perceived her coming toward him he quickly dismounted from his war-horse and he went forward for to meet her with the bridle-rein over his arm. And when he had come nigh to her, he perceived that she was extraordinarily beautiful, and that her face was like wax for clearness, and that her eyes were perfectly black, and that they were as bright and glistening as though they were two jewels set in ivory. And he perceived that her hair was like silk and as black as it was possible to be, and so long that it reached unto the ground as she walked. And the lady was clad all in green – only that a fine cord of crimson and gold was interwoven into the plaits of her hair. And around her neck there hung a very beautiful necklace of several strands of opal stones and emeralds, set in cunningly wrought gold; and around her wrists were bracelets of the like sort – of opal stones and emeralds set into gold. So when King Arthur beheld her wonderful appearance, that it was like to an ivory statue of exceeding beauty clad all in green, he immediately kneeled before her in the midst of all those flowers as he said, "Lady, I do certainly perceive that thou art no mortal damoiselle, but that thou art Fay. Also that this place, because of its extraordinary beauty, can be no other than some land of Faerie into which I have entered."

And the Lady replied, "King Arthur, thou sayest soothly, for I am indeed Faerie. Moreover, I may tell thee that my name is Nymue, and that I am the chiefest of those Ladies of the Lake of whom thou mayst have heard people speak. Also thou art to know that what thou beholdest yonder as a wide lake is, in truth, a plain like unto this, all bedight with flowers. And likewise thou art to know that in the midst of that plain there standeth a castle of white marble and of ultramarine illuminated with gold. But, lest mortal eyes should behold our dwelling-place, my sisters and I have caused it to be that this appearance as of a lake should extend all over that castle so that it is entirely hidden from sight. Nor may any mortal man cross that lake, saving in one way – otherwise he shall certainly perish therein."

"Lady," said King Arthur, "that which thou tellest me causes me to wonder a very great deal. And, indeed, I am afraid that in coming hitherward I have been doing amiss for to intrude upon the solitude of your dwelling-place."

"Nay, not so, King Arthur," said the Lady of the Lake, "for, in truth, thou art very welcome hereunto. Moreover, I may tell thee that I have a greater friendliness for thee and those noble knights of thy court than thou canst easily wot of. But I do beseech thee of thy courtesy for to tell me what it is that brings thee to our land?"

"Lady," quoth the King, "I will tell thee the entire truth. I fought of late a battle with a certain sable knight, in the which I was sorely and grievously wounded, and wherein I burst my spear and snapped my sword and lost even my misericordia, so that I had not a single thing left me by way of a weapon. In this extremity Merlin, here, told me of Excalibur, and of how he is continually upheld by an arm in the midst of this magical lake. So I came hither and, behold, I find it even as he hath said. Now, Lady, an it be possible, I would fain achieve that excellent sword, that, by means of it I might fight my battle to its entire end."

"Ha! my lord King," said the Lady of the Lake, "that sword is no easy thing for to achieve, and, moreover, I may tell thee that several knights have lost their lives by attempting that which thou has a mind to do. For, in sooth, no man may win yonder sword unless he be without fear and without reproach."

"Alas, Lady!" quoth King Arthur, "that is indeed a sad saying for me. For, though I may not lack in knightly courage, yet, in truth, there be many things wherewith I do reproach myself withal. Ne'theless, I would fain attempt this thing, even an it be to my great endangerment. Wherefore, I prithee tell me how I may best undertake this adventure."

"King Arthur," said the Lady of the Lake, "I will do what I say to aid thee in thy wishes in this matter." Whereupon she lifted a single emerald that hung by a small chain of gold at her girdle and, lo! the emerald was cunningly carved into the form of a whistle. And she set the whistle to her lips and blew upon it very shrilly. Then straightway there appeared upon the water, a great way off, a certain thing that shone very brightly. And this drew near with great speed, and as it came nigh, behold! it was a boat all of carven brass. And the prow of the boat was carved into the form of a head of a beautiful woman, and upon either side were wings like the wings of a swan. And the boat moved upon the water like a swan – very swiftly – so that long lines, like to silver threads, stretched far away behind, across the face of the water, which otherwise was like unto glass for smoothness. And when the brazen boat had reached the bank it rested there and moved no more.

Then the Lady of the Lake bade King Arthur to enter the boat, and so he entered it. And immediately he had done so, the boat moved away from the bank as swiftly as it had come thither. And Merlin and the Lady of the Lake stood upon the margin of the water, and gazed after King Arthur and the brazen boat.

And King Arthur beheld that the boat floated swiftly across the lake to where was the arm uplifting the sword, and that the arm and the sword moved not but remained where they were.

Then King Arthur reached forth and took the sword in his hand, and immediately the arm disappeared beneath the water, and King Arthur held the sword and the scabbard thereof and the belt thereof in his hand and, lo! they were his own.

Then verily his heart swelled with joy an it would burst within his bosom, for Excalibur was an hundred times more beautiful than he had thought possible. Wherefore his heart was nigh breaking for pure joy at having obtained that magic sword.

Then the brazen boat bore him very quickly back to the land again and he stepped ashore where stood the Lady of the Lake and Merlin. And when he stood upon the shore, he gave the Lady great thanks beyond measure for all that she had done for to aid him in his great undertaking; and she gave him cheerful and pleasing words in reply.

Then King Arthur saluted the lady, as became him, and, having mounted his war-horse, and Merlin having mounted his palfrey, they rode away thence upon their business – the King's heart still greatly expanded with pure delight at having for his own that beautiful sword – the most beautiful and the most famous sword in all the world.

That night King Arthur and Merlin abided with the holy hermit at the forest sanctuary, and when the next morning had come (the King having bathed himself in the ice-cold forest fountain, and being exceedingly refreshed thereby) they took their departure, offering thanks to that saintly man for the harborage he had given them.

Anon, about noon-tide, they reached the valley of the Sable Knight, and there were all things appointed exactly as when King Arthur had been there before: to wit, that gloomy castle, the lawn of smooth grass, the apple-tree covered with shields, and the bridge whereon hung that single shield of sable.

"Now, Merlin," quoth King Arthur, "I do this time most strictly forbid thee for to interfere in this quarrel. Nor shalt thou, under pain of my displeasure, exert any of thy arts of magic in my behalf. So hearken thou to what I say, and heed it with all possible diligence."

Thereupon, straightway, the King rode forth upon the bridge and, seizing the brazen mall, he smote upon the sable shield with all his might and main. Immediately the portcullis of the castle was let fall as afore told, and, in the same manner as that other time, the Sable Knight rode forth therefrom, already bedight and equipped for the encounter. So he came to the bridge-head and there King

Arthur spake to him in this wise: "Sir Pellinore, we do now know each other entirely well, and each doth judge that he hath cause of quarrel with the other: thou, that I, for mine own reasons as seemed to me to be fit, have taken away from thee thy kingly estate, and have driven thee into this forest solitude: I, that thou has set thyself up here for to do injury and affront to knights and lords and other people of this kingdom of mine. Wherefore, seeing that I am here as an errant Knight, I do challenge thee for to fight with me, man to man, until either thou or I have conquered the other."

Unto this speech King Pellinore bowed his head in obedience, and thereupon he wheeled his horse, and, riding to some little distance, took his place where he had afore stood. And King Arthur also rode to some little distance, and took his station where he had afore stood. At the same time there came forth from the castle one of those tall pages clad all in sable, pied with crimson, and gave to King Arthur a good, stout spear of ash-wood, well seasoned, and untried in battle; and when the two Knights were duly prepared, they shouted and drave their horses together, the one smiting the other so fairly in the midst of his defences that the spears shivered in the hand of each, bursting all into small splinters as they had aforetime done.

Then each of these two knights immediately voided his horse with great skill and address, and drew each his sword. And thereupon they fell to at a combat, so furious and so violent, that two wild bulls upon the mountains could not have engaged in a more desperate encounter.

But now, having Excalibur for to aid him in his battle, King Arthur soon overcame his enemy. For he gave him several wounds and yet received none himself, nor did he shed a single drop of blood in all that fight, though his enemy's armor was in a little while all stained with crimson. And at last King Arthur delivered so vehement a stroke that King Pellinore was entirely benumbed thereby, wherefore his sword and his shield fell down from their defence, his thighs trembled beneath him and he sank unto his knees upon the ground, Then he called upon King Arthur to have mercy, saying, "Spare my life and I will yield myself unto thee."

And King Arthur said, "I will spare thee and I will do more than that. For now that thou hast yielded thyself unto me, lo! I will restore unto thee thy power and estate. For I bear no ill-will toward thee, Pellinore, ne'theless, I can brook no rebels against my power in this realm. For, as God judges me, I do declare that I hold singly in my sight the good of the people of my kingdom. Wherefore, he who is against me is also against them, and he who is against them is also against me. But now that thou hast acknowledged me I will take thee into my favor. Only as a pledge of thy good faith toward me in the future, I shall require it of thee that thou shalt send me as hostage of thy good-will, thy two eldest sons, to wit: Sir Aglaval and Sir Lamorack. Thy younger son, Dornar, thou mayest keep with thee for thy comfort.

So those two young knights above mentioned came to the Court of King Arthur, and they became very famous knights, and by and by were made fellows in great honor of the Round Table.

And King Arthur and King Pellinore went together into the castle of King Pellinore, and there King Pellinore's wounds were dressed and he was made comfortable. That night King Arthur abode in the castle of King Pellinore, and when the next morning had come, he and Merlin returned unto the Court of the King, where it awaited him in the forest at that place where he had established it.

Now King Arthur took very great pleasure unto himself as he and Merlin rode together in return through that forest; for it was the leafiest time of all the year, what time the woodlands decked themselves in their best apparel of clear, bright green. Each bosky dell and dingle was full of the perfume of the thickets, and in every tangled depth the small bird sang with all his might and main, and as though he would burst his little throat with the melody of his singing. And the ground beneath the horses' feet was so soft with fragrant moss that the ear could not hear any sound of hoof-beats upon the earth. And the bright yellow sunlight came down through the leaves so that all the ground was scattered over with a great multitude of trembling circles as of pure yellow gold. And, anon, that sunlight would fall down upon the armed knight as he rode, so that every little while his armor appeared to catch fire with a great glory, shining like a sudden bright star amid the dark shadows of the woodland.

So it was that King Arthur took great joy in that forest land, for he was without ache or pain of any sort and his heart was very greatly elated with the wonderfulness of the success of that adventure into which he had entered. For in that adventure he had not only won a very bitter enemy into a friend who should be of great usefulness and satisfaction to him, but likewise, he had obtained for himself a sword, the like of which the world had never before beheld. And whenever he would think of that singularly splendid sword which now hung by his side, and whenever he remembered that land of Faëry into which he had wandered, and of that which had befallen him therein, his heart would become so greatly elated with pure joyousness that he hardly knew how to contain himself because of the great delight that filled his entire bosom.

And, indeed, I know of no greater good that I could wish for you in all of your life than to have you enjoy such happiness as cometh to one when he hath done his best endeavor and hath succeeded with great entirety in his undertaking. For then all the world appears to be filled as with a bright shining light, and the body seemeth to become so elated that the feet are uplifted from heaviness and touch the earth very lightly because of the lightness of the spirit within. Wherefore, it is, that if I could have it in my power to give you the very best that the world hath to give, I would wish that you might win your battle as King Arthur won his battle at that time, and that you might ride homeward in such triumph and joyousness as filled him that day, and that the sunlight might shine around you as it shone around him, and that the breezes might blow and that all the little birds might sing with might and main as they sang for him, and that your heart also might sing its song of rejoicing in the pleasantness of the world in which you live.

Now as they rode thus through the forest together, Merlin said to the King: "Lord, which wouldst thou rather have, Excalibur, or the sheath that holds him?" To which King Arthur replied, "Ten thousand times would I rather have Excalibur than his sheath." "In that thou art wrong, my Lord," said Merlin, "for let me tell thee, that though Excalibur is of so great a temper that he may cut in twain either a feather or a bar of iron, yet is his sheath of such a sort that he who wears it can suffer no wound in battle, neither may he lose a single drop of blood. In witness whereof, thou mayst remember that, in thy late battle with King Pellinore, thou didst suffer no wound, neither didst thou lose any blood."

Then King Arthur directed a countenance of great displeasure upon his companion and he said, "Now, Merlin, I do declare that thou hast taken from me the entire glory of that battle which I have lately fought. For what credit may there be to any knight who fights his enemy by means of enchantment such as thou tellest me of? And, indeed, I am minded to take this glorious sword back to that magic lake and to cast it therein where it belongeth; for I believe that a knight should fight by means of his own strength, and not by means of magic."

"My Lord," said Merlin, "assuredly thou art entirely right in what thou holdest. But thou must bear in mind that thou art not as an ordinary errant knight, but that thou art a King, and that thy life belongeth not unto thee, but unto thy people. Accordingly thou hast no right to imperil it, but shouldst do all that lieth in thy power for to preserve it. Wherefore thou shouldst keep that sword so that it may safeguard thy life."

Then King Arthur meditated that saying for a long while in silence; and when he spake it was in this wise: "Merlin, thou art right in what thou sayest, and, for the sake of my people, I will keep both Excalibur for to fight for them, and likewise his sheath for to preserve my life for their sake. Ne'theless, I will never use him again saving in serious battle." And King Arthur held to that saying, so that thereafter he did no battle in sport excepting with lance and a-horseback.

King Arthur kept Excalibur as the chiefest treasure of all his possessions. For he said to himself, "Such a sword as this is fit for a king above other kings and a lord above other lords. Now, as God hath seen fit for to intrust that sword into my keeping in so marvellous a manner as fell about, so must He mean that I am to be His servant for to do unusual things. Wherefore I will treasure this noble weapon not more for its excellent worth than because it shall be unto me as a sign of those great things that God, in His mercy, hath evidently ordained for me to perform for to do Him service."

So King Arthur had made for Excalibur a strong chest or coffer, bound around with many bands of wrought iron, studded all over with great nails of iron, and locked with three great padlocks. In this strong-box he kept Excalibur lying upon a cushion of crimson silk and wrapped in swathings of fine linen, and very few people ever beheld the sword in its glory excepting when it shone like a sudden flame in the uproar of battle.

For when the time came for King Arthur to defend his realm or his subjects from their enemies, then he would take out the sword, and fasten it upon the side of his body; and when he did so he was like unto a hero of God girt with a blade of shining lightning. Yea; at such times Excalibur shone with so terrible a brightness that the very sight thereof would shake the spirits of every wrong-doer with such great fear that he would, in a manner, suffer the pangs of death ere ever the edge of the blade had touched his flesh.

So King Arthur treasured Excalibur and the sword remained with him for all of his life, wherefore the name of Arthur and Excalibur are one. So, I believe that that sword is the most famous of any that ever was seen or heard tell of in all the Courts of Chivalry.

As for the sheath of the blade, King Arthur lost that through the treachery of one who should, by rights, have been his dearest friend (as you shall hear of anon), and in the end the loss of that miraculous sheath brought it about that he suffered a very great deal of pain and sorrow.

All that also you shall read of, God willing, in due season.

So endeth the story of the winning of Excalibur, and may God give unto you in your life, that you may have His truth to aid you, like a shining sword, for to overcome your enemies; and may He give you Faith (for Faith containeth Truth as a scabbard containeth its sword), and may that Faith heal all your wounds of sorrow as the sheath of Excalibur healed all the wounds of him who wore that excellent weapon. For with Truth and Faith girded upon you, you shall be as well able to fight all your battles as did that noble hero of old, whom men called King Arthur.

PART III

# THE WINNING OF A QUEEN

*So, having told you how King Arthur obtained that very excellent sword, Excalibur, for a weapon of defence, I shall now presently recount sundry other noble and knightly adventures whereby he won for himself a most beautiful and gentle lady for his Queen.*

*For, though all the world is very well acquainted with the renown of that perfectly gracious dame, the Lady Guinevere, yet I do not think that the whole story of those adventures by the which King Arthur won her good favor hath ever yet been told.*

*So as the matter hereinafter to be related contains not only the narrative of that affair, but also the account of a certain enchanted disguise which King Arthur assumed for his purposes, as well as sundry adventures of very knightly daring which he undertook, I have great hope that he who reads what I have written shall find it both an agreeable and an entertaining history.*

## Chapter First

# How King Arthur Disguised Himself for a Certain Purpose

Now, upon a certain day King Arthur proclaimed a high feast, which was held at Carleon upon Usk. Many noble guests were bidden, and an exceedingly splendid Court gathered at the King's castle. For at that feast there sat seven kings and five queens in royal state, and there were high lords and beautiful ladies of degree, to the number of three score and seven; and there were a multitude of those famous knights of the King's Court who were reckoned the most renowned in arms in all of Christendom. And of all this great gathering of kings, lords, and knights, not one man looked askance at his neighbor, but all were united in good fellowship. Wherefore, when the young King looked about him and beheld such peace and amity among all these noble lords where, aforetime, had been discord and ill-regard: "Certes," quoth he to himself, "it is wonderful how this reign of mine hath knit men together in kindness and good fellowship!" And because of such thoughts as these, his spirit took wings like unto a bird and sang within him.

Now while the King said: "Speak, and tell me, what is thy message?"

To which the herald made reply: "I come from King Leodegrance of Cameliard, who is in sore trouble. For thus it is: His enemy and thine enemy, King Ryence of North Wales (he who at one time in contempt of thee commanded thee to send him thy beard for to trim his mantle), doth make sundry demands of my master, King

Leodegrance, which demands King Leodegrance is altogether loath to fulfil. And King Ryence of North Wales threateneth to bring war into Cameliard because King Leodegrance doth not immediately fulfil those demands. Now King Leodegrance hath no such array of knights and armed men as he one time had gathered about him for to defend his kingdom against assault. For, since thou in thy majesty hath brought peace to this realm and hath reduced the power of all those kings under thee, those knights who once made the Court of King Leodegrance so famous have gone elsewhither for to seek better opportunities for their great valor and prowess at arms than his peaceful Court may afford. Wherefore my master, King Leodegrance, doth beseech aid of thee, who art his King and Overlord."

To these things that the herald-messenger said, King Arthur, and all that Court that feasted with him, listened in entire silence. And the King's countenance, which erstwhiles had been expanded with cheerfulness, became overcast and dark with anger. "Ha!" he cried, "this is, verily, no good news that thou hast brought hither to our feast. Now I will give what aid I am able to thy master, King Leodegrance, in this extremity, and that right speedily. But tell me, sir herald, what things are they that King Ryence demandeth of thy master?"

"That I will tell you, Lord," quoth the herald-messenger. "Firstly, King Ryence maketh demand upon my master of a great part of those lands of Cameliard that march upon the borders of North Wales. Secondly, he maketh demand that the Lady Guinevere, the King's daughter, be delivered in marriage unto Duke Mordaunt of North Umber, who is of kin unto King Ryence, and that Duke, though a mighty warrior, is so evil of appearance, and so violent of temper, that I believe that there is not his like for ugliness or for madness of humor in all of the world."

Now when King Arthur heard this that the messenger said he was immediately seized with an extraordinary passion of anger. For his eyes appeared, an it were, to shoot forth sparks of pure light, his face flamed like fire, and he ground his teeth together like the stones of a quern. Then he immediately rose from the chair where he sat and went forth from that place, and all those who beheld his anger shuddered thereat and turned their eyes away from his countenance.

Then King Arthur went into an inner room of the castle by himself, and there he walked up and down for a great while, and in that time no one of his household dared to come nigh to him. And the reason of the King's wrath was this: that ever since he had lain wounded and sick nigh unto death in the forest, he bare in mind how the Lady Guinevere had suddenly appeared before him like some tall, straight, shining angel who had descended unto him out of Paradise – all full of pity, and exceedingly beautiful. Wherefore, at thought of that wicked, mad Duke Mordaunt of North Umber making demand unto marriage with her, he was seized with a rage so violent that it shook his spirit like a mighty wind.

So, for a long while, he walked up and down in his wrath as aforesaid, and no one durst come nigh unto him, but all stood afar off, watching him from a distance.

Then, after a while, he gave command that Merlin, and Sir Ulfius, and Sir Kay should come to him at that place where he was. And when they had come thither he talked to them for a considerable time, bidding Merlin for to make ready to go upon a journey with him, and bidding Sir Ulfius and Sir Kay for to gather together a large army of chosen knights and armed men, and to bring that army straightway into those parts coadjacent to the royal castle of Tintagalon, which same standeth close to the borders of North Wales and of Cameliard.

So Sir Ulfius and Sir Kay went about to do as King Arthur commanded, and Merlin also went about to do as he commanded; and the next day King Arthur and Merlin, together with certain famous knights of the King's Court who were the most approved at arms of all those about him – to wit, Sir Gawaine, and Sir Ewaine (who were nephews unto the King), and Sir Pellias and Sir Geraint, the son of Erbin – set forth for Tintagalon across the forest-land of Usk.

So they travelled for all that day and a part of the next, and that without adventure or misadventure of any sort. So they came, at last, to that large and noble castle, hight Tintagalon, which guards the country bordering upon Cameliard and North Wales. Here King Arthur was received with great rejoicing; for whithersoever the King went the people loved him very dearly. Wherefore the folk of Tintagalon were very glad when he came unto them.

Now the morning after King Arthur had come unto Tintagalon (the summer night having been very warm), he and Merlin were glad to arise betimes to go abroad for to enjoy the dewy freshness of the early daytime. So, in the cool of the day, they walked together in the garden (which was a very pleasant place), and beneath the shadow of a tall, straight tower. And all around about were many trees with a good shade, where the little birds sang sweetly in the cheerfulness of the summer weather.

And here King Arthur opened his mind very freely to Merlin, and he said: "Merlin, I do believe that the Lady Guinevere is the fairest lady in all of the world; wherefore my heart seems ever to be entirely filled with love for her, and that to such a degree that I think of her continually by day (whether I be eating, or drinking, or walking, or sitting still, or going about my business), and likewise I dream of her many times at night. And this has been the case with me, Merlin, ever since a month ago, when I lay sick in that hermit's cell in the forest, what time she came and stood beside me like a shining angel out of Paradise. So I am not willing that any other man than I should have her for his wife.

"Now I know very well that thou art wonderfully cunning in those arts of magic that may change a man in his appearance so that even those who know him best may not recognize him. Wherefore I very greatly desire it of thee that thou wilt so disguise me that I may go, unknown of any man, into Cameliard, and that I may dwell there in such a way that I may see the Lady Guinevere every day. For I tell thee very truly that I greatly desire to behold her in such a wise that she may not be in any way witting of my regard. Likewise I would fain see for myself how great may be the perils that encompass King Leodegrance – the King being my right good friend."

"My Lord King," said Merlin, "it shall be as thou desirest, and this morning I will cause thee to be so disguised that no one in all the world shall be able to know thee who thou art."

So that morning, a little before the prime, Merlin came unto the King where he was and gave him a little cap. And the cap was of such a sort that when the King set it upon his head he assumed, upon the instant, the appearance of a rude and rustic fellow from the country-side. Then the King commanded that a jerkin of rough frieze should be brought to him, and with this he covered his royal and knightly vestments, and with it he hid that golden collar and its jewel, pendent, which he continually wore about his neck. Then, setting the cup upon his head, he assumed at once the guise of that peasant hind.

Whereupon, being thus entirely disguised, he quitted Tintagalon unknown of any man, and took his way a-foot unto the town of Cameliard.

Now toward the slanting of the day he drew nigh to that place, and lo! he beheld before him a large and considerable town of many comely houses with red walls and shining windows. And the houses of the town sat all upon a high, steep hill, the one overlooking the other, and the town itself was encompassed around about by a great wall, high and strong. And a great castle guarded the town, and the castle had very many towers and roofs. And all round about the tower were many fair gardens and lawns and meadows, and several orchards and groves of trees with thick and pleasing shade. Now at that time of the day the sky behind the tower was all, as it were, an entire flame of fire, so that the towers and the battlements of the castle and the roofs and the chimneys thereof stood altogether black against the brightness of the light. And, behold! great flocks of pigeons encircled the towers of the castle in a continual flight against that fiery sky. So, because King Arthur was a-weary with walking for all that day, it appeared to him that he had hardly ever beheld in all of his life so fair and pleasing a place as that excellent castle with its gardens and lawns and groves of trees.

Thus came King Arthur unto the castle of Cameliard, in the guise of a poor peasant from the country-side, and no man in all of the world knew him who he was.

So, having reached the castle, he made inquiries for the head gardener thereof; and when he had speech with the gardener he besought him that he might be taken into service into that part of the garden that appertained to the dwelling-place of the Lady Guinevere. Then the gardener looked upon him and saw that he was tall and strong and well framed, wherefore he liked him very well and took him into service even as he desired.

And thus it was that King Arthur of Britain became a gardener's boy at Cameliard.

Now the King was very glad to be in that garden; for in this pleasant summer season the Lady Guinevere came every day to walk with her damsels among the flowers, and King Arthur, all disguised as a peasant gardener boy, beheld her very many times when she came thither.

So King Arthur abode at that place for above a week, and he took no care that in all that time he enjoyed none of his kingly estate, but was only gardener's boy in the castle garden of Cameliard.

Now it happened upon a day when the weather was very warm, that one of the damsels who was in attendance upon the Lady Guinevere, arose all in the early morning whiles the air was still cool and refreshing. So, leaving the Lady Guinevere still sleeping, this damsel, whose name was Mellicene of the White Hand, went into the ante-room and, opening the casement thereof, looked forth into that garden of roses which adjoined the Lady Guinevere's bower.

Now there was at that place a carven marble figure of a youth, holding in his arms a marble ewer, and a fountain of water, as clear as crystal, flowed out from the ewer into a basin of marble. And the figure, and the fountain, and the marble basin into which the fountain flowed lay beneath the shadow of a linden-tree. And all around was a thick growth of roses, so that the place was entirely hidden, saving only from those windows of the castle that were above.

So it befell that as the damsel looked down thitherward out of the window, she beheld a very wonderful sight. For, lo! a strange knight kneeled beside the fountain and bathed his face and his bosom in the crystal water thereof. And the damsel saw that the sunlight fell down through the leaves of the linden-tree and lay upon that strange knight. And she perceived that his hair and his beard were of the color of red gold – shining surpassingly in the brightness of the morning. And she beheld that his brow and his throat and his bosom were white like alabaster. And she beheld that around his neck and shoulders there hung a golden collar of marvellous beauty, so that when the sunlight shone upon it it flashed like pure lightning.

So, beholding this strange appearance – as it were a vision – the damsel Mellicene stood for a long while, all entranced with wonder and with pleasure, and wist not whether that which she saw was a dream or no dream, nor whether he who sat there was a spirit, or whether he was a man of flesh and blood.

Then, by and by, recovering somewhat from her astonishment, she withdrew herself softly from the casement, and, turning about, ran fleetly down the turret stairs, and so came out thence into that fair and blooming garden at the foot of the tower. So she ran through the garden with all speed and silence, and thus came down an alley-way and to the marble fountain and the linden-trees and the rose-trees around about where she had anon beheld that strange knight bathing himself in the crystal waters.

But King Arthur had heard the coming of that damsel, and had speedily set the cap upon his head again. So that when the damsel Mellicene came thither, she found no one by the fountain but the gardener's boy. Of him she demanded: "Who art thou, fellow? And why sittest thou here by the fountain?"

And unto her he replied: "I am the gardener's lad who came a short time ago to take service at this place."

"Then tell me, fellow," quoth she, "and tell me truly. Who was that young knight who was here beside the fountain but now, and whither hath he gone?" "Lady, whereunto," he said, "there has been no one at this fountain this day, but only I."

"Nay, fellow," she cried, "thou art deceiving me, for I do assure thee that with mine own eyes I beheld but now, where a strange young knight sat bathing himself in the waters of this fountain." And the gardener's boy said, "Lady, that which I have told you is the very truth, for indeed there hath no one been here this morn but only I. Wherefore, an thou deemst thou hast seen anyone else, thou art certainly mistaken."

At this the damsel set her look upon him, in great perplexity. Likewise, she marvelled very greatly, for she could not altogether disbelieve him. Not yet could she entirely believe him either, because her eyes had beheld that which she had beheld, and she wotted that she had not been mistaken. Therefore she knew not what to think, and, because of her perplexity, she felt a very great displeasure at that gardener's boy. "Truly, wherefore," she said, "if thou art deceiving me, I shall certainly cause thee to suffer a great deal of pain, for I shall have thee whipped with cords." Thereupon she turned and went away from that place, much marvelling at that strange thing, and wondering what it all signified.

That morning she told unto the Lady Guinevere all that she had seen, but the Lady Guinevere only laughed at her and mocked her, telling her that she had been asleep and dreaming, when she beheld that vision. And, indeed, the damsel herself had begun to think this must be the case. Nevertheless, she thereafter looked out every morning from her casement window, albeit she beheld nothing for a great while, for King Arthur came not soon to that place again.

So, by and by, there befell another certain morning when she looked out of the casement and, lo! there sat that strange knight by the fountain once more as he had aforetime sat. And he bathed his face and his bosom in the water as he had aforetime done. And he appeared as comely and as noble as he had appeared before; and his hair and his young beard shone like gold as they had shone before in the sun. And this time she beheld that his collar of gold lay upon the brink of the fountain beside him, and it sparkled with great splendor in the sunlight the whiles he bathed his bosom. Then, after that damsel had regarded him for a considerable time, she ran with all speed to the chamber where the Lady Guinevere still lay, and she cried in a loud voice, "Lady! lady! arouse thee and come with me! For, lo! that same young knight whom I beheld before, is even now bathing himself at the fountain under the linden-tree."

Then the Lady Guinevere, greatly marvelling, aroused herself right quickly, and, dighting herself with all speed, went with the damsel unto that casement window which looked out into that part of the garden.

And there she herself beheld the young knight where he laved himself at the fountain. And she saw that his hair and his beard shone like gold in the sunlight; and she saw that his undervestment was of purple linen threaded with gold; and she saw that beside him lay that cunningly wrought collar of gold inset with many jewels of various colors, and the collar shone with great splendor where it lay upon the marble verge of the fountain.

Somewhiles she gazed, exceedingly astonished; then she commanded the damsel Mellicene for to come with her, and therewith she turned and descended the turret stairs, and went quickly out into the garden, as her damsel had done aforetime. Then, as that damsel had done, she straightway hastened with all speed down the alley-way toward the fountain.

But, behold! when she had come there, she found no young knight, but only the gardener boy, exactly as had happened with the damsel Mellicene aforetime. For King Arthur had heard her coming, and had immediately put that enchanted cap upon his head. Then the Lady Guinevere marvelled very greatly to find there only the gardener's boy, and she wist not what to think of so strange a thing. Wherefore she demanded of him, even as Mellicene had done, whither had gone the young knight whom she had beheld anon there at the fountain. And unto her the gardener lad made answer as aforetime: "Lady! there hath been no one at this place at any time this morning, but only I."

Now when King Arthur had donned his cap at the coming of the Lady, he had, in his great haste, forgotten his golden collar, and this Guinevere beheld where it lay shining very brightly, beside the margin of the fountain. "How now!" quoth she. "Wouldst thou dare to make a mock of me? Now tell me, thou fellow, do gardeners' boys in the land whence thou didst come wear golden collars about their necks like unto that collar that lieth yonder beside the fountain? Now, an I had thee well whipped, it would be thy rightful due. But take thou that bauble yonder and give it unto him to whom it doth rightfully belong, and tell him from me that it doth ill become a true belted knight for to hide himself away in the privy gardens of a lady." Then turned she with the damsel Mellicene, and left she that place and went back again into her bower.

Yet, indeed for all that day, as she sat over her 'broidery, she did never cease to marvel and to wonder how it was possible that that strange young knight should so suddenly have vanished away and left only the poor gardener's boy in his stead. Nor, for a long time, might she unriddle that strange thing.

Then, of a sudden, at that time when the heat of the day was sloping toward the cooler part of the afternoon, she aroused herself because of a thought that had come in an instant unto her. So she called the damsel Mellicene to come to her, and she bade her to go and tell the gardener's lad for to fetch her straightway a basket of fresh roses for to adorn her tower chamber.

So Mellicene went and did as she bade, and after considerable time the gardener's lad came bearing a great basket of roses. And, lo! he wore his cap upon his head. And all the damsels in waiting upon the Lady Guinevere, when they saw how he wore his cap in her presence, cried out upon him, and Mellicene of the White Hand demanded of him: "What! How now, Sir boor! Dost thou know so little of what is due unto a king's daughter that thou dost wear thy cap even in the presence of the Lady

Guinevere? Now I bid thee straightway to take thy cap off thy head."

And to her King Arthur made answer: "Lady, I cannot take off my cap."

Quoth the Lady Guinevere: "And why canst thou not take off thy cap, thou surly fellow?"

"Lady," said he, "I cannot take off my cap, because I have an ugly place upon my head."

"Then wear thy cap," quoth the Lady Guinevere. "Only fetch thou the roses unto me."

And so at her bidding, he brought the roses to her. But when he had come nigh unto the lady, she, of a sudden, snatched at the cap and plucked it off from his head. Then, lo! he was upon the instant transformed; for instead of the gardener's boy there stood before the Lady Guinevere and her damsel the appearance of a noble young knight with hair and beard like threads of gold. Then he let fall his basket of roses so that the flowers were scattered all over the floor, and he stood and looked at all who were there. And some of those damsels in attendance upon the Lady Guinevere shrieked, and others stood still from pure amazement and wist not how to believe what their eyes beheld. But not one of those ladies knew that he whom she beheld was King Arthur. Nevertheless the Lady Guinevere remembered that this was the knight whom she had found so sorely wounded, lying in the hermit's cell in the forest.

Then she laughed and flung him back his cap again. "Take thy cap," quoth she, "and go thy ways, thou gardener's boy who hath an ugly place upon his head." Thus she said because she was minded to mock him.

But King Arthur did not reply to her, but straightway, with great sobriety of aspect, set his cap upon his head again. So resuming his humble guise once more, he turned and quitted that place, leaving those roses scattered all over the floor even as they had fallen.

And after that time, whenever the Lady Guinevere would come upon the gardener's lad in the garden, she would say unto her damsel in such a voice that he might hear her speech: "Lo! yonder is the gardener's lad who hath an ugly place upon his head so that he must always wear his cap for to hide it."

Thus she spake openly, mocking at him; but privily she bade her damsels to say naught concerning these things, but to keep unto themselves all those things which had befallen.

## CHAPTER SECOND

# HOW KING ARTHUR FOUGHT WITH THE DUKE OF NORTH UMBER

Now, upon a certain day at this time there came a messenger to the Court of King Leodegrance, with news that King Ryence of North Wales and Duke Mordaunt of North Umber were coming thither and that they brought with them a very noble and considerable Court of knights and lords. At this news King Leodegrance was much troubled in spirit, for he wist not what such a visit might betoken; and yet he greatly feared that it boded ill for him. So on that day when King Ryence and the Duke of North Umber appeared before the castle, King Leodegrance went forth to greet them and they three met together in the meadows that lie beneath the castle walls of Cameliard.

There King Leodegrance bade those others welcome in such manner as was fitting, desiring them that they should come into the castle with him so that he might entertain them according to their degree.

But to this courtesy upon the part of King Leodegrance, King Ryence deigned no pleasing reply. "Nay," quoth he, "we go not with thee into thy castle, King Leodegrance, until we learn whether thou art our friend or our enemy. For just now we are, certes, no such good friends with thee that we care to sit down at thy table and eat of thy salt. Nor may we be aught but enemies of thine until thou hast first satisfied our demands; to wit, that thou givest to me those lands which I demand of thee and that thou givest unto my cousin, Duke Mordaunt of North Umber, the Lady Guinevere to be his wife. In these matters thou hast it in thy power to make us either thy friends or thine enemies. Wherefore we shall abide here, outside of thy castle, for five days, in the which time thou mayst frame thine answer, and so we may know whether we shall be friends or enemies."

"And in the meantime," quoth Duke Mordaunt of North Umber, "I do hold myself ready for to contest my right unto the hand of the Lady Guinevere with any knight of thy Court who hath a mind to deny my just title thereto; and if thou hast no knight in all thy Court who can successfully assay a bout of arms with me, thou thyself canst hardly hope to succeed in defending thyself against that great army of knights whom King Ryence hath gathered together to bring against thee in case thou denyest us that which we ask."

Then was King Leodegrance exceedingly cast down in his spirits, for he feared those proud lords and he wist not what to say in answer to them. Wherefore he turned and walked back into his castle again, beset with great anxiety and sorrow of spirit. And King Ryence, and Duke Mordaunt and their Court of lords and knights pitched their pavilions in those meadows over against the castle, so that the plain was entirely covered with those pavilions. And there they took up their inn with great rejoicing and with the sound of feasting and singing and merry-making, for it was an exceeding noble Court King Ryence had gathered about him.

And when the next morning had come Duke Mordaunt of North Umber went forth clad all in armor of proof. And he rode up and down the field before the castle and gave great challenge to those within; daring any knight to come forth for to meet him in knightly encounter. "Ho!" he cried, "how now, ye Knights of Cameliard! Is there no one to come forth to meet me? How then may ye hope to contend with the Knights of North Wales, an ye fear to meet with one single Knight from North Umber?" So he scoffed at them in his pride, and none dared to come forth from Cameliard against him. For the Duke of North Umber was one of the most famous knights of his day, and one of exceeding strength and success at arms, and there was now, in these times of peace, no one of King Leodegrance's Court who was at all able to face a warrior of his approved skill and valor. Wherefore, no one took up that challenge which the Duke of North Umber gave to the Court of Cameliard. Meantime many people gathered upon the walls of Cameliard and gazed down therefrom upon that proud and haughty duke, all bedight in his splendid armor, and all were grieved and ashamed that there was no one in that peaceful town to go out against him. And all the lords and knights of King Ryence's Court came and stood in front of the King's pavilion and laughed and clapped their hands together, and cheered Duke Mordaunt, as he so rode up and down before them. And the greater they were expanded with mirth, the more abashed were the people of Cameliard. "Ho! Ho!" cried that proud Duke. "How now! Will no one come forth to meet me? How then may ye of Cameliard hope to face the King of North Wales and all his knightly array of which I am but one man?" And the people of Cameliard, gathered upon the walls, listened to him with shame and sorrow.

Now all this while King Arthur digged in the garden; but, nevertheless, he was well aware of everything that passed and of how that the Duke of North Umber rode up and down so proudly before the castle walls. So, of a sudden, it came to him that he could not abide this any longer. Wherefore he laid aside his spade and went out secretly by a postern way, and so up into the town.

Now there was in Cameliard an exceedingly rich merchant, by name Ralph of Cardiff, and the renown of his possessions and his high estate had reached even unto King Arthur's ears at Carleon. Accordingly it was unto his house that King Arthur directed his steps.

And while he was in a narrow way, not far from the merchant's house, he took off his magic cap of disguise and assumed somewhat of his noble appearance once more, for he was now of a mind to show his knightliness unto those who looked upon him. Accordingly, when he stood before the rich merchant in his closet, and when the merchant looked up into his face, he wist not what to think to behold so noble a lord clad all in frieze. For though King Arthur was a stranger to the good man, so that he knew not his countenance, yet that merchant wist that he was no ordinary knight, but that he must assuredly be one of high degree and in authority, even though he was clad in frieze.

Then King Arthur opened the breast of his jerkin and showed the merchant the gold collar that hung around his neck. And also he showed beneath the rough coat of frieze how that there was an undergarment of fine purple silk embroidered with gold. And then he showed to the good man his own signet ring, and when the merchant saw it, he knew it to be the ring of the King of Britain. Wherefore, beholding these tokens of high and lordly authority, the merchant arose and stood before the King and doffed his cap.

"Sir Merchant," quoth the King, "know that I am a stranger knight in disguise in this place. Ne'theless, I may tell thee that I am a very good friend to King Leodegrance and wish him exceeding well. Thou art surely aware of how the Duke of North Umber rides continually up and down before the King's castle, and challenges anyone within to come forth for to fight against him in behalf of the Lady Guinevere. Now I am of a mind to assay that combat mine own self, and I hope a very great deal that I shall succeed in upholding the honor of Cameliard and of bringing shame upon its enemies.

"Sir Merchant, I know very well that thou hast several suits of noble armor in thy treasury, for the fame of them hath reached unto mine ears though I dwell a considerable distance from this place. Wherefore I desire that thou shalt provide me in the best manner that thou art able to do, so that I may straightway assay a bout of arms with that Duke of North Umber. Moreover, I do pledge thee my knightly word that thou shalt be fully recompensed for the best suit of armor that thou canst let me have, and that in a very little while."

"My Lord," said Master Ralph, "I perceive that thou art no ordinary errant knight, but rather someone of extraordinary estate; wherefore it is a very great pleasure to fulfil all thy behests. But even an thou wert other than thou art, I would be altogether willing to equip thee with armor, seeing that thou hast a mind to ride forth against yonder duke."

Upon this he rang a little silver bell that stood nigh to him, and in answer to its sound several attendants immediately appeared. Into their hands he intrusted the person of the King, bidding them to do him extraordinary honor. Accordingly, certain of those attendants prepared for the King a bath of tepid water perfumed with ambergris, very grateful to the person. And after he was bathed in this bath and was wiped with soft linen towels, other attendants conducted him to a hall all hung with tapestries and 'broideries, and at this place a noble feast had been spread ready for his refreshment. Here that lordly merchant himself ministered to the King's wants, serving him with various meats – very dainty, and of several sorts – and likewise with fine white bread. And he poured him wine of various countries – some as red as ruby, others as yellow as gold; and indeed the King had hardly ever enjoyed a better feast than that which the merchant, Ralph of Cardiff, had thus spread for him.

And after he had entirely refreshed himself with eating, there came six pages richly clad in sarsanet of azure, and these, taking the King to an apartment of great state, they there clad him in a suit of Spanish armor, very cunningly wrought and all inlaid with gold. And the like of that armor was hardly to be found in all of the land. The juppon and the several trappings of the armor were all of satin and as white as milk. And the shield was white, and altogether without emblazonment or device of any sort. Then these attendants conducted the King into the courtyard, and there stood a noble war-horse, as white as milk, and all the trappings of the horse were of milk-white cloth without emblazonment or adornment of any sort; and the bridle and the bridle rein were all studded over with bosses of silver.

Then after the attendants had aided King Arthur to mount this steed, the lordly merchant came forward and gave him many words of good cheer, and so the king bade him adieu and rode away, all shining in white and glittering in fine armor, wherefore he resembled the full moon in harvest season.

And as he drave down the stony streets of the town, the people turned and gazed after him, for he made a very noble appearance as he passed along the narrow way between the houses of the town.

So King Arthur directed his way to the postern gate of the castle, and, having reached that place, he dismounted and tied his horse. Then he straightway entered the garden, and there, finding an attendant, he made demand that he should have present speech with the Lady Guinevere. So the attendant, all amazed at his lordly presence, went and delivered the message, and by and by the Lady Guinevere came, much wondering, and passed along a gallery with several of her damsels, until she had come over above where King Arthur was. And when King Arthur looked up and saw her above him, he loved her exceeding well. And he said to her: "Lady, I have great will to do thee such honor as I am able. For I go forth now to do combat with that Duke of North Umber who rides up and down before this castle. Moreover, I hope and verily believe that I shall encompass his downfall; accordingly, I do beseech of thee some token, such as a lady may give unto a knight for to wear when that knight rides forth to do her honor."

Then the Lady Guinevere said: "Certes, Sir Knight, I would that I knew who thou art. Yet, though I know not, nevertheless I am altogether willing for to take thee for my champion as thou offerest. So, touching that token thou speakest of, if thou wilt tell me what thing it is that thou desirest, I will gladly give it to thee."

"An that be so, Lady," said King Arthur, "I would fain have that necklace that thou wearest about thy throat. For, meseems that if I had that tied about my arm, I would find my valor greatly increased thereby."

"Pardee, Sir Knight," said the Lady, "what thou desirest of me thou shalt assuredly have." Thereupon speaking, she took from her long, smooth neck the necklace of pearls which she wore, and dropped the same down to King Arthur where he stood.

And King Arthur took the necklace and tied it about his arm, and he gave great thanks for it. Then he saluted the Lady Guinevere with very knightly grace, and she saluted him, and then, straightway, he went forth from that place, greatly expanded with joy that the Lady Guinevere had shown him such favor.

Now the report had gone about Cameliard that a knight was to go forth to fight the Duke of North Umber. Wherefore great crowds gathered upon the walls, and King Leodegrance and the Lady Guinevere and all the Court of the King came to that part of the castle walls overlooking the meadow where the Duke of North Umber defended. Wherefore, so great a concourse was presently assembled, that any knight might be encouraged to do his utmost before such a multitude as that which looked down upon the field.

Then of a sudden the portcullis of the castle was lifted, and the bridge let fall, and the White Champion rode forth to that encounter which he had undertaken. And, as he drave across that narrow bridge, the hoofs of his war-horse smote the boards with a noise like to thunder, and when he came out into the sunlight, lo! his armor flamed of a sudden like unto lightning, and when the people saw him they shouted aloud.

Then when the Duke of North Umber beheld a knight all clad in white, he rode straightway to him and spoke to him with words of knightly greeting. "Messire," he said, "I perceive that thou bearest no crest upon thy helm, nor hast thou a device of any sort upon thy shield, wherefore I know not who thou art. Ne'theless, I do believe that thou art a knight of good quality and of approved courage, or else thou wouldst not have thus come to this place."

"Certes, Sir Knight," said King Arthur, "I am of a quality equal to thine own. And as for my courage, I do believe that it hath been approved in as many encounters as even thine own hath been."

"Sir Knight," quoth the Duke of Umber, "thou speakest with a very large spirit. Ne'theless, thou mayst make such prayers as thou art able, for I shall now presently so cast thee down from thy seat, so that thou shalt never rise again; for so have I served better men than ever thou mayst hope to be."

To this King Arthur made answer with great calmness of demeanor: "That shall be according to the will of Heaven, Sir Knight, and not according to thy will."

So each knight saluted the other and rode to his assigned station, and there each dressed his spear and his shield, and made him ready for the encounter. Then a silence fell upon all so great that a man might hear his own heart beat in the stillness. So, for a small space, each knight sat like a statue made of iron. Then, of a sudden, each shouted to his war-horse, and drave spurs into his flank, and launched forth from his station. And so they met in the midst of the course with a noise like unto a violent thunder-clap. And lo! the spear of the Duke of North Umber burst into splinters unto the very truncheon thereof; but the spear of King Arthur broke not, but held, so that the Duke was cast out of his saddle like a windmill – whirling in the air and smiting the earth so that the ground shuddered beneath him. And indeed he rolled full three times over and over ere he ceased to fall.

Then all the people upon the wall shouted with might and main, so that the noise thereof was altogether astonishing; for they had hardly hoped that their champion should have proved so extraordinarily strong and skilful.

Meanwhile, those of King Ryence's Court ran immediately to the Duke of Umber where he lay upon the earth, and they straightway unlaced his helm for to give him air. And first they thought that he was dead, and then they thought that he was like to die; for, behold! he lay without any life or motion. Nor did he recover from that swoon wherein he lay for the space of full two hours and more.

Now whilst the attendants were thus busied about Duke Mordaunt of North Umber, King Arthur sat his horse, very quietly, observing all that they did. Then, perceiving that his enemy was not dead, he turned him about and rode away from that place.

Nor did he return unto Cameliard at that time, for he deemed that he had not yet entirely done with these enemies to the peace of his realm, wherefore he was minded not yet to return the horse and the armor to the merchant, but to keep them for a while for another occasion.

So he bethought him of how, coming to Cameliard, he had passed through an arm of the forest where certain wood-choppers were at work felling the trees. Wherefore, remembering that place, he thought that he would betake him thither and leave his horse and armor in the care of those rude folk until he would need those things once more. So now he rode away into the country-side, leaving behind him the town and the castle and all the noise of shouting and rejoicing; nor did he once so much as turn his head to look back toward that place where he had so violently overthrown his enemy.

And now you shall presently hear of certain pleasant adventures of a very joyous sort that befell him ere he had accomplished all his purposes. For when a man is a king among men, as was King Arthur, then is he of such a calm and equal temper that neither victory nor defeat may cause him to become either unduly exalted in his own opinion or so troubled in spirit as to be altogether cast down into despair. So if you would become like to King Arthur, then you shall take all your triumphs as he took this victory, for you will not be turned aside from your final purposes by the great applause that many men may give you, but you will first finish your work that you have set yourself to perform, ere you give yourself ease to sit you down and to enjoy the fruits of your victory.

Yea, he who is a true king of men, will not say to himself, "Lo! I am worthy to be crowned with laurels;" but rather will he say to himself, "What more is there that I may do to make the world the better because of my endeavors?"

CHAPTER THIRD

# HOW KING ARTHUR ENCOUNTERED FOUR KNIGHTS

Now, the day was extraordinarily sweet and pleasant unto one so lusty of frame and so lithe of heart as was good King Arthur. For the bright clouds swam smoothly across the blue sky in prodigious volumes of vapor, and the wind blew across the long grass of the meadow lands, and across the fields of growing wheat, so that a multitude of waves travelled over the hills and valleys like an it were across an entire sea of green. And now all the earth would be darkened with wide shadows from those clouds, and, anon, everything would burst out, of a sudden, into a wonderful radiance of sunlight once more. And the little birds they sang all gayly in the hedge-rows and the leafy thickets as though they would burst their tiny throats with singing, and the cock crowed, strong and lusty, from the farm croft, and all was so blithe and comely that the young King, with the visor of his helmet uplifted to the refreshment of the gentle breeze, would sometimes carol very joyously in his journeying. So travelled King Arthur in all that gay and tender summer season, when the earth was young and the time was of long-gone-by.

Now, you are to remember that when King Arthur had come from Carleon unto the castle of Tintagalon, he had brought with him four young knights for to bear him company. And those knights aforesaid were as follows: There was Sir Gawaine, the son of King Lot and of Queen Margaise, and there was Sir Ewaine, the son of King

Uriens and of Queen Morgana la Fay (and these two were nephews, half in blood, unto the King), and there was Sir Pellias, and there was Sir Geraint, the son of Erbin. These were the four noble young knights who had come with King Arthur from Camelot unto Tintagalon.

Now it befell, as King Arthur rode all gayly in the summer time as aforesaid, that he came to a certain part of the road where he beheld before him a tall and comely tower that stood upon a green hillock immediately by the roadside. And lo! there stood upon the balcony of that tower three fair demoiselles, clad all in green taffeta. And on the high road in front of the castle there was a knight clad all in very fine armor. And the knight sat upon a noble war-horse, and in his hands he held a lute, and he played upon the lute and sang in a voice of extraordinary sweetness. Whiles he sang those three ladies in green taffeta listened to him with great cheerfulness of mien. And whenever that knight would stint his singing, then those three ladies would clap their hands together with great acclaim, and would bid him to sing to them again; and so he would do with great readiness of spirit.

All this King Arthur beheld, and it appeared to him to be a very pleasant sight, wherefore he rejoiced at it exceedingly.

And as he drew nigh, lo! he beheld that the knight who thus sat upon his horse and played upon the lute and sang unto the accompaniment thereof, was none other than Sir Geraint, the son of Erbin. For that knight wore upon his crest the figure of a gryphon, and the device upon his shield was two gryphons rampant facing one another upon a field azure, and King Arthur knew that this was the crest and the device of Sir Geraint. And when the King perceived who was the knight who sat there and sang, he laughed unto himself and straightway closed his visor and made him ready for such encounter as might, perchance, befall. So he drew nigh to where the knight sang and the ladies listened.

Now when Sir Geraint perceived King Arthur approach, he ceased singing and hung up his lute behind him across his shoulder. Then, casting upward his look to those three ladies above him, quoth he: "Mesdames, ye have been pleased to listen to that singing which I have assayed altogether in your honor. Now, likewise, in your honor, I will perform a deed of knightly prowess which I very much hope shall bring great glory to you. For, if ye will be pleased to lend me that encouragement which your very great beauty can so easily afford, ye shall behold me, I doubt not, overthrow yonder knight completely, and that to your great credit and renown."

"Sir Knight," said that lady who spoke for the others, "you are, truly, a lord of noble bearing and exceedingly pleasing of address, wherefore we do wish you great success in this undertaking; and we do believe that you will succeed in that which you assay to do."

Upon these Sir Geraint gave those three demoiselles great thanks for their words, and thereupon he closed the visor of his helmet. So, dressing his spear and shield, and saluting those three ladies with great humility of demeanor, he went forth to meet

King Arthur where he now sat at a little distance, very quietly and soberly awaiting his pleasure.

Now Sir Geraint knew not King Arthur because he wore no crest upon his helm and no device upon his shield, wherefore as he saluted him he made speech to him in this wise: "Ha! Messire, I know not who thou art, seeing that thou bearest neither crest nor device. Ne'theless, I am minded to do thee such honor as I may in running a tilt with thee upon that balcony. For I do affirm, and am ready to maintain the same with my knightly person, that those ladies are fairer than thy lady, whomsoever she may be."

"Sir Knight," quoth King Arthur, "I will gladly run a course with thee in honor of my lady; for, I may tell thee, she is a princess, and is held by many to be the most beautiful dame in all of the world. But I will only contend with thee upon one condition, and the condition is this – that he who is overthrown shall yield himself as servant unto the other for seven days, and in that time he shall do all that may be required of him."

"I will accept thy gage, Sir Unknown Knight," quoth Sir Geraint, "and when I have overthrown thee, I will yield thee unto those fair ladies yonder for to be their servant for seven days. And I do tell thee that there are a great many knights who would certainly regard that as being both a pleasant and an honorable task."

"And should I so chance as to overthrow thee," said King Arthur, "I will send thee for to serve my lady for that same period of time, and that will be even a pleasanter and a more honorable task than that which thou hast a mind for me to perform."

So each knight saluted the other, and thereupon each took such a stand as should cast the encounter immediately beneath where those three fair demoiselles looked down from the balcony. Then each knight dressed his spear and his shield, and, having made ready for the encounter, each sat for a small space entirely prepared. Then each shouted to his war-horse, and drave spur into its flank, and launched forth with wonderful speed to the assault. So they met in the very midst of the course with a force so vehemently that the noise thereof was wonderfully appalling for to hear. And each knight smote the other in the very centre of his defences. And, lo! the spear of Sir Geraint burst into small pieces, even to the truncheon thereof; but the spear of King Arthur held, and Sir Geraint was cast so violently backward that both he and his horse were overthrown into the dust with a tumult like to a monstrous roaring of thunder.

And when Sir Geraint had recovered his footing, he was, for awhile, so astonished that he wist not where he stood, for never had he been so overthrown in all of his life before. Then, coming quickly unto himself again, he straightway drew forth his sword and called upon King Arthur with exceeding vehemence for to come down from out of his saddle, and to fight him afoot.

"Nay, not so, Sir Knight," said King Arthur, "I will not have to do with thee in that way. Moreover, thou art not to forget that thou hast promised to give thyself unto me as my servant for seven days, for, assuredly, I have entirely overcome thee in this encounter, and now thou art pledged unto me to be my servant."

Then Sir Geraint knew not what to say, being altogether abashed with shame and vexation at his overthrow. Ne'theless, he perceived that he must uphold his knightly word unto that which he had pledged himself to do; wherefore, he put up his sword again, though with exceeding discontent. "Sir Knight," said he, "I do acknowledge myself to have been overcome in this encounter, wherefore I yield myself now unto thy commands, according to my plighted word."

"Then I do place my commands upon thee in this wise," quoth King Arthur. "My command is, that thou goest straightway unto the Lady Guinevere at Cameliard, and that thou tellest her that thou hast been overthrown by that knight to whom she gave her necklace as a token. Moreover, I do desire that thou shalt obey her in everything that she may command thee to do, and that for the space of seven days to come."

"Sir Knight," quoth Sir Geraint, "that which thou biddest me to do, I will perform according to thy commands."

Thereupon he mounted his horse and went his way. And King Arthur went his way. And those three ladies who stood upon the balcony of the castle were exceedingly glad that they had beheld so noble an assay-at-arms as that which they had looked down upon.

Now, after King Arthur had travelled forward for the distance of two or three leagues or more, he came to a certain place of moorlands, where were many ditches of water, and where the heron and the marsh-hen sought harborage in the sedge. And here, at sundry points, were several windmills, with their sails all turning slowly in the sunlight before a wind which blew across the level plains of ooze. And at this place there was a long, straight causeway, with two long rows of pollard willows, one upon either hand. Now, when he had come nigh the middle of this causeway, King Arthur perceived two knights, who sat their horses in the shade of a great windmill that stood upon one side of the roadway. And a large shadow of the sails moved ever and anon across the roadway as the wheel of the mill turned slowly afore the wind. And all about the mill, and everywhere about, were great quantities of swallows that darted hither and thither like bees about a hive in midsummer. And King Arthur saw that those two knights, as they sat in the shadow of the mill, were eating of a great loaf of rye bread, fresh baked and of brittle crust; and they ate fair white cheese, which things the miller, all white with dust, served to them. But when these two knights perceived King Arthur, they immediately ceased eating that bread and cheese, and straightway closed their helmets. As for the miller, when he saw them thus prepare themselves, he went quickly back into the mill and shut the door thereof, and then went and looked out of a window which was over above where the knights were standing.

But King Arthur made very merry unto himself when he perceived that those two knights were Sir Gawaine and Sir Ewaine. For he knew that the one was Sir Gawaine because that the crest of his helmet was a leopard rampant, and because he bore upon his shield the device of a leopard rampant upon a field gules; and he knew that the other was Sir Ewaine, because he bore upon his crest an unicorn, and because the device upon his shield was that of a lady holding a naked sword in her hand, which same was upon a field or. Accordingly, whiles he was yet at some distance, King Arthur closed his helmet so that those two young knights might not know who he was.

So, when he had come anear to the two knights, Sir Gawaine rode forward for a little distance for to meet him. "Sir Knight," quoth he, "thou must know that this is soothly parlous ground whereon thou hast ventured; for there is no byway hence across the morass, and thou mayst not go forward without trying a tilt with me."

"Sir Knight," said King Arthur, "and I am very willing to run a tilt with thee. Ne'theless, I will only encounter thee upon one condition, and that is this: that he who is overthrown shall serve the other entirely for the space of seven full days."

"I do accept thy gage, Sir Knight," quoth Sir Gawaine. For he said unto himself, "Of a surety, so exceedingly strong and skilful a knight as I shall easily encompass the overthrow of this unknown knight."

So each knight immediately took his appointed station, and having dressed his spear and his shield, and having fully prepared himself in every manner, and having rested for a little space, each suddenly shouted to his horse, and drave spur into the flanks thereof, and so rushed to the encounter. And each knight smote the other in the midst of his defence, and lo! the spear of Sir Gawaine burst into fragments. But the spear of King Arthur held, so that Sir Gawaine was lifted entirely out of his saddle and over the crupper of his horse. And indeed he fell with wonderful violence into the dust. Nor could he immediately rise from that fall, but lay all bedazed for a little while. And when he did arise, he perceived that the white knight who had overthrown him sat nigh to him upon his horse.

Then King Arthur spake and said: "Sir Knight, I have altogether overthrown thee, and so thou must now serve me according to thy knightly word."

Then up spake Sir Ewaine, who sat nearby upon his horse. "Not so, Sir Knight," he said; "not so, nor until thou hast had to do with me. For I do make demand of thee that thou shalt straightway joust with me. And if I overthrow thee I will claim of thee that thou shalt release my cousin from that servitude unto which he hath pledged himself. But if thou overthrowst me, then will I serve thee even as he hath pledged himself to serve thee."

"Sir Knight," said King Arthur, "I do accept thy gage with all readiness of spirit!"

So each knight took his assigned place and dressed himself for the encounter. Then they shouted, and drave together, rushing the one upon the other like unto two rams upon the hillside. And the spear of Sir Ewaine was also shivered into pieces. But King Arthur's spear held, so that the girths of Sir Ewaine's saddle were burst apart, and both the saddle and the knight were swept off the horse's back with such violence that a tower falling could not have made a greater noise than did Sir Ewaine when he smote the dust of that causeway.

Then Sir Ewaine arose to his feet and gazed upon him, all filled with entire amazement. To him came King Arthur, and bespake him thus: "Ha, Sir Knight, meseems that thou hast been fairly overcome this day. And so, according to your promises, both thou and yonder other knight must fulfil all my commands for the space of full seven days to come. Now this is the command that I set upon ye both: that ye shall straightway go unto the Lady Guinevere at Cameliard and shall take her greeting from her knight. And ye shall say to her that her knight unto whom she gave her necklace, hath sent ye, who are King's sons, for to do obedience unto her. And all that she shall command ye to do in the space of these seven days that are to come, that shall ye perform even unto the smallest grain."

"Sir Knight," said Sir Gawaine, "so we will do according to thy commands, having pledged ourselves thereunto. But when these seven days are passed, I do make my vow that I shall seek thee out and shall carry this combat unto its entire extremity. For it may happen to any knight to be unhorsed as I have been, yet I do believe that I may have a better success with thee an I battle with thee to the extremity of my endeavor."

"Sir Knight," said King Arthur, "it shall be even as thou desirest. Yet I do verily believe that when these seven days are passed thou wilt not have such a great desire for to fight with me as thou now hast."

Having so spoken, King Arthur saluted those two knights and they saluted him. And then he turned his horse and went his way. And whenever he bethought him of how those two good knights had fallen before his assault, and when he thought of how astonished and abashed they had been at their overthrow, he laughed aloud for pure mirth, and vowed unto himself that he had never in all of his life engaged in so joyous an adventure as this.

So when Sir Ewaine had mended the girths of his saddle then he and Sir Gawaine mounted their horses and betook their way toward Cameliard much cast down in spirits.

Then the miller came forth from the mill once more, greatly rejoiced at having beheld such a wonderfully knightly encounter from so safe a place as that from which he had beheld it.

And so King Arthur rode onward with great content of mind until the slanting of the afternoon had come, and by that time he had come nigh to that arm of the forest-land which he had in mind as the proper place where he might leave his horse and his armor.

Now as he drew nigh to this part of the forest skirts, he perceived before him at the roadside a gnarled and stunted oak-tree. And he perceived that upon the oak-tree there hung a shield, and that underneath the shield were written these words in fair large letters:

"Whoso smiteth upon this shield
Doeth so at the peril of his body."

Then King knight was filled with a great spirit, and, uplifting his spear, he smote upon that shield so that it rang like thunder.

Then immediately King Arthur heard a voice issue out of the forest crying, "Who hath dared to assail my shield!" And straightway there came out thence a knight of large frame, riding upon a horse white, like that which King Arthur himself rode. And the trappings of the horse and of the knight were all white like unto the trappings of King Arthur and his horse. And the knight bore upon his helmet as his crest a swan with outspread wings, and upon his shield he bore the emblazonment of three swans upon a field argent. And because of the crest and the emblazonment of the shield, King Arthur knew that this knight was Sir Pellias, who had come with him from Camelot to Tintagalon.

So when Sir Pellias had come nigh to where King Arthur waited for him, he drew rein and bespake him with great sternness of voice: "Ho! Ho! Sir Knight," quoted he. "Why didst thou dare to smite upon my shield! Verily, that blow shall bring thee great peril and dole. Now, prepare to defend thyself straightway because of what thou hast done."

"Stay! Stay! Sir Knight," said King Arthur, "it shall be as thou wouldst have it; and I will do combat with thee. Yet will I not assay this adventure until thou hast agreed that the knight who is overcome in the encounter shall serve the other in whatsoever manner that other may desire, for the space of one se'night from this time."

"Sir Knight," said Sir Pellias, "I do accept that risk, wherefore I bid thee now presently to prepare thyself for the encounter."

Thereupon each knight took his station and dressed his spear and shield. And when they had prepared themselves, they immediately launched together with a violence like to two stones cast from a catapult. So they met in the midst of the course, and again King Arthur was entirely successful in that assault which he made. For the spear of Sir Pellias burst to pieces, and the spear of King Arthur held; and Sir Pellias was cast with passing violence out of his saddle for the distance of more than half a spear's length behind the crupper of his horse. Nor did he altogether recover from that fall for a long time, so that King Arthur had to wait beside him for a considerable while ere he was able to lift himself up from the ground whereon he lay.

"Ha! Sir Knight," said King Arthur, "assuredly it hath not gone well with thee this day, for thou hast been entirely overthrown and now thou must straightway redeem thy pledge to serve me for seven days hereafter. Wherefore, I now set it upon thee as my command, that thou shalt go straightway unto Cameliard, and that thou shalt greet the Lady Guinevere from me, telling her that her knight unto whom she gave her necklace hath been successful in battle with thee. Likewise I set it upon thee that thou shalt obey her for the space of seven days in whatsoever she may command thee to do."

"Sir Knight," said Sir Pellias, "it shall even be as thou dost ordain. Yet I would that I knew who thou art, for I do declare that I have never yet in all my life been overthrown as thou hast overthrown me. And, indeed, I think that there are very few men in the world who could serve me as thou hast served me."

"Sir Knight," said King Arthur, "some time thou shalt know who I am. But, as yet, I am bound to entire secrecy."

Thereupon he saluted Sir Pellias and turned and entered the forest and was gone.

And Sir Pellias mounted his horse and betook him to Cameliard, much cast down and disturbed in spirit, yet much marvelling who that knight could be who had served him as he had been served.

So that day there came to Cameliard, first Sir Geraint and then Sir Gawaine and Sir Ewaine, and last of all there came Sir Pellias. And when these four beheld one another they were all abashed so that one scarce dared to look the other in the face. And when they came before the Lady Guinevere and made their condition known to her, and told her how that knight who wore her necklace had overthrown them all and had sent them thither to serve her for a se'night, and when she reckoned how great and famous were those four knights in deeds of chivalry, she was exceedingly exalted that her knight should have approved himself so great in those deeds of arms which he had undertaken to perform. But she greatly marvelled who that champion could be, and debated those things in her own mind. For it was a thing altogether unheard of that one knight, in one day, and with a single spear, should have overthrown five such well proved and famous knights as Duke Mordaunt of North Umber, Sir Geraint, Sir Gawaine, Sir Ewaine, and Sir Pellias. So she gave herself great joy that she had bestowed the gift of her necklace upon so worthy a knight, and she was exceedingly uplifted with extraordinary pleasure at the thought of the credit he had endowed her withal.

Now after King Arthur had entered the forest, he came by and by to where those wood-choppers, afore spoken of, plied their craft. And he abided with them for that night; and when the next morning had come, he intrusted them with his horse and armor, charging them to guard those things with all care, and that they should be wonderfully rewarded therefor. Then he took his departure from that place with intent to return unto Cameliard. And he was clad in that jerkin of frieze which he had worn ever since he had left Tintagalon.

And when he had reached the outskirts of the forest, he set his cap of disguise upon his head and so resumed his mean appearance once more. So, his knightliness being entirely hidden, he returned to Cameliard for to be gardener's boy as he had been before.

CHAPTER FOURTH

# HOW THE FOUR KNIGHTS SERVED THE LADY GUINEVERE

Now, when King Arthur returned to Cameliard once more (which fell upon the afternoon of a second day), he found the gardener waiting for him, exceedingly filled with wrath. And the gardener had a long birchen rod which he had fetched thither for to punish his boy withal, when that he should have returned to the garden again. So when he saw King Arthur he said: "Thou knave! wherefore didst thou quit thy work to go a-gadding?" And King Arthur laughed and said: "Touch me not." At this, the gardener waxed so exceeding wroth, that he catched the King by the collar of his jerkin with intent to beat him, saying: "Dost thou laugh at me, knave, and make a mock at me? Now I will beat thee well for the offence thou hast committed."

Then, when King Arthur felt that man's hand laid upon him, and when he heard the words that the gardener spake in his wrath, his royal spirit waxed very big within him and he cried out: "Ha, wretch! wouldst thou dare to lay thy hands upon my sacred person?" So saying, he seized the gardener by the wrists, and took the rod straight away from him, and struck him with it across the shoulders. And when that poor knave felt himself thus in the powerful grasp of the angry King, and when he felt the rod upon his shoulders, he straightway lifted up a great outcry, albeit the blow hurt him not a whit. "Now get thee gone!" quoth King Arthur, "and trouble me no more; else will I serve thee in a way that will not at all belike thee." Herewith he loosed that poor man and let him go; and the gardener was so bemazed with terror, that both the earth and the sky swam before him. For King Arthur's eyes had flashed upon him like lightning, and those two hands had held his wrists with wonderful power. Wherefore, when the King let him go he gat him away as quickly as might be, all trembling and sweating with a great fear.

So he went straight to the Lady Guinevere and complained to her of the manner in which he had been treated. "Lady," quoth he, weeping with the memory of his terror, "my boy goeth away for a day or more, I know not whither; and when I would whip him for quitting his work he taketh the rod straight away from me and beateth me with it. Wherefore, now, I prithee, deal with him as is fitting, and let several strong men drive him away from this place with rods."

Then the Lady Guinevere laughed. "Let be!" she said, "and meddle with him no more; for, indeed, he appeareth to be a very saucy fellow. As for thee! take thou no heed of his coming or his going, and haply I will deal with him in such a way as shall be fitting."

Whereupon the gardener went his way, greatly marvelling that the Lady Guinevere should be so mild in dealing with that toward knave. And the Lady Guinevere went her way, very merry. For she began to bethink her that there was soothly some excellent reason why it should happen that when the White Champion, who did such wonderful deeds, should come thither; then that gardener's boy should go; and that when that same Champion should go, then the gardener's boy should come thitherward again. Wherefore she suspected many things, and was wonderfully merry and cheerful in spirit.

Now, that day, in the afternoon, the Lady Guinevere chanced to walk in the garden with her damsels, and with her walked those four noble knights who had been sent thither by her White Champion, to wit, Sir Gawaine, Sir Ewaine, Sir Geraint, and Sir Pellias. And the gardener's lad was digging in the gardens; and as they passed by where he was the Lady Guinevere laughed aloud and cried out: "Look! Look! Messires and Ladies! Yonder is a very saucy fellow for to be a gardener's lad, for he continually weareth his cap, even when he standeth in the presence of lords and ladies."

Then Sir Gawaine up and spake, saying: "Is it even so? Now will I straightway go to yonder knave, and will take his hat off for him, and that in a way so greatly to his misliking, that I do not believe that he will ever offend by wearing it in our presence again."

At this the Lady Guinevere laughed a very great deal. "Let be!" she said, "let be! Sir Gawaine! it would ill beseem one so gentle as thou art to have to do with yonder saucy fellow. Moreover, he doth assure us all that he hath an ugly place upon his head, wherefore let him wear his cap in God's mercy."

Thus the Lady Guinevere, though she suspected a very great deal, was yet pleased to make a mock of him whom she suspected.

Now that day Duke Mordaunt of North Umber had entirely recovered from those sore hurts that he had suffered from his overthrow at the hands of the White Champion. Wherefore, the next morning having come, he appeared again before the castle as he had appeared aforetime – clad all in complete armor. So this time there rode before him two heralds, and when the duke and the two heralds had come to that part of the meadows that lay immediately before the castle of Cameliard, the heralds blew their trumpets exceedingly loud. So at the sound of the trumpets many people came and gathered upon the walls; and King Leodegrance came, and took stand upon a lesser tower that looked down upon the plain where were the Duke of North Umber and the two heralds. Then the Duke of North Umber lifted up his eyes and beheld King Leodegrance where he stood over above him upon the top of that tower, and he cried out in a loud voice: "What ho! King Leodegrance! Thou shalt not think because I suffered a fall from my horse through the mischance of an assault at arms, that thou art therefore quit of me. Yet, ne'theless, I do now make this fair proffer unto thee. To-morrow day I shall appear before this castle with six knights'companion. Now if thou hast any seven knights who are able to stand against me and my companions in an assault at arms – whether with spears or swords, or ahorse or afoot – then shall I engage myself for to give over all pretence whatsoever unto the hand of the Lady Guinevere. But if thou canst not provide such champions to contend successfully against me and my knights-companion, then shall I not only lay claim to Lady Guinevere, but I shall likewise seize upon and shall hold for mine own, three certain castles of thine that stand upon the borders of North Umber. And, likewise, I shall seize upon and shall hold for mine own all the lands and glebes appertaining unto those same castles. Moreover, this challenge of mine shall hold only until to-morrow at set of sun; after the which time it shall be null and void. Wherefore, King Leodegrance, thou hadst best look to it straightway to provide thee with such champions as may defend thee from these demands aforesaid.

Hereupon those two heralds blew their trumpets once more, and Duke Mordaunt of North Umber turned his horse about and went away from that place. Then King Leodegrance also went his way, very sorrowful and downcast in his spirits. For he said to himself: "Is it at all likely that another champion shall come unto me like that wonderful White Champion who came two days since, I know not whence, for to defend me against mine enemies? And, touching that same White Champion; if I know not whence he came, so also I know not whither he hath departed; how then shall I know where to seek him to beseech his further aid in this time of mine extremity?" Wherefore he went his way, very sorrowful, and wist not what he was to do for to defend himself. So being thus exceedingly troubled in his spirit, he went straight unto his own room, and there shut himself therein; nor would he see any man nor speak unto anyone, but gave himself over entirely unto sorrow and despair.

Now in this extremity the Lady Guinevere bethought her of those four knights who had been pledged for to serve her for seven days. So she went unto them where they were and she bespoke them in this wise: "Messires, ye have been sent hither pledged for to serve me for seven days. Now I do ordain it of thee that you will take this challenge of Duke Mordaunt upon you at my behest, and I do much desire that you go forth to-morrow-day for to meet this Duke of North Umber and his knights-companion in battle. For ye are terribly powerful knights, and I do believe you may easily defend us against our enemies."

But Sir Gawaine said, "Not so, Lady; not so! For though we are pledged unto thy service, yet are we not pledged unto the service of King Leodegrance, thy father. Nor have we quarrel of any sort with this Duke of North Umber, nor with his six knights-companion. For we are knights of King Arthur, his Court, nor may we, except at his command, take any foreign quarrel upon us in the service of another king."

Then was the Lady Guinevere exceedingly angry, wherefore she said with great heat: "Either thou art a wonderfully faithful lord unto thy King, Sir Gawaine, or else thou fearest to meet this Duke of North Umber and his knights'companion."

And at this speech of the Lady Guinevere's, Sir Gawaine was also exceedingly wroth, wherefore he made reply: "An thou wert a knight and not a lady, Dame Guinevere, thou wouldst think three or four times ere thou wouldst find courage to speak those words unto me." Whereupon he arose and went out from that place with a countenance all inflamed with wrath. And the Lady Guinevere went away also from that place and to her bower, where she wept a very great deal, both from sorrow and from anger.

Now all this while King Arthur had been very well aware of everything that passed; wherefore he by and by arose and went out and found the gardener. And he took the gardener strongly by the collar of his coat and held him where he was. And he said to him: "Sirrah! I have a command to set upon thee, and thou shalt perform that command to the letter, else, an thou perform it not, a very great deal of pain may befall thee." Herewith speaking, he thrust his hand into the bosom of his jerkin and brought forth thence that necklace of pearls which the Lady Guinevere had given him from about her neck. And he said further unto the gardener: "Thou shalt take this necklace to the Lady Guinevere and thou shalt say to her thus: that she is to send me forth with bread and meat and wine and comfits from her own table. And thou shalt say unto her that I desire her to summon those four knights – to wit, Sir Gawaine, Sir Ewaine, Sir Geraint, and Sir Pellias – and that she is to bid those four for to come and serve me with those things for my refreshment. And thou art to say unto her that she is to lay her commands upon those knights that they are further to serve me according as I may command, and that they are henceforth to be my servants and not her servants. And these are the commands that I lay upon thee; that thou art to say these things unto the Lady Guinevere."

Now when the gardener heard those words he was so astonished that he wist not what to think, for he deemed that the gardener's lad had gone altogether mad. Wherefore he lifted up his voice and cried aloud, "How now! What is this thou sayest! Verily, should I do such a thing as this thou bidst me to do, either it will cost me my life or else it will cost thee thy life. For who would dare for to say such words unto the Lady Guinevere?"

But King Arthur said: "Ne'theless, thou shalt surely do as I command thee, sirrah. For if thou disobey in one single point, then I do assure thee it will go exceedingly ill with thee. For I have it in my power for to make thee suffer as thou hast never suffered before."

And upon this the gardener said, "I will go." For he said unto himself, "If I do as this fellow biddeth me, then will the Lady Guinevere have him punished in great measure, and so I shall be revenged upon him for what he did unto me yesterday. Moreover, it irks me exceedingly that I should have a lad for to work in the garden who behaves as this fellow does. Wherefore," he said, "I will go." So he took that necklace of pearls that King Arthur gave him, and he went forth and, after awhile, he found the Lady Guinevere where she was. And when he had found her, he bespoke her in this wise:

"Lady, my garden boy hath assuredly gone entirely mad. For, under the threat of certain great harm he would do unto me an I performed not his errand, he hath sent me to offer a very grievous affront unto thee. For he hath sent me with this string of large beads for to give to thee; and he bids me to tell thee that thou art to send to him bread and meat and sweetmeats and wine, such as thou usest at thine own table; and he bids me to tell thee that these things are to be served to him by the four noble knights who came hither the day before yesterday. And he saith that thou art to command those same knights that they are to obey him in whatsoever he may command, for that they are henceforth to be his servants and not thine. And, indeed, Lady, he would listen to naught that I might say to him contrariwise, but he hath threatened me with dire injury an I came not hither and delivered this message unto thee."

Now when the Lady Guinevere heard what the gardener said, and when she beheld the necklace which she had given unto that White Champion, and when she wist that the White Champion and the gardener's boy were indeed one, she was uplifted with an exceeding joy; wherefore she knew not whether to laugh or whether to weep for that pure joy. So she arose and took the necklace of pearls, and she bade the gardener for to come with her. Then she went forth until she found those four knights, and when she had found them she spake unto them thus:

"My Lords, awhile sin when I commanded you to take my quarrel with Duke Mordaunt of North Umber upon you for my sake, ye would not do so. And thou, my lord Gawaine, didst speak such angry words as are not fitting that one who serveth should speak unto his mistress, far less that a knight should speak unto the daughter of a king. Accordingly I have it in my mind that ye shall perform a certain thing by way of a penance, which, an ye refuse to do, I will know very well that ye do not intend to fulfil that word which ye plighted to my knight when he overthrew you all four in fair combat. Now my command is this: that ye take certain food prepared for my table – meats and white bread and sweetmeats and wine – and that ye take that food unto my gardener's boy, whose cap, Sir Gawaine, thou didst threaten so valorously for to take away from him this very morning. And ye four are to serve the food unto him as though he were a royal knight. And when ye have so served him, ye are to obey him in whatsoever he may ordain. And this I put upon ye as a penalty because ye took not my quarrel upon ye as true knights should, for hereafter ye are to be servants unto that gardener's boy and not unto me. Wherefore ye are now to go unto the buttery of the castle, and ye are to bid the sewer for to give you meats such as are served upon mine own table. And the food ye are to serve upon silver plates, and the wine ye are to serve in silver cups and goblets. And ye are to minister unto that gardener's boy as though he were a great lord of exceeding fame and renown."

Thus spake the Lady Guinevere, and when she had spoken, she turned and left those four knights, and she took with her the gardener, who was so astonished at that which he had heard, that he wist not whether he had gone mad or whether the Lady Guinevere had gone mad. And the Lady Guinevere bade the gardener to go to the gardener's boy and to tell him that all things should be fulfilled according to his commands. And so the gardener did as he was told.

Now turn we to those four knights whom the Lady Guinevere had left. For they were bemazed and abashed at the singular commands she had set upon them. And when they recovered from their amazement, they were inflamed with exceeding indignation that, for the time, they wist not whether that which they saw with their eyes was the light of day, or whether it was altogether darkness. Nor could one of them look at another in the face, so overcome were they with shame at the affront that had been put upon them. Then up and spake Sir Gawaine, and his voice so trembled with his exceeding anger that he could scarce contain it for to speak his words. "Messires," quoth he, "do ye not see how that this lady hath wantonly put a great affront upon us because we would not take up her quarrel against the Duke of North Umber? Now we will indeed serve this gardener's boy even as she hath ordained. For we will serve him with meat and drink as she hath commanded; and we will render our service unto him as she hath bidden us to do. But observe ye; we are no longer her servants, but we are his servants; wherefore we may serve him as we choose for to do. So, when we have fulfilled her commands and have served him with meat and drink, and when we have obeyed all the behests he layeth upon us; then do I make my vow that I, with mine own hand, shall slay that gardener's boy. And when I have slain him, I will put his head into a bag, and I will send that bag unto the Lady Guinevere by the meanest carrier whom I can find for that purpose. And so this proud lady shall receive an affront which she hath put upon us." And they all said that that which Sir Gawaine had planned should be exactly as he had said.

So those four lords went unto the sewer of the castle, and they asked for the best of that food which was to be served unto the Lady Guinevere – meats and bread and sweetmeats and wine. Then they took them silver plates and platters and they placed the food upon them; and they took silver cups and silver goblets and they poured the wine into them; and they went forth with these things. And when they had come back of the castle nigh to the stables, they found the gardener's boy, and they bade him sit down and eat and to drink. And they waited upon him as though he had been some great lord. And not one of those four knights wist who he was, nor that he was the great King whose servant they, soothly, were. For he wore his cap of disguise upon his head, wherefore they deemed him to be only a poor peasant fellow.

Now when Sir Ewaine beheld that he still wore his cap before them, he spake unto him with great indignation, saying: "Ha, villain! Wouldst thou wear thy cap even in the presence of great princes and lords such as we be?"

Unto this Sir Gawaine said, "Let be, it matters not." And then he said very bitterly unto the gardener's boy: "Eat thou well, sirrah! For thou shalt hardly eat another meal of food upon this earth."

To this the gardener's boy made reply: "Sir Knight, that, haply, shall lie unto another will than thine for to determine. For maybe, I shall eat many other meals than this. And, maybe, ye shall serve at them as ye are serving me now." And those four lords were astonished beyond measure that he should bespeak them thus so calmly and without any appearance of fear.

Then, after he had eaten, the gardener's boy said unto those knights, "Behold, Messires, I have had enough and am done; and now I have other commands for you to fulfil. And my next command is that ye shall make ready straightway to go abroad with me, and to that end ye shall clothe yourselves with complete armor. And thou, Sir Gawaine, shalt go to the head stable-keeper of this castle, and thou shalt demand of him that he shall make ready the Lady Guinevere's palfrey so that I may straightway ride forth upon it. And when ye are all encased in your armor, and when everything is duly appointed according to my command, ye shall bring that palfrey unto the postern gate of the castle, and there I shall meet ye for to ride forth with you."

And Sir Gawaine said: "It shall be done in every way according as thou dost command. But when we ride forth from this castle it shall be a sorry journey for thee."

And the gardener's boy said: "I think not so, Sir Gawaine."

Then those four went away and did according as the gardener's boy commanded. And when they had made themselves ready in full array of armor, and when they had obtained the Lady Guinevere's palfrey, they went unto the postern gate and there the gardener's boy met them. And when he saw that they sat their horses and that they moved not at his coming, he said: "Ha, Messires! would ye so entreat him whom ye have been ordained to serve? Now I do bid ye, Sir Gawaine and Sir Ewaine, for to come down and to hold my stirrup for me; and I bid ye, Sir Geraint and Sir Pellias, for to come down and to hold my palfrey for me whiles I mount."

Then those four noble knights did as they were commanded. And Sir Gawaine said: "Thou mayst command as thou dost list, and I do bid thee to make the most of it whiles thou mayst do so; for thou shalt have but a little while longer for to enjoy the great honor that hath fallen upon thee. For that honor which hath fallen upon thee – lo! it shall presently crush thee unto death."

And the gardener's boy said: "Not so; I believe I shall not die yet whiles." And again those four lords were greatly astonished at the calmness of his demeanor.

And so they rode forth from that place; and the gardener's boy would not permit that they should ride either before him or beside him, but he commanded them that they should ride behind him whiles they were still servants unto him.

So they rode as he assigned them for a considerable way. Then after they had gone forward a great distance, they drew nigh to a gloomy and dismal woodland that lay entirely beyond the country coadjacent to Cameliard. Then, when they had come nigh unto this woodland, Sir Gawaine rode a little forward, and he said: "Sir Gardener's Boy, seest thou yonder woodland? Now when we come into it thou shalt immediately die, and that by a sword that hath never yet been touched by any but noble or knightly blood."

And King Arthur turned him about in his saddle, and he said: "Ha! Sir Gawaine! Wouldst thou ride forward thus when I bid thee to ride behind me?"

And as he spake he took the cap from his head, and, lo! they all beheld that it was King Arthur who rode with them.

Then a great silence of pure astonishment fell upon them all, and each man sat as though he were turned into an image of stone. And it was King Arthur who first spake. And he said: "Ha! how now, Sir Knights? Have ye no words of greeting for to pay to me? Certes, ye have served me with a very ill grace this day. Moreover, ye have threatened to slay me; and now, when I speak to you, ye say naught in reply."

Then those four knights immediately cried out aloud; and they leaped down from off their horses, and they kneeled down into the dust of the road. And when King Arthur beheld them kneeling there, he laughed with great joyfulness of spirit, and he bade them for to mount their horses again, for the time was passing by when there was much to do.

So they mounted their horses and rode away, and as they journeyed forward the King told them all that had befallen him, so that they were greatly amazed, and gave much acclaim unto the knightliness with which he had borne himself in those excellent adventures through which he had passed. And they rejoiced greatly that they had a king for to rule over them who was possessed of such a high and knightly spirit.

So they rode to that arm of the forest where King Arthur had left his horse and his armor.

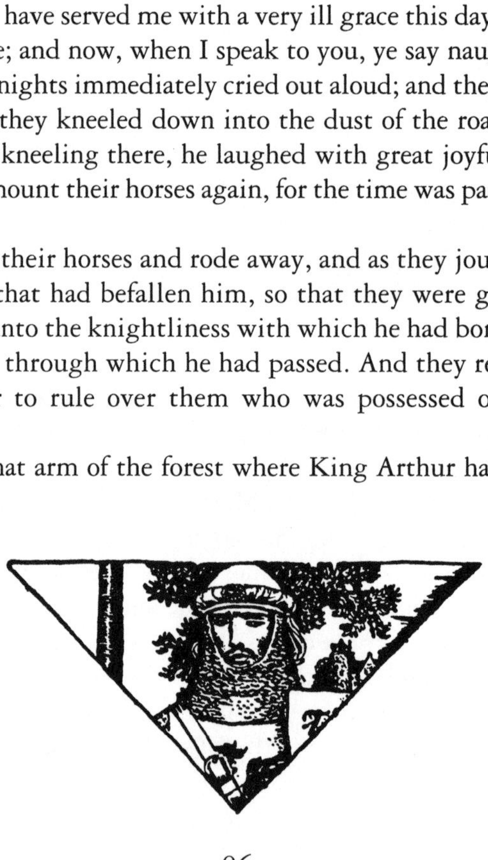

CHAPTER FIFTH

# How King Arthur Overcame the Enemies of King Leodegrance

Now, when the next day had come, the Duke of North Umber and six knights-companion appeared upon the field in front of the castle of Cameliard as he had duly declared that he and they would do. And those seven champions appeared in very great estate; for in front of them there rode seven heralds with trumpets and tabards, and behind them there rode seven esquires, each esquire bearing the spear, the shield, the crest, and the banneret of the knight who was his lord and master. And the seven heralds blew their trumpets so exceedingly loud that the sound thereof penetrated unto the utmost parts of Cameliard, so that the people came running from everywhere. And while the heralds blew their trumpets the seven esquires shouted, and waved the spears and the bannerets. So those seven knights rode in such proud estate that those who looked upon them had hardly ever beheld such a splendid presentment of chivalry.

So they paraded up and down that field three times for its entire length, and, meantime, a great crowd of people, called thither by the blowing of the herald's trumpets, stood upon the walls and gazed therefrom at that noble spectacle. And all the Court of King Ryence came, and stood upon the plain in front of the King's pavilion, and they shouted and cheered the Duke of North Umber and his six knights-companion.

Meanwhile, King Leodegrance of Cameliard was so cast down with trouble and shame that he did not choose to show his face, but hid himself away from all his Court. Nor would he permit anyone for to come into his presence at that time.

Nevertheless, the Lady Guinevere, with sundry of her damsels, went unto the King's closet where he was, and knocked upon the door thereof, and when the King denied her to come in to him, she spake to him through the door, giving him words of good cheer, saying: "My lord knight and father, I prithee for to look up and to take good cheer unto thyself. For I do assure thee that there is one who hath our cause in his hands, and that one is, certes, a very glorious champion. And he shall assuredly come by and by ere this day is done, and when he cometh, he shall certainly overthrow our enemies."

But King Leodegrance opened not the door, but he said: "My daughter, that which thou sayest thou sayest for to comfort me. For there is no other help for me in this time of trouble only God, His good strong help and grace." And she said: "Nay, I say that which is the truth; and the help that God shall send unto thee he shall certainly send through a worthy champion who at this moment hath our cause in his hand."

So spake the Lady Guinevere, so that whilst King Leodegrance came not forth, yet he was greatly comforted at that which she said to him.

Thus passed all that morning and a part of the afternoon, and yet no one appeared for to take up that challenge which the seven knights had declared. But, whilst the sun was yet three or four hours high, there suddenly appeared at a great distance a cloud of dust. And in that cloud of dust there presently appeared five knights, riding at great speed, thitherward. And when these had come nigh unto the walls, lo! the people beheld that he who rode foremost of all was the same White Champion who had aforetime overthrown the Duke of North Umber. Moreover, they perceived that the four knights who rode with that White Champion were very famous knights and of great prowess and glory of arms. For the one was Sir Gawaine, and the other was Sir Ewaine, and the other was Sir Geraint, and the other was Sir Pellias. For the people of the castle and the town knew those four knights, because they had dwelt for two days at Cameliard, and they were of such exceeding renown that folk crowded from far and near for to look upon them whensoever they appeared for to walk abroad.

So when the people upon the walls beheld who those knights were, and when they perceived that White Champion who had aforetime brought them such exceeding honor, they shouted aloud for the second time with a voice mightier than that with which they had the first time shouted.

Now King Leodegrance heard the people shouting, whereupon hope awoke of a sudden within him. So he straightway came forth with all speed for to see what was ado, and there he beheld those five noble champions about to enter into the field below the castle walls.

And the Lady Guinevere also heard the shouting and she came forth likewise and, behold! there was that White Champion and those four other knights. So when she beheld that White Knight and his four companions-at-arms, her heart was like to break within her for pure joy and gladness, wherefore she wept for the passion thereof, and laughed the whiles she wept. And she waved her kerchief unto those five noble lords and kissed her hand unto them, and the five knights saluted her as they rode past her and into the field.

Now, when the Duke of North Umber was made aware that those five knights had come against him and his knights-companion for to take up his challenge, he straightway came forth from his pavilion and mounted his horse. And his knights-companion came forth and mounted their horses, and he and they went forth for to meet those who had come against them.

And when the Duke of North Umber had come nigh enough, he perceived that the chiefest of those five knights was the White Champion who had aforetime overthrown him. Wherefore he said unto that White Champion: "Sir Knight, I have once before condescended unto thee who art altogether unknown to me or to anybody else that is here. For without inquiring concerning thy quality, I ran a course with thee and, lo! by the chance of arms thou didst overthrow me. Now this quarrel is more serious than that, wherefore I and my companions-at-arms will not run a course with thee and thy companions; nor will we fight with thee until I first know what is the quality of him against whom I contend. Wherefore, I bid thee presently declare thyself, who thou art and what is thy condition."

Then Sir Gawaine opened the umbril of his helmet, and he said: "Sir Knight, behold my face, and know that I am Gawaine, the son of King Lot. Wherefore thou mayst perceive that my condition and estate are even better than thine own. Now I do declare unto thee that yonder White Knight is of such a quality that he condescends unto thee when he doeth combat with thee, and that thou dost not condescend unto him."

"Ho, Sir Gawaine!" quoth the Duke of Umber. "What thou sayest is a very strange thing, for, indeed, there are few in this world who are so exalted that they may condescend unto me. Ne'theless, since thou dost avouch for him, I may not gainsay that which thou sayest. Yet, there is still another reason why we may not fight with ye. For, behold! we are seven well-approved and famous knights, and ye are but five; so, consider how unequal are our forces, and that you stand in great peril in undertaking so dangerous an encounter."

Then Sir Gawaine smiled right grimly upon that Duke of North Umber. "Gramercy for thy compassion, and for the tenderness which thou showeth concerning our safety, Sir Duke," quoth he. "But ne'theless, thou mayst leave that matter unto us with entire content of spirit upon thy part. For I consider that the peril in which ye seven stand is fully equal to our peril. Moreover, wert thou other than a belted knight, a simple man might suppose that thou wert more careful of thine own safety in this matter, than thou art of ours."

Now at these words the countenance of the Duke of North Umber became altogether covered with red, for he wist that he had, indeed, no great desire for this battle, wherefore he was ashamed because of the words which Sir Gawaine spake to him. So, each knight closed his helmet, and all turned their horses, and the one party rode unto one end of the field, and the other party rode to the other end of the field, and there each took stand in the place assigned unto them.

And they arranged themselves thus: In the middle was King Arthur, and upon either hand were two knights; and in the middle was the Duke of North Umber, and upon either hand were three knights. So, when they had thus arrayed themselves they dressed their spears and their shields, and made them altogether ready for the onset. Then King Arthur and Duke Mordaunt each shouted aloud, and the one party hurled upon the other party with such violence that the ground shook and thundered beneath the hoofs of the horses, and the clouds of dust rose up against the heavens.

And so they met in the middle of the field with an uproar of such dreadful violence that one might have heard the crashing thereof for the distance of more than a mile away.

And when the one party had passed the other, and the dust of the encounter had arisen, lo! three of the seven had been overthrown, and not one of the five had lost his seat.

And one of those who had been overthrown was Duke Mordaunt of North Umber. And, behold! he never more arose again from the ground whereon he lay. For King Arthur had directed his spear into the very midst of his defences, and the spear had held, wherefore the point thereof had pierced the shield of the Duke of North Umber, and had pierced his body armor, and so violent was the stroke, that the Duke of North Umber had been lifted entirely out of his saddle, and had been cast a full spear's length behind the crupper of his horse. Thus died that wicked man, for as King Arthur drave past him, the evil soul of him quitted his body with a weak noise like to the squeaking of a bat, and the world was well rid of him.

Now when King Arthur turned him about at the end of the course and beheld that there were but four knights left upon their horses of all those seven against whom he and his companions had driven, he uplifted his spear, and drew rein upon his horse, and bespake his knights in this wise: "Messires, I am aweary of all this coil and quarrelling, and do not care to fight any more to-day, so go ye straightway and engage those knights in battle. As for me, I will abide here, and witness your adventure."

"Lord," said they, "we will do our endeavor as thou dost command."

So those four good knights did as he commanded, and they went forth straightway against those other four, much encouraged that their King looked upon their endeavor. And King Arthur sat with the butt of his spear resting upon his instep, and looked upon the field with great content of spirit, and a steadfast countenance.

As for those four knights-companion that remained of the Duke of North Umber's party, they came not forth to this second encounter with so much readiness of spirit as they had done aforetime. For they were now well aware of how great was the excellent prowess of those other knights, and they beheld that their enemies came forth to this second encounter very fiercely, and with great valor and readiness of spirit. Wherefore their hearts melted away within them with doubt and anxiety as to the outcome of this second encounter.

Nevertheless, they prepared themselves with such resolve as might be, and came forth as they were called upon to do.

Then Sir Gawaine drave straight up to the foremost knight, who was a very well-known champion, hight Sir Dinador of Montcalm. And when he had come sufficiently nigh to him, he lifted himself up in his stirrups and he smote Sir Dinador so fierce a blow that he cleft the shield of that knight asunder, and he cleft his helmet, and a part of the blade of his sword brake away and remained therein.

And when Sir Dinador felt that blow, his brains swam like water, and he was fain to catch the horn of his saddle for to save himself from falling therefrom. Then a great terror straightway fell upon him, so that he drew rein violently to one side. So he fled away from that place with the terror of death hanging above him like to a black cloud of smoke. And when his companions beheld that stroke that Sir Gawaine delivered, and when they beheld Sir Dinador flee away from before him, they also drew rein to one side and fled away with all speed, pursued with an entire terror of their enemies. And Sir Gawaine and Sir Ewaine and Sir Geraint and Sir Pellias pursued them as they fled. And they chased them straight through the Court of King Ryence, so that the knights and nobles of that Court scattered hither and thither like chaff at their coming. And they chased those fleeing knights in among the pavilions of King Ryence's Court, and no man stayed them; and when they had chased those knights entirely away, they returned to that place where King Arthur still held his station, steadfastly awaiting them.

Now when the people of Cameliard beheld the overthrow of their enemies, and when they beheld how those enemies fled away from before the faces of their champions, they shouted with might and main, and made great acclaim. Nor did they stint their loud shouting when those four knights returned from pursuing their enemies and came back unto the White Champion again. And still more did they give acclaim when those five knights rode across the drawbridge and into the gateway of the town and into the town.

Thus ended the great bout-at-arms, which was one of the most famous in all the history of chivalry of King Arthur's Court.

Now when King Arthur had thus accomplished his purposes, and when he had come into the town again, he went unto that merchant of whom he had obtained the armor that he wore, and he delivered that armor back to him again. And he said, "To-morrow-day, Sir Merchant, I shall send thee two bags of gold for the rent of that armor which thou didst let me have."

To this the merchant said: "Lord, it is not needed that thou shouldst recompense me for that armor, for thou hast done great honor unto Cameliard by thy prowess."

But King Arthur said: "Have done, Sir Merchant, nor must thou forbid what I say. Wherefore take thou that which I shall send unto thee."

Thereupon he went his way, and, having set his cap of disguise upon his head, he came back into the Lady Guinevere's gardens again.

Now when the next morning had come the people of Cameliard looked forth and, lo! King Ryence had departed entirely away from before the castle. For that night he had struck his pavilions, and had withdrawn his Court, and had gone away from that place where he and his people had sat down for five days past. And with him he had taken the body of the Duke of North Umber, conveying it away in a litter surrounded by many lighted candles and uplifted by a peculiar pomp of ceremony. But when the people of Cameliard beheld that he was gone, they were exceedingly rejoiced, and made merry, and shouted and sang and laughed. For they wist not how deeply enraged King Ryence was against them; for his enmity aforetime toward King Leodegrance was but as a small flame when compared unto the anger that now possessed him.

Now that morning Lady Guinevere walked into her garden, and with her walked Sir Gawaine and Sir Ewaine, and lo! there she beheld the gardener's boy again.

Then she laughed aloud, and she said unto those two knights, "Messires behold! Yonder is the gardener's boy, who weareth his cap continually because he hath an ugly place upon his head."

Then those two knights, knowing who that gardener's boy was, were exceedingly abashed at her speech, and wist not what to say or whither to look. And Sir Gawaine spake, aside unto Sir Ewaine, and quoth he: "'Fore Heaven, that lady knoweth not what manner of man is yonder gardener's boy; for, an she did, she would be more sparing of her speech."

And the Lady Guinevere heard Sir Gawaine that he spoke, but she did not hear his words. So she turned unto Sir Gawaine, and she said: "Sir Gawaine, haply it doth affront thee that the gardener's boy should wear his cap before us, and maybe thou wilt go and take it off from his head as thou didst offer to do two or three days since."

And Sir Gawaine said: "Peace, Lady! Thou knowest not what thou sayest. Yonder gardener's boy could more easily take my head from off my shoulders than I could take his cap from off his head."

At this the Lady Guinevere made open laughter; but in her heart she secretly pondered that saying and greatly marvelled what Sir Gawaine meant thereby.

Now about noon of that day there came an herald from King Ryence of North Wales, and he appeared boldly before King Leodegrance where the King sat in his hall with a number of his people about him. And the herald said: "My lord King: my master, King Ryence of North Wales, is greatly displeased with thee. For thou didst set certain knights upon Duke Mordaunt of North Umber, and those knights have slain that excellent nobleman, who was close kin unto King Ryence. Moreover, thou hast made no reply to those demands that my master, King Ryence, hath made touching the delivery unto him of certain lands and castles bordering upon North Wales. Wherefore my master is affronted with thee beyond measure. So my master, King Ryence, bids me to set forth to thee two conditions, and the conditions are these: Firstly, that thou dost immediately deliver into his hands that White Knight who slew the Duke of North Umber; secondly, that thou makest immediate promise that those lands in question shall be presently delivered unto King Ryence."

Then King Leodegrance arose from where he sat and spake to that herald with great dignity of demeanor. "Sir Herald," quoth he, "the demands that King Ryence maketh upon me pass all bounds for insolence. That death which the Duke of North Umber suffered, he suffered because of his own pride and folly. Nor would I deliver that White Knight into thy master's hands, even an I were able to do so. As for those lands that thy master demandeth of me, thou mayst tell King Ryence that I will not deliver unto him of those lands so much as a single blade of grass, or a single grain of corn that groweth thereon."

And the herald said: "If, so be, that is then answer, King Leodegrance, then am I bidden for to tell thee that my master, King Ryence of North Wales, will presently come hither with an array of a great force of arms, and will take from thee by force those things which thou wilt not deliver unto him peacefully." Whereupon, so saying, he departed thence and went his way.

Now after the herald had departed, King Leodegrance went into his closet, and when he had come there he sent, privily, for the Lady Guinevere. So the Lady Guinevere came to him where he was. And King Leodegrance said to her: "My daughter, it hath happened that a knight clad all in white, and bearing no crest or device of any sort, hath twice come to our rescue and hath overthrown our enemies. Now it is said by everybody that that knight is thine own particular champion, and I hear say that he wore thy necklace as a favor when he first went out against the Duke of North Umber. Now I prithee, daughter, tell me who that White Champion is, and where he may be found."

Then the Lady Guinevere was overwhelmed with a confusion, wherefore she looked away from her father's countenance; and she said: "Verily, my Lord, I know not who that knight may be."

Then King Leodegrance spake very seriously to the Lady Guinevere, and he took her by the hand and said: "My daughter, thou art now of an age when thou must consider being mated unto a man who may duly cherish thee and protect thee from thine enemies. For, lo! I grow apace in years, and may not hope to defend thee always from those perils that encompass one of our estate. Moreover, since King Arthur (who is a very great King indeed) hath brought peace unto this realm, all that noble court of chivalry which one time gathered about me has been scattered elsewhither where greater adventures may be found than in my peaceful realm. Wherefore (as all the world hath seen this week past) I have now not one single knight whom I may depend upon to defend us in such times of peril as these which now overshadow us. Now, my daughter, it doth appear to me that thou couldst not hope to find anyone who could so well safeguard thee as this White Knight; for he doth indeed appear to be a champion of extraordinary prowess and strength. Wherefore it would be well if thou didst feel thyself to incline unto him as he appeareth to incline unto thee."

Then the Lady Guinevere became all rosy red as with a fire even unto her throat.

And she laughed, albeit the tears overflowed her eyes and ran down upon her cheeks. So she wept, yet laughed in weeping. And she said unto King Leodegrance: "My Lord and father, an I give my liking unto any one in the manner thou speaketh of, I will give it only unto the poor gardener's boy who digs in my garden."

Then, at these words, the countenance of King Leodegrance became contracted with violent anger, and he cried out: "Ha, Lady! Wouldst thou make a mock and a jest of my words?"

Then the Lady Guinevere said: "Indeed, my Lord! I jest not and I mock not. Moreover, I tell thee for verity that that same gardener's boy knoweth more concerning the White Champion than anybody else in all of the world." Then King Leodegrance said: "What is this that thou tellest me?" And the Lady Guinevere said: "Send for that gardener's boy and thou shalt know." And King Leodegrance said: "Verily, there is more in this than I may at present understand."

So he called to him the chief of his pages, hight Dorisand, and he said to him: "Go, Dorisand, and bring hither the gardener's boy from the Lady Guinevere's garden."

So Dorisand, the page, went as King Leodegrance commanded, and in a little while he returned, bringing with him that gardener's boy. And with them came Sir Gawaine, and Sir Ewaine, and Sir Pellias and Sir Geraint. And those four lords stood over against the door, where they entered; but the gardener's boy came and stood beside the table where King Leodegrance sat. And the King lifted up his eyes and looked upon the gardener's boy, and he said: "Ha! Wouldst thou wear they cap in our presence?"

Then the gardener's boy said: "I cannot take off my cap."

But the Lady Guinevere, who stood beside the chair of King Leodegrance, spake and said: "I do beseech thee, Messire, for to take off thy cap unto my father."

Whereupon the gardener's boy said: "At thy bidding I will take it off."

So he took the cap from off his head, and King Leodegrance beheld his face and knew him. And when he saw who it was who stood before him, he made a great outcry from pure amazement. And he said: "My Lord and my King! What is this!" Thereupon he arose from where he sat, and he went and kneeled down upon the ground before King Arthur. And he set the palms of his hands together and he put his hands within the hands of King Arthur, and King Arthur took the hands of King Leodegrance within his own. And King Leodegrance said: "My Lord! My Lord! Is it then thou who hast done all these wonderful things?"

Then King Arthur said: "Yea; such as those things were, I have done them." And he stooped and kissed King Leodegrance upon the cheek and lifted him up unto his feet and gave him words of good cheer.

Now the Lady Guinevere, when she beheld those things that passed, was astonished beyond measure. And lo! she understood of a sudden all these things with amazing clearness. Wherefore a great fear fell upon her so that she trembled exceedingly, and said unto herself: "What things have I said unto this great King, and how have I made a mock of him and a jest of him before all those who were about me!" And at the thought thereof, she set her hand upon her side for to still the extreme disturbance of her heart. So, whilst King Arthur and King Leodegrance gave to one another words of royal greeting and of compliment, she withdrew herself and went and stood over against the window nigh to the corner of the wall.

Then, by and by, King Arthur lifted up his eyes and beheld her where she stood afar off. So he went straightway unto her and he took her by the hand, and he said: "Lady, what cheer?"

And she said: "Lord, I am afraid of thy greatness." And he said: "Nay, Lady. Rather it is I who am afeared of thee. For thy kind regard is dearer unto me than anything else in all the world, else had I not served for these twelve days as a gardener's boy in thy garden all for the sake of thy good will." And she said: "Thou hast my good will, Lord." And he said: "Have I thy good will in great measure?" And she said: "Yea, thou hast it in great measure."

Then he stooped his head and kissed her before all those who were there, and thus their troth was plighted.

Then King Leodegrance was filled with such an exceeding joy that he wist not how to contain himself therefore.

Now, after these things, there followed a war with King Ryence of North Wales. For Sir Kay and Sir Ulfius had gathered together a great army as King Arthur had bidden them to do, so that when King Ryence came against Cameliard he was altogether routed, and his army dispersed, and he himself chased, an outcast, into his mountains.

Then there was great rejoicing in Cameliard. For, after his victory, King Arthur remained there for awhile with an exceedingly splendid Court of noble lords and of beautiful ladies. And there was feasting and jousting and many famous bouts at arms, the like of which those parts had never before beheld. And King Arthur and the Lady Guinevere were altogether happy together.

Now, one day, whiles King Arthur sat at feast with King Leodegrance – they two being exceedingly expanded with cheerfulness – King Leodegrance said unto King Arthur: "My Lord, what shall I offer thee for a dowery with my daughter when thou takest her away from me for to be they Queen?"

The King Arthur turned to Merlin, who stood nigh to him, and he said: "Ha, Merlin! What shall I demand of my friend by way of that dowery?"

Unto him Merlin said: "My lord King, thy friend King Leodegrance hath one thing, the which, should he bestow it upon thee, will singularly increase the glory and renown of thy reign, so that the fame thereof shall never be forgotten."

And King Arthur said: "I bid thee, Merlin, tell me what is that thing."

So Merlin said: "My lord King, I will tell thee a story:

"In the days of thy father, Uther-Pendragon, I caused to be made for him a certain table in the shape of a ring, wherefore men called it the ROUND TABLE. Now, at this table were seats for fifty men, and these seats were designed for the fifty knights who were the most worthy knights in all the world. These seats were of such a sort, that whenever a worthy knight appeared, then his name appeared in letters of gold upon that seat that appertained unto him; and when that knight died, then would his name suddenly vanish from that seat which he had aforetime occupied.

"Now, forty-and-nine of these seats, except one seat, were altogether alike (saving only one that was set aside for the King himself, which same was elevated above the other seats, and was cunningly carved and inlaid with ivory and with gold), and the one seat was different from all the others, and it was called the SEAT PERILOUS. For this seat was unlike the others both in its structure and its significance; for it was cunningly inset with gold and silver of curious device, and it was covered with a canopy of satin embroidered with gold and silver; and it was altogether of a wonderful magnificence of appearance. And no name ever appeared upon this seat, for only one knight in all of the world could hope to sit therein with safety unto himself. For, if any other dared to sit therein, either he would die a sudden and violent death within three days' time, or else a great misfortune would befall him. Hence that seat was called the SEAT PERILOUS.

"Now, in the days of King Uther-Pendragon, there sat seven-and-thirty knights at the ROUND TABLE. And when King Uther-Pendragon died, he gave the ROUND TABLE unto his friend, King Leodegrance of Cameliard.

"And in the beginning of King Leodegrance's reign, there sat four-and-twenty knights at the ROUND TABLE.

"But times have changed since then, and the glory of King Leodegrance's reign hath paled before the glory of thy reign, so that his noble Court of knights have altogether quitted him. Wherefore there remaineth now not one name, saving only the name of King Leodegrance, upon all those fifty seats that surround the ROUND TABLE. So now that ROUND TABLE lieth beneath its pavilion altogether unused.

"Yet if King Leodegrance will give unto thee, my lord King, that ROUND TABLE for a dower with the Lady Guinevere, then will it lend unto thy reign its greatest glory. For in thy day every seat of that TABLE shall be filled, even unto the SEAT PERILOUS, and the fame of the knights who sit at it shall never be forgotten."

"Ha!" quoth King Arthur. "That would indeed be a dower worthy for any king to have with his queen."

"Then," King Leodegrance said, "that dower shalt thou have with my daughter; and if it bring thee great glory, then shall thy glory be my glory, and thy renown shall be my renown. For if my glory shall wane, and thy glory shall increase, behold! is not my child thy wife?"

And King Arthur said: "Thou sayest well and wisely."

Thus King Arthur became the master of that famous ROUND TABLE. And the ROUND TABLE was set up at Camelot (which some men now call Winchester). And by and by there gathered about it such an array of knights as the world had never beheld before that time, and which it shall never behold again.

Such was the history of the beginning of the ROUND TABLE in King Arthur's reign.

CHAPTER SIXTH

# How King Arthur was Wedded and the Round Table Established

And now was come the early fall of the year; that pleasant season when the meadow-land and the wold were still green with summer that had only just passed; when the sky likewise was as of summer-time – extraordinarily blue and full of large floating clouds; when a bird might sing here and another there, a short song in memory of spring-time, when all the air was tempered with warmth and yet the leaves were everywhere turning brown and red and gold, so that when the sun shone through them it was as though a cloth of gold, broidered with brown and crimson and green, hung above the head. At this season of the year it is exceedingly pleasant to be a-field among the nut-trees with hawk and hound, or to travel abroad in the yellow world, whether it be a-horse or a-foot.

Now this was the time of year in which had been set the marriage of King Arthur and the Lady Guinevere at Camelot, and at that place was extraordinary pomp and glory of circumstance. All the world was astir and in a great ferment of joy, for everybody was exceedingly glad that King Arthur was to have him a Queen.

In preparation for that great occasion the town of Camelot was bedight very magnificently, for the stony street along which the Lady Guinevere must come to the royal castle of the King was strewn thick with fresh-cut rushes smoothly laid. Moreover it was in many places spread with carpets of excellent pattern such as might be fit to lay upon the floor of some goodly hall. Likewise all the houses along the way were hung with fine hangings of woven texture interwoven with threads of azure and crimson, and everywhere were flags and banners afloat in the warm and gentle breeze against the blue sky, wherefore that all the world appeared to be alive with bright colors, so that when one looked adown that street, it was as though one beheld a crooked path of exceeding beauty and gayety stretched before him.

Thus came the wedding-day of the King – bright and clear and exceedingly radiant.

King Arthur sat in his hall surrounded by his Court awaiting news that the Lady Guinevere was coming thitherward. And it was about the middle of the morning when there came a messenger in haste riding upon a milk-white steed. And the raiment of that messenger and the trappings of his horse were all of cloth of gold embroidered with scarlet and white, and the tabard of the messenger was set with many jewels of various sorts so that he glistened from afar as he rode, with a singular splendor of appearance.

So this herald-messenger came straight into the castle where the King abided waiting, and he said: "Arise, my lord King, for the Lady Guinevere and her Court draweth nigh unto this place."

Upon this the King immediately arose with great joy, and straightway he went forth with his Court of Knights, riding in great state. And as he went down that marvellously adorned street, all the people shouted aloud as he passed by, wherefore he smiled and bent his head from side to side; for that day he was passing happy and loved his people with wonderful friendliness.

Thus he rode forward unto the town gate, and out therefrom, and so came thence into the country beyond where the broad and well-beaten highway ran winding down beside the shining river betwixt the willows and the osiers.

And, behold! King Arthur and those with him perceived the Court of the Princess where it appeared at a distance, wherefore they made great rejoicing and hastened forward with all speed. And as they came nigh, the sun falling upon the apparels of silk and cloth of gold, and upon golden chains and the jewels that hung therefrom, all of that noble company that surrounded the Lady Guinevere her litter flashed and sparkled with surpassing radiance.

For seventeen of the noblest knights of the King's Court, clad in complete armor, and sent by him as an escort unto the lady, rode in great splendor, surrounding the litter wherein the Princess lay. And the framework of that litter was of richly gilded wood, and its curtains and its cushions were of crimson silk embroidered with threads of gold. And behind the litter there rode in gay and joyous array, all shining with many colors, the Court of the Princess – her damsels in waiting, gentlemen, ladies, pages, and attendants.

So those parties of the King and the Lady Guinevere drew nigh together until they met and mingled the one with the other.

Then straightway King Arthur dismounted from his noble horse and, all clothed with royalty, he went afoot unto the Lady Guinevere's litter, whiles Sir Gawaine and Sir Ewaine held the bridle of his horse. Thereupon one of her pages drew aside the silken curtains of the Lady Guinevere's litter, and King Leodegrance gave her his hand and she straightway descended therefrom, all embalmed, as it were, in exceeding beauty. So King Leodegrance led her to King Arthur, and King Arthur came to her and placed one hand beneath her chin and the other upon her head and inclined his countenance and kissed her upon her smooth cheek – all warm and fragrant like velvet for softness, and without any blemish whatsoever. And when he had thus kissed her upon the cheek, all those who were there lifted up their voices in great acclaim, giving loud voice of joy that those two noble souls had thus met together.

Thus did King Arthur give welcome unto the Lady Guinevere and unto King Leodegrance her father upon the highway beneath the walls of the town of Camelot, at the distance of half a league from that place. And no one who was there ever forgot that meeting, for it was full of extraordinary grace and noble courtliness.

Then King Arthur and his Court of Knights and nobles brought King Leodegrance and the Lady Guinevere with great ceremony unto Camelot and unto the royal castle, where apartments were assigned to all, so that the entire place was alive with joyousness and beauty.

And when high noon had come, the entire Court went with great state and ceremony unto the cathedral, and there, surrounded with wonderful magnificence, those two noble souls were married by the Archbishop.

And all the bells rang right joyfully, and all the people who stood without the cathedral shouted with loud acclaim, and lo! the King and the Queen came forth all shining, like unto the sun for splendor and like unto the moon for beauty.

In the castle a great noontide feast was spread, and there sat thereat four hundred, eighty and six lordly and noble folk – kings, knights, and nobles – with queens and ladies in magnificent array. And near to the King and the Queen there sat King Leodegrance and Merlin, and Sir Ulfius, and Sir Ector the trustworthy, and Sir Gawaine, and Sir Ewaine, and Sir Kay, and King Ban, and King Pellinore and many other famous and exalted folk, so that no man had ever beheld such magnificent courtliness as he beheld at that famous wedding-feast of King Arthur and Queen Guinevere.

And that day was likewise very famous in the history of chivalry, for in the afternoon the famous Round Table was established, and that Round Table was at once the very flower and the chiefest glory of King Arthur's reign.

For about mid of the afternoon the King and Queen, preceded by Merlin and followed by all that splendid Court of kings, lords, nobles and knights in full array, made progression to that place where Merlin, partly by magic and partly by skill, had caused to be builded a very wonderful pavilion above the Round Table where it stood.

And when the King and the Queen and the Court had entered in thereat they were amazed at the beauty of that pavilion, for they perceived, an it were, a great space that appeared to be a marvellous land of Fay. For the walls were all richly gilded and were painted with very wonderful figures of saints and of angels, clad in ultramarine and crimson, and all those saints and angels were depicted playing upon various musical instruments that appeared to be made of gold. And overhead the roof of the pavilion was made to represent the sky, being all of cerulean blue sprinkled over with stars. And in the midst of that painted sky was an image, an it were, of the sun in his glory. And under foot was a pavement all of marble stone, set in squares of black and white, and blue and red, and sundry other colors.

In the midst of the pavilion was a Round Table with seats thereat exactly sufficient for fifty persons, and at each of the fifty places was a chalice of gold filled with fragrant wine, and at each place was a paten of gold bearing a manchet of fair white bread. And when the King and his Court entered into the pavilion, lo! music began of a sudden for to play with a wonderful sweetness.

Then Merlin came and took King Arthur by the hand and led him away from Queen Guinevere. And he said unto the King, "Lo! this is the Round Table."

Then King Arthur said, "Merlin, that which I see is wonderful beyond the telling."

After that Merlin discovered unto the King the various marvels of the Round Table, for first he pointed to a high seat, very wonderfully wrought in precious woods and gilded so that it was exceedingly beautiful, and he said, "Behold, lord King, yonder seat is hight the 'Seat Royal,' and that seat is thine for to sit in." And as Merlin spake, lo! there suddenly appeared sundry letters of gold upon the back of that seat, and the letters of gold read the name,

ARTHUR, KING.

And Merlin said, "Lord, yonder seat may well be called the center seat of the Round Table, for, in sooth, thou art indeed the very centre of all that is most worthy of true knightliness. Wherefore that seat shall be called the centre seat of all the other seats."

Then Merlin pointed to the seat that stood opposite to the Seat Royal, and that seat also was of a very wonderful appearance as afore told in this history. And Merlin said unto the King: "My lord King, that seat is called the Seat Perilous, for no man but one in all this world shall sit therein, and that man is not yet born upon the earth. And if any other man shall dare to sit therein that man shall either suffer death or a sudden and terrible misfortune for his temerity. Wherefore that seat is called the Seat Perilous."

"Merlin," quoth the King, "all that thou tellest me passeth the bound of understanding for marvellousness. Now I do beseech thee in all haste for to find forthwith a sufficient number of knights to fill this Round Table so that my glory shall be entirely complete."

Then Merlin smiled upon the King, though not with cheerfulness, and said, "Lord, why art thou in such haste? Know that when this Round Table shall be entirely filled in all its seats, then shall thy glory be entirely achieved and then forthwith shall thy day begin for to decline. For when any man hath reached the crowning of his glory, then his work is done and God breaketh him as a man might break a chalice from which such perfect ichor hath been drunk that no baser wine may be allowed to defile it. So when thy work is done and ended shall God shatter the chalice of thy life."

Then did the King look very steadfastly into Merlin's face, and said, "Old man, that which thou sayest is ever of great wonder, for thou speakest words of wisdom. Ne'theless, seeing that I am in God His hands, I do wish for my glory and for His good will to be accomplished even though He shall then entirely break me when I have served His purposes."

"Lord," said Merlin, "thou speakest like a worthy king and with a very large and noble heart. Ne'theless, I may not fill the Round Table for thee at this time. For, though thou hast gathered about thee the very noblest Court of Chivalry in all of Christendom, yet are there but two and thirty knights here present who may be considered worthy to sit at the Round Table."

"Then, Merlin," quoth King Arthur, "I do desire of thee that thou shalt straightway choose me those two and thirty."

"So will I do, lord King," said Merlin.

Then Merlin cast his eyes around and lo! he saw where King Pellinore stood at a little distance. Unto him went Merlin and took him by the hand. "Behold, my lord King," quoth he. "Here is the knight in all the world next to thyself who at this time is most worthy for to sit at this Round Table. For he is both exceedingly gentle of demeanor unto the poor and needy and at the same time is so terribly strong and skilful that I know not whether thou or he is the more to be feared in an encounter of knight against knight."

Then Merlin led King Pellinore forward and behold! upon the high seat that stood upon the left hand of the Royal Seat there appeared of a sudden the name,

PELLINORE.

And the name was emblazoned in letters of gold that shone with extraordinary lustre. And when King Pellinore took his seat, great and loud acclaim long continued was given him by all those who stood round about.

Then after that Merlin had thus chosen King Arthur and King Pellinore he chose out of the Court of King Arthur the following knights, two and thirty in all, and these were the knights of great renown in chivalry who did first establish the Round Table. Wherefore they were surnamed "The Ancient and Honorable Companions of the Round Table."

To begin, there was Sir Gawaine and Sir Ewaine, who were nephews unto the King, and they sat nigh to him upon the right hand; there was Sir Ulfius (who held his seat but four years and eight months unto the time of his death, after which Sir

Geheris – who was esquire unto his brother, Sir Gawaine – held that seat); and there was Sir Kay the Seneschal, who was foster brother unto the King; and there was Sir Baudwain of Britain (who held his seat but three years and two months until his death, after the which Sir Agravaine held that seat); and there was Sir Pellias and Sir Geraint and Sir Constantine, son of Sir Caderes the Seneschal of Cornwall (which same was king after King Arthur); and there was Sir Caradoc and Sir Sagramore, surnamed the Desirous, and Sir Dinadan and Sir Dodinas, surnamed the Savage, and Sir Bruin, surnamed the Black, and Sir Meliot of Logres, and Sir Aglaval and Sir Durnure, and Sir Lamorac (which three young knights were sons of King Pellinore), and there was Sir Griflet and Sir Ladinas and Sir Persavant of Ironside, and Sir Dinas of Cornwall, and Sir Brian of Listinoise, and Sir Palomides and Sir Degraine and Sir Epinogres, the son of the King of North Umberland and brother unto the enchantress Vivien, and Sir Lamiel of Cardiff, and Sir Lucan the Bottler and Sir Bedevere his brother (which same bare King Arthur unto the ship of Fairies when he lay so sorely wounded nigh unto death after the last battle which he fought). These two and thirty knights were the Ancient Companions of the Round Table, and unto them were added others until there were nine and forty in all, and then was added Sir Galahad, and with him the Round Table was made entirely complete.

Now as each of these knights was chosen by Merlin, lo! as he took that knight by the hand, the name of that knight suddenly appeared in golden letters, very bright and shining, upon the seat that appertained to him.

But when all had been chosen, behold! King Arthur saw that the seat upon the right hand of the Seat Royal had not been filled, and that it bare no name upon it. And he said unto Merlin: "Merlin, how is this, that the seat upon my right hand hath not been filled, and beareth no name?"

And Merlin said: "Lord, there shall be a name thereon in a very little while, and he who shall sit therein shall be the greatest knight in all the world until that the knight cometh who shall occupy the Seat Perilous. For he who cometh shall exceed all other men in beauty and in strength and in knightly grace."

And King Arthur said: "I would that he were with us now." And Merlin said: "He cometh anon."

Thus was the Round Table established with great pomp and great ceremony of estate. For first the Archbishop of Canterbury blessed each and every seat, progressing from place to place surrounded by his Holy Court, the choir whereof singing most musically in accord, whiles others swung censers from which there ascended an exceedingly fragrant vapor of frankincense, filling that entire pavilion with an odor of Heavenly blessedness.

And when the Archbishop had thus blessed every one of those seats, the chosen knight took each his stall at the Round Table, and his esquire came and stood behind him, holding the banneret with his coat-of-arms upon the spear-point above the knight's head. And all those who stood about that place, both knights and ladies, lifted up their voices in loud acclaim.

Then all the knights arose, and each knight held up before him the cross of the hilt of his sword, and each knight spake word for word as King Arthur spake. And this was the covenant of their Knighthood of the Round Table: That they would be gentle unto the weak; that they would be courageous unto the strong; that they would be terrible unto the wicked and the evil-doer; that they would defend the helpless who should call upon them for aid; that all women should be held unto them sacred; that they would stand unto the defence of one another whensoever such defence should be required; that they would be merciful unto all men; that they would be gentle of deed, true in friendship, and faithful in love. This was their covenant, and unto it each knight sware upon the cross of his sword, and in witness thereof did kiss the hilt thereof. Thereupon all who stood thereabouts once more gave loud acclaim.

Then all the knights of the Round Table seated themselves, and each knight brake bread from the golden pattern, and quaffed wine from the golden chalice that stood before him, giving thanks unto God for that which he ate and drank.

Thus was King Arthur wedded unto Queen Guinevere, and thus was the Round Table established.

# CONCLUSION

*So endeth this Book of King Arthur which hath been told by me with such joyousness of spirit that I find it to be a very great pleasure, in closing this first volume of my work, to look forward to writing a second volume, which now presently followeth.*

*In that volume there shall be told the history of several very noble worthies who were of the Court of the King, and it seems to me to be a good thing to have to do with the history of such noble and honorable knights and gentlemen. For, indeed, it might well please anyone to read such an history, and to hear those worthies speak, and to behold in what manner they behaved in times of trial and tribulation. For their example will doubtless help us all to behave in a like manner in a like case.*

# The Book of Three Worthies

# FOREWORD

*Here beginneth the Second Book of the History of King Arthur, called The Book of Three Worthies, because it has to do with three very excellent, honorable Lords of the Court of King Arthur.*

*Of these three, the first is Merlin the Wise, the second is Sir Pellias, surnamed the Gentle Knight, and the third is Sir Gawaine, the son of King Lot of Orkney and the Isles.*

*So now presently follows the story of the passing of Merlin the Wise; in the which you shall see how the very wisdom that Merlin possessed in such great measure was the cause of his own undoing. Wherefore I do hope that you yourselves may take that story unto heart so that you shall see that those gifts of mind or person which God assigns unto you may not be so misused by you or others that they shall become the means of compassing your own downfall.*

*For it shall not excuse you in any wise that, as you journey forward in your life, you shall find many men who, like Merlin, have been endowed by the grace of God with very great gifts of talent which they might very easily use to the great benefit of mankind, but which they so misuse as to bring the greater ruin upon themselves and the greater harm unto other men. For, if you shall prove so weak or so wicked as to misuse your talents in that manner unto the harm of others and of yourself, it shall not make your fault the less that others shall have done greater evil than yourself.*

*Wherefore, let this story of Merlin be a warning unto you, I pray you all. For, though I do not believe that Merlin intended that his talents of magic should do harm unto others, yet, because of his folly, they did as great harm as though he himself had designed to do evil by means of them. Yea; it is hard to tell whether the wickedness or the follies of men do the greater harm in the world; therefore seek to guard yourself well, not only against sin, but against folly and weakness likewise.*

# Prologue

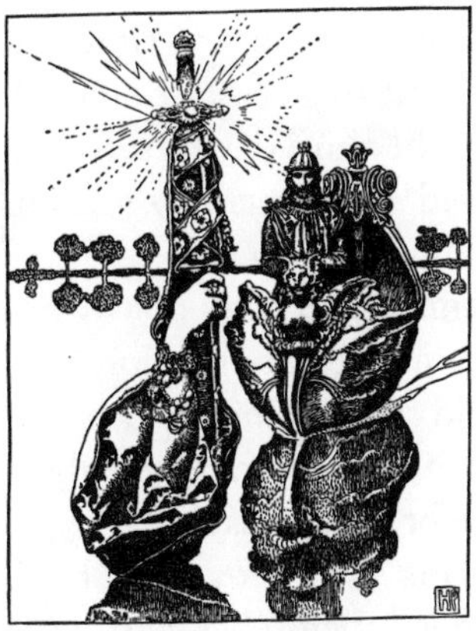

Upon a certain day King Arthur sat in the Royal Hall of Camelot with the Queen and all of his Court and all of her Court. And there was great joy and mirth at that place.

Whiles they sat there, there suddenly came an armed knight into the Hall, and his armor was all covered with blood and dust, and he had a great many wounds upon his body. Then all they who were at that place were astonished and affrighted at the aspect of that knight, for his appearance boded no good news to King Arthur. The knight-messenger came to where the King was, and he was nearly fainting with weakness and with the many wounds he had received, and he brought news unto those who were there present that five kings, enemies to King Arthur, had suddenly come into that land and that they were burning and harrying the country upon every side.

And the knight-messenger said that these five kings were the King of Denmark, the King of Ireland, the King of Soleyse, the King of the Vale, and the King of Longtinaise. These had brought with them a great host and were laying waste the land all around about, so that all the realm was in sore travail and sorrow because of their devastations.

Upon this news, King Arthur smote his palms together with great vehemence and cried out, "Alas! who would be a king! Will the time never come when these wars and disturbances shall cease and we shall have entire peace in this land!" Therewith he arose in great agitation and went out from that place, and all who were there were in sore trouble.

So King Arthur immediately sent messengers to two friendly kings who were nearest to him – to wit, to King Pellinore and to King Uriens of Gore – and he bade them to come to his aid without any loss of time. Meantime he himself gathered together a large army with intent to go forth to meet his enemies forthwith.

So he went forth and upon the third day he came with his army unto the forest of Tintagalon and there he stayed with intent to rest for a little until King Pellinore and King Uriens should have joined him.

But the five kings, his enemies, had news that King Arthur was at that place, and thereupon they made a forced march through North Wales with intent to strike him ere those other two kings could come to his aid. So they came by night to where King Arthur was, and they fell upon him so unexpectedly that there was great danger of his army being put to rout before that assault.

But King Arthur drew his army together by his own courage and large-heartedness, and so they defended themselves with a great spirit until King Pellinore appeared with his army and joined in that battle.

So in the end King Arthur won a great victory over his enemies; for they were put to rout and scattered in every direction. Likewise by means of that war, and because of the submissions of these five kings, King Arthur recovered all that realm that had once been his father's, and more besides.

Now in that war eight of the knights of the Round Table lost their lives and King Arthur mourned their loss with great dolor; for these were the first knights of the Round Table who had lost their lives in doing battle in his defence.

Whilst King Arthur was grieving very sorely for these eight knights, Merlin came unto him, and said, "Be not downcast, lord, for lo! thou hast many excellent knights still left about thee and thou canst certainly not have a very great deal of trouble in filling those eight places that have been thus made empty by death. Now if thou followest my counsel, thou must choose some very worthy adviser from the knights-companion of thy Round Table, and thou wilt consult with him in this matter (for the counsel of two is better than the counsel of one), and between ye ye may fill those places made vacant by war."

This counsel appeared very good to King Arthur, so he did as Merlin advised. For that morning he summoned King Pellinore to his privy closet and laid the matter before him and they two communed together thereupon. In that consultation King Pellinore advised King Arthur in this wise: That there should be four old and worthy knights chosen to fill four of those empty seats, and that there should be four young and ardent knights chosen to fill the other four seats, and in that manner all those eight seats should be filled.

Now that advice appeared to King Arthur to be good, wherefore he said, "Let it be that way." So first they two chose the four old knights as follows: There was King Uriens of Gore, and King Lac, and Sir Hervise de Reuel, and Sir Galliar of Rouge. And from the younger knights of the Court they chose Sir Marvaise of Leisle and Sir Lionel, the son of King Ban of Benwick, and Sir Cadar of Cornwall. So that there was one place yet to be filled.

Now it was a very hard thing to determine who should fill that place, for there were at that time two very honorable young knights at the Court. One of these was Sir Baudemagus, a young knight, brother of Sir Ewaine and son of King Uriens of Gore and Queen Morgana le Fay (which lady was half-sister unto King Arthur as hath been aforetold). And the other young knight was Sir Tor who, though late come to Court, had performed several very famous adventures. And Sir Tor was a son of King Pellinore (though not of his Queen), and King Pellinore loved him a very great deal.

Then King Pellinore said to King Arthur, "Lord, there are certainly but two knights in all thy Court to choose from for to fill this eighth seat at the Round Table: one of these is thy sister's son, Sir Baudemagus, and the other is my son, Sir Tor. Now I may not advise thee in this matter, wherefore do thou, Lord, choose the one or the other of these young knights to fill that place. But this I may say, that it will please me very greatly if thy favor should fall upon Sir Baudemagus, for then will all the world believe that I have been above reproach in my dealings in this affair, whereas should Sir Tor be chosen all men would say that I favored mine own son."

Then King Arthur meditated upon this matter for a long while and by and by he spoke and said, "Sir, I have weighed this whole affair, and it is my belief that Sir Tor is the better knight of those twain. For he hath performed several very excellent adventures, whilst Sir Baudemagus, though a worthy knight, hath not yet made manifest any very great achievement in the fields of chivalry. So, in God's name, let Sir Tor be seated as companion of the Round Table."

Then King Pellinore said, "So be it," and thereupon they both arose and went forth from that place.

And, lo! that very moment the names of those eight worthies so chosen appeared each upon the back of the seat at the Round Table that appertained unto him, and so the decision of those two knights was confirmed in the sight of all the world in that manner.

Now when the word of all this reached the ears of Queen Morgana le Fay she was greatly affronted that Sir Baudemagus, her son, should have been passed by and that another should have been chosen in his stead. Wherefore she cried out against King Arthur in the hearing of several people, saying: "Ha! how is this! is blood and kinship of no account in the eyes of this King that he passes by so worthy a knight as his own nephew to choose one who is not of lawful birth in his stead? Now, my husband's house has suffered many grievous ills at the hands of King Arthur, for, lo! he hath taken away our royal power and hath made us all little better than captives in his own Court. This in itself is as great an affront as though we were his bitter enemies instead of his nigh of kin. But this that he hath now done to my son in thus passing him by is a greater affront than that other."

And Queen Morgana le Fay spoke in this wise not only to King Uriens, who was her husband, but to Sir Ewaine and Sir Baudemagus, who were her sons. But King Uriens of Gore rebuked her for her speech, for he had grown to love King Arthur very much because of the high nobility of his nature, and likewise Sir Ewaine rebuked her saying that he would listen to no ill thing said of King Arthur, for that not only did he love King Arthur better than anyone else in all the world, but that the King was at once the looking-glass of all knighthood and likewise the very fountain-head of honor.

So spake these two; but Sir Baudemagus hearkened to what his mother, Queen Morgana said, for he was very angry with King Arthur because the King had passed him by. Wherefore he took his departure from the Court without asking leave of King Arthur and went errant in quest of adventure, and at this King Arthur was very sorry.

Now, as aforesaid, Queen Morgana le Fay spake her indignation to several other people of the Court, so that word thereof came at last to the ears of King Arthur and grieved him a very great deal. So when Queen Morgana came to him one day and besought his leave for to quit the Court, he spake to her with great sadness of spirit, saying, "My sister, I am very sorry that you are not pleased with what I have done in this matter, for God knows that I have endeavored to do to the best of my power. And though I would rather a great deal that Sir Baudemagus were fellow of the Round Table, yet it was my very honest belief that, for several reasons, Sir Tor had the best right to a seat at that Table. Now if I chose otherwise than according to my right judgment, what virtue would the Round Table have, seeing that I should have shown favor unto a man because of his kinship to me?"

Then Queen Morgana le Fay said with great heat, "Sir, all that you say only adds to the affront that our house hath sustained at your hands. For now you not only deny my son that seat, but you belittle him by comparing him to his disadvantage with this low-born knight whom you have chosen. Now, the only pleasure that I can have in talking to you is to beseech you to let me go away from this place."

Then King Arthur, speaking with great dignity, said, "Lady, it shall be as you would have it, and you shall go whithersoever it pleases you. For God forbid that I should stay you in your wishes. Moreover, I shall see to it that you shall not depart from this place without such a Court for company as may very well befit one who is the wife of one king and the sister of another."

And so he did as he said he would do, for he sent Queen Morgana le Fay away from his Court with great honor and in high estate of circumstance. But the more patient King Arthur was with her and the more he showed her favor, the more angry Queen Morgana le Fay was with him and the more she hated him.

So she betook her way to an estuary of the sea and there she dismissed those whom the King had sent with her and embarked with her own Court in several ships, betaking her way to that enchanted isle, hight Avalon, which was her home.

This island of Avalon was a very strange, wonderful land, such as was not to be seen anywhere else in all the world. For it was like a Paradise for beauty, being covered all over with divers gardens of flowers, intermingled with plantations of fair trees, some bearing fruit and others all a-bloom with blossoms. And besides these were many terraces of lawns, overlooking the sea from tall white walls of pure marble. And in the midst of these gardens and orchards and plantations and lawns and terraces, were a multitude of castles and towers built up the one above the other – some as white as snow and others very gay with many colors.

And the greatest marvel of that wonderful island was this: that in the midst of all those castles and towers was a single tower built entirely of loadstone. And in that lay the great mystery of that place.

For the island floated upon the surface of the water, and that tower of loadstone possessed such a potency that Avalon would float from place to place according to the will of Queen Morgana le Fay, so that sometimes it would be here, and sometimes it would be there, as that royal lady willed it to be.

Nor was there a very many people who had seen that island, for somewhiles it would be all covered over with a mist of enchantment like to silver, so that no eyes could behold it unless they were fay. But sometimes it had been seen, as it were a vision of Paradise. What time he who beheld it would hear gay voices sounding from its lawns and plantations – very thin and clear because of the great distance (for no one ever came nigh to Avalon unless by authority of Queen Morgana le Fay), and he would hear music of so sweet a sort that it was likely that his soul would grow all faint because of the music. Then Avalon would suddenly disappear very marvellously, and he who had seen it would be aware that it was not likely that he would ever see it again.

Such was the island of Avalon, and if you would read of it more particularly you shall find much about it in a certain book written in French and called "Ogier le Danois."

Queen Morgana le Fay loved this island a very great deal, and it is said by many that King Arthur is yet alive in that place, lying there very peacefully and tranquilly whiles he awaits that certain time when he shall return unto the world to make right all that is wrong therein. So it is I have told you of it with these particulars at this place.

PART I

# THE STORY OF MERLIN

~

*Here followeth a particular account of the enchantment of Morgana le Fay by a certain damsel, hight Vivien, and of all the circumstances thereunto appertaining.*

*Likewise it is to be narrated how King Arthur was betrayed by his own sister, and of how he would certainly have been slain only for the help of that same enchantress Vivien who was the cause of Merlin's undoing.*

*Also it shall be told how the sheath of Excalibur was lost at that time.*

CHAPTER FIRST

# How Queen Morgana le Fay Meditated Evil Against King Arthur

Now Morgana le Fay was a very cunning enchantress, and was so much mistress of magic that she could, by means of potent spells, work her will upon all things, whether quick or dead. For Merlin himself had been her master in times past, and had taught her his arts whilst she was still a young damsel at the Court of Uther-Pendragon. So it was that, next to Merlin, she was, at that time, the most potent enchanter in all the world. Nevertheless she lacked Merlin's foreknowledge of things to happen and his gift of prophecy thereupon, for these things he could not impart unto anyone, wherefore she had not learned them of him.

Now, after Queen Morgana le Fay had come to the Island of Avalon as aforetold, she brooded a great deal over that affront which she deemed King Arthur had placed upon her house; and the more she brooded upon it the more big did it become in her mind. Wherefore, at last, it seemed to her that she could have no pleasure in life unless she could punish King Arthur for that which he had done. Yea; she would have been glad to see him dead at her feet because of the anger that she felt against him.

But Queen Morgana was very well aware that she could never do the King, her brother, an injury so long as Merlin was there to safeguard him, for Merlin would certainly foresee any danger that might threaten the King, and would counteract it, wherefore she was aware that if she would destroy the King, she must first destroy Merlin.

Now, there was at the Court of Queen Morgana le Fay, a certain damsel of such marvellous and bewitching beauty that her like was hardly to be seen in all of the world. This damsel was fifteen years old and of royal blood, being the daughter of the King of Northumberland; and her name was Vivien. This damsel, Vivien, was both wise and cunning beyond all measure for one so young. Moreover, she was without any heart, being cold and cruel to all who were contrary-minded to her wishes. So, because she was so cunning and wise, Queen Morgana liked her and taught her many things of magic and sorcery which she knew. But, notwithstanding all that Queen Morgana did for her, this maiden did not feel any love for her mistress, being altogether devoid of heart.

One day this damsel and Queen Morgana le Fay sat together in a garden of that magic island of Avalon, and the garden was upon a very high terrace and overlooked the sea. And the day was very fair and the sea so wonderfully blue that it appeared to be as though the blue sky had melted into water and the water into the sky. As Vivien and the Queen sat in this beautiful place, the Queen said to the damsel, "Vivien, what wouldst thou rather have than anything else in all the world?" To which Vivien replied, "Lady, I would rather have such wisdom as thou hast, than anything else."

Then Queen Morgana laughed and said, "It is possible for thee to be as wise as I am, and wiser too, if so be thou wilt do according to my ordination. For I know a way in which thou mayst obtain wisdom."

"How may I obtain that wisdom, Lady?" said Vivien.

Then Queen Morgana le Fay said, "Hearken and I will tell thee. Thou must know that Merlin, whom thou hast several times seen at the Court of King Arthur, is the master of all the wisdom that it is possible for anyone to possess in this world. All that I know of magic Merlin hath taught me, and he knoweth many things that he did not teach me, but which he withheld from me. For Merlin taught me, when I was a young damsel at the Court of my mother's husband, because I was beautiful in his eyes. For Merlin loveth beauty above all things else in the world, and so he taught me many things of magic and was very patient with me.

"But Merlin hath a gift which belongeth to him and which he cannot communicate to anyone else, for it is instinct with him. That gift is the gift of foreseeing into the future and the power of prophesying thereupon.

"Yet though he may foresee the fate of others, still he is blind to his own fate. For so he confessed to me several times: that he could not tell what was to happen in his own life when that happening concerned himself alone.

"Now thou, Vivien, art far more beautiful than I was at thine age. Wherefore I believe that thou wilt easily attract the regard of Merlin unto thee. And if I give thee, besides, a certain charm which I possess, I may cause it to be that Merlin may love thee so much that he will impart to thee a great deal more of his wisdom than ever he taught me when I was his disciple.

"But thou art to know, Vivien, that in winning this gift of knowledge from Merlin thou wilt put thyself in great peril. For, by and by, when the charm of thy beauty shall have waned with him, then he may easily regret what he hath done in imparting his wisdom to thee; in the which case there will be great danger that he may lay some spell upon thee to deprive thee of thy powers; for it would be impossible that both thou and he could live in the same world and each of ye know so much cunning of magic."

Now unto all this Vivien listened with a great deal of attention, and when Queen Morgana had ended the damsel said, "Dear Lady, all that thou tellest me is very wonderful, and I find myself possessed with a vehement desire to attain such knowledge in magic as that. Wherefore, if thou wilt help me in this matter so that I may beguile his wisdom from Merlin, thou wilt make of me a debtor unto thee for as long as I may live. And touching the matter of any danger that may fall to me in this affair, I am altogether willing to assume that; for I have a great hope that I may be able so to protect myself from Merlin that no harm shall befall me. For when I have drawn all the knowledge that I am able to obtain from him, then I will use that same knowledge to cast such a spell upon him that he shall never be able to harm me or anyone else again. In this I shall play my wit against his wisdom and my beauty against his cunning, and I believe that I shall win at that game."

Then Queen Morgana fell a-laughing beyond all measure, and when she had stinted her laughter, she cried, "Hey, Vivien! certes thou art cunning beyond anything that I ever heard tell of, and I believe that thou art as wicked as thou art cunning. For whoever heard of a child of fifteen years old who would speak such words as thou hast just now spoken; or whoever could suppose that so young a girl could conceive the thought of compassing the downfall of the wisest magician who hath ever lived."

Then Queen Morgana le Fay set to her lips a small whistle of ivory and gold and blew very shrilly upon it, and in reply there came running a young page of her Court. Queen Morgana commanded him to bring to her a certain casket of alabaster, cunningly carved and adorned with gold and set with several precious stones. And Queen Morgana opened the box and took from within it two rings of pure yellow gold, beautifully wrought and set, the one ring with a clear white stone of extraordinary brilliancy, and the other with a stone as red as blood. Then Queen Morgana said, "Vivien, behold these two rings! They possess each a spell of wonderful potency. For if thou wearest that ring with the white stone, whoever weareth the ring with the red stone shall love thee with such a passion of love that thou mayst do with him whatever thou hast a will to do. So take these rings and go to King Arthur's Court and use them as thy cunning may devise."

So Vivien took the two rings and gave Queen Morgana le Fay thanks beyond all measure for them.

Now King Arthur took much pleasure in holding a great feast each Pentecost, at which time his Court was gathered about him with much mirth and rejoicing. At such times it delighted him to have some excellent entertainment for to amuse himself and his Court, wherefore it befell that nearly always something happened that gave much entertainment to the King. So came the Feast of Pentecost, and King Arthur sat at the table with a great many noble and lordly folk and several kings and queens. Now as they all sat at that feast, their spirits greatly expanded with mirth and good cheer, there suddenly came into the hall a very beautiful young damsel, and with her a dwarf, wonderfully misshapen and of a very hideous countenance. And the maiden was dressed all in flame-colored satin, very rich, and with beautiful embroidery of gold and embroidery of silver. And her hair, which was red like gold, was coiled into a net of gold. And her eyes were black as coals and extraordinarily bright and glistening. And she had about her throat a necklace of gold of three strands, so that with all that gold and those bright garments she shone with wonderful splendor as she entered the hall. Likewise, the dwarf who accompanied her was clad all in flame-colored raiment, and he bore in his hands a cushion of flame-colored silk with tassels of gold, and upon the cushion he bare a ring of exceeding beauty set with a red stone.

So when King Arthur beheld this beautiful maiden he supposed nothing else, than that there was some excellent entertainment, and at that he rejoiced a very great deal.

But when he looked well at the damsel it appeared to him that he knew her face, wherefore he said to her, "Damsel, who art thou?" "Sir," she said, "I am the daughter of the King of Northumberland, and my name is Vivien," and thereat King Arthur was satisfied.

Then King Arthur said to her, "Lady, what is that thou hast upon yonder cushion,and why hast thou honored us by coming hitherward?" To the which Vivien made reply, "Lord, I have here a very good entertainment for to give you pleasure at this Feast of Pentecost. For here is a ring of such a sort that only he who is the most wise and the most worthy of all men here present may wear it." And King Arthur said, "Let us see the ring."

So Vivien took the ring from the cushion which the dwarf held and she came and brought it unto King Arthur, and the King took the ring into his own hand. And he perceived that the ring was exceedingly beautiful, wherefore he said, "Maiden, have I thy leave to try this ring upon my finger?" And Vivien said, "Yea, lord."

So King Arthur made attempt to place the ring upon his finger; but, lo! the ring shrank in size so that it would not pass beyond the first joint thereof. Wherefore King Arthur said, "It would appear that I am not worthy to wear this ring."

Then the damsel, Vivien, said, "Have I my lord's leave to offer this ring to others of his Court?" And King Arthur said, "Let the others try the ring." So Vivien took the ring to the various folk of the Court, both lords and ladies, but not one of these could wear the ring. Then last of all Vivien came to the place where Merlin sat, and she kneeled upon the ground before him and offered the ring to him; and Merlin, because this concerned himself, could not forecast into the future to know that harm was intended to him. Nevertheless he looked sourly upon the damsel and he said, "Child,

*King Arthur was to have him a Queen (First Book, Part III, Chapter Sixth)*

*So she betook her way (Second Book, Prologue)*

what is this silly trick thou offerest me?" "Sir," quoth Vivien, "I beseech you for to try this ring upon your finger." Then Merlin regarded the damsel more closely, and he perceived that she was very beautiful, wherefore his heart softened toward her a great deal. So he spake more gently unto her and he said, "Wherefore should I take the ring?" To the which she made reply, "Because I believe that thou art the most wise and the most worthy of any man in all this place, wherefore the ring should belong to thee."

Then Merlin smiled, and took the ring and placed it upon his finger, and, lo! it fitted the finger exactly. Thereupon Vivien cried out, "See! the ring hath fitted his finger and he is the most wise and the most worthy." And Merlin was greatly pleased that the ring which the beautiful damsel had given him had fitted his finger in that way.

Then, after a while, he would have withdrawn the ring again but, behold! he could not, for the ring had grown to his finger as though it were a part of the flesh and the bone thereof. At this Merlin became much troubled in spirit and very anxious, for he did not understand what might be meant by the magic of the ring. So he said, "Lady, whence came this ring?" And Vivien said, "Sir, thou knowest all things; dost thou then not know that this ring was sent hitherward from Morgana le Fay?" Then again Merlin was greatly a-doubt, and he said, "I hope there may be no evil in this ring." And Vivien smiled upon him and said, "What evil could there be in it?"

Now by this time the great magic that was in the ring began to work upon Merlin's spirit, wherefore he regarded Vivien very steadily, and suddenly he took great pleasure in her beauty. Then the magic of the ring gat entire hold upon him and, lo! a wonderful passion immediately seized upon his heart and wrung it so that it was pierced as with a violent agony.

And Vivien beheld what passed in Merlin's mind, and she laughed and turned away. And several others who were there also observed the very strange manner in which Merlin regarded her, wherefore they said among themselves, "Of a surety Merlin is bewitched by the beauty of that young damoiselle."

So, after that time the enchantment of the ring of Morgana le Fay so wrought upon Merlin's spirit that he could in no wise disentangle himself from Vivien's witchery; for from that day forth, whithersoever she went, there he might be found not far away; and if she was in the garden, he would be there; and if she was in the Hall, he also would be there; and if she went a-hawking he would also be a-horseback. And all the Court observed these things and many made themselves merry and jested upon it. But, Vivien hated Merlin with all her might, for she saw that they all made merry at that folly of Merlin's, and he wearied her with his regard. But she dissembled this disregard before his face and behaved to him in all ways as though she had a great friendship for him.

Now it happened upon a day that Vivien sat in the garden, and it was wonderfully pleasant summer weather, and Merlin came into the garden and beheld Vivien where she sat. But when Vivien perceived Merlin coming she suddenly felt so great a disregard for him that she could not bear for to be nigh him at that time, wherefore she arose in haste with intent to escape from him. But Merlin hurried and overtook her and he said to her, "Child, do you then hate me?" And Vivien said, "Sir, I do not hate you." But Merlin said, "In very truth I believe that you do hate me." And Vivien was silent.

Then in a little Merlin said, "I would that I knew what I might do for you so that you would cease to hate me, for I find that I have a wonderful love for you." Upon this Vivien looked at Merlin very strangely, and by and by she said, "Sir, if you would only impart your wisdom and your cunning unto me, then I believe that I could love you a very great deal. For, behold! I am but as a young child in knowledge and thou art so old and so wise that I am afraid of thee. If thou wouldst teach me thy wisdom so that I might be thine equal, then haply I might grow to have such a regard for thee as thou wouldst have me feel."

Upon this Merlin looked very steadily at Vivien and he said, "Damsel, thou art, certes, no such foolish child as thou dost proclaim thyself to be; for I see that thine eyes are very bright with a cunning beyond thy years. Now I misdoubt that if I should teach thee the wisdom which thou dost desire to possess, either it would be to thy undoing or else it would be to my undoing."

Then Vivien cried out with a very loud and piercing voice, "Merlin, if thou dost love me, teach me thy wisdom and the cunning of thy magic and then I will love thee beyond anyone else in all the world!"

But Merlin sighed very deeply, for his heart misgave him. Then by and by he said, "Vivien, thou shalt have thy will and I will teach thee all those things of wisdom and magic that thou desirest to know."

Upon this Vivien was filled with such vehement agony of joy that she did not dare to let Merlin look into her countenance lest he should read what was therein written. Wherefore she cast down her eyes and turned her face away from him. Then in a little while she said, "Master, when wilt thou teach me that wisdom?"

To this Merlin made reply, "I shall not teach thee to-day nor to-morrow nor at this place; for I can only teach thee those knowledges in such solitude that there shall be nothing to disturb thy studies. But to-morrow thou shalt tell King Arthur that thou must return unto thy father's kingdom. Then we will depart together accompanied by thy Court; and when we have come to some secluded place, there I will build a habitation by the means of my magic and we shall abide therein until I have instructed thee in wisdom."

Then Vivien made great joy, and she caught Merlin's hand in hers and she kissed his hand with great passion.

So the next day Vivien besought King Arthur that he would give her leave to return unto her father's Court, and upon the third day she and Merlin and a number of attendants who were in service upon the damsel, quitted the Court of King Arthur and departed as though to go upon their way to the Kingdom of Northumberland.

But after they had gone some little distance from the Court of the King, they turned to the eastward and took their way toward a certain valley of which Merlin was acquainted, and which was so fair and pleasant a place that it was sometimes called the Valley of Delight, and sometimes the Valley of Joyousness.

## Chapter Second

# How Merlin Met His Downfall

So, Merlin and Vivien and those who were with them travelled for three days to the eastward, until, toward the end of the third day, they reached the confines of a very dark and dismal forest. And there they beheld before them trees so thickly interwoven together that the eyes could not see anything at all of the sky because of the thickness of the foliage. And they beheld the branches and the roots of the trees that they appeared like serpents all twisted together. Wherefore Vivien said, "Sir, this is a very dismal woodland." "Yea," said Merlin, "so it appeareth to be. Ne'theless there lieth within this forest that place which is called by some the Valley of Joyousness, and by others the Valley of Delight, because of the great beauty of that place. And there are several pathways extending through this forest by the means of which that valley may be reached by a man, whether a-horse or afoot."

And after a while they found it was as Merlin said, for they came by and by upon one of those pathways and entered it and penetrated into the forest. And, lo! within that doleful woodland it was so dark that it appeared as though night-time had fallen, although it was bright daylight beyond the borders thereof, wherefore many of that party were very much afraid. But Merlin ever gave them good cheer and so they went forward upon their way. So, by and by, they came out at last from that place and into the open again, whereat they were greatly rejoiced and took much comfort.

Now, by this time, the evening had come, very peaceful and tranquil, and they beheld beneath them a valley spread out in that light and it was wonderfully beautiful. And in the centre of the valley was a small lake so smooth and clear, like to crystal, that it appeared like an oval shield of pure silver laid down upon the ground. And all about the margin of the lake were level meadows covered over with an incredible multitude of flowers of divers colors and kinds, very beautiful to behold.

When Vivien saw this place she cried unto Merlin, "Master, this is, indeed, a very joyous valley, for I do not believe that the blessed meadows of Paradise are more beautiful than this." And Merlin said, "Very well; let us go down into it." So they went down and, as they descended, the night fell apace and the round moon arose into the sky and it was hard to tell whether that valley was the more beautiful in the daytime or whether it was the more beautiful when the moon shone down upon it in that wise.

So they all came at last unto the borders of the lake and they perceived that there was neither house nor castle at that place.

Now upon this the followers of Merlin murmured amongst themselves, saying, "This enchanter hath brought us hitherward, but how will he now provide for us that we may find a resting-place that may shelter us from the inclement changes of the weather. For the beauty of this spot cannot alone shelter us from rain and storm." And Merlin overheard their murmurings and he said, "Peace! take ye no trouble upon that matter, for I will very soon provide ye a good resting-place." Then he said to them, "Stand ye a little distance aside till I show ye what I shall do." So they withdrew a little, as he commended them, and he and Vivien remained where they were. And Vivien said, "Master, what wilt thou do?" And Merlin said, "Wait a little and thou shalt see."

Therewith he began a certain very powerful conjuration so that the earth began for to tremble and to shake and an appearance as of a great red dust arose into the air. And in this dust there began to appear sundry shapes and forms, and these shapes and forms arose very high into the air and by and by those who gazed thereon perceived that there was a great structure apparent in the midst of the cloud of red dust.

Then, after a while, all became quiet and the dust slowly disappeared from the air, and, behold! there was the appearance of a marvellous castle such as no one there had ever beheld before, even in a dream. For the walls thereof were of ultramarine and vermilion and they were embellished and adorned with figures of gold, wherefore that castle showed in the moonlight like as it were a pure vision of great glory.

Now Vivien beheld all that Merlin had accomplished and she went unto him and kneeled down upon the ground before him and took his hand and set it to her lips. And while she kneeled thus, she said, "Master, this is assuredly the most wonderful thing in the world. Wilt thou then teach me such magic that I may be able to build a castle like this castle out of the elements?" And Merlin said, "Yea; all this will I teach thee and more besides; for I will teach thee not only how thou mayst create such a structure as this out of invisible things, but will also teach thee how thou mayst, with a single touch of thy wand, dissipate that castle instantly into the air; even as a child, with a stroke of a straw, may dissipate a beautiful shining bubble, which, upon an instant is, and upon another instant is not. And I will teach thee more than that, for I will teach thee how to change and transform a thing into the semblance of a different thing; and I will teach thee spells and charms such as thou didst never hear tell of before."

Then Vivien cried out, "Master, thou art the most wonderful man in all of the world!" And Merlin looked upon Vivien and her face was very beautiful in the moonlight and he loved her a very great deal. Wherefore he smiled upon her and said, "Vivien, dost thou still hate me?" And she said, "Nay, master."

But she spake not the truth, for in her heart she was evil and the heart of Merlin was good, and that which is evil will always hate that which is good. Wherefore, though Vivien lusted for the knowledge of necromancy, and though she spake so lovingly with her lips, yet in her spirit she both feared and hated Merlin because of his wisdom. For she wist right well that, except for the enchantment of that ring which he wore, Merlin would not love her any longer in that wise. Wherefore she said in her heart, "If Merlin teaches me all of his wisdom, then the world cannot contain both him and me."

Now Merlin abided with Vivien in that place for a year and a little more, and in that time he taught her all of magic that he was able to impart. So at the end of that time he said unto her, "Vivien, I have now taught thee so much that I believe there is no one in all of the world who knoweth more than thou dost of these things of magic which thou hast studied in this time. For not only hast thou such power of sorcery that thou canst make the invisible elements take form at thy will, and not only canst thou transform at thy will one thing into the appearance of an altogether different thing, but thou hast such potent magic in thy possession that thou mayst entangle any living soul into the meshes thereof, unless that one hath some very good talisman to defend himself from they wiles. Nor have I myself very much more power than this that I have given to thee."

So said Merlin, and Vivien was filled with great joy. And she said in her heart, "Now, Merlin, if I have the good fortune to entangle thee in my spells, then shalt thou never behold the world again."

Now, when the next day had come, Vivien caused a very noble feast to be prepared for herself and Merlin. And by means of the knowledge which Merlin had imparted to her she produced a certain very potent sleeping-potion which was altogether without taste. This potion she herself infused into a certain noble wine, and the wine she poured into a golden chalice of extraordinary beauty.

So when that feast was ended, and whiles she and Merlin sat together, Vivien said,

"Master, I have a mind to do thee a great honor." And Merlin said, "What is it?" "Thou shalt see," said Vivien. Therewith she smote her hands together and there immediately came a young page unto where they were, and he bare that chalice of wine in his hand and gave it unto Vivien. Then Vivien took the chalice and she went to where Merlin sat and kneeled down before him and said, "Sir, I beseech thee to take this chalice and to drink the wine that is within it. For as that wine is both very noble and very precious, so is thy wisdom both very noble and very precious; and as the wine is contained within a chalice of priceless cost, so is thy wisdom contained within a life that hath been beyond all value to the world." Therewith she set her lips to the chalice and kissed the wine that was in it.

Then Merlin suspected no evil, but he took the chalice and quaffed of the wine with great cheerfulness.

After that, in a little, the fumes of that potent draught began to arise into the brains of Merlin and it was as though a cloud descended upon his sight, and when this came upon him he was presently aware that he was betrayed, wherefore he cried out thrice in a voice, very bitter and full of agony, "Woe! Woe! Woe!" And then he cried out, "I am betrayed!" And therewith he strove to arise from where he sat but he could not.

That while Vivien sat with her chin upon her hands and regarded him very steadily, smiling strangely upon him. So presently Merlin ceased his struggles and sank into a sleep so deep that it was almost as though he had gone dead. And when that had happened Vivien arose and leaned over him and set a very powerful spell upon him. And she stretched out her forefinger and wove an enchantment all about him so that it was as though he was entirely encompassed with a silver web of enchantment. And when she had ended, Merlin could move neither hand nor foot nor even so much as a finger-tip, but was altogether like some great insect that a cunning and beautiful spider had enmeshed in a net-work of fine, strong web.

Now, when the next morning had come, Merlin awoke from his sleep and he beheld that Vivien sat over against him regarding him very narrowly. And they were in the same room in which he had fallen asleep. And when Vivien perceived that Merlin was awake, she laughed and said, "Merlin, how is it with thee?" And Merlin groaned with great passion, saying, "Vivien, thou hast betrayed me."

At this Vivien laughed again very shrilly and piercingly, and she said, "Behold! Merlin, thou art altogether in my power; for thou art utterly inwoven in those enchantments which thou, thyself, hast taught me. For lo! thou canst not move a single hair without my will. And when I leave thee, the world shall see thee no more and all thy wisdom shall be my wisdom and all thy power shall be my power,and there shall be no other in the whole world who shall possess the wisdom which I possess."

Then Merlin groaned with such fervor that it was as though his heart would burst asunder. And he said, "Vivien, thou hast brought me to such shame that even were I released from this spell I could not endure that any man should ever see my face again. For I grieve not for my undoings so much as I grieve at the folly that hath turned mine own wisdom against me to my destruction. So I forgive thee all things that thou hast done to me to betray me; yet there is one thing alone which I crave of thee."

And Vivien said, "Does it concern thee?" And Merlin said, "No, it concerns another." Thereupon Vivien said, "What is it?"

Then Merlin said, "It is this: Now I have received my gift of foresight again, and I perceive that King Arthur is presently in great peril of his life. So I beseech thee Vivien that thou wilt straightway go to where he is in danger, and that thou wilt use thy powers of sorcery for to save him. Thus, by fulfilling this one good deed, thou shalt haply lessen the sin of this that thou hast done to betray me."

Now at that time Vivien was not altogether bad as she afterward became, for she still felt some small pity for Merlin and some small reverence for King Arthur. Wherefore now she laughed and said, "Very well, I will do thy desire in this matter. Whither shall I go to save that King?"

Then Merlin replied, "Go into the West country and unto the castle of a certain knight hight Sir Domas de Noir, and when thou comest there then thou shalt immediately see how thou mayst be of aid to the good King." Upon this Vivien said, "I will do this thing for thee, for it is the last favor that anyone may ever render unto thee in this world."

Therewith Vivien smote her hands together and summoned many of her attendants. And when these had come in she presented Merlin before them, and she said, "Behold how I have bewitched him. Go! See for yourselves! Feel of his hands and his face and see if there be any life in him." And they went to Merlin and felt of him; his hands and arms and his face, and even they plucked at his beard, and Merlin could not move in any wise but only groan with great dolor. So they all laughed and made them merry at his woful state.

Then Vivien caused it by means of her magic that there should be in that place a great coffer of stone. And she commanded those who were there that they should lift Merlin up and lay him therein and they did as she commanded. Then she caused it that, by means of her magic, there should be placed a huge slab of stone upon that coffer such as ten men could hardly lift, and Merlin lay beneath that stone like one who was dead.

Then Vivien caused it to be that the magic castle should instantly disappear and so it befell as she willed. Then she caused it that a mist should arise at that place, and the mist was of such a sort that no one could penetrate into it, or sever it asunder, nor could any human eye see what was within. Then, when she had done all this, she went her way with all of her Court from that valley, making great joy in that she had triumphed over Merlin.

Nevertheless she did not forget her promise, but went to the castle of Sir Domas de Noir, and after a while it shall all be told how it befell at that place.

Such was the passing of Merlin, and God grant it that you may not so misuse the wisdom He giveth you to have, that it may be turned against you to your undoing. For there can be no greater bitterness in the world than this: That a man shall be betrayed by one to whom he himself hath given the power of betraying him.

And now turn we unto King Arthur to learn how it fell with him after Merlin had thus been betrayed to his undoing.

CHAPTER THIRD

# HOW QUEEN MORGANA LE FAY RETURNED TO CAMELOT

Now, after Merlin had quitted the Court with Vivien in that manner aforetold, Queen Morgana le Fay returned again to Camelot. There she came unto King Arthur and kneeled before him, bowing her face, with an appearance of great humility. And she said, "Brother, I have meditated much upon these matters that have passed and I perceive that I have done very ill to talk against thee as I have done, and to be so rebellious against thy royalty. Wherefore I crave of thee to forgive me my evil words and thoughts against thee."

Then King Arthur was very much moved and he came to Queen Morgana and took her by the hand and lifted her up upon her feet and kissed her brow, and her eyes, saying, "My sister, I have no ill-will against thee, but nothing but love for thee in my heart." And so, Queen Morgana le Fay abode at the Court in the same manner as she had aforetime done, for King Arthur believed that they were reconciled.

Now one day, Queen Morgana and the King fell into a friendly talk concerning Excalibur, and Queen Morgana le Fay expressed a very great desire to see that noble weapon more closely than she had yet done, and King Arthur said he would sometime show it to her. So the next day he said, "Sister, come with me and I will show thee Excalibur." Therewith he took Queen Morgana by the hand and led her into another apartment where was a strong wooden coffer bound with bands of iron.

Then the King opened the coffer and therein Queen Morgana le Fay beheld Excalibur where he lay in his sheath. Then King Arthur said to her, "Lady, take this sword and examine it as you please." Therewith Queen Morgana took Excalibur into her hands and lifted him out of the coffer. And she drew the sword out of the sheath and, lo! the blade flashed like lightning. Then she said, "Sir, this is a very beautiful sword and I would that I might take it hence and keep it for a little so that I might enjoy it in full measure."

Now King Arthur was of a mind to show the Queen great courtesy at this time of their reconciliation, wherefore he said to her, "Take it, and be thou its keeper for as long as thou wilt." So Queen Morgana took Excalibur and his sheath and bare them away with her to her inn, and she hid the sword in the bed in which she slept.

Then Queen Morgana sent for sundry goldsmiths, eight in number, and for certain armorsmiths, eight in number, and for certain cunning jewellers, eight in number, and she said unto them, "Make me a sword in every particular like this sword that I have here." And thereupon she showed them Excalibur in his sheath. So these goldsmiths and armorsmiths and lapidaries labored with great diligence, and in a fortnight they had made a sword so exactly like Excalibur that no eye could have told the difference betwixt the one and the other. And Queen Morgana le Fay kept both swords by her until her purposes should have been fulfilled.

It befell upon a certain day that King Arthur proclaimed a hunt, and he and all of his Court were party thereunto.

Now the day before this hunt took place Queen Morgana le Fay came to King Arthur and said, "Brother, I have here for thee a very beautiful and noble horse which I intend to give thee as a gift of love." Therewith she called aloud and there came two grooms bringing a horse as black as jet and all beset with trappings and harness of silver. And the horse was of such extraordinary beauty that neither King Arthur nor anybody who was with him had ever before seen its like for beauty. So a wonderful delight possessed the King at sight of the horse and he said, "Sister, this is the noblest gift I have had given to me for this long time." "Ha! brother," quoth Queen Morgana, "doth that horse then belike thee?" "Yea," said King Arthur, "it belikes me more than any horse that I ever beheld before." "Then," quoth Queen Morgana, "consider it as a gift of reconciliation betwixt thee and me. And in sign of that reconciliation I beg of thee that thou wilt ride that horse forth upon the hunt to-morrow day." And King Arthur said, "I will do so."

So the next day he rode forth to the hunt upon that horse as he said that he would do.

Now it happened some time after noon that the hounds started a hart of extraordinary size, and the King and all of his Court followed the chase with great eagerness. But the horse of King Arthur soon outstripped all the other horses saving only that of a certain very honorable and worthy knight of the Court hight Sir Accalon of Gaul. So Sir Accalon and the King rode at a great pace through the forest, and they were so eager with the chase that they wist not whither they were riding. And at last they overtook the hart and found that it was embushed in a certain very thick and tangled part of the forest, and there King Arthur slew the stag, and so the chase was ended.

Now after this had come to pass, the King and Sir Accalon would have retraced their way whither they had come, but in a little they perceived that they were lost in the mazes of the woodland and wist not where they were. For they had followed the chase so far that they were in an altogether strange country. So they wandered hither and thither at great length until eventide, at which time they were oppressed with hunger and weariness. Then King Arthur said to Sir Accalon, "Messire, meseems we shall have nowhere to rest ourselves to-night unless it be beneath a tree in this forest."

To this Sir Accalon made reply, "Lord, if thou wilt follow my counsel thou wilt let our horses seek their own way through this wilderness, so, haply, because of the instinct of such creatures, they shall bring us unto some place of habitation."

Now this advice appeared to be very good to King Arthur, wherefore he did as Sir Accalon advised and let loose his bridle-rein and allowed his horse to travel as it listed. So King Arthur's horse went along a certain path, and Sir Accalon followed after the King. And they went a great pass in this wise, and the night was descending upon them in the forest.

But, before it was entirely dark, they emerged out of that forest and into an open place where they beheld before them a very wide estuary, as it were an inlet of the sea. And before them was a beach of sand, very smooth, and white, and they two went down to that beach and stood upon the shore, and they wist not what to do, for there was no habitation in sight in any direction.

Now, whiles they stood there a-doubt, they suddenly perceived a ship at a very great distance away. And this ship approached where they were, sailing very rapidly. As the ship drew nigh to that place they perceived that it was of a very strange and wonderful appearance, for it was painted in many divers colors, very gaudy and brilliant, and the sails were all of cloth of silk, woven in divers colors and embroidered with figures like to the figures of a tapestry; and King Arthur was very greatly amazed at the appearance of that ship.

Now, as they stood so watching the ship, they perceived that it drew nigher and nigher to that place where they were, and in a little it beached itself upon the shore of sand not very far away from them.

Then King Arthur said to Sir Accalon, "Sir, let us go forward to the shore where we may look into this ship, for never did I see its like before in all of my life, wherefore I have a thought that maybe it is fay."

So they two went to where the ship was and they stood upon the shore and looked down into it, and at first they thought that there was no one upon board of the ship, for it appeared to be altogether deserted. But as they stood there marvelling at the wonderfulness of that ship and at the manner in which it had come thither, they beheld, of a sudden, that certain curtains that hung before an apartment at the farther extremity of the ship were parted asunder and there came forth from that place twelve very beautiful damsels. Each of these was clad in a rich garment of scarlet satin very bright and shining, and each wore around her head a circlet of gold, and each had many bracelets of gold upon her arms. These damsels came forward unto where the two knights were and they said, "Welcome, King Arthur!" And they said, "Welcome, Sir Accalon!"

At this King Arthur was very much astonished that they should know him, and he said, "Fair ladies, how is this? Ye appear to know me very well, but I know ye not. Who are ye that know me and my companion and call us by name?"

Unto this the chiefest of those damsels made reply, "Sir, we are part fay and we know all about you; and we know how that ye have been following a very long chase; and we know that ye are aweary, anhungered, and athirst. Wherefore we beseech ye that ye come aboard of this ship and rest and refresh yourselves with food and drink."

Now, this appeared to King Arthur to be a very bel-adventure, wherefore he said to Sir Accalon, "Messires, I have a great mind for to go aboard this ship and to follow out this adventure." And Sir Accalon said, "Lord, if thou goest, I will go also."

So those ladies let fall a gangplank from the ship and King Arthur and Sir Accalon drave their horses up the gangplank and aboard the ship, and immediately they did so, the ship withdrew itself from the sands and sailed away as it had come – very swiftly – and it was now the early night-time with the moon very round and full in the sky like to a disk of pure shining silver.

Then those twelve damoiselles aided King Arthur and Sir Accalon to dismount; and some took their horses away and others led them into a fair chamber at the end of the ship. And in this chamber King Arthur beheld that a table had been placed as though for their entertainment, spread with a linen cloth and set with divers savory meats, and with manchets of white bread and with several different sorts of excellent wines. And at the sight King Arthur and Sir Accalon were very much rejoiced, for they were very greatly anhungered.

So they immediately sat themselves down at that table and they ate and drank with great heartiness, and whiles they did so some of those damsels served them with food, and others held them in pleasant discourse, and others made music upon lutes and citterns for their entertainment. So they feasted and made very merry.

But, after a while, a very great drowsiness of sleep began to descend upon King Arthur; albeit, he deemed that that drowsiness had come upon him because of the weariness of the chase. So presently he said, "Fair damsels, ye have refreshed us a very great deal and this hath been a very pleasant adventure. But I would now that ye had a place for us to sleep."

Unto this the chiefest of the damsels replied, "Lord, this boat hath been prepared for your refreshment, wherefore all things have been made ready for you with entire fulness."

Therewith some of those twelve damsels conducted King Arthur into a sleeping‘chamber that had been prepared for him, and others led Sir Accalon into another chamber prepared for him. And King Arthur marvelled at the beauty of his chamber, for he thought that he had never beheld a more excellently bedight bedchamber than that one into which he had now entered. So King Arthur laid himself down with much comfort to his body, and straightway he fell into deep and gentle sleep, without dream or disturbance of any sort.

Now when King Arthur awoke from that sleep, he was astonished beyond all measure so that he wist not whether he was still asleep and dreaming, or whether he was awake. For, lo! he lay upon a pallet in a very dark and dismal chamber all of stone. And he perceived that this chamber was a dungeon, and all about him he heard the sound of many voices in woful complaint. Then King Arthur said to himself, "Where is that ship in which I was last night, and what hath become of those ladies with whom I spake?"

Upon this he looked about him and, behold! he saw that he was indeed in a dungeon and that there were many knights in very sad estate all about him. Wherefore he perceived that they also were captives and that it was they who had made that sound of woful lamentation which he had heard when awaking.

Then King Arthur aroused himself from where he lay and he saw that all those knights who were prisoners there were strangers unto him, and he knew not them and they knew not him. And of these knights there were two and twenty who were prisoners in that place.

Then King Arthur said, "Messires, who are you and where am I at these present?" To the which the chiefest of those knights who were prisoners made reply, "Sir, we are, like yourself, prisoners in a dungeon of this castle, and the castle belongeth to a certain knight, hight Sir Domas, surnamed le Noir."

Then King Arthur made great marvel at what had befallen him, wherefore he said, "Messires, here is a very singular thing hath happened to me, for last night I was asleep in a very wonderful ship that I believe was fay, and with me was a knight-companion, and, lo! this morning I awake alone in this dungeon, and know not how I came hither."

"Sir," said the knight who spake for the others, "thou wert last night brought hither by two men clad in black, and thou wert laid down upon yonder pallet without awakening, wherefore it is very plain to me that thou art in the same case that we are in, and that thou art a prisoner unto this Sir Domas le Noir."

Then King Arthur said, "Tell me, who is this Sir Domas, for I declare that I never before heard of him." "I will tell you," said the captive knight, and therewith he did so as follows:

"I believe," said he, "that this Sir Domas is the falsest knight that liveth, for he is full of treason and leasing, and is altogether a coward in his heart. Yet he is a man of very great estate and very powerful in these parts.

"Now there are two brothers, and Sir Domas is one and the other is hight Sir

Ontzlake, and Sir Domas is the elder and Sir Ontzlake is the younger. When the father of these two knights died, he left the one an equal patrimony with the other. But now it hath come about that Sir Domas hath nearly all of those estates and that Sir Ontzlake hath only one castle, which same he now holdeth by the force of arms and because of his own courage. For, though Sir Domas is altogether a coward in his heart, yet he hath cunning and guile beyond any man of whom I ever heard tell; wherefore it hath so come about that of his father's patrimony Sir Domas hath everything and Sir Ontzlake hath nothing saving only that one castle and the estate thereunto appertaining.

"Now it would appear to be very strange that Sir Domas is not satisfied with all this, yet he is not satisfied, but he covets that one castle and that small estate that is his brother's, so that he can hardly have any pleasure in life because of his covetousness. Yet he knoweth not how to obtain that estate from his brother, for Sir Ontzlake is a very excellent knight, and the only way that Sir Domas can lay hands upon that estate is by having to do with his brother as man to man in a contest at arms, and this he is afraid to attempt.

"So, for a long time, Sir Domas hath been in search of a knight who may take up his case for him, and do battle against Sir Ontzlake in his behalf. Wherefore all the knights whom he can arrest he bringeth to this castle and giveth them their choice, either to take up his case against his brother, or else to remain in this place as his prisoner without ransom. So he hath arrested all of us, and hath made demand of each that he should do battle in his behalf. But not one of us will take up the case of such an evil-conditioned knight as Sir Domas, so we all remain his prisoners."

"Well," quoth King Arthur, "this is a very wonderful case. But methinks that if Sir Domas maketh his appeal to me, I will take up his case. For I would rather do that than remain a prisoner here for all my life. But if I should take upon me this battle and be successful therein, then I will afterward have to do with Sir Domas himself in such a manner as I do not believe would be very much to his liking."

Now a little while after this the door of that prison-house was opened by the porter, and there entered a very fair young damsel. And this damsel came to King Arthur and she said to him, "What cheer?" "I cannot tell," quoth King Arthur, "but meseems I am in a very sorry pass in this place." "Sir," said the damsel, "I am grieved to see so noble-appearing a knight in so dolorous a case. But if you will undertake to defend the cause of the lord of this castle with your person against his enemy, then you shall have leave to go whithersoever you please." To this King Arthur made reply, "Lady, this is a very hard case, that either I must fight a battle I care not for, or else remain a prisoner here without ransom for all of my days. But I would liever fight than live here all my life, and so I will undertake that adventure as thou wouldst have me do. But if I do battle for the lord of this castle, and if I should have Grace of Heaven to win that battle, then it must be that all these, my companions in imprisonment, shall also go forth with me into freedom."

To this the damsel said, "Very well, be it so, for that shall content the master of this castle."

Then King Arthur looked more closely at the maiden, and he said, "Damsel, meseems I should know thy face, for I think I have seen thee somewhere before this."

"Nay, sir," said she, "that can hardly be, for I am the daughter of the lord of this castle."

But in this she was false, for she was one of the damsels of Morgana le Fay; and she was one of those who had beguiled King Arthur into the ship the night before; and it was she who had brought him to that castle and had delivered him into the hands of Sir Domas. And all these things she had done upon command of Queen Morgana le Fay.

Then King Arthur said, "But if I do this battle, thou must carry a message for me unto the Court of King Arthur, and that message must be delivered unto Queen Morgana le Fay into her own hands. Then, when that is done, I will do this battle for the cause of Sir Domas." And the damsel said, "It shall be done so."

So King Arthur wrote a sealed letter to Queen Morgana le Fay that she should send to him his sword Excalibur; and he sent that message to her. And when Queen Morgana received that letter she laughed and said, "Very well, he shall have a sword that shall please his eye as well as Excalibur." And therewith she sent him that other sword that she had had made exactly like Excalibur.

So Sir Domas sent word unto his brother Sir Ontzlake, that he had now a champion for to do battle in his behalf to recover all that portion of their patrimony which Sir Ontzlake still withheld from him.

Now when Sir Ontzlake received this message he was thrown into great trouble of spirit, for a little while before he had been very sorely wounded in a tournament in the which a spear had been thrust through both his thighs, so that he was then abed with that wound and without power to arise therefrom. Wherefore he wist not what to do in this case, for he could not do battle upon his own behalf, and he had no one to do battle for him.

CHAPTER FOURTH

# How King Arthur Came Nigh to Losing His Life

Here followeth the account of what happened unto Sir Accalon the morning after he went aboard that magic ship with King Arthur as aforetold.

Now when Sir Accalon awoke from that same sleep it was with him as it had been with King Arthur; for, at first, he wist not whether he was still asleep and dreaming or whether he was awake. For, lo! he found himself to be lying beside a marble basin of clear water that gushed up very high from a silver tube. And he perceived that not far from this fountain was a large pavilion of parti-colored silk which stood upon the borders of a fair meadow of grass.

So Sir Accalon was altogether astonished to find himself in this place when he had fallen asleep on board that ship, wherefore he was afraid that all this was the fruit of some very evil spell. So he crossed himself and said, "God save King Arthur from any harm, for it seems to me that those damsels upon that ship have wrought some magic upon us for to separate us the one from the other." So saying, he arose from where he lay with intent to inquire further into that matter.

Now, as he made some noise in bestirring himself, there came forth from that pavilion aforementioned a very hideous dwarf, who saluted him with all civility and with high respect. Then Sir Accalon said to the dwarf, "Sirrah, who are you?" Unto which the dwarf made answer, "Messire, I belong unto the lady of yonder pavilion, and she hath sent me to bid you welcome to this place, and to invite you in for to partake of a repast with her." "Ha!" quoth Sir Accalon, "and how was it I came hither?" "Sir," said the dwarf, "I do not know, but when we looked forth this morning we saw you lying here by the fountain side."

Then Sir Accalon made great marvel at that which had happened to him, and by and by he said, "Who is thy lady?" To which the dwarf replied, "She is hight the Lady Gomyne of the Fair Hair, and she will be passingly glad of your company in her pavilion."

Upon this Sir Accalon arose, and, having laved himself at the fountain and so refreshed himself, he went with the dwarf unto the pavilion of that lady. And when he had come there he saw that in the center of the pavilion was a table of silver spread with a fair white cloth and covered with very excellent food for a man to break his fast withal.

Now immediately Sir Accalon came into the pavilion, the curtains upon the further side thereof were parted and there entered from a further chamber a very beautiful lady and gave Sir Accalon welcome to that place. And Sir Accalon said to her, "Lady, methinks thou art very civil to invite me thus into thy pavilion." "Nay, sir," said the lady, "it took no great effort to be civil unto a knight so worthy as thou." Then she said to Sir Accalon, "Sir, wilt thou sit here at the table with me and break thy fast?"

At this Sir Accalon was very glad, for he was anhungered, and the beauty of the lady pleased him a very great deal, wherefore it afforded him great joy for to be in her company.

So they two sat at the table with a very cheerful and pleasant spirit and the dwarf waited upon them.

Now after Sir Accalon and the Lady of the Pavilion had broken their fasts she spake to him in this wise, "Sir knight, thou appearest to be a very strong and worthy lord and one very well used to feats of arms and to prowess in battle."

To this Sir Accalon made reply, "Lady, it does not beseem me to bespeak of my own worth, but this much I may freely say; I have engaged in several affrays at arms in such measure as a knight with belt and spurs may do, and I believe that both my friends and mine enemies have had reason to say that I have at all times done my devoirs to the best of my powers."

Then the damoiselle said, "I believe you are a very brave and worthy knight, and being such you might be of service to a good worthy knight who is in sad need of such service as one knight may render unto another."

To this Sir Accalon said, "What is that service?" And the damoiselle replied, "I will tell thee: There is, dwelling not far from this place, a certain knight hight Sir Ontzlake, who hath an elder brother hight Sir Domas. This Sir Domas hath served Sir Ontzlake very ill in many ways, and hath deprived him of well nigh all of his patrimony, so that only a little is left to Sir Ontzlake of all the great possessions that were one time his father's. But even such a small holding as that Sir Domas begrudges Sir Ontzlake, so that Sir Ontzlake must needs hold what he hath by such force of arms as he may himself maintain. Now Sir Domas hath found himself a champion who is a man of a great deal of strength and prowess, and through this champion Sir Domas challenges Sir Ontzlake's right to hold even that small part of those lands which were one time his father's; wherefore if Sir Ontzlake would retain what is his he must presently do battle therefore.

"Now this is a very sad case for Sir Ontzlake, for a short time since he was wounded by a spear at a tournament and was pierced through both of his thighs, wherefore he is not now able to sit upon his horse and to defend his rights against assault. Wherefore meseems that a knight could have no better cause to show his prowess than in the defence of so sad a case as this."

So spake that lady, and to all she said Sir Accalon listened with great attention, and when she had ended he said, "Lady, I would be indeed right willing to defend Sir Ontzlake's right, but, lo! I have no armor nor have I any arms to do battle withal."

Then that damoiselle smiled very kindly upon Sir Accalon and she said to him, "Sir, Sir Ontzlake may easily fit thee with armor that shall be altogether to thy liking. And as for arms, I have in this pavilion a sword that hath but one other fellow in all the world."

Upon this she arose and went back into that curtained recess from which she had come, and thence she presently returned, bringing a certain thing wrapped in a scarlet cloth. And she opened the cloth before Sir Accalon's eyes, and lo! that which she had there was King Arthur's sword Excalibur in his sheath. Then the damoiselle said, "This sword shall be thine if thou wilt assume this quarrel upon behalf of Sir Ontzlake."

Now when Sir Accalon beheld that sword he wist not what to think, and he said to himself, "Certes, either this is Excalibur or else it is his twin brother." Therewith he drew the blade from out of its shield and it shined with extraordinary splendor. Then Sir Accalon said, "I know not what to think for pure wonder, for this sword is indeed the very image of another sword I wot of." When he so spake that damoiselle smiled upon him again, and she said, "I have heard tell that there is in the world another sword like to this."

Then Sir Accalon said, "Lady, to win this sword for myself I would be willing to fight in any battle whatsoever." And the damoiselle replied, "Then if thou wilt fight this battle for Sir Ontzlake thou art free to keep that sword for thine own," at the which Sir Accalon was rejoiced beyond all measure of gladness.

So it came about that, by the wiles of Queen Morgana le Fay, King Arthur was brought to fight a battle unknowingly with a knight very much beloved by him, and that that knight had Excalibur to use against his master. For all these things had come to pass through the cunning of Morgana le Fay.

Now a fair field was prepared for that battle in such a place as was convenient both to Sir Domas and to Sir Ontzlake, and thither they came upon the day assigned, each with his knight-champion and his attendants, Sir Ontzlake being brought thither in a litter because of the sore wound in his thighs. Also a great many other folk came to behold the combat, for the news thereof had gone forth to a great distance around about that place. So, all being in readiness, the two knights that were to do battle in that field were brought within the barriers of combat, each fully armed and each mounted upon a very good horse.

Now King Arthur was clad all in armor of Sir Domas, and Sir Accalon was clad in armor that belonged to Sir Ontzlake, and the head of each was covered by his helmet so that neither of those two knew the other.

Then the herald came forth and announced that the battle was toward, and each knight immediately put himself in readiness for the assault. Thereupon, the word for assault being given, the two rushed forth, each from his station, with such speed and fury that it was wonderful to behold. And so they met in the midst of the course with a roar as of thunder, and the spear of each knight was burst all into small pieces unto the truncheon which he held in his hand. Upon this each knight voided his horse with great skill and address, and allowed it to run at will in that field. And each threw aside the truncheon of his spear and drew his sword, and thereupon came, the one against the other, with the utmost fury of battle.

It was at this time that Vivien came to that place upon the behest of Merlin, and she brought with her such a Court and state of beauty that a great many people took notice of her with great pleasure. So Vivien and her Court took stand at the barriers whence they might behold all that was toward. And Vivien regarded those two knights and she could not tell which was King Arthur and which was his enemy, wherefore she said, "Well, I will do as Merlin desired me to do, but I must wait and see this battle for a while ere I shall be able to tell which is King Arthur, for it would be a pity to cast my spells upon the wrong knight."

So these two knights came together in battle afoot, and first they foined and then they both struck at the same time and, lo! the sword of King Arthur did not bite into the armor of Sir Accalon, but the sword of Sir Accalon bit very deeply into the armor of King Arthur and wounded him so sorely that the blood ran down in great quantities into his armor. And after that they struck very often and very powerfully, and as it was at first so it was afterward, for the sword of Sir Accalon ever bit into the armor of King Arthur, and the sword of King Arthur bit not at all into his enemy's armor. So in a little while it came that King Arthur's armor was stained all over red with the blood that flowed out from a great many wounds, and Sir Accalon bled not at all because of the sheath of Excalibur which he wore at his side. And the blood of King Arthur flowed down upon the ground so that all the grass around about was ensanguined with it. So when King Arthur beheld how all the ground was wet with his own blood, and how his enemy bled not at all, he began to fear that he would die in that battle; wherefore he said to himself, "How is this? Hath the virtue departed out of Excalibur and his sheath? Were it not otherwise I would think that that sword which cutteth me so sorely is Excalibur and that this sword is not Excalibur."

Upon this a great despair of death came upon him, and he ran at Sir Accalon and smote him so sore a blow upon the helm that Sir Accalon nigh fell down upon the ground.

But at that blow the sword of King Arthur broke short off at the cross of the handle and fell into the grass among the blood, and the pommel thereof and the cross thereof was all that King Arthur held in his hand.

Now at that blow Sir Accalon waxed very mad, so he ran at King Arthur with intent to strike him some dolorous blow. But when he saw that King Arthur was without weapon, he paused in his assault and he said, "Sir Knight, I see that thou art without weapon and that thou hast lost a great deal of blood. Wherefore I demand thee to yield thyself unto me as recreant."

Then King Arthur was again very much a-dread that his death was near to him; yet, because of his royalty, it was not possible for him to yield to any knight. So he said, "Nay, Sir Knight, I may not yield myself unto thee for I would liever die with honor than yield myself without honor. For though I lack a weapon, there are peculiar reasons why I may not lack worship. Wherefore thou mayst slay me as I am without weapon and that will be thy shame and not my shame."

"Well," said Sir Accalon, "as for the shame I will not spare thee unless thou dost yield to me." And King Arthur said, "I will not yield me." Thereupon Sir Accalon said, "Then stand thou away from me so that I may strike thee." And, when King Arthur had done as Sir Accalon bade him, Sir Accalon smote him such a woful blow that the King fell down upon his knees. Then Sir Accalon raised Excalibur with intent to strike King Arthur again, and with that all the people who were there cried out upon him to spare so worshipful a knight. But Sir Accalon would not spare him.

Then Vivien said unto herself, "Certes, that must be King Arthur who is so near to his death, and I do make my vow that it would be a great pity for him to die after he hath fought so fiercely." So when Sir Accalon raised his sword that second time with intent to strike his enemy, Vivien smote her hands with great force, and emitted at the same time a spell of such potency that it appeared to Sir Accalon upon the instant as though he had received some very powerful blow upon his arm. For with that spell his arm was benumbed all from the finger-tips unto the hollow of his armpit, and thereupon Excalibur fell out of Sir Accalon's hands and into the grass.

Then King Arthur beheld the sword and he perceived that it was Excalibur and therewith he knew that he had been betrayed. Wherefore he cried out thrice, in a very loud voice, "Treason! Treason! Treason!" and with that he set his knee upon the blade and before Sir Accalon could stay him he had seized it into his hands.

Then it appeared to King Arthur that a great virtue had come into him because of that sword. Wherefore he arose from his knees and ran at Sir Accalon and smote him so sorely that the blade penetrated his armor to the depth of half a palm's breadth. And he smote him again and again and Sir Accalon cried out in a loud voice, and fell down upon his hands and knees. Then King Arthur ran to him and catched the sheath of Excalibur and plucked it away from Sir Accalon and flung it away, and thereupon the wounds of Sir Accalon burst out bleeding in great measure. Then King Arthur catched the helmet of Sir Accalon and rushed it off his head with intent to slay him.

Now because King Arthur was blinded with his own blood he did not know Sir Accalon, wherefore he said, "Sir Knight, who art thou who hast betrayed me?" And Sir Accalon said, "I have not betrayed thee. I am Sir Accalon of Gaul and I am knight in good worship of King Arthur's Court."

But when King Arthur heard this he made great outcry and he said, "How is this? Know you who I am?" And Sir Accalon said, "Nay, I know you not." Then King Arthur said, "I am King Arthur who am thy master." And upon this he took off his helmet and Sir Accalon knew him.

And when Sir Accalon beheld King Arthur he swooned away and lay like one dead upon the ground, and King Arthur said, "Take him hence."

Then when those who were there were aware who King Arthur was, they burst over the barriers and ran toward him with great outcry of pity. And King Arthur would have left this place but upon that he also swooned away because of the great issue of blood that had come from him, wherefore all those who were round about took great sorrow, thinking that he was dying, wherefore they bewailed themselves without stint.

Then came Vivien out into that field and she said, "Let me have him, for I believe that I shall be able to cure his hurts." So she commanded that two litters should be brought and she placed King Arthur in one of the litters and she placed Sir Accalon in the other, and she bore them both away to a priory of nuns that was at no great distance from that place.

So when Vivien had come there she searched the wounds of King Arthur and bathed them with a very precious balsam, so that they immediately began to heal. As for Sir Accalon, she would not have to do with his wounds, but let one of her attendants bathe him and dress his hurts.

Now when the next morning had come, King Arthur was so much recovered that he was able to rise, though very weak and sick nigh unto death. So he got up from his couch and he would not permit anyone to stay him, and he wrapped a cloak about him and went to the place where Sir Accalon lay. When he had come there he questioned Sir Accalon very narrowly and Sir Accalon told him all that had happened to him after he had left that ship, and how the strange damsel had given him a sword for to fight with. So when King Arthur heard all that Sir Accalon had to tell him, he said, "Messire, I think that thou art not to be blamed in this matter, but I much do fear me that there is treachery here to compass my ruin."

Then he went out from that place and he found Vivien and he said to her, "Damsel, I beseech thee to dress the wounds of that knight with the same balsam that thou didst use to dress my wounds." "Lord," said Vivien, "I cannot do so, for I have no more of that balsam." But what she said was false, for she did have more of that balsam, but she did not choose to use it upon Sir Accalon.

So that afternoon Sir Accalon died of his wounds which he had received in his battle with King Arthur.

And that day King Arthur summoned Sir Domas and Sir Ontzlake into his presence and they came and stood before him, so filled with the terror of his majesty, that they had not the power to stand, but fell down upon their knees unto him.

Then King Arthur said, "I will pardon you, for ye knew not what ye did. But thou, Sir Domas, I believe, art a very false and treasonable knight, wherefore I shall deprive thee of all thy possessions but that one single castle which thy brother had and that I shall give unto thee, but all thy possessions I shall give unto Sir Ontzlake. And I shall further ordain that thou shalt never hereafter have the right to ride upon any horse but a palfrey, for thou art not worthy to ride upon a courser as a true knight hath a right to do. And I command it of thee that thou shalt presently liberate all those knights who were my companions in captivity, and thou shalt recompense them for all the injury that thou hast done to them according as it shall be decided by a Court of Chivalry."

Therewith he dismissed those two knights, and they were very glad that he had dealt so mercifully with them.

# Conclusion

Now shortly after that combat betwixt King Arthur and Sir Accalon the news thereof was brought to Queen Morgana le Fay, and the next day thereafter she heard that Sir Accalon was dead, and she wist not how it could be that her designs could have so miscarried. Then she was a-doubt as to how much King Arthur might know of her treachery, so she said to herself, "I will go and see my brother, the King, and if he is aware of my treason I will beseech him to pardon my transgression." So, having made diligent inquiry as to where it was that King Arthur lay, she gathered together her Court of knights and esquires and went thitherward.

So she came to that place upon the fifth day after the battle, and when she had come there she asked of those who were in attendance what cheer the King had. They answered her, "He is asleep and he must not be disturbed." To the which Queen Morgana le Fay replied, "No matter, I am not to be forbidden, for I must presently see him and speak with him." So they did not dare to stay her because she was the King's sister.

So Queen Morgana went into the chamber where the King lay and he did not waken at her coming. Then Queen Morgana was filled full of hatred and a great desire for revenge, wherefore she said to herself, "I will take Excalibur and his shield and will carry them away with me to Avalon, and my brother shall never see them again." So she went very softly to where King Arthur lay, and she looked upon him as he slept and perceived that he had Excalibur beside him and that he held the handle of the sword in his hand while he slept. Then Queen Morgana said, "Alas, for this, for if I try to take Excalibur away from him, haply he will awake and he will slay me for my treason." Then she looked and perceived where the sheath of Excalibur lay at the foot of the couch. So she took the sheath of Excalibur very softly and she wrapped it up in her mantle and she went out thence, and King Arthur did not awaken at her going.

So Queen Morgana came out from the King's chamber and she said to those in attendance, "Do not waken the King, for he sleepeth very soundly." Therewith she mounted her horse and went her way from that place.

Now, after a considerable while, King Arthur awoke and he looked for the sheath of Excalibur, but he perceived that it was gone, wherefore he said immediately, "Who hath been here?" They in attendance made answer, "Queen Morgana le Fay had been here and she came in and saw you and went her way without waking you." Then King Arthur's heart misgave him, and he said, "I fear me that she hath dealt treacherously with me from the beginning to the end of these adventures."

Whereupon he arose and summoned all his knights and esquires and mounted his horse for pursuit of Queen Morgana, although he was still passing sick and faint from his sore wounds and loss of blood.

Now, as the King was about ready to depart, Vivien came to him where he was, and she said, "Lord, take me with thee, for if thou dost not do so thou wilt never recover Excalibur his sheath, nor wilt thou ever overtake Queen Morgana le Fay." And King Arthur said, "Come with me, damsel, in God's name." So Vivien went with him in pursuit of Queen Morgana.

Now, by and by, as she fled, Queen Morgana le Fay looked behind her and therewith she perceived that Vivien was with the party of King Arthur, wherefore her heart failed her and she said, "I fear me that I am now altogether ruined, for I have aided that damsel to acquire such knowledge of magic that I shall have no spells to save myself from her counter-spell. But at any rate it shall be that King Arthur shall never have the sheath of Excalibur again for to help him in his hour of need."

Now at that time they were passing beside the margin of a lake of considerable size. So Queen Morgana le Fay took the sheath of Excalibur in both her hands and swung it by its belt above her head and she threw it a great distance out into the water.

Then, lo! a very singular miracle occurred, for there suddenly appeared a woman's arm out of the water and it was clad in white. And it was adorned with many bracelets. And the hand of the arm catched the sheath of Excalibur and drew it underneath the water and no one ever beheld that sheath again.

So the sheath of Excalibur was lost, and that was a grievous thing for King Arthur in after time, as you may some time read.

Now after Queen Morgana le Fay had thus thrown the sheath of Excalibur into the lake, she went on a little farther to where was a very lonely place with a great many rocks and stones lying about upon the ground. And when she had come to that place she exercised very potent spells of magic that Merlin had taught her. So, by means of those spells, she transformed herself and all of her Court and all of their horses into large round stones of divers sizes.

Then in a little while came King Arthur to that place with his knights and esquires, and he was exceedingly heavy of heart, for he had beheld from a great distance how Queen Morgana le Fay had thrown the sheath of Excalibur into that lake.

Now when the King and his Court had come to that spot the damsel Vivien called out upon him to stop and she said to him, "Lord, dost thou behold all those great round stones?" "Yea," said the King, "I do see them." Then Vivien said, "Lo! those stones are Queen Morgana le Fay and the Court who were with her. For this magic that she hath done to change herself and them into stones was a certain thing that Merlin had taught her. Now I myself know that magic, and I also know how to remove that magic at my will. Wherefore, if thou wilt promise to immediately punish that wicked woman for all her treason by depriving her of her life, then will I bring her back unto her true shape again so that thou mayst have her in thy power."

Then King Arthur looked upon Vivien with great displeasure, and he said, "Damsel, thou hast a cruel heart! Thou thyself hast suffered no injury at the hands of Queen Morgana; wherefore, then, wouldst thou have me slay her? Now, but for all thou hast done for me I would be very much affronted with thee. As for her, I forgive her all of this, and I shall forgive her again and again and yet again if she sin against me. For her mother was my mother, and the blood which flows in her veins and in my veins cometh from the same fountain-head, wherefore I will do no evil thing against her. Let us return again whence we came."

Then Vivien looked upon King Arthur very bitterly, and she laughed with great scorn, and said, "Thou art both a fool and a dotard," and therewith she vanished from the sight of all.

And after that, because King Arthur had rebuked her for her wickedness in the presence of others, she hated him even more than Morgana le Fay had hated him.

Some time after that, King Arthur heard how Merlin had been beguiled by Vivien, and he sorrowed with great bitterness that Merlin was lost unto the world in that wise.

So endeth the story of the passing of Merlin.

## Part II

# The Story of Sir Pellias

*Here followeth the story of Sir Pellias, surnamed by name the Gentle Knight. For Sir Pellias was of such a sort that it was said of him that all women loved him without disadvantage to themselves, and that all men loved him to their great good advantage.*

*Wherefore, when in the end he won for his beloved that beautiful Lady of the Lake, who was one of the chiefest damoiselles of Faëry, and when he went to dwell as lord paramount in that wonderful habitation which no other mortal than he and Sir Launcelot of the Lake had ever beheld, then were all men rejoiced at his great good fortune – albeit all the Court of King Arthur grieved that he had departed so far away from them never to return again.*

*So I believe that you will have pleasure in reading the history of the things concerning Sir Pellias hereinafter written for your edification.*

CHAPTER FIRST

# HOW QUEEN GUINEVERE WENT A-MAYING AND SIR PELLIAS TOOK UPON HIM A QUEST

Now it befell upon a pleasant day in the spring-time, that Queen Guinevere went a-Maying with a goodly company of Knights and Ladies of her Court. And among those Knights were Sir Pellias, and Sir Geraint, and Sir Dinadan, and Sir Aglaval, and Sir Agravaine, and Sir Constantine of Cornwall, and sundry others, so that the like of that Court was hardly to be found in all of the world, either then or before or since.

The day was exceedingly pleasant with the sunlight all yellow, like to gold, and the breeze both soft and gentle. The small birds they sang with very great joy, and all about there bloomed so many flowers of divers sorts that the entire meadows were carpeted with their tender green. So it seemed to Queen Guinevere that it was very good to be abroad in the field and beneath the sky at such a season.

Now as the Queen and her Court walked in great joy among the blossoms, one of the damsels attendant upon the Lady Guinevere cried out of a sudden, "Look! Look! Who is that cometh yonder?" Thereupon Queen Guinevere lifted up her eyes, and she beheld that there came across the meadows a damsel riding upon a milk-white palfrey, accompanied by three pages clad in sky-blue raiment. That damsel was also clad entirely in azure, and she wore a finely wrought chain of gold about her neck and a fillet of gold about her brows, and her hair, which was as yellow as gold, was wrapped all about with the bands of blue ribbon embroidered with gold. And one of the pages that followed the damsel bare a square frame of no very great size, and that the frame was enveloped and covered with a curtain of crimson satin.

Now when the Queen beheld that goodly company approaching, she bade one of the knights attendant upon her for to go forth to meet the damsel. And the knight who went forth in obedience to her command was Sir Pellias.

So when Sir Pellias met the damsel and her three pages, he spake to her in this wise: "Fair damsel, I am commanded by yonder lady for to greet you and to crave of you the favor of your name and purpose."

"Sir Knight," said the damsel, "I do perceive from your countenance and address that you are some lord of very high estate and of great nobility, wherefore I will gladly tell to you that my name is Parcenet, and that I am a damsel belonging to the Court of a certain very high dame who dwelleth at a considerable distance from here, and who is called the Lady Ettard of Grantmesnle. Now I come hitherward desiring to be admitted into the presence of Queen Guinevere. Accordingly, if you can tell me whereabouts I may find that noble lady, I shall assuredly be very greatly beholden unto you."

"Ha, Lady!" quoth Sir Pellias, "thou shalt not have very far to go to find Queen Guinevere; for, behold! yonder she walketh, surrounded by her Court of Lords and Ladies." Then the damsel said, "I prithee bring me unto her."

So Sir Pellias led Parcenet unto the Queen, and Queen Guinevere received her with great graciousness of demeanor, saying, "Damsel, what is it that ye seek of us?"

"Lady," quoth the damsel, "I will tell you that very readily. The Lady Ettard, my mistress, is considered by all in those parts where she dwelleth to be the most beautiful lady in the world. Now, of late, there hath come such a report of your exceeding beauty that the Lady Ettard hath seen fit for to send me hitherward to see with mine own eyes if that which is recorded of you is soothly true. And indeed, Lady, now that I stand before you, I may not say but that you are the fairest dame that ever mine eyes beheld unless it be the Lady Ettard aforesaid."

Then Queen Guinevere laughed with very great mirth. And she said, "It appears to me to be a very droll affair that thou shouldst have travelled so great a distance for so small a matter." Then she said, "Tell me, damsel, what is that thy page beareth so carefully wrapped up in that curtain of crimson satin?"

"Lady," quoth the damsel, "it is a true and perfect likeness of the Lady Ettard, who is my mistress."

Then Queen Guinevere said, "Show it to me."

Upon this the page who bore the picture dismounted from his palfrey and, coming to Queen Guinevere, he kneeled down upon one knee and uncovered the picture so that the Queen and her Court might look upon it. Thereupon they all beheld that that picture was painted very cunningly upon a panel of ivory framed with gold and inset with many jewels of divers colors. And they saw that it was the picture of a lady of such extraordinary beauty that all they who beheld it marvelled thereat. "Hey, damsel!" quoth Queen Guinevere, "thy lady is, indeed, graced with wonderful beauty. Now if she doth in sooth resemble that picture, then I believe that her like to loveliness is not to be found anywhere in the world."

Upon this Sir Pellias spake out and said, "Not so, Lady; for I do protest, and am willing to maintain my words with the peril of my body, that thou thyself art much more beautiful than that picture."

"Hey day, Sir Knight!" quoth the damsel Parcenet, "it is well that thou dost maintain that saying so far away from Grantmesnle; for at that place is a certain knight, hight Sir Engamore of Malverat, who is a very strong knight indeed, and who maintaineth the contrary to thy saying in favor of the Lady Ettard against all comers who dare to encounter him."

Then Sir Pellias kneeled down before Queen Guinevere, and set his palms together. "Lady," he said, "I do pray thee of thy grace that thou wilt so far honor me as to accept me for thy true knight in this matter. For I would fain assay an adventure in thy behalf if I have thy permission for to do so. Wherefore, if thou grantest me leave, I will straightway go forth to meet this knight of whom the damsel speaketh, and I greatly hope that when I find him I shall cause his overthrow to the increasing of thy glory and honor."

Then Queen Guinevere laughed again with pure merriment. "Sir," quoth she, "it pleases me beyond measure that thou shouldst take so small a quarrel as this upon thee in my behalf. For if, so be, thou dost assume so small a quarrel, then how much more wouldst thou take a serious quarrel of mine upon thee? Wherefore I do accept thee very joyfully for my champion in this affair. So go thou presently and arm thyself in such a way as may be fitting for this adventure."

"Lady," said Sir Pellias, "if I have thy leave, I will enter into this affair clad as I am. For I entertain hopes that I shall succeed in winning armor and accoutrements upon the way, in the which case this adventure will be still more to thy credit than it would otherwise be."

At this the Queen was very much pleased, that her knight should undertake so serious an adventure clad only in holiday attire; wherefore she said, "Let it be as thou wouldst have it." Thereupon she bade her page, Florian, for to go fetch the best horse that he might obtain for Sir Pellias; and Florian, running with all speed, presently returned with a noble steed, so black of hue that I believe there was not a single white hair upon him.

Then Sir Pellias gave adieu to Queen Guinevere, and her merry Maycourt, and they gave him adieu and great acclaim, and thereupon he mounted his horse and rode away with the damsel Parcenet and the three pages clad in blue.

Now when these had gone some distance the damsel Parcenet said, "Sir, I know not thy name or thy condition, or who thou art?"

Unto this Sir Pellias said, "Damsel, my name is Pellias and I am a knight of King Arthur's Round Table."

At that Parcenet was very much astonished, for Sir Pellias was held by many to be the best knight-at-arms alive, saving only King Arthur and King Pellinore.

Wherefore she cried out, "Messire, it will assuredly be a very great honor for Sir Engamore to have to do with so famous a knight as thou." Unto this Sir Pellias said, "Damsel, I think there are several knights of King Arthur's Round Table who are better knights than I." But Parcenet said, "I cannot believe that to be the case."

Then after awhile Parcenet said to Sir Pellias, "Messire, how wilt thou get 'thyself armor for to fight Sir Engamore?" "Maiden," said Sir Pellias, "I do not know at these present where I shall provide me armor; but before the time cometh for me to have to do with Sir Engamore, I have faith that I shall find armor fit for my purpose. For thou must know that it is not always the defence that a man weareth upon his body that bringeth him success, but more often it is the spirit that uplifteth him unto his undertakings."

Then Parcenet said, "Sir Pellias, I do not believe that it is often the case that a lady hath so good a knight as thou for to do battle in her behalf." To which Sir Pellias said very cheerfully, "Damsel, when thy time cometh I wish that thou mayst have a very much better knight to serve thee than I." "Sir," quoth Parcenet, "such a thing as that is not likely to befall me." At the which Sir Pellias laughed with a great lightness of heart. Then Parcenet said, "Heigh ho! I would that I had a good knight for to serve me."

To this Sir Pellias made very sober reply, "Maiden, the first one that I catch I will give unto thee for thy very own. Now wouldst thou have him fair or dark, or short or tall? For if thou wouldst rather have him short and fair I will let the tall, dark one go; but if thou wouldst have him tall and dark, I will let go the other sort."

Then Parcenet looked very steadily at Sir Pellias, and she said, "I would have him about as tall as thou art, and with the same color of hair and eyes, and with a straight nose like unto thine, and with a good wit such as thou hast."

"Alas!" said Sir Pellias, "I would that thou hadst told me this before we had come so far from Camelot; for I could easily have got thee such a knight at that place. For they have them there in such plenty that they keep them in wicker cages, and sell them two for a farthing." Whereat Parcenet laughed very cheerfully, and said, "Then Camelot must be a very wonderful place, Sir Pellias."

So, with very merry discourse they journeyed upon their way with great joy and good content, taking much pleasure in the spring-time and the pleasant meadows whereon they travelled, being without care of any sort, and heart-full of cheerfulness and good-will.

That night they abided at a very quaint, pleasant hostelry that stood at the outskirts of the Forest of Usk, and the next morning they departed betimes in the freshness of the early day, quitting that place and entering into the forest shadows.

Now, after they had travelled a considerable distance in that forest, the damsel Parcenet said to Sir Pellias, "Sir, do you know what part of the woods this is?" "Nay," said Sir Pellias. "Well," said Parcenet, "this part of the woodland is sometimes called Arroy, and is sometimes called the Forest of Adventure. For I must tell you it is a

*"Then stand thou away from me so that I may strike thee."*
*(Second Book, Part I, Chapter Fourth)*

*The knight could not uplift himself above the flood (Second Book, Part II, Chapter Fourth)*

very wonderful place, full of magic of sundry sorts. For it is said that no knight may enter into this forest but some adventure shall befall him."

"Damsel," said Sir Pellias, "that which thou tellest me is very good news. For, maybe, if we should fall in with some adventure at this place I may then be able to obtain armor suitable for my purpose."

So they entered the Forest of Adventure forthwith, and then travelled therein for a long way, marvelling greatly at the aspect of that place into which they were come. For the Forest was very dark and silent and wonderfully strange and altogether different from any other place that they had ever seen. Wherefore it appeared to them that it would not be at all singular if some extraordinary adventure should befall them.

So after they had travelled in this wise for a considerable pass they came of a sudden out of those thicker parts of the woodland to where was an opening of considerable extent. And there they beheld before them a violent stream of water that flowed very turbulently and with great uproar of many noises. And they saw that by the side of the stream of water there was a thorn-tree, and that underneath the thorn-tree was a bank of green moss, and that upon the bank of moss there sat an aged woman of a very woful appearance. For that old woman was extraordinarily withered with age, and her eyes were all red as though with a continual weeping of rheum, and many bristles grew upon her cheeks and her chin, and her face was covered with such a multitude of wrinkles that there was not any place that was free from wrinkles.

Now when that old woman beheld Sir Pellias and Parcenet and the three pages approaching where she sat, she cried out in a loud voice, "Sir, wilt thou not bear me over this water upon thy horse? For, lo! I am very old and feeble and may not cross this river by myself."

Then Parcenet rebuked the old woman, saying, "Peace, be still! Who art thou to ask this noble knight for to do thee such a service as that?"

Then Sir Pellias was not pleased with Parcenet, wherefore he said, "Damsel, thou dost not speak properly in this matter, for that which beseemeth a true knight is to give succor unto anyone soever who needeth his aid. For King Arthur is the perfect looking-glass of knighthood, and he hath taught his knights to give succor unto all who ask succor of them, without regarding their condition." So saying Sir Pellias dismounted from his horse and lifted the old woman up upon the saddle thereof. Then he himself mounted once more and straightway rode into the ford of the river and so came across the torrent with the old woman in safety to the other side. And Parcenet followed him, marvelling very greatly at his knightliness, and the three pages followed her.

Now when they had reached the other side of the water, Sir Pellias dismounted with intent to aid the old woman to alight from the horse. But she waited not for his aid, but immediately leaped down very lightly from where she was. And, lo! Sir Pellias beheld that she whom he had thought to be only an aged and withered beldame was, in truth, a very strange, wonderful lady of extraordinary beauty. And, greatly marvelling, he beheld that she was clad in apparel of such a sort as neither he nor any who were there had ever beheld before. And because of her appearance he was aware that she was not like any ordinary mortal, but that she was doubtless of enchantment. For he perceived that her face was of a wonderful clearness, like to ivory for whiteness, and that her eyes were very black and extraordinarily bright, like unto two jewels set into ivory; and he perceived that she was clad all in green from head to foot and that her hair was long and perfectly black and like to fine silk for softness and for glossiness; and he perceived that she had about her neck a collar of opal stones and emeralds inset into gold, and that about her wrists were bracelets of finely wrought gold inset with opal stones and emeralds. Wherefore from all these circumstances he knew that she must be fay.

(For thus was the Lady Nymue of the Lake; and so had she appeared unto King Arthur, and so did she appear unto Sir Pellias and those who were with him.)

So, beholding the wonderful magical quality of that lady, Sir Pellias kneeled down before her and set his hands together, palm to palm. But the Lady of the Lake said, "Sir, why dost thou kneel to me?" "Lady," quoth Sir Pellias, "because thou art so wonderfully strange and beautiful." "Messire," said the Lady of the Lake, "thou hast done a very good service to me and art, assuredly, a very excellent knight. Wherefore, arise and kneel no longer!" So Sir Pellias arose from his knees and stood before her, and he said, "Lady, who art thou?" To the which she made reply, "I am one who holdeth an exceedingly kind regard toward King Arthur and all his knights. My name is Nymue and I am the chiefest of those Ladies of the Lake of whom they mayst have heard tell. I took upon me that form of a sorry old woman for to test thy knightliness, and, lo! I have not found thee amiss in worthy service." Then Sir Pellias said, "Lady, thou hast assuredly done me great favor in these." Upon that the Lady of the Lake smiled upon Sir Pellias very kindly, and she said, "Sir, I have a mind to do thee a greater favor than that."

Therewith, so saying, she immediately took from about her neck that collar of opal stones, of emeralds and gold, and hung it about the shoulders of Sir Pellias, so that it hung down upon his breast with a very wonderful glory of variegated colors.

"Keep this," she said, "for it is of very potent magic."

Upon that she vanished instantly from the sight of those who were there, leaving them astonished and amazed beyond measure at what had befallen.

And Sir Pellias was like one who was in a dream, for he wist not whether that which he had beheld was a vision, or whether he had seen it with his waking eyes. Wherefore he mounted upon his horse in entire silence, as though he knew not what he did. And likewise in entire silence he led the way from that place. Nor did any of those others speak at that time; only after they had gone a considerable distance Parcenet said, speaking in a manner of fear, "Messire, that was a very wonderful thing that befell us." To which Sir Pellias said, "Yea, maiden."

Now that necklace which the Lady of the Lake had hung about the neck of Sir Pellias possessed such a virtue that whosoever wore it was beloved of all those who looked upon him. For the collar was enchanted with that peculiar virtue; but Sir Pellias was altogether unaware of that circumstance, wherefore he only took joy to himself because of the singular beauty of the jewel which the Lady of the Lake had given him.

CHAPTER SECOND

# How Sir Pellias Overcame a Red Knight

Now, after that wonderful happening, they journeyed continuously for a great while. Nor did they pause at any place until they came, about an hour after the prime of the day, to a certain part of the forest where charcoal-burners were plying their trade. Here Sir Pellias commanded that they should draw rein and rest for a while, and so they dismounted for to rest and to refresh themselves, as he had ordained that they should do.

Now as they sat there refreshing themselves with meat and drink, there came of a sudden from out of the forest a sound of great lamentation and of loud outcry, and almost immediately there appeared from the thickets, coming into that open place, a lady in woful array, riding upon a pied palfrey. And behind her rode a young esquire, clad in colors of green and white and seated upon a sorrel horse. And he also appeared to be possessed of great sorrow, being in much disarray and very downcast of countenance. And the lady's face was all beswollen and inflamed with weeping, and her hair hung down upon her shoulders with neither net nor band for to stay it in place, and her raiment was greatly torn by the brambles and much stained with forest travel. And the young esquire who rode behind her came with a drooping head and a like woful disarray of apparel, his cloak dragging behind him and made fast to his shoulder by only a single point.

Now when Sir Pellias beheld the lady and the esquire in such sad estate, he immediately arose from where he sat and went straightway to the lady and took her horse by the bridle and stayed it where it was. And the lady looked at him, yet saw him not, being altogether blinded by her grief and distraction. Then Sir Pellias said to her, "Lady, what ails thee that thou sorrowest so greatly?" Whereunto she made reply, "Sir, it matters not, for thou canst not help me." "How know ye that?" said Sir Pellias. "I have a very good intention for to aid thee if it be possible for me to do so."

Then the lady looked more narrowly at Sir Pellias, and she perceived him as though through a mist of sorrow. And she beheld that he was not clad in armor, but only in a holiday attire of fine crimson cloth. Wherefore she began sorrowing afresh, and that in great measure, for she deemed that here was one who could give her no aid in her trouble. Wherefore she said, "Sir, thy intentions are kind, but how canst thou look to give me aid when thou hast neither arms nor defences for to help thee in taking upon thee such a quarrel?" But Sir Pellias said, "Lady, I know not how I may aid thee until that thou tellest me of thy sorrow. Yet I have good hope that I may serve thee when I shall know what it is that causes thee such disorder of mind." Thereupon, still holding the horse by the bridle, he brought the lady forward to that place where Parcenet still sat beside the napkin spread with food with which they had been refreshing themselves. And when he had come to that place, he, with all gentleness, constrained the lady for to dismount from her horse. Then, with equal gentleness, he compelled her to sit down upon the grass and to partake of the food. And when she had done so, and had drunk some of the wine, she found herself to be greatly refreshed and began to take to herself more heart of grace. Thereupon, beholding her so far recovered, Sir Pellias again demanded of her what was her trouble and besought her that she would open her heart unto him.

So, being encouraged by his cheerful words, she told to Sir Pellias the trouble that had brought her to that pass.

"Sir Knight," she said, "the place where I dwell is a considerable distance from this. Thence I came this morning with a very good knight, hight Sir Brandemere, who is my husband. We have been married but for a little over four weeks, so that our happiness until this morning was as yet altogether fresh with us. Now this morning Sir Brandemere would take me out a-hunting at the break of day, and so we went forth with a brachet of which my knight was wonderfully fond. So, coming to a certain place in the forest, there started up of a sudden from before us a doe, which same the brachet immediately pursued with great vehemence of outcry. Thereupon, I and my lord and this esquire followed thereafter with very great spirit and enjoyment of the chase. Now, when we had followed the doe and the hound for a great distance – the hound pursuing the doe with a great passion of eagerness – we came to a certain place where we beheld before us a violent stream of water which was crossed by a long and narrow bridge. And we beheld that upon the other side of the stream there stood a strong castle with seven towers, and that the castle was built up upon the rocks in such a way that the rocks and the castle appeared to be altogether like one rock.

"Now, as we approached the bridge aforesaid, lo! the portcullis of the castle was lifted up and the drawbridge was let fall very suddenly and with a great noise, and there immediately issued forth from out of the castle a knight clad altogether in red. And all the trappings and the furniture of his horse were likewise of red; and the spear which he bore in his hand was of ash-wood painted red. And he came forth very terribly, and rode forward so that he presently stood at the other end of that narrow bridge. Thereupon he called out aloud to Sir Brandemere, my husband, saying: 'Whither wouldst thou go, Sir Knight?' And unto him Sir Brandemere made reply: 'Sir, I would cross this bridge, for my hound, which I love exceedingly, hath crossed here in pursuit of a doe.' Then that Red Knight cried out in a loud voice, 'Sir Knight, thou comest not upon this bridge but at thy peril; for this bridge belongeth unto me, and whosoever would cross it must first overthrow me or else he may not cross.'

"Now, my husband, Sir Brandemere, was clad at that time only in a light raiment such as one might wear for hunting or for hawking; only that he wore upon his head a light bascinet enwrapped with a scarf which I had given him. Ne'theless, he was so great of heart that he would not abide any challenge such as that Red Knight had given unto him; wherefore, bidding me and this esquire (whose name is Ponteferet) to remain upon the farther side of the bridge, he drew his sword and rode forward to the middle of the bridge with intent to force a way across if he was able so to do. Whereupon, seeing that to be his intent, that Red Knight, clad all in complete armor, cast aside his spear and drew his sword and rode forward to meet my knight. So they met in the middle of the bridge, and when they had thus met that Red Knight lifted himself in his stirrup and smote my husband, Sir Brandemere, upon the crown of his bascinet with his sword. And I beheld the blade of the Red Knight's sword that it cut through the bascinet of Sir Brandemere and deep into his brain-pan, so that the blood ran down upon the knight's face in great abundance. Then Sir Brandemere straightway fell down from his horse and lay as though he were gone dead.

"Having thus overthrown him, that Red Knight dismounted from his horse and lifted up Sir Brandemere upon the horse whence he had fallen so that he lay across the saddle. Then taking both horses by the bridles the Red Knight led them straight back across the bridge and so into his castle. And as soon as he had entered into the castle the portcullis thereof was immediately closed behind him and the drawbridge was raised. Nor did he pay any heed whatever either to me or to the esquire Ponteferet, but he departed leaving us without any word of cheer; nor do I now know whether my husband, Sir Brandemere, is living or dead, or what hath befallen him."

And as the lady spake these words, lo! the tears again fell down her face in great abundance.

Then Sir Pellias was very much moved with compassion, wherefore he said, "Lady, thy case is, indeed, one of exceeding sorrowfulness, and I am greatly grieved for thee. And, indeed, I would fain aid thee to all the extent that is in my power. So, if thou wilt lead me to where is this bridge and that grimly castle of which thou speakest, I make thee my vow that I will assay to the best of my endeavor to learn of the whereabouts of thy good knight, and as to what hath befallen him."

"Sir," said the lady, "I am much beholden unto thee for thy good will. Yet thou mayst not hope for success shouldst thou venture to undertake so grave an adventure as that without either arms or armor for to defend thyself. For consider how grievously that Red Knight hath served my husband, Sir Brandemere, taking no considered as to his lack of arms or defence. Wherefore, it is not likely that he will serve thee any more courteously." And to the lady's words Parcenet also lifted up a great voice, bidding Sir Pellias not to be so unwise as to do this thing that he was minded to do. And so did Ponteferet, the esquire, also call out upon Sir Pellias, that he should not do this thing, but that he should at least take arms to himself ere he entered upon this adventure.

But to all that they said Sir Pellias replied, "Stay me not in that which I would do, for I do tell you all that I have several times undertaken adventures even more perilous than this and yet I have 'scaped with no great harm to myself." Nor would he listen to anything that the lady and the damsel might say, but, arising from that place, he aided the lady and the damsel to mount their palfreys. Then mounting his own steed, and the esquire and the pages having mounted their steeds, the whole party immediately departed from that place.

So they journeyed for a great distance through the forest, the esquire, Ponteferet, directing them how to proceed in such a way as should bring them by and by to the castle of the Red Knight. So, at last they came to a more open place in that wilderness where was a steep and naked hill before them. And when they had reached to the top of that hill they perceived beneath them a river, very turbulent and violent. Likewise they saw that the river was spanned by a bridge, exceedingly straight and narrow, and that upon the farther side of the bridge and of the river there stood a very strong castle with seven tall towers. Moreover the castle and the towers were built up upon the rocks, very lofty and high, so that it was hard to tell where the rocks ceased and the walls began, wherefore the towers and the walls appeared to be altogether one rock of stone.

Then the esquire, Ponteferet, pointed with his finger, and said, "Sir Knight, yonder is the castle of the Red Knight, and into it he bare Sir Brandemere after he had been so grievously wounded." Then Sir Pellias said unto the lady, "Lady, I will presently inquire as to thy husband's welfare."

Therewith he set spurs to his horse and rode down the hill toward the bridge with great boldness. And when he had come nigher to the bridge, lo! the portcullis of the castle was lifted and the drawbridge was let fall with a great noise and tumult, and straightway there issued forth from out of the castle a knight clad all in armor and accoutrements of red, and this knight came forward with great speed toward the bridge's head. Then, when Sir Pellias saw him approaching so threateningly, he said unto those who had followed him down the hill: "Stand fast where ye are and I will go forth to bespeak this knight, and inquire into the matter of that injury which he hath done unto Sir Brandemere." Upon this the esquire, Ponteferet, said unto him, "Stay, Sir Knight, thou wilt be hurt." But Sir Pellias said, "Not so, I shall not be hurt."

So he went forth very boldly upon the bridge, and when the Red Knight saw him approach, he said, "Ha! who art thou who darest to come thus upon my bridge?"

Unto him Sir Pellias made reply, "It matters not who I am, but thou art to know, thou discourteous knight, that I am come to inquire of thee where thou hast disposed of that good knight Sir Brandemere, and to ask of thee why thou didst entreat him so grievously a short time since."

At this the Red Knight fell very full of wrath. "Ha! ha!" he cried vehemently, "that thou shalt presently learn to thy great sorrow, for as I have served him, so shall I quickly serve thee, so that in a little while I shall bring thee unto him; then thou mayst ask him whatsoever thou dost list. But seeing that thou art unarmed and without defence, I would not do thee any bodily ill, wherefore I demand of thee that thou shalt presently surrender thyself unto me, otherwise it will be very greatly to thy pain and sorrow if thou compellest me to use force for to constrain thy surrender."

Then Sir Pellias said, "What! what! Wouldst thou thus assail a knight who is altogether without arms or defence as I am?" And the Red Knight said, "Assuredly shall I do so if thou dost not immediately yield thyself unto me."

"Then," quoth Pellias, "thou art not fit for to be dealt with as beseemeth a tried knight. Wherefore, should I encounter thee, thy overthrow must be of such a sort as may shame any belted knight who weareth golden spurs."

Thereupon he cast about his eyes for a weapon to fit his purpose, and he beheld how that a certain huge stone was loose upon the coping of the bridge. Now this stone was of such a size that five men of usual strength could hardly lift it. But Sir Pellias lifted it forth from its place with great ease, and, raising it with both hands, he ran quickly toward that Red Knight and flung the rock at him with much force. And the stone of the blow drave the knight backward from his saddle, so that he fell down to the earth from his horse with a terrible tumult and lay upon the bridgeway like one who was altogether dead.

And when they within the castle who looked forth therefrom, saw that blow, and when they beheld the overthrow of the Red Knight, they lifted up their voices in great lamentation so that the outcry thereof was terrible to hear.

But Sir Pellias ran with all speed to the fallen knight and set his knee upon his breast. And he unlaced his helmet and lifted it. And he beheld that the face of the knight was strong and comely and that he was not altogether dead.

So when Sir Pellias saw that the Red Knight was not dead, and when he perceived that he was about to recover his breath from the blow that he had suffered, he drew that knight's misericordia from its sheath and set the point to his throat, so that when the Red Knight awoke from his swoon he beheld death, in the countenance of Sir Pellias and in the point of the dagger.

So when the Red Knight perceived how near death was to him he besought Sir Pellias for mercy, saying, "Spare my life unto me!" Whereunto Sir Pellias said, "Who art thou?" And the knight said, "I am hight Sir Adresack, surnamed of the Seven Towers." Then Sir Pellias said to him, "What hast thou done unto Sir Brandemere and how doth it fare with that good knight?" And the Red Knight replied, "He is not so seriously wounded as you suppose."

Now when Sir Brandemere's lady heard this speech she was greatly exalted with joy, so that she smote her hands together, making great cry of thanksgiving.

But Sir Pellias said, "Now tell me, Sir Adresack, has thou other captives beside that knight, Sir Brandemere, at thy castle?" To which Sir Adresack replied, "Sir Knight, I will tell thee truly; there are in my castle one and twenty other captives beside him: to wit, eighteen knights and esquires of degree and three ladies. For I have defended this bridge for a long time and all who have undertaken to cross it, those have I taken captive and held for ransom. Wherefore I have taken great wealth and gained great estate thereby."

Then Sir Pellias said, "Thou art soothly a wicked and discourteous knight so to serve travellers that come thy way, and I would do well for to slay thee where thou liest. But since thou hast besought mercy of me I will grant it unto thee, though I will do so only with great shame unto thy knighthood. Moreover, if I spare to thee thy life there are several things which thou must perform. First thou must go unto Queen Guinevere at Camelot, and there must thou say unto her that the knight who left her unarmed hath taken thine armor from thee and hath armed himself therewith for to defend her honor. Secondly, thou must confess thy faults unto King Arthur as thou hast confessed them unto me and thou must beg his pardon for the same, craving that he, in his mercy, shall spare thy life unto thee. These are the things that thou must perform."

To this Sir Adresack said, "Very well, these things do I promise to perform if thou wilt spare my life."

Then Sir Pellias permitted him to arise and he came and stood before Sir Pellias. And Sir Pellias summoned the esquire, Ponteferet, unto him, and he said, "Take thou this knight's armor from off of his body and put it upon my body as thou knowest how to do." And Ponteferet did as Sir Pellias bade him. For he unarmed Sir Adresack and he clothed Sir Pellias in Sir Adresack's armor, and Sir Adresack stood ashamed before them all. Then Sir Pellias said unto him, "Now take me into thy castle that I may there liberate those captives that thou so wickedly holdest as prisoners." And Sir Adresack said, "It shall be done as thou dost command."

Thereupon they all went together unto the castle and into the castle, which was an exceedingly stately place. And there they beheld a great many servants and attendants, and these came at the command of Sir Adresack and bowed themselves down before Sir Pellias. Then Sir Pellias bade Sir Adresack for to summon the keeper of the dungeon, and Sir Adresack did so. And Sir Pellias commanded the keeper that he should conduct them unto the dungeon, and the keeper bowed down before him in obedience.

Now when they had come to that dungeon they beheld it to be a very lofty place and exceedingly strong. And there they found Sir Brandemere and those others of whom Sir Adresack had spoken.

But when that sorrowful lady perceived Sir Brandemere, she ran unto him with great voice of rejoicing and embraced him and wept over him. And he embraced her and wept and altogether forgot his hurt in the joy of beholding her again.

And in the several apartments of that part of the castle, there were in all eighteen knights and esquires, and three ladies besides Sir Brandemere. Moreover, amongst those knights were two from King Arthur's Court: to wit, Sir Brandiles and Sir Mador de la Porte. Whereupon these beholding that it was Sir Pellias who had liberated them, came to him and embraced him with great joy and kissed him upon either cheek.

And all those who were liberated made great rejoicing and gave Sir Pellias such praise and acclaim that he was greatly contented therewith.

Then when Sir Pellias beheld all those captives who were in the dungeon he was very wroth with Sir Adresack, wherefore he turned unto him and said, "Begone, Sir Knight, for to do that penance which I imposed upon thee to perform, for I am very greatly displeased with thee, and fear me lest I should repent me of my mercy to thee."

Thereupon Sir Adresack turned him away and he immediately departed from that place. And he called to him his esquire and he took him and rode away to Camelot for to do that penance which he had promised Sir Pellias to do.

Then, after he was gone, Sir Pellias and those captives whom he had liberated, went through the divers parts of the castle. And there they found thirteen chests of gold and silver money and four caskets of jewels – very fine and of great brilliancy – all of which treasure had been paid in ransom by those captives who had aforetime been violently held prisoners at that place.

And Sir Pellias ordained that all those chests and caskets should be opened, and when those who were there looked therein, the hearts of all were wonderfully exalted with joy at the sight of that great treasure.

Then Sir Pellias commanded that all that treasure of gold and silver should be divided into nineteen equal parts, and when it had been so divided, he said, "Now let each of you who have been held captive in this place, take for his own one part of that treasure as a recompense for those sorrows which he hath endured." Moreover, to each of the ladies who had been held as captives in that place, he gave a casket of jewels, saying unto her, "Take thou this casket of jewels as a recompense for that sorrow which thou hast suffered. And unto Sir Brandemere's lady he gave a casket of the jewels for that which she had endured.

But then those who were there beheld that Sir Pellias reserved no part of that great treasure for himself, they all cried out upon him: "Sir Knight! Sir Knight! How is this? Behold, thou hast set aside no part of this treasure for thyself."

Then Sir Pellias made answer: "You are right, I have not so. For it needs not that I take any of this gold and silver, or any of these jewels,for myself. For, behold! ye have suffered much at the hands of Sir Adresack, wherefore ye should receive recompense therefore, but I have suffered naught at his hands, wherefore I need no such recompense."

Then were they all astonished at his generosity and gave him great praise for his largeness of heart. And all those knights vowed unto him fidelity unto death.

Then, when all these things were accomplished, Sir Brandemere implored all who were there that they would come with him unto his castle, so that they might refresh themselves with a season of mirth and good faring. And they all said that they would go with him, and they did go. And at the castle of Sir Brandemere there was great rejoicing with feasting and jousting for three days.

And all who were there loved Sir Pellias with an astonishing love because of that collar of emeralds and opals and of gold. Yet no one knew of the virtue of that collar, nor did Sir Pellias know of it.

So Sir Pellias abided at that place for three days. And when the fourth day was come he arose betimes in the morning and bade saddle his horse, and the palfrey of the damsel Parcenet, and the horses of their pages.

Then when all those who were there saw that he was minded to depart, they besought him not to go, but Sir Pellias said, "Stay me not, for I must go."

Then came to him those two knights of Arthur's Court, Sir Brandiles and Sir Mador de la Porte, and they besought him that he would let them go with him upon that adventure. And at first Sir Pellias forbade them, but they besought him the more, so that at last he was fain to say, "Ye shall go with me."

So he departed from that place with his company, and all those who remained gave great sorrow that he had gone away.

## CHAPTER THIRD

# HOW SIR PELLIAS DID BATTLE WITH SIR ENGAMORE

Now, Sir Pellias and his party and the damsel Parcenet and her party travelled onward until after awhile in the afternoon they came unto the utmost boundaries of the forest, where the woodlands ceased altogether and many fields and meadows, with farms and crofts and plantations of trees all a-bloom with tender leaves and fragrant blossoms, lay spread out beneath the sky.

And Sir Pellias said, "This is indeed a very beautiful land into which we have come." Whereat the damsel Parcenet was right well pleased, for she said, "Sir, I am very glad that that which thou seest belikes thee; for all this region belongeth unto the Lady Ettard, and it is my home. Moreover, from the top of yonder hill one mayst behold the castle of Grantmesnle which lieth in the valley beneath." Then Sir Pellias said, "Let us make haste! For I am wonderfully desirous of beholding that place."

So they set spurs to their horses and rode up that hill at a hand gallop. And when they had reached the top thereof, lo! beneath them lay the Castle of Grantmesnle in such a wise that it was as though upon the palm of a hand. And Sir Pellias beheld that it was an exceedingly fair castle, built altogether without of a red stone, and containing many buildings of red brick within the wall. And behind the walls there lay a little town, and from where they stood they could behold the streets thereof, and the people coming and going upon their businesses.

So Sir Pellias, beholding the excellence of that castle, said, "Certes, maiden, yonder is a very fair estate."

"Yea," said Parcenet; "we who dwell there do hold it to be a very excellent estate."

Then Sir Pellias said to Parcenet: "Maiden, yonder glade of young trees nigh unto the castle appeareth to be a very cheerful spot. Wherefore at that place I and my companions in arms will take up our inn. There, likewise, we will cause to be set up three pavilions for to shelter us by day and by night. Meantime, I beseech of thee, that thou wilt go unto the lady, thy mistress, and say unto her that a knight hath come unto this place, who, albeit he knoweth her not, holdeth that the Lady Guinevere of Camelot is the fairest lady in all of the world. And I beseech thee to tell the lady that I am here to maintain that saying against all comers at the peril of my body. Wherefore, if the lady have any champion for to undertake battle in her behalf, him will I meet in yonder field to-morrow at mid-day a little before I eat my mid-day meal. For at that time I do propose for to enter into yonder field, and to make parade therein until my friends bid me for to come in to my dinner; and I shall take my stand in that place in honor of the Lady Guinevere of Camelot."

"Sir Pellias," said the damsel, "I will even do as thou desirest of me. And, though I may not wish that thou mayst be the victor in that encounter, yet am I soothly sorry for to depart from thee. For thou art both a very valiant and a very gentle knight, and I find that I have a great friendship for thee."

Then Sir Pellias laughed, and he said, "Parcenet, thou art minded to give me praise that is far beyond my deserving." And Parcenet said, "Sir, not so, for thou dost deserve all that I may say to thy credit."

Thereupon they twain took leave of one another with very good will and much kindness of intention, and the maiden and the three pages went the one way, and Sir Pellias and his two companions and the several attendants they had brought with them went into the glade of young trees as Sir Pellias had ordained.

And there they set up three pavilions in the shade of the trees; the one pavilion of fair white cloth, the second of green cloth, and the third of scarlet cloth. And over each pavilion they had set a banner emblazoned with the device of that knight unto whom the pavilion appertained: above the white pavilion was the device of Sir Pellias: to wit, three swans displayed upon a field argent; above the red pavilion, which was the pavilion of Sir Brandiles, was a red banner emblazoned with his device: to-wit, a mailed hand holding in its grasp a hammer; above the green pavilion, which was that of Sir Mador de la Porte, was a green banner bearing his device, which was that of a carrion crow holding in one hand a white lily flower and in the other a sword.

So when the next day had come, and when mid-day was nigh at hand, Sir Pellias went forth into that field before the castle as he had promised to do, and he was clad all from head to foot in the red armor which he had taken from the body of Sir Adresack, so that in that armor he presented a very terrible appearance. So he rode up and down before the castle walls for a considerable while crying in a loud voice,

"What ho! What ho! Here stands a knight of King Arthur's Court and of his Round Table who doth affirm, and is ready to maintain the same with his body, that the Lady Guinevere, King Arthur's Queen of Camelot, is the most beautiful lady in all of the world, barring none whomsoever. Wherefore, if any knight maintaineth otherwise, let him straightway come forth for to defend his opinion with his body."

Now after Sir Pellias had thus appeared in that meadow there fell a great commotion within the castle, and many people came upon the walls thereof and gazed down upon Sir Pellias where he paraded that field. And after a time had passed, the drawbridge of the castle was let fall, and there issued forth a knight, very huge of frame and exceedingly haughty of demeanor. This knight was clad altogether from head to foot in green armor, and upon either arm he wore a green sleeve, whence he was sometimes entitled the Knight of the Green Sleeves.

So that Green Knight rode forward toward Sir Pellias, and Sir Pellias rode forward unto the Green Knight, and when they had come together they gave salute with a great deal of civility and knightly courtesy. Then the Green Knight said unto Sir Pellias, "Sir Knight, wilt thou allow unto me the great favor for to know thy name?"

Then the Green Knight made reply, "Ha, Sir Pellias, it is a great honor for me to have to do with so famous a knight, for who is there in Courts of Chivalry who hath not heard of thee? Now, if I have the good fortune for to overthrow thee, then will all thy honor become my honor. Now, in return for thy courtesy for making proclamation of thy name, I give unto thee my name and title, which is Sir Engamore of Malverat, further known as the Knight of the Green Sleeves. And I may furthermore tell thee that I am the champion unto the Lady Ettard of Grantmesnle, and that I have defended her credit unto peerless beauty for eleven months, and that against all comers, wherefore if I do successfully defend it for one month longer, then do I become lord of her hand and of all this fair estate. So I am prepared to do the uttermost in my power in her honor."

Then Sir Pellias said, "Sir Knight, I give thee gramercy for thy words of greeting, and I too will do my uttermost in this encounter." Thereupon each knight saluted each other with his lance, and each rode to his appointed station.

Now a great concourse of people had come down to the lower walls of the castle and of the town for to behold the contest of arms that was toward, wherefore it would be hard to imagine a more worthy occasion where knights might meet in a glorious contest of friendly jousting, wherefore each knight prepared himself in all ways, and dressed him his spear and his lance with great care and circumspection. So when all had been prepared for that encounter, an herald, who had come forth from the castle into the field, give the signal for assault. Thereupon in an instant, each knight drave spurs into his horse and rushed the one against the other, with such terrible speed that the ground shook and trembled beneath the beating of their horses' feet. So they met exactly in the centre of the field of battle, the one knight smiting the other in the midst of his defences with a violence that was very terrible to behold. And the spear of Sir Engamore burst into as many as thirty pieces, but the spear of Sir Pellias held so that the Green Knight was hurtled so violently from out of his saddle that he smote the earth above a spear's length behind the crupper of his horse.

Now when those who had stood upon the walls beheld how entirely the Green Knight was overthrown in the encounter, they lifted up their voices in great outcry; for there was no other such knight as Sir Engamore in all those parts. And more especially did the Lady Ettard make great outcry; for Sir Engamore was very much beloved by her; wherefore, seeing him so violently flung down upon the ground, she deemed that perhaps he had been slain.

Then three esquires ran to Sir Engamore and lifted him up and unlaced his helm for to give him air. And they beheld that he was not slain, but only in a deep swoon. So by and by he opened his eyes, and at that Sir Pellias was right glad, for it would have grieved him had he slain that knight. Now when Sir Engamore came back unto his senses once more, he demanded with great vehemence that he might continue that contest with Sir Pellias afoot and with swords. But Sir Pellias would not have it so. "Nay, Sir Engamore," quoth he, "I will not fight thee so serious a quarrel as that, for I have no such despite against thee." And at that denial Sir Engamore fell a weeping from pure vexation and shame of his entire overthrow.

Then came Sir Brandiles and Sir Mador de la Porte and gave Sir Pellias great acclaim for the excellent manner in which he had borne himself in the encounter, and at the same time they offered consolation unto Sir Engamore and comforted him for the misfortune that had befallen him. But Sir Engamore would take but little comfort in their words.

Now whiles they thus stood all together, there issued out from the castle the Lady Ettard and an exceedingly gay and comely Court of esquires and ladies, and these came across the meadow toward where Sir Pellias and the others stood.

Then when Sir Pellias beheld that lady approach, he drew his misericordia and cut the thongs of his helmet, and took the helmet off of his head, and thus he went forward, bareheaded, for to meet her.

But when he had come nigh to her he beheld that she was many times more beautiful than that image of her painted upon the ivory panel which he had aforetime beheld, wherefore his heart went forth unto her with a very great strength of liking. So therewith he kneeled down upon the grass and set his hands together palm to palm, before her, and he said: "Lady, I do very greatly crave thy forgiveness that I should thus have done battle against thy credit. For, excepting that I did that endeavor for my Queen, I would rather, in another case, have been thy champion than that of any lady whom I have ever beheld."

Now at that time Sir Pellias wore about his neck the collar of emeralds and opal stones and gold which the Lady of the Lake had given to him. Wherefore, when the Lady Ettard looked upon him, that necklace drew her heart unto him with very great enchantment. Wherefore she smiled upon Sir Pellias very cheerfully and gave him her hand and caused him to arise from that place where he kneeled. And she said to him, "Sir Knight, thou art a very famous warrior; for I suppose there is not anybody who knoweth aught of chivalry but hath heard of the fame of Sir Pellias, the Gentle Knight. Wherefore, though my champion Sir Engamore of Malverat hath heretofore overthrown all comers, yet he need not feel very much ashamed to have been overthrown by so terribly strong a knight."

Then Sir Pellias was very glad of the kind words which the Lady Ettard spake unto him, and therewith he made her known unto Sir Brandiles and Sir Mador de la Porte. Unto these knights also, the Lady Ettard spake very graciously, being moved thereto by the extraordinary regard she felt toward Sir Pellias. So she besought those knights that they would come into the castle and refresh themselves, with good cheer, and with that, the knights said that they would presently do so. Wherefore they returned each knight unto his pavilion, and there each bedight himself with fine raiment and with ornaments of gold and silver in such a fashion that he was noble company for any Court. Then those three knights betook themselves unto the castle of Grantmesnle, and when they had come thither everybody was astonished at the nobility of their aspect.

But Sir Engamore, who had by now recovered from his fall, was greatly cast down, for he said unto himself, "Who am I in the presence of these noble lords?" So he stood aside and was very downcast of heart and oppressed in his spirits.

Then the Lady Ettard set a very fine feast and Sir Pellias and Sir Brandiles and Sir Mador de la Porte were exceedingly glad thereof. And upon her right hand she placed Sir Pellias, and upon her left hand she placed Sir Engamore. And Sir Engamore was still more cast down, for, until now, he had always sat upon the right hand of the Lady Ettard.

Now because Sir Pellias wore that wonderful collar which the Lady of the Lake had given unto him, the Lady Ettard could not keep her regard from him. So after they had refreshed themselves and had gone forth into the castle pleasaunce for to walk in the warm sunshine, the lady would have Sir Pellias continually beside her. And when it came time for those foreign knights to quit the castle, she besought Sir Pellias that he would stay a while longer. Now Sir Pellias was very glad to do that, for he was pleased beyond measure with the graciousness and the beauty of the Lady Ettard.

So by and by Sir Brandiles and Sir Mador de la Porte went back unto their pavilions, and Sir Pellias remained in the castle of Grantmesnle for a while longer.

Now that night the Lady Ettard let to be made a supper for herself and Sir Pellias, and at that supper she and Sir Pellias alone sat at the table, and the damsel Parcenet waited in attendance upon the lady. Whiles they ate, certain young pages and esquires played very sweetly upon harps, and certain maidens who were attendant upon the Court of the lady sang so sweetly that it expanded the heart of the listener to hear them. And Sir Pellias was so enchanted with the sweetness of the music, and with the beauty of the Lady Ettard, that he wist not whether he were indeed upon the earth or in Paradise, wherefore, because of his great pleasure, he said unto the Lady Ettard, "Lady, I would that I might do somewhat for thee to show unto thee how high is the regard and the honor in which I hold thee."

Now as Sir Pellias sat beside her, the Lady Ettard had continually held in observation that wonderful collar of gold and of emerald and of opal stones which hung about his neck; and she coveted that collar exceedingly. Wherefore, she now said unto Sir Pellias, "Sir Knight, thou mayst indeed do me great favor if thou hast a mind for to do so." "What favor may I do thee, Lady?" said Sir Pellias. "Sir," said the Lady Ettard, "thou mayst give unto me that collar which hangeth about thy neck."

At this the countenance of Sir Pellias fell, and he said, "Lady, I may not do that; for that collar came unto me in such an extraordinary fashion that I may not part it from me."

Then the Lady Ettard said, "Why mayst thou not part it from thee, Sir Pellias?"

Thereupon Sir Pellias told her all of that extraordinary adventure with the Lady of the Lake, and of how that fairy lady had given the collar unto him.

At this the Lady Ettard was greatly astonished, and she said, "Sir Pellias, that is a very wonderful story. Ne'theless, though thou mayst not give that collar unto me, yet thou mayst let me wear it for a little while. For indeed I am charmed by the beauty of that collar beyond all manner of liking, wherefore I do beseech thee for to let me wear it for a little."

Then Sir Pellias could refuse her no longer, so he said, "Lady, thou shalt have it to wear for a while." Thereupon he took the collar from off of his neck, and he hung it about the neck of the Lady Ettard.

Then, after a little time the virtue of that jewel departed from Sir Pellias and entered into the Lady Ettard, and the Lady Ettard looked upon Sir Pellias with altogether different eyes than those with which she had before regarded him. Wherefore she said unto herself: "Hah! what ailed me that I should have been so enchanted with that knight to the discredit of my champion who hath served me so faithfully? Hath not this knight done me grievous discredit? Hath he not come hitherward for no other reason than for that purpose? Hath he not overthrown mine own true knight in scorn of me? What then hath ailed me that I should have given him such regard as I have bestowed upon him?" But though she thought all this, yet she made no sign thereof unto Sir Pellias, but appeared to laugh and talk very cheerfully. Nevertheless, she immediately began to cast about in her mind for some means whereby she might be revenged upon Sir Pellias; for she said unto herself, "Lo! is he not mine enemy and is not mine enemy now in my power? Wherefore should I not take full measure of revenge upon him for all that which he hath done unto us of Grantmesnle?"

So by and by she made an excuse and arose and left Sir Pellias. And she took Parcenet aside, and she said unto the damsel Parcenet, "Go and fetch me hither presently a powerful sleeping-draught." Then Parcenet said, "Lady, what would you do?" And the Lady Ettard said, "No matter." And Parcenet said, "Would you give unto that noble knight a sleeping-draught?" And the lady said, "I would." Then Parcenet said, "Lady, that would surely be an ill thing to do unto one who sitteth in peace at your table and eateth of your salt." Whereunto the Lady Ettard said, "Take thou no care as to that, girl, but go thou straightway and do as I bid thee."

Then Parcenet saw that it was not wise for her to disobey the lady. Wherefore she went straightway and did as she was bidden. So she brought the sleeping-draught to the lady in a chalice of pure wine, and the Lady Ettard took the chalice and said to Sir Pellias, "Take thou this chalice of wine, Sir Knight, and drink it unto me according to the measure of that good will thou hast unto me." Now Parcenet stood behind her lady's chair, and when Sir Pellias took the chalice she frowned and shook her head at him. But Sir Pellias saw it not, for he was intoxicated with the beauty of the Lady Ettard, and with the enchantment of the collar of emeralds and opal stones and gold which she now wore. Wherefore he said unto her, "Lady, if there were poison in that chalice, yet would I drink of the wine that is in it at thy command."

At that the Lady Ettard fell a-laughing beyond measure, and she said, "Sir Knight, there is no poison in that cup."

So Sir Pellias took the chalice and drank the wine, and he said, "Lady, how is this? The wine is bitter." To which the Lady Ettard made reply, "Sir, that cannot be."

Then in a little while Sir Pellias his head waxed exceedingly heavy as if it were of lead, wherefore he bowed his head upon the table where he sat. That while the Lady Ettard remained watching him very strangely, and by and by she said, "Sir Knight, dost thou sleep?" To the which Sir Pellias replied not, for the fumes of the sleeping-draught had ascended into his brains and he slept.

Then the Lady Ettard arose laughing, and she smote her hands together and summoned her attendants. And she said to them, "Take this knight away, and convey him into an inner apartment, and when ye have brought him thither, strip him of his gay clothes and of his ornaments so that only his undergarments shall remain upon him. And when ye have done that, lay him upon a pallet and convey him out of the castle and into that meadow beneath the walls where he overthrew Sir Engamore, so that when the morning shall arise he shall become a mock and a jest unto all who shall behold him. Thus shall we humiliate him in that same field wherein he overthrew Sir Engamore, and his humiliation shall be greater than the humiliation of Sir Engamore hath been."

Now when the damsel Parcenet heard this she was greatly afflicted, so that she withdrew herself apart and wept for Sir Pellias. But the others took Sir Pellias and did unto him as the Lady Ettard had commanded.

Now when the next morning had come, Sir Pellias awoke with the sun shining into his face. And he wist not at all where he was, for his brains were befogged by the sleeping-draught which he had taken. So he said unto himself, "Am I dreaming, or am I awake? for certes the last that I remember was that I sat at supper with the Lady Ettard, yet here I am now in an open field with the sun shining upon me."

So he raised himself upon his elbow, and behold! he lay beneath the castle walls nigh to the postern gate. And above him, upon the top of the wall, was a great concourse of people, who, when they beheld that he was awake, laughed at him and mocked at him. And the Lady Ettard also gazed down at him from a window and he saw that she laughed at him and made herself merry. And lo! he beheld that he lay there clad only in his linen undervestment, and that he was in his bare feet as though he were prepared to sleep at night. So he sat upon the cot, saying unto himself, "Certainly this must be some shameful dream that oppresses me." Nor was he at all able to recover from his bewilderment.

Now, as he sat thus, the postern gate was opened of a sudden, and the damsel Parcenet came out thence. And her face was all be-wet with tears, and she bare in her hand a flame-colored mantle. Straightway she ran to Sir Pellias, and said, "Thou good and gentle knight, take thou this and wrap thyself in it."

Upon this Sir Pellias wist that this was no dream, but a truth of great shame; wherefore he was possessed with an extreme of agony of shame, so that he fell to trembling, whilst his teeth chattered as though with an ague. Then he said to Parcenet, "Maiden, I thank thee." And he could find no more words to say. So he took the mantle and wrapped himself in it.

Now when the people upon the walls beheld what Parcenet had done, they hooted her and reviled her with many words of ill-regard. So the maiden ran back again into the castle, but Sir Pellias arose and went his way toward his pavilion wrapped in that mantle. And as he went he staggered and tottered like a drunken man, for a great burden of shame lay upon him almost more than he could carry.

So when Sir Pellias had reached his pavilion, he entered it and threw himself on his face upon his couch and lay there without saying anything. And by and by Sir Brandiles and Sir Mador de la Porte heard of that plight into which Sir Pellias had fallen, and thereupon they hastened to where he lay and made much sorrow over him. Likewise, they were exceedingly wroth at the shame that had been put upon him; wherefore they said, "We will get us aid from Camelot, and we will burst open yonder castle and we will fetch the Lady Ettard hither to crave thy pardon for this affront. This we will do even if we have to drag her hither by the hair of her head."

But Sir Pellias lifted not his head, only he groaned and he said, "Let be, Messires; for under no circumstances shall ye do that thing, she being a woman. As it is, I would defend her honor even though I died in that defence. For I know not whether I am bewitched or what it is that ails me, but I love her with a very great passion and I cannot tear my heart away from her."

At this Sir Brandiles and Sir Mador de la Porte were greatly astonished, wherefore they said the one to the other, "Certes, that lady hath laid some powerful spell upon him."

Then after a while Sir Pellias bade them go away and leave him, and they did so, though not with any very good will.

So Sir Pellias lay there for all that day until the afternoon had come. Then he aroused himself and bade his esquire for to bring him his armor. Now when Sir Brandiles and Sir Mador de la Porte heard news of this they went to where he was and said, "Sir, What have ye a mind to do?" To this Sir Pellias said, "I am going to try to win me unto the Lady Ettard's presence." Then they said, "What madness is this?" "I know not," said Sir Pellias, "but, meseems, that if I do not behold the Lady Ettard and talk with her I shall surely die of longing to see her." And they say, "Certes, this is madness." Whereunto he replied, "I know not whether it is madness or whether I am caught in some enchantment."

So the esquire fetched unto Sir Pellias his armor as he had commanded, and he clad Sir Pellias in it so that he was altogether armed from head to foot. Thereupon straightway Sir Pellias mounted his horse and rode out toward the castle of Grantmesnle.

Now when the Lady Ettard beheld Sir Pellias again parading the meadow below the castle, she called unto her six of her best knights,and she said unto them, "Behold, Messires, yonder is that knight who brought so much shame upon us yesterday. Now I bid ye for to go forth against him and to punish him as he deserveth."

So those six knights went and armed themselves, and when they had done so they straightway rode forth against Sir Pellias.

Now, when Sir Pellias beheld these approach, his heart overflowed with fury and he shouted in a great voice and drave forward against them. And for a while they withstood him, but he was not to be withstood, but fought with surpassing fury, wherefore they presently brake from before him and fled. So he pursued them with great fury about that field and smote four of them down from their horses. Then, when there were but two of those knights remaining, Sir Pellias of a sudden ceased to fight, and he cried out unto those two knights, "Messires, I surrender myself unto ye."

Now at that those two knights were greatly astonished, for they were entirely filled with the fear of his strength, and wist not why he should yield to them. Nevertheless they came and laid hands upon him and took him toward the castle. Upon this Sir Pellias said unto himself, "Now they will bring me unto the Lady Ettard, and I shall have speech with her." For it was for this that he had suffered himself to be taken by those two knights.

But it was not to be as Sir Pellias willed it. For when they had brought him close under the castle, the Lady Ettard called unto them from a window in the wall. And she said, "What do you with that knight?" They say, "We bring him to you, Lady." Upon this she cried out very vehemently, "Bring him not to me, but take him and tie his hands behind his back and tie his feet beneath his horse's belly, and send him back unto his companions."

Then Sir Pellias lifted up his eyes unto that window and he cried out in a great passion of despair, "Lady, it was unto thee I surrendered, and not unto these unworthy knights."

But the Lady Ettard cried out all the more vehemently, "Drive him hence, for I do hate the sight of him."

So those two knights did as the Lady Ettard said; they took Sir Pellias and bound him hand and foot upon his horse. And when they had done so they allowed his horse for to bear him back again unto his companions in that wise.

Now when Sir Brandiles and Sir Mador de la Porte beheld how Sir Pellias came unto them with his hands bound behind his back and his feet tied beneath his horse's belly, they were altogether filled with grief and despair. So they loosed those cords from about his hands and feet, and they cried out upon Sir Pellias, "Sir Knight, Sir Knight, art thou not ashamed to permit such infamy as this?" And Sir Pellias shook and trembled as though with an ague,and he cried out in great despair, "I care not what happens unto me!" They said, "Not unto thyself, Sir Knight; but what shame dost thou bring upon King Arthur and his Round Table!" Upon this Sir Pellias cried aloud, with a great and terrible voice, "I care not for them, either."

All of this befell because of the powerful enchantment of the collar of emeralds and opal stones and of gold which Sir Pellias had given unto the Lady Ettard, and which she continually wore. For it was beyond the power of any man to withstand the enchantment of that collar. So it was that Sir Pellias was bewitched and brought to that great pass of shame.

CHAPTER FOURTH

# HOW QUEEN GUINEVERE QUARRELLED WITH SIR GAWAINE

Now, in the same measure that Queen Guinevere felt high regard for Sir Pellias, in that same degree she felt misliking for Sir Gawaine. For, though Sir Gawaine was said of many to have a silver tongue, and whiles he could upon occasion talk in such a manner as to beguile others unto his will, yet he was of a proud temper and very stern and haughty. Wherefore he would not always brook that the Lady Guinevere should command him unto her will as she did other knights of that Court. Moreover, she could not ever forget how Sir Gawaine did deny her that time at Cameliard when she besought him and his companions for aid, in her time of trouble, nor how discourteous his speech had been to her upon that occasion. So there was no great liking between these two proud souls, for Queen Guinevere held to her way and Sir Gawaine held to his way under all circumstances.

Now it happened upon an occasion that Sir Gawaine and Sir Griflet and Sir Constantine of Cornwall sat talking with five ladies of the Queen's Court in a pleached garden that lay beneath the tower of the Lady Guinevere, and they made very pleasant discourse together. For some whiles they would talk and make them merry with jests and contes, and other whiles one or another would take a lute that they had with them and would play upon it and would sing.

Now while these lords and ladies sat thus enjoying pleasant discourse and singing in that manner, Queen Guinevere sat at a window that overlooked the garden, and which was not very high from the ground, wherefore she could overhear all that they said. But these lords and ladies were altogether unaware that the Queen could overhear them, so that they talked and laughed very freely, and the Queen greatly enjoyed their discourse and the music that they made.

That day was extraordinarily balmy, and it being well toward the sloping of the afternoon, those lords and ladies were clad in very gay attire. And of all who were there Sir Gawaine was the most gayly clad, for he was dressed in sky-blue silk embroidered with threads of silver. And Sir Gawaine was playing upon the lute and singing a ballad in an exceedingly pleasing voice so that Queen Guinevere, as she sat at the window beside the open casement, was very well content for to listen to him.

Now there was a certain greyhound of which Queen Guinevere was wonderfully fond; so much so that she had adorned its neck with a collar of gold inset with carbuncles. At that moment the hound came running into that garden and his feet were wet and soiled with earth. So, hearing Sir Gawaine singing and playing upon the lute that hound ran unto him and leaped upon him. At this Sir Gawaine was very wroth, wherefore he clinched his hand and smote the hound upon the head with the knuckles thereof, so that the hound lifted up his voice with great outcry.

But when Queen Guinevere beheld that blow she was greatly offended, wherefore she called out from her window, "Why dost thou smite my dog, Messire?" And those lords and ladies who were below in the garden were very much surprised and were greatly abashed to find that the Queen was so nigh unto them as to overhear all that they had said and to behold all that they did.

But Sir Gawaine spake up very boldly, saying, "Thy dog affronted me, Lady, and whosoever affronteth me, him I strike."

Then Queen Guinevere grew very angry with Sir Gawaine, wherefore she said, "Thy speech is over-bold, Messire," and Sir Gawaine said, "Not over-bold, Lady; but only bold enough for to maintain my rights."

At this speech the Lady Guinevere's face flamed like fire and her eyes shone very bright and she said, "I am sure that thou dost forget unto whom thou speakest, Sir Knight," at the which Sir Gawaine smiled very bitterly and said, "And thou, Lady, dost not remember that I am the son of a king so powerful that he needs no help from any other king for to maintain his rights."

At these words all those who were there fell as silent as though they were turned into stones, for that speech was exceedingly bold and haughty. Wherefore all looked upon the ground, for they durst not look either upon Queen Guinevere nor upon Sir Gawaine. And the Lady Guinevere, also, was silent for a long time, endeavoring to recover herself from that speech, and when she spake, it was as though she was half smothered by her anger. And she said, "Sir Knight, thou art proud and arrogant beyond measure, for I did never hear of anyone who dared to give reply unto his Queen as thou hast spoken unto me. But this is my Court, and I may command in it as I choose; wherefore I do now bid thee for to begone and to show thy face no more, either here nor in Hall nor any of the places where I hold my Court. For thou art an offence unto me, wherefore in none of these places shalt thou have leave to show thy face until thou dost ask my pardon for the affront which thou hast put upon me." Then Sir Gawaine arose and bowed very low to the Queen Guinevere and he said, "Lady, I go. Nor will I return thitherward until thou art willing for to tell me that thou art sorry for the discourteous way in which thou hast entreated me now and at other times before my peers."

So saying, Sir Gawaine took his leave from that place, nor did he turn his head to look behind him. And Queen Guinevere went into her chamber and wept in secret for anger and for shame. For indeed she was greatly grieved at what had befallen; yet she was so proud that she would in no wise have recalled the words that she had spoken, even had she been able for to have done so.

Now when the news of that quarrel had gone about the castle it came unto the ears of Sir Ewaine, wherefore Sir Ewaine went straightway unto Sir Gawaine, and asked him what was ado, and Sir Gawaine, who was like one distraught and in great despair, told him everything. Then Sir Ewaine said: "Thou wert certainly wrong for to speak unto the Queen as thou didst. Nevertheless, if thou art banished from this Court, I will go with thee, for thou art my cousin-german and my companion, and my heart cleaveth unto thee." So Sir Ewaine went unto King Arthur, and he said, "Lord, my cousin, Sir Gawaine, hath been banished from this Court by the Queen. And though I may not say that he hath not deserved that punishment, yet I would fain crave thy leave for to go along with him."

At this King Arthur was very grieved, but he maintained a steadfast countenance, and said, "Messire, I will not stay thee from going where it pleases thee. As for thy kinsman, I daresay he gave the Queen such great offence that she could not do otherwise than as she did."

So both Sir Ewaine and Sir Gawaine went unto their inns and commanded their esquires for to arm them. Then they, with their esquires, went forth from Camelot, betaking their way toward the forest lands.

There those two knights and their esquires travelled for all that day until the gray of the eventide, what time the birds were singing their last songs ere closing their eyes for the night. So, finding the evening drawing on apace, those knights were afraid that they would not be able to find kindly lodging ere the night should descend upon them, and they talked together a great deal concerning that thing. But as they came to the top of a certain hill, they beheld below them a valley, very fair and well tilled, with many cottages and farm-crofts. And in the midst of that valley was a goodly abbey very fair to look upon; wherefore Sir Gawaine said unto Sir Ewaine: "If yonder abbey is an abbey of monks, I believe we shall find excellent lodging there for to-night."

So they rode down into that valley and to the abbey, and they found a porter at the wicket of whom they learned that it was indeed an abbey of monks. Wherefore they were very glad and made great rejoicing.

But when the abbot of that abbey learned who they were and of what quality and high estate, he was exceedingly pleased for to welcome them wherefore he brought them into that part of the abbey where he himself dwelt. There he bade them welcome and had set before them a good supper, whereat they were very much rejoiced. Now the abbot was merry of soul, and took great pleasure in discourse with strangers, so he diligently inquired of those two knights concerning the reason why they were errant. But they told him naught concerning that quarrel at Court, but only that they were in search of adventure. Upon this the abbot said, "Ha, Messires, if ye are in search of adventures, ye may find one not very far from this place."

So Sir Gawaine said, "What adventure is that?" And the abbot replied, "I will tell ye; if ye will travel to the eastward from this place, ye will come, after a while, to a spot where ye shall find a very fair castle of gray stone. In front of that castle ye will find a good level meadow, and in the midst of the meadow a sycamore-tree, and upon the sycamore-tree a shield to which certain ladies offer affront in a very singular manner. If ye forbid those ladies to affront that shield you will discover a very good adventure."

Then Sir Gawaine said, "That is a very strange matter. Now, to-morrow morning we will go to that place and will endeavor to discover of what sort that adventure may be." And the abbot said, "Do so," and laughed in great measure.

So when the next morning had come, Sir Gawaine and Sir Ewaine gave adieu unto the abbot, and took their leave of that place, riding away unto the eastward, as the abbot had advised. And after they had ridden in that direction for two or three hours or more they beheld before them the borders of a forest all green and shady with foliage, and very cheerful in the warmth of the early summer day. And, lo! immediately at the edge of the woodland there stood a fair, strong castle of gray stone, with windows of glass shining very bright against the sky.

Then Sir Gawaine and Sir Ewaine beheld that everything was as the abbot had said; for in front of the castle was a smooth, level meadow with a sycamore-tree in the midst thereof. And as they drew near they perceived that a sable shield hung in the branches of the tree, and in a little they could see that it bore the device of three white goshawks displayed. But that which was very extraordinary was that in front of that shield there stood seven young damsels, exceedingly fair of face, and that these seven damsels continually offered a great deal of insult to that shield. For some of those damsels smote it ever and anon with peeled rods of osier, and others flung lumps of clay upon it, so that the shield was greatly defaced therewith. Now nigh to the shield was a very noble-appearing knight clad all in black armor, and seated upon a black war-horse, and it was very plain to be seen that the shield belonged unto that knight, for otherwise he had no shield. Yet, though that was very likely his shield, yet the knight offered no protest either by word or by act to stay those damoiselles from offering affront thereunto.

Then Sir Ewaine said unto Sir Gawaine, "Yonder is a very strange thing that I behold; belike one of us is to encounter yonder knight." And Sir Gawaine said,

"Maybe so." Then Sir Ewaine said, "If it be so then I will undertake the adventure." "Not so," said Sir Gawaine, "for I will undertake it myself, I being the elder of us twain, and the better seasoned in knighthood." So Sir Ewaine said, "Very well. Let it be that way, for thou art a very much more powerful knight than I, and it would be a pity for one of us to fail in this undertaking." Thereupon Sir Gawaine said, "Let be, then, and I will undertake it."

So he set spurs to his horse and he rode rapidly to where those damsels offered affront in that way to the sable shield. And he set his spear in rest and shouted in a loud voice, "Get ye away! Get ye away!" So when those damsels beheld the armed knight riding at them in that wise they fled away shrieking from before him.

Then the Sable Knight, who sat not a great distance away, rode forward in a very stately manner unto Sir Gawaine, and he said, "Sir Knight, why dost thou interfere with those ladies?" Whereunto Sir Gawaine replied, "Because they offered insult unto what appeared to me to be a noble and knightly shield." At this the Sable Knight spake very haughtily, saying, "Sir Knight, that shield belongeth unto me and I do assure thee that I am very well able for to take care of it without the interference of any other defender." To which Sir Gawaine said, "It would appear not, Sir Knight."

Then the Sable Knight said, "Messire, an thou thinkest that thou art better able to take care of that shield than I, I think that thou wouldst do very well to make thy words good with thy body." To this Sir Gawaine said, "I will do my endeavor to show thee that I am better able to guard that shield than thou art who ownest it."

Upon this the Sable Knight, without further ado, rode unto the sycamore-tree, and took down from thence the shield that hung there. And he dressed the shield upon his arm and took his spear in hand and made him ready for defence, and then each knight took such station upon the field as appeared unto him to be fitting.

Now, when the people of that castle perceived that a combat of arms was toward, they crowded in great numbers to the walls, so that there were as many as twoscore ladies and esquires and folk of different degrees looking down upon that field of battle from the walls.

So when those knights were altogether prepared, Sir Ewaine gave the signal for encounter and each knight shouted aloud and drave spurs into his charger and rushed forward to the assault with a noise like thunder for loudness.

Now, Sir Gawaine thought that he should easily overcome his adversary in this assault and that he would be able to cast him down from out of his saddle without much pains, for there was hardly any knight in that realm equal to Sir Gawaine for prowess. And, indeed, he had never yet been unhorsed in combat excepting by King Arthur. So when those two rode to the assault, the one against the other, Sir Gawaine thought of a surety that his adversary would fall before him. But it was not so, for in that attack Sir Gawaine's spear was broken into many pieces, but the spear of the Sable Knight held, so that Sir Gawaine was cast with great violence out of the saddle, smiting the dust with a terrible noise of falling. And so astonished was he at that fall that it appeared unto him not as though he fell from his saddle, but as though the earth rose up and smote him. Wherefore he lay for a while all stunned with the blow and with the astonishment thereof.

But when he heard the shouts of the people upon the castle wall, he immediately aroused himself from where he lay in the dust, and he was so filled with rage and shame that he was like one altogether intoxicated. Wherefore he drew his sword and rushed with great fury upon his enemy with intent to hew him down by main strength. Then that other knight, seeing him come thus at him, immediately voided his own saddle and drew his sword and put himself in posture either for assault or for defence. So they lashed together, tracing this way and that, and smiting with such fury that the blows they gave were most terrible for to behold. But when Sir Ewaine beheld how fierce was that assault, he set spurs unto his horse and pushed him between the knights'contestant, crying out aloud, "Sir Knights! Sir Knights! what is this? Here is no cause for such desperate battle." But Sir Gawaine cried out very furiously, "Let be! let be! and stand aside! for this quarrel concerns thee not." And the Sable Knight said, "A-horse or afoot, I am ready to meet that knight at any time."

But Sir Ewaine said, "Not so; ye shall fight no more in this quarrel. For shame, Gawaine! For shame to seek such desperate quarrel with a knight that did but meet thee in a friendly fashion in a fair contest!"

Then Sir Gawaine was aware that Sir Ewaine was both just and right; wherefore he put up his sword in silence, albeit he was like to weep for vexation at the shame of his overthrow. And the Sable Knight put up his sword also, and so peace was made betwixt those two.

Then the Sable Knight said, "I am glad that this quarrel is ended, for I perceive, Messires, that ye are assuredly knights of great nobility and gentleness of breeding; wherefore I would that we might henceforth be friends and companions instead of enemies. Wherefore I do beseech ye for to come with me a little ways from here where I have taken up my inn, so that we may rest and refresh ourselves in my pavilion."

Unto this Sir Ewaine said, "I give thee gramercy for thy courtesy, Sir Knight; and we will go with thee with all the pleasure that it is possible to feel." And Sir Gawaine said, "I am content." So these three knights straightway left the field of battle.

And when they had come to the edge of the forest Sir Gawaine and Sir Ewaine perceived a very fine pavilion of green silk set up beneath the tree. And about that pavilion were many attendants of divers sorts all clad in colors of green and white. So Sir Gawaine perceived that the knight who had overthrown him was certainly someone of very high estate, wherefore he was very greatly comforted. Then the esquires of those three knights came and removed the helmet, each esquire from his knight, so that the knight might be made comfortably thereby. And when this was done Sir Gawaine and Sir Ewaine perceived that the Sable Knight was very comely of countenance, being ruddy of face and with hair like to copper for redness. Then Sir

Ewaine said unto the knight, "Sir Unknown Knight, this knight, my companion, is Sir Gawaine, son of King Urien of Gore, and I am Ewaine, the son of King Lot of Orkney. Now I crave of thee that wilt make thyself known unto us in like manner."

"Ha," said the other; "I am glad that ye are such very famous and royal knights, for I am also of royal blood, being Sir Marhaus, the son of the King of Ireland."

Then Sir Gawaine was very glad to discover how exalted was the quality of that knight who overthrew him and he said unto Sir Marhaus, "Messire, I make my vow, that thou art one of the most terrible knights in the world. For thou hast done unto me this day what only one knight in all the world hath ever done, and this is King Arthur, who is my uncle and my lord. Now thou must certainly come unto the Court of King Arthur, for he will be wonderfully glad for to see thee, and maybe he will make thee a Knight of his Round Table – and there is no honor in all of the world that can be so great as that." Thus he spoke unthinkingly; and then he remembered. Wherefore he smote his fist against his forehead, crying out, "Aha! aha! who am I for to bid thee to come unto the Court of King Arthur, who only yesterday was disgraced and banished therefrom?"

Then Sir Marhaus was very sorry for Sir Gawaine, and he inquired concerning the trouble that lay upon him, and Sir Ewaine told Sir Marhaus all about that quarrel; at that Sir Marhaus was still more sorry for Sir Gawaine, wherefore he said, "Messires, I like ye both wonderfully well, and I would fain become your companion in the adventures ye are to undertake. For now I need remain here no longer. Ye must know that I was obliged to defend those ladies who assailed my shield until I had overthrown seven knights in their behalf. And I must tell ye that Sir Gawaine was the seventh knight I have overthrown. Wherefore, since I have now overthrown him, I am now released from my obligation and may go with ye."

Then Sir Gawaine and Sir Ewaine were very much astonished that any knight should lie beneath so strange an obligation as that – to defend those who assailed his shield – and they besought Sir Marhaus to tell them why he should have been obliged to fulfil such a pledge. So Sir Marhaus said, "I will tell ye. The case was this: Some whiles ago I was travelling in these parts with a hawk upon my wrist. At that time I was clad very lightly in holiday attire, to wit: I wore a tunic of green silk, and hosen one of green and one of white. And I had nothing upon me by way of defence but a light buckler and a short sword. Now, coming unto a certain stream of water, very deep and rapid, I perceived before me a bridge of stone crossing that stream, but so narrow that only one horseman might cross the bridge at a time. So I entered upon that bridge and was part way across it, when I perceived a knight in armor coming the other way. And behind the knight there sat upon a pillion a very fair lady with golden hair and very proud of demeanor. Now, when that knight perceived me upon the bridge, he cried aloud, 'Get back! get back! and suffer me to pass!' But this I would not do, but said, 'Not so, Sir Knight, for, having advanced so far upon this bridge, I have certes the right of way to complete my passage, and it is for you to wait and to permit me to cross.' But the knight would not do so, but immediately put himself in posture of offence and straightway came against me upon the bridge with intent either to slay me or to drive me back unto the other extremity of the bridge. But this he was not able to do, for I defended myself very well with my light weapons. And I so pushed my horse against his horse that I drave him backward from off the bridge and into the water, whereinto the horse and the knight and the lady all of them fell with a terrible uproar.

"At this the lady shrieked in great measure and both she and the knight were like to drown in the water, the knight being altogether clad in armor, so that he could not uplift himself above the flood. Wherefore, beholding their extremity, I leaped from off my horse and into the water, and with great ado and with much danger unto myself, I was able to bring them both unto the land.

"But that lady was very greatly offended with me, for her fair raiment was altogether wet and spoiled by the water, wherefore she upbraided me with great vehemence. So I kneeled down before her and besought her pardon with all humility, but she still continued to upbraid me. Then I offered unto her for to perform any penance that she might set upon me. At this the lady appeared to be greatly mollified, for she said, 'Very well, I will set thee a penance,' and when her knight had recovered she said, 'Come with us,' and so I mounted my horse and followed them. So after we had gone a considerable distance we came to this place and here she commanded me as follows: 'Sir Knight,' quoth she, 'this castle belongeth unto me and unto this knight who is my lord. Now, this shall be the penance for the affront thou hast given me: thou shalt take thy shield and hang it up in yonder sycamore-tree and every day I will send certain damsels of mine own out from the castle. And they shall offend against that shield and thou shalt not only suffer whatever offence they may offer, but thou shalt defend them against all comers until thou hast overcome seven knights.'

"So I have done until this morning, when thou, Sir Gawaine, camest hither. Thou art the seventh knight against whom I have contended, and as I have overcome thee, my penance is now ended and I am free."

Then Sir Gawaine and Sir Ewaine gave Sir Marhaus great joy that his penance was completed, and they were very well satisfied each party with the other. So Sir Gawaine and Sir Ewaine abided that night in the pavilion of Sir Marhaus and the next morning they arose and, having laved themselves in a forest stream, they departed from that place where they were.

So they entered the forest land once more and made their way by certain paths, they knew not whitherward; and they travelled all that morning and until the afternoon was come.

Now, as they travelled thus Sir Marhaus said of a sudden, "Messires, know ye where we are come to?" "Nay," they said, "we know not." Then Sir Marhaus said, "This part of the forest is called Arroy and it is further called 'The Forest of Adventure.' For it is very well known that when a knight, or a party of knights enter this forest, they will assuredly meet with an adventure of some sort, from which some come forth with credit while others fail therein." And Sir Ewaine said, "I am glad that we have come hither. Now let us go forward into this forest."

So those three knights and their esquires continued onward in that woodland where was silence so deep that even the tread of their horses upon the earth was scarcely to be heard. And there was no note of bird and no sound of voice and hardly did any light penetrate into the gloom of that woodland. Wherefore those knights said unto one another, "This is soothly a very strange place and one, maybe, of enchantment."

Now when they had come into the very midst of these dark woodlands, they perceived of a sudden, in the pathway before them, a fawn as white as milk. And round the neck of the fawn was a collar of pure gold. And the fawn stood and looked at them, but when they had come nigh to it, it turned and ran along a very narrow path. Then Sir Gawaine said, "Let us follow that fawn and see where it goeth." And the others said, "We are content." So they followed that narrow path until of a sudden they came to where was a little open lawn very bright with sunlight. In the midst of the lawn was a fountain of water, and there was no fawn to be seen, but, lo! beside the fountain there sat a wonderfully beautiful lady, clad all in garments of green. And the lady combed her hair with a golden comb, and her hair was like to the wing of a raven for blackness. And upon her arms she wore very wonderful bracelets of emeralds and of opal stones inset into cunningly wrought gold. Moreover, the face of the lady was like ivory for whiteness and her eyes were bright like jewels set in ivory. Now, when this lady perceived the knights she arose and laid aside her golden comb and bound up the locks of her hair with ribbons of scarlet silk, and thereupon, she came to those knights and gave them greeting.

Then those three knights gat them down straightway from off their horses, and Sir Gawaine said, "Lady, I believe that thou art not of mortal sort, but that thou art of faërie." Unto this the lady said, "Sir Gawaine, thou art right," and Sir Gawaine marvelled that she should know his name so well. Then he said to her, "Lady, who art thou?" and she made answer, "My name is Nymue and I am the chiefest of those Ladies of the Lake of whom thou mayst have heard. For it was I who gave unto King Arthur his sword Excalibur; for I am very friendly unto King Arthur and to all the noble Knights of his Court. So it is that I know ye all. And I know that thou, Sir Marhaus, shall become one of the most famous Knights of the Round Table." And all they marvelled at the lady's words. Then she said, "I prithee tell me what it is that ye seek in these parts?" And they say, "We seek adventure." "Well," said she, "I will bring you unto adventure, but it is Sir Gawaine who must undertake it." And Sir Gawaine said, "That is very glad news." Then the lady said, "Take me behind you upon your saddle, Sir Gawaine, and I will show unto you that adventure." So Sir Gawaine took the lady up behind him upon the saddle, and lo! she brought with her a fragrance such as he had never known before; for that fragrance was so subtle that it seemed to Sir Gawaine that the forest gave forth that perfume which the Lady of the Lake brought with her.

So the Lady of the Lake brought them by many devious ways out from that part of the forest; and she brought them by sundry roads and paths until they came out into an open country, very fruitful and pleasant to behold; and she brought them up a very high hill, and from the top of the hill they looked down upon a fruitful and level plain as upon a table spread out before them. And they beheld that in the midst of the plain was a noble castle built all of red stone and of red brick; and they beheld that there was a small town built also of red bricks.

Now as they sat their horses there on top of the hill they perceived of a sudden a knight clad all in red armor who came forth from a glade of trees. And they saw that the knight paraded the meadow that lay in front of the castle, and they saw that he gave challenge to those within the castle. Then they perceived that the drawbridge of the castle was let fall of a sudden and that there issued from thence ten knights clad in complete armor. And they beheld those ten knights assail the one knight in red armor, and they beheld the one knight assail the ten. And they beheld that for a while those ten withstood the one, but that he assailed them so terribly that he smote down four of them very quickly. Then they beheld that the rest brake and fled from before that one, and that the Red Knight pursued the others about the meadow with great fury. And they saw that he smote down one from out his saddle and another and another until but two of those knights were left.

Then Sir Gawaine said, "That is certainly a very wonderful sight for to see." But the Lady of the Lake only smiled and said, "Wait a little."

So they waited and they saw that when the Red Knight had smitten down all of his enemies but those two, and that when he had put those two in great peril of their lives, he of a sudden sheathed his sword and surrendered himself unto them. And they saw that those two knights brought the Red Knight to the castle, and that when they had brought him there a lady upon the wall thereof bespake that Red Knight as with great violence of language. And they beheld that those two knights took the Red Knight and bound his hands behind his back, and that they bound his feet beneath his horse's belly, and that they drave him away from that place.

All this they beheld from the top of the hill, and the Lady of the Lake said unto Sir Gawaine, "There thou shalt find thy adventure, Sir Gawaine." And Sir Gawaine said, "I will go," and the Lady of the Lake said, "Do so."

Thereupon, lo! she vanished from their sight and they were greatly amazed.

## Chapter Fifth

# How Sir Gawaine met Sir Pellias and Promised to Aid Him

Now, after that wonderful lady had disappeared from their sight in that manner, those three knights stood for a little while altogether astonished, for they wist not how to believe what their eyes had beheld. Then, by and by, Sir Gawaine spake, saying, "Certes, that was a very wonderful thing that happened to us, for in all my life I never knew so strange a miracle to befall. Now, it is very plain that some excellent adventure lieth in what we have seen, wherefore let us descend into yonder valley, for there we shall doubtless discover what that signifies which we have just now beheld. For I make my vow that I have hardly ever seen so terribly powerful a knight as he who has just now fought yonder battle, wherefore I can in no wise understand why, when he should so nearly have obtained a victory over his enemies, he should have surrendered himself to them as he did."

And Sir Ewaine and Sir Marhaus agreed that it would be well to go down and inquire what was the meaning of that which they had beheld.

So they three and their attendants rode down into the valley.

And they rode forward until they had come to a certain glade of trees and there they beheld three goodly pavilions that stood there: the one pavilion of white cloth, the second pavilion of green cloth, and the third pavilion of scarlet cloth.

Now, as the three knights-companion drew nigh to the pavilions, there came forth two knights to meet them. And when Sir Gawaine and Sir Ewaine saw the shields of the two, they immediately knew that they were Sir Brandiles and Sir Mador de la Porte. And in the same manner Sir Brandiles and Sir Mador de la Porte knew Sir Gawaine and Sir Ewaine,and each party was very much astonished at thus meeting the other in so strange a place. So when they came together they gave one another very joyful greeting and clasped hands with strong love and good fellowship.

Then Sir Gawaine and Sir Marhaus acquainted with Sir Brandiles and Sir Mador de la Porte and thereupon the five knights all went together into those three pavilions, discoursing the while with great amity and pleasure. And when they had come into the pavilion of Sir Brandiles they found there spread a good refreshment of white bread and wine of excellent savor.

Then after a while Sir Gawaine said to Sir Brandiles and Sir Mador de la Porte, "Messires, we observed a little while ago a very singular thing; for, as we stood together at the top of yonder hill and looked down into this plain we beheld a single knight clad all in red armor who did battle with ten knights. And that one knight in red armor combated the ten with such fury that he drave them all from before him, though they were so many and he but one. And truly I make my vow that I have hardly ever seen a knight show such great prowess in arms as he. Yet, when he had overcome all but two of those knights, and was in fair way to win a clear victory, he suddenly yielded himself unto the two and suffered them to take him and bind him and drive him with great indignity from the field. Now, I pray ye, tell me what was the meaning of that which we beheld, and who was that knight who fought so great a battle and yet yielded himself so shamefully."

At this Sir Brandiles and Sir Mador de la Porte made no answer, but directed their looks another way, for they knew not what to say. But when Sir Gawaine beheld that they were abashed he began more than ever to wonder what that thing meant; wherefore he said, "What is this? Why do ye not answer me? I bid ye tell me what is the meaning of your looks, and who is that red knight!"

Then after a while Sir Mador de la Porte said, "I shall not tell you, but you may come and see."

Then Sir Gawaine began to think maybe there was something in this that it would be better not to publish, and that, haply, he had best examine further into the matter alone. So he said unto the other knights, "Bide ye here a little, Messires, and I will go with Sir Mador de la Porte."

So Sir Gawaine went with Sir Mador de la Porte, and Sir Mador led him unto the white pavilion. And when they had come there Sir Mador drew aside the curtains of the pavilion, and he said, "Enter!" and Sir Gawaine entered.

Now, when he had come into the pavilion he perceived that a man sat upon a couch of rushes covered with an azure cloth, and in a little he perceived that man was Sir Pellias. But Sir Pellias saw not him immediately, but sat with his head bowed, like one altogether overwhelmed by a great despair.

*"I yet hope that thou wilt give us the pleasure of thy company awhile." (Second Book, Part II, Chapter Fifth)*

*"I believe that thou has slain this knight." (Second Book, Part II, Chapter Sixth)*

But when Sir Gawaine beheld who it was that sat upon the couch, he was greatly amazed and cried out, "Ha! is it thou, Sir Pellias? is it thou?"

But when Sir Pellias heard Sir Gawaine's voice, and when he perceived who it was that spake to him, he emitted an exceedingly bitter cry. And sprang to his feet and ran as far away as the walls of the pavilion would let him, and turned his face unto the walls thereof.

Then, after a while, Sir Gawaine spoke very sternly to Sir Pellias, saying, "Messire, I am astonished and very greatly ashamed that a Knight of King Arthur's Round Table should behave in so dishonorable a manner as I saw thee behave this day. For it is hardly to be believed that a knight of such repute and nobility as thou would suffer himself to be taken and bound by two obscure knights as thou didst suffer thyself this day. How couldst thou bring thyself to submit to such indignity and insult? Now, I do demand of thee that thou wilt explain this matter unto me."

But Sir Pellias was silent and would not make any reply. Then Sir Gawaine cried out very fiercely, "Ha! wilt thou not answer me?" and Sir Pellias shook his head.

Then Sir Gawaine said, still speaking very fiercely, "Messire! thou shalt answer me one way or another! For either thou shalt tell me the meaning of thy shameful conduct, or else thou shalt do extreme battle with me. For I will not suffer it that thou shalt bring such shame upon King Arthur and his Round Table without myself defending the honor and the credit of him and of it. One while thou and I were dear friends, but unless thou dost immediately exculpate thyself I shall hold thee in contempt, and shall regard thee as an enemy."

Upon this Sir Pellias spake like unto one that was nigh distracted, and he said, "I will tell thee all." Then he confessed everything unto Sir Gawaine, telling all that had befallen since that time when he had left the May Court of Queen Guinevere to enter upon this adventure, and Sir Gawaine listened unto him with great amazement. And when Sir Pellias had made an end of telling all that had befallen him, Sir Gawaine said, "Certes, this is very wonderful. Indeed, I cannot understand how thou camest to be so entangled in the charms of this lady unless she hath bewitched thee with some great enchantment."

Unto this Sir Pellias said, "Yea, I believe that I have been bewitched, for I am altogether beside myself in this, and am entirely unable to contain my passion."

Then Sir Gawaine bethought him for a long while, considering that matter very seriously; and by and by he said, "I have a plan, and it is this: I will go unto the Lady Ettard myself, and will inquire diligently into this affair. And if I find that anyone hath entangled thee in enchantments, it will go hard with me but I will punish that one with great dolor. For I shall not have it that another enchanter shall beguile thee as one hath already beguiled Merlin the Wise."

Then Sir Pellias said unto Sir Gawaine, "How wilt thou accomplish this matter so as to gain into the presence of the Lady Ettard?"

Thereupon Sir Gawaine replied, "That I will tell thee. We twain shall exchange armor, and I will go unto the castle in thy armor. When I have come there I shall say that I have overcome thee in an encounter, and have taken thine armor away from thee. Then they will haply admit me into the castle to hear my story, and I shall have speech with her."

Then Sir Pellias said, "Very well; it shall be as thou dost ordain."

So Sir Pellias summoned an esquire, and Sir Gawaine summoned his esquire, and those two removed the armor from Sir Pellias, and clad Sir Gawaine therein. After they had done that Sir Gawaine mounted upon the horse of Sir Pellias, and rode openly into that field wherein Sir Pellias had aforetime paraded.

Now, it happened that the Lady Ettard was at that time walking upon a platform within the castle walls, from which place she looked down into that meadow. So when she beheld a red knight parading in the meadow, she thought it was Sir Pellias come thither again, and at that she was vexed and affronted beyond all measure. Wherefore she said unto those nigh her, "That knight vexes me so wofully that I fear me I shall fall ill of vexation if he cometh here many more times. I would that I knew how to rid myself of him; for already, and only an hour ago, I sent ten good knights against him, and he overcame them all with great despatch and with much dishonor unto them and unto me."

So she beckoned to the Red Knight, and when he had come nigh to the walls of the castle, she said to him, "Sir Knight, why dost thou come hitherward to afflict me and to affront me thus? Canst thou not understand that the more often thou comest to tease me in this manner, the more do I hate thee?"

Then Sir Gawaine opened the umbril of his helmet and showed his face, and the Lady Ettard saw that the Red Knight was not Sir Pellias. And Sir Gawaine said, "Lady, I am not that one whom thou supposest me to be, but another. For, behold! I have thine enemy's armor upon my body, wherefore thou mayst see that I have overcome him. For thou mayst suppose that it is hardly to be thought that I could wear his armor unless I took it from him by force of arms. Wherefore thou needst trouble thyself no more about him."

Then the Lady Ettard could not think otherwise than this knight (whom she knew not) had indeed overthrown Sir Pellias in a bout of arms, and had taken his armor away from him. And indeed she was exceedingly astonished that such a thing could have happened; for it appeared to her that Sir Pellias was one of the greatest knights in the world; wherefore she marvelled who this knight could be who had overthrown him in battle. So she gave command to sundry of those in attendance upon her that they should go forth and bring that red knight into the castle and that they should pay him great honor; for that he must assuredly be one of the very greatest champions in the world.

Thus Sir Gawaine came into the castle and was brought before the Lady Ettard where she stood in a wonderfully large and noble hall. For that hall was illuminated by seven tall windows of colored glass, and it was hung around with tapestries and hangings, very rich and of a most excellent quality, wherefore Sir Gawaine was greatly astonished at the magnificence of all that he beheld in that place.

Now, Sir Gawaine had taken the helmet from off his head, and he bore it under his arm and against his hip, and his head was bare so that all who were there could see his face very plainly. Wherefore they all perceived that he was exceedingly comely, that his eyes were as blue as steel, his nose high and curved, and his hair and beard very dark and rich in color. Moreover, his bearing was exceedingly steadfast and haughty, so that those who beheld him were awed by the great knightliness of his aspect.

Then the Lady Ettard came to Sir Gawaine and gave him her hand, and he kneeled down and set it to his lips. And the lady bespoke him very graciously, saying, "Sir Knight, it would give me a great deal of pleasure if thou wouldst make us acquainted with thy name, and if thou wouldst proclaim thy degree of estate unto us."

Unto this Sir Gawaine made reply, "Lady, I cannot inform you of these things at these present, being just now vowed unto secrecy upon those points, wherefore I do crave your patience for a little."

Then the Lady Ettard said, "Sir Knight, it is a great pity that we may not know thy name and degree; ne'theless, though we are as yet in ignorance as to thy quality, I yet hope that thou wilt give us the pleasure of thy company awhile, and that thou wilt condescend to remain within this poor place for two days or three, whiles we offer thee such refreshment as we are able to do."

Now here a very untoward thing befell. To wit, it was this: The Lady Ettard had come to love that necklace of emeralds and of opal stones and of gold that she had borrowed from Sir Pellias, and that to such a degree that she never let it depart from her whether by day or by night. Wherefore she wore it at that moment hanging about her neck and her throat. So, as she talked to Sir Gawaine, he looked upon that necklace, and the enchantment thereof began to take a very great hold upon him. For he presently began to feel as though his heart was drawn with exceeding ardency out of his bosom and unto the Lady Ettard; so much so that, in a little while, he could not at all keep his regard withdrawn from her. And the more that he looked upon the necklace and the lady the more did the enchantment of the jewel take hold upon his spirits. Accordingly, when the Lady Ettard spake so graciously unto him, he was very glad to accept of her kindness; wherefore he said, gazing very ardently at her the whiles, "Lady, thou art exceedingly gentle to extend so great a courtesy unto me; wherefore I shall be glad beyond measure for to stay with thee for a short while."

At these words the Lady Ettard was very greatly pleased, for she said to herself, "Certes, this knight (albeit I know not who he may be) must be a champion of extraordinary prowess and of exalted achievement. Now, if I can persuade him to remain in this castle as my champion, then shall I doubtless gain very great credit thereby; for I shall have one for to defend my rights who must assuredly be the greatest knight in all the world." Wherefore she set forth every charm and grace of demeanor to please Sir Gawaine, and Sir Gawaine was altogether delighted by the kindness of her manner.

Now, Sir Engamore was there present at that time, wherefore he was very greatly troubled in spirit. For in the same degree that Sir Gawaine received courtesy from the Lady Ettard, in that same degree Sir Engamore was cast down into great sorrow and distress – so much so that it was a pity for to see him. For Sir Engamore said to himself, "Aforetime, ere these foreign knights came hitherward, the Lady Ettard was very kind to me, and was willing to take me for her champion and lord. But first came Sir Pellias and overthrew me, and now cometh this strange knight and overthroweth him, wherefore, in the presence of such a great champion as this, I am come to be as nothing in her sight." So Sir Engamore withdrew himself from that place and went unto his closet, where he sat himself down alone in great sorrow.

Now the Lady Ettard had given command that a very noble and splendid feast should be prepared for Sir Gawaine and for herself, and whilst it was preparing she and Sir Gawaine walked together in the pleasaunce of the castle. For there was a very pleasant shade in the place, and flowers grew there in great abundance, and many birds sang very sweetly in among the blossoms of the trees. And as Sir Gawaine and the lady walked thus together, the attendants stood at a little distance and regarded them. And they said to one another, "Assuredly it would be a very good thing if the Lady Ettard would take this knight for her champion, and if he should stay here in Grantmesnle forever."

So Sir Gawaine and the lady walked together, talking very cheerfully, until sunset, and at that time the supper was prepared and they went in and sat down to it. And as they supped, a number of pages, very fair of face, played upon harps before them; and sundry damsels sang very sweetly in accord to that music, so that the bosom of Sir Gawaine was greatly expanded with joy. Wherefore he said to himself, "Why should I ever leave this place? Lo! I have been banished from King Arthur's Court; why then should I not establish here a Court of mine own that might, in time, prove to be like to his for glory?" And the Lady Ettard was so beautiful in his eyes that this seemed to him to be a wonderfully pleasant thought.

Now turn we unto Sir Pellias:

For after Sir Gawaine had left him, the heart of Sir Pellias began to misgive him that he had not been wise; and at last he said to himself, "Suppose that Sir Gawaine should forget his duty to me when he meeteth the Lady Ettard. For it seems that haply she possesses some potent charm that might well draw the heart of Sir Gawaine unto her. Wherefore if Sir Gawaine should come within the circle of such enchantment as that, he may forget his duty unto me and may transgress against the honor of his knighthood."

And the more that Sir Pellias thought of this the more trouble he grew in his mind. So at last, when evening had fallen, he called an esquire unto him and he said, "Go, and fetch me hither the garb of a black friar, for I would fain go unto the castle of Grantmesnle in disguise." So the esquire went as he commanded and brought him such a garb, and Sir Pellias clad himself therein.

Now, by that time, the darkness had come entirely over the face of the earth so that it would not have been possible for anyone to know Sir Pellias, even if they had seen his face. So he went unto the castle, and they who were there, thinking that he was a black friar, as he appeared to be, admitted him into the castle by the postern gate.

So, as soon as Sir Pellias had come into the castle, he began to make diligent inquiry concerning where he might find that knight who had come thither in the afternoon, and those within the castle, still thinking him to be a friar of black orders, said unto him, "What would ye with that knight?" To the which Sir Pellias said, "I have a message for him." They of the castle said, "Ye cannot come at that knight just now, for he is at supper with the Lady Ettard, and he holds her in pleasant discourse."

At this Sir Pellias began to wax very angry, for he greatly misliked the thought that Sir Gawaine should then make merry with the Lady Ettard. So he said, speaking very sternly, "I must presently have speech with that knight, wherefore I bid ye to bring me unto him without delay." Then they of the castle said, "Wait and we will see if that knight is willing to have you come to him."

So one of the attendants went unto that place where Sir Gawaine sat at supper with the Lady Ettard, and he said, "Sir Knight, there hath come hither a black friar who demandeth to have present speech with thee, and he will not be denied, but continually maketh that demand.

At this Sir Gawaine was greatly troubled in his conscience, for he knew that he was not dealing honorably by Sir Pellias, and he pondered whether or not this black friar might be a messenger from his friend. But yet he could not see how he might deny such a messenger speech with him. So, after a while of thought, he said, "Fetch the black friar hither and let him deliver his message to me."

So Sir Pellias, in the garb of a black friar, was brought by the attendants into the outer room of that place where Sir Gawaine sat at supper with the lady. But for a little time Sir Pellias did not enter the room, but stood behind the curtain of the ante-room and looked upon them, for he desired to make sure as to whether or no Sir Gawaine was true to him.

Now everything in that room where the knight and the lady sat was bedight with extraordinary splendor, and it was illuminated by a light of several score of waxen tapers that sent forth a most delightful perfume as they burned. And as Sir Pellias stood behind the curtains, he beheld Sir Gawaine and the Lady Ettard as they sat at the table together, and he saw that they were filled with pleasure in the company of one another. And he saw that Sir Gawaine and the lady quaffed wine out of the same chalice and that the cup was of gold. And as he saw those two making merry with one another, he was filled with great anger and indignation, for he now perceived that Sir Gawaine had betrayed him.

So, by and by, he could contain himself no longer, wherefore he took five steps into that room and stood before Sir Gawaine and the Lady Ettard. And, when they looked upon him in great surprise, he cast back the hood from his face and they knew him. Then the Lady Ettard shrieked with great vehemence, crying out, "I have been betrayed!" and Sir Gawaine sat altogether silent, for he had not a single word to say either to the lady or to Sir Pellias.

Then Sir Pellias came close to the Lady Ettard with such a fell countenance that she could not move for fear. And when he had come nigh to her he catched that necklace of emeralds and opal stones and gold with such violence that he brake the clasp thereof and so plucked it from her neck. Then he said, "This is mine and thou hast no right to it!" And therewith he thrust it into his bosom. Then he turned upon Sir Gawaine where he sat, and he said, "Thou art false both unto thy knighthood and unto thy friendship, for thou hast betrayed me utterly." Thereupon he raised his arm and smote Sir Gawaine upon the face with the back of his hand so violently that the mark of his fingers was left in red all across the cheek of Sir Gawaine.

Then Sir Gawaine fell as pale as ashes and he cried out, "Sir, I have in sooth betrayed thee, but thou hast offered such affront to me that our injury is equal." To the which Sir Pellias made reply, "Not so; for the injury I gave to thee is only upon thy cheek, but the injury thou gavest to me is upon my heart. Ne'theless, I will answer unto thee for the affront I have done thee. But thou also shalt answer unto me for the offence thou hast done unto me, in that thou hast betrayed me."

Then Sir Gawaine said, "I am willing to answer unto thee in full measure." And Sir Pellias said, "Thou shalt indeed do so." Thereupon he turned and left that place, nor did he so much as look again either at Sir Gawaine or at the Lady Ettard.

But, now that the Lady Ettard no longer had the magic collar about her neck, Sir Gawaine felt nothing of the great enchantment that had aforetime drawn him so vehemently unto her. Accordingly, he now suffered a misliking for her as great as that liking which had aforetime drawn him unto her. Wherefore he said to himself, "How was it possible that for this lady I could have so betrayed my knighthood and have done so much harm unto my friend!" So he pushed back his chair very violently and arose from that table with intent to leave her.

But when the Lady Ettard saw his intent she spake to him with very great anger, for she was very much affronted in that he had deceived her when he said that he had overcome Sir Pellias. Wherefore she said with great heat, "Thou mayst go, and I am very willing for to have thee do so, for thou didst say false when thou didst tell me that thou hadst overcome Sir Pellias. For now I perceive that he is both a stronger and nobler knight than thou. For he smote thee as though thou wert his servant, and thou yet bearest the marks of his fingers upon thy cheek."

At this Sir Gawaine was exceedingly wroth and entirely filled with the shame of that which had befallen him, wherefore he said, "Lady, I think thou hast bewitched me to bring me to such a pass of dishonor. As for Sir Pellias, look forth into that meadow to-morrow and see if I do not put a deeper mark upon him than ever he hath put upon me." Thereupon he left that place and went down into the court-yard and called upon the attendants who were there for to fetch him his horse. So they did as he commanded and he straightway rode forth into the night.

And he was very glad of the darkness of the night, for it appeared to him that it was easier to bear his shame in the darkness, wherefore when he had come to the glade of trees he would not enter the pavilion where his friends were. And also, when Sir Ewaine and Sir Marhaus came out unto him and bade him to come in, he would not do so, but stayed without in the darkness; for he said unto himself, "If I go in where is a light, haply they will behold the mark of Sir Pellias his hand upon my face."

So he stayed without in the darkness and bade them to go away and leave him alone.

But when they had gone he called his esquire unto him and he said, "Take this red armor off me and carry it into the pavilion of Sir Pellias, for I hate it." So the esquire did as Sir Gawaine commanded, and Sir Gawaine walked up and down for the entire night, greatly troubled in spirit and in heart.

CHAPTER SIXTH

# How the Lady of the Lake Took Back Her Necklace

Now, when the next morning had come, Sir Gawaine summoned his esquire unto him and said, "Fetch hither my armor and case me in it." And the esquire did so. Then Sir Gawaine said, "Help me unto my horse," and the esquire did so. And the morning was still very early, with the grass all lustrous and sparkling with dew, and the little birds singing with such vehemence that it might have caused anyone great joy to be alive. Wherefore, when Sir Gawaine was seated a-horseback and in armor, he began to take more courage unto himself, and the dark vapors that had whilom overshadowed him lifted themselves a little. So he bespoke his esquire with stronger voice, saying, "Take this glove of mine and bear it to Sir Pellias and tell him that Sir Gawaine parades in the meadow in front of the castle and that he there challenges Sir Pellias for to meet him a-horse or afoot, howsoever that knight may choose."

At these that esquire was very much astonished, for Sir Gawaine and Sir Pellias had always been such close friends that there was hardly their like for friendship in all that land, wherefore their love for one another had become a byword with all men. But he held his peace concerning his thoughts and only said, "Wilt thou not eat food ere thou goest to battle?" And Sir Gawaine said, "Nay, I will not eat until I have fought. Wherefore do thou go and do as I have bid thee."

So Sir Gawaine's esquire went to Sir Pellias in his pavilion and he gave unto that knight the glove of Sir Gawaine, and he delivered Sir Gawaine's message to him. And Sir Pellias said, "Tell thy master that I will come forth to meet him as soon as I have broken my fast."

Now, when the news of that challenge had come to the ears of Sir Brandiles and Sir Mador de la Porte and Sir Ewaine and Sir Marhaus, those knights were greatly disturbed thereat, and Sir Ewaine said to the others, "Messires, let us go and make inquiries concerning this business." So the four knights went to the white pavilion where Sir Pellias was breaking his fast.

And when they had come into the presence of Sir Pellias, Sir Ewaine said to him, "What is this quarrel betwixt my kinsman and thee?" And Sir Pellias made reply, "I will not tell thee, so, let be and meddle not with it."

Then Sir Ewaine said, "Wouldst thou do serious battle with thy friend?" To which Sir Pellias said, "He is a friend to me no longer."

Then Sir Brandiles cried out, "It is a great pity that a quarrel should lie betwixt such friends as thou and Sir Gawaine. Wilt thou not let us make peace betwixt you?" But Sir Pellias replied, "Ye cannot make peace, for this quarrel cannot be stayed until it is ended."

Then those knights saw that their words could be of no avail and they went away and left Sir Pellias.

So when Sir Pellias had broken his fast, he summoned an esquire named Montenoir, and he bade him case him in that red armor that he had worn for all this time, and Montenoir did so. Then, when Sir Pellias was clad in that armor, he rode forth into the meadow before the castle where Sir Gawaine paraded. And when he had come thither those four other knights came to him again and besought him that he would let peace be made betwixt him and Sir Gawaine, but Sir Pellias would not listen to them, and so they went away again and left him, and he rode forth into the field before the castle at Grantmesnle.

Now a great concourse of people had come down upon the castle walls for to behold that assault-at-arms, for news thereof had gone all about that place. And it had also come to be known that the knight that would do combat with Sir Pellias was that very famous royal knight hight Sir Gawaine, the son of King Lot of Orkney, and a nephew of King Arthur; wherefore all the people were very desirous to behold so famous a knight do battle.

Likewise the Lady Ettard came down to the walls and took her stand in a lesser tower that overlooked the field of battle. And when she had taken her stand at that place she beheld that Sir Pellias wore that necklace of emeralds and opal stones and gold above his body armor, and her heart went out to him because of it, wherefore she hoped that he might be the victor in that encounter.

Then each knight took his station in such place as seemed to him to be fitting, and they dressed each his spear and his shield and made him ready for the assault. Then, when they were in all ways prepared, Sir Marhaus gave the signal for that assault. Thereupon each knight instantly quitted that station which he held, dashing against the other with the speed of lightning, and with such fury that the earth thundered and shook beneath their horses' hoofs. So they met fairly in the centre of the course, each knight striking the other in the very midst of his defences. And in that encounter the spear of Sir Gawaine burst even to the hand-guard, but the spear of Sir Pellias held, so that Sir Gawaine was cast out of his saddle with terrible violence, smiting the earth with such force that he rolled thrice over in the dust and then lay altogether motionless as though bereft of life.

At this, all those people upon the walls shouted with a great voice, for it was an exceedingly noble assault-at-arms.

Then the four knights who stood watching that encounter made all haste unto Sir Gawaine where he lay; and Sir Pellias also rode back and sat his horse nigh at hand. Then Sir Ewaine and Sir Gawaine's esquire unlaced the helmet of Sir Gawaine with all speed, and, behold! his face was the color of ashes and they could not see that he breathed.

Thereupon Sir Marhaus said, "I believe that thou has slain this knight, Sir Pellias," and Sir Pellias said, "Dost thou think so?" "Yea," quoth Sir Marhaus, "and I deem it a great pity." Unto which Sir Pellias made reply, "He hath not suffered more than he deserved."

At these words Sir Ewaine was filled with great indignation, wherefore he cried out, "Sir Knight, I think that thou forgettest the quality of this knight. For not only is he a fellow-companion of the Round Table, to whom thou hast vowed entire brotherhood, but he is also the son of a king and the nephew of King Arthur himself."

But to this Sir Pellias maintained a very steadfast countenance and replied, "I would not repent me of this were that knight a king in his own right instead of the son of a king."

Then Sir Ewaine lifted up his head with great indignation, crying out upon Sir Pellias, "Begone! or a great ill may befall thee." "Well," said Sir Pellias, "I will go."

Upon this he turned his horse and rode away from that place and entered the woodland and so was gone from their sight.

Then those others present lifted up Sir Gawaine and bare him away unto the pavilion late of Sir Pellias, and there they laid him upon the couch of Sir Pellias. But it was above an hour ere he recovered himself again; and for a great part of that while those nigh unto him believed him to have been dead.

But not one of those knights wist what was the case; to wit, that Sir Pellias had been so sorely wounded in the side in that encounter that it was not to be hoped that he could live for more than that day. For, though the spear of Sir Gawaine had burst, and though Sir Pellias had overthrown him entirely, yet the head of Sir Gawaine's spear had pierced the armor of Sir Pellias, and had entered his side and had there broken off, so that of the iron of the spear, the length of the breadth of a palm had remained in the body of Sir Pellias a little above the midriff. Wherefore, while Sir

Pellias sat there talking so steadfastly unto those four knights, he was yet whiles in a great passion of pain, and the blood ran down into his armor in abundance. So, what with the loss of the blood, and of the great agony which he suffered, the brain of Sir Pellias swam as light as a feather all the time that he held talk with those others. But he said not a word unto them concerning the grievous wound he had received, but rode away very proudly into the forest.

But when he had come into the forest he could not forbear him any longer, but fell to groaning very sorely, crying out, "Alas! alas! I have certes got my death-wound in this battle!"

Now it chanced that morn that the damsel Parcenet had ridden forth to fly a young gerfalcon, and a dwarf belonging to the Lady Ettard had ridden with her for company. So, as the damsel and the dwarf rode through a certain part of the forest skirt, not a very great distance from Grantmesnle, where the thicker part of the woodland began and the thinner part thereof ceased, the damsel heard a voice in the woodlands, lamenting with very great dolor. So she stopped and harkened, and by and by she heard that voice again making a great moan. Then Parcenet said to the dwarf, "What is that I hear? Certes, it is the voice of someone in lamentation. Now let us go and see who it is that maketh such woful moan." And the dwarf said, "It shall be as thou sayest."

So the damsel and the dwarf went a little way farther and there they beheld a knight sitting upon a black horse beneath an oak-tree. And that knight was clad altogether in red armor, wherefore, Parcenet knew that it must be Sir Pellias. And she saw that Sir Pellias leaned with the butt of his spear upon the ground and so upheld himself upon his horse from which he would otherwise have fallen because of his great weakness, and all the while he made that great moan that Parcenet had heard. So, seeing him in this sorry condition, Parcenet was overcome with great pity, and she made haste to him crying out, "Alas! Sir Pellias, what ails thee?"

Then Sir Pellias looked at her as though she were a great way removed from him, and, because of the faintness of his soul, he beheld her, as it were, through thin water. And he said, very faintly, "Maiden, I am sore hurt." Thereupon she said, "How art thou hurt, Sir Pellias?" And he replied, "I have a grievous wound in my side, for a spear's point standeth therein nigh a palm's breadth deep so that it reaches nearly to my heart, wherefore, meseems that I shall not live for very long."

Upon this the maiden cried out, "Alas! alas! what is this!" and she made great lament and smote her hands together with sorrow that that noble knight should have come to so grievous an extremity.

Then the dwarf that was with Parcenet, seeing how greatly she was distracted by sorrow, said, "Damsel, I know of a certain place in this forest (albeit it is a considerable distance from this) where there dwelleth a certain very holy hermit who is an extraordinarily skilful leech. Now, an we may bring this knight unto the chapel where that hermit dwelleth, I believe that he may be greatly holpen unto health and ease again."

Upon this Parcenet said, "Gansaret" – for Gansaret was the dwarf's name - "Gansaret, let us take this knight unto that place as quickly as we are able. For I tell thee sooth when I say that I have a very great deal of love for him." "Well," said the dwarf, "I will show thee where that chapel is."

So the dwarf took the horse of Sir Pellias by the bridle-rein and led the way through that forest, and Parcenet rode beside Sir Pellias and upheld him upon his saddle. For some whiles Sir Pellias fainted with sickness and with pain so that he would else have fallen had she not upheld him. Thus they went forward very sorrowfully and at so slow a pace that it was noontide ere they came to that certain very dense and lonely part of the forest where the hermit abided.

And when they had come unto that place the dwarf said, "Yonder, damsel, is the chapel whereof I spake."

Then Parcenet lifted up her eyes and she beheld where was a little woodland chapel built in among the leafy trees of the forest. And around this chapel was a little open lawn bedight with flowers, and nigh to the door of the hermitage was a fountain of water as clear as crystal. And this was a very secret and lonely place and withal very silent and peaceful, for in front of the chapel they beheld a wild doe and her fawn browsing upon the tender grass and herbs without any fear of harm. And when the dwarf and the maiden and the wounded knight drew nigh, the doe and the fawn looked up with great wide eyes and spread their large ears with wonder, yet fled not, fearing no harm, but by and by began their browsing again. Likewise all about the chapel in the branches of the trees were great quantities of birds, singing and chirping very cheerfully. And those birds were waiting for their mid-day meal that the hermit was used to cast unto them.

(Now this was the same forest sanctuary whereunto King Arthur had come that time when he had been so sorely wounded by Sir Pellinore as hath been aforetold in this history.)

As the maiden and the dwarf and the wounded knight drew nigh to this chapel, a little bell began ringing very sweetly so that the sound thereof echoed all through those quiet woodlands, for it was now the hour of noon. And Sir Pellias heard that bell as it were a great way off, and first he said, "Whither am I come?" and then he made shift to cross himself. And Parcenet crossed herself and the dwarf kneeled down and crossed himself. Then when the bell had ceased ringing, the dwarf cried out in a loud voice, "What ho! what ho! here is one needing help!"

Then the door of the sanctuary was opened and there came forth from that place a very venerable man with a long white beard as it were of finely carded wool. And, lo! as he came forth, all those birds that waited there flew about him in great quantities, for they thought that he had come forth for to feed them; wherefore the hermit was compelled to brush those small fowls away with his hands as he came unto where the three were stationed.

And when he had come unto them he demanded of them who they were and why they had come thither with that wounded knight. So Parcenet told him how it was with them, and of how they had found Sir Pellias so sorely wounded in the forest that morning and had brought him hitherward.

Then, when the hermit had heard all of her story, he said, "It is well and I will take him in." So he took Sir Pellias into his cell, and when they had helped lay him upon the couch, Parcenet and the dwarf went their way homeward again.

After they had gone, the hermit examined the hurt of Sir Pellias, and Sir Pellias lay in a deep swoon. And the swoon was so deep that the hermit beheld that it was the death-swoon, and that the knight was nigh to his end. So he said, "This knight must assuredly die in a very little while, for I can do naught to save him." Wherefore he immediately quitted the side of Sir Pellias and set about in haste to prepare the last sacrament such as might be administered unto a noble knight who was dying.

Now whiles the hermit was about this business the door opened of a sudden and there came into that place a very strange lady clad all in green and bedight around the arms with armlets of emeralds and opal stones inset into gold. And her hair, which was very soft, was entirely black and was tied about with a cord of crimson ribbon. And the hermit beheld that her face was like to ivory for whiteness and that her eyes were bright, like unto jewels set into ivory, wherefore he knew that she was no ordinary mortal.

And this lady went straight to Sir Pellias and leaned over him so that her breath touched his forehead. And she said, "Alas! Sir Pellias, that thou shouldst lie so." "Lady," said the hermit, "thou mayst well say 'Alas,' for this knight hath only a few minutes to live." To this the lady said, "Not so, thou holy man, for I tell thee that this knight shall have a long while yet to live." And when she had said this she stooped and took from about his neck that necklace of emeralds and opal stones and gold that encircled it and she hung it about her own neck.

Now when the hermit beheld what she did, he said, "Lady, what is this that thou dost take that ornament from a dying man?"

But the lady made reply very tranquilly, "I gave it unto him, wherefore I do but take back again what is mine own. But now I prithee let me be with the knight for a little while, for I have great hope that I may bring back life unto him again."

Then the hermit was a-doubt and he said, "Wilt thou endeavor to heal him by magic?" And the lady said, "If I do, it will not be by magic that is black."

So the hermit was satisfied and went away, and left the lady alone with Sir Pellias.

Now when the lady was thus alone with the wounded knight she immediately set about doing sundry very strange things. For first she brought forth a loadstone of great power and potency and this she set to the wound. And, lo! the iron of the spear-head came forth from the wound; and as it came Sir Pellias groaned with great passion. And when the spear-point came forth there burst out a great issue of blood like to a fountain of crimson. But the lady immediately pressed a fragrant napkin of fine cambric linen to the wound and stanched the blood, and it bled no more, for she held it within the veins by the very potent spells of magic. So, the blood being stanched in this wise, the lady brought forth from her bosom a small crystal phial filled with an elixir of blue color and of a very singular fragrance. And she poured some of this elixir between the cold and leaden lips of the knight; and when the elixir touched his lips the life began to enter into his body once more; for, in a little while, he opened his eyes and gazed about him with a very strange look, and the first thing that he beheld was that lady clad in green who stood beside him, and she was so beautiful that he thought that haply he had died and was in Paradise, wherefore he said, "Am I then dead?"

"Nay, thou art not dead," said the lady, "yet hast thou been parlously nigh to death." "Where then am I?" said Sir Pellias. And she replied, "Thou art in a deep part of the forest, and this is the cell of a saint-like hermit of the forest." At this Sir Pellias said, "Who is it that hath brought me back to life?" Upon this the lady smiled and said, "It was I."

Now for a little while Sir Pellias lay very silent, then by and by he spake and said, "Lady, I feel very strangely." "Yea," said the lady, "that is because thou hast now a different life." Then Sir Pellias said, "How is it with me?" And the lady said, "It is thus: that to bring thee back to life I gave thee to drink of a certain draught of an *elixir vitae* so that thou art now only half as thou wert before; for if by the one half thou art mortal, by the other half thou art fay."

Then Sir Pellias looked up and beheld that the lady had about her neck the collar of emeralds and opal stones and gold which he had aforetime worn. And, lo! his heart went out to her with exceeding ardor, and he said, "Lady, thou sayest that I am half fay, and I do perceive that thou art altogether fay. Now, I pray thee to let it be that henceforth I may abide nigh unto where thou art." And the lady said, "It shall be as thou dost ask, for it was to that end I have suffered thee nearly to die, and then have brought thee back unto life again."

Then Sir Pellias said, "Where may I go with thee?" And she said, "In a little when thou hast had to drink." "How may that be?" said Sir Pellias, "seeing that I am but yet like unto a little child for weakness." To the which the lady made reply, "When thou hast drunk of water thy strength shall return unto thee, and thou shalt be altogether well and whole again."

So the Lady of the Lake went out, and presently returned, bearing in her hand an earthen crock filled with water from the fountain near at hand. And when Sir Pellias had drunk that water he felt, of a sudden, his strength come altogether back to him.

Yet he was not at all as he had been before, for now his body felt as light as air, and his soul was dilated with a pure joy such as he had never felt in his life before that time. Wherefore he immediately uprose from his couch of pain, and he said, "Thou hast given life unto me again, now do I give that life unto thee forever."

Then the lady looked upon him and smiled with great loving-kindness. And she said, "Sir Pellias, I have held thee in tender regard ever since I beheld thee one day in thy young knighthood drink a draught of milk at a cottager's hut in this forest. For the day was warm and thou hadst set aside thy helmet, and a young milkmaid, brown of face and with bare feet, came and brought thee a bowl of milk, which same thou didst drink of with great appetite. That was the first time that I beheld thee – although thou didst not see me. Since that time I have had great friendship for all thy fellowship of King Arthur's Court and for King Arthur himself, all for thy sake."

Then Sir Pellias said, "Lady, wilt thou accept me for thy knight?" and she said, "Aye." Then Sir Pellias said, "May I salute thee?" And she said, "Yea, if it pleasures thee." So Sir Pellias kissed her upon the lips, and so their troth was plighted.

Now return we unto Parcenet and the dwarf:

After those two had left that hermitage in the woodland, they betook their way again toward Grantmesnle, and when they had come nigh out of the forest at a place not far from the glade of trees wherein those knights-companion had taken up their inn, they met one of those knights clad in half-armor, and that knight was Sir Mador de la Porte. Then Parcenet called upon him by name, saying, "Alas! Sir Mador, I have but this short time quitted a hermit's cell in the forest where I left Sir Pellias sorely wounded to death, so I fear me he hath only a little while to live."

Then Sir Mador de la Porte cried out, "Ha! maiden, what is this thou tellest me? That is a very hard thing to believe; for when Sir Pellias quitted us this morn he gave no sign of wound or disease of any sort."

But Parcenet replied, "Ne'theless, I myself beheld him lying in great pain and dole, and, ere he swooned his death-swoon, he himself told me that he had the iron of a spear in his side."

Then Sir Mador de la Porte said, "Alas! alas! that is sorry news! Now, damsel, by thy leave and grace, I will leave thee and hasten to my companions to tell them this news." And Parcenet said, "I prithee do so."

So Sir Mador de la Porte made haste to the pavilion where were his companions, and he told them the news that he had heard.

Now at this time Sir Gawaine was altogether recovered from the violent overthrow he had suffered that morning, wherefore when he heard the news that Sir Mador de la Porte brought to him, he smote his hands together and cried out aloud, "Woe is me! what have I done! For first I betrayed my friend, and now I have slain him. Now I will go forth straightway to find him and to crave his forgiveness ere he die."

But Sir Ewaine said, "What is this that thou wouldst do? Thou art not yet fit to undertake any journey."

Sir Gawaine said, "I care not, for I am determined to go and find my friend." Nor would he suffer any of his companions to accompany him; but when he had summoned his esquire to bring him his horse, he mounted thereon and rode away into the forest alone, betaking his way to the westward, and lamenting with great sorrow as he journeyed forward.

Now when the afternoon had fallen very late, so that the sun was sloping to its setting, and the light fell as red as fire through the forest leaves, Sir Gawaine came to that hermit's cell where it stood in the silent and solitary part of the forest woodland. And he beheld that the hermit was outside of his cell digging in a little garden of lentils. So when the hermit saw the armed knight come into that lawn all in the red light of the setting sun, he stopped digging and leaned upon his trowel. Then Sir Gawaine drew nigh, and, as he sat upon his horse, he told the holy man of the business whereon he had come.

To this the hermit said, "There came a lady hither several hours ago, and she was clad all in green, and was of a very singular appearance, so that it was easy to see that she was fay. And by means of certain charms of magic that lady cured thy friend, and after she had healed him, the two rode away into the forest together."

Then Sir Gawaine was very much amazed, and he said, "This is a very strange thing that thou tellest me, that a knight who is dying should be brought back to life again in so short a time, and should so suddenly ride forth from a bed of pain. Now, I prithee tell me whither they went." The hermit said, "They went to the westward." Whereupon, when Sir Gawaine heard this, he said, "I will follow them."

So he rode away and left the hermit gazing after him. And as he rode forward upon his way, the twilight began to fall apace, so that the woodlands after a while grew very dark and strange all around him. But as the darkness descended a very singular miracle happened, for, lo! there appeared before Sir Gawaine, a light of a pale blue color, and it went before him and showed him the way, and he followed it, much marvelling.

Now after he had followed the light for a very long time he came at last, of a sudden, to where the woodland ceased, and where there was a wide, open plain of very great extent. And this plain was illuminated by a singular radiance which was like that of a clear full moonlight, albeit no moon was shining at that time. And in that pale and silver light Sir Gawaine could see everything with wonderful distinctness; wherefore he beheld that he was in a plain covered all over with flowers of divers sorts, the odors whereof so filled the night that it appeared to press upon the bosom with a great pleasure. And he beheld that in front of him lay a great lake, very wide and still. And all those things appeared so strange in that light that Sir Gawaine wotted that he had come into a land of faëry. So he rode among tall flowers toward that lake in a sort of fear, for he wist not what was to befall him.

Now as he drew near the lake he perceived a knight and a lady approaching him; and when they had come nigh he beheld that the knight was Sir Pellias, and that his countenance was exceedingly strange. And he beheld that the lady was she whom he had aforetime seen all clad in green apparel when he had travelled in the Forest of Adventure with Sir Ewaine and Sir Marhaus.

Now when Sir Gawaine first beheld Sir Pellias he was filled with a great fear, for he thought it was a spirit that he saw. But when he perceived that Sir Pellias was alive, there came into his bosom a joy as great as that fear had been; wherefore he made haste toward Sir Pellias. And when he had come near to Sir Pellias, he leaped from off his horse, crying out, "Forgive! Forgive!" with great vehemence of passion. Then he would have taken Sir Pellias into his arms, but Sir Pellias withdrew himself from the contact of Sir Gawaine, though not with any violence of anger. And Sir Pellias spake in a voice very thin and of a silvery clearness as though it came from a considerable distance, and he said, "Touch me not, for I am not as I was aforetime, being not all human, but part fay. But concerning my forgiveness: I do forgive thee whatsoever injury I may have suffered at thy hands. And more than this I give unto thee my love, and I greatly hope for thy joy and happiness. But now I go away to leave thee, dear friend, and haply I shall not behold thee again, wherefore I do leave this with thee as my last behest; to wit, that thou dost go back to King Arthur's Court and make thy peace with the Queen. So thou mayst bring them news of all that hath happened unto me."

Then Sir Gawaine cried out in great sorrow, "Whither wouldst thou go?"

And Sir Pellias said, "I shall go to yonder wonderful city of gold and azure which lieth in yonder valley of flowers."

Then Sir Gawaine said, "I see no city but only a lake of water."

Whereupon Sir Pellias replied, "Ne'theless, there is a city yonder and thither I go, wherefore I do now bid thee farewell."

Then Sir Gawaine looked into the face of Sir Pellias and beheld again that strange light that it was of a very singular appearance, for, lo! it was white like to ivory and his eyes shone like jewels set in ivory, and a smile lay upon his lips and grew neither more nor less, but always remained the same. (For those who were of that sort had always that singular appearance and smiled in that manner – to wit, the Lady of the Lake, and Sir Pellias, and Sir Launcelot of the Lake.)

Then Sir Pellias and the Lady of the Lake turned and left Sir Gawaine where he stood, and they went toward the lake, and they entered the lake, and when the feet of the horse of Sir Pellias had touched the water of the lake, lo! Sir Pellias was gone and Sir Gawaine beheld him no more, although he stood there for a long time weeping with great passion.

So endeth the story of Sir Pellias.

But Sir Gawaine returned unto the Court of King Arthur as he had promised Sir Pellias to do, and he made his peace with Queen Guinevere and, thereafter, though the Queen loved him not, yet there was a peace betwixt them. And Sir Gawaine published these things to the Court of King Arthur and all men marvelled at what he told.

And only twice thereafter was Sir Pellias ever seen of any of his aforetime companions.

And Sir Marhaus was made a Companion of the Round Table and became one of the foremost knights thereof.

And the Lady Ettard took Sir Engamore into favor again, and that summer they were wedded and Sir Engamore became lord of Grantmesnle.

So endeth this story.

## Part III

# The Story of Sir Gawaine

*Here followeth the story of Sir Gawaine and of how he discovered such wonderful faithfulness unto King Arthur, who was his lord, that I do not believe that the like of such faithfulness was ever seen before.*

*For indeed, though Sir Gawaine was at times very rough and harsh in his manner, and though he was always so plain-spoken that his words hid the gentle nature that lay within him, yet, under this pride of manner, was much courtesy; and at times he was so urbane of manner and so soft of speech that he was called by many the Knight of the Silver Tongue.*

*So here ye shall read how his faithfulness unto King Arthur brought him such high reward that almost anyone in all the world might envy him his great good fortune.*

## Chapter First

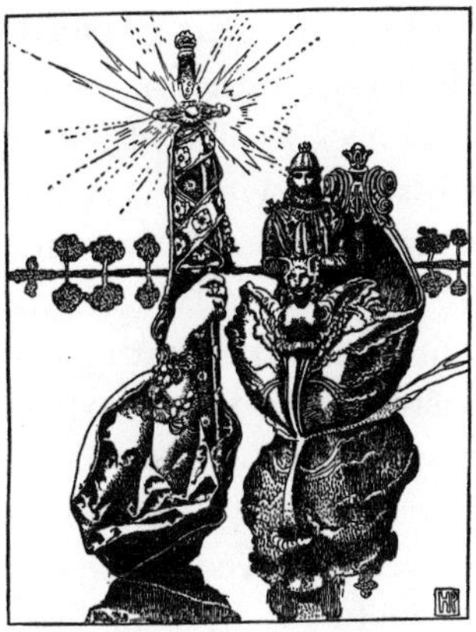

# How a White Hart Appeared before King Arthur

Upon a certain time King Arthur, together with Queen Guinevere and all of his Court, were making progression through that part of his kingdom which was not very near to Camelot. At this time the King journeyed in very great state, and Queen Guinevere had her Court about her, so there were many esquires and pages; wherefore, what with knights, lords, and ladies in attendance, more than six score of people were with the King and Queen.

Now it chanced that at this time the season of the year was very warm, so that when the middle of the day had come the King commanded that a number of pavilions should be spread for their accommodation, wherein that they might rest there until the heat of the day had passed. So the attendants spread three pavilions in a pleasant glade upon the outskirts of the forest.

When this had been done, the King gave command that the tables, whereat they were to eat their mid-day meal, should be spread beneath the shadow of that glade of trees; for there was a gentle wind blowing and there were many birds singing, so that it was very pleasant to sit in the open air.

Accordingly the attendants of the Court did as the King commanded, and the tables were set upon the grass beneath the shade, and the King and Queen and all the lords and ladies of their Courts sat down to that cheerful repast.

Now whiles they sat there feasting with great content of spirit, and with much mirth and goodly talk among themselves, there came of a sudden a great outcry from the woodland that was near by, and therewith there burst forth from the cover of that leafy wilderness a very beautiful white hart pursued by a white brachet of equal beauty. And there was not a hair upon either of these animals that was not as white as milk, and each wore about its neck a collar of gold very beautiful to behold.

The hound pursued the white hart with a very great outcry and bellowing, and the hart fled in the utmost terror. In this wise they ran thrice around the table where King Arthur and his Court sat at meat, and twice in that chase the hound caught the hart and pinched it on its haunch, and therewith the hart leaped away, and all they who sat there observed that there was blood at two places upon its haunch where the hound had pinched it. But each time the hart escaped from the hound, and the hound followed after it with much outcry of yelling so that King Arthur and Queen Guinevere and all their Court were annoyed at the noise and tumult that those two creatures made. Then the hart fled away into the forest again by another path, and the hound pursued it and both were gone, and the baying of the hound sounded more and more distant as it ran away into the woodland.

Now, ere the King and Queen and their Court had recovered from their astonishment at these things, there suddenly appeared at that part of the forest whence the hart and the hound had emerged, a knight and a lady, and the knight was of very lordly presence and the lady was exceedingly beautiful. The knight was clad in half-armor, and the lady was clad in green as though for the chase; and the knight rode upon a charger of dapple gray, and the lady upon a piebald palfrey. With them were two esquires, also clad for the chase.

These, seeing the considerable company gathered there, paused as though in surprise, and whilst they stood so, there suddenly appeared another knight upon a black horse, clad in complete armor, and he seemed to be very angry. For he ran upon the half-armed knight and smote him so sorry a blow with his sword, that the first knight fell down from his horse and lay upon the ground as though dead; whereat the lady who was with him shrieked with great dolor.

Then the full-armed knight upon the black horse ran to the lady and catched her, and he lifted her from her palfrey and laid her across the horn of his saddle, and thereupon he rode back into the forest again. The lady screamed with such vehemence of violent outcry, that it was a great pity to hear her, but the knight paid no attention to her shrieking, but bore her away by main force into the forest.

Then, after he and the lady had gone, the two esquires came and lifted up the wounded knight upon his horse, and then they also went away into the forest and were gone.

All this King Arthur and his Court beheld from a distance, and they were so far away that they could not stay that knight upon the black horse from doing what he did to carry away that lady into the forest; nor could they bring succor to that other knight in half-armor whom they had beheld struck down in that wise. So they were very greatly grieved at what they had beheld and knew not what to think of it. Then King Arthur said to his Court, "Messires, is there not some one of you who will follow up this adventure and discover what is the significance of that which we have seen, and compel that knight to tell why he behaved as he did?"

Upon this Sir Gawaine said, "Lord, I shall be very glad indeed to take upon me this adventure if I have thy leave to do so." And King Arthur said, "Thou hast my leave." Then Sir Gawaine said, "Lord, I would that thou would also let me take my younger brother, Gaheris, with me as mine esquire in this undertaking, for he groweth apace unto manhood, and yet he hath never beheld any considerable adventure at arms." So King Arthur said, "Thou hast my leave to take thy brother with thee."

At this Gaheris was very glad, for he was of an adventurous spirit, wherefore the thought of going with his brother upon this quest gave him great pleasure.

So they two went to the pavilion of Sir Gawaine, and there Gaheris aided Sir Gawaine as his esquire to don his armor. Then they rode forth upon that quest which Sir Gawaine had undertaken.

Now they journeyed onward for a very considerable distance, following that direction which they had seen the hart take when it had sped away from before the hound, and when, from time to time, they would meet some of the forest folk, they would inquire of them whither had fled that white brachet and the white hart, and whither had fled the knight and the lady, and so they followed that adventure apace.

By and by, after a long pass – it being far advanced in the afternoon – they were suddenly aware of a great uproar of conflict, as of a fierce battle in progress. So they followed this sound, and after a while they came to an open meadow-land with very fair and level sward. Here they beheld two knights fighting with great vehemence of passion, and with a very deadly purpose. Then Sir Gawaine said, "What is this? Let us go see." So he and Gaheris rode forward to where those two knights were engaged, and as they approached, the two knights paused in their encounter, and rested upon their weapons. Then Sir Gawaine said, "Ha! Messires, what is to do and why do ye fight with such passion, the one against the other, in that wise?" Then one of the knights said to Sir Gawaine, "Sir, this does not concern you;" and the other said, "Meddle not with us, for this battle is of our own choosing."

"Messires," said Sir Gawaine, "I would be very sorry to interfere in your quarrel, but I am in pursuit of a white hart and a white brachet that came this way, and also of a knight who hath carried off a lady upon the same pass. Now I would be greatly beholden to ye if you would tell me if ye have seen aught of one or the other."

Then that knight who had first spoken said, "Sir, this is a very strange matter, for it was upon account of that very white hart and that brachet, and of the knight and the lady that we two were just now engaged in that battle as thou didst behold. For the case is this: We two are two brothers, and we were riding together in great amity when that hart and that hound came hitherward. Then my brother said he very greatly hoped that the white hart would escape from the hound, and I said that I hoped that the hound would overtake the hart and bring it to earth. Then came that knight with that lady, his captive, and I said that I would follow that knight and rescue the lady, and my brother said that he would undertake that adventure.

"Upon these points we fell into dispute; for it appeared to me that I felt great affection for that hound, and my brother felt as extraordinary regard for the white hart, and that as I had first spoken I should have the right to follow that adventure; but my brother felt affection for the hart, and he considered that as he was the elder of us twain, he had the best right to the adventure. So we quarrelled, and by and by we fell to upon that fight in which thou did see us engaged."

At this Sir Gawaine was very greatly astonished, and he said, "Messires, I cannot understand how so great a quarrel should have arisen from so small a dispute; and, certes, it is a great pity for two brothers to quarrel as ye have done, and to give one another such sore cuts and wounds as I perceive you have both received."

"Messires," said the second knight, "I think thou art right, and I now find myself to be very much ashamed of that quarrel." And the other said, "I too am sorry for what I have done."

Then Sir Gawaine said, "Sirs, I would be very glad indeed if you would tell me your names." And the one knight said, "I am called Sir Sorloise of the Forest." And the other said, "I am called Sir Brian of the Forest."

Then Sir Sorloise said, "Sir Knight, I would deem it a very great courtesy if thou wouldst tell me who thou art."

"I would be very glad to do that," said Sir Gawaine, and therewith he told them his name and condition. Now, when they heard who Sir Gawaine was, those two knights were very greatly astonished and pleased; for no one in all the courts of chivalry was more famous than Sir Gawaine, the son of King Lot of Orkney. Wherefore those two brothers said, "It is certainly a great joy to us to meet so famous a knight as thou art, Sir Gawaine."

Then Sir Gawaine said, "Sir Knights, that hart and that hound came only a short while ago to where King Arthur and Queen Guinevere and their Courts of lords and ladies were at feast, and there, likewise, all we beheld that knight seize upon the lady and make her captive. Wherefore, I and my brother have come forth upon command of King Arthur for to discover what is the meaning of that which we beheld. Now I shall deem it a very great courtesy upon your part if you will cease from this adventure and will go in amity unto the Court of the King, and will tell him of what ye beheld and of how you quarrelled and of how we met. For otherwise I myself will have to engage ye both, and that would be a great pity; for ye are weary with battle and I am fresh."

Then these two knights said, "Sir, we will do as you desire, for we have no wish to have to do with so powerful a knight as you."

Thereupon those two knights departed and went to the Court of King Arthur as Sir Gawaine ordained, and Sir Gawaine and his brother rode forward upon their adventure.

Now, by and by they came nigh to a great river, and there they beheld before them a single knight in full armor, who carried a spear in his hand and a shield hanging to his saddle-bow. Thereupon Sir Gawaine made haste forward and he called aloud to the knight, and the knight paused and waited until Sir Gawaine had overtaken him. And when Sir Gawaine came up to that knight he said, "Sir Knight, hast thou seen a white hart and a white hound pass by this way? And hast thou seen a knight bearing off a captive lady?"

Unto this the knight said, "Yea, I beheld them both, and I am even now following after them with intent to discover whither they are bound." Then Sir Gawaine said, "Sir Knight, I bid thee not to follow this adventure farther, for I myself am set upon it. Wherefore I desire thee for to give it over so that I may undertake it in thy stead." "Sir," said the other knight, speaking with a very great deal of heat, "I know not who thou art, nor do I care a very great deal. But touching the pursuance of this adventure, I do tell thee that I myself intend to follow it to the end and so will I do, let who will undertake to stay me."

Thereupon Sir Gawaine said, "Messire, thou shalt not go forward upon this adventure unless thou hast first to do with me." And the knight said, "Sir, I am very willing for that."

So each knight took such stand upon that field as appeared to him to be best, and each put himself into a posture of defence and dressed his shield and his spear. Then, when they were thus prepared in all ways, they immediately launched forth, the one against the other, rushing together with great speed and with such an uproar that the ground trembled and shook beneath them. So they met together in the midst of the course and the spear of the strange knight burst all into small pieces, but the spear of Sir Gawaine held; wherefore he hurled that knight out of his saddle with such violence that he smote the ground with a blow like an earthquake.

Then Sir Gawaine rode back to where his enemy was (for that knight was unable to rise), and he removed the helmet from the head of the fallen knight and beheld that he was very young and comely.

Now, when the fresh air smote upon the knight's face, he presently awoke from the swoon and came back unto his senses again, whereupon Sir Gawaine said, "Dost thou yield unto me?" And the knight said, "I do so." Then Sir Gawaine said, "Who art thou?" And the knight said, "I am called Sir Alardin of the Isles." "Very well," said Sir Gawaine; "then I lay my command upon thee in this wise: that thou shalt go to the Court of King Arthur and deliver thyself to him as a captive of my prowess. And thou art to tell him all that thou knowest of the hart and the hound and the knight and the lady. And thou shalt tell him all that hath befallen thee in this assault."

So the knight said that he would do that, and thereupon they parted, the one party going the one way and the other party going the other way.

After that Sir Gawaine and his brother, Gaheris, rode a considerable distance until they came, by and by, through a woodland into an open plain, and it was now about the time of sunset. And they beheld in the midst of the plain a very stately and noble castle with five towers and of very great strength.

And right here they saw a sight that filled them with great sorrow, for they beheld the dead body of that white brachet lying beside the road like any carrion. And they saw that the hound was pierced through with three arrows, wherefore they wist that it had been slain very violently.

Now when Sir Gawaine beheld that beautiful hound lying dead in that wise, he was filled with great sorrow. "What a pity it is," he cried, "that this noble hound should be slain in this wise; for I think that it was the most beautiful hound that ever I saw in all my life. Here hath assuredly been great treachery against it; for it hath been foully dealt with because of that white hart which it pursued. Now, I make my vow that if I can find that hart I will slay it with mine own hands, because it was in that chase that this hound met its death."

After that they rode forward toward that castle, and as they drew nigh, lo! they beheld that white hart with the golden collar browsing upon the meadows before the castle.

Now, as soon as the white hart beheld those two strangers, it fled with great speed toward the castle, and it ran into the court-yard of the castle. And when Sir Gawaine beheld the stag, he gave chase in pursuit of it with great speed, and Gaheris followed after his brother.

So Sir Gawaine pursued the white hart into the court-yard of the castle and from thence it could not escape. Then Sir Gawaine leaped him down from his horse and drew his sword and slew the hart with a single blow of his weapon.

This he did in great haste, but when he had done that and it was too late to mend it, he repented him of what he had done very sorely.

Now with all this tumult, there came out the lord and the lady of that castle; and the lord was one of very haughty and noble aspect, and the lady was extraordinarily graceful and very beautiful of appearance. And Sir Gawaine looked upon the lady and he thought he had hardly ever seen so beautiful a dame, wherefore he was more sorry than ever that, in his haste, he had slain that white hart.

But when the lady of the castle beheld the white hart, that it lay dead upon the stone pavement of the court-yard, she smote her hands together and shrieked with such shrillness and strength, that it pierced the ears to hear her. And she cried out, "Oh, my white hart, art thou then dead?" And therewith she fell to weeping with great passion. Then Sir Gawaine said, "Lady, I am very sorry for what I have done, and I would that I could undo it." Then the lord of that castle said to Sir Gawaine, "Sir, didst thou slay that stag?" "Yea," said Sir Gawaine. "Sir," said the lord of the castle, "thou hast done very ill in this matter, and if thou wilt wait a little I will take full vengeance upon thee." Unto which Sir Gawaine said, "I will wait for thee as long as it shall please thee."

Then the lord of the castle went into his chamber and clad himself in his armor, and in a little while he came out very fiercely. "Sir," said Sir Gawaine, "what is thy quarrel with me?" And the lord of the castle said, "Because thou hast slain the white hart that was so dear to my lady." To the which Sir Gawaine said, "I would not have slain the white hart only that because of it the white brachet was so treacherously slain." Upon this the lord of the castle was more wroth than ever, and he ran at Sir Gawaine and smote him unawares, so that he clave through the epaulier of his armor and cut through the flesh and unto the bone of the shoulder, so that Sir Gawaine was put to a great agony of pain at the stroke. Then Sir Gawaine was filled with rage at the pain of the wound, wherefore he smote the knight so woful a blow that he cut through his helmet and into the bone beneath, and thereupon the knight fell down upon his knees because of the fierceness of the blow, and he could not rise up again. Then Sir Gawaine catched his helmet and rushed it off from his head.

Upon this the knight said in a weak voice, "Sir Knight, I crave mercy of you, and yield myself to you."

But Sir Gawaine was very furious with anger because of that unexpected blow which he had received and because of the great agony of the wound, wherefore he would not have mercy, but lifted up his sword with intent to slay that knight.

Then the lady of the castle beheld what Sir Gawaine was intent to do, and she brake away from her damsels and ran and flung herself upon the knight so as to shield him with her own body. And in that moment Sir Gawaine was striking and could not stay his blow; nevertheless, he was able to turn his sword in his hand so that the edge thereof did not smite the lady. But the flat of the sword struck her upon the neck a very grievous blow, and the blade cut her a little, so that the blood ran down her smooth white neck and over her kerchief; and with the violence of the blow the lady fell down and lay upon the ground as though she were dead.

Now when Sir Gawaine beheld that, he thought that he had slain that lady in his haste, and he was all a-dread at what he had done, wherefore he cried, "Woe is me! what have I done?"

"Alas!" said Gaheris, "that was a very shameful blow that thou didst strike; and the shame of it is mine also because thou art my brother. Now I wish I had not come with thee to this place."

Then Sir Gawaine said to the lord of that castle, "Sir, I will spare thy life, for I am very sorry for what I have done in my haste."

But the knight of the castle was filled with great bitterness, because he thought that his lady was dead, wherefore he cried out as in despair, "I will not now have thy mercy, for thou art a knight without mercy and without pity. And since thou hast slain my lady, who is dearer to me than my life, thou mayst slay me also. For that is the only service which thou canst now render me."

But by now the damsels of the lady had come to her where she lay, and the chiefest of these cried out to the lord of the castle, "Ha, sir, thy lady is not dead, but only in a swoon from which she will presently recover."

Then when the lord of the castle heard that, he fell to weeping in great measure from pure joy; for now that he knew his lady was alive he could not contain himself for joy. Therewith Sir Gawaine came to him and lifted him up from the ground where he was, and kissed him upon the cheek. Then certain others came and bare the lady away into her chamber, and there in a little while she recovered from that swoon and was but little the worse for the blow she had received.

That night Sir Gawaine, and his brother, Gaheris, abided with the knight and the lady, and when the knight learned who Sir Gawaine was, he felt it great honor to have so famous a knight in that place. So they feasted together that evening in great amity.

Now, after they had refreshed themselves, Sir Gawaine said, "I beseech you, sir, to tell me what was the meaning of the white hart and the white brachet which led me into this adventure?"

To this the lord of the castle (whose name was Sir Ablamor of the Marise) said, "I will do so." And therewith he spake as follows:

"You must know, sir, that I have a brother who hath always been very dear to me, and when I took this, my lady, unto wife, he took her sister as his wife.

"Now, my brother dwelt in a castle nigh to this, and we held commerce together in great amity. But it befell upon a day that my lady and my brother's lady were riding through this forest together discoursing very pleasantly. What time there appeared a lady unto them, exceedingly beautiful, and of very strange appearance, for I do not think that either my lady or her sister ever beheld her like before.

"This strange lady brought unto those two ladies a white hart and a white brachet, and the hart and the hound she held each by a silver chain attached to a golden collar that encircled its neck. And the white hart she gave unto my lady and the white brachet she gave unto my lady's sister. And then she went away leaving them very glad.

"But their gladness did not last for very long, for ever since that time there hath been nothing else but discord between my brother and myself, and between my lady and her sister, for the white hound hath ever sought the white hart for to destroy it, wherefore I and my lady have entertained very great offence against my brother and his lady because they did not keep the white brachet at home. So it has come to pass that a number of times we have sought to destroy the hound, so that my brother and his lady have held equal offence against us.

"Now this day it chanced I was toward the outskirts of the forest to the east of us, when I heard a great outcry in the woodland, and by and by the white hart that belonged to my lady came fleeing through the woodland, and the white brachet that belonged to my brother's lady was in pursuit of it; and my brother and his lady and two esquires followed rapidly after the hart and the brachet.

"Then I was very greatly angered, for it seemed to me that they were chasing that white hart out of despite of my lady and myself, wherefore I followed after them with all speed.

"So I came upon them at the outskirts of the woodland, nigh to where there were a number of pavilions pitched in the shade of a glade of trees in the midst of the meadow, and there, in mine anger, I struck my brother a great blow so that I smote him down from his horse. And I catched his lady and I threw her across the horn of my saddle and I bore her here away to this castle, and here I have held her out of revenge because they pursued the white hart which belonged to the lady. For my lady loved that hart as she loved nothing else in the world, excepting myself."

"Sir," said Sir Gawaine, "this is a very strange matter. Now I beseech thee to tell me of what appearance was that lady who gave the white hart and the white hound unto those two ladies?" "Messire," said the knight, "she was clad all in crimson, and about her throat and arms were a great many ornaments of gold beset with stones of divers colors, and her hair was red like gold and was enmeshed in a net of gold, and her eyes were very black and shone with exceeding brightness, and her lips were like coral, so that she possessed a very strange appearance."

"Ha!" said Sir Gawaine, "from this description methinks that lady could have been none other than the sorceress Vivien. For now she spendeth all of her time in doing such mischief as this by means of her enchantment, out of pure despite. And, indeed, I think it would be a very good thing if she were put out of this world so that she could do no more such mischief. But tell me, Messire, where now is that lady, thy wife's sister?" "Sir," said the knight, "she is in this castle and is a prisoner of honor." "Well," quoth Sir Gawaine, "since now both the hart and the hound are dead, ye can assuredly bear no more enmity toward her and your brother, wherefore I do beseech you that you will let her go free, and will enter again into a condition of amity and good-will the one with the other, in such a manner as hath afore obtained between you." And the lord of the castle said, "Sir, it shall be so."

And so he set the lady free at that time, and thereafter there was amity between them as Sir Gawaine had ordained.

And the next day Sir Gawaine and his brother, Gaheris, returned unto this Court of the King and he told King Arthur and his Court all that had befallen, hiding nothing from them.

Now, Queen Guinevere was very much displeased when she heard how Sir Gawaine would show no mercy to that knight and how he had struck the lady with his sword. Wherefore she said aside to one of those who stood nigh to her, "It seems to me to be a very strange thing for a belted knight to do, to refuse to give mercy unto a fallen enemy and to strike a lady with his sword; for I should think that any sword that had drawn blood from a lady in such wise would be dishonored for aye; and I cannot think that anyone who would strike a lady in that wise would hold himself guiltless unto his vow of knighthood."

This Sir Gawaine overheard and he was exceedingly wroth thereat. But he concealed his anger at that time. Only after he had gone away he said to Gaheris, his brother, "I believe that lady hateth me with all her heart; but some time I will show to her that I have in me more courtesy and am more gentle than she believes me to be. As for my sword, since she deemeth it to be dishonored by that blow, I will not use it any more." So he took the sword out of its sheath and brake it across his knee and flung it away.

Now all this hath been told to set forth that which follows; for there ye shall learn what great things of nobility Sir Gawaine could do when it behooved him to do them. For, haply, ye who have read this story may feel as Queen Guinevere did, that Sir Gawaine was not rightwise courteous as a belted knight should have been in that adventure aforetold.

## Chapter Second

# How King Arthur Became Lost in the Forest

Now, it befell upon a time some while after this, that King Arthur was at Tintagalon upon certain affairs of state. And Queen Guinevere and her Court and the King's Court made progression from Camelot unto Carleon, and there they abided until the King should be through his business at Tintagalon and should join them at Carleon.

Now that time was the spring of the year, and all things were very jolly and gay, wherefore King Arthur became possessed with a great desire for adventure. So he called unto him a certain favorite esquire, hight Boisenard, and he said to him, "Boisenard, this day is so pleasant that I hardly know how I may contain myself because of the joy I take in it, for it seems to be that my heart is nigh ready to burst with a great pleasure of desiring. So I am of a mind to go a-gadding with only thee for companion."

To this Boisenard said, "Lord, I know of nothing that would give to me a greater pleasure than that."

So King Arthur said, "Very well, let us then go away from this place in such a manner that no one will be aware of our departure. And so we will go to Carleon and surprise the Queen by coming unexpectedly to that place."

So Boisenard brought armor, without device, and he clad the King in that armor; and then they two rode forth together, and no one wist that they had left the castle.

And when they came forth into the fields, King Arthur whistled and sang and jested and laughed and made himself merry; for he was as a war-horse turned forth upon the grass that taketh glory in the sunshine and the warm air and becameth like unto a colt again.

So by and by they came into the forest and rode that way with great content of spirit; and they took this path and they took that path for no reason but because the day was so gay and jolly. So, by and by, they lost their way in the mazes of the woodland and knew not where they were.

Now when they found themselves to be lost in that wise they journeyed with more circumspection, going first by this way and then by that, but in no manner could they find their way out from their entanglement. And so fell night-time and they knew not where they were; but all became very dark and obscure, with the woodland full of strange and unusual sounds around about them.

Then King Arthur said, "Boisenard, this is a very perplexing pass and I do not know how we shall find lodging for this night."

To this Boisenard said, "Lord, if I have thy permission to do so, I will climb one of these trees and see if I can discover any sign of habitation in this wilderness." And King Arthur said, "Do so, I pray thee."

So Boisenard climbed a very tall tree and from the top of the tree he beheld a light a great distance away, and he said, "Lord, I see a light in that direction." And therewith he came down from the tree again.

So King Arthur and Boisenard went in the direction that Boisenard had beheld the light, and by and by they came out of the forest and into an open place where they beheld a very great castle with several tall towers, very grim and forbidding of appearance. And it was from this castle that the light had appeared that Boisenard had seen. So they two rode up to the castle and Boisenard called aloud and smote upon the gate of the castle. Then immediately there came a porter and demanded of them what they would have. Unto him Boisenard said, "Sirrah, we would come in to lodge for to-night, for we are a-weary." So the porter said, "Who are you?" and speaking very roughly and rudely to them, for he could not see of what condition they were because of the darkness. Then Boisenard said, "This is a knight of very good quality and I am his esquire, and we have lost our way in the forest and now we come hither seeking shelter."

"Sir," said the porter, "if ye know what is good for you, ye will sleep in the forest rather than come into this place, for this is no very good retreat for errant knights to shelter themselves."

Upon this King Arthur bespake the porter, for that which the porter said aroused great curiosity within him. So he said, "Nay, we will not go away from here and we demand to lodge here for this night."

Then the porter said, "Very well; ye may come in." And thereupon he opened the gate and they rode into the court-yard of that castle.

Now at the noise of their coming, there appeared a great many lights within the castle, and there came running forth divers attendants. Some of these aided King Arthur and Boisenard to dismount, and others took the horses, and others again brought basins of water for them to wash withal. And after they had washed their faces and hands, other attendants brought them into the castle.

Now as they came into the castle, they were aware of a great noise of very many people talking and laughing together, with the sound of singing and of harping. And so they came into the hall of the castle and beheld that it was lighted with a great number of candles and tapers and torches. Here they found a multitude of people gathered at a table spread for a feast, and at the head of the table there sat a knight, well advanced in years and with hair and beard white as milk. Yet he was exceedingly strong and sturdy of frame, having shoulders of wonderful broadness and a great girth of chest. This knight was of a very stern and forbidding appearance, and was clad altogether in black, and he wore around his neck a chain of gold, with a locket of gold hanging pendant from it.

Now when this knight beheld King Arthur and Boisenard come into the hall, he called aloud to them in a very great voice bidding them to come and sit with him at the head of the table; and they did so, and those at the head of the table made place for them, and thus they sat there beside the knight.

Now King Arthur and Boisenard were exceedingly hungry, wherefore they ate with great appetite and made joy of the entertainment which they received, and meantime the knight held them in very pleasant discourse, talking to them of such things as would give them the most entertainment. So after a while the feast was ended and they ceased from eating.

Then, of a sudden, the knight said to King Arthur, "Messire, thou art young and lusty of spirit and I doubt not but thou hath a great heart within thee. What say you now to a little sport betwixt us two?" Upon this King Arthur regarded that knight very steadily and he believed that his face was not so old as it looked; for his eyes were exceedingly bright and shone like sparks of light; wherefore he was a-doubt and he said, "Sir, what sport would you have?" Upon this the knight fell a-laughing in great measure and he said, "This is a very strange sport that I have in mind, for it is this: That thou and I shall prove the one unto the other what courage each of us may have." And King Arthur said, "How shall we prove that?" Whereunto the knight made reply, "This is what we shall do: Thou and I shall stand forth in the middle of this hall, and thou shalt have leave to try to strike off my head; and if I can receive that blow without dying therefrom, then I shall have leave to strike thy head off in a like manner."

Upon this speech King Arthur was greatly a-dread and he said, "That is very strange sport for two men to engage upon."

Now when King Arthur said this, all those who were in the hall burst out laughing beyond all measure and as though they would never stint from their mirth. Then, when they had become in a measure quiet again, the knight of that castle said,

"Sir, art thou afraid of that sport?" Upon which King Arthur fell very angry and he said, "Nay, I am not afeared, for no man hath ever yet had reason to say that I showed myself afeared of anyone." "Very well," said the knight of the castle; "then let us try that sport of which I spake." And King Arthur said, "I am willing."

Then Boisenard came to King Arthur where he was, and he said, "Lord, do not thou enter into this thing, but rather let me undertake this venture in thy stead, for I am assured that some great treachery is meditated against thee." But King Arthur said, "Nay; no man shall take my danger upon himself, but I will assume mine own danger without calling upon any man to take it." So he said to the knight of the castle, "Sir, I am ready for that sport of which thou didst speak, but who is to strike that first blow and how shall we draw lots therefor?" "Messire," said the knight of the castle, "there shall be no lots drawn. For, as thou art the guest of this place, so shall thou have first assay at that sport."

Therewith that knight arose and laid aside his black robe, and he was clad beneath in a shirt of fine linen very cunningly worked. And he wore hosen of crimson. Then he opened that linen undergarment at the throat and he turned down the collar thereof so as to lay his neck bare to the blow. Thereupon he said, "Now, Sir Knight, thou shalt have to strike well if thou wouldst win at this sport."

But King Arthur showed no dread of that undertaking, for he arose and drew Excalibur so that the blade of the sword flashed with exceeding brightness. Then he measured his distance, and lifted the sword, and he smote the knight of the castle with all his might upon the neck. And, lo! the blade cut through the neck of the knight of the castle with wonderful ease, so that the head flew from the body to a great distance away.

But the trunk of the body of that knight did not fall, but instead of that it stood, and it walked to where the head lay, and the hands of the trunk picked up the head and they set the head back upon the body, and, lo! that knight was as sound and whole as ever he had been in all his life.

Upon this all those of the castle shouted and made great mirth, and they called upon King Arthur that it was now his turn to try that sport. So the King prepared himself, laying aside his surcoat and opening his undergarment at the throat, as the knight of the castle had done. And at that Boisenard made great lamentation. Then the knight of the castle said, "Sir, art thou afeared?" And King Arthur said, "No, I am not afeared, for every man must come to his death some time, and it appears that my time hath now come, and that I am to lay down my life in this foolish fashion for no fault of mine own."

Then the knight of the castle said, "Well, stand thou away a little distance so that I may not strike thee too close, and so lose the virtue of my blow."

So King Arthur stood forth in the midst of the hall, and the knight of the castle swung his sword several times, but did not strike. Likewise, he several times laid the blade of the sword upon King Arthur's neck, and it was very cold. Then King Arthur cried out in great passion, "Sir, it is thy right to strike, but I beseech thee not to torment me in this manner." "Nay," said the knight of the castle, "it is my right to strike when it pleases me, and I will not strike any before that time. For if it please me I will torment thee for a great while ere I slay thee." So he laid his sword several times more upon King Arthur's neck, and King Arthur said no more, but bore that torment with a very steadfast spirit.

Then the knight of the castle said, "Thou appearest to be a very courageous and honorable knight, and I have a mind to make a covenant with thee." And King Arthur said, "What is that covenant?" "It is this," said the knight of the castle, "I will spare thee thy life for a year and a day if thou wilt pledge me thy knightly word to return hither at the end of that time."

Then King Arthur said, "Very well; it shall be so." And therewith he pledged his knightly word to return at the end of that time, swearing to that pledge upon the cross of the hilt of Excalibur.

Then the knight of the castle said, "I will make another covenant with thee." "What is it?" said King Arthur. "My second covenant is this," quoth the knight of the castle, "I will give to thee a riddle, and if thou wilt answer that riddle when thou returnest hither, and if thou makest no mistake in that answer, then will I spare thy life and set thee free." And King Arthur said, "What is that riddle?" To which the knight made reply, "The riddle is this: What is it that a woman desires most of all in the world?"

"Sir," said King Arthur, "I will seek to find the answer to that riddle, and I give thee gramercy for sparing my life for so long a time as thou hast done, and for giving me the chance to escape my death." Upon this the knight of the castle smiled very sourly, and he said, "I do not offer this to thee because of mercy to thee, but because I find pleasure in tormenting thee. For what delight canst thou have in living thy life when thou knowest that thou must, for a surety, die at the end of one short year? And what pleasure canst thou have in living even that year when thou shalt be tormented with anxiety to discover the answer to my riddle?"

Then King Arthur said, "I think thou art very cruel." And the knight said, "I am not denying that."

So that night King Arthur and Boisenard lay at the castle, and the next day they took their way thence. And King Arthur was very heavy and troubled in spirit; ne'theless he charged Boisenard that he should say nothing concerning that which had befallen, but that he should keep it in secret. And Boisenard did as the King commanded, and said nothing concerning that adventure.

Now in that year which followed, King Arthur settled his affairs. Also he sought everywhere to find the answer to that riddle. Many there were who gave him answers in plenty, for one said that a woman most desired wealth, and another said she most desired beauty, and one said she desired power to please, and another said that she most desired fine raiment; and one said this, and another said that; but no answer appeared to King Arthur to be good and fitting for his purpose.

So the year passed by, until only a fortnight remained; and then King Arthur could not abide to stay where he was any longer, for it seemed to him his time was very near at hand, and he was filled with a very bitter anxiety of soul, wherefore he was very restless to be away.

So he called Boisenard to him, and he said, "Boisenard, help me to arm, for I am going away."

Then Boisenard fell a-weeping in very great measure, and he said, "Lord, do not go."

At this King Arthur looked very sternly at his esquire, and said, "Boisenard, how is this? Wouldst thou tempt me to violate mine honor? It is not very hard to die, but it would be very bitter to live my life in dishonor; wherefore tempt me no more, but do my bidding and hold thy peace. And if I do not return in a month from this time, then mayst thou tell all that hath befallen. And thou mayst tell Sir Constantine of Cornwall that he is to search the papers in my cabinet, and that there he will find all that is to be done should death overtake me."

So Boisenard put a plain suit of armor upon King Arthur, though he could hardly see what he was about for the tears that flowed down out of his eyes in great abundance. And he laced upon the armor of the King a surcoat without device, and he gave the King a shield without device. Thereupon King Arthur rode away without considering whither his way took him. And of everyone whom he met he inquired what that thing was that a woman most desired, and no one could give him an answer that appeared to him to be what it should be, wherefore he was in great doubt and torment of spirit.

Now the day before King Arthur was to keep his covenant at that castle, he was wandering through the adjacent forest in great travail of soul, for he wist not what he should do to save his life. As he wandered so, he came of a sudden upon a small hut built up under an overhanging oak-tree so that it was very hard to tell where the oak-tree ended and the hut began. And there were a great many large rocks all about covered with moss, so that the King might very easily have passed by the hut only that he beheld a smoke to arise therefrom as from a fire that burned within. So he went to the hut and opened the door and entered. At first he thought there was no one there, but when he looked again he beheld an old woman sitting bent over a small fire that burned upon the hearth. And King Arthur had never beheld such an ugly beldame as that one who sat there bending over that fire, for her ears were very huge and flapped, and her hair hung down over her head like to snakes, and her face was covered all over with wrinkles so that there were not any places at all where there was not a wrinkle; and her eyes were bleared and covered over with a film, and the eyelids were red as with the continual weeping of her eyes, and she had but one tooth in her mouth, and her hands, which she spread out to the fire, were like claws of bone.

Then King Arthur gave her greeting and she gave the King greeting, and she said to him, "My lord King, whence come ye? and why do ye come to this place?"

Then King Arthur was greatly astonished that the old woman should know him, who he was, and he said, "Who are you that appeareth to know me?" "No matter," said she, "I am one who meaneth you well; so tell me what is the trouble that brings you here at this time?" So the King confessed all his trouble to that old woman, and he asked her if she knew the answer to that riddle, "What is it that a woman most desires?" "Yea," said the old woman, "I know the answer to that riddle very well, but I will not tell it to thee unless thou wilt promise me something in return."

At this King Arthur was filled with very great joy that the old woman should know the answer to that riddle, and he was filled with doubt of what she would demand of him, wherefore he said, "What is it thou must have in return for that answer?"

Then the old woman said, "If I aid thee to guess thy riddle aright, thou must promise that I shall become wife unto one of the knights of thy Court, whom I may choose when thou returnest homeward again."

"Ha!" said King Arthur, "how may I promise that upon the behalf of anyone?" Upon this the old woman said, "Are not the knights of thy Court of such nobility that they will do that to save thee from death?" "I believe they are," said King Arthur. And with that he meditated a long while, saying unto himself, "What will my kingdom do if I die at this time? I have no right to die." So he said to the old woman, "Very well, I will make that promise."

Then she said unto the King, "This is the answer to that riddle: That which a woman most desires is to have her will." And the answer seemed to King Arthur to be altogether right. Then the old woman said, "My lord King, thou hast been played upon by that knight who hath led thee into this trouble, for he is a great conjurer and a magician of a very evil sort. He carrieth his life not within his body, but in a crystal globe which he weareth in a locket hanging about his neck; wherefore it was that when thou didst cut the head from off his body, his life remained in that locket and he did not die. But if thou hadst destroyed that locket, then he would immediately have died."

"I will mind me of that," said King Arthur.

So King Arthur abided with that old woman for that night, and she refreshed him with meat and drink and served him very well. And the next morning he set forth unto that castle where he had made his covenant, and his heart was more cheerful than it had been for a whole year.

Chapter Third

# How King Arthur Overcame the Knight-enchanter

Now, when King Arthur came to the castle, the gateway thereof was immediately opened to him and he entered. And when he had entered, sundry attendants came and conducted him into the hall where he had aforetime been. There he beheld the knight of that castle and a great many people who had come to witness the conclusion of the adventure. And when the knight beheld King Arthur he said to him, "Sir, hast thou come to redeem thy pledge?" "Yea," said King Arthur, "for so I made my vow to thee." Then the knight of the castle said, "Sir, hast thou guessed that riddle?" And King Arthur said, "I believe that I have." The knight of the castle said, "Then let me hear thy answer thereto. But if thou makest any mistake, or if thou dost not guess aright, then is thy life forfeit." "Very well," said King Arthur, "let it be that way. Now this is the answer to thy riddle: That which a woman most desires is to have her will."

Now when the lord of the castle heard King Arthur guess aright he wist not what to say or where to look, and those who were there also perceived that the King had guessed aright.

Then King Arthur came very close to that knight with great sternness of demeanor, and he said, "Now, thou traitor knight! thou didst ask me to enter into thy sport with thee a year ago, so at these present it is my turn to ask thee to have sport with me. And this is the sport I will have, that thou shalt give me that chain and locket that hang about thy neck, and that I shall give thee the collar which hangeth about my neck."

At this, the face of that knight fell all pale, like to ashes, and he emitted a sound similar to the sound made by a hare when the hound lays hold upon it. Then King Arthur catched him very violently by the arm, and he catched the locket and brake it away from about the knight's neck, and upon that the knight shrieked very loud, and fell down upon his knees and besought mercy of the King, and there was great uproar in that place. Then King Arthur opened the locket and lo! there was a ball as of crystal, very clear and shining. And King Arthur said, "I will have no mercy," and therewith he flung the ball violently upon the stone of the pavement so that it brake with a loud noise. Then, upon that instant, the knight-conjurer gave a piercing bitter cry and fell down upon the ground; and when they ran to raise him up, behold! he was entirely dead.

Now when the people of that castle beheld their knight thus suddenly dead, and when they beheld King Arthur how he stood in the fury of his kingly majesty, they were greatly afeared so that they shrunk away from the King where he stood. Then the King turned and went out from that castle and no one stayed him, and he mounted his horse and rode away, and no one gave him let or hindrance in his going.

Now when the King had left the castle in that wise, he went straight to the hut where was the old beldame and he said to her, "Thou hast holpen me a very great deal in mine hour of need, so now will I fulfil that pledge which I made unto thee, for I will take thee unto my Court and thou shalt choose one of my knights for thy husband. For I think there is not one knight in all my Court but would be very glad to do anything that lieth in his power to reward one who hath saved me as thou hast done this day."

Therewith he took that old woman and he lifted her up upon the crupper of his horse; then he himself mounted upon his horse and so they rode away from that place. And the King comported himself to that aged beldame all ways with the utmost consideration as though she had been a beautiful dame of the highest degree in the land. Likewise he showed her such respect that had she been a lady of royal blood, he could not have shown greater respect to her.

So in due time they reached the Court, which was then at Carleon. And they came there nigh about mid-day.

Now about that time it chanced that the Queen and a number of the lords of the Court, and a number of the ladies of the Court, were out in the fields enjoying the pleasantness of the Maytime; for no one in all the world, excepting the esquire, Boisenard, knew anything of the danger that beset King Arthur; hence all were very glad of the pleasantness of the season. Now as King Arthur drew nigh to that place, these lifted up their eyes and beheld him come, and they were astonished beyond all measure to see King Arthur come to them across that field with that old beldame behind him upon the saddle, wherefore they stood still to wait until King Arthur reached them.

But when King Arthur had come to them, he did not dismount from his horse, but sat thereon and regarded them all very steadfastly; and Queen Guinevere said, "Sir, what is this? Hast thou a mind to play some merry jest this day that thou hast brought hither that old woman?"

"Lady," said King Arthur, "excepting for this old woman it were like to have been a very sorry jest for thee and for me; for had she not aided me I would now have been a dead man and in a few days you would doubtless all have been in great passion of sorrow."

Then all they who were there marvelled very greatly at the King's words. And the Queen said, "Sir, what is it that hath befallen thee?"

Thereupon King Arthur told them all that had happened to him from the very beginning when he and Boisenard had left the castle of Tintagalon. And when he had ended his story, they were greatly amazed.

Now there were seventeen lords of the Court there present. So when King Arthur had ended his story, he said unto these, "Messires, I have given my pledge unto this aged woman that any one of you whom she may choose, shall take her unto him as his wife, and shall treat her with all the regard that it is possible for him to do; for this was the condition that she laid upon me. Now tell me, did I do right in making unto her my pledge that I would fulfil that which she desired?" And all of those who were present said, "Yea, lord, thou didst right, for we would do all in the world for to save thee from such peril as that from which thou hast escaped."

Then King Arthur said to that old woman, "Lady, is there any of these knights here whom you would choose for to be your husband?" Upon this, the old woman pointed with her very long, bony finger unto Sir Gawaine, saying, "Yea, I would marry that lord, for I see by the chain that is around his neck and by the golden circlet upon his hair and by the haughty nobility of his aspect, that he must be the son of a king."

Then King Arthur said unto Sir Gawaine, "Sir, art thou willing to fulfil my pledge unto this old woman?" And Sir Gawaine said, "Yea, lord, whatsoever thou requirest of me, that will I do." So Sir Gawaine came to that old woman and took her hand into his and set it to his lips; and not one of all those present so much as smiled. Then they all turned their faces and returned unto the King's castle; and they were very silent and downcast, for this was sore trouble that had come upon that Court.

Now after they had returned unto the Court, they assigned certain apartments therein to that old woman, and they clad her in rich raiment such as a queen might wear, and they assigned unto her a Court such as was fit for a queen; and it seemed to all the Court that, in the rich robes which she wore, she was ten times more ugly than she was before. So when eleven days had passed, Sir Gawaine was wedded to that old woman in the chapel of the King's Court with great ceremony and pomp of circumstance, and all of those who were there were as sad and as sorrowful as though Sir Gawaine had been called upon to suffer his death.

Afterward that they were married, Sir Gawaine and the old woman went to Sir Gawaine's house and there Sir Gawaine shut himself off from all the world and suffered no one to come nigh him; for he was proud beyond all measure, and in this great humiliation he suffered in such a wise that words cannot tell how great was that humiliation. Wherefore he shut himself away from the world that no one might behold his grief and his shame.

And all the rest of that day he walked continually up and down his chamber, for he was altogether in such despair that it came unto his mind that it would be well if he took his own life; for it seemed to him impossible for to suffer such shame as that which had come upon him. So after a while it fell the dark of the early night and therewith a certain strength came to Sir Gawaine and he said, "This is a shame for me to behave in this way; for since I have married that lady she is my true wedded wife and I do not treat her with that regard unto which she hath the right." So he went out of that place and sought the apartment of that old woman who was his wife, and by that time it was altogether dark. But when Sir Gawaine had come into that place where she was, that old woman upbraided him, crying out upon him, "So, Sir! You have treated me but ill upon this our wedding-day, for you have stayed all the afternoon away from me and now only come to me when it is dark night." And Sir Gawaine said, "Lady, I could not help it, for I was very sore oppressed with many cares. But if I have disregarded thee this day, I do beseech thy forgiveness therefore, and I will hold myself willing to do all that is in my power to recompense thee for any neglect that I have placed upon thee." Then the lady said, "Sir, it is very dark in this place; let us then have a light. "It shall be as thou dost desire," said Sir Gawaine, "and I, myself, will go and fetch a light for thee."

So Sir Gawaine went forth from that place and he brought two waxen tapers, one in either hand, and he bore them in candlesticks of gold; for he was minded to show all respect unto that old woman. And when he came into the room he perceived that she was at the farther end of the apartment and he went toward her, and she arose and stood before him as he approached.

But when the circle of light fell upon that old woman, and when Sir Gawaine beheld her who stood before him, he cried out aloud in a very great voice because of the great marvel and wonder of that which he saw. For, instead of that old woman whom he had left, he beheld a lady of extraordinary beauty and in the very flower of her youth. And he beheld that her hair was long and glossy and very black, and that her eyes were likewise black like to black jewels, and that her lips were like coral, and her teeth were like pearls. So, for a while, Sir Gawaine could not speak, and then he cried out, "Lady! lady! who art thou?"

Then that lady smiled upon Sir Gawaine with such loving-kindness that he wist not what to think, other than that this was an angel who had descended to that place out of paradise. Wherefore he stood before her for a long time and could find no more words to say, and she continued to smile upon him very kindly in that wise. Then by and by Sir Gawaine said to her, "Lady, where is that dame who is my wife?" And the lady said, "Sir Gawaine, I am she." "It is not possible," cried out Sir Gawaine, "for she was old and extraordinarily ugly, but I believe that thou art beautiful beyond any lady whom I have beheld." And the lady said, "Nevertheless, I am she and because thou hast taken me for thy wife with thine own free will and with great courtesy, so is a part of that enchantment that lay upon me removed from me. For I will now be able to appear before thee in mine own true shape. For whiles I was a little while ago so ugly and foul as thou didst behold me to be, now am I to be as thou seest me, for one-half the day – and the other half thereof I must be ugly as I was before."

Then Sir Gawaine was filled beyond all words with great joy. And with that joy there came an extreme passion of loving regard for that lady. So he cried out aloud several times, "This is surely the most wonderful thing that ever befell any man in all the world." Therewith he fell down upon his knees and took that lady's hands into his own hands, and kissed her hands with great fervor, and all the while she smiled upon him as she had done at first.

Then again the lady said, "Come, sit thee down beside me and let us consider what part of the day I shall be in the one guise, and what part of the day I shall be in the other guise; for all day I may have the one appearance, and all night I may have the other appearance."

Then Sir Gawaine said, "I would have thee in this guise during the night time, for then we are together at our own inn; and since thou art of this sort that I now see thee, I do not at all reckon how the world may regard thee."

Upon this the lady spake with great animation, saying, "No, sir, I would not have it in that wise, for every woman loveth the regard of the world, and I would fain enjoy such beauty as is mine before the world, and not endure the scorn and contempt of men and women."

To this Sir Gawaine said, "Lady, I would have it the other way."

And she said, "Nay, I would have it my way."

Then Sir Gawaine said, "So be it. For since I have taken thee for my wife, so must I show thee respect in all matters; wherefore thou shalt have thy will in this and in all other things."

Then that lady fell a-laughing beyond all measure and she said, "Sir, I did but put this as a last trial upon thee, for as I am now, so shall I always be."

Upon this Sir Gawaine was so filled with joy that he knew not how to contain himself.

So they sat together for a long time, hand in hand. Then after a while Sir Gawaine said, "Lady, who art thou?" Unto which she made reply, "I am one of the Ladies of the Lake; but for thy sake I have become mortal like to other women and have quit that very beautiful home where I one time dwelt. I have kept thee in my heart for a considerable while, for I was not very far distant at that time when thou didst bid adieu to Sir Pellias beside the lake. There I beheld how thou didst weep and bewail thyself when Sir Pellias left thee, wherefore my heart went out to thee with great pity. So, after a while, I quitted that lake and became mortal for thy sake. Now, when I found the trouble into which King Arthur had fallen I took that occasion to have him fetch me unto thee so that I might test the entire nobility of thy knighthood; and, lo! I have found it all that I deemed it possible to be. For though I appeared to thee so aged, so ugly, and so foul, yet hast thou treated me with such kind regard that I do not believe that thou couldst have behaved with more courtesy to me had I been the daughter of a king. Wherefore it doth now afford me such pleasure for to possess thee for my knight and my true lord, that I cannot very well tell thee how great is my joy therein."

Then Sir Gawaine said, "Lady, I do not think it can be so great as my joy in possessing thee." And thereupon he came to her and laid his hand upon her shoulder and kissed her upon the lips.

Then, after that, he went forth and called with a great voice all through that house, and the people of the house came running from everywhere. And he commanded that the people should bring lights and refreshments, and they brought the lights, and when they had brought them and beheld that beautiful lady instead of the aged dame, they were filled with great wonder and joy; wherefore they cried out aloud and clapped their hands together and made much sound of rejoicing. And they set a great feast for Sir Gawaine and his lady, and in place of the sorrow and darkness that had been, there was joy and light, and music and singing; wherefore those of the King's Court, beholding this from a distance, said, "It is very strange that Sir Gawaine should have taken so much joy of having wedded that old beldame."

But when the next morning had come, that lady clad herself in raiment of yellow silk, and she hung about her many strands of precious stones of several colors, and she set a golden crown upon her head. And Sir Gawaine let call his horse, and he let call a snow-white palfrey for the lady, and thereupon they rode out from that place and entered the Court of the King. But when the King and the Queen and their several Courts beheld that lady, they were filled with such great astonishment that they wist not what to say for pure wonder. And when they heard all that had happened, they gave great joy and loud acclaim so that all their mourning was changed into rejoicing. And, indeed, there was not one knight there of all that Court who would not have given half his life to have been so fortunate in that matter as was Sir Gawaine, the son of King Lot of Orkney.

Such is the story of Sir Gawaine, and from it I draw this significance: as that poor ugly beldame appeared unto the eyes of Sir Gawaine, so doth a man's duty sometimes appear to him to be ugly and exceedingly ill-favored unto his desires. But when he shall have wedded himself unto that duty so that he hath made it one with him as a bridegroom maketh himself one with his bride, then doth that duty become of a sudden very beautiful unto him and unto others.

So may it be with ye that you shall take duty unto yourselves no matter how much it may mislike ye to do so. For indeed a man shall hardly have any real pleasure in his life unless his inclination becometh wedded unto his duty and cleaveth unto it as a husband cleaveth unto his wife. For when inclination is thus wedded unto duty, then doth the soul take great joy unto itself as though a wedding had taken place betwixt a bridegroom and a bride within its tabernacle.

Likewise, when you shall have become entirely wedded unto your duty, then shall you become equally worthy with that good knight and gentleman Sir Gawaine; for it needs not that a man shall wear armor for to be a true knight, but only that he shall do his best endeavor with all patience and humility as it hath been ordained for him to do. Wherefore, when your time cometh unto you to display your knightness by assuming your duty, I do pray that you also may approve yourself as worthy as Sir Gawaine approved himself in this story which I have told you of as above written.

# Conclusion

*So endeth this volume wherein hath been told, with every circumstance of narration, the history of those Three Worthies who were of the Court of King Arthur.*

*And now, if God will give me the grace to do so, I will some time, at no very great time from this, write the further history of sundry other knights and worthies of whom I have not yet spoken.*

*And among the first of these shall be Sir Launcelot, whom all the world knoweth to have been the greatest knight in prowess of arms of any who has lived, excepting Sir Galahad, who was his son. And I shall tell you the story of Sir Ewaine and Sir Geraint, and of Sir Percival and of sundry others.*

*But of this another time. For now, with great regret I bid you adieu and bring this history unto a close.*

*So may God grant us to come together at another time with such happiness and prosperity that you may have a free and untroubled heart to enjoy the narrated history of those excellent men which I shall then set before you. Amen.*

# The Merry Adventures of Robin Hood

Howard Pyle

*Illustrated by*
Roland Wheelwright and Howard Pyle

# CONTENTS

# Colour Illustrations

# Prologue

In merry England in the time of old, when good King Henry the Second ruled the land, there lived within the green glades of Sherwood Forest, near Nottingham Town, a famous outlaw whose name was Robin Hood. No archer ever lived that could speed a gray goose shaft with such skill and cunning as his, nor were there ever such yeomen as the sevenscore merry men that roamed with him through the greenwood shades. Right merrily they dwelt within the depths of Sherwood Forest, suffering neither care nor want, but passing the time in merry games of archery or bouts of cudgel play, living upon the King's venison, washed down with draughts of ale of October brewing.

Not only Robin himself but all the band were outlaws and dwelt apart from other men, yet they were beloved by the country people round about, for no one ever came to jolly Robin for help in time of need and went away again with an empty fist.

And now I will tell how it first came about that Robin Hood fell afoul of the law.

When Robin was a youth of eighteen, stout of sinew and bold of heart, the Sheriff of Nottingham proclaimed a shooting-match and offered a prize of a butt of ale to whomsoever should shoot the best shaft in Nottinghamshire. "Now," quoth Robin, "will I go too, for fain would I draw a string for the bright eyes of my lass, and a butt of good October brewing." So up he got and took his good stout yew bow and a score or more of broad clothyard arrows, and started off from Locksley Town through Sherwood Forest to Nottingham.

It was at the dawn of the day in the merry May-time, when hedgerows are green and flowers bedeck the meadows; daisies pied and yellow cuckoo buds and fair primroses all along the briery hedges; when apple buds blossom and sweet birds sing, the lark at dawn of day, the throstle cock and cuckoo; when lads and lasses look upon each other with sweet thoughts; when busy housewives spread their linen to bleach upon the bright green grass. Sweet was the greenwood as he walked along its paths, and bright the green and rustling leaves, amid which the little birds sang with might and main: and blithely Robin whistled as he trudged along, thinking of Maid Marian and her bright eyes, for at such times a youth's thoughts are wont to turn pleasantly upon the lass that he loves the best.

As thus he walked along with a brisk step and a merry whistle, he came suddenly upon some foresters seated beneath a great oak tree. Fifteen there were in all, making themselves merry with feasting and drinking as they sat around a huge party, to which each man helped himself, thrusting his hands into the pie, and washing down that which they ate with great horns of ale which they drew all foaming from a barrel that stood nigh. Each man was clad in Lincoln green, and a fine show they made, seated upon the sward beneath that fair, spreading tree. Then one of them with his mouth full, called out to Robin, –

"Hulloa, where goest thou, little lad, with thy one penny bow and thy farthing shafts?"

Then Robin grew angry, for no stripling likes to be taunted with his green years.

"Now," quoth he, "my bow and eke mine arrows are as good as thine; and moreover, I go to the shooting-match at Nottingham Town, which same has been proclaimed by our good Sheriff of Nottinghamshire; there I will shoot with other stout yeomen, for a prize has been offered of a fine butt of ale."

Then one who held a horn of ale in his hand, said, "Ho! listen to the lad! Why, boy, thy mother's milk is yet scarce dry upon thy lips, and yet thou pratest of standing up with good stout men at Nottingham butts, thou who art scarce able to draw one string of a two stone bow."

"I'll hold the best of you twenty marks," quoth bold Robin, "that I hit the clout at threescore rods, by the good help of Our Lady fair."

At this all laughed aloud, and one said, "Well boasted, thou fair intent, well boasted! and well thou knowest that no target is nigh to make good thy wager."

And another cried, "He will be taking ale with his milk next."

At this Robin grew right mad. "Hark ye," said he; "yonder, at the glade's end, I see a herd of deer, even more than threescore rods distant. I'll hold you twenty marks that, by leave of Our Lady, I cause the best hart among them to die."

"Now done!" cried he who had spoken first. "And here are twenty marks. I wager that thou causest no beast to die, with or without the aid of Our Lady."

Then Robin took his good yew bow in his hand, and placing the tip at his instep, he strung it right deftly; then he nocked a broad clothyard arrow, and, raising the bow, drew the gray goose-feather to his ear; the next moment the bow-string rang and the arrow sped down the glade as a sparrowhawk skims in a northern wind. High leaped the noblest hart of all the herd, only to fall dead, reddening the green path with his heart's blood.

"Ha!" cried Robin, "how likest thou that shot, good fellow? I wot the wager were mine, in it were three hundred pounds."

Then all the foresters were filled with rage, and he who had spoken the first and had lost the wager was more angry than all.

"Nay," cried he, "the wager is none of thine, and get thee gone, straightway, or, by all the saints of heaven, I'll baste thy sides until thou wilt ne'er be able to walk again."

"Knowest thou not," said another, "that thou hast killed the King's deer, and, by the laws of our gracious lord and sovereign, King Harry, thine ears should be shaven close to thy head?"

"Catch him!" cried a third.

"Nay," said a fourth, "let him e'en go because of his tender years."

Never a word said Robin Hood, but he looked at the foresters with a grim face; then, turning on his heel, strode away from them down the forest glade. But his heart was bitterly angry, for his blood was hot and youthful and prone to boil.

Now, well would it have been for him who had first spoken had he left Robin Hood alone; but his anger was hot, both because the youth had gotten the better of him and because of the deep draughts of ale that he had been quaffing. So, of a sudden, without any warning, he sprang to his feet, and seized upon his bow and fitted it to a shaft. "Ay," cried he, "and I'll hurry thee anon;" and he sent the arrow whistling after Robin.

It was well for Robin Hood that that same forester's head was spinning with ale, or else he would never have taken another step; as it was, the arrow whistled within three inches of his head. Then he turned around and quickly drew his own bow, and sent an arrow back in return.

"Ye said I was no archer," cried he aloud, "but say so now again!"

The shaft flew straight; the archer fell forward with a cry, and lay on his face upon the ground, his arrows rattling about him from out of his quiver, the gray goose shaft wet with his heart's blood. Then, before the others could gather their wits about them, Robin Hood was gone into the depths of the greenwood. Some started after him, but not with much heart, for each feared to suffer the death of his fellow; so presently they all came and lifted the dead man up and bore him away to Nottingham Town.

Meanwhile Robin Hood ran through the greenwood. Gone was all the joy and brightness from everything, for his heart was sick within him, and it was borne in upon his soul that he had slain a man.

"Alas!" cried he, "thou hast found me an archer that will make thy wife to wring!

I would that thou hadst ne'er said one word to me, or that I had never passed thy way, or e'en that my right forefinger had been stricken off ere that this had happened! In haste I smote, but grieve I sore at leisure!" And then, even in his trouble, he remembered the old saw that "What is done is done; and the egg cracked cannot be cured."

And so he came to dwell in the greenwood that was to be his home for many a year to come, never again to see the happy days with the lads and lasses of sweet Locksley Town; for he was outlawed, not only because he had killed a man, but also because he had poached the King's deer, and two hundred pounds were set upon his head, as a reward for whoever would bring him to the court of the King.

Now the Sheriff of Nottingham swore that he himself would bring this knave, Robin Hood, to justice, and for two reasons: first, because he wanted the two hundred points, and next, because the forester that Robin Hood had killed was of kin to him.

But Robin Hood lay hidden in Sherwood Forest for one year, and in that time there gathered around him many others like himself, cast out from other folk for this cause and for that. Some had shot deer in hungry winter time, when they could get no other food, and had been seen in the act by the foresters, but had escaped, thus saving their ears; some had been turned out of their inheritance, that their farms might be added to the King's lands in Sherwood Forest; some had been despoiled by a great baron or a rich abbot or a powerful esquire, – all, for one cause or another, had come to Sherwood to escape wrong and oppression.

So, in all that year, fivescore or more good stout yeomen gathered about Robin Hood, and chose him to be their leader and chief. Then they vowed that even as they themselves had been despoiled they would despoil their oppressors, whether baron, abbot, knight, or squire, and that from each they would take that which had been wrung from the poor by unjust taxes, or land, rents, or in wrongful fines; but to the poor folk they would give a helping hand in need and trouble, and would return to them that which had been unjustly taken from them. Beside this, they swore never to harm a child nor to wrong a woman, be she maid, wife, or widow; so that, after a while, when the people began to find that no harm was meant to them, but that money or food came in time of want to many a poor family, they came to praise Robin and his merry men, and to tell many tales of him and of his doings in Sherwood Forest, for they felt him to be one of themselves.

Up rose Robin Hood one merry morn when all the birds were singing blithely among the leaves, and up rose all his merry men, each fellow washing his head and hands in the cold brown brook that leaped laughing from stone to stone. Then said Robin: "For fourteen days have we seen no sport, so now I will go abroad to seek adventures forthwith. But tarry ye, my merry men all, here in the greenwood; only see that ye mind well my call. Three blasts upon the bugle horn I will blow in my hour of need; then come quickly, for I shall want your aid."

So saying, he strode away through the leafy forest glades, until he had come to the verge of Sherwood. There he wandered for a long time, through highway and byway, through dingly dell and forest skirts. Now he met a fair buxom lass in a shady lane, and each gave the other a merry word and passed their way; now he saw a fair lady upon an ambling pad, to whom he doffed his cap, and who bowed sedately in return to the fair youth; now he saw a fat monk on a pannier-laden ass; now a gallant knight, with spear and shield and armor that flashed brightly in the sunlight; now a page clad in crimson; and now a stout burgher from good Nottingham Town, pacing along with serious footsteps; all these sights he saw, but adventure found he none. At last he took a road by the forest skirts; a bypath that dipped toward a broad, pebbly stream spanned by a narrow bridge made of a log of wood. As he drew nigh this bridge he saw a tall stranger coming from the other side. Thereupon Robin quickened his pace, as did the stranger likewise; each thinking to cross first.

"Now stand thou back," quoth Robin, "and let the better man cross first."

"Nay," answered the stranger, "then stand back thine own self, for the better man, I wot, am I."

"That will we presently see," quoth Robin; "and meanwhile stand thou where thou art, or else, by the bright brow of Saint Ælfrida, I will show thee right good Nottingham play with a clothyard shaft betwixt thy ribs."

"Now," quoth the stranger, "I will tan thy hide till it be as many colors as a beggar's cloak, if thou darest so much as touch a string of that same bow that thou holdest in thy hands."

"Thou pratest like an ass," said Robin, "for I could send this shaft clean through thy proud heart before a curtal friar could say grace over a roast goose at Michaelmastide."

"And thou pratest like a coward," answered the stranger, "for thou standest there with a good yew bow to shoot at my heart, while I have nought in my hand but a plain blackthorn staff wherewith to meet thee."

"Now," quoth Robin, "by the faith of my heart, never have I had a coward's name in all my life before. I will lay by my trusty bow and eke my arrows, and if thou darest abide my coming, I will go and cut a cudgel to test thy manhood withal."

"Ay, marry, that will I abide thy coming, and joyously, too," quoth the stranger; whereupon he leaned sturdily upon his staff to await Robin.

Then Robin Hood stepped quickly to the coverside and cut a good staff of ground oak, straight, without flaw, and six feet in length, and came back trimming away the tender stems from it, while the stranger waited for him, leaning upon his staff, and whistling as he gazed around him from top to toe from out the corner of his eye, and thought that he had never sen a lustier or a stouter man. Tall was Robin, but taller was the stranger by a head and a neck, for he was seven feet in height. Broad was Robin across the shoulders, but broader was the stranger by twice the breadth of a palm, while be measured at least an ell around the waist.

"Nevertheless," said Robin to himself, "I will baste thy hide right merrily, my good fellow;" then, aloud, "Lo, here is my good staff, lusty and tough. Now wait my coming, an thou darest, and meet me, an thou fearest not; then we will fight until one or the other of us tumble into the stream by dint of blows."

"Marry, that meeteth my whole heart!" cried the stranger, twirling his staff above his head, betwixt his fingers and thumb, until it whistled again.

Never did the Knights of Arthur's Round Table meet in a stouter fight than did these two. In a moment Robin stepped quickly upon the bridge where the stranger stood; first he made a feint, and then delivered a blow at the stranger's head that, had it met its mark, would have tumbled him speedily into the water; but the stranger turned the blow right deftly, and in return gave one as stout, which Robin also turned as the stranger had done. So they stood, each in his place, neither moving a finger's breadth back, for one good hour, and many blows were given and received by each in that time, till here and there were sore bones and bumps, yet neither thought of crying "Enough," or seemed likely to fall from off the bridge. Now and then they stopped to rest, and each thought that he never had seen in all his life before such a hand at quarter-staff. At last Robin gave the stranger a blow upon the ribs that made his jacket smoke like a damp straw thatch in the sun. So shrewd was the stroke that the stranger came within a hair's breadth of falling off the bridge; but he regained himself right quickly, and, by a dexterous blow, gave Robin a crack on the crown, that caused the blood to flow. Then Robin grew mad with anger, and smote with all his might at the other; but the stranger warded the blow, and once again thwacked Robin, and this time so fairly that he fell heels over head into the water, as the queen pin falls in a game of bowls.

"And where art thou now, good lad?" shouted the stranger, roaring with laughter.

"Oh, in the flood and floating adown with the tide," cried Robin; nor could he forbear laughing himself at his sorry plight. Then, gaining his feet, he waded to the bank, the little fish speeding hither and thither, all frightened at his splashing.

"Give me thy hand," cried he, when he had reached the bank. "I must needs own thou art a brave and a sturdy soul, and, withal, a good stout stroke with the cudgels. By this and by that, my head hummeth like to a hive of bees on a hot June day."

Then he clapped his horn to his lips, and winded a blast that went echoing sweetly down the forest paths. "Ay, marry," quoth he again, "thou art a tall lad, and eke a brave one, for ne'er, I trow, is there a man betwixt here and Canterbury Town could do the like to me that thou hast done."

"And thou," quoth the stranger, laughing, "takest thy cudgelling like a brave heart and a stout yeoman."

But now the distant twigs and branches rustled with the coming of men, and suddenly a score or two of good stout yeomen, all clad in Lincoln green, burst from out the covert, with merry Will Stutely at their head.

"Good master," cried Will, "how is this? Truly thou art all wet from head to foot, and that to the very skin."

"Why, marry," answered jolly Robin, "you stout fellow hath tumbled me neck and crop into the water, and hath given me a drubbing beside."

"Then shall he not go without a ducking and else a drubbing himself!" cried Will Stutely. Have at him, lads!"

Then Will and a score of yeomen leaped upon the stranger, but though they sprang quickly they found him ready and felt him strike right and left with his stout staff, so that, though he went down and press of numbers, some of them rubbed cracked crowns before he was overcome.

"Nay, forbear!" cried Robin, laughing until his sore sides ached again; "he is a right good man and true, and no harm shall befall him. Now hark ye, good youth, wilt thou stay with me and be one of my band? Three suits of Lincoln green shalt thou have each year, beside forty marks in fee, and share with us whatsoever shall befall us. Thou shalt eat sweet venison and quaff the stoutest ale, and mine own good right-hand man shalt thou be, for never did I see such a cudgel-player in all my life before. Speak! wilt thou be one of my good merry men?"

"That know I not," quoth the stranger, surlily, for he was angry at being so tumbled about. "If ye handle yew bow and apple shaft no better than ye do oaken cudgel, I wot ye are not fit to be called yeomen in my country; but if there be any man here that can shoot a better shaft than I, then will I bethink me of joining with you."

"Now by my faith," said Robin, "thou art a right saucy varlet, sirrah; yet I will stoop to thee as I never stooped to man before. Good Stutely, cut thou a fair white piece of bark four fingers in breadth, and set it forescore yards distant on yonder oak. Now, stranger, hit that fairly with a gray goose shaft and call thyself an archer."

"Ay, marry, that will I," answered he. "Give me a god stout bow and a fair broad arrow, and if I hit it not strip me and beat me blue with bowstrings."

Then he chose the stoutest bow amongst them all, next to Robin's own, and a straight gray goose shaft, well-feathered and smooth, and stepping to the mark – while all the band, sitting or lying upon the greensward, watched to see him shoot – he drew the arrow to his cheek and loosed the shaft right deftly, sending it so straight down the path that it clove the mark in the very centre. "Aha!" cried he, "mend thou that if thou canst;" while even the yeomen clapped their hands at so fair a shot.

"That is a keen shot, indeed," quoth Robin, "mend it I cannot, but mar it I may, perhaps."

Then taking up his own good stout bow and nocking an arrow with care he shot with his very greatest skill. Straight flew the arrow, and so true that it hit fairly upon the stranger's shaft and split it into splinters. Then all the yeomen leaped to their feet and shouted for joy that their master had shot so well.

"Now by the lusty yew bow of good Saint Withold," cried the stranger, "that is a shot indeed, and never saw I the like in all my life before! Now truly will I be thy man henceforth and for aye. Good Adam Bell[1] was a fair shot, but never shot he so!"

"Then have I gained a right good man this day," quoth jolly Robin. "What name goest thou by, good fellow."

"Men call me John Little whence I came," answered the stranger.

Then Will Stutely, who loved a good jest, spoke up. "Nay, fair little stranger," said he, "I like not thy name and fain would I have it otherwise. Little art thou indeed, and small of bone and sinew, therefore shalt thou be christened Little John, and I will by thy godfather."

Then Robin Hood and all his band laughed aloud until the stranger began to grow angry.

"An thou make a jest of me," quoth he to Will Stutely, "thou wilt have sore bones and little pay, and that in short season."

"Nay, good friend," said Robin Hood, "bottle thine anger for the name fitteth thee well. Little John shall thou be called henceforth, and Little John shall it be. So come, my merry men, and we will go and prepare a christening feast for this fair infant."

So turning their backs upon the stream, they plunged into the forest once more, through which they traced their steps till they reached the spot where they dwelt in the depths of the woodland. There had they built huts of bark and branches of trees, and made couches of sweet rushes spread over with skins of fallow deer. Here stood a great oak tree with branches spreading broadly around, beneath which was a seat of green moss where Robin Hood was wont to sit at feast and at merrymaking with his stout men about him. Here they found the rest of the band, some of whom had come in with a brace of fat does. Then they all built great fires and after a time roasted the does and broached a barrel of humming ale. Then when the feast was ready they all sat down, but Robin Hood placed Little John at his right hand, for he was henceforth to be the second in the band.

Then when the feast was done Will Stutely spoke up. "It is now time, I ween, to christen our bonny babe, is it not so, merry boys?" And "Aye! Aye!" cried all, laughing till the woods echoed with their mirth."

Then seven sponsors shall we have," quoth Will Stutely; and hunting among all the band he chose the seven stoutest men of them all.

"Now by Saint Dunstan," cried Little John, springing to his feet, "more than one of you shall rue it an you lay finger upon me."

But without a word they all ran upon him at once, seizing him by his legs and arms and holding him tightly in spite of his struggles, and they bore him forth while all stood around to see the sport. Then one came forward who had been chosen to play the priest because he had a bald crown, and in his hand he carried a brimming pot of ale. "Now who bringeth this babe?" asked he right soberly.

"That do I," answered Will Stutely.

"And what name callest thou him?"

---

[1] Adam Bell, Clym o' the Clough, and William of Cloudesly were three noted north-country bowmen whose names have been celebrated in many ballads of the olden time.

"Little John call I him."

"Now Little John," quoth the mock priest, "thou hast not lived heretofore, but only got thee along through the world, but henceforth thou wilt live indeed. When thou livedst not thou wast called John Little, but now that thou dost live indeed, Little John shalt thou be called, so christen I thee." And at these last words he emptied the pot of ale upon Little John's head.

Then all shouted with laughter as they saw the good brown ale stream over Little John's beard and trickle from his nose and chin, while his eyes blinked with the smart of it. At first he was of a mind to be angry, but found he could not because the others were so merry; so he, too; laughed with the rest. Then Robin took this sweet, pretty bebe, clothed him all anew from top to toe in Lincoln green, and gave him a good stout bow, and made him a member of the merry band.

And thus it was that Robin Hood became outlawed; thus a band of merry companions gathered about him, and thus he gained his right-hand man, Little John; and so the prologue ends. And now I will tell how the Sheriff of Nottingham three times sought to take Robin Hood, and how he failed each time.

# PART FIRST

*Telling how the Sheriff of Nottingham swore that he would deal dole to Robin Hood. Also, how he made three trials thereat, but missed each time by a good bow's length.*

CHAPTER ONE

# Robin Hood and the Tinker

Now it was told before how two hundred pounds were set upon Robin Hood's head, and how the Sheriff of Nottingham swore that he himself would seize Robin, both because he would fain have the two hundred pounds and because the slain man was a kinsman of his own. Now the Sheriff did not yet know what a force Robin had about him in Sherwood, but thought that he might serve a warrant for his arrest as he could upon any other man that had broken the laws; therefore he offered fourscore golden angels to any one who would serve this warrant. But men of Nottingham Town knew more of Robin Hood and his doings than the Sheriff did, and many laughed to think of serving a warrant upon the bold outlaw, knowing well that all they would get for such service would be cracked crowns; so that no one came forward to take the matter in hand. Thus a fortnight passed, in which time none came forward to do the Sheriff's business. Then said he: "A right good reward have I offered to whomsoever would serve my warrant upon Robin Hood, and I marvel that no one has come to undertake the task."

Then one of his men who was near him said: "Good master, thou wettest not the force that Robin Hood has about him and how little he cares for warrant of king or sheriff. Truly, no one likes to go on this service, for fear of cracked crowns and broken bones."

"Then I hold all Nottingham men to be cowards," said the Sheriff. "And let me see the man in all Nottinghamshire that dare disobey the warrant of our sovereign lord, King Harry, for, by the shrine of Saint Edmund, I will hang him forty cubits high! But if no man in Nottingham dare win fourscore angels, I will send elsewhere, for there should be men of mettle somewhere in this land."

Then he called up a messenger in whom he placed great trust, and bade him saddle his horse and make ready to go to Lincoln Town to see whether he could find anyone there that would do his bidding, and win the reward. So that morning the messenger started forth upon his errand.

Bright shone the sun upon the dusty highway that led from Nottingham to Lincoln, stretching away all white over hill and dale. Dusty was the highway and dusty the throat of the messenger, so that his heart was glad when he saw before him the sign of the Blue Boar Inn, when somewhat more than half his journey was done. The inn looked fair to his eyes, and the shade of the oak trees that stood around it seemed cool and pleasant, so he alighted from his horse to rest himself for a time, calling for a pot of ale to refresh his thirsty throat.

There he saw a party of right jovial fellows seated beneath the spreading oak that shaded the greensward in front of the door. There was a tinker, two barefoot friars and a party of six of the King's foresters all clad in Lincoln green, and all them were quaffing humming ale and singing merry ballads of the good old times. Loud laughed the foresters, as jests were bandied about between the singing, the louder laughed the friars, for they were lusty men with beards that curled like the wool of black rams; but loudest of all laughed the Tinker, and he sang more sweetly than any of the rest. His bag and his hammer hung upon a twig of the oak tree, and near by leaned his good stout cudgel, as thick as his wrist and knotted at the end.

"Come," cried one of the foresters to the tired messenger, "come join us for this shot. Ho, landlord! bring a fresh pot of ale for each man."

The messenger was glad enough to sit down along with the others who were there, for his limbs were weary and the ale was good.

"Now what news bearest thou so fast?" quoth one, "and whither ridest thou to-day?"

The messenger was a chatty soul and loved a bit of gossip dearly; beside the pot of ale warmed his heart; so that, settling himself in an easy corner of the inn bench, while the host leaned upon the doorway and the hostess stood with her hands beneath her apron, he unfolded his budget of news with great comfort. He told all from the very first: how Robin Hood had slain the forester, and how he had hidden in the greenwood to escape the law; how that he lived therein, all against the law, God wot, slaying his Majesty's deer and levying toll on fat abbot, knight, and esquire, so that none dare travel even on broad Watling Street or the Foss Way for fear of him; how that the Sheriff, Heaven save his worship, who paid him, the messenger, sixpence every Saturday night, of good broad money stamped with the King's head, beside ale at Michaelmus and a fat goose at Christmas-tide, had a mind to serve the king's warrant upon this same rogue, though little would he mind either warrant of King or Sheriff, for he was far from being a law-abiding man. Then he told how none could be found in all Nottingham Town to serve this warrant, for fear of cracked pates and broken bones, and how that he, the messenger, was now upon his way to Lincoln Town to find of what mettle the Lincoln men might be, and whether there were any there that dared serve this same warrant; wherefore was he now sitting among the prettiest lads he had ever known, and the ale was the best ale he had tasted in all his life.

To this discourse they listened with open mouths and eyes, for it was a fair piece of gossip to them. Then when the messenger had done the jolly Tinker broke silence.

"Now come I, forsooth, from good Banbury Town," said he, "and no one nigh Nottingham – nor Sherwood either, an that be the mark – can hold cudgel with my grip. Why lads, did I not meet that wag, Simon of Ely, even at the famous Fair at Hertford Town, and beat him in the ring at that place before Sir Robert of Leslie and his lady? This same Robin Hood, of whom, I wot, I never heard before, is a right merry blade, but gin he be strong, am not I stronger? and gin he be sly, am not I slyer? Now by the bright eyes of Nan o' the Mill, and by mine own name, and that's Wat o' the Crabstaff, and by mine own mother's son, and that's myself, will I, even I, Wat o' the Crabstaff, meet this same sturdy rogue and gin he mind not the seal of our glorious sovereign, King Harry, and the warrant of the good Sheriff of Nottinghamshire, I will so bruise, beat, and bemaul his pate, that he shall never move finger or toe again! Hear ye that, bully boys? Come, let us have another bout."

"Now art thou the man for my farthing," cried the messenger. "And back thou goest with me to Nottingham Town."

"Nay," quoth the Tinker, shaking his head slowly from side to side, "Go I with no man gin it be not with mine own free will."

"Nay, nay," said the messenger, "no man is there in Nottinghamshire could make thee go against thy will, thou brave fellow."

"Ay, that be I brave," said the Tinker.

"Ay, marry," said the messenger, thou art a brave lad; but our good Sheriff hath offered fourscore angels of bright gold to whosoever shall serve the warrant upon Robin Hood; though little good will it do."

"Then I will go with thee, lad. Do but wait till I get my bag, and hammer, and my cudgel. Ay, let me but meet this same Robin Hood, and let me see whether he will not mind the King's warrant." So, after having paid their score, the messenger, with the Tinker striding beside his nag, started back to Nottingham again.

One bright morning soon after this time, Robin Hood started off to Nottingham Town to find what was a-doing there, walking merrily along the roadside where the grass was sweet with daisies, his eyes wandering and his thoughts also. His bugle-horn hung at his hip and his bow and arrows at his back, while in his hand he bore a good stout oaken staff, which he twirled with his fingers as he strolled along.

As thus he walked down a shady lane he saw a tinker coming, trolling a merry song as he drew nigh. On his back hung his bag and his hammer, and in his hand he carried a right stout crabstaff full six feet long, and thus sang he?-

*"In peascod time, when hound to horn*
*Gives ear till buck be killed,*
*And little lads with pipes of corn*
*Sit keeping beasts afield"* –

"Halloa, good friend!" cried Robin.

*"I want to gather strawberries"* -

"Halloa!" cried Robin again,

*"By woods and groves full fair"* –

"Halloa! art thou deaf, man? Good friend, say I!"

"And who art thou dost so boldly check a fair song?" quoth the Tinker, stopping in his singing. "Halloa, thine own self, whether thou be good friend or no. But let me tell thee, thou stout fellow, gin thou be a good friend it were well for us both; but gin thou be no good friend it were ill for thee."

"Then let us be good friends," quoth jolly Robin, "for ill would it be to be ill, and like I thine oaken staff full well to make it but well, so good friends let us be."

"Ay, marry, then let us be," said the Tinker. "But, good youth, thy tongue runneth so nimbly that my poor and heavy wits can but ill follow it, so talk more plainly, I pray, for I am a plain man, forsooth."

"And whence comest thou, my lusty blade?" quoth Robin.

"I come from Banbury," answered the Tinker.

"Alas!" quoth Robin, "I hear there is sad news this merry more."

"Ha! is it indeed so?" cried the Tinker, eagerly. "Prythee tell it speedily, for I am a tinker by trade, as thou seest, and as I am in my trade I am greedy for news, even as a priest is greedy for farthings."

"Well then," quoth Robin, "list thou and I will tell, but bear thyself up bravely, for the news is sad, I wot. Thus it is: I hear that two tinkers are in the stocks for drinking ale and beer!"

"Now a murrain seize thee and thy news, thou scurvy dog," quoth the Tinker, "for thou speakest but ill of good men. But sad news is it indeed, gin there bee two stout fellows in the stocks."

"Nay," said Robin, "thou hast missed the mark and dost but weep for the wrong sow. The sadness of the news lieth in that there be but two in the stocks, for the others do roam the country at large."

"Now by the pewter platter of Saint Dunstan," cried the Tinker, "I have a good part of a mind to baste thy hide for thine ill jest. But gin men be put in the stocks for drinking ale and beer, I trow thou wouldst not lose thy part."

Loud laughed Robin and cried: "Now well taken, Tinker, well taken! Why, thy wits are like beer, and do froth up most when they grow sour! But right art thou, man, for I love ale and beer right well. Therefore come straightway with me hard by to the sign of the Blue Boar, and if thou drinkest as thou appearest, – and I wot thou wilt not belie thy looks, – I will drench thy throat with as good homebrewed as ever was tapped in all broad Nottinghamshire."

"Now by my faith," said the Tinker, "thou art a right good fellow in spite of thy scurvy jests. I love thee, my sweet chuck, and gin I go not with thee to that same Blue Boar thou mayst call me a heathen Jew."

"Tell me thy news, good friend, I Prythee," quoth Robin as they trudged along together, "for tinkers, I ween, are all as full of news as an egg of meat."

"Now I love thee as my brother, my bully blade," said the Tinker, "else I would not tell thee my news; for sly am I, man, and I have in hand a grave undertaking that doth call for all my wits, for I come to seek a bold outlaw that men, hereabouts, call Robin Hood. Within my pouch I have a warrant, all fairly written out on parchment, forsooth, with a great red seal for to make it lawful. Could I but meet this same Robin Hood I would serve it upon his dainty body, and if he minded it not I would beat him till every one of his ribs would cry Amen. But thou livest hereabouts, mayhap thou knowest Robin Hood thyself, good fellow."

"Ay, marry, that do I somewhat," quoth Robin, "and I have seen him this very morn. But, Tinker, men say that he is but a sad, sly thief. Thou hadst better watch thy warrant, man, or else he may steal it out of the very pouch."

"Let him but try!" cried the Tinker. "Sly may he be, but sly am I, too. I would I had him here now, man to man!" And he made his heavy cudgel to spin again. "But what manner of man is he, lad?"

"Much like myself," said Robin, laughing, "and in height and build and age nigh the same; and he hath blue eyes, too, like mine."

"Nay," quoth the Tinker, "thou art but a green youth. I thought him to be a great bearded man, Nottingham, men feared him so."

"Truly, he is not so old nor so stout as thou art," said Robin. "But men do call him a right deft hand at quarterstaff."

"That may be," said the Tinker, right sturdily, "but I am more deft than he, for did I not overcome Simon of Ely in a fair bout in the ring at Hertford Town? But if thou knowest him, my jolly blade, wilt thou go with me and bring me to him? Fourscore bright angels hath the Sheriff promised me if I serve the warrant upon the knave's body, and ten of them will I give to thee if thou showest me him."

"Ay, that will I," quoth Robin; "but show me thy warrant, man, until I see whether it be good or no."

"That will I not do, even to mine own brother," answered the Tinker. "No man shall see my warrant till I serve it upon yon fellow's own body."

"So be it," quoth Robin. "An thou show it not to me I know not to whom thou wilt show it. But here we are at the sign of the Blue Boar, so let us in and taste his brown October."

No sweeter inn could be found in all Nottinghamshire than that of the Blue Boar. None had such lovely trees standing around, or was so covered with trailing clematis and sweet woodbine; none had such good beer and such humming ale; nor, in winter time, when the north wind howled and snow drifted around the hedges, was there to be found, elsewhere, such a roaring fire as blazed upon the hearth of the Blue Boar. At such times might be found a goodly company of yeomen or country folk seated around the blazing hearth, bandying merry jests, while roasted crabs[1] bobbed in bowls of ale upon the hearthstone. Well known was the inn to Robin Hood and his band, for there had he and such merry companions as Little John or Will Stutely or young David of Doncaster often gathered when all the forest was filled with snow. As for mine host, he knew how to keep a still tongue in his head, and to swallow his words before they passed his teeth, for he knew very well which side of his bread was spread with butter, for Robin and his band were the best of customers, and paid their scores without having them chalked up behind the door. So now, when Robin Hood and the Tinker came thereto and called aloud for two great pots of ale, none would have known from look or speech that the host had ever set eyes upon the outlaw before.

"Bide thou here," quoth Robin to the Tinker, "while I go and see that mine host draweth ale from the right butt, for he had good October, I know, and that brewed by Withold of Tamworth." So saying, he went within and whispered to the host to add a measure of Flemish strong waters to the good English ale; which the latter did and brought it to them.

"By Our Lady," said the Tinker, after a long draught of the ale, "you same Withold of Tamworth – a right good Saxon name, too, I would have thee know – breweth the most humming ale that e'er passed the lips of ~Wat o' the Crabstaff."

"Drink, man, drink," cried Robin, only wetting his own lips meanwhile. "Ho, landlord! bring my friend another pot of the same. And now for a song, my jolly blade."

"Ay, that will I give thee a song, my lovely fellow," quoth the Tinker, "for I never tasted such ale in all my days before. By'r Lady, it doth make my head hum, even now! Hey, Dame Hostess, come listen, an thou wouldst hear a song; and thou too, thou bonny lass, for never sing I so well as when bright eyes do look upon me the while."

Then he sang an ancient ballad of the time of good King Arthur, called the Marriage of Sir Gawaine, which you may some time read, yourself, in stout English of early times; and as he sang, all listened to that noble tale of noble knight and his sacrifice to his king. But long before the Tinker came to the last verse his tongue began to trip and his head to spin, because of the strong waters mixed with the ale.

---

[1]Small sour apples.

First his tongue tripped, then it grew thick of sound; then his head wagged from side to side, until at last he fell asleep as though he never would waken again.

Then Robin Hood laughed aloud, and quickly took the warrant from out the Tinker's pouch with his deft fingers. "Sly art thou, Tinker," quoth he, "but not yet, I trow, art thou as sly as that same sly thief, Robin Hood."

Then he called the host to him and said, "Here, good man, are ten broad shillings for the entertainment thou hast given us this day. See that thou takest good care of thy fair guest there, and when he wakes thou mayst again charge him ten shillings also, and if he hath it not, thou mayst take his bag and hammer, and even his coat, in payment. Thus do I punish those that come into the greenwood to deal dole to me. As for thine own self, never knew I landlord yet that would not charge twice an he could."

At this the host smiled slyly, as though saying to himself the rustic saw, "Teach a magpie to suck eggs."

The Tinker slept until the afternoon drew to a close and the shadows grew long beside the woodland edge, then he awoke. First he looked up, then he looked down, then he looked east, then he looked west, for he was gathering his wits together, like barley-straws blown apart by the wind. First he thought of his merry companion, but he was gone. Then he thought of his stout crabstaff, and that he had within his hand. Then of his warrant, and of the fourscore angels he was to gain for serving it upon Robin Hood. He thrust his hand into his pouch, but not a scrap nor a farthing was there. Then he sprang to his feet in a rage.

"Ho, landlord!" cried he, "whither hath that knave gone that was with me but now?"

"'What knave meaneth your worship!" quoth the landlord, calling the Tinker worship to soothe him, as a man would pour oil upon angry water; "I saw no knave with your worship, for I swear no man would dare call that man knave so nigh to Sherwood Forest. A right stout yeoman I saw with your worship, but I thought that your worship knew him, for few there be about here that pass him by and know him not."

"Now, how should I, that ne'er have squealed in your sty, know all the swine therein? Who was he, then, an thou knowest him so well?"

"Why, yon same is a right stout fellow whom men hereabouts do call Robin Hood; which same –"

"Now, by'r Lady!" cried the Tinker hastily, and in a deep voice like an angry bull, "thou didst see me come into thine inn, I, a staunch, honest craftsman, and never told me who my company was, well knowing thine own self who he was. Now, I have a right round piece of a mind to crack thy knave's pate for thee!" Then he took up his cudgel and looked at the landlord as though he would smite him where he stood.

"Nay," cried the host, throwing up his elbow, for he feared the blow, "how knew I that thou knewest him not?"

"Well and truly thankful mayst thou be," quoth the Tinker, "that I be a patient man, and so do spare thy bald crown, else wouldst thou ne'er cheat customer again.

But as this same knave, Robin Hood, I go straightway to seek him, and if I do not score his knave's pate, cut my staff into faggots and call me woman." So saying, he gathered himself together to depart.

"Nay," quoth the landlord, standing in front of him and holding out his arms like a gooseherd driving his flock, for money made him bold, "thou goest not till thou hast paid me my score."

"But did not he pay thee?"

"Not so much as one farthing; and ten good shillings' worth of ale have ye drunk this day. Nay, I say, thou goest not away without paying me, else shall our good sheriff know of it."

"But nought have I to pay thee with, good fellow," quoth the Tinker.

"'Good Fellow' not me," said the landlord. "Good fellow am I not when it cometh to lose ten shillings! Pay me that thou owest me in broad money, or else leave thy coat and bag and hammer; yet, I wot they are not worth ten shillings, and I shall lose thereby. Nay, an thou stirrest, I have a great dog within and I will loosen him upon thee. Maken, open thou the door and let forth Brian if this fellow stirs one step."

"Nay," quoth the Tinker, – for, by roaming the country, he had learned what dogs were, – "take thou what thou wilt have, and let me depart in peace, and may a murrain go with thee. But oh, landlord! an I catch yon scurvy varlet, I swear he shall pay full with usury for that he hath had!"

So saying, he strode away toward the forest, talking to himself, while the landlord and his worthy dame and Maken stood looking after him, and laughed when he had fairly gone.

"Robin and I have stripped yon ass of his pack main neatly," quoth the landlord.

Now it happened about this time that Robin Hood was going through the forest to Foss Way, to see what was to be seen there, for the moon was full and the night gave promise of being bright. In his hand he carried his stout oaken staff, and at his side hung his bugle horn. As thus he walked up a forest path, whistling, down another path came the Tinker, muttering to himself and shaking his head like an angry bull; and so, at a sudden bend, they met sharply face to face. Each stood still for a time, and then Robin spoke:-

"Halloa, my sweet bird," said be, laughing merrily, "how likest thou thine ale? Wilt not sing to me another song?"

The Tinker said nothing at first, but stood looking at Robin with a grim face. "Now,"quoth he at last, "I am right glad I have met thee, and if I do not rattle thy bones within thy hide this day, I give thee leave to put thy foot upon my neck."

"With all my heart," cried merry Robin; "rattle my bones, an thou canst." So saying, he gripped his staff and threw himself upon his guard. Then the Tinker spat upon his hands, and, grasping his staff, came straight at the other. He struck two or three blows, but soon found that he had met his match, for Robin warded and parried all of them, and, before the Tinker thought, he gave him a rap upon the ribs in return. At this Robin laughed aloud, and the Tinker grew more angry than ever, and smote again with all his might and main. Again Robin warded two of the strokes, but at the third, his staff broke beneath the mighty blows of the Tinker. "Now, ill betide thee, traitor staff," cried Robin, as it fell from his hands; "a foul stick art thou to serve me thus in mine hour of need."

"Now yield thee," quoth the Tinker, "for thou art my captive; and if thou do not, I will beat thy pate to a pudding."

To this Robin Hood made no answer, but, clapping his horn to his lips, he blew three blasts, loud and clear.

"Ay," quoth the Tinker, "blow thou mayest, but go thou must with me to Nottingham Town, for the Sheriff would fain see thee there. Now wilt thou yield thee, or shall I have to break thy pretty head?"

"An I must drink sour ale, I must," quoth Robin; "but never have I yielded me to man before, and that without wound or mark upon my body. Nor, when I bethink me, will I yield now. Ho, my merry men! come quickly!"

Then from out the forest leaped Little John and six stout yeomen clad in Lincoln green.

"How now, good master," cried Little John, "what need hast thou that thou dost wind thy horn so loudly?"

"There stands a tinker," quoth Robin, "that would fain take me to Nottingham, there to hang upon the gallows tree."

"Then shall he himself hang forthwith," cried Little John; and he and the others made at the Tinker, to seize him.

"Nay, touch him not," said Robin "for a right stout man is he. A metal man he is by trade, and a mettled man by nature; moreover, he doth sing a lovely ballad. Say, good fellow, wilt thou join my merry men all? Three suits of Lincoln green shalt thou have a year, beside twenty marks in fee; thou shalt share all with us and lead a right merry life in the greenwood; for cares have we not and misfortune cometh not upon us within the sweet shades of Sherwood, where we shoot the dun deer, and feed upon venison and sweet oaten cakes, and curds and honey. Wilt thou come with me?"

"Ay, marry, will I join with you all," quoth the Tinker, "for I love a merry life, and I love thee, good master, though thou didst thwack my ribs and cheat me into the bargain. Fain am I to own thou art both a stouter and a slyer man than I; so I will obey thee and be thine own true servant."

So all turned their steps to the forest depths, where the Tinker was to live henceforth. For many a day he sang ballads to the band, until the famous Allan a Dale joined them, before whose sweet voice all others seemed as harsh as a raven's; but of him we will learn hereafter.

CHAPTER TWO

# THE SHOOTING-MATCH AT NOTTINGHAM TOWN

Then the Sheriff was very wroth because of this failure to take jolly Robin, for it came to his ears, as ill news always does, that the people laughed at him and made a jest of his thinking to serve a warrant upon such a one as the bold outlaw; and a man hates nothing so much as being made a jest of; so he said: "Our gracious Lord and Sovereign King himself shall know of this, and how his laws are perverted and despised by this band of rebel outlaws. As for yon traitor Tinker, him will I hang, if I catch him, upon the very highest gallows tree in all Nottinghamshire."

Then he bade all his servants and retainers to make ready to go to London Town, to see and speak with the King.

At this there was bustling at the Sheriff's castle, and men ran hither and thither upon this business and upon that, while the forge fires of Nottingham glowed red far into the night like twinkling stars, for all the smiths of the town were busy making or mending armor for the Sheriff's troop of escort. For two days this labor lasted, then, on the third, all was ready for the journey. So forth they started in the bright sunlight, from Nottingham Town to Fosse Way and thence to Watling Street; and so they journeyed for two days, until they saw at last the spires and towers of great London Town; and many folks stopped, as they journeyed along, and gazed at the show they made riding along the highways with their flashing armor, and gay plumes and trappings.

In London King Henry and his fair Queen Elinor held their Court, gay with ladies in silks and satins and velvets and cloth of gold, and also brave knights and gallant courtiers. Thither came the Sheriff and was shown into the King's presence.

"A boon, a boon," quoth he, as he knelt upon the ground.

"Now what wouldst thou have?" said the King. "Let us hear what may be thy desires."

"O good my Lord and Sovereign," spoke the Sheriff, "in Sherwood Forest, in our own good shire of Nottingham, liveth a bold outlaw whose name is Robin Hood."

"In good sooth," said the King, "his doings have reached even our own royal ears. He is a saucy, rebellious varlet, yet, I am fain to own, a right merry soul withal."

"But hearken, O my most gracious Sovereign," said the Sheriff. "I sent a warrant to him with thine own royal seal attached, by a right lusty knave, but he beat the messenger and stole the warrant. And he killeth thy deer and robbeth thine own liege subjects even upon the great highways."

"Why, how now," quoth the King, wrathfully. "What wouldst thou have me do? Comest thou not to me with a great array of men-at-arms and retainers, and yet art not able to take a single band of lusty knaves without armor on breast, in thine own county! What wouldst thou have me do? Art thou not my Sheriff? Are not my laws in force in Nottinghamshire? Canst thou not take thine own course against those that break the laws or do an injury to thee or thine? Go, get thee gone, and think well; devise some plan of thine own but trouble me no further. But look well to it, master Sheriff, for I will have my laws obeyed by all men within my kingdom, and if thou art not able to enforce them thou art no sheriff for me. So look well to thyself, I say, or ill may befall thee as well as all the thieving knaves in Nottinghamshire. When the flood cometh it sweepeth away grain as well as chaff."

Then the Sheriff turned away with a sore and troubled heart, and sadly he rued his fine show of retainers, for he saw that the King was angry because he had so many men about him and yet could not enforce the laws. So, as they all rode slowly back to Nottingham, the Sheriff was thoughtful and full of care. Not a word did he speak to any one, and no one of his men spoke to him, but all the time he was busy devising some plan to take Robin Hood.

"Aha!" cried he suddenly, smiting his hand upon his thigh, "I have it now! Ride on, my merry men all, and let us get back to Nottingham Town as speedily as we may. And mark well my words: before a fortnight is passed, that evil knave, Robin Hood, will be safely clapped into Nottingham gaol."

But what was the Sheriff's plan?

As a Jew takes each one of a bag of silver angels, feeling each coin to find whether it be clipped or not, so the Sheriff, as all rode slowly and sadly back toward Nottingham, took up thought after thought in turn, feeling around the edges of each but finding in every one some flaw. At last he thought of the daring soul of jolly

Robin and how, as he the Sheriff knew, he often came even within the walls of Nottingham.

"Now," thought the Sheriff, "could I but persuade Robin nigh to Nottingham Town so that I could find him, I warrant I would lay hands upon him so stoutly that he would never get away again." Then of a sudden it came to him like a flash that were he to proclaim a great shooting-match and offer some grand prize, Robin Hood might be over-persuaded by his spirit to come to the butts; and it was this thought which caused him to cry "Aha!" and smite his palm upon his thigh.

So, as soon as he had returned safely to Nottingham, he sent messengers north and south, and east and west, to proclaim through town, hamlet, and countryside, this grand shooting-match, and every one was bidden that could draw a long bow, and the prize was to be an arrow of pure beaten gold.

When Robin Hood first heard the news of this he was in Lincoln Town, and hastening back to Sherwood Forest he soon called all his merry men about him and spoke to them thus:-

"Now hearken, my merry men all, to the news that I have brought from Lincoln Town to-day. Our friend the Sheriff of Nottingham hath proclaimed a shooting-match, and hath sent messengers to tell of it through all the country side, and the prize is to be a bright golden arrow. Now I fain would have one of us win it, both because of the fairness of the prize and because our sweet friend the Sheriff hath offered it. So we will take our bows and shafts and go there to shoot, for I know right well that merriment will be a-going. What say ye, lads?"

Then young David of Doncaster spoke up and said: "Now listen, I pray thee, good master, unto what I say. I have come straight from our friend Eadom o' the Blue Boar, and there I heard the full news of this same match. But, master, I know from him, and he got it from the Sheriff's man Ralph o' the Scar, that this same knavish Sheriff hath but laid a trap for thee in this shooting-match and wishes nothing so much as to see thee there. So go not, good master, for I know right well he doth seek to beguile thee, but stay within the greenwood lest we all meet dole and woe."

"Now," quoth Robin, 'thou art a wise lad and keepest thine ears open and thy mouth shut, as becometh a wise and crafty woodsman. But shall we let it be said that the Sheriff of Nottingham did cow bold Robin Hood and sevenscore as fair archers as are in all merry England? Nay, good David, what thou tellest me maketh me to desire the prize even more than I else should do. But what sayeth our good gossip Swanthold? is it not 'A hasty man burneth his mouth, and the fool that keepeth his eyes shut falleth into the pit?' Thus he says, truly, therefore we must meet guile with guile. Now some of you clothe yourselves as curtal friars, and some as rustic peasants, and some as tinkers, or as beggars, but see that each man taketh a good bow or broadsword, in case need should arise. As for myself, I will shoot for this same golden arrow, and should I win it, we will hang it to the branches of our good greenwood tree for the joy of all the band. How like you the plan, my merry men all?"

Then "good, good!" cried all the band right heartily.

A fair sight was Nottingham Town on the day of the shooting-match. All along upon the green meadow beneath the town wall stretched a row of benches, one above the other, which were for knight and lady, squire and dame, and rich burghers and their wives; for none but those of rank and quality were to sit there. At the end of the range, near the target, was a raised seat bedecked with ribbons and scarfs and garlands of flowers, for the Sheriff of Nottingham and his dame. The range was two score paces broad. At one end stood the target, at the other a tent of striped canvas, from the pole of which fluttered many-colored flags and streamers. In this booth were casks of ale, free to be broached by any of the archers who might wish to quench their thirst.

Across the range from where the seats for the better folk were raised was a railing to keep the poorer people from crowding in front of the target. Already, while it was early, the benches were beginning to fill with people of quality, who kept constantly arriving in little carts, or upon palfreys that curveted gayly to the merry tinkle of silver bells at bridle-reins; with these came also the poorer folk, who sat or lay upon the green grass near the railing that kept them off the range. In the great tent the archers were gathering by twos and threes; some talking loudly of the fair shots each man had made in his day; some looking well to their bows, drawing a string betwixt the fingers to see that there was no fray upon it, or inspecting arrows, shutting one eye and peering down a shaft to see that it was not warped, but straight and true, for neither bow nor shaft should fail at such a time and for such a prize. And never were such a company of yeomen as were gathered at Nottingham Tower that day, for the very best archers of merry England had come to this shooting-match. There was Gill o' the Red Cap, the Sheriff's own head archer, and Diccon Cruikshank of Lincoln Town, and Adam o' the Dell, a man of Tamworth, of threescore years and more, yet hale and lusty still, who in his time had shot in the famous match at Woodstock, and had there beaten that renowned archer, Clym o' the Clough. And many more famous men of the long bow were there, whose names have been handed down to us in goodly ballads of the olden time.

But now all the benches were filled with guests, lord and lady, burgher and dame, when at last the Sheriff came with his lady, he riding with stately mien upon his milk-white horse and she upon her brown filly. Upon his head he wore a purple velvet cap, and purple velvet was his robe, all trimmed about with rich ermine; his jerkin and hose were of sea-green silk, and his shoes of black velvet, the pointed toes fastened to his garters with golden chains. A golden chain hung about his neck, and at his collar was a great carbuncle set in red gold. His lady was dressed in blue velvet, all trimmed with swan's down. So they made a gallant sight as they rode along side by side, and all the people shouted from where they crowded across the space from the gentlefolk; so the Sheriff and his lady came to their place, where men-at-arms, with hauberk and spear, stood about, waiting for them.

Then when the Sheriff and his dame had sat down, he bade his herald wind upon his silver horn; who thereupon sounded three blasts that came echoing cheerily back from the gray walls of Nottingham. Then the archers stepped forth to their places, while all the folk shouted with a mighty voice, each man calling upon his favorite yeoman. "Red Cap!" cried some; "Cruikshank!" cried others; "Hey for William o' Leslie!" shouted others yet again; while ladies waved silken scarfs to urge each yeoman to do his best.

Then the herald stood forth and loudly proclaimed the rules of the game as follows:-

"Shoot each man from yon mark, which is sevenscore yards and ten from the target. One arrow shooteth each man first, and from all the archers shall the ten that shooteth the fairest shafts be chosen for to shoot again. Two arrows shooteth each man of these ten, then shall the three that shoot the fairest shafts be chosen for to shoot again. Three arrows shooteth each man of those three, and to him that shooteth the fairest shafts shall the prize be given."

Then the Sheriff leaned forward, looking keenly among the press of archers to find whether Robin Hood was amongst them; but no one was there clad in Lincoln green, such as was worn by Robin and his band. "Nevertheless," said the Sheriff to himself, "he may still be there, and I miss him among the crowd of other men. But let me see when but ten men shoot, for I wot he will be among the ten, or I know him not."

And now the archers shot, each man in turn, and the good folk never saw such archery as was done that day. Six arrows were within the clout, four within the black, and only two smote the outer ring; so that when the last arrow sped and struck the target, all the people shouted aloud, for it was noble shooting.

And now but ten men were left of all those that had shot before, and of these ten, six were famous throughout the land, and most of the folk gathered there knew them. These six men were Gilbert o' the Red Cap, Adam o' the Dell, Diccon Cruikshank, William o' Leslie, Hubert o' Cloud, and Swithin o' Hertford. Two others were yeomen of merry Yorkshire, another was a tall stranger in blue, who said he came from London Town, and the last was a tattered stranger in scarlet, who wore a patch over one eye.

"Now," quoth the Sheriff to a man-at-arms who stood near him, "seest thou Robin Hood amongst those ten?"

"Nay, that do I not, your worship," answered the man. "Six of them I know right well. Of those Yorkshire yeomen, one is too tall and the other too short for that bold knave. Robin's beard is as yellow as gold, while yon tattered beggar in scarlet hath a beard of brown, besides being blind of one eye. As for the stranger in blue, Robin's shoulders, I ween, are three inches broader than his."

"Then," quoth the Sheriff, smiting his thigh angrily, "yon knave is a coward as well as a rogue, and dares not show his face among good men and true."

Then, after they had rested a short time, those ten stout men stepped forth to shoot again. Each man shot two arrows, and as they shot, not a word was spoken, but all the crowd watched with scarce a breath of sound; but when the last had shot his arrow another great shout arose, while many cast their caps aloft for joy of such marvellous shooting.

"Now by our gracious Lady fair," quoth old Sir Amyas o' the Dell, who, bowed with fourscore years and more, sat near the Sheriff, "ne'er saw I such archery in all my life before, yet have I seen the best hands at the long bow for threescore years and more."

And now but three men were left of all those that had shot before. One was Gill o' the Red Cap, one the tattered stranger in scarlet, and one Adam o' the Dell of Tamworth Town. Then all the people called aloud, some crying, "Ho for Gilbert o' the Red Cap! " and some, "Hey for stout Adam o' Tamworth!" but not a single man in the crowd called upon the stranger in scarlet.

"Now shoot thou well, Gilbert," cried the Sheriff, "and if thine be the best shaft, fivescore broad silver pennies will I give to thee beside the prize."

"Truly I will do my best," quoth Gilbert, right sturdily. "A man cannot do aught but his best, but that will I strive to do this day." So saying, he drew forth a fair smooth arrow with a broad feather and fitted it deftly to the string, then drawing his bow with care he sped the shaft. Straight flew the arrow and lit fairly in the clout, a finger breadth from the center. "A Gilbert, a Gilbert!" shouted all the crowd; and, "Now, by my faith," cried the Sheriff, smiting his hands together, "that is a shrewd shot."

Then the tattered stranger stepped forth, and all then people laughed as they saw a yellow patch that showed beneath his arm when he raised his elbow to shoot, and also to see him aim with but one eye. He drew the good yew bow quickly, and quickly loosed a shaft; so short was the time that no man could draw a breath betwixt the drawing and the shooting; yet his arrow lodged nearer the centre than the other by twice the length of a barleycorn.

"Now by all the saints in Paradise!" cried the Sheriff, "that is a lovely shaft in very truth!"

Then Adam o' the Dell shot, carefully and cautiously, and his arrow lodged close beside the stranger's. Then after a short space they all three shot again, and once more each arrow lodged within the clout, but this time Adam o' the Dell's was farthest from the center, and again the tattered stranger's shot was the best. Then, after another time of rest, they all shot for the third time. This time Gilbert took great heed to his aim, keenly measuring the distance and shooting with shrewdest care. Straight flew the arrow, and all shouted till the very flags that waved in the breeze shook with the sound, and the rooks and daws flew clamoring about the roofs of the old gray tower, for the shaft had lodged close beside the spot that marked the very center.

"Well done, Gilbert!" cried the Sheriff, right joyously. "Fain am I to believe the prize is thine, and right fairly won. Now, thou ragged knave, let me see thee shoot a better shaft than that."

Naught spake the stranger but took his place, while all was hushed, and no one spoke or even seemed to breathe, so great was the silence for wonder what he would do. Meanwhile, also, quite still stood the stranger holding his bow in his hand, while one could count five; then he drew his trusty yew, holding it drawn but a moment, then loosed the string. Straight flew the arrow, and so true that it smote a gray goose feather from off Gilbert's shaft, which fell fluttering through the sunlit air as the stranger's arrow lodged close beside his of the red cap, and in the very centre. No one spoke a word for a while and no one shouted, but each man looked into his neighbor's face amazedly.

"Nay," quoth old Adam o' the Dell presently, drawing a long breath and shaking his head as he spoke; "twoscore years and more have I shot shaft, and maybe not all times bad, but I shoot no more this day, for no man can match with yon stranger, whosoe'er he may be." Then he thrust his shaft into his quiver, rattling, and unstrung his bow without another word.

Then the Sheriff came down from his dais and drew near, in all his silks and velvets, to where the tattered stranger stood leaning upon his stout bow, whilst the good folk crowded around to see the man who shot so wonderfully well. "Here, good fellow," quoth the Sheriff, "take thou the prize, and well and fairly hast thou won it, I trow. What me be thy name, and whence comest thou?"

"Men do call me Jock o' Teviotdale, and thence am I come," said the stranger.

"Then, by Our Lady, Jock, thou art the fairest archer that e'er mine eyes beheld, and if thou wilt join my service I will clothe thee with a better coat than that thou hast upon thy back; thou shalt eat and drink of the best, and at every Christmas-tide fourscore marks shall be thy wage. I trow thou drawest better bow than that same coward knave, Robin Hood, that dared not show his face here this day. Say, good fellow, wilt thou join my service?"

"Nay, that will I not," quoth the stranger, roughly. "I will be mine own, and no man in all merry England shall be my master."

"Then get thee gone, and a murrain seize thee!" cried the Sheriff, and his voice trembled with anger. "And by my faith and troth I have a good part of a mind to have thee beaten for thine insolence!" Then he turned upon his heel and strode away.

It was a right motley company that gathered about the noble greenwood tree in Sherwood's depths that same day. A score and more of barefoot friars were there, and some that looked like tinkers, and some that seemed to be sturdy beggars and rustic hinds; and seated upon a mossy couch was one all clad in tattered scarlet, with a patch over one eye; and in his hand he held the golden arrow that was the prize of the great shooting-match. Then, amidst a noise of talking and laughter, he took the patch from off his eye and stripped away the scarlet rags from off his body and showed himself all clothed in fair Lincoln green, and quoth he: "Easy come these things away, but walnut stain cometh not so speedily from yellow hair." Then all laughed louder than before, for it was Robin Hood himself that had won the prize from the Sheriff's very hands.

Then all sat down to the woodland feast and talked amongst themselves of the merry jest that had been played upon the Sheriff, and of the adventures that had befallen each member of the band in his disguise. But when the feast was done, Robin Hood took Little John apart and said, "Truly am I vexed in my blood, for I heard the Sheriff say to-day, 'Thou shootest better than that coward knave, Robin Hood, that dared not show his face here this day.' I would fain let him know who it was who won the golden arrow from out his hand, and also that I am no coward such as he takes me to be."

Then Little John said, "Good master, take thou me and Will Stutely and we will send yon fat Sheriff news of all this by a messenger such as he doth not expect."

That day the Sheriff sat at meat in the great hall of his house at Nottingham Town. Long tables stood down the hall, at which sat men-at-arms and household servants and good stout villains,[1] in all fourscore and more. There they talked of the day's shooting as they ate their meat and quaffed their ale. The Sheriff sat at the head of the table upon a raised seat under a canopy, and beside him sat his dame.

"By my troth," said he, "I did reckon full roundly that that knave, Robin Hood, would be at the game to-day. I did not think that he was such a coward. But who could that saucy knave be who answered me to my beard so bravely? I wonder that I did not have him beaten; but there was something about him that spoke of other things than rags and tatters."

Then, even as he finished speaking, something fell rattling among the dishes on the table, while those that sat near started up wondering what it might be. After a while one of the men-at-arms gathered courage enough to pick it up and bring it to the Sheriff. Then every one saw that it was a blunted gray goose shaft, with a fine scroll, about the thickness of a goose quill, tied near to its head. The Sheriff opened the scroll and glanced at it, while the veins upon his forehead swelled and his cheeks grew ruddy with rage as he read, for this was what he saw:-

*"Now Heaven bless thy grace this day,*
*Say all in sweet Sherwood,*
*For thou didst give the prize away*
*To merry Robin Hood."*

"Whence came this?" cried the Sheriff in a mighty voice.

"Even through the window, your worship," quoth the man who had handed the shaft to him.

[1]Bond-servants.

## CHAPTER THREE

# WILL STUTELY RESCUED BY HIS GOOD COMPANIONS

Now when the Sheriff found that neither law nor guile could overcome Robin Hood, he was much perplexed, and said to himself, "Fool that I am! Had I not told our King of Robin Hood, I would not have gotten myself into such a coil; but now I must either take him captive or have wrath visited upon my head from his most gracious Majesty. I have tried law, and I have tried guile, and I have failed in both; so I will try what may be done with might."

Thus communing within himself, he called his constables together and told them what was in his mind. "Now take ye each four men, all armed in proof," said he, "and get ye gone to the forest, at different points, and lay in wait for this same Robin Hood. But if any constable finds too many men against him, let him sound a horn, and then let each band within hearing come with all speed and join the party that calls them. Thus, I think, shall we take this green-clad knave. Furthermore, to him that first meeteth with Robin Hood shall one hundred pounds of silver money be given, if he be brought to me, dead or alive; and to him that meeteth with any of his band shall twoscore pounds be given, if such be brought to me dead or alive. So, be ye bold and be ye crafty."

So thus they went in threescore companies of five to Sherwood Forest, to take Robin Hood, each constable wishing that he might be the one to find the bold outlaw, or at least one of his band. For seven days and nights they hunted through the forest glades, but never saw so much as a single man in Lincoln green; for tidings of all this had been brought to Robin Hood by trusty Eadom o' the Blue Boar.

When he first heard the news, Robin said, "If the Sheriff dare send force to meet force, woe will it be for him and many a better man beside, for blood will flow, and there will be great trouble for all. But fain would I shun blood and battle, and fain would I not deal sorrow to women folk and wives because good stout yeomen lose their lives. Once I slew a man, and never do I wish to slay a man again, for it is bitter for the soul to think thereon. So now we will abide silently in Sherwood Forest, so that it may be well for all; but should we be forced to defend ourselves, or any of our band, then let each man draw bow and brand with might and main."

At this speech many of the band shook their heads, and said to themselves, "Now the Sheriff will think that we are cowards, and folk will scoff throughout the countryside, saying that we fear to meet these men." But they said nothing aloud, swallowing their words, and doing as Robin bade them.

Thus they hid in the depths of Sherwood Forest for seven days and seven nights, and never showed their faces abroad in all that time; but early in the morning of the eighth day Robin Hood called the band together and said, "Now who will go and find what the Sheriff's men are at by this time? for I know right well they will not bide forever within Sherwood shades."

At this a great shout arose, and each man waved his bow aloft and cried that he might be the one to go. Then Robin Hood's heart was proud when he looked around on his stout, brave fellows, and he said, "Brave and true are ye all, my merry men, and a right stout band of good fellows are ye; but ye cannot all go, so I will choose one from amongst you, and it shall be good Will Stutely, for he is as sly as e'er an old dog fox in Sherwood Forest."

Then Will Stutely leaped high aloft and laughed loudly, clapping his hands, for pure joy that he should have been chosen from amongst them all. "Now thanks, good master," quoth he, "and if I bring not news of those knaves to thee, call me no more thy sly Will Stutely."

Then he clad himself in a friar's gown, and underneath the robe he hung a good broadsword in such a place that he could easily lay hands upon it. Thus clad, he set forth upon his quest, until he came to the verge of the forest, and so to the highway. He saw two bands of the Sheriff's men, yet he turned neither to the right nor the left, but only drew his cowl the closer over his face, folding his hands as if in meditation. So at last he came to the Sign of the Blue Boar. "For," quoth he to himself, "our good friend Eadom will tell me all the news."

At the Sign of the Blue Boar he found a band of the Sheriff's men drinking right lustily; so, without speaking to any one, he sat down upon a distant bench, his staff in his hand, and his head bowed forward as though he were meditating. Thus he sat waiting until he might see the landlord apart, and Eadom did not know him, but thought him to be some poor tired friar, so he let him sit without saying a word to him or molesting him, though he liked not the cloth; "for," said he to himself, "it is a hard heart that kicks the lame dog from off the sill."

As Stutely sat thus, there came a great house cat and rubbed against his knee, raising his robe a palm's breadth high. Stutely pushed his robe quickly down again, but the constable who commanded the Sheriff's men saw what had passed, and saw also fair Lincoln green beneath the friar's robe. He said nothing at the time, but communed within himself in this wise: "Yon is no friar of orders gray, and also, I wot, no honest yeoman goeth about in priest's garb, nor doth a thief go so for naught. Now I think in good sooth that is one of Robin Hood's own men." So, presently, he said aloud:-

"O holy father, wilt thou not take a good pot of March beer to slake thy thirsty soul withal?" But Stutely shook his head silently, for he said to himself, "Maybe there be those here who know my voice."

Then the constable said again, "Wither goest thou, holy friar, upon this hot summer's day?"

"I go a pilgrim to Canterbury Town," answered Will Stutely, speaking gruffly, so that none might know his voice.

Then the constable said, for the third time, "Now tell me, holy father, do pilgrims to Canterbury wear good Lincoln green beneath their robes? Ha! by my faith, I take thee to be some lusty thief, and perhaps one of Robin Hood's own band! Now, by Our Lady's grace, if thou movest hand or foot, I will run thee through the body with my sword!"

Then he flashed forth his bright sword and leaped upon Will Stutely, thinking he would take him unaware; but Stutely had his own sword tightly held in his hand, beneath his robe, so he drew it forth before the constable came upon him. Then the stout constable struck a mighty blow; but he struck no more in all that fight, for Stutely, parrying the blow right deftly, smote the constable back again with all his might. Then he would have escaped, but could not, for the other, all dizzy with the wound and with the flowing blood, seized him by the knees with his arms even as he reeled and fell. Then the others rushed upon him, and Stutely struck again at another of the Sheriff's men, but the steel cap glanced the blow, and though the blade bit deep, it did not kill. Meanwhile, the constable, fainting as he was, drew Stutely downward, and the others, seeing the yeoman hampered so, rushed upon him again, and one smote him a blow upon the crown so that the blood ran down his face and blinded him. Then, staggering, he fell, and all sprang upon him, though he struggled so manfully that they could hardly hold him fast. Then they bound him with stout hempen cords, so that he could not move either hand or foot, and thus they overcame him. But it was a doleful day's doings for two of that band; for the constable was sorely wounded, and the other, that Stutely smote upon the crown, lay sick for many a day ere he was the stout man that he had been before this famous fight.

Robin Hood stood under the greenwood tree, thinking of Will Stutely and how he might be faring, when suddenly he saw two of his stout yeomen come running down the forest path, and betwixt them ran buxom Maken of the Blue Boar. Then Robin's heart fell, for he knew they were the bearers of ill tidings.

"Will Stutely hath been taken," cried they, when they had come to where he stood.

"And is it thou that hast brought such doleful news?" said Robin to the lass.

"Ay, marry, for I saw it all,' cried she, panting as the hare pants when it has escaped the hounds; "and I fear he is wounded sore, for one smote him main shrewdly i' the crown. They have bound him and taken him to Nottingham Town, and ere I left the Blue Boar I heard that he should be hanged to-morrow day."

"He shall not be hanged to-morrow day," cried Robin; or, if he be, full many a one shall gnaw the sod, and many shall have cause to cry Alack-a-day!"

Then he clapped his horn to his lips and blew three blasts right loudly, and presently his good yeomen came running through the greenwood until sevenscore bold blades were gathered around him.

"Now hark you all!" cried Robin. "Our dear companion, Will Stutely, hath been taken by that vile Sheriff's men, therefore doth it behoove us to take bow and brand in hand to bring him off again; for I wot that we ought to risk life and limb for him, as he hath risked life and limb for us. Is it not so, my merry men all?" Then all cried, "Ay!" with a great voice.

"Now," quoth Robin again, "if there be any here that care not to risk life and limb, let them bide within Sherwood shades, for I constrain no man to my will; to-morrow I will bring Will Stutely back or I will die with him."

Then up spake stout Little John. "Thinkest thou, good master," he said, "that there be one among us all that would not risk life and limb for fellow in trouble? If such there be, then do not I know every man in this company of stout yeomen. And, moreover, if there be such, I wot he should be stripped and beaten from out our merry woodlands. Is it not so, good friends?"

Then all cried, "Ay!" again, for there was not one man amongst them all that would not venture everything for a friend in need.

So the next day they all wended their way from Sherwood Forest, but by different paths, for it behooved them to be very crafty; so the band separated into parties of twos and threes, which were all to meet again in a tangled dell that lay near to Nottingham Town. Then, when they had all gathered together at the place of meeting, Robin spoke to them thus:-

"Now we will lie here in ambush until we can get news, for it doth behoove us to be cunning and wary if we would bring our friend, Will Stutely, off from the Sheriff's clutches."

So they lay hidden a long time, until the sun stood high in the sky. The day was warm and the dusty road was bare of travellers, except an aged palmer who walked slowly along the high-road that led close beside the gray castle wall of Nottingham Town. When Robin saw that no other wayfarer was within sight, he called young David of Doncaster, who was a shrewd man for his years, and said to him, "Now get thee forth, young David, and speak to yonder palmer that walks beside the town wall, for he hath come but now from Nottingham Town, and may tell thee news of good Stutely, perchance."

So David strode forth, and when he came up to the pilgrim, he saluted him and said: "Good morrow, holy father, and canst thou tell me when Will Stutely will be hanged upon the gallows tree? I fain would not miss the sight, for I have come from afar to see so sturdy a rogue hanged."

"Now, out upon thee, young man," cried the Palmer, "that thou shouldst speak so when a good stout man is to be hanged for nothing but guarding his own life!" and he struck his staff upon the ground in anger. "Alas, say I, that this thing should be! for even this day, toward evening, when the sun falleth low, he shall be hanged, fourscore rods from the great town gate of Nottingham, where three roads meet; for there the Sheriff sweareth he shall die as a warning to all outlaws in Nottinghamshire. But yet, I say again, Alas! for, though Robin Hood and his band may be outlaws, yet he taketh only from the rich and the strong and the dishonest man, while there is not a poor widow nor a peasant with many children, nigh to Sherwood, but has barley-flour enough all the year long through him. It grieves my heart to see one as gallant as this Stutely die, for I have been a good Saxon yeoman in my day, ere I turned palmer, and well I know a stout hand and one that smiteth shrewdly at a cruel Norman or a proud abbot with fat money-bags. Had good Stutely's master but known how his man was compassed about with perils, perchance he might send succor to bring him out of the hand of his enemies."

"Ay, marry, that is true," cried the young man. "If Robin and his men be nigh this place, I wot right well they will strive to bring him forth from his peril. But fare thee well, thou good old man, and believe me, that, if Will Stutely die, he shall be right well avenged."

Then he turned and strode rapidly away; but the Palmer looked after him, muttering, "I wot that youth is no country hind that hath come to see a good man die. Well, well, perchance Robin Hood is not so far away but that there will be stout doings this day." So he went upon his way, muttering to himself.

When David of Doncaster told Robin Hood what the Palmer had said to him, Robin called the band around him and spoke to them thus:

"Now let us get straightway into Nottingham Town, and mix ourselves with the people there; but keep ye one another in sight, pressing as near the prisoner and his guards as ye can, when they come outside the walls. Strike no man without need, for I would fain avoid bloodshed, but if ye do strike, strike hard, and see that there be no need to strike again. Then keep all together until we come again to Sherwood, and let no man leave his fellows."

The sun was low in the western sky when a bugle-note sounded from the castle wall. Then all was bustle in Nottingham Town and crowds filled the streets, for all knew that the famous Will Stutely was to be hanged that day. Presently then castle gates opened wide and a great array of men-at-arms came forth with noise and clatter, the Sheriff, all clad in shining mail of linked chain, riding at their head. In the midst of all the guard, in a cart, with a halter about his neck, rode Will Stutely. His face was pale with his wound and with loss of blood, like the moon in broad daylight, and his fair hair was clotted in points upon his forehead, where the blood had hardened. When he came forth from the castle he looked up and he looked down, but though he saw some faces that showed pity and some that showed friendliness, he saw none that he knew. Then his heart sank within him like a plummet of lead, but nevertheless he spoke up boldly.

"Give a sword into my hand, Sir Sheriff," said he, "and wounded man though I be, I will fight thee and all thy men till life and strength be gone."

"Nay, thou naughty varlet," quoth the Sheriff, turning his head and looking right grimly upon Will Stutely, "thou shalt have no sword but shall die a mean death, as beseemeth a vile thief like thee."

"Then do but untie my hands and I will fight thee and thy men with no weapon but only my naked fists. I crave no weapon, but let me not be meanly hanged this day."

Then the Sheriff laughed aloud. "Why, how now," quoth he, "is thy proud stomach quailing? Shrive thyself, thou vile knave, for I mean that thou shalt hang this day, and that where three roads meet, so that all men shall see thee hang, for carrion crows and daws to peck at."

"O thou dastard heart!" cried Will stutely, gnashing his teeth at the Sheriff. "Thou coward hind! If ever my good master meet thee thou shalt pay dearly for this day's work! He doth scorn thee, and so do all brave hearts. Knowest thou not that thou and thy name are jests upon the lips of every brave yeoman? Such a one as thou art, thou wretched craven, will never be able to subdue bold Robin Hood."

"Ha!" cried the Sheriff, in a rage, "is it even so? Am I a jest with thy master, as thou callest him? Now I will make a jest of thee and a sorry jest withal, for I will quarter thee limb from limb, after thou art hanged." Then he spurred his horse forward, and said no more to Stutely.

At last they came to the great town gate, through which Stutely saw the fair country beyond, with hills and dales all clothed in verdure, and far away the dusky line of Sherwood's skirts. Then when he saw the slanting sunlight lying on field and fallow, shining redly here and there on cot and farmhouse, and when he heard the sweet birds singing their vespers, and the sheep bleating upon the hillside, and beheld the swallows flying in the bright air, there came a great fulness to his heart so that all things blurred to his sight through salt tears, and he bowed his head lest the folk should think him unmanly when they saw the tears in his eyes. Thus he kept his head bowed till they had passed through the gate and were outside the walls of the town. But when he looked up again he felt his heart leap within him and then stand still for pure joy, for he saw the face of one of his own dear companions of merry Sherwood; then glancing quickly around he saw well-known faces upon all sides of him crowding closely upon the men-at-arms who were guarding him. Then of a sudden the blood sprang to his cheeks, for he saw for a moment his own good master in the press, and, seeing him, knew that Robin Hood and all his band were there. Yet betwixt him and them was a line of men-at-arms.

"Now, stand back!" cried the Sheriff in a mighty voice, for the crowd pressed around on all sides. "What means ye, varlets, that ye push upon us so? Stand back, I say!"

Then came a bustle and a noise, and one strove to push between the men-at-arms so as to reach the cart, and Stutely saw that it was Little John that made all that stir.

"Now stand thou back!" cried one of the men-at-arms whom Little John pushed with his elbows.

"Now stand thou back thine own self," quoth Little John, and straightway smote the man a buffet beside his head that felled him as a butcher fells an ox, and then he leaped to the cart where Stutely sat.

"I pray thee take leave of thy friends ere thou diest, Will," quoth he, "or maybe I will die with thee if thou must die, for I could never have better company." Then with one stroke he cut the bonds that bound the other's arms and legs, and Stutely leaped straightway from the cart.

"Now as I live," cried the Sheriff, "you varlet I know right well is a sturdy rebel! Take him, I bid you all, and let him not go!"

So saying he spurred his horse upon Little John, and rising in his stirrups smote with might and main, but Little John ducked quickly underneath the horse's belly and the blow whistled harmlessly over his head.

"Nay, good Sir Sheriff, cried he, leaping up again when the blow had passed, "I must e'en borrow thy most worshipful sword." Thereupon he twitched the weapon deftly from out the Sheriff's hand. "Here, Stutely," he cried, "the Sheriff hath lent thee his sword! Back to back with me, man, and defend thyself, for help is nigh!"

"Down with them!" bellowed the Sheriff in a voice like an angry bull; and he spurred his horse upon the two who now stood back to back, forgetting in his rage that he had no weapon with which to defend himself.

"Stand back, Sheriff!" cried Little John; and even as he spoke, a bugle-horn sounded shrilly, and a clothyard shaft whistled within an inch of the Sheriff's head. Then there came a swaying hither and thither and oaths and cries and groans and clashing of steel, and swords flashed in the setting sun, and a score of arrows whistled through the air: and some cried "Help, help!" and some, 'A rescue, a rescue!"

"Treason!" cried the Sheriff in a loud voice. "Bear back! bear back! else we be all dead men!" Thereupon he reined his horse backward through the thickest of the crowd.

Now Robin Hood and his band might have slain half of the Sheriff's men had they desired to do so, but they let them push out of the press and get them gone, only sending a bunch of arrows after them in their flight.

"Oh stay!" shouted Will Stutely after the Sheriff. "Thou wilt never catch bold Robin Hood if thou dost not stand to meet him face to face." But the Sheriff, bowing along his horse's back, made no answer but only spurred the faster.

Then Will Stutely turned to Little John and looked him in the face till the tears ran down from his eyes and he wept aloud, and kissing his friend's cheeks, "O Little John!" quoth he, "mine own true friend, and he that I love better than man or woman in all the world beside! Little did I reckon to see thy face this day, or to meet thee this side Paradise." And Little John could make no answer, but wept also.

Then Robin Hood gathered his band together in a close rank, with Will Stutely in the midst, and thus they moved slowly away toward Sherwood, and were gone, as a storm-cloud moves away from the spot where a tempest has swept the land. But they left ten of the Sheriff's men lying along the ground wounded – some more, some less – yet no one knew who smote them down.

Thus the Sheriff of Nottingham tried thrice to take Robin Hood and failed each time; and the last time he was frightened, for he felt how near he had come to losing his life; so he said: "These men fear neither God nor man, nor King nor King's officers. I would sooner lose mine office than my life, so I will trouble them no more." So he kept close within his castle for many a day and dared not show his face outside of his own household, and all the time he was gloomy and would speak to no one, for he was ashamed of what had happened that day.

# PART SECOND

*In which shall be told how Robin Hood turned Butcher, and how he revenged himself upon the Sheriff. Also, of the famous adventures that befel Little John at the Nottingham Archery Match, and how he entered the Sheriff's service.*

## Chapter One

# Robin Hood Turns Butcher

Now after all these things had happened, and it became known to Robin Hood how the Sheriff had tried three times to make him captive, he said to himself: "If I have the chance, I will make our worshipful Sheriff pay right well for that which he hath done to me. Maybe I may bring him some time into Sherwood Forest, and have him to a right merry feast with us." For when Robin Hood caught a baron or a squire, or a fat abbot or bishop, he brought them to the greenwood tree and feasted them before he lightened their purses.

But in the mean time Robin Hood and his band lived quietly in Sherwood Forest, without showing their faces abroad, for Robin knew that it would not be wise for him to be seen in the neighborhood of Nottingham, those in authority being very wroth with him. But though they did not go abroad, they lived a merry life within the woodlands, spending the days in shooting at garlands hung upon a willow wand at the end of the glade, the leafy aisles ringing with merry jests and laughter: for whoever missed the garland was given a sound buffet, which, if delivered by Little John, never failed to topple over the unfortunate yeoman. Then they had bouts of wrestling and of cudgel play, so that every day they gained in skill and strength.

Thus they dwelt for nearly a year, and in that time Robin Hood often turned over in his mind many means of making an even score with the Sheriff. At last he began to fret at his confinement; so one day he took up his stout cudgel and set forth to seek adventure, strolling blithely along until he came to the edge of Sherwood. There, as he rambled along the sunlit road, he met a lusty young Butcher driving a fine mare, and riding in a stout new cart, all hung about with meat. Merrily whistled the Butcher as he jogged along, for he was going to the market, and the day was fresh and sweet, making his heart blithe within him.

"Good morrow to thee, jolly fellow," quoth Robin; "thou seemest happy this merry morn."

"Ay, that am I," quoth the jolly Butcher; "and why should I not be so? Am I not hale in wind and limb? Have I not the bonniest lass in all Nottinghamshire? And lastly, am I not to be married to her on Thursday next in sweet Locksley Town?"

"Ha," said Robin, "comest thou from Locksley Town? Well do I know that fair place for miles about, and well do I know each hedgerow and gentle pebbly stream, and even all the bright little fishes therein, for there I was born and bred. Now, where goest thou with thy meat, my fair friend?"

"I go to the market at Nottingham Town to sell my beef and my mutton," answered the Butcher. "But who art thou that comest from Locksley Town?"

"A yeoman am I, good friend, and men do call me Robin Hood."

"Now, by Our Lady's grace, cried the Butcher, "well do I know thy name, and many a time have I heard thy deeds both sung and spoken of. But Heaven forbid that thou shouldst take ought of me! An honest man am I, and have wronged neither man nor maid; so trouble me not, good master, as I have never troubled thee."

"Nay, Heaven forbid, indeed," quoth Robin, "that I should take from such as thee, jolly fellow! Not so much as one farthing would I take from thee, for I love a fair Saxon face like thine right well; more especially when it cometh from Locksley Town, and most especially when the man that owneth it is to marry a bonny lass on Thursday next. But come, tell me for what price thou wilt sell all thy meat and thy horse and cart."

"At four marks do I value meat, cart, and mare," quoth the Butcher; "but if I do not sell all my meat I will not have four marks in value."

Then Robin Hood plucked the purse from his girdle, and quoth he, "Here in this purse are six marks. Now, I would fain be a butcher for the day and sell my meat in Nottingham Town, and thou close a bargain with me and take six marks for thine outfit?"

"Now may the blessings of all the saints fall on thine honest head!" cried the Butcher right joyfully, as he leaped down from his cart and took the purse that Robin held out to him.

"Nay," quoth Robin, laughing loudly, "many do like me and wish me well, but few call me honest. Now get thee gone back to thy lass, and give her a sweet kiss from me." So saying, he donned the Butcher's apron, and, climbing into the cart, he took the reins in his hand, and drove off through the forest to Nottingham Town.

When he came to Nottingham, he entered that part of the market where butchers stood, and took up his inn[1] in the best place he could find. Next, he opened his stall and spread his meat upon the bench, then, taking his cleaver and steel and clattering them together, he trolled aloud, in merry tones:-

*"Now come, ye lasses, and eke, ye dames,*
*And buy your meat from me;*
*For three pennyworths of meat I sell*
*For the charge of one penny.*

*"Lamb have I that hath fed upon nought*
*But the dainty daisies pied,*
*And the violet sweet, and the daffodil*
*That grow fair streams beside.*

*"And beef have I from the heathery wolds,*
*And mutton from dales all green,*
*And veal as white as a maiden's brow,*
*With its mother's milk, I ween.*

*"Then come, ye lasses, and eke, ye dames,*
*Come, buy your meat from me;*
*For three pennyworths of meat I sell*
*For the charge of one penny."*

Thus he sang blithely, while all who stood near listened amazedly; then, when he had finished, he clattered the steel and cleaver still more loudly, shouting lustily, "Now, who'll buy? Four fixed prices have I. Three pennyworths of meat I sell to a fat friar or priest for sixpence, for I want not their custom; stout aldermen I charge threepence, for it doth not matter to me whether they buy or not; to buxom dames I sell three pennyworths of meat for one penny, for I like their custom well; but to the bonny lass that hath a liking for a good tight butcher I charge nought but one fair kiss, for I like her custom the best of all."

Then all began to stare and wonder, and crowd around, laughing, for never was such selling heard of in all Nottingham Town; but when they came to buy they found it as he had said, for he gave good wife or dame as much meat for one penny as they could buy elsewhere for three, and when a widow or a poor woman came to him, he gave her flesh for nothing; but when a merry lass came and gave him a kiss, he charged not one penny for his meat; and many such came to his stall, for his eyes were as blue as the skies of June, and he laughed merrily, giving to each full measure. Thus he sold his meat so fast that no butcher that stood near him could sell anything.

Then they began to talk among themselves, and some said, "This must be some thief who has stolen cart, horse, and meat;" but others said, "Nay, when did ye ever see a thief who parted with his goods so freely and merrily? This must be some prodigal who hath sold his father's land, and would fain live merrily while the money

[1]Stand for selling.

lasts." And these latter being the greater number, the others came round, one by one, to their way of thinking.

Then some of the butchers came to him to make his acquaintance. "Come, brother," quoth one who was the head of them all, "we be all of one trade, so wilt thou go dine with us? For this day the Sheriff hath asked all the Butchers Guild to feast with him at the Guild Hall. There will be stout fare and much to drink, and that thou likest, or I much mistake thee."

"Now, beshrew his heart," quoth jolly Robin, "that would deny a butcher. And, moreover, I will go dine with you all, my sweet lads, and that as fast as I can hie." Whereupon, having sold all his meat, he closed his stall, and went with them to the great Guild Hall.

There the Sheriff had already come in state, and with him many butchers. When Robin and those that were with him came in, all laughing at some merry jest he had been telling them, those that were near the Sheriff whispered to him, "Yon is a right mad blade, for he hath sold more meat for one penny this day than we could sell for three, and to whatsoever merry lass gave him a kiss he gave meat for nought." And others said, "He is some prodigal that hath sold his land for silver and gold, and meaneth to spend all right merrily."

Then the Sheriff called Robin to him, not knowing him in his butcher's dress, and made him sit close to him on his right hand; for he loved a rich young prodigal – especially when he thought that he might lighten that prodigal's pockets into his own most worshipful purse. So he made much of Robin, and laughed and talked with him more than with any of the others.

At last the dinner was ready to be served and the Sheriff bade Robin say grace, so Robin stood up and said: "Now Heaven bless us all and eke good meat and good sack within this house, and may all butchers be and remain as honest men as I am."

At this all laughed, the Sheriff loudest of all, for he said to himself, "Surely this is indeed some prodigal, and perchance I may empty his purse of some of the money that the fool throweth about so freely." Then he spake aloud to Robin, saying: "Thou art a jolly young blade, and I love thee mightily;" and he smote Robin upon the shoulder.

Then Robin laughed loudly too. "Yea," quoth he, "I know thou dost love a jolly blade, for didst thou not have jolly Robin Hood at thy shooting-match and didst thou not gladly give him a bright golden arrow for his own?"

At this the Sheriff looked grave and all the guild of butchers too, so that none laughed but Robin, only some winked slyly at each other.

"Come, fill us some sack!" cried Robin. "Let us e'er be merry while we may, for man is but dust, and he hath but a span to live here till the worm getteth him, as our good gossip Swanthold sayeth; so let life be merry while it lasts, say I. Nay, never look down i' the mouth, Sir Sheriff. Who knowest but that thou mayest catch Robin Hood yet if thou drinkest less good sack and Malmsey, and bringest down the fat about thy paunch and the dust from out thy brain. Be merry, man."

Then the Sheriff laughed again, but not as though he liked the jest, while the butchers said, one to another, "Before Heaven, never have we seen such a mad rollicking blade. Mayhap, though, he will make the Sheriff mad."

"How now, brothers," cried Robin, "be merry! nay, never count over your farthings, for by this and by that I will pay this shot myself, e'en though it cost two hundred pounds. So let no man draw up his lip, nor thrust his forefinger into his purse, for I swear that neither butcher nor Sheriff shall pay one penny for this feast."

"Now thou art a right merry soul," quoth the Sheriff, "and I wot thou must have many a head of horned beasts and many an acre of land, that thou dost spend thy money so freely."

"Ay, that have I," quoth Robin, laughing loudly again, "five hundred and more horned beasts have I and my brothers, and none of them have we been able to sell, else I might not have turned butcher. As for my land, I have never asked my steward how many acres I have."

At this the Sheriff's eyes twinkled, and he chuckled to himself. "Nay, good youth," quoth he, "if thou canst not sell thy cattle it may be I will find a man that will lift them from thy hands; perhaps that man may be myself, for I love a merry youth and would help such a one along the path of life. Now how much dost thou want for thy horned cattle?"

"Well," quoth Robin, "they are worth at least five hundred pounds."

"Nay," answered the Sheriff, slowly, and as if he were thinking within himself; "well do I love thee, and fain would I help thee along, but five hundred pounds in money is a good round sum; beside I have it not by me. Yet I will give thee three hundred pounds for them all, and that in good hard silver and gold."

"Now thou old Jew!" quoth Robin; "well thou knowest that so many horned cattle are worth seven hundred pounds and more, and even that is but small for them, and yet thou, with thy gray hairs and one foot in the grave, wouldst trade upon the folly of a wild youth."

At this the Sheriff looked grimly at Robin. "Nay," quoth Robin, "look not on me as though thou hadst sour beer in thy mouth, man. I will take thine offer, for I and my brothers do need the money. We lead a merry life, and no one leads a merry life for a farthing, so I will close the bargain with thee. But mind that thou bringest a good three hundred pounds with thee, for I trust not one that driveth so shrewd a bargain."

"I will bring the money," said the Sheriff. "But what is thy name, good youth?"

"Men call me Robert o' Locksley," quoth bold Robin.

"Then, good Robert o' Locksley," quoth then Sheriff, "I will come this day to see thy horned beasts. But first my clerk shall draw up a paper in which thou shalt be bound to the sale, for thou gettest not my money without I get thy beasts in return."

Then Robin Hood laughed again. "So be it," he cried, smiting his palm upon the Sheriff's hand. "Truly my brothers will be thankful to thee for thy money."

Thus the bargain was closed; but many of the butchers talked among themselves of the Sheriff, saying that it was but a scurvy trick to beguile a poor spendthrift youth in this way.

The afternoon had come when the Sheriff mounted his horse and joined Robin Hood, who stood outside the gateway of the paved court waiting for him, for he had sold his horse and cart to a trader for two marks. Then they set forth upon their way, the Sheriff riding upon his horse and Robin running beside him. Thus they left Nottingham Town and travelled forward along the dusty highway, laughing and jesting together as though they had been old friends; but all the time the Sheriff said within himself, "Thy jest to me of Robin Hood shall cost thee dear, good fellow, even four hundred pounds, thou fool." For he thought he would make at least that much by his bargain.

So they journeyed onward till they came within the verge of Sherwood Forest, when presently the Sheriff looked up and down and to the right and to the left of him and then grew quiet and ceased his laughter. "Now," quoth he, "may Heaven and its saints preserve us this day from a rogue man call Robin Hood."

Then Robin laughed aloud. "Nay," said he, "thou mayst set thy mind at rest, for well do I know Robin Hood and well do I know that thou art in no more danger from him this day than thou art from me."

At this the Sheriff looked askance at Robin, saying to himself, "I like not that thou seemest so well acquainted with this bold outlaw, and I wish that I were well out of Sherwood Forest."

But still they travelled deeper into the forest shades, and the deeper they went the more quiet grew the Sheriff. At last they came to where the road took a sudden bend, and before them a herd of dun deer went tripping across the path. Then Robin Hood came close to the Sheriff and pointing his finger he said, "These are my horned beasts, good Master Sheriff. How dost thou like them? Are they not fat and fair to see?"

At this the Sheriff drew rein quickly. "Now fellow," quoth he, "I would I were well out of this forest, for I like not thy company. Go thou thine own path, good friend, and let me but go mine."

But Robin only laughed and caught the Sheriff's bridle rein. "Nay," cried he, "stay a while, for I would thou shouldst see my brothers who own these fair horned beasts with me." So saying he clapped his bugle to his mouth and winded three merry notes, and presently up the path came leaping fivescore good stout yeomen with Little John at their head.

"What wouldst thou have, good master?" quoth Little John.

"Why," answered Robin, "dost thou not see that I have brought goodly company to feast with us to-day? Fye, for shame! do you not see out good and worshipful master, the Sheriff of Nottingham? Take thou his bridle, Little John, for he has honored us to-day by coming to feast with us."

Then all doffed their hats humbly, without smiling, or seeming to be in jest, whilst Little John took the bridle rein and led the palfrey still deeper into the forest, all marching in order, with Robin Hood walking beside the Sheriff, hat in hand.

All this time the Sheriff said never a word but only looked about him like one suddenly awakened from sleep; but when he found himself going within the very depth of Sherwood his heart sank within him, for he thought, "Surely my three hundred pounds will be taken from me, even if they take not my life itself, for I have plotted against their lives more than once." But all seemed humble and meek and not a word was said of danger, either to life or money.

So at last they came to that part of Sherwood Forest where a noble oak spread its branches wide, and beneath it was a seat all made of moss, on which Robin sat down, placing the Sheriff at his right hand. "Now busk ye, my merry men all," quoth he, "and bring forth the best we have, both of meat and wine, for his worship, the Sheriff, hath feasted me in Nottingham Guild Hall to-day, and I would not have him go back empty."

All this time nothing had been said of the Sheriff's money, so presently he began to pluck up heart; "For," said he to himself, "maybe Robin Hood hath forgotten all about it."

Then, whilst beyond in the forest bright fires crackled and savory smells of sweetly roasting venison and fat capons filled the glade, and brown pasties warmed beside the blaze, did Robin Hood entertain the Sheriff right royally. First, several couples stood forth at quarterstaff, and so shrewd were they at the game, and so quickly did they give stroke and parry, that the Sheriff, who loved to watch all lusty sports of the kind, clapped his hands, forgetting where he was, and crying aloud, "Well struck! well struck, thou fellow with the black beard!" little knowing that the man he called upon was the Tinker that tried to serve his warrant upon Robin Hood.

Then the best archers of the band set up a fair garland of flowers at eightscore paces distance, and shot at it with the cunningest archery practice. But the Sheriff grew grave, for he did not like this so well, the famous meeting at the butts in Nottingham Town being still green in his memory, and the golden arrow that had been won there hanging close behind him. Then, when Robin saw what was in the Sheriff's mind, he stopped the sport, and called forth some of his band, who sang merry ballads, while others made music upon the harp.

When this was done, several yeomen came forward and spread cloths upon the green grass, and placed a royal feast; while others still broached barrels of sack and Malmsey and good stout ale, and set them in jars upon the cloth, with drinking-horns about them. Then all sat down and feasted and drank merrily together until the sun was low and the half-moon glimmered with a pale light betwixt the leaves of the trees overhead.

Then the Sheriff arose and said, "I thank you all, good yeomen, for the merry entertainment ye have given me this day. Right courteously have ye used me, showing therein that ye have much respect for our glorious King and his deputy in brave Nottinghamshire. But the shadows grow long, and I must away before darkness comes, lest I lose myself within the forest."

Then Robin Hood and all his merry men arose also, and Robin said to the Sheriff, "If thou must go, worshipful sir, go thou must; but thou hast forgotten one thing."

"Nay, I forgot nought," said the Sheriff; yet all the same his heart sank within him.

"But I say thou hast forgot something," quoth Robin. "We keep a merry inn here in the greenwood, but whoever becometh our guest must pay his reckoning."

Then the Sheriff laughed, but the laugh was hollow. "Well, jolly boys," quoth he, "we have had a merry time together to-day, and even if ye had not asked me, I would have given you a score of pounds for the sweet entertainment I have had."

"Nay," quoth Robin seriously, "it would ill beseem us to treat your worship so meanly. By my faith, Sir Sheriff, I would be ashamed to show my face if I did not reckon the King's deputy at three hundred pounds. Is it not so, my merry men all?"

Then "Ay!" cried all, in a loud voice.

"Three hundred devils!" roared the Sheriff. "Think ye that your beggarly feast was worth three pounds, let alone three hundred?"

"Nay," quoth Robin, gravely. "Speak not so roundly, your worship. I do love thee for the sweet feast thou hast given me this day in merry Nottingham Town; but there be those here who love thee not so much. If thou wilt look down the cloth thou wilt see Will Stutely, in whose eyes thou hast no great favor; then two other stout fellows are there here that thou knowest not, that were wounded in a brawl nigh Nottingham Town, some time ago – thou wottest when; one of them was sore hurt in one arm, yet he hath got the use of it again. Good Sheriff, be advised by me; pay the score without more ado, or maybe it may fare ill with thee."

As he spoke the Sheriff's ruddy cheeks grew pale, and he said nothing more but looked upon the ground and gnawed his nether lip. Then slowly he drew forth his fat purse and threw it upon the cloth in front of him.

"Now take the purse, Little John," quoth Robin Hood, "and see that the reckoning be right. We would not doubt our Sheriff, but he might not like it if he should find he had not paid his full score."

Then Little John counted the money, and found that the bag held three hundred pounds in silver and gold. But to the Sheriff it seemed as if every clink of the bright money was a drop of blood from his veins; and when he saw it all counted out in a heap of silver and gold, filling a wooden platter, he turned away and silently mounted his horse.

"Never have we had so worshipful a guest before!" quoth Robin; "and, as the day waxeth late, I will send one of my young men to guide thee out of the forest depths."

"Nay, heaven forbid!" cried the Sheriff, hastily. "I can find mine own way, good man, without aid."

"Then I will put thee on the right track mine own self," quoth Robin; and, taking the Sheriff's horse by the bridle rein, he led him into the main forest path; then, before he let him go, he said, "Now, fare thee well, good Sheriff, and when next thou thinkest to despoil some poor prodigal, remember thy feast in Sherwood Forest. 'Ne'er buy a horse, good friend, without first looking into its mouth,' as our good gaffer Swanthold says. And so, once more, fare thee well." Then he clapped his hand to the horse's back, and off went nag and Sheriff through the forest glades.

Then bitterly the Sheriff rued the day that first he meddled with Robin Hood, for all men laughed at him and many ballads were sung by folk throughout the country, of how the Sheriff went to shear and came home shorn to the very quick. For thus men sometimes overreach themselves through greed and guile.

*"We will fight until one of us tumble into the stream." (Prologue)*

*The shaft flew straight, the archer fell forward with a cry*
*(Prologue)*

## Chapter Two

# Little John goes to the Fair at Nottingham Town

Now we will tell of the merry adventures that befell Little John at the shooting-match at Nottingham, and how he overcame Eric o' Lincoln in the famous bout at quarterstaff in that town; also how he entered the Sheriff's service, and of his merry encounter with the Sheriff's cook. So listen to what follows.

Spring had gone since the Sheriff's feast in Sherwood, and summer also, and the mellow month of October had come. All the air was cool and fresh; the harvests were gathered home, the young birds were full fledged, the hops were plucked, and apples were ripe. But though time had so smoothed things over that men no longer talked of the horned beasts that the Sheriff wished to buy, he was still sore about the matter and could not bear to hear Robin Hood's name spoken in his presence.

With October had come the time for holding the great Fair which was celebrated every five years at Nottingham Town, to which folk came from far and near throughout the country. At such times archery was always the main sport of the day, for the Nottinghamshire yeomen were the best hand at the longbow in all Merry England; but this year the Sheriff hesitated a long time before he issued a proclamation of the Fair, fearing lest Robin Hood and his band might come to it. At first he had a great part of a mind not to proclaim the Fair, but second thought told him that men would laugh at him and say among themselves that he was afraid of Robin Hood, as he put that thought by. At last he fixed in his mind that he would offer such a prize as they would not care to shoot for. At such times it had been the custom to offer a half score of marks or a tin of ale, so this year he proclaimed that a prize of two fat steer should be given to the best bowman.

When Robin Hood heard what had been proclaimed he was vexed, and said, "Now beshrew this Sheriff that he should offer such a prize that none but shepherd hinds will care to shoot for it! I would have loved nothing better than to have had another bout at merry Nottingham Town, but if I should win this prize naught would it pleasure or profit me."

Then up spoke Little John: "Nay, hearken, good master," said he, "only to-day Will Stutely, young David of Doncaster, and I were at the sign of the Blue Boar, and there we heard all the news of this merry Fair, and also that the Sheriff hath offered this prize that we of Sherwood might not care to come to the Fair; so, good master, if thou wilt, I would fain go and strive to win even this poor thing among the stout yeomen who will shoot at Nottingham Town."

"Nay, Little John," quoth Robin, "thou art a sound stout fellow, yet thou lackest the cunning that good Stutely hath, and I would not have harm befall thee for all Nottinghamshire. Nevertheless if thou wilt go, take some disguise lest there be those there who may know thee."

"So be it, good master," quoth Little John; "yet all the disguise that I wish is a good suit of scarlet instead of this of Lincoln green. I will draw the cowl of my jacket about my head so that it will hide my brown hair and beard, and then, I trust, no one will know me."

"It is much against my will," said Robin Hood, "ne'ertheless, if thou dost wish it, get thee gone, but bear thyself seemingly, Little John, for thou art mine own right hand man and I could ill bear to have harm befall thee."

So Little John clad himself all in scarlet, and started off to the Fair at Nottingham Town.

Right merry were these Fair days at Nottingham, when the green before the great town gate was dotted with booths standing in rows, with tents of many-colored canvas, hung about with streamers and garlands of flowers, and the folk came from all the countryside, both gentle and common. In some booths there was dancing to merry music, in others flowed ale and beer, and in others yet again sweet cakes and barley sugar were sold; and sport was going outside the booths also, where some minstrel sang ballads of the olden time, playing a second upon the harp, or where the wrestlers struggled with one another within the sawdust ring; but the people gathered most of all around a raised platform where stout fellows played at quarterstaff.

So Little John came to the Fair. All scarlet were his hose and jerkin, and scarlet was his cowled cap, with a scarlet feather stuck in the side of it. Over his shoulders was slung a stout bow of yew, and across his back hung a quiver of good round arrows. Many turned to look after such a stout, tall fellow, for his shoulders were broader by a palm's breadth than any that were there, and he stood a head taller than all the other men. The lasses, also, looked at him askance, thinking they had never seen a lustier youth.

First of all he went to the booth where stout ale was sold, and, standing aloft on a bench, he called to all that were near to come and drink with him. "Hey, sweet lads!" cried he, "who will drink ale with a stout yeoman? Come, all! come, all! Let us be merry, for the day is sweet and the ale is tingling. Come hither, good yeoman, and thou, and thou; for not a farthing shall one of you pay. Nay, turn hither, thou lusty beggar, and thou jolly tinker, for all shall be merry with me."

Thus he shouted, and all crowded around, laughing, while the brown ale flowed; and they called Little John a brave fellow, each swearing that he loved him as his own brother; for when one has entertainment with nothing to pay, one loves the man that gives it to one.

The next place Little John went to was the dancing booth, where three men made sweet music with bagpipes. Here he laid aside his bow and his quiver, and joined in the sport, dancing so long that none could stand against him. A score of lasses came, one after another, and strove to dance him down, but could not do so; for Little John leaped so high, snapping his fingers the while, and shouted so loud, that every lass vowed that she had never seen so sweet a lad in all her life before.

Then, after he had danced a long time, he strolled to the platform where they were at cudgel-play, for he loved a bout at quarterstaff as he loved meat and drink; and here befell an adventure that was sung in ballads throughout the mid-country for many a day.

One fellow there was that cracked crowns of every one who threw cap into the ring. This was Eric o' Lincoln, of great renown, whose name had been sung in ballads throughout the countryside. When Little John reached the stand he found none fighting, but only bold Eric walking up and down the platform, swinging his staff and shouting lustily: "Now, who will come and strike a stroke for the lass he loves the best, with a good Lincolnshire yeoman? How now, lads? step up! step up! or else thy lasses' eyes are not bright hereabouts, or the blood of Nottingham youth is sluggish and cold. Lincoln against Nottingham, say I! for no one hath put foot upon the boards this day such as we of Lincoln call a cudgel-player."

At this, one would nudge another with his elbow, saying "Go thou, Ned!" or "Go thou, Thomas!" but no lad cared to gain a cracked crown for nothing.

Presently Eric saw where Little John stood among the others, a head and shoulders above them all, and he called to him loudly, "Halloa, thou long-legged fellow in scarlet! Broad are thy shoulders and thick thy head; is not thy lass fair enough for thee to take cudgel in hand for her sake? In truth, I believe that Nottingham men do turn to bone and sinew, for neither heart nor courage have they! Now, thou great lout, wilt thou not twirl staff for Nottingham?"

"Ay," quoth Little John, "had I but mine own good staff here, it would pleasure me hugely to crack thy knave's pate, thou saucy braggart! I wot it would be well for thee an thy cock's comb were cut!" Thus he spoke, slowly at first, for he was slow to move; but his wrath gathered headway like a great stone rolling down a hill, so that at the end he was full of anger.

Then Eric o' Lincoln laughed aloud. "Well spoken for one who fears to meet me fairly, man to man," said he. "Saucy art thou thine own self, and, if thou puttest foot upon these boards, I will make thy saucy tongue rattle within thy teeth!"

"Now," quoth Little John, "is there never a man here that will lend me a good stout stuff till I try the mettle of yon fellow?" At this, half a score reached him their staves, and he took the stoutest and heaviest of them all. Then, looking up and down the cudgel, he said, "Now, I have in my hand but a splint of wood, – a barley-straw, an it were, – yet, I trow it will have to serve me; so here goeth." Thereupon he cast the cudgel upon the stand, and, leaping lightly after it, snatched it up in his hand again.

Then each man stood in his place and measured the other with fell looks until he that directed the sport cried, "Play!" At this they stepped forth, each grasping his staff tightly in the middle. Then those that stood around saw the stoutest game of quarterstaff that e'er Nottingham Town beheld. At first Eric o' Lincoln thought that he would gain an easy advantage, so he came forth as if he would say, "Watch, good people, how that I carve you this cockerel right speedily;" but he presently found it to be no such speedy matter. Right deftly he struck, and with great skill of fence, but he had found his match in Little John. Once, twice, thrice he struck, and three times Little John turned the blows to the left hand and to the right. Then quickly and with a dainty backhanded blow he rapped Eric beneath his guard so shrewdly that it made his head ring again. Then Eric stepped back to gather his wits, while a great shout went up and all were glad that Nottingham had cracked Lincoln's crown; and thus ended the first bout of the game.

Then presently the director of the sport cried, "Play!" and they came together again; but now Eric played warily, for he found his man was of right good mettle, and also he had no sweet memory of the blow that he had got; so this bout neither Little John nor the Lincoln man caught a stroke within his guard; then, after a while, they parted again, and this made the second bout.

Then for the third time they came together, and at first Eric strove to be wary, as he had been before; but, growing mad at finding himself so foiled, he lost his wits, and began to rain blows so fiercely and so fast that they rattled like hail on penthouse roof; but, in spite of all, he did not reach within Little John's guard. Then at last Little John saw his chance and seized it right cleverly. Once more, with a quick blow, he rapped Eric beside the head, and ere he could regain himself, Little John slipped his right hand down to his left, and, with a swinging blow, smote the other so sorely upon the crown that down he fell as though he would never move again.

Then the people shouted so loud that folk came running from all about to see what was the ado; while Little John leaped down from the stand and gave the staff back to him that had lent it to him. And thus ended the famous bout between Little John and Eric o' Lincoln of great renown.

But now the time had come when those who were to shoot with the long bow were to take their places, so the people began flocking to the butts where the shooting was to be. Near the target, in a good place, sat the Sheriff, upon a raised dais, with many gentlefolk around him. When the archers had taken their places, the herald came forward and proclaimed the rules of the game, and how each should shoot three shots, and to him that should shoot the best the prize of two fat steers was to belong. A score of brave shots were gathered there, and among them some of the keenest hands at the long bow in Lincoln and Nottinghamshire; and among them Little John stood taller than all the rest. "Who is yon stranger clad all in scarlet?" said some; and others answered, "It is he that hath but now so soundly cracked the crown of Eric o' Lincoln." Thus the people talked among themselves until at last it reached even the Sheriff's ears.

And now each man stepped forward and shot in turn; but though each shot well, Little John was the best of all, for three times he struck the clout, and once only the length of a barleycorn from the center. "Hey for the tall archer!" shouted the crowd; and some among them shouted, "Hey for Reynold Greenleaf!" for this was the name that Little John had called himself that day.

Then the Sheriff stepped down from the raised seat and came to where the archers stood, while all doffed their caps that saw him coming. He looked keenly at Little John, but did not know him, though he said, after a while, "How now, good fellow, methinks there is that about thy face that I have seen erewhile."

"Mayhap it may be so," quoth Little John, "for often have I seen your worship;" and, as he spoke, he looked steadily into the Sheriff's eyes, so that the latter did not suspect who he was.

"A brave blade art thou, good friend," said the Sheriff, "and I hear that thou hast well upheld the skill of Nottinghamshire against that of Lincoln this day. What may be thy name, good fellow?"

"Men do call me Reynold Greenleaf, your worship," said Little John; and the old ballad that tells of this, adds, "So, in truth, was he a green leaf, but of what manner of tree the Sheriff wotted not."

"Now, Reynold Greenleaf," quoth the Sheriff, "thou art the fairest hand at the long bow that mine eyes ever beheld, next to that false knave, Robin Hood, from whose wiles Heaven forfend me! Wilt thou join my service, good fellow? Thou shalt be paid right well, for three suits of clothes shalt thou have a year, with good food and as much ale as thou canst drink; and, beside this, I will pay thee forty marks each Michaelmastide."

"Then here stand I a free man, and right gladly will I enter thy household," said Little John; for he thought he might find some merry jest, should he enter the Sheriff's service.

"Fairly hast thou won the fat steers," said the Sheriff, "and thereunto I will add a butt of good March beer, for joy of having gotten such a man, for, I wot, thou shootest as fair a shaft as Robin Hood himself."

"Then," said Little John, "for joy of having gotten myself into thy service, I will give fat steers and brown ale to all these good folk to make them merry withal." At this arose a great shout, many casting their caps aloft, for joy of the gift.

Then some built great fires and roasted the steers, and others broached the butt of ale, with which all made themselves merry; then, when they had eaten and drunk as much as they could, and when the day faded and the great moon arose, all red and round, over the spires and towers of Nottingham Town, they joined hands and danced around the fires, to the music of bagpipes and harps. But long before this merrymaking had begun, the Sheriff and his new servant, Reynold Greenleaf, were in the Castle of Nottingham.

CHAPTER THREE

# HOW LITTLE JOHN LIVED AT THE SHERIFF'S HOUSE

Thus Little John entered into the Sheriff's service, and found the life he led there easy enough, for the Sheriff made him right-hand man, and held him in great favor. He sat nigh the Sheriff at meat, and he ran beside his horse when he went a-hunting; so that, what with hunting and hawking a little, and eating rich dishes and drinking good sack and sleeping until late hours in the morning, he grew as fat as a stall-fed ox. Thus things floated easily along with the tide, until one day when the Sheriff went a-hunting, there happened that which broke the smooth surface of things.

This morning the Sheriff and many of his men set forth to meet certain lords, to go a-hunting. He looked all about him for his good man, Reynold Greenleaf, but, not finding him, was vexed, for he wished to show Little John's skill to his noble friends. As for Little John, he lay abed, snoring lustily, till the sun was high in the heavens. At last he opened his eyes and looked about him, but did not move to arise. Brightly shone the sun in at the window, and all the air was sweet with the scent of woodbine that hung in sprays about the wall without, for the cold winter was past and spring was come again, and Little John lay still, thinking how sweet was everything on this fair morn. Just then he heard, faint and far away, a distant bugle-note sounding thin and clear. The sound was small, but, like a little pebble dropped into a glassy fountain, it broke all the smooth surface of his thoughts, until his whole soul was filled with disturbance. His spirit seemed to awaken from its sluggishness, and his memory brought back to him all the merry greenwood life – how the birds were singing blithely there this bright morning, and how his loved companions and friends were feasting and making merry, or perhaps talking of him with sober speech; for when he first entered the Sheriff's service he did so in jest; but the hearthstone was warm during the winter, and the fare was full, and so he had abided, putting off from day to day his going back to Sherwood, until six long months had passed. But now he thought of his good master, and of Will Stutely, whom he loved better than any one in all the world, and of young David of Doncaster, whom he had trained so well in all manly sports, till there came over his heart a great and bitter longing for them all, so that his eyes filled with tears. Then he said aloud: "Here I grow fat like a stall-fed ox and all my manliness departeth from me while I become a sluggard and dolt. But I will arouse me and go back to mine own dear friends once more, and never will I leave them again till life doth leave my lips." So saying, he leaped from bed, for he hated his sluggishness now.

When he came down-stairs he saw the Steward standing near the pantry door – a great, fat man, with a huge bundle of keys hanging to his girdle. Then Little John said, "Ho, Master Steward, a hungry man am I, for nought have I had for all this blessed morn. Therefore, give me to eat."

Then the steward looked grimly at him and rattled the keys in his girdle, for he hated Little John because he had found favor with the Sheriff. "So, Master Reynold Greenleaf, thou art an hungered , art thou?" quoth he. "But, fair youth, if thou livest long enough, thou wilt find that he who getteth overmuch sleep for an idle head goeth with an empty stomach. For what sayeth the old saw, Master Greenleaf? is it not 'The late fowl findeth but ill faring?'"

"Now, thou great purse of fat!" cried Little John, "I ask thee not for fool's wisdom, but for bread and meat. Who art thou, that thou shouldst deny me to eat? By Saint Dunstan, thou hadst best tell me where my breakfast is, if thou wouldst save broken bones!"

"Thy breakfast, Master Fireblaze, is in the pantry," answered the Steward.

"Then fetch it hither!" cried Little John, who waxed angry by this time.

"Go thou and fetch it thine own self," quoth the Steward. "Am I thy slave, to fetch and carry for thee?"

"I say, go thou, bring it me!"

"I say, go thou, fetch it for thyself!"

"Ay, marry, that will I, right quickly!" quoth Little John, in a rage; and, so saying, he strode to the pantry and tried to open the door; but found it locked, whereat the Steward laughed and rattled his keys. Then the wrath of Little John boiled over, and, lifting his clenched fist, he smote the pantry door, bursting out three panels, and making so large an opening that he could easily stoop and walk through it.

When the Steward saw what was done, he waxed mad with rage; and, as Little John stooped to look within the pantry, he seized him from behind by the nape of the neck, pinching him sorely and smiting him over the head with his keys till the yeoman's ears rang again. At this Little John turned upon the Steward and smote him such a buffet that the fat man fell to the floor and lay there as though he would never move again. "There," quoth Little John, "think well of that stroke and never keep a good breakfast from a hungry man again."

So saying, he crept into the pantry and looked about him to see if he could find something to appease his hunger. He saw a great venison pasty and two roasted capons, beside which was a platter of plover's eggs; moreover, there was a flask of sack and one of canary, – a sweet sight to a hungry man. These he took down from the shelves and placed upon a sideboard, and prepared to make himself merry.

Now the Cook, in the kitchen across the courtyard, heard the loud talking between Little John and the Steward, and also the blow that Little John struck the other, so he came running across the court and up the stairway to where the Steward's pantry was, bearing in his hands the spit with the roast still upon it. Meanwhile the Steward had gathered his wits about him and risen to his feet, so that when the Cook came to the steward's pantry he saw him glowering through the broken door at Little John, who was making ready for a good repast, as one dog glowers at another that has a bone. When the Steward saw the Cook, he came to him, and, putting one arm over his shoulder, "Alas, sweet friend!" quoth he – for the Cook was a tall, stout man – "seest thou what that vile knave, Reynold Greenleaf, hath done? He hath broken in upon our master's goods, and hath smitten me a buffet upon the ear, so that I thought I was dead. Good Cook, I love thee well, and thou shalt have a good postle of our master's best wine every day, for thou art an old and faithful servant. Also, good Cook, I have ten shillings that I mean to give as a gift to thee. But hatest thou not to see a vile upstart like this Reynold Greenleaf taking it upon him so bravely?"

"Ay, marry, that do I," quoth the Cook boldly, for he liked the Steward because of his talk of the wine and of the ten shillings. "Get thee gone straightway to thy room, and I will bring out this knave by his ears." So saying, he laid aside his spit and drew the sword that hung by his side; whereupon the Steward left as quickly as he could, for he hated the sight of naked steel.

Then the Cook walked straightway to the broken pantry door, through which he saw Little John tucking a napkin beneath his chin, and preparing to make himself merry.

"Why, how now, Reynold Greenleaf?" said the Cook; "thou art no better than a thief, I wot. Come thou straight forth, men, or I will carve thee as I would carve a sucking pig."

"Nay, good Cook, bear thou thyself more seemingly, or else I will come forth to thy dole. At most times I am as a yearling lamb, but when one cometh between me and my meat, I am a raging lion, as it were."

"Lion or no lion," quoth the valorous Cook, "come thou straight forth, else thou art a coward heart as well as a knavish thief."

"Ha!" cried Little John, "coward's name have I never had; so, look to thyself, good Cook, for I come forth straight, the roaring lion I did speak of but now."

Then he, too, drew his sword and came out of the pantry; then, putting themselves into position, they came slowly together, with grim and angry looks; but suddenly Little John lowered his point. "Hold, good Cook!" said he. "Now, I bethink me it were ill of us to fight with good victuals standing so nigh, and such a feast as would befit two stout fellows such as we are. Marry, good friend, I think we should enjoy this fair feast ere we fight. What sayest thou, jolly Cook?"

At this speech the Cook looked up and down, scratching his head in doubt, for he loved good feasting. At last he drew a long breath, and said to Little John, "Well, good friend, I like thy plan right well; so, pretty boy, say I, let us feast, with all my heart, for one of us may sup in Paradise before nighfall."

So each thrust his sword back into the scabbard, and entered the pantry; then, after they had seated themselves, Little John drew his dagger and thrust it into the pie. "A hungry man must be fed," quoth he, "so, sweet chuck, I help myself without leave." But the Cook did not lag far behind, for straightway his hands also were deeply thrust within the goodly pasty. After this, neither of them spoke further, but used their teeth to better purpose. But though neither spoke, they looked at one another, each thinking within himself that he had never sen a more lusty fellow than the one across the board.

At last, after a long time had passed, the Cook drew a full, deep breath, as though of much regret, and wiped his hands upon the napkin, for he could eat no more. Little John, also, had enough, for he pushed the pasty aside, as though he would say, "I want thee by me no more, good friend." Then he took the pottle of sack, and said he, "Now, good fellow, I swear by all that is bright, that thou art the stoutest companion at eating that ever I had. Lo! I drink thy health." So saying, he clapped the flask to his lips and cast his eyes aloft, while the good wine flooded his throat. Then he passed the pottle to the Cook, who also said, "Lo, I drink my health, sweet fellow!" Nor was he behind Little John in drinking any more than in eating.

"Now," quoth Little John, "thy voice is right round and sweet, jolly lad; I doubt not thou canst sing a ballad most blithely; canst thou not?"

"Truly, I have trolled one now and then," quoth the Cook; "yet I would not sing alone."

"Nay, truly," said Little John, "that were but ill courtesy. Strike up thy ditty, and I will afterwards sing one to match it, if I can."

"So be it, pretty boy," quoth the Cook. "And hast thou e'er heard the song of the deserted Shepherdess?"

"Truly, I know not," answered Little John; "but sing thou away and let me hear."

Then the Cook took another draught from the pottle, and, clearing his throat, sang right sweetly –

*THE SONG OF THE DESERTED SHEPHERDESS*

*"In Lenten time, when leaves wax green,*
*And pretty birds begin to mate,*
*When lark doth sing, and thrush, I ween,*
*And stockdove cooeth soon and late,*
*Fair Phillis sat beside a stone,*
*And thus I heard her make her moan:*
*'O willow, willow, willow, willow!*
*I'll take me of thy branches fair*
*And twine a wreath to deck my hair.*

*"'The thrush hath taken him a she,*
*The robin, too, and eke the dove;*
*My Robin hath deserted me,*
*And left me for another love.*
*So here, by brookside, all alone,*
*I sit me down and make my moan.*
*O willow, willow, willow, willow!*
*I'll take me of thy branches fair*
*And twine a wreath to deck my hair.'*

*"But ne'er came herring from the sea,*
*But good as he were in the tide;*
*Young Corydon came o'er the lea,*
*And sat him Phillis down beside.*
*So, presently, she changed her tone,*
*And 'gan to cease her from her moan,*
*'O willow, willow, willow, willow!*
*Thou mayst e'en keep thy garlands fair,*
*I want them not to deck my hair."'*

"Now, by my faith," cried Little John, "that same is a right good song, and hath truth in it, also."

"Glad am I thou likest it, sweet lad," said the Cook; "now sing thou one also, for ne'er should a man be merry alone, or sing and list not."

"Then I will sing thee a song of a right good knight of Arthur's court, and how he cured his heart's wound without running upon the dart again, as did thy Phillis; for I wot she did but cure one smart by giving herself another. So, list thou while I sing –

*THE GOOD KNIGHT AND HIS LOVE*

*"When Arthur, King, did rule this land,*
*A goodly king was he,*
*And had he of stout knights a band*
*Of merry company.*

*"Among them all, both great and small,*
*A good stout knight was there,*
*A lusty childe, and eke a tall,*
*That loved a lady fair.*

*"But nought would she to do with he,*
*But turned her face away;*
*So gat he gone to far countrye,*
*And left that lady gay.*

*"There all alone he made his moan,*
*And eke did sob and sigh,*
*And weep till it would move a stone,*
*And he was like to die.*

*"But still his heart did feel the smart,*
*And eke the dire distress,*
*And rather grew his pain more sharp*
*As grew his body less.*

*"Then got he back where was good sack*
*And merry companye,*
*And soon did cease to cry 'Alack!'*
*When blithe and gay was he.*

*"From which I hold, and feel full bold*
*To say, and eke believe,*
*That gin the belly go not cold*
*The heart will cease to grieve."*

"Now, by my faith," cried the Cook, as he rattled the pottle against the sideboard, "I like that same song hugely, and eke the motive of it, which lieth like a sweet kernel in a hazel-nut."

"Now thou art a man of shrewd opinions," quoth Little John, "and I love thee truly as thou wert my brother."

"And I love thee, too. But the day draweth on, and I have my cooking to do ere our master cometh home; so let us e'en go and settle this brave fight we have in hand."

"Ay, marry," quoth Little John, "and that right speedily. Never have I been more laggard in fighting than in eating and drinking. So come thou straight forth into the passage-way, where there is good room to swing a sword, and I will try to serve thee."

Then they both stepped forth into the broad passage that led to the Steward's pantry, where each man drew his sword again, and without more ado fell upon the other as though he would hew his fellow limb from limb. Then their swords clashed upon one another with great din, and sparks flew from each blow in showers. So they fought up and down the hall for an hour and more, neither striking the other a blow, though they strove their best to do so; for both were skilful at the fence; so nothing came of all their labor. Ever and anon they rested, panting; then, after getting their wind, at it they would go again more fiercely than ever. At last Little John cried aloud, "Hold, good Cook!" whereupon each rested upon his sword, panting.

"Now will I make my vow," quoth Little John, "thou art the very best swordsman that ever mine eyes beheld. Truly, I had thought to carve thee ere now."

"And I had thought to do the same by thee," quoth the Cook; "but I have missed the mark somehow."

"Now I have been thinking within myself," quoth Little John, "what we are fighting for; but albeit I do not rightly know."

"Why, no more do I," said the Cook. "I bear no love for that pursy steward, but I thought that we had engaged to fight with one another, and that it must be done."

"Now," quoth Little John, "it doth seem to me that instead of striving to cut one another's throats, it were better for us to be boon companions. What sayst thou, jolly Cook, wilt thou go with me to Sherwood Forest and join with Robin Hood's band? Thou shalt live a merry life within the woodlands, and sevenscore good companions shoult thou have, one of whom is mine own self. Thou shalt have two suits of Lincoln green each year, and forty marks in pay."

"Now, thou art a man after mine own heart!" cried the Cook right heartily; "and, as thou speakest of it, that is the very service for me. I will go with thee, and that right gladly. Give me thy palm, sweet fellow, and I will be thine own companion from henceforth. What may be thy name, lad?"

"Men do call me Little John, good fellow."

"How? And art thou indeed Little John, and Robin Hood's own right-hand man? Many a time and oft have I heard of thee, but never did I hope to set eyes upon thee. And thou art indeed the famous Little John!" And the Cook seemed lost in amazement, and looked upon his companion with open eyes.

"I am Little John, indeed, and I will bring to Robin Hood this day a right stout fellow to join his merry band. But ere we go, good friend, it seemeth to me to be a vast pity that, as we have had so much of the good Sheriff's food, we should not also carry off some of his silver plate to Robin Hood, as a present from his worship."

'Ay, marry is it," said the Cook. And so they began hunting about, and took as much silver as they could lay hands upon, clapping it into a bag, and when they had filled the sack they set forth to Sherwood Forest.

Plunging into the woods, they came at last to the greenwood tree, where they found Robin Hood and threescore of his merry men lying upon the fresh green grass. When Robin and his men saw who it was that came, they leaped to their feet. "Now welcome!" cried Robin Hood, "Now welcome, Little John! for long hath it been since we have heard from thee, though we all knew that thou hadst joined the Sheriff's service. And how has thy fared all these long days?"

"Right merrily have I lived at the Lord Sheriff's," answered Little John, "and I have come straight thence. See, good master! I have brought thee his cook, and even his silver plate." Thereupon he told Robin Hood and his merry men that were there all that had befallen him since he had left them to go to the Fair at Nottingham Town. Then all shouted with laughter, except Robin Hood; but he looked grave.

"Nay, Little John," said he, "thou art a brave blade and a trusty fellow. I am glad thou hast brought thyself back to us, and with such a good companion as the Cook, whom we all welcome to Sherwood. But I like not so well that thou hast stolen the Sheriff's plate like some paltry thief. The sheriff hath been punished by us, and hath lost three hundred pounds, even as he sought to despoil another; but he hath done nought that we should steal his household plate from him."

Though Little John was vexed with this, he strove to pass it off with a jest. "Nay, good master," quoth he, "if thou thinkest the Sheriff gave us not the plate, I will fetch him, that he may tell us with his own lips he giveth it all to us." So saying, he leaped to his feet, and was gone before Robin Hood could call him back.

Little John ran for full five miles till he came to where the Sheriff of Nottingham and a gay company were hunting near the forest. When Little John came to the Sheriff he doffed his cap and bent his knee. "God save thee, good master," quoth he.

"Why, Reynold Greenleaf!" cried the Sheriff, "whence comest thou and where hast thou been?"

"I have been in the forest," answered Little John, speaking amazedly, "and there I saw a sight such as ne'er before man's eyes beheld! Yonder I saw a young hart all in green from top to toe, and about him was a herd of threescore deer, and they, too, were all of green from head to foot. Yet I dared not shoot, good master, for fear lest they should slay me."

"Why, how now, Reynold Greenleaf," cried the Sheriff; "art thou dreaming, or art thou mad, that thou dost bring me such a tale?"

"Nay, I am not dreaming nor am I mad," said Little John; "and if thou wilt come with me, I will show thee this fair sight, for I have seen it with mine own eyes. But thou must come alone, good master, lest the others frighten them and they get away."

So the party all rode forward, and Little John led them downward into the forest.

"Now, good master," quoth he at last, "we are nigh where I saw this herd."

Then the Sheriff descended from his horse and bade them wait for him until he should return; and Little John led him forward through a close copse until suddenly they came to a great open glade, at the end of which Robin Hood sat beneath the shade of the great oak tree, with his merry men all about him. "See, good Master Sheriff," quoth Little John, "yonder is the hart of which I spake to thee."

At this the Sheriff turned to Little John, and said bitterly, "Long ago I thought I remembered thy face, but now I know thee. Woe betide thee, Little John, for thou hast betrayed me this day."

Then Little John laughed aloud. "Good Master Sheriff," said he, "thou dost indeed know me, and I am Little John. But let me tell thee, all this would not have happened had not thy beggarly Steward starved me, and had he given me food to eat when I asked it. But if he gave none to me, the green hart will give thee another feast, and when thou goest back, tell thy Steward the time will come when he and I shall have a reckoning."

In the mean time Robin Hood had come to them. "Now welcome, Master Sheriff," said he. "Hast thou come to-day to take another feast with me?"

"Nay, heaven forbid!" said the Sheriff, in tones of deep earnest. "I care for no feast and have no hunger to-day."

"Nevertheless," quoth Robin, "if thou hast no hunger, maybe thou hast thirst, and well I know thou wilt take a cup of sack with me. But I am grieved that thou wilt not feast with me, for thou couldst have victuals to thy liking, for there stands thy Cook."

Then he led the Sheriff, will-he-nill-he, to the seat he knew so well beneath the greenwood tree.

"Ho, lads"" cried Robin, "fill our good friend, the Sheriff, a right brimming cup of sack and fetch it hither, for he is faint and weary."

Then one of the band brought the Sheriff a cup of sack, bowing low as he handed it to him; but the Sheriff could not touch the wine, for he saw it served in one of his own silver flagons, on one of his own silver plates.

"How now," quoth Robin, "dost thou not like our new silver service? We have gotten a bag of it this day." So saying, he held up the sack of silver that Little John and the Cook had brought with them.

Then the Sheriff's heart was bitter within him; but, not daring to say anything, he only gazed upon the ground. Robin looked keenly at him for a time before he spoke again; then said he, "Now, Master Sheriff, the last time thou camest to Sherwood Forest thou didst come seeking to despoil a poor spend-thrift, and thou wert despoiled thine own self; but now thou comest seeking to do no harm, nor do I know that thou hast despoiled any man. I take my tithes from fat priests and lordly squires, to help those that they despoil and to raise up those that they bow down; but I know not that thou hast tenants of thine own whom thou hast wronged in any way. Therefore, take thou thine own again, nor will I dispossess thee to-day of so much as one farthing. Come with me, and I will lead thee from the forest back to thine own party again."

Then, slinging the bag upon his shoulder, he turned away, the Sheriff following him, all too perplexed in mind to speak. So they went forward until they came to within a furlong of the spot where the Sheriff's companions were waiting for him. Then Robin Hood gave the sack of silver back to the Sheriff. "Take thou thine own again" he said, "and, hearken to me, good Sheriff,take thou a piece of advice with it. Try thy servants well ere thou dost engage them again so readily." Then, turning, he left the other standing bewildered, with the sack in his hands.

The company that waited for the Sheriff were all amazed to see him come out of the forest bearing a heavy sack upon his shoulders; but though they questioned him, he answered never a word, acting like one who walks in a dream. Without a word, he placed the bag across his nag's back, and then, mounting, rode away, all following him; but all the time there was a great turmoil of thoughts within his head, tumbling one over the other. And thus ends the merry tale of Little John and how he entered the Sheriff's service.

# Part Third

*Recounting three merry adventures that befel Robin Hood and certain others, by which he gained sore bones and three good merry men, all in one day.*

## Chapter One

# Little John and the Tanner of Blyth

It often comes about in this world that unlucky happenings fall upon one in such measure that it seems, as the saying is, that every cat that one strokes flies in one's face. Thus it was with Robin Hood and Little John one bright day in the merry Maytime; so listen and you shall hear how Dame Luck so buffeted them that their bones were sore for many a day thereafter.

One fine day, not long after Little John had left abiding with the Sheriff and had come back, with his worship's cook, to the merry greenwood, as has just been told, Robin Hood and a few chosen fellows of his band lay upon the soft sward beneath the greenwood tree where they dwelt. The day was warm and sultry, so that whilst most of the band were scattered through the forest upon this mission and upon that, these few stout fellows lay lazily beneath the shade of the tree, in the soft afternoon, passing jests among themselves and telling merry stories, with laughter and mirth.

All the air was laden with the bitter fragrance of the May, and all the bosky shades of the woodlands beyond rang with the sweet song of birds, – the throstle-cock, the cuckoo, and the wood-pigeon, – and with the song of birds mingled the cool sound of the gurgling brook that leaped out of the forest shades, and ran fretting amid its rough, gray stones across the sunlit open glade before the trysting-tree. And a fair sight was that halfscore of tall, stout yeomen, all clad in Lincoln green, lying beneath the broad-spreading branches of the great oak tree, amid the quivering leaves of which the sunlight shivered and fell in dancing patches upon the grass.

The good old times have gone by when such men grow as grew then; when sturdy quarterstaff and long bow toughened a man's thews till they were like leather. Around Robin Hood that day there lay the very flower of English yeomanrie. Here the great Little John, with limbs as tough as the gnarled oak, yet grown somewhat soft from good living at the Sheriff's house in Nottingham Town; there Will Stutely, his face as brown as a berry from the sun and wind, but, for all that, the comeliest yeoman in the midcountry, only excepting Allan a Dale, the minstrel, of whom you shall hear anon. Beside these was Will Scathelock, as lank as a greyhound, yet as fleet of foot as a buck of three years' growth; young David of Doncaster, with great stout limbs only less than those of Little John in size, the tender beard of early youth now just feathering his chin, and others of great renown both far and near.

Suddenly Robin Hood smote his knee.

"By Saint Dunstan," quoth he, "I had nigh forgot that quarter-day cometh on apace, and yet no cloth of Lincoln green in all our store. It must be looked to, and that in quick season. Come, busk thee, Little John! stir those lazy bones of thine, for thou must get thee straightway to our good gossip, the draper, Hugh Longshanks of Ancaster. Bid him send us straightway twentyscore yards of fair cloth of Lincoln green; and mayhap the journey may take some of the fat from off thy bones, that thou hast gotten from lazy living at our dear Sheriff's."

"Nay," muttered Little John (for he had heard so much upon this score that he was sore upon the point), "nay, truly, mayhap I have more flesh upon my joints than I once had, yet, flesh or no flesh, I doubt not that I could still hold my place and footing upon a narrow bridge against e'er a yeoman in Sherwood, or Nottinghamshire, for the matter of that, even though he had no more fat about his bones than thou hast, good master."

At this reply a great shout of laughter went up, and all looked at Robin Hood, for each man knew that Little John spake of a certain fight that happened between their master and himself, through which they first became acquainted.

"Nay," quoth Robin Hood, laughing louder than all, "Heaven forbid that I should doubt thee, for I care for no taste of thy staff myself, Little John. I must needs own that there are those of my band can handle a seven-foot staff more deftly than I; yet no man in all Nottinghamshire can draw gray-goose shaft with my fingers. Nevertheless, a journey to Ancaster may not be ill for thee; so go thou, as I bid, and thou hadst best go this very evening, for since thou hast abided at the Sheriff's many know thy face, and if thou goest in broad daylight, thou mayst get thyself into a coil with some of his worship's men-at-arms. Bide thou here till I bring thee money to pay our good Hugh. I warrant he hath no better customers in all Nottinghamshire than we." So saying, Robin left them and entered the forest.

Not far from the trysting tree was a great rock in which a chamber had been hewn, the entrance being barred by a massive oaken door two palms' breadth in thickness, studded about with spikes, and fastened with a great padlock. This was the treasure-house of the band, and thither Robin Hood went, and, unlocking the door, entered the chamber from which he brought forth a bag of gold, which he gave to Little John, to pay Hugh Longshanks withal, for the cloth of Lincoln green.

Then up got Little John, and, taking the bag of gold, which he thrust into his bosom, he strapped a girdle about his loins, took a stout pikestaff full seven feet long in his hand, and set forth upon his journey.

So he strode whistling along the leafy forest path that led to Fosse Way, turning neither to the right hand nor the left, until at last he came to where the path branched, leading on the one hand onward to Fosse Way, and on the other, as well Little John knew, to the merry Blue Boar Inn. Here Little John suddenly ceased whistling, and stopped in the middle of the path. First he looked up and then he looked down, and then, tilting his cap over one eye, he slowly scratched the back part of his head. For thus it was: at the sight of these two roads, two voices began to alarum within him, the one crying, "There lies the road to the Blue Boar Inn, a can of brown October, and a merry night with sweet companions such as thou mayst find there;" the other, "There lies the way to Ancaster and the duty thou art sent upon." Now the first of these two voices was far the louder, for Little John had grown passing fond of good living through abiding at the Sheriff's house; so, presently, looking up into the blue sky, across which bright clouds were sailing like silver boats, and swallows skimming in circling flight, quoth he, "I fear me it will rain this evening, so I'll e'en stop at the Blue Boar till it passes by, for I know my good master would not have me wet to the skin." So, without more ado, off he strode down the path that lay the way of his likings. Now there was no sign of any foul weather, but when one wishes to do a thing, as Little John did, one finds no lack of reasons for the doing.

Four merry wags were at the Blue Boar Inn; a butcher, a beggar, and two barefoot friars. Little John heard them singing from afar, as he walked through the hush of the mellow twilight that was now falling over hill and dale. Right glad were they to welcome such a merry blade as Little John. Fresh cans of ale were brought, and with jest and song and merry tales the hours slipped away on fleeting wings. None thought of time or tide till the night was so far gone that Little John put by the thought of setting forth upon his journey again that night, and so bided at the Blue Boar Inn until the morrow.

Now it was an ill piece of luck for Little John that he left his duty for his pleasure, and he paid a great score for it, as we are all apt to do in the same case, as you shall see.

Up he rose at the dawn of the next day, and, taking his stout pikestaff in his hand, he set forth upon his journey once more, as though he would make up for lost time.

In the good town of Blyth there lived a stout tanner, celebrated far and near for feats of strength and many tough boats at wrestling and the quarterstaff. For five years he had held the midcountry champion belt for wrestling, till the great Adam o' Lincoln cast him in the ring and broke one of his ribs; but at quarterstaff he had never yet met his match in all the country about. Beside all this, he dearly loved the long bow, and a sly jaunt in the forest when the moon was full and the dun deer in season; so that the King's rangers kept a shrewd eye upon him and his doings, for Arthur a Bland's house was apt to have a plenty of meat in it that was more like venison than the law allowed.

Now Arthur had been to Nottingham Town the day before Little John set forth on his errand, there to sell a halfscore of tanned cowhides. At the dawn of the same day that Little John left the inn, he started from Nottingham, homeward for Blyth. His way led, all in the dewy morn, past the verge of Sherwood Forest, where the birds were welcoming the lovely day with a great and merry jubilee. Across the Tanner's shoulders was slung his stout quarterstaff, ever near enough to him to be gripped quickly, and on his head was a cap of double cowhide, so tough that it could hardly be cloven even by a broadsword.

"Now," quoth Arthur a Bland to himself, when he had come to that part of the road that cut through a corner of the forest, "no doubt at this time of year the dun deer are coming from the forest depths nigher to the open meadow lands. Mayhap I may chance to catch a sight of the dainty brown darlings thus early in the morn." For there was nothing he loved better than to look upon a tripping herd of deer, even when he could not tickle their ribs with a clothyard shaft. Accordingly, quitting the path, he went peeping this way and that through the underbush, spying now here and now there, with all the wiles of a master of woodcraft, and of one who had more than once donned a doublet of Lincoln green.

Now as Little John stepped blithely along, thinking of nothing but of such things as the sweetness of the hawthorn buds that bedecked the hedgerows, or the crab-trees that stood here and there all covered with fair pink blossoms, or gazing upward at the lark, that, springing from the dewy grass, hung aloft on quivering wings in the yellow sunlight, pouring forth its song that fell like a falling star from the sky, his luck led him away from the highway, not far from the spot where Arthur a Bland was peeping this way and that through the leaves of the thickets. Hearing a rustling of the branches, Little John stopped, and presently caught sight of the brown cowhide cap of the Tanner moving amongst the bushes.

"I do much wonder," quoth Little John to himself, "what yon knave is after, that he should go thus peeping and peering about. I verily believe that yon scurvy varlet is no better than a thief, and cometh here after our own and the good King's dun deer." For by much roving in the forest, Little John had come to look upon all the deer in Sherwood as belonging to Robin Hood and his band as much as to good King Harry. "Nay," quoth he again, after a time, "this matter must e'en be looked into."

So, quitting the high-road, he also entered the thickets, and began spying around after stout Arthur a Bland.

So for a long time they both of them went hunting about, Little John after the Tanner, and the Tanner after the deer. At last Little John trod upon a stick, which snapped under his foot, whereupon, hearing the noise, the Tanner turned quickly and caught sight of the yeoman. Seeing that the Tanner had spied him out, Little John put a bold face upon the matter.

"Hilloa," quoth he, "what art thou doing here, thou naughty fellow? Who art thou that comest ranging Sherwood's paths? In very sooth thou hast an evil cast of countenance, and I do think, truly, that thou art no better than a thief, and comest after our good King's deer."

"Nay," quoth the Tanner boldly, – for, though taken by surprise, he was not a man to be frightened by big words, – "thou liest in thy teeth. I am no thief, but an honest craftsman. As for my countenance, it is what it is; and, for the matter of that, thine own is none too pretty, thou saucy fellow."

"Ha!" quoth Little John, in a great loud voice, "wouldst thou give me back-talk? Now I have a great part of a mind to crack thy pate for thee. I would have thee know, fellow, that I am, as it were, one of the King's foresters. Leastwise," muttered he to himself, "I and my friends do take good care of our good sovereign's deer."

"I care not who thou art," answered the bold Tanner, "and unless thou hast many more of thy kind by thee, thou canst never make Arthur a Bland cry 'A mercy.'"

"Is it so?" cried Little John, in a rage. "Now, by my faith, thou saucy rogue, thy tongue hath led thee into a pit thou wilt have a sorry time getting out of; for I will give thee such a drubbing as ne'er hast thou had in all thy life before. Take thy staff in thy hand, fellow, for I will not smite an unarmed man."

"Marry come up with a murrain!" cried the Tanner, for he, too, had talked himself into a fume. "Big words ne'er killed so much as a mouse. Who art thou that talkest so freely of cracking the head of Arthur a Bland? If I do not tan thy hide this day as ne'er I tanned a calf's hide in all my life before, split my staff into skewers for lamb's flesh and call me no more brave man! Now look to thyself, fellow!"

"Stay!" said Little John; "let us first measure our cudgels. I do reckon my staff longer than thine, and I would not take vantage of thee by even so much as an inch."

"Nay, I pass not for length," answered the Tanner. "My staff is long enough to knock down a calf; so look to thyself, fellow, I say again."

So, without more ado, each gripped his staff in the middle, and, with fell and angry looks, they came slowly together.

Now news had been brought to Robin Hood how that Little John, instead of doing his bidding, had passed by duty for pleasure, and so had stopped over night with merry company at the Blue Boar Inn, instead of going straight to Ancaster. So, being vexed to his heart by this, he set forth at dawn of day to seek Little John at the Blue Boar, or at least to meet the yeoman on the way, and ease his heart of what he thought of the matter. As thus he strode along in anger, putting together the words he would use to chide Little John, he heard, of a sudden, loud and angry voices, as of men in a rage, passing fell words back and forth from one to the other. At this, Robin Hood stopped and listened. "Surely," quoth he to himself, "that is Little John's voice, and he is talking in anger also. Methinks the other is strange to my ears. Now Heaven forfend that my good trusty Little John should have fallen into the hands of the King's rangers. I must see to this matter, and that quickly."

Thus spoke Robin Hood to himself, all his anger passing away like a breath from the window-pane, at the thought that perhaps his trusty right-hand man was in some danger of his life. So cautiously he made his way through the thickets whence the voices came, and, pushing aside the leaves, peeped into the little open space where the two men, staff in hand, were coming slowly together.

"Ha!" quoth Robin to himself, "here is merry sport afoot. Now I would give three golden angels from my own pocket if yon stout fellow would give Little John a right sound drubbing! It would please me to see him well thumped for having failed in my bidding. I fear me, though, there is but poor chances of my seeing such a pleasant sight." So saying, he stretched himself at length upon the ground, that he might not only see the sport the better, but that he might enjoy the merry sight at his ease.

As you may have seen two dogs that think to fight, walking slowly round and round each other, neither cur wishing to begin to combat, so those two stout yeomen moved slowly around, each watching for a chance to take the other unaware, and so get in the first blow. At last Little John struck like a flash, and, "rap," the Tanner met the blow and turned it aside, and then smote back at Little John, who also turned the blow; and so this mighty battle began. Then up and down and back and forth they tried, the blows falling so thick and fast that, at a distance, one would have thought that half a score of men were fighting. Thus they fought for nigh a half an hour, until the ground was all ploughed up with the digging of their heels, and their breathing grew labored like the ox in the furrow. But Little John suffered the most, for he had become unused to such stiff labor, and his joints were not as supple as they had been before he went to dwell with the Sheriff.

All this time Robin Hood lay beneath the bush, rejoicing at such a comely bout of quarterstaff. "By my faith!" quoth he to himself, "never had I thought to see Little John so evenly matched in all my life. Belike, though, he would have overcome yon stout fellow before this had he been in his former trim."

At last Little John saw his chance, and, throwing all the strength he felt going from him into one blow that might have felled an ox, he struck at the Tanner with might and main. And now did the Tanner's cowhide cap stand him in good stead, and but for it he might never have held staff in hand again. As it was, the blow he caught beside the head was so shrewd that it sent him staggering across the little glade, so that, if Little John had had the strength to follow up his vantage, it would have been ill for stout Arthur. But he regained himself quickly, and, at arm's length, struck back a blow at Little John, and this time the stroke reached its mark, and down went Little John at full length, his cudgel flying from his hand as he fell. Then, raising his staff, stout Arthur dealt him another blow upon the ribs.

"Hold!" roared Little John. "Wouldst thou strike a man when he is down?"

"Ay, marry would I," quoth the Tanner, giving him another thwack with his staff.

"Stop!" roared Little John. "Help! hold, I say! I yield me! I yield me, I say, good fellow!"

"Hast thou had enough?" asked the Tanner, grimly, holding his staff aloft.

"Ay, marry, and more than enough."

"And thou dost own that I am the better man of the two!"

"Yes, truly, and a murrain seize thee!" said Little John, the first aloud and the last to his beard.

"Then thou mayst go thy ways; and thank thy patron saint that I am a merciful man," said the Tanner.

"A plague of such mercy as thine!" said Little John, sitting up and feeling his ribs where the Tanner had cudgelled him. "I make my vow, my ribs feel as though every one of them were broken in twain. I tell thee, good fellow, I did think there was never a man in all Nottinghamshire could do to me what thou hast done this day."

"And so thought I, also," cried Robin Hood, bursting out of the thicket and shouting with laughter till the tears ran down his cheeks. "O man, man!" said he, as well as he could for his mirth, "'a didst go over like a bottle knocked from a wall. I did see the whole merry bout, and never did I think to see thee yield thyself so, hand and foot, to any man in all merry England. I was seeking thee, to chide thee for leaving my bidding undone; but thou hast been paid all I owed thee, full measure, pressed down and overflowing, by this good fellow. Marry, 'a did reach out his arm full length whilst thou stood gaping at him, and, with a pretty rap, tumbled thee over as never have I seen one tumbled before." So spoke bold Robin, and all the time Little John sat upon the ground, looking as though he had sour curds in his mouth. "What may be thy name, good fellow?" said Robin, next, turning to the Tanner.

"Men do call me Arthur a Bland," spoke up the Tanner, boldly; "and now what may be thy name?"

"Ha! Arthur a Bland!" quoth Robin, "I have heard thy name before, good fellow. Thou didst break the crown of a friend of mine at the fair at Ely last October. The folk there call him Jock o' Nottingham; we call him Will Scathelock. This poor fellow whom thou hast so belabored is counted the best hand at the quarterstaff in all merry England. His name is Little John, and mine Robin Hood."

"How!" cried the Tanner, "art thou indeed the great Robin Hood, and is this the famous Little John? Marry, had I known who thou art, I would never have been so bold as to lift my hand against thee. Let me help thee to thy feet, good Master Little John, and let me brush the dust from off thy coat."

"Nay," quoth Little John, testily, at the same time rising carefully, as though his bones had been made of glass, "I can help myself, good fellow, without thy aid; and, let me tell thee, had it not been for that vile cowskin cap of thine, it would have been ill for thee this day."

At this Robin laughed again, and, turning to the Tanner, he said, "Wilt thou join my band, good Arthur? for I make my vow thou art one of the stoutest men that ever mine eyes beheld."

"Will I join thy band?" cried the Tanner, joyfully; "ay, marry, will I! Hey for a merry life!" cried he, leaping aloft and snapping his fingers, "and hey for the life I love! Away with tanbark and filthy vats and foul cowhides! I will follow thee to the ends of the earth, good master, and not a herd of dun deer in all the forest but shall know the sound of the twang of my bowstring."

"As for thee, Little John," said Robin, turning to him and laughing, "thou wilt start once more for Ancaster, and we will go part way with thee, for I will not have thee turn again to either the right hand or the left till thou hast fairly gotten away from Sherwood. There are other inns that thou knowest yet, hereabouts." Thereupon, leaving the thickets, they took once more to the highway, and departed upon their business.

CHAPTER TWO

# ROBIN HOOD AND WILL SCARLET

Thus they travelled along the sunny road, three stout fellows such as you could hardly match anywhere else in all merry England. Many stopped to gaze after them as they strode along, so broad were their shoulders and so sturdy their gait.

Quoth Robin Hood to Little John, "Why didst thou not go straight to Ancaster, yesterday, as I told thee? Thou hadst not gotten thyself into such a coil hadst thou done as I ordered."

"I feared the rain that threatened," said Little John in a sullen tone, for he was vexed at being so chafed by Robin with what had happened to him.

"The rain!" cried Robin, stopping of a sudden in the middle of the road, and looking at Little John in wonder. "Why, thou great oaf! not a drop of rain has fallen these three days, neither has any threatened, nor hath there been a sign of foul weather in earth or sky or water."

"Nevertheless," growled Little John, "the holy Saint Swithin holdeth the waters of the heavens in his pewter pot, and he could have poured them out, had he chosen, even from a clear sky; and wouldst thou have had me wet to the skin?"

At this Robin Hood burst into a roar of laughter. "O Little John!" said he, "what butter wits hast thou in that head of thine! Who could hold anger against such a one as thou art?"

So saying, they all stepped out once more, with the right foot foremost, as the saying is.

After they had travelled some distance, the day being warm and the road dusty, Robin Hood waxed thirsty; so, there being a fountain of water as cold as ice, just behind the hedgerow, they crossed the stile and came to where the water bubbled up from beneath a mossy stone. Here, kneeling and making cups of the palms of their hands, they drank their fill, and then, the spot being cool and shady, they stretched their limbs and rested them for a space.

In front of them, over beyond the hedge, the dusty road stretched away across the plain; behind them the meadow lands and bright green fields of tender young corn lay broadly in the sun, and overhead spread the shade of the cool, rustling leaves of the beechen tree. Pleasantly to their nostrils came the tender fragrance of the purple violets and wild thyme that grew within the dewy moisture of the edge of the little fountain, and pleasantly came the soft gurgle of the water; all else was sunny silence, broken only now and then by the crow of a distant cock, borne up to them on the wings of the soft and gentle breeze, or the drowsy drone of the humble-bee burrowing in the clover blossoms that grew in the sun, or the voice of the busy housewife in the nearest farmhouse. All was so pleasant and so full of the gentle joy of the bright Maytime, that for a long time neither of the three cared to speak, but each lay on his back, gazing up through the trembling leaves of the trees to the bright sky overhead. At last, Robin, whose thoughts were not quite so busy wool-gathering as those of the others, and who had been gazing around him now and then, broke the silence.

"Heyday!" quoth he, "yon is a gayly-feathered bird, I take my vow."

The others looked and saw a young man walking slowly down the highway. Gay was he, indeed, as Robin had said, and a fine figure he cut, for his doublet was of scarlet silk and his stockings also; a handsome sword hung by his side, the embossed leathern scabbard being picket out with fine threads of gold; his cap was of scarlet velvet, and a broad feather hung down behind and back of one ear. His hair was long and yellow and curled upon his shoulders, and in his hand he bore an early rose which he smelt at daintily now and then.

"By my life!" quoth Robin Hood, laughing, "saw ye e'er such a pretty, mincing fellow?"

"Truly, his clothes have overmuch prettiness for my taste," quoth Arthur a Bland; "but, ne'ertheless, his shoulders are broad and his loins are narrow, and seest thou, good master, how that his arms hang from his body? They dangle not down like spindles, but hang stiff and bend at the elbow. I take my vow, there be no bread and milk limbs in those fine clothes, but stiff joints and tough thews."

"Methinks thou art right, friend Arthur," said Little John. "I do verily think that yon is no such rose-leaf and whipped cream gallant as he would have one take him to be."

"Pah!" quoth Robin Hood, "the sight of such a fellow doth put a nasty taste into my mouth! Look how he doth hold that fair flower betwixt his thumb and finger, as he would say, 'Good rose, I like thee not so ill but I can bear thy odor for a little while.' I take it ye are both wrong, and verily believe that were a furious mouse to run across his path, he would cry, 'La!' or 'Alack-a-day!' and fall straightway into a swoon. I wonder who he may be."

"Some great baron's son, I doubt not," answered Little John, "with good and true men's money lining his purse."

"Ay, marry, that is true, I make no doubt," quoth Robin. "What a pity that such men as he, that have no thought but to go abroad in gay clothes, should have good fellows, whose shoes they are not fit to tie, dancing at their bidding. By Saint Dunstan, Saint Alfred, Saint Withold, and all the good men in the Saxon calendar, it doth make me mad to see such gay lordlings from over the sea go stepping on the necks of good Saxons who owned this land before ever their great-grandsires chewed rind of brawn! By the bright bow of Heaven, I will have their ill-gotten gains from them, even though I hang for it as high as e'er a forest tree in Sherwood!"

"Why, how now, master," quoth Little John, "what heat is this? Thou doest set thy pot a-boiling, and mayhap no bacon to cook! Methinks yon fellow's hair is over light for Norman locks. He may be a good man and true for aught thou knowest."

"Nay," said Robin, "my head against a leaden farthing, he is what I say. Whenever saw ye Saxon mince along like that, as though he feared to muddy the toes of his shoes? At least, I will go forth and stop him, and see whether his purse be free of foul money. If I am wrong, then he may go forward upon his journey without the loss of so much as a groat; but if I am right, I will pluck him as close as ever a goose was plucked for live feathers in midsummer. Thou sayst he is a sturdy fellow, Little John. Lie thou here and watch till I show thee how woodland life toughens a man, as easy living, such as thine hath been of late, drags him down. So, lie ye both here, I say, till I show you how I drub this fellow." So saying, Robin Hood stepped forth from the shade of the beech tree, crossed the stile, and stood in the middle of the road, with his hands on his hips, in the stranger's path.

Meantime the stranger, who had been walking so slowly that all this talk was held before he came opposite the place where they were, neither quickened his pace nor seemed to see that such a man as Robin Hood was in the world. So Robin stood in the middle of the road, waiting while the other walked slowly forward, smelling his rose, and looking this way and that, and everywhere except at Robin.

"Hold!" cried Robin, when at last the other had come close to him. "Hold! stand where thou art!"

"Wherefore should I hold, good fellow?" said the stranger in soft and gentle voice; "and wherefore should I stand where I am? Ne'ertheless, as thou dost desire that I should stay, I will abide for a short time, that I may hear what thou mayst have to say to me."

"Then," quoth Robin, "as thou dost so fairly do as I tell thee, and dost give me such soft speech, I will also treat thee with all due courtesy. I would have thee know, fair friend, that I am, as it were, a votary at the shrine of Saint Wilfred, who, thou mayst know, took, willy-nilly, all their gold from the heathen, and melted it up into candlesticks. Wherefore, upon such as come hereabouts, I levy a certain toll, which I use for a better purpose, I hope, than to make candlesticks withal. Therefore, sweet chuck, I would have thee deliver to me thy purse, that I may look into it, and judge, to the best of my poor powers, whether thou hast more wealth about thee than our law allows. For, as our good Gaffer Swanthold sayeth, 'He who is fat from overliving must needs lose blood.'"

All this time the youth had been sniffing at the rose that he held betwixt his thumb and finger. "Nay," said he with a gentle smile, when Robin Hood had done, "I do love to hear thee talk, thou pretty fellow, and if, haply, thou art not yet done, finish, I beseech thee. I have yet some little time to stay."

"I have said all," quoth Robin; "and now, if thou wilt give me thy purse, I will let thee go thy way without let or hindrance so soon as I shall see what it may hold. I will take none from thee if thou hast but little."

"Alas! it doth grieve me much," said the other, "that I cannot do as thou dost wish. I have nothing to give thee. Let me go my way, I prythee. I have done thee no harm."

"Nay, thou goest not," quoth Robin, "till thou hast shown me thy purse."

"Good friend," said the other, gently, "I have business elsewhere. I have given thee much time and have heard thee patiently. Prythee, let me now depart in peace."

"I have spoken to thee, friend," said Robin, sternly, "and I now tell thee again, that thou goest not one step forward till thou hast done as I bid thee." So saying, he raised his quarterstaff above his head in a threatening way.

"Alas!" said the stranger, sadly, "it doth grieve me that this thing must be. I fear much that I must slay thee, thou poor fellow!" So saying, he drew his sword.

"Put by thy weapon," quoth Robin; "I would take no vantage of thee. Thy sword cannot stand against an oaken staff such as mine. I could snap it like a barley straw. Yonder is a good oaken thicket by the roadside; take thee a cudgel thence and defence thyself fairly, if thou hast a taste for a sound drubbing."

First the stranger measured Robin with his eye, and then he measured the oaken staff. "Thou art right, good fellow," said he presently; "truly, my sword is no match for that cudgel of thine. Bide thee a while till I get me a staff. So saying, he threw aside the rose that he had been holding all this time, thrust his sword back into the scabbard, and, with a more hasty step than he had yet used, stepped to the roadside where grew the little clump of ground oaks Robin had spoken of. Choosing among them, be presently found a sapling to his liking. He did not cut it, but, rolling up his sleeves a little way, he laid hold of it, placed his heel against the ground, and, with one mighty pull, plucked the young tree up by the roots from out the very earth. Then he came back, trimming away the roots and tender stems with his sword as quietly as if he had done naught to speak of.

Little John and the Tanner had been watching all that passed, but when they saw the stranger drag the sapling up from the earth, and heard the rending and snapping of its roots, then Tanner pursed his lips together, drawing his breath between them in a long inward whistle.

"By the breath of my body!" said Little John, as soon as he could gather his wits from their wonder, "sawest thou that, Arthur? Marry, I think our poor master will stand but an ill chance with yon fellow. By Our Lady, he plucked up yon green tree as it were a barley straw."

Whatever Robin Hood thought, he stood his ground, and now he and the stranger in scarlet stood face to face.

Well did Robin Hood hold his own that day as a midcountry yeoman. This way and that they fought, and back and forth, Robin's skill against the stranger's strength. The dust of the highway rose up around them like a cloud, so that at times Little John and the Tanner could see nothing, but only hear the rattle of the staves against one another. Thrice Robin Hood struck the stranger; once upon the arm and twice upon the ribs, and yet had he warded all the other's blows, only one of which, had it met its mark, would have laid stout Robin lower in the dust than he had ever gone before. At last the stranger struck Robin's cudgel so fairly in the middle that he could hardly hold his staff in his hand; again he struck, and Robin bent beneath the blow; a third time he struck, and now not only fairly beat down Robin's guard, but gave him such a rap, also, that down he tumbled into the dusty road.

"Hold!" cried Robin Hood, when he saw the stranger raising his staff once more. "I yield me!"

"Hold!" cried Little John, bursting from his cover, with the Tanner at his heels. "Hold! give over, I say!"

"Nay," answered the stranger quietly, "if there be two more of you, and each as stout as this good fellow, I am like to have my hands full. Nevertheless, come on, and I will strive my best to serve you all."

"Stop!" cried Robin Hood, "we will fight no more. I take my vow, this is an ill day for thee and me, Little John. I do verily believe that my wrist, and eke my arm, are palsied by the jar of the blow that this stranger struck me."

Then Little John turned to Robin Hood. "Why, how now, good master," said he, "Alas! thou art in an ill plight. Marry, thy jerkin is all befouled with the dust of the road. Let me help thee to arise."

"A plague on thy aid!" cried Robin, angrily. "I can get to my feet without thy help, good fellow."

"Nay, but let me at least dust thy coat for thee. I fear thy poor bones are mightily sore," quoth Little John, soberly, but with a sly twinkle in his eyes.

"Give over, I say!" quoth Robin in a fume. "My coat hath been dusted enough already, without aid of thine." Then, turning to the stranger, he said, "What may be thy name, good fellow?"

"My name is Gamwell," answered the other.

"Ha!" cried Robin, "is it even so? I have near kin of that name. Whence camest thou, fair friend?"

"From Maxfield Town I come," answered the stranger. "There was I born and bred, and thence I come to seek my mother's young brother, whom men call Robin Hood. So, if perchance thou mayst direct me" –

"Ha! Will Gamwell!" cried Robin, placing both hands upon the other's shoulders and holding him off at arm's length. "Surely, it can be none other! I might have known thee by that pretty maiden air of thine' – that dainty, finicking manner of gait. Dost thou not know me, lad? Look upon me well."

"Now, by the breath of my body!" cried the other, "I do believe from my heart that thou art mine own Uncle Robin. Nay, certain it is so!" and each flung his arms around the other, kissing him upon the cheek. Then once more Robin held his kinsman off at arm's length and scanned him keenly from top to toe. "Why, how now," quoth he, "what change is here? Verily, some eight or ten years ago I left thee a stripling lad, with great joints and ill-hung limbs, and lo! here thou art, as tight a fellow as e'er I set mine eyes upon. Dost thou not remember, lad, how I showed thee the proper way to nip the goose feather betwixt thy fingers and throw out thy bow arm steadily? Thou gavest great promise of being a keen archer. And dost thou not mind how I taught thee to fend and parry with the cudgel?"

"Yea," said young Gamwell," and I did so look up to thee, and thought thee so above all other men that, I make my vow, had I known who thou wert, I would never have dared to lift hand against thee this day. I trust I did thee no great harm."

"No, no," quoth Robin, hastily, and looking sideways at Little John, "thou didst not harm me. But say no more of that, I prythee. Yet I will say, lad, that I hope I may never feel again such a blow as thou didst give me. By'r Lady, my arm doth tingle yet from finger-nail to elbow. Truly, I thought that I was palsied for life. I tell thee, coz, that thou art the strongest man that ever I laid mine eyes upon. I take my vow, I felt my stomach quake when I beheld thee pluck up yon green tree as thou didst. But tell me, how camest thou to leave Sir Edward and thy mother?"

"Alas!" answered young Gamwell, "it is an ill story, uncle, that I have to tell thee. My father's steward, who came to us after old Giles Crookleg died, was ever a saucy varlet, and I know not why my father kept him, saying that he did oversee with great judgment. It used to gall me to hear him speak up so boldly to my father, who, thou knowest, was ever a patient man to those about him, and slow to anger and harsh words. Well, one day – and an ill day it was for that saucy fellow – he sought to berate my father, I standing by. I could stand it no longer, good uncle, so, stepping forth, I gave him a box o' the ear, and – wouldst thou believe it? – the fellow straightway died o't. I think they said I broke his neck, or something o' the like. So off they packed me to seek thee and escape the law. I was on my way when thou sawest me, and here I am."

"Well, by the faith of my heart," quoth Robin Hood, "for any one escaping the law, thou wast taking it the most easily that ever I beheld in all my life. Whenever did any one in all the world see one who had slain a man, and was escaping because of it, tripping along the highway like a dainty court damsel, sniffing at a rose the while?"

"Nay, uncle," answered Will Gamwell, "over haste never churned good butter, as the old saying hath it. Moreover, I do verily believe that this over-strength of my body hath taken the nimbleness out of my heels. Why, thou didst but just now rap me thrice, and I thee never a once, save by overbearing thee by my strength."

"Nay," quoth Robin, "let us say no more on that score. I am right glad to see thee, Will, and thou wilt add great honor and credit to my band of merry fellows. But thou must change thy name, for warrants will be out presently against thee; so, because of thy gay clothes, thou shalt henceforth and for aye be called Will Scarlet."

"Will Scarlet," quoth Little John, stepping forward and reaching out his great palm, which the other took, "Will Scarlet, the name fitteth thee well. Right glad am I to welcome thee amongst us. I am called Little John; and this is a new member who has just joined us, a stout tanner named Arthur a Bland. Thou art like to achieve fame, Will, let me tell thee, for there will be many a merry ballad sung about the country, and many a merry story in Sherwood of how Robin Hood taught Little John and Arthur a Bland the proper way to use a quarterstaff; likewise, as it were, how our good master bit off so large a piece of cake that he choked on it."

"Nay, good Little John," quoth Robin, gently, for he liked ill to have such a jest told of him, "Why should we speak of this little matter? Prythee, let us keep this day's doings amongst ourselves."

"With all my heart," quoth Little John. "But, good master, I thought that thou didst love a merry story, because thou hast so often made a jest about a certain increase of fatness on my joints, of flesh gathered by my abiding with the Sheriff of" –

"Nay, good Little John," said Robin, hastily, "I do bethink me I have said full enough on that score."

"It is well," quoth Little John, "for in truth I myself have tired of it somewhat. But now I bethink me, thou didst also seem minded to make a jest of the rain that threatened last night; so" –

"Nay, then," said Robin Hood, testily, "I was mistaken. I remember me now it did seem to threaten rain."

"Truly, I did think so myself," quoth Little John; "therefore, no doubt, thou dost think it was wise of me to abide all night at the Blue Boar Inn, instead of venturing forth in such stormy weather; dost thou not?"

"A plague of thee and thy doings!" cried Robin Hood. "If thou wilt have it so, thou wert right to abide whenever thou didst choose."

"Once more, it is well," quoth Little John. "As for myself, I have been blind this day. I did not see thee drubbed; I did not see thee tumbled heels over head in the dust; and if any man says that thou wert, I can with a clear conscience rattle his lying tongue betwixt his teeth."

"Come," cried Robin, biting his nether lip, while the others could not forbear laughing, "We will go no farther to-day, but will return to Sherwood, and thou shalt go to Ancaster another time, Little John."

So said Robin, for now that his bones were sore, he felt as though a long journey would be an ill thing for him. So, turning their backs, they retraced their steps whence they came.

Chapter Three

# The Merry Adventure with Midge the Miller

When the four yeomen had travelled for a long time toward Sherwood again, high noontide being past, they began to wax hungry. Quoth Robin Hood, "I would that I had somewhat to eat. Methinks a good loaf of white bread, with a piece of snow-white cheese, washed down with a draught of humming ale, were a feast for a king."

"Since thou speakest of it," said Will Scarlet, "methinks it would not be amiss myself. There is that within me crieth out, 'Victuals, good friend, victuals!'"

"I know a house near by," said Arthur a Bland, "and, had I but the money, I would bring ye that ye speak of; to wit, a sweet loaf of bread, a fair cheese, and a skin of brown ale."

"For the matter of that, thou knowest I have money by me, good master," quoth Little John.

"Why, so thou hast, Little John," said Robin. "How much money will it take, good Arthur, to buy us meat and drink?"

"I think that six broad pennies will buy food enow for a dozen men," said the Tanner.

"Then give him six pennies, Little John," quoth Robin, "for methinks food for three men will about fit my need. Now get thee gone, Arthur, with the money, and bring the food here, for there is a sweet shade in that thicket yonder, beside the road, and there will we eat our meal."

So Little John gave Arthur the money, and the others stepped to the thicket, there to await the return of the Tanner.

After a time he came back, bearing with him a great brown loaf of bread and a fair, round cheese, and a goat-skin full of stout March beer, slung over his shoulders. Then Will Scarlet took his sword and divided the loaf and the cheese into four fair portions, and each man helped himself. Then Robin Hood took a deep pull at the beer. "Aha!" said he, drawing in his breath, "never have I tasted sweeter drink than this."

After this no man spake more, but each munched away at his bread and cheese lustily, with ever and anon a pull at the beer.

At last Will Scarlet looked at a small piece of bread he still held in his hand, and quoth he, "Methinks I will give this to the sparrows," So, throwing it from him, he brushed the crumbs from his jerkin.

"I, too," quoth Robin, "have had enough, I think." As for Little John and the Tanner, they had by this time eaten every crumb of their bread and cheese.

"Now, sweet friends," quoth Robin, gathering up the skin of beer, that was not yet nearly empty, "I do wish that ye may ever have such happiness as a good stout meal like this bringeth to my heart. Thus pledging you all, I drink to your health, that it may ever remain such as it is this day." So saying, he took a long, hearty pull at the stout beer. Next Will Scarlet took the skin, then Little John, and, last of all, the stout Tanner. A good full skin of beer, as fat as a town tradesman, began the round; a poor, flabby hide came forth, as weak and limp as an aged man.

"Now," quoth Robin, "I do feel myself another man, and would fain enjoy something pleasant before going farther upon our journey. I do bethink me, Will, that thou didst use to have a pretty voice, and one that tuned sweetly upon a song. Prythee, give us one ere we journey farther."

"Truly, I do not mind turning a tune," answered Will Scarlet; "but I would not sing alone."

"Nay, others will follow. Strike up, lad," quoth Robin.

"In that case, 't is well," said Will Scarlet. "I do call to mind a song that a certain minstrel used to sing in my father's hall, upon occasion. I know no name for it, and so can give you none; but thus it is." Then, clearing his throat, he sang as follows:-

*"In the merry blossom time,*
*When love-longings flood the breast,*
*When the flower is on the lime,*
*When the small fowl builds her nest,*
*Sweetly sings the nightingale*
*And the throstle-cock so bold;*
*Cuckoo in the dewy dale,*
*And the turtle in the wild.*

*But the robin I love dear,*
*For he singeth through the year.*
*Robin! Robin!*
*Merry Robin!*
*So I'd have my true love be:*
*Not to fly*
*At the night*
*Sign of cold adversity.*

*"When the Spring brings sweet delights,*
*When aloft the lark doth rise,*
*Lovers woo o' mellow nights,*
*And youths peep in maidens' eyes,*
*That time blooms the eglantine,*
*Daisies pied upon the hill,*
*Cowslips fair and columbine,*
*Dusky violets by the rill.*
*But the Ivy green doth grow*
*When the north wind bringeth snow.*
*Ivy! Ivy!*
*Stanch and true!*
*Thus I'd have her love to be;*
*Not to die*
*At the nigh*
*Breath of cold adversity."*

"Tis well sung," quoth Robin; "but, cousin, I tell thee plain, I would rather hear a stout fellow like thee sing some lusty ballad than a finicking song of flowers and birds and what not. Yet, thou didst sing it fair, and 't is none so bad a snatch of a song, for the matter of that. Now, Tanner, it is thy turn next."

"I know not," quoth Arthur, smiling, with his head on one side, like a budding lass that is asked to dance, "I know not that I can match our sweet friend's song; moreover, I do verily think that I have caught a cold and have a certain tickling and huskiness in the windpipe."

"Nay, sing up, friend," quoth Little John, who sat next to him, patting him upon the shoulder. "Thou hast a fair, round, mellow voice; let us have a touch of it."

"Nay, an ye will ha' a poor thing," said Arthur, "I will do my best. Have ye ever heard of the wooing of Sir Keith, the stout young Cornish knight, in good King Arthur's time?"

"Methinks I have heard somewhat of it," said Robin; "but ne'ertheless strike up thy ditty and let us hear it, for, as I do remember me, it is a gallant song; so out with it, good fellow."

Thereupon, clearing his throat, the Tanner, without more ado, began to sing the ballad of –

*THE WOOING OF SIR KEITH*

*"King Arthur sat in his royal hall,
And about on either hand
Was many a noble lordling tall,
The greatest in the land.*

*"Sat Lancelot with raven locks,
Gawaine with golden hair,
Sir Tristram, Kay who kept the locks,
And many another there.*

*"And through the stained windows bright,
From o'er the red tiled eaves,
The sunlight blazed with colored light
On golden helms and greaves.*

*"But suddenly a silence came
About the Table Round,
For up the hall there walked a dame
Bent nigh unto the ground.*

*"Her nose was hooked, her eyes were bleared,
Her locks were lank and white;
Upon her chin there grew a beard;
She was a grewsome sight.*

*"And so with crawling step she came
And kneeled at Arthur's feet;
Quoth Kay, 'She is the foulest dame
That e'er my sight did greet.'*

*" 'O mighty King! of thee I crave
A boon on bended knee;'
'Twas thus she spake. 'What wouldst thou have,'
Quoth Arthur, King 'of me?'*

*"Quoth she, 'I have a foul disease
Doth gnaw my very heart,
And but one thing can bring me ease
Or cure my bitter smart.*

*" 'There is no rest, no ease for me
North, east, or west, or south,
Till Christian knight will willingly
Thrice kiss me on the mouth.*

*" 'Nor wedded may this childe have been
That giveth ease to me;
Nor may he be constrained, I ween,
But kiss me willingly.*

*" 'So is there here one Christian knight*
*Of such a noble strain*
*That he will give a tortured wight*
*Sweet ease of mortal pain?'*

*" 'A wedded man,' quoth Arthur, King,*
*'A wedded man I be,*
*Else would I deem it noble thing*
*To kiss thee willingly.*

*" 'Now, Lancelot, in all men's sight*
*Thou art the head and chief*
*Of chivalry. Come, noble knight,*
*And give her quick relief.'*

*"But Lancelot he turned aside*
*And looked upon the ground,*
*For it did sting his haughty pride*
*To hear them laugh around.*

*" 'Come thou, Sir, Tristram,' quoth the King.*
*Quoth he, 'It cannot be,*
*For ne'er can I my stomach bring*
*To do it willingly.'*

*" 'Wilt thou, Sir Kay, thou scornful wight?'*
*Quoth Kay, 'Nay, by my troth!*
*What noble dame would kiss a knight*
*That kissed so foul a mouth?'*

*" 'Wilt thou, Gawaine?' 'I cannot, King.'*
*'Sir Geraint?' 'Nay, not I,*
*My kisses no relief could bring,*
*For sooner would I die.'*

*"Then up and spake the youngest man*
*Of all about the board,*
*'Now such relief as Christian can*
*I'll give to her, my lord.'*

*"It was Sir Keith, a youthful knight,*
*Yet strong of limb and bold,*
*With beard upon his chin as light*
*As finest threads of gold.*

*"Quoth Kay, 'He hath no mistress yet*
*That he may call his own,*
*But here is one that's quick to get,*
*As she herself has shown.'*

*"He kissed her once, he kissed her twice,*
*He kissed her three times o'er,*
*A wundrous change came in a trice.*
*And she was foul no more.*

*"Her cheeks grew red as any rose,*
*Her brow as white as lawn,*
*Her bosom like the winter snows,*
*Her eyes like those of fawn.*

*"Her breath grew sweet as summer breeze*
*That blows the meadows o'er;*
*Her voice grew soft as rustling trees,*
*And cracked and harsh no more.*

*"Her hair grew glittering like the gold,*
*Her hands as white as milk;*
*Her filthy rags, so foul and old,*
*Were changed to robes of silk.*

*"In great amaze the knights did stare.*
*Quoth Kay, 'I make my vow*
*If it will please thee, lady fair,*
*I'll gladly kiss thee now.'*

*"But young Sir Keith kneeled on one knee*
*And kissed her robes so fair,*
*'O let me bye thy slave,' said he,*
*'For none to thee compare.'*

*"She bent her down, she kissed his brow,*
*She kissed his lips and eyes.*
*Quoth she, 'Thou art my master now,*
*My lord, my love, arise!*

*" 'And all the wealth that is mine own,*
*My lands, I give to thee,*
*For never knight hath lady shown*
*Such noble courtesy.*

*" 'Bewitched was I, in bitter pain,*
*But thou hast set me free,*
*So now I am myself again,*
*I give myself to thee.' "*

"Yea, truly," quoth Robin Hood, when the Tanner had made an end of singing, "it is as I remember it, a fair ditty, and a ballad with a pleasing tune of a song."

"It hath oftentimes seemed to me," said Will Scarlet, "that it hath a certain motive in it, e'en such as this: That a duty which seemeth to us sometimes ugly and harsh, when we do kiss it fairly upon the mouth, so to speak, is no such foul thing after all."

"Methinks thou art right," quoth Robin, "and, contrariwise, that when we kiss a pleasure that appeareth gay it turneth foul to us; is it not so, Little John? Truly such a thing hath brought thee sore thumps this day. Nay, man, never look down in the mouth. Clear thy pipes and sing us a ditty."

"Nay," said Little John, "I have none as fair as that merry Arthur has trolled. They are all poor things that I know. Moreover, my voice is not in tune to-day, and I would not spoil even a tolerable song by ill singing."

Upon this all pressed Little John to sing, so that when he had denied them a proper length of time, such as is seemly in one that is asked to sing, he presently yielded. Quoth he, "Well, an ye will ha' it so, I will give you what I can. Like to fair Will, I have no title to my ditty, but thus it runs." Then clearing his voice he sang:-

*"O Lady mine, the spring is here,*
*With a hey nonny nonny;*
*The sweet love season of the year,*
*With a ninny ninny nonny;*
*Now lad and lass*
*Lie in the grass*
*That groweth green*
*With flowers between.*
*The buck doth rest,*
*The leaves do start,*
*The cock doth crow,*
*The breeze doth blow,*
*And all things laugh in" –*

"Who may yon fellow be coming along the road?" said Robin, breaking into the song.

"I know not," quoth Little John, in a surly voice. "But this I do know, that it is an ill thing to do to check the flow of a good song."

"Nay, Little John," said Robin, "be not vexed, I prythee; but I have been watching him coming along, bent beneath that great bag over his shoulder, ever since thou didst begin thy song. Look, Little John, I pray, and see if thou knowest him."

Little John looked whither Robin Hood pointed. "Truly," quoth he, after a time, "I think your fellow is a certain young miller I have seen now and then around the edge of Sherwood; a poor wight, methinks, to spoil a good song about."

"Now thou speakest of him," quoth Robin Hood, "methinks I myself have seen him now and then. Hath he not a mill over beyond Nottingham Town, night to the Salisbury road?"

"Thou art right; that is the man," said Little John.

"A good stout fellow," quoth Robin. "I saw him crack Ned o' Bradford's crown about a fortnight since, and never saw I hair lifted more neatly in all my life before."

By this time the young miller had come so near that they could see him clearly. His clothes were dusted with flour, and over his back he carried a great sack of meal, bending so as to bring the whole weight upon his shoulders, and across the sack was a thick quarterstaff. His limbs were stout and strong, and he strode along the dusty road right sturdily with the heavy sack across his shoulders. His cheeks were ruddy as a winter hip, his hair was flaxen in color, and on his chin was a downy growth of flaxed beard.

"A good honest fellow," quoth Robin Hood, "and such an one as is a credit to English yeomanrie. Now let us have a merry jest with him. We will forth as though we were common thieves and pretend to rob him of his honest gains. Then will we take him into the forest and give him a feast such as his stomach never held in all his life before. We will flood his throat with good canary and send him home with crowns in his purse for every penny he hath. What say ye, lads?"

"Truly, it is a merry thought," said Will Scarlet.

"It is well planned," quoth Little John, "but all the saints preserve us from any more drubbings this day! Marry, my poor bones ache so that I" –

"Prythee peace, Little John," quoth Robin. "Thy foolish tongue will get us both well laughed at yet."

"My foolish tongue, forsooth," growled Little John to Arthur a Bland. "I would it could keep our master from getting us into another coil this day."

But now the Miller, plodding along the road, had come opposite to where the yeomen lay hidden, whereupon all four of them ran at him and surrounded him.

"Hold, friend!"cried Robin to the Miller; whereupon he turned slowly, with the weight of the bag upon his shoulder, and looked at each in turn all bewildered, for though a good stout man his wits did not skip like roasting chestnuts.

"Who bids me stay?" said the Miller in a voice deep and gruff, like the growl of a great dog.

"Marry that do I," quoth Robin; "and let me tell thee, friend, thou hadst best mind my bidding."

"And who art thou, good friend?" said the Miller, throwing the great sack of meal from his shoulder to the ground; "and who are those with thee?"

"We be four good Christian men," quoth Robin, "and would fain help thee by carrying part of thy heavy load for thee."

"I give you all thanks," said the Miller, "but my bag is none that heavy that I cannot carry it e'en by myself."

"Nay, thou dost mistake," quoth Robin, "I meant that thou mightest perhaps have some heavy farthings or pence about thee, not to speak of silver and gold. Our good Guffer Swanthold sayeth that gold is an over heavy burden for a two-legged ass to carry; so we would e'en lift some of this load from thee."

"Alas!" cried the Miller; "what would ye do to me? I have not about me so much as a clipped groat. Do me no harm, I pray you, but let me depart in peace. Moreover, let me tell you that ye are upon Robin Hood's ground, and should he find you seeking to rob an honest craftsman, he will clip your ears to your heads and scourge you even to the walls of Nottingham."

"In truth I fear Robin Hood no more than I do myself," quoth jolly Robin. "Thou must this day give up to me every penny thou hast about thee. Nay, if thou dost budge an inch I will rattle this staff about thine ears."

"Nay, smite me not!" cried the Miller, throwing up his elbow as though he feared the blow. "Thou mayst search me if thou wilt, but thou wilt find nothing upon me, pouch, pocket, or skin."

"Is it so?" quoth Robin Hood, looking keenly upon him. "Now I believe that what thou tellest is no true tale. If I am not much mistook thou hast somewhat in the bottom of that fat sack of meal. Good Arthur, empty the bag upon the ground; I warrant thou wilt find a shilling or two in the flour."

"Alas!" cried the Miller, falling upon his knees, "spoil not all my good meal! It can better you not, and will ruin me. Spare it, and I will give up the money in the bottom of the bag."

"Ha!" quoth Robin, nudging Will Scarlet, "Is it so? And have I found where thy money lies? Marry, I have a wondrous nose for the blessed images of good King Harry. I thought that I smelt gold and silver beneath the barley meal. Bring it straight forth, Miller."

Then slowly the Miller arose to his feet, and slowly and unwillingly he untied the mouth of the bag, and slowly thrust his hands into the meal and began fumbling about with his arms buried to the elbows in the barley flour. The others gathered round him, their heads together, looking and wondering what he would bring forth.

So they stood, all with their heads close together, gazing down into the sack. But while he pretended to be searching for the money, the Miller gathered two great handfuls of meal, "Ha," quoth he, "here they are, the beauties." Then, as the others leaned still more forward to see what he had, he suddenly cast the meal into their faces, filling their eyes and noses and mouths with the flour, blinding and half choking them. Arthur a Bland was worse off than any, for his mouth was open, agape with wonder of what was to come, so that a great cloud of flour flew down his throat, setting him a-coughing till he could scarcely stand.

Then, while all four stumbled about, roaring with the smart of the meal in their eyeballs, and while they rubbed their eyes till the tears made great channels on their faces through the meal, the Miller seized another handful of flour and another and another, throwing it in their faces, so that even had they had a glimmering of light before they were now as blind as ever a beggar in Nottinghamshire, while their hair and beards and clothes were as white as snow.

Then catching up his great crab staff, the Miller began laying about him as though he were clean gone mad. This way and that skipped the four, like peas on a drumhead, but they could neither see to defend themselves nor to run away. Thwack! thwack! went the Miller's cudgel across their backs, and at every blow great white clouds of flour rose in the air from their jackets and went drifting down the breeze.

"Stop!" roared Robin at last. "Give over, good friend, I am Robin Hood!"

"Thou liest, thou knave," cried the Miller, giving him a rap on the ribs, that sent up a great cloud of flour like a puff of smoke. "Stout Robin never robbed an honest tradesman. Ha! thou wouldst have my money, wouldst thou?" And he gave him another blow. "Nay, thou are not getting thy share, thou long-legged knave. Share and share alike." And he smote Little John across the shoulders so that he sent him skipping half across the road. "Nay, fear not, it is thy turn now, black beard." And he gave the Tanner a crack that made him roar for all his coughing. "How now, red coat, let me brush the dust from thee!" cried he, smiting Will Scarlet. And so he gave them merry words and blows until they could scarcely stand, and whenever he saw one like to clear his eyes he threw more flour in his face.

At last Robin Hood found his horn, and clapping it to his lips blew three loud blasts upon it.

Now it chanced that Will Stutely and a party of Robin's men were in the glade not far from where this merry sport was going forward. Hearing the hubbub of voices, and blows that sounded like the noise of a flail in the barn in winter time, they stopped, listening, and wondering what was toward. Quoth Will Stutely, "Now if I mistake not there is some stout battle with cudgels going forward not far hence. I would fain see this pretty sight." So saying, he and the whole party turned their steps whence the noise came. When they had come near where all the tumult sounded they heard the three blasts of Robin's bugle horn.

"Quick!" cried young David of Doncaster. "Our master is in sore need!" So, without stopping a moment, they dashed forward with might and main and burst forth from the covert into the high-road.

But what a sight was that which they saw. The road was all white with meal, and five men stood there also white with meal from top to toe, for much of the barley flour had fallen back upon the Miller.

"What is thy need, master?" cried Will Stutely. "And what doth all this mean?"

"Why," quoth Robin in a mighty passion, "yon traitor fellow hath come as nigh slaying me as e'er a man in all the world. Hadst thou not come quickly, good Stutely, thy master had been dead."

Hereupon, whilst he and the three others rubbed the meal from their eyes, and Will Stutely and his men brushed their clothes clean, he told them all; how that he had meant to pass a jest upon the Miller, which same had turned so grievously upon them.

"Quick, men, seize the vile Miller!" cried Stutely, who was nigh choking with laughter as were the rest; whereupon several ran upon the stout fellow, and seizing him bound his arms behind his back with bowstrings.

"Ha!" cried Robin, when they brought the trembling Miller to him. "Thou wouldst murder me, wouldst thou? By my faith" – Here he stopped and stood glaring upon the Miller with a grim look. But Robin's anger could not hold, so first his eyes twinkled, and then in spite of all he broke into a laugh.

Now when they saw their master laugh, the yeomen who stood around could contain themselves no longer, and a mighty shout of laughter went up from all. Many could not stand, but rolled upon the ground from pure merriment.

"What is thy name, good fellow?" said Robin at last to the Miller, who stood gaping and as though he were in a maze.

"Alas, sir, I am Midge, the Miller's son," said he in a frightened voice.

"I make my vow," quoth merry Robin, smiting him upon the shoulder, "thou art the mightiest Midge that e'er mine eyes beheld. Now wilt thou leave thy dusty mill and come and join my band? By my faith, thou art too stout a man to spend thy days betwixt the hopper and the till."

"Then truly, if thou dost forgive me for the blows I struck, not knowing who thou wast, I will join with thee right merrily," said the Miller.

"Then have I gained this day," quoth Robin, "the three stoutest yeomen in all Nottinghamshire. We will get us away to the greenwood tree, and there hold a merry feast in honor of our new friends, and mayhap a cup or two of good sack and canary may mellow the soreness of my poor joints and bones, though I warrant it will be many a day before I am again the man I was." So saying, he turned and led the way, the rest following, and so they entered the forest once more and were lost to sight.

So that night all was ablaze with crackling fires in the woodlands, for though Robin and those others spoken of, only excepting Midge, the Miller's son, had many a sore bump and bruise here and there on their bodies, they were still not so sore in the joints that they could not enjoy a jolly feast given all in welcome to the new members of the band. Thus with songs and jesting and laughter that echoed through the deeper and more silent nooks of the forest, the night passed quickly along, as such merry times are wont to do, until at last each man sought his couch and silence fell on all things and all things seemed to sleep.

Thus came about three merry adventures in one day, the one stepping upon the heels of another.

But Little John's tongue was ever one that was not easy of guidance, so that, inch by inch, the whole story of his fight with the Tanner and Robin's fight with Will Scarlet leaked out. And so I have told it that you may laugh at the merry tale along with me.

Now happenings so come upon us in this world that the serious things of this world become so mixed up with the merry things that our life is all of a jumble of black and white, like the boards of checkered black and white upon which country folk play draughts at the inn beside the blazing fire of a winter's night.

So things fell out with Robin Hood, for this day of merry sport, through which we have just trudged and buffeted with him and certain other mad wags, was speedily followed by one in which, though merriment was a-doing, more weighty matters were undertaken. So listen to what follows.

# Part Fourth

*In which it is told how Allan a Dale was brought to Robin Hood, who promised to help him in trouble. Also how Robin sought the curtal Friar of Fountain Abbey with that aim in view. Likewise it is recounted how Robin Hood brought two true lovers together that would else have been made unhappy all their lives.*

## Chapter One

# Robin Hood and Allan a Dale

It has just been told how three unlucky adventures fell upon Robin Hood and Little John all in one day, bringing them sore ribs and aching bones. So next we will tell how they made up for those ill happenings by a good action that came about not without some small pain to Robin.

Two days had passed by, and somewhat of the soreness had passed away from Robin Hood's joints, yet still, when he moved of a sudden and without thinking, pain here and there would, as it were jog him, crying, "Thou hast had a drubbing, good fellow."

The day was bright and jocund, and the morning dew still lay upon the grass. Under the greenwood tree sat Robin Hood; on one side was Will Scarlet, lying at full length upon his back, gazing up into the clear sky, with hands clasped behind his head; upon the other side sat Little John, fashioning a cudgel out of a stout crab-tree limb; elsewhere upon the grass sat or lay many others of the band.

Will Scathelock, who was as full of tales and legends as an egg is of meat, was telling of the adventures that befell brave Sir Carodoc of the Shrunken Arm, of King Arthur's time, and of his love to his one true maid, and of what they dared and suffered for each other's sake. That noble story you yourself may read some time, for it has been written and sung in more than one ancient tale and ballad, both in courtly and in homely phrase. To this all listened without a word, and when it was done many drew deep breaths, being carried away by the tale of knightly daring and noble sacrifice.

"It doth make a man better," quoth Robin Hood, "to hear of those noble men that lived so long ago. When one doth list to such tales, his soul doth say, 'Put by thy poor little likings and seek to do likewise.' Truly, one may not do as nobly one's self, but in the striving one is better. I mind me our good Gaffer Swanthold was wont to say, 'He who jumps for the moon and gets it not leaps higher than he who stoops for a penny in the mud.'"

"Truly," quoth Will Stutely, "it is a fine thought, but, nevertheless, good master, the one gets a penny and the other gets nought, and, without the penny, one is like to go with an empty stomach. These same stories are well to listen to but ill to follow, say I."

"By the faith of my heart," quoth merry Robin, "thou dost ever trip up a lofty thought that gazes in the sky, and dost bring its nose in the dust. Nevertheless, thou hast a shrewd wit in thy head, good Stutely; and now that thou bringest me to things of the world, I do bethink me that we have had no one to dine with us for this long time. Our money groweth low in the purse, for no one hath come to pay a reckoning for many a day. Now busk thee, good Stutely, and choose thee six men, and get thee gone to Fosse Way or thereabouts, and see that thou bringest some one to eat with us this evening. Meantime we will prepare a grand feast to do whosoever may come the greater honor. And stay, good Stutely. I would have thee take Will Scarlet with thee, for it is meet that he should become acquaint with the ways of the forest."

"Now do I thank thee, good master," quoth Stutely, springing to his feet, "that thou hast chosen me for this adventure. Truly, my limbs do grow slack through abiding idly here. As for two of my six, I will choose Midge the Miller, and Arthur a Bland, for, as well thou knowest, good master, they are stout fists at the quarterstaff. Is it not so, Little John?"

At this all laughed but Little John, and Robin, who twisted up his face. "I can speak for Midge," said he, "and likewise for my cousin Scarlet. This very blessed morn I looked at my ribs and found them as many colors as a beggar's cloak."

So, having chosen four more stout fellows, Will Stutely and his band set forth to Fosse Way, to find whether they might not come across some rich guest to feast that day in Sherwood with Robin and his band.

For all the livelong day they abided near this highway. Each man had brought with him a good store of cold meat and a bottle of stout March beer to stay his stomach till the home-coming. So when high noontide had come they sat them down upon the soft grass, beneath a green and wide-spreading hawthorn bush, and held a hearty and jovial feast. After this, one kept watch while the others napped, for it was a still and sultry day.

Thus they passed the time pleasantly enow, but no guest such as they desired showed his face in all the time that they lay hidden there. Many passed along the dusty road in the glare of the sun: now it was a bevy of chattering damsels merrily tripping along; now it was a plodding tinker; now a merry shepherd lad; now a sturdy farmer; all gazing ahead along the road, unconscious of the seven stout fellows that lay hidden so near them. Such were the travellers along the way; but fat abbot, rich esquire, or money-laden usurer came there none.

At last the sun began to sink low in the heavens; the light grew red and the shadows long. The air grew full of silence, the birds twittered sleepily, and from afar came, faint and clear, the musical song of the milkmaid calling the kine home to the milking.

Then Stutely arose from where he was lying. "A plague of such ill luck!" quoth he. "Here have we abided all day, and no bird worth the the shooting, so to speak, hath come within reach of our bolt. Had I gone forth on an innocent errand, I had met a dozen stout priests or a score of pursy money-lenders. But it is ever thus: the dun deer are never so scarce as when one has a gray goose feather nipped betwixt the fingers. Come, lads, let us pack up and home again, say I." Accordingly, the others arose, and, coming forth from out the thicket, they all turned their toes back again to Sherwood.

After they had gone some distance, Will Stutely, who headed the party, suddenly stopped. "Hist!" quoth he, for his ears were as sharp as those of a five-year-old fox. "Hark, lads! Methinks I hear a sound." At this all stopped and listened with bated breath, albeit for a time they could hear nothing, their ears being duller than Stutely's. At length they heard a faint and melancholy sound, like some one in lamentation.

"Ha!" quoth Will Scarlet, "this must be looked into. There is some one in distress nigh to us here."

"I know not," quoth Will Stutely, shaking his head doubtfully, "our master is ever rash about thrusting his finger into a boiling pot; but, for my part, I see no use in getting ourselves into mischievous coils. Yon is a man's voice, if I mistake not, and a man should be always ready to get himself out from his own pothers." Thus spoke Will Stutely, yet, in truth, only half meant what he said. Nevertheless, since he had escaped so narrowly from out the Sheriff's clutches he had grown somewhat over-cautious.

Then out spake Will Scarlet boldly. "Now out upon thee, to talk in that manner, Stutely! Stay, if thou dost list. I go to see what may be the trouble of this poor creature."

"Nay," quoth Stutely, "thou doest lean so quickly thou'lt tumble into the ditch. Who said I would not go? Come along, say I." Thus saying, he led the way, the others following, till, after they had gone a short distance, they came to a little opening in the woodland, whence a brook, after gurgling out from under the tangle of overhanging bushes, spread out into a broad and glassy pebbled pool. By the side of this pool, and beneath the branches of a willow, lay a youth upon his face, weeping aloud, the sound of which had first caught the quick ears of Stutely. His golden locks were tangled, his clothes were all awry, and everything about him betokened sorrow and woe. Over his head, from the branches of the osier, hung a beautiful harp of polished wood inlaid with gold and silver in fantastic devices. Beside him lay a stout ashen bow and half a score of fair, smooth arrows.

"Halloa!" shouted Will Stutely, when they had come out from the forest into the little open spot. "Who are thou, fellow, that liest there killing all the green grass with salt water?"

Hearing the voice, the stranger sprang to his feet, and, snatching up his bow and fitting a shaft, held himself in readiness for whatever ill might befall him.

"Truly," said one of the yeomen, when they had seen the young stranger's face, "I do know that lad right well. He is a certain minstrel that I have seen hereabouts more than once. It was only a week ago I saw him skipping across the hill like a yearling doe. A fine sight he was then, with a flower at his ear and a cock's plume stuck in his cap; but now, methinks, our cockerel is shorn of his gay feathers."

"Pah!"cried Will Stutely, coming up to the stranger, "wipe thine eyes man! I do hate to see a tall, stout fellow so snivelling like a girl of fourteen over a dead tomtit. Put down thy bow, man! we mean thee no harm."

But Will Scarlet, seeing how the stranger, who had a young and boyish look, was stung by the words that Stutely had spoken, came to him and put his hand upon the youth's shoulder. "Nay, thou art in trouble, poor boy!" said he, kindly. "Mind not what these fellows have said. They are rough, but they mean thee well. Mayhap they do not understand a lad like thee. Thou shalt come with us, and perchance we may find a certain one that can aid thee in thy perplexities, whatsoever they may be."

"Yea, truly, come along." said Will Stutely, gruffly. "I meant thee no harm, and may mean thee some good. Take down thy singing tool from off this fair tree, and away with us."

The youth did as he was bidden, and, with bowed head and sorrowful step, accompanied the others, walking beside Will Scarlet.

So they wended their way through the forest. The bright light faded from the sky and a glimmering gray fell over all things. From the deeper recesses of the forest the strange whispering sounds of night-time came to the ear; all else was silent, saving only for the rattling of their footsteps amid the crisp, dry leaves of the last winter. At last a ruddy glow shone before them here and there through the trees; a little farther and they came to the open glade, now bathed in the pale moonlight. In the centre of the open crackled a great fire, throwing a red glow on all around. At the fire were roasting juicy steaks of venison, pheasants, capons, and fresh fish from the river. All the air was filled with the sweet smell of good things cooking.

The little band made its way across the glade, many yeomen turning with curious looks and gazing after them, but none speaking or questioning them. So, with Will Scarlet upon one side and Will Stutely upon the other, the stranger came to where Robin Hood sat on a seat of moss under the greenwood tree, with Little John standing beside him.

"Good even, fair friend," said Robin Hood, rising as the other drew near. "And hast thou come to feast with me this day?"

"Alas! I know not," said the lad, looking around him with dazed eyes, for he was bewildered with all that he saw. "Truly, I know not whether I be in a dream," said he to himself in a low voice.

"Nay, marry," quoth jolly Robin, laughing; "thou art awake, as thou wilt presently find, for a fine feast is a-cooking for thee. Thou art our honored guest this day."

Still the young stranger looked about him, as though in a dream. Presently he turned to Robin. "Methinks," said he, "I know now where I am and what hath befallen me. Art not thou the great Robin Hood?"

"Thou hast hit the bull's eye," quoth Robin, clapping him upon the shoulder. "Men hereabouts do call me by that name. Sin' thou knowest me, thou knowest also that he who feasteth with me must pay his reckoning. I trust thou hast a full purse with thee, fair stranger."

"Alas!" said the stranger, "I have no purse nor no money either, saving only the half of a sixpence, the other half of which mine own dear love doth carry in her bosom, hung about her neck by a strand of silken thread."

At this speech a great shout of laughter went up from those around, whereat the poor boy looked as he would die of shame; but Robin Hood turned sharply to Will Stutely. "Why, how now," quoth he, "is this the guest that thou hast brought us to fill our purse? Methinks thou hast brought but a lean cock to the market."

"Nay, good master," answered Will Stutely, grinning, "he is no guest of mine; it was Will Scarlet that brought him thither. Nevertheless, as thou mayst remember a certain talk this morning of duty and what not being better than a penny plucked from the dust, methinks here is a fine chance for practising charity."

Then up spoke Will Scarlet, and told how they had found the lad in sorrow, and how he had brought him to Robin, thinking that he might perchance aid him in his trouble. Then Robin Hood turned to the youth, and, placing his hand upon the other's shoulder, held him off at arm's length, scanning his face closely.

"A young face," quoth he in a low voice, half to himself, "a kind face, a good face. 'T is like a maiden's for purity, and, withal, the fairest that e'er mine eyes did see; but, if I may judge fairly by thy looks, grief cometh to young as well as to old." At these words, spoken so kindly, the poor lad's eyes brimmed up with tears. "Nay, nay," said Robin, hastily, "cheer up, lad; I warrant thy case is not so bad that it cannot be mended. What may be thy name?"

"Allan a Dale is my name, good master."

"Allan a Dale," repeated Robin, musing. "Allan a Dale. It doth seem to me that the name is not altogether strange to mine ears. Yea, surely thou art the minstrel of whom we have been hearing lately, whose voice so charmeth all men. Dost thou not come from the Dale of Rotherstream, over beyond Stavely?"

"Yea, truly," answered Allan, "I do come thence."

"How old art thou, Allan?" said Robin.

"I am but twenty years of age."

"Methinks thou art over young to be perplexed with trouble," quoth Robin, kindly; then, turning to the others, he cried, "Come, lads, busk ye and get our feast ready; only thou, Will Scarlet, and thou, Little John, stay here with me."

Then, when the others had gone, each man about his business, Robin turned once more to the youth. "Now, lad," said he, "tell us thy troubles, and speak freely. A flow of words doth ever ease the heart of sorrows; it is like opening the waste weir when the mill-dam is over full. Come, sit thou here beside me, and speak at thine ease."

Then straightway the youth told the three yeomen all that was in his heart; at first in broken words and phrases, then freely and with greater ease when he saw that all listened closely to what he said. So he told them how he had come from York to the sweet vale of Rother, travelling the country through as a minstrel, stopping now at castle, now at hall, and now at farmhouse; how he had spend one sweet evening in a certain broad, low farmhouse, where he sang before a stout franklin and a maiden as pure and lovely as the first snowdrop of spring; how he had played and sung to her, and how sweet Ellen o' the Dale had listened to him and had loved him. Then, in a low, sweet voice, scarcely louder than a whisper, he told how he had watched for her and met her now and then when she went abroad, but was all too afraid in her sweet presence to speak to her, until at last, beside the banks of Rother, he had spoken of his love, and she had whispered that which had made his heartstrings quiver for joy. Then they broke a sixpence between them, and vowed to be true to one another forever.

Next he told how her father had discovered what was a-doing, and had taken her away from him so that he never saw her again, and his heart was sometimes like to break; how this morn, only one short month and a half from the time that he had seen her last, he had heard and knew it to be so, that she was to marry old Sir Stephen of Trent, two days hence for Ellen's father thought it would be a grand thing to have his daughter marry so high, albeit she wished it not; nor was it wonder that a knight should wish to marry his own sweet love, who was the most beautiful maiden in all the world.

To all this the yeomen listened in silence, the clatter of many voices, jesting and laughing, sounding around them, and the red light of the fire shining on their faces and in their eyes. So simple were the poor boy's words, and so deep his sorrow, that even Little John felt a certain knotty lump rise in his throat.

"I wonder not," said Robin, after a moment's silence, "that thy true love loved thee, for thou hast surely a silver cross beneath thy tongue, even like good Saint Francis, that could charm the birds of the air by his speech."

"By the breath of my body," burst forth Little John, seeking to cover his feelings with angry words, "I have a great part of a mind to go straightway and cudgel the nasty life out of the body of that same vile Sir Stephen. Marry, come up, say I – what a plague – does an old weazen think that tender lasses are to be bought like pullets o' a market day? Out upon him! – I – but no matter, only let him look to himself."

Then up spoke Will Scarlet. "Methinks it seemeth but ill done of the lass that she should so quickly change at others' bidding, more especially when it cometh to the marrying of a man as old as this same Sir Stephen. I like it not in her, Allan."

"Nay," said Allan, hotly, "thou dost wrong her. She is as soft and gentle as a stockdove. I know her better than any one in all the world. She may do her father's bidding, but if she marries Sir Stephen, her heart will break and she will die. My own sweet dear, I" – He stopped and shook his head, for he could say nothing further.

Whilst the others were speaking, Robin Hood had been sunk in thought. "Methinks I have a plan might fit thy case, Allan," said he. "But tell me first, thinkest thou, lad, that thy true love hath spirit enough to marry thee were ye together in church, the banns published, and the priest found, even were her father to say her nay?"

"Ay, marry would she," cried Allan, eagerly.

"Then if her father be the man that I take him to be, I will undertake that he shall give you both his blessing as wedded man and wife, in the place of old Sir Stephen, and upon his wedding morn. But stay, now I bethink me, there is one thing reckoned not upon – the priest. Truly, those of the cloth do not love me overmuch, and when it comes to doing as I desire in such a matter, they are as like as not to prove stiff-necked. As to the lesser clergy, they fear to do me a favor because of abbot or bishop."

"Nay," quoth Will Scarlet, laughing, "so far as that goeth, I know of a certain friar that, couldst thou but get on the soft side of him would do thy business even though Pope Joan herself stood forth to ban him. He is known as the Curtal Friar of Fountain Abbey, and dwelleth in Fountain Dale."

"But," quoth Robin, "Fountain Abbey is a good hundred miles from here. An we would help this lad, we have no time to go thither and back before his true love will be married. Naught is to be gained there, coz."

"Yea," quoth Will Scarlet, laughing again, "but this Fountain Abbey is not so far away as the one of which thou speakest, uncle. The Fountain Abbey of which I speak is no such rich and proud place as the other, but a simple little cell; yet, withal, as cosy a spot as ever stout anchorite dwelt within. I know the place well, and can guide thee thither, for, though it is a goodly distance, yet methinks a stout pair of legs could carry a man there and back in one day."

"Then give me thy hand, Allan," cried Robin, "and let me tell thee, I swear by the bright hair of Saint Ælfrida that this time two days hence Ellen a Dale shall be thy wife. I will seek this same Friar of Fountain Abbey to-morrow day, and I warrant I will get upon the soft side of him, even if I have to drub one soft."

At this Will Scarlet laughed again. "Be not too sure of that, good uncle," quoth he; "nevertheless, from what I know of him, I think this curtal friar will gladly join two such fair lovers, more especially if there be good eating and drinking afoot thereafter."

But now one of the band came to say that the feast was spread upon the grass; so,

Robin leading the way, the others followed to where the goodly feast was spread. Merry was the meal. Jest and story passed freely, and all laughed till the forest rang again. Allan laughed with the rest, for his cheeks were flushed with the hope that Robin Hood had given him.

At last the feast was done, and Robin Hood turned to Allan, who sat beside him. "Now, Allan," quoth he, "so much has been said of thy singing that we would fain have a taste of thy skill ourselves. Canst thou not give us something?"

"Surely," answered Allan, readily; for he was no third-rate songster that must be asked again and again, but said "yes" or "no" at the first bidding; so, taking up his harp, he ran his fingers lightly over the sweetly-sounding strings, and all was hushed about the cloth. Then, backing his voice with sweet music on his harp, he sang

*MAY ELLEN'S WEDDING*

(*Giving an account of how she was beloved by a fairy prince, who took her to his own home.*)

1.

*"May Ellen sat beneath a thorn,*
*And in a shower around*
*The blossoms fell at every breeze*
*Like snow upon the ground,*
*And in a lime-tree near was heard*
*The sweet song of a strange, wild bird.*

2.

*"O sweet, sweet, sweet, O piercing sweet,*
*O lingering sweet the strain!*
*May Ellen's heart within her breast*
*Stood still with blissful pain:*
*And so, with listening, upturned face,*
*She sat as dead in that fair place.*

3.

*" 'Come down from out the blossoms, bird!*
*Come down from out the tree,*
*And on my heart I'll let thee lie,*
*And love thee tenderly!'*
*Thus cried May Ellen, soft and low,*
*From where the hawthorn shed its snow.*

4.

*"Down dropped the bird on quivering wing,*
*From out the blossoming tree,*
*And nestled in her snowy breast.*
*'My love! my love!' cried she;*
*Then straightway home, 'mid sun and flower,*
*She bare him to her own sweet bower.*

5.

*"The day hath passed to mellow night,*
*The moon floats o'er the lea,*
*And in its solemn, pallid light*
*A youth stands silently:*
*A youth of beauty strange and rare,*
*Within May Ellen's bower there.*

6.

*"He stood where o'er the pavement cold*
*The glimmering moonbeams lay.*
*May Ellen gazed with wide, scared eyes,*
*Nor could she turn away,*
*For, as in mystic dreams we see*
*A spirit, stood he silently.*

7.

*"All in a low and breathless voice,*
*'Whence comest thou?' said she;*
*'Art thou the creature of a dream,*
*Or a vision that I see?'*
*Then soft spake he, as night winds shiver*
*Through straining reeds beside the river.*

8.

*" 'I came, a bird on feathered wing,*
*From distant Faery land*
*Where murmuring waters softly sing*
*Upon the golden strand,*
*Where sweet trees are forever green;*
*And there my mother is the queen.'*

9.

*"No more May Ellen leaves her bowere*
*To grace the blossoms fair;*
*But in the hushed and midnight hour*
*They hear her talking there,*
*Or, when the moon is shining white,*
*They hear her singing through the night.*

10.

*" 'Oh don thy silks and jewels fine,'*
*May Ellen's mother said,*
*'For hither comes the Lord of Lyne*
*And thou this lord must wed.'*
*May Ellen said, 'It may not be.*
*He ne'er shall find his wife in me.'*

11.

*"Up spoke her brother, dark and grim:*
*'Now by the bright blue sky:*
*E'er yet a day hath gone for him*
*Thy wicked bird shall die!*
*For he hath wrought thee bitter harm,*
*By some strange art or cunning charm.'*

12.

*"Then, with a sad and mournful song,*
*Away the bird did fly,*
*And o'er the castle eaves, and through*
*The gray and windy sky.*
*'Come forth?' then cried the brother grim,*
*'Why dost thou gaze so after him?'*

13.

*"It is May Ellen's wedding day,*
*The sky is blue and fair,*
*And many a lord and lady gay*
*In church are gathered there.*
*The bridegroom was Sir Hugh the Bold,*
*All clad in silk and cloth of gold.*

14.

*"In came the Bride in samite white,*
*With a white wreath on her head;*
*Her eyes were fixed with a glassy look,*
*Her face was as the dead,*
*And when she stood among the throng,*
*She sang a wild and wondrous song.*

15.

*"Then came a strange and rushing sound*
*Like the coming wind doth bring,*
*And in the open windows shot*
*Nine swans on whistling wing,*
*And high above the heads they flew,*
*In gleaming flight the darkness through.*

16.

*"Around May Ellen's head they flew*
*In wide and windy flight,*
*And three times round the circle drew,*
*The guests shrank in affright,*
*And the Priest beside the altar there,*
*Did cross himself with muttered prayer.*

17.

*"But the third time they flew around,*
*Fair Ellen straight was gone,*
*And in her place, upon the ground,*
*There stood a snow-white swan.*
*Then, with a wild and lovely song,*
*It joined the swift and winged throng.*

18.

*"There's ancient men at weddings been,*
*For sixty years and more,*
*But such a wondrous wedding day,*
*They never saw before.*
*But none could check and one could stay,*
*The swans that bore the Bride away."*

Not a sound broke the stillness when Allan a Dale had done, but all sat gazing at the handsome singer, for so sweet was his voice and so sweet the music that each man sat with bated breath, lest one drop more should come and he should lose it.

"By my faith and my troth," quoth Robin at last, drawing a deep breath, "lad," thou art – Thou must not leave our company, Allan! Wilt thou not stay with us here in the sweet green forest? Truly, I do feel my heart go out toward thee with great love."

Then Allan took Robin's hand and kissed it. "I will stay with thee always, dear master," said he, "for never have I known such kindness as thou hast shown me this day."

Then Will Scarlet stretched forth his hand and shook Allan's in token of fellowship, as did Little John likewise. And thus the famous Allan a Dale became one of Robin Hood's band.

## Chapter Two

# Robin Seeketh the Curtal Friar of the Fountain

The stout yeomen of Sherwood Forest were ever early risers of a morn, more especially when the summer time had come, for then in the freshness of the dawn the dew was always the brightest, and the song of the small birds the sweetest.

Quoth Robin, "Now I will go to seek this same Friar of Fountain Abbey of whom we spoke yesternight, and I will take with me four of my good men, and these four shall be Little John, Will Scarlet, David of Doncaster, and Arthur a Bland. Bide the rest of you here, and Will Stutely shall be your chief whilst I am gone."

Then straightway Robin Hood donned a fine steel coat of chain mail, over which he put on a light jacket of Lincoln green. Upon his head he clapped a steel cap, and this he covered by one of soft white leather, in which stood a nodding cock's plume. By his side he hung a good broadsword of tempered steel, the bluish blade marked all over with strange figures of dragons, winged women, and what not. A gallant sight was Robin so arrayed, I wot, the glint of steel showing here and there as the sunlight caught brightly the links of polished mail that showed beneath his green coat.

So, having arrayed himself, he and the four yeomen set forth upon their way, Will Scarlet taking the lead, for he knew better than the others whither to go. Thus, mile after mile, they strode along, now across a brawling stream, now along a sunlit road, now adown some sweet forest path, over which the trees met in green and rustling canopy, and at the end of which a herd of startled deer dashed away, with rattle of leaves and crackle of branches. Onward they walked with song and jest and laughter till high noontide was passed, when at last they came to the banks of a wide, glassy, and lily-padded stream. Here a broad beaten path stretched along beside the banks, on which path labored the horses that tugged at the slow moving barges, laden with barley-meal or what not, from the countryside to the many-towered town. But now, in the hot silence of the midday, no horse was seen nor any man beside themselves. Behind them and before them stretched the ricer, its placid bosom ruffled here and there by the purple dusk of a small breeze. Sweet green osiers bordered the banks, and far away the red-tiled eaves of some tall tower glimmered in the sun, the weather-vane a spark against the blue sky. And now they travelled more easily, for the road was level and hard. Around them and over the surface of the water skimmed and dipped the swallows, gay dragon-flies darted hither and thither glistening in the sun, and now and then a solitary heron rose splashing and with startled cry from its hiding place among the reeds and sedges that grew in the shallow margin of the stream.

"Now, good uncle," quoth Will Scarlet at last, when they had walked for a long time beside this sweet bright river, "just beyond yon bend ahead of us is a shallow ford which in no place is deeper than thy mid-thigh, and upon the other side of the stream is a certain little hermitage hidden amidst the bosky tangle of the thickets wherein dwelleth the Friar of Fountain Dale. Thither will I lead thee, for I know the way; albeit it is not overhard to find."

"Nay," quoth jolly Robin, stopping suddenly, "had I thought that I should have had to wade water, even were it so crystal a stream as this, I had donned other clothes than I have upon me. But no matter now, for after all a wetting will not wash the skin away, and what must be must. But hide ye here, lads, for I would enjoy this merry adventure alone. Nevertheless, listen well, and if ye hear me sound upon my bugle-horn, come quickly."

"'T is ever thus," said Little John, half muttering; "thou dost always seek these ventures alone, whilst we, whose lives are but of small worth beside thine, and who would be but too glad to enter upon them, must sit, as it were, twiddling our thumbs in idleness."

"Nay, Little John," quoth jolly Robin, "this venture, I wot, is without danger to me. I know thou art overready to peril thyself; nevertheless, bide thou here this time as I bid thee." So saying he turned and left them, striding onward alone.

Robin had walked no farther than where the bend of the road hid his good men from his view, when he stopped suddenly, for the thought that he heard voices. He stood still and listened, and presently heard words passed back and forth betwixt what seemed to be two men, and yet the two voices were wondrously alike. The sound came from over behind the bank, that here was steep and high, dropping from the edge of the road a half a score of feet to the sedgy verge of the river.

"'T is strange," muttered Robin to himself after a space, when the voices had ceased their talking; "surely there be two people that spoke the one to the other, and yet methinks their voices are mightily alike. I make my vow that never have I heard the like in all my life before. Truly, if this twain are to be judged by their voices no two peas were ever more alike. I will look into this matter." So saying, he came softly to the river bank, and laying him down upon the grass peered over the edge and down below.

All was cool and shady beneath the bank. A stout osier grew, not straight upward, but leaning across the water, shadowing the spot with its soft foliage. All around grew a mass of feathery ferns such as hide and nestle in cool places, and up to Robin's nostrils came the tender odor of the wild thyme, that loves the moist verges of running streams. Here, with his broad back against the rugged trunk of the willow tree, and half hidden by the soft ferns around him, sat a stout, brawny fellow, but no other man was there. His head was as round as a ball, and covered with a mat of close-clipped curly black hair that grew low down on his forehead. But his crown was shorn as smooth as the palm of one's hand, which, together with his loose robe, cowl, and string of beads, showed that which his looks never would have done that he was a Friar. His cheeks were as red and shining as a winter crab, albeit they were nearly covered over with a close curly black beard, as were his chin and upper lip likewise. His neck was thick like that of a north country bull, and his round head closely set upon shoulders e'en a match for those of Little John himself. Beneath his bushy black brows danced a pair of little gray eyes that could not stand still for very drollery of humor. No man could look into his face and not feel his heartstrings tickled by the merriment of their look. By his side lay a steel cap, which he had laid off for the sake of the coolness to his crown. His legs were stretched wide apart, and betwixt his knees he held a great pasty compounded of juicy meats of divers kinds made savory with tender young onions, both meat and onions being mingled with a good rich gravy. In his right fist he held a great piece of brown crust at which he munched sturdily, and every now and then he thrust his left hand into the pie and drew it forth full of meat; anon he would take a mighty pull at a great bottle of Malmsley that lay beside him.

"By my faith," quoth Robin to himself, "I do verily believe that this is the merriest feast, the merriest wight, the merriest place, and the merriest sight in all merry England. Methought there was another here, but it must have been this holy man talking to himself."

So Robin lay watching the Friar, and the Friar, all unknowing that he was so overlooked, ate his meal placidly. At last he was done, and, having first wiped his greasy hands upon the ferns and wild thyme (and sweeter napkin ne'er had king in all the world), he took up his flask and began talking to himself as though he were another man, and answering himself as though he were somebody else.

"Dear lad, thou art the sweetest fellow in all the world, I do love thee as a lover loveth his lass. La, thou dost make me shamed to speak so to me in this solitary place, no one being by, and yet if thou wilt have me say so, I do love thee as thou lovest me. Nay then, wilt thou not take a drink of good Malmsey? After thee, lad, after thee. Nay, I beseech thee, sweeten the draught with thy lips (here he passed the flask from his right hand to his left). An thou wilt force it on me so I must needs do thy bidding, yet with the more pleasure do I so as I drink thy very great health (here he took a long, deep draught). And now, sweet lad, 't is thy turn next (here he passed the bottle from his left hand back again to his right). I take it, sweet chuck, and here's wishing thee as much good as thou wishest me." Saying this he took another draught, and truly he drank enough for two.

All this time merry Robin lay upon the bank and listened, while his stomach so quaked with laughter that he was forced to press his palm across his mouth to keep it from bursting forth; for, truly, he would not have spoiled such a goodly jest for the half of Nottinghamshire.

Having gotten his breath from his last draught, the Friar began talking again in this wise: "Now, sweet lad, canst thou not sing me a song? La, I know not, I am but in an ill voice this day; prythee ask me not; dost thou not hear how I croak like a frog? Nay, nay, thy voice is as sweet as any bullfinch; come, sing, I prythee, I would rather hear thee sing than eat a fair feast. Alas, I would fain not sing before one that can pipe so well and hath heard so many goodly songs and ballads, ne'ertheless, an thou wilt have it so, I will do my best. But now methinks that thou and I might sing some fair song together; dost thou not know a certain dainty little catch called "The Loving Youth and the Scornful Maid"? Why, truly, methinks I have heard it ere now. Then dost thou not think that thou couldst take the lass's part if I take the lad's? I know not but I will try; begin thou with the lad and I will follow with the lass."

Then, singing first with a voice deep and gruff, and anon in one high and squeaking, he blithely trolled the merry catch of –

*THE LOVING YOUTH AND THE SCORNFUL MAID*

*HE*

*"Ah, it's wilt thou come with me, my love?*
*And it's wilt thou, love, be mine?*
*For I will give unto thee, my love,*
*Gay knots and ribbons so fine.*
*I'll woo thee, love, on my bended knee,*
*And I'll pipe sweet songs to none but thee.*
*Then it's hark! hark! hark!*
*To the winged lark.*
*And it's hark to the cooing dove!*
*And the bright daffodil*
*Groweth down by the rill,*
*So come thou and be my love.*

*SHE*

*"Now get thee away, young man so fine;*
*Now get thee away, I say;*
*For my true love shall never be thine,*
*And so thou hadst better not stay.*
*Thou art not a fine enough lad for me,*
*So I'll wait till a better young man I see.*
*For it's hark! hark! hark!*
*To the winged lark,*
*And it's hark to the cooing dove!*
*And the bright daffodil*
*Groweth down by the rill,*
*Yet never I'll be thy love.*

*HE*

*"Then straight will I ask for another fair she,*
*For many a maid can be found,*
*And as thou wilt never have aught of me,*
*By the will I never be bound.*
*For never is a blossom in the field so rare,*
*But others are found that are just as fair.*
*So it's hark! hark! hark!*
*To the joyous lark,*
*And it's hark to the cooing dove!*
*And the bright daffodil*
*Groweth down by the rill,*
*And I'll seek me another dear love.*

*SHE*

*"Young man, turn not so very quick away*
*Another fair lass to find.*
*Methinks I have spoken in haste to-day,*
*Nor have I made up my mind,*
*And if you only wilt stay with me,*
*I'll love no other, sweet lad, but thee."*

Here Robin could contain himself no longer but burst forth into a mighty roar of laughter; then, the holy Friar keeping on with the song, he joined in the chorus, and together they sang, or, as one might say, bellowed:

*"So it's hark! hark! hark!*
*To the joyous lark,*
*And it's hark to the cooing dove!*
*For the bright daffodil*
*Groweth down by the rill,*
*And I'll be thine own true love."*

So they sang together, for the stout Friar did not seem to have heard Robin's laughter, neither did he seem to know that the yeoman had joined in with the song, but, with eyes half closed, looking straight before him and wagging his round head from side to side in time to the music, he kept on bravely to the end, he and Robin finishing up with a mighty roar that might have been heard a mile. But no sooner had the last word been sung than the holy man seized his steel cap, clapped it on his head, and springing to his feet cried in a great voice, "What spy have we here? Come forth, thou limb of evil, and I will carve thee into as fine pudding-meat as e'er a wife in Yorkshire cooked of a Sunday." Hereupon he drew from beneath his robes a great broadsword full as stout as was Robin's.

"Nay, put up thy pinking iron, friend," quoth Robin, standing up with the tears of laughter still on his cheeks. "Folk who have sung so sweetly together should not fight thereafter." Hereupon he leaped down the bank to where the other stood. "I tell thee, friend," said he, "my throat is as parched with that song as e'er a barley stubble in October. Hast thou haply any Malmsey left in that stout pottle?"

"Truly," said the Friar in a glum voice, "thou dost ask thyself freely where thou art not bidden. Yet I trust I am too good a Christian to refuse any man drink that is athirst. Such as there is o't thou art welcome to a drink of the same." And he held the pottle out to Robin.

Robin took it without more ado, and putting it to his lips tilted his head back, while that which was within said "glug! glug! glug!" for more than three winks, I wot. The stout Friar watched Robin anxiously the while, and when he was done took the pottle quickly. He shook it, held it betwixt his eyes and the light, looked reproachfully at the yeoman, and straightway placed it at his own lips. When it came away again there was naught within it.

"Dost thou know the country hereabouts, thou good and holy man?" asked Robin, laughing.

"Yea, somewhat," answered the other, dryly.

"And dost thou know a a certain spot called Fountain Abbey?"

"Yea, somewhat."

"Then perchance thou knowest also of a certain one who goeth by the name of the Curtal Friar of Fountain Abbey."

"Yea, somewhat."

"Well then, good fellow, holy father, or whatever thou art," quoth Robin, "I would know whether this same Friar is to be found upon this side of the river or the other."

"Truly, the river hath no side but the other," said the Friar.

"How dost thou prove that?" asked Robin.

"Why thus;" said the Friar, noting the points upon his fingers. "The other side of the river is then other, thou grantest?"

"Yea, truly."

"Yet the other side is but one side, thou dost mark?"

"No man could gainsay that," said Robin.

"Then if the other side is one side, this side is the other side. But the other side is the other side, therefore both sides of the river are the other side Q. E. D."

"'T is well and pleasantly argued," quoth Robin; "yet I am still in the dark as to whether this same Curtal Friar is upon the side of the river on which we stand or upon the side of the river on which we do not stand."

"That," quoth the Friar, "is a practical question upon which the cunning rules appertaining to logic touch not. I do advise thee to find that out by the aid of thine own five senses; sight, feeling, and what not."

"I do wish much," quoth Robin, looking thoughtfully at the stout priest, "to cross your ford and strive to find this same good Friar."

"Truly," said the other, piously, "it is a goodly wish on the part of one so young. Far be it from me to check thee in so holy a quest. Friend, the river is free to all."

"Yea, good father," said Robin; "but thou seest that my clothes are of the finest and I fain would not get them wet. Methinks thy shoulders are stout and broad; couldst thou not find it in thy heart to carry me across?"

"Now, by the white hand of the holy Lady of the Fountain!" burst forth the Friar in a mighty rage; "dost thou, thou poor puny stripling, thou kiss-my-lady-la poppenjay; thou – thou – What shall I call thee? Dost thou ask me, the holy Tuck to carry thee? Now I swear" – Here he paused suddenly, then slowly the anger passed from his face, and his little eyes twinkled once more. "But why should I not?" quoth he, piously: "Did not the holy Saint Christopher ever carry the stranger across the river? and should I, poor sinner that I am, be ashamed to do likewise? Come with me, stranger, and I will do thy bidding in an humble frame of mind." So saying he clambered up the bank, closely followed by Robin, and led the way to the shallow pebbly ford, chuckling to himself the while as though he were enjoying some goodly jest within himself.

Having come to the ford, he girded up his robes about his loins, tucked his good broadsword beneath his arm, and stooped his back to take Robin upon it. Suddenly he straightened up. "Methinks," quoth he, "thou'lt get thy weapon wet. Let me tuck it beneath mine arm along with mine own."

"Nay, good father," said Robin, "I would not burden thee with aught of mine but myself."

"Dost thou think," said the Friar, mildly, "that the good Saint Christopher would ha' sought his own ease so? Nay, give my thy tool as I bid thee, for I would carry it as a penance to my pride."

Upon this, without more ado, Robin Hood unbuckled his sword from his side and handed it to the other, who thrust it with his own beneath his arm. Then once more the Friar bent his back, and, Robin having mounted upon it, he stepped sturdily into the water, and so strode onward, splashing in the shoal, and breaking all the smooth surface into ever-widening rings. At last he reached the other side and Robin leaped lightly from his back.

"Many thanks, good father," quoth he. "Thou art indeed a good and holy man. Prythee give me my sword and let me away, for I am in haste."

At this the stout Friar looked upon Robin for a long time, his head on one side, and with a most waggish twist to his face; then he slowly winked his right eye. "Nay, good youth," said he, gently. "I doubt not that thou art in haste with thine affairs, yet thou dost think nothing of mine. Thine are of a carnal nature; mine are of a spiritual nature, a holy work, so to speak; moreover, mine affairs do lie upon the other side of this stream. I see by the quest of this same holy recluse that thou art a good young man and most reverent to the cloth. I did get wet coming hither, and am sadly afraid that should I wade the water again I might get certain cricks and pains i' the joints that would mar my devotions for many a day to come. I know that since I have so humbly done thy bidding thou wilt carry me back again. Thou seest how Saint Godrick that holy hermit whose natal day this is, hath placed in my hands two swords and in thine never a one. Therefore be persuaded, good youth, and carry me back again."

Robin Hood looked up and he looked down, biting his nether lip. Quoth he, "Thou cunning Friar, thou hast me fair and fast enow. Let me tell thee that not one of thy cloth hath so hoodwinked me in all my life before. I might have known from thy looks that thou wert no such holy man as thou didst pretend to be."

"Nay," interrupted the Friar, "I bid thee speak not so scurrilously neither, lest thou mayst perchance feel the prick of an inch or so of blue steel!"

"Tut, tut," said Robin, "speak not so, Friar; the loser hath ever the right to use his tongue as he doth list. Give me my sword; I do promise to carry thee back straightway. Nay, I will not lift the weapon against thee."

"Marry, come up," quoth the Friar, "I fear thee not, fellow. Here is thy skewer; and get thyself presently ready, for I would hasten back."

So Robin took his sword again and buckled it at his side; then he bent his stout back and took the Friar upon it.

Now I wot Robin Hood had a heavier load to carry in the Friar than the Friar had in him. Moreover he did not know the ford, so he went stumbling among the stones, now stepping into a deep hole, and now nearly tripping over a bowlder, while the sweat ran down his face in beads from the hardness of his journey and the heaviness of his load. Meantime, the Friar kept digging his heels into Robin's sides and bidding him hasten, calling him many ill names the while. To all this Robin answered never a word, but, having softly felt around till he found the buckle of the belt that held the Friar's sword, he worked slyly at the fastenings, seeking to loosen them. Thus it came about that, by the time he had reached the other bank with his load, the Friar's sword-belt was loose albeit he knew it not; so when Robin stood on dry land and the Friar leaped from his back, the yeoman gripped hold of the sword so that blade, sheath, and strap came away from the holy man, leaving him without a weapon.

"Now then," quoth merry Robin, panting as he spake and wiping the sweat from his brow, "I have thee, fellow. This time that same Saint of whom thou didst speak but now hath delivered two swords into my hand and hath stripped thine away from

*he... gave Robin a crack on the crown (Prologue)*

*A noble oak spread its branches wide (Part II, Chapter 1)*

thee. Now if thou dost not carry me back, and that speedily, I swear I will prick thy skin till it is as full of holes as a slashed doublet."

The good Friar said not a word for a while, but he looked at Robin with a grim look. "Now," said he at last, "I did think that thy wits were of the heavy sort and knew not that thou wert so cunning. Truly, thou hast me upon the hip. Give me my sword, and I promise not to draw it against thee save in self-defense; also I promise to do thy bidding and take thee upon my back and carry thee."

So jolly Robin gave him his sword again, which then Friar buckled to his side, and this time looked to it that it was more secure in its fastenings; then tucking up his robes once more, he took Robin Hood upon his back and without a word stepped into the water, and so waded on in silence while Robin sat laughing upon his back. At last he reached the middle of the ford where the water was deepest. Here he stopped for a moment, and then, with a sudden lift of his hand and heave of his shoulders, fairly shot Robin over his head as though he were a sack of grain.

Down went Robin into the water with a mighty splash. "There," quoth the holy man, calmly turning back again to the shore, "let that cool thy hot spirit, if it may."

Meantime, after much splashing, Robin had gotten to his feet and stood gazing about him all bewildered, the water running from him in pretty little rills. At last he shot the water our of his ears and spar some out of his mouth, and gathering his scattered wits together, saw the stout Friar standing on the bank and laughing. Then, I wot, was Robin Hood a mad man. "Stay, thou villain!" roared he, "I am after thee straight, and if I do not carve thy brawn for thee this day, may I never lift finger again!" So saying, he dashed, splashing, to the bank.

"Thou needst not hasten thyself unduly," quoth the stout Friar. "Fear not; I will abide here, and if thou dost not cry 'Alack-a-day' ere long time is gone, may I never more peep through the brake at a fallow deer."

And now Robin, having reached the bank, began, without more ado, to roll up his sleeves above his wrists. The Friar, also, tucked his robes more about him, showing a great, stout arm on which the muscles stood out like humps of an aged tree. Then Robin saw, what he had not wotted of before, that the Friar had also a coat of chain mail beneath his gown.

"Look to thyself," cried Robin, drawing his good sword.

"Ay, marry," quoth the Friar, who held his already in his hand. So, without more ado, they came together, and thereupon began a fierce and mighty battle. Right and left, and up and down, and back and forth they fought! The swords flashed in the sun and then met with a clash that sounded far and near. I wot this was no playful bout at quarterstaff, but a grim and serious fight of real earnest. Thus they strove for an hour or more, pausing every now and then to rest, at which times each looked at the other with wonder, and thought that never had he seen so stout a fellow; then once again they would go at it more fiercely than ever. Yet in all this time neither had harmed the other nor caused his blood to flow. At last merry Robin cried, "Hold thy hand, good friend!" whereupon both lowered their swords.

"Now I crave a boon ere we begin again," quoth Robin, wiping the sweat from his brow; for they had striven so long that he began to think that it would be an ill-done thing either to be smitten himself or to smite so stout and brave a fellow.

"What wouldst thou have of me?" asked the Friar.

"Only this," quoth Robin; "that thou wilt let me blow thrice upon my bugle horn."

The Friar bent his brows and looked shrewdly at Robin Hood. "Now I do verily think that thou hast some cunning trick in this," quoth he. "Ne'ertheless, I fear thee not, and will let thee have thy wish, providing thou wilt also let me blow thrice upon this little whistle."

"With all my heart," quoth Robin; "so, here goes for one." So saying, he raised his silver horn to his lips, and blew thrice upon it, clear and high.

Meantime, the Friar stood watching keenly for what might come to pass, holding in his fingers the while a pretty silver whistle, such as knights use for calling their hawks back to their wrists, which whistle always hung at his girdle along with his rosary.

Scarcely had the echo of the last note of Robin's bugle come winding back from across the river, when four tall men in Lincoln green came running around the bend of the road, each with a bow in his hand and an arrow ready nocked upon the string,

"Ha! is it thus, thou traitor knave!" cried the Friar. "Then, merry, look to thyself!" so saying, he straightway clapped the hawk's whistle to his lips and blew a blast that was both loud and shrill. And now there came a crackling of the bushes that lined the other side of the road, and presently forth from the covert burst four great, shaggy hounds.

"At 'em Sweet Lips! at 'em, Bell Throat! at 'em, Beauty! at 'em, Fangs!" cried the Friar, pointing at Robin.

And now it was well for that yeoman that a tree stood nigh him beside the road, else had he had an ill chance of it. Ere one could say "Gaffer Downthe-dale" the hounds were upon him, and he had only time to drop his sword and leap lightly into the tree, around which the hounds gathered, looking up at him as though he were a cat on the eaves. But the Friar quickly called off his dogs. "At 'em!" cried he, pointing down the road to where the yeomen were standing stock still with wonder of what they saw. As the hawk darts down upon its quarry, so sped the four dogs at the yeomen; but when the four men saw the hounds so coming, all with one accord, saving Will Scarlet, drew each man his goose feather to his ear and let fly his shaft.

And now the old ballad telleth of a wondrous thing that happened, for this it says, that each dog so shot at leaped lightly aside, and as the arrow passed him whistling, caught it in his mouth and bit it in twain. Now it would have been an ill day for these four good fellows had not Will Scarlet stepped before the others and met the hounds as they came rushing. "Why, how now, Fangs!" cried he, sternly. "Down, Beauty!, down sirrah! What means this?"

At the sound of his voice each dog shrank back quickly, and then straightway came to him and licked his hands and fawned upon him, as is the wont of dogs that meet one they know. Then the four yeomen came forward, the hounds leaping around Will Scarlet joyously. "Why, how now!" cried the stout Friar, "what means this? Art thou wizard to turn those wolves into lambs? Ha!" cried he, when they had come still nearer, "can I trust mine eyes? What means it that I see young Master William Gamwell in such company?"

"Nay, Tuck," said the young man, as the four came forward to where Robin was now clambering down from the tree in which he had been roosting, he having seen that all danger was over for the time; "nay, Tuck, my name is no longer Will Gamwell, but Will Scarlet; and this is my good uncle, Robin Hood, with whom I am abiding just now."

"Truly, good master," said the Friar, looking somewhat abashed and reaching out his great palm to Robin, "I ha' oft heard thy name both sung and spoken of, but I never thought to meet thee in battle. I crave thy forgiveness, and do wonder not that I found so stout a man against me."

"Truly, most holy father," said Little John, "I am more thankful than e'er I was in all my life before that our good friend Scarlet knew thee and thy dogs. I tell thee seriously that I felt my heart crumble away from me when I saw my shaft so miss its aim, and those great beasts of thine coming straight at me."

"Thou mayst indeed be thankful, friend," said the Friar, gravely. "But, Master Will, how cometh it that thou dost now abide in Sherwood?"

"Why, Tuck, dost thou not know of my ill happening with my father's steward?" answered Scarlet.

"Yea, truly, yet I knew not that thou wert in hiding because of it. Marry, the times are all awry when a gentleman must lie hidden for so small a thing."

"But we are losing time," quoth Robin, "and I have yet to find that same curtal Friar."

"Why, uncle, thou hast not far to go," said Will Scarlet, pointing to the Friar, "for there he stands beside thee."

"How?" quoth Robin, "art thou the man that I have been at such pains to seek all day, and have got such a ducking for?"

"Why, truly," said the Friar, demurely, "some do call me the curtal Friar of Fountain Dale; others again call me in jest the Abbot of Fountain Abbey; others still again call me simple Friar Tuck."

"I like the last name best," quoth Robin, "for it doth slip more glibly off the tongue. But why didst thou not tell me thou wert he I sought, instead of sending me searching for black moonbeams?"

"Why, truly, thou didst not ask me, good master," quoth stout Tuck; "but what didst thou desire of me?"

"Nay," quoth Robin, "the day groweth late, and we cannot stand longer talking here. Come back with us to Sherwood, and I will unfold all to thee as we travel along."

So, without tarrying longer, they all departed, with the stout dogs at their heels, and wended their way back to Sherwood again; but it was long past nightfall ere they reached the greenwood tree.

Now listen, for next I will tell how Robin Hood compassed the happiness of two young lovers, aided by the merry Friar Tuck of Fountain Dale.

## Chapter Three

# Robin Hood Compasseth the Marriage to Two True Lovers

And now had come the morning when fair Ellen was to be married, and on which merry Robin had sworn that Allan a Dale should, as it were, eat out of the platter that had been filled for Sir Stephen of Trent. Up rose Robin Hood, blithe and gay, up rose his merry men one and all, and up rose last of all stout Friar Tuck, winking the smart of sleep from out his eyes. Then, whilst the air seemed to brim over with the song of many birds, all blended together and all joying in the misty morn, each man laved face and hands in the leaping brook, and so the day began.

"Now," quoth Robin, when they had broken their fast, and each man had eaten his fill, "it is time for us to set forth upon the undertaking that we have in hand for to-day. I will choose me one score of my good men to go with me, for I may need aid; and thou, Will Scarlet, wilt abide here and be the chief whiles I am gone." Then searching through all the band, each man of whom crowded forward eager to be chosen, Robin called such as he wished by name, until he had a score of stout fellows, the very flower of his yeomanrie. Beside Little John and Will Stutely were nigh all those famous lads of whom I have already told you. Then, while those so chosen ran leaping, full of joy, to arm themselves with bow and shaft and broadsword, Robin Hood stepped aside into the covert, and there donned a gay coat such as might have been worn by some strolling minstrel, and slung a harp across his shoulder, the better to carry out that part.

And now I warrant Robin Hood was a sight to make all men stare. His hose were of green, but his jerkin was of mixed red and yellow, all hung about with streamers and knots and tags and ribbons of red and yellow also. Upon his head he wore a tall hat of red leather, and thrust therein was a nodding peacock's plume.

All the band stared and many laughed, for never had they seen their master in such a fantastic guise before. Little John walked all around him, seriously observing him narrowly, with his neck craned and his head on one side. As you may have seen the barnyard cock walk slowly round some unwonted thing, such as a sleeping cat or what not, pausing anon and anon, moving again with doubtful step, wondering the while and clucking to himself; so walked Little John around Robin with such words as, "La! Look ye there now! is it sooth? 't is pretty, I wot!" At last he stopped in front of Robin, "By my soul," said he, "this same is a dainty and pretty dress that thou hast upon thee, good master. Never hath sweeter bodily clothing been seen sin' good Saint Wolfhad, the martyr, saw one sitting upon a rock painting his tail purple and green."

"Truly," quoth Robin, holding up his arms and looking down at himself, "I do think it be somewhat of a gay, gaudy, grasshopper dress; but it is a pretty thing for all that, and doth not ill befit the turn of my looks, albeit I wear it but for the nonce. But stay, Little John, here are two bags that I would have thee carry in thy pouch for the sake of safe-keeping. I can ill care for them myself beneath this motley."

"Why, master," quoth Little John, taking the bags and weighing them in his hand, "here is the chink of gold."

"Well, what an there be," said Robin; "it is mine own coin, and the band is none the worse for what is there. Come, busk ye, lads;" and he turned quickly away, "get ye ready straightway." Then gathering the score together in a close rank, in the midst of which were Allan a Dale and Friar Tuck, he led them forth upon their way from the forest shades.

So they walked on for a long time till they had come out of Sherwood and to the vale of Rother stream. Here were different sights from what one saw in the forest; hedge-rows, broad fields of barley corn, pasture lands rolling upward till they met the sky and all dotted over with flocks of white sheep, hayfields whence came the odor of new-mown hay that lay in smooth swathes over which skimmed the swifts in rapid flight; such they saw, and different was it, I wot, from the tangled depths of the sweet woodlands, but full as fair. Thus Robin led his band, walking blithely with chest thrown out and head thrown back, snuffing the odors of the gentle breeze that came drifting from over the hayfields.

"Truly," quoth he, "the dear world is as fair here as in the woodland shades. Who calls it a vale of tears? Methinks it is but the darkness in our minds that bringeth gloom to the world. For what sayeth that merry song thou singest, Little John? is it not thus? –

> *"For when my love's eyes do shine, do shine*
> *And when her lips smile so rare,*
> *The day it is jocund and fine, so fine,*
> *Though let it be wet or be fair,*
> *And when the stout ale is all flowing so fast,*
> *Our sorrows and troubles are things of the past."*

"Nay," said Friar Tuck piously, "ye do think of profane things and of naught else; yet, truly, there be better safe-guards against care and woe than ale drinking and bright eyes, to wit, fasting and meditation. Look upon me, have I the likeness of a sorrowful man?"

At this a great shout of laughter went up from all around, for the night before the stout Friar had emptied twice as many canakins of ale as any one of all the merry men.

"Truly," quoth Robin, when he could speak for laughter, "I should say that thy sorrows were about equal to thy goodliness."

So they stepped along, talking, singing, jesting, and laughing, until they had come to a certain little church that belonged to the great estates owned by the rich Priory of Emmet. Here it was that fair Ellen was to be married on that morn, and here was the spot toward which the yeomen had pointed their toes. On the other side of the road from where the church stood with waving fields of barley around, ran a stone wall along the roadside. Over the wall from the highway was a fringe of young trees and bushes, and here and there the wall itself was covered by a mass of blossoming woodbine that filled all the warm air far and near with its sweet summer odor. Then straightway the yeomen leaped over the wall, alighting on the tall soft grass upon the other side, frightening a flock of sheep that lay there in the shade so that they scampered away in all directions. Here was a sweet cool shadow both from the wall and from the fair young trees and bushes, and here sat the yeomen down, and glad enough they were to rest after their long tramp in the morning.

"Now," quoth Robin, "I would have one of you watch and tell me when he sees any one coming to the church, and the one I choose shall be young David of Doncaster. So get thee upon the wall, David, and hide beneath the woodbine so as to keep watch."

Accordingly young David did as he was bidden, the others stretching themselves at length upon the grass, some talking together and others sleeping. Then all was quiet save only for the low voices of those that talked together, and for Allan's restless footsteps pacing up and down, for his soul was so full of disturbance that he could not stand still, and saving, also, for the mellow snoring of Friar Tuck, who enjoyed his sleep with a noise as of one sawing soft wood very slowly. Robin lay upon his back and gazed aloft into the leaves of the trees, his thought leagues away, and so a long time passed.

Then up spoke Robin: "Now tell us, young David of Doncaster, what dost thou see?"

Then David answered, "I see the white clouds floating and I feel the wind a-blowing and three black crows are flying over the wold; but naught else do I see, good master."

So silence fell again and another time passed, broken only as I have said, till Robin, growing impatient, spake again. "Now tell me, young David, what does thou see by this?"

And David answered, "I see the windmills swinging and three tall poplar trees swaying against the sky, and a flock of field-fares are flying over the hill; but naught else do I see, good master."

So another time passed, till at last Robin asked young David once more what he saw; and David said, "I hear the cuckoo singing, and I see how the wind makes waves in the barley field; and now over the hill to the church cometh an old friar, and in his hands he carries a great bunch of keys; and lo! now he cometh to the church door."

Then up rose Robin Hood and shook Friar Tuck by the shoulder. "Come, rouse thee, holy man!" cried he; whereupon, with much grunting, the stout Tuck got to his feet. "Marry, bestir thyself," quoth Robin, "for yonder, in the church door, is one of thy cloth. Go thou and talk to him, and so get thyself into the church, that thou mayst be there when thou art wanted; meantime, Little John, Will Stutely, and I will follow thee anon."

So Friar Tuck clambered over the wall, crossed the road, and came to the church, where the old Friar was still laboring with the great key, the lock being somewhat rusty and he somewhat old and feeble.

"Hilloa, brother," quoth Tuck, "let me aid thee." So saying, he took the key from the other's hand, and quickly opened the door with a turn of it.

"Who art thou, good brother?" asked the old Friar, in a high, wheezing voice. "Whence comest thou, and whither art thou going?" And he winked and blinked at stout Friar Tuck like an owl at the sun.

"Thus do I answer thy questions, brother," said the other. "My name is Tuck, and I go no farther than this spot, if thou wilt haply but let me stay while this same wedding is going forward. I come from Fountain Dale, and, in truth, am a certain poor hermit, as one may say, for I live in a cell beside the fountain blessed by that holy Saint Ethelrada, which same suffered the sharpest martyrdom that ever befell a woman, to wit, she had her tongue cut out, so that she could speak no more words than a dead jackdaw, as it were. But what befell? Marry, listen. Straight came this blessed woman to that same fountain, – so it was, and yet I am fain to confess that ne'er ha I got much good from the waters thereof; for cold water doth ever stir my inward parts with certain gripings and what not."

"But," piped the old brother, in his high, wheezing voice, "I do much wish to know what befell this holy woman upon coming to that same blessed fountain."

"Marry, a' drank o' the waters, and straightway regained that which an evil-minded fellow might say, and many might think, was no such heavenly gift, and that was her powers of speech. But, if I understand aught, there is to be a gay wedding here to-day; so, if thou minded not, I would fain rest me in the cool shade within, for I would like to see this fine sight."

"Truly, thou art welcome, brother," said the old man, leading the way within. Meantime, Robin Hood, in his guise of harper, together with Little John and Will Stutely, had come to the church. Robin sat him down on a bench beside the door, but Little John, carrying the two bags of gold, went within, as did Will Stutely.

So Robin sat by the door, looking up the road and down the road to see who might come, till, after a time, he saw six horsemen come riding sedately and slowly, as became them, for they were churchmen in high orders. Then, when they had come nearer, Robin saw who they were, and knew them. The first was the Bishop of Hereford, and a fine figure he cut, I wot. His vestments were of the richest silk, and around his neck was a fair chain of beaten gold! The cap that hid his tonsure was of black velvet, and around the edges of it were rows of jewels that flashed in the sunlight, each stone being set in gold. His hose were of flame-colored silk, and his shoes of black velvet, the long, pointed toes being turned up and fastened to his knees, and on either instep was embroidered a cross in gold thread. Beside the Bishop rode the Prior of Emmet upon a mincing palfrey. Rich were his clothes also, but not so gay as the stout Bishop's. Behind these were two of the higher brethren of Emmet, and behind these again two retainers belonging to the Bishop; for the Lord Bishop of Hereford strove to be as like the great barons as was in the power of one in holy orders.

When Robin saw this train drawing near, with flash of jewels and silk and jingle of silver bells on the trappings of the nags, he looked sourly upon them. Quoth he to himself, "Yon Bishop is overgaudy for a holy man. I do wonder whether his patron, who, methinks, was Saint Thomas, was given to wearing golden chains about his neck, silk clothing upon his body, and pointed shoes upon his feet; the money for all of which, God wot, hath been wrung from the sweat of poor tenants. Bishop, Bishop, thy pride may have a fall ere thou wottest of it."

So the holy men came to the church; the Bishop and the Prior jesting and laughing between themselves about certain fair dames, their words more befitting the lips of laymen, methinks, than holy clerks. Then they dismounted, and the Bishop, looking around, presently caught side of Robin standing in the doorway. "Hilloa, good fellow," quoth he, in a jovial voice, "who art thou that struttest in such gay feathers?"

"A harper am I from the North country," quoth Robin; "and I can touch the springs, I wot, as never another man in all merry England can do. Truly, good Lord Bishop, many a knight and burgher, clerk and layman, have danced to my music, willy nilly, and most times greatly against their will; such is the magic of my harping. Now this day, my Lord Bishop, if I may play at this wedding, I do promise that I will cause the fair bride to love the man she married with a love that shall last as long as that twain shall live together."

"Ha! is it so?" cried the Bishop. "Meanest thou this in sooth?" and he looked keenly at Robin, who gazed boldly back again into his eyes. "Now, if thou wilt cause this maiden (who had verily bewitched my poor cousin Stephen) thus to love the man she is to marry, as thou sayst thou canst, I will give thee whatsoever thou wilt ask me in due measure. Let me have a taste of thy skill, fellow."

"Nay," quoth Robin, "my music cometh not without I choose, even at a lord bishop's bidding. In sooth I will not play until the bride and bridegroom come."

"Now, thou art a saucy varlet to speak so to my crest," quoth the Bishop, frowning on Robin. "Yet, I must needs bear with thee. Look, Prior, hither cometh our cousin, Sir Stephen, and his lady-love."

And now, around the bend of the high-road, came others, riding upon horses. The first of all was a tall, thin man, of knightly bearing, dressed all in black silk, with a black velvet cap upon his head, turned up with scarlet. Robin looked, and had no doubt that this was Sir Stephen, both because of his knightly carriage and of his gray hairs. Beside him rode a stout Saxon franklin, Ellen's father, Edward of Deirwold; behind those two came a litter borne by two horses, and therein was a maiden whom Robin knew must be Ellen. Behind this litter rode six men-at-arms, the sunlight flashing on their steel caps as they came jingling up the dusty road.

So these also came to the church, and there Sir Stephen leaped from his horse, and, coming to the litter, handed fair Ellen out therefrom. Then Robin Hood looked at her, and could wonder no longer how it came about that so proud a knight as Sir Stephen of Trent wished to marry a common franklin's daughter; nor did he wonder that no ado was made about the matter, for she was the fairest maiden that ever he had beheld. Now, however, she was all pale and drooping, like a fair white lily snapped at the stem; and so, with bent head and sorrowful look, she went within the church, Sir Stephen leading her by the hand.

"Why dost thou not play, fellow?" quoth the Bishop, looking sternly at Robin.

"Marry," said Robin, calmly, "I will play in greater wise than your lordship thinks; but not till the right time hath come."

Said the Bishop to himself, while he looked grimly at Robin, "When this wedding is gone by I will have this fellow well whipped for his saucy tongue and bold speech."

And now fair Ellen and Sir Stephen stood before the altar, and the Bishop himself came in his robes and opened his book, wherest fair Ellen looked up and about her in bitter despair, like the fawn that finds the hounds on her haunch. Then, in all his fluttering tags and ribbons of red and yellow, Robin Hood strode forward. Three steps he took from the pillar, whereby he leaned, and stood between the bride and bridegroom.

"Let me look upon this lass," he said in a loud voice. "Why, how now! what have we here? Here be lilies in the cheeks, and not roses such as befit a bonny bride. This is no fit wedding. Thou, Sir Knight, so old, and she so young, and thou thinkest to make her thy wife? I tell thee it may not be, for thou art not her own true love."

At this all stood amazed, and knew not where to look nor what to think or say, for they were all bewildered with the happening; so, whilst every one looked at Robin as though they had been changed to stone, he clapped his bugle-horn to his lips and blew three blasts so loud and clear, they echoed from floor to rafter as though they were sounded by the trump of doom. Then straightway Little John and Will Stutely came leaping and stood upon either side of Robin Hood, and quickly drew their broadswords, the while a mighty voice rolled over the heads of all; "Here be I, good master, when thou wantest me;" for it was Friar Tuck that so called from the organ loft.

And now all was hubbub and noise. Stout Edward strode forward raging, and would have seized his daughter to drag her away, but Little John stepped between and thrust him back. "Stand back, old man," said he; "thou art a hobbled horse this day."

"Down with the villains!" cried Sir Stephen, and felt for his sword, but it hung not beside him on his wedding day.

Then the men-at-arms drew their swords, and it seemed like that blood would wet the stones; but suddenly came a bustle at the door and loud voices, steel flashed in the light, and the crash of blows sounded. The men-at-arms fell back, and up the aisle came leaping eighteen stout yeomen all clad in Lincoln green, with Allan a Dale at their head. In his hand he bore Robin Hood's good stout trusty bow of yew, and this he gave to him, kneeling the while upon one knee.

Then up spake Edward of Deirwold in a deep voice of anger: "Is it thou, Allan a Dale, that hath bred all this coil in a church?"

"Nay," quoth merry Robin, "that have I done, and I care not who knoweth it, for my name is Robin Hood."

At this name a sudden silence fell. The Prior of Emmet and those that belonged to him gathered together like a flock of frightened sheep when the scent of the wolf is nigh, while the Bishop of Hereford, laying aside his book, crossed himself devoutly. "Now Heaven keep us this day," said he, "from that evil man!"

"Nay," quoth Robin, "I mean you no harm; but here is fair Ellen's betrothed husband, and she shall marry him or pain will be bred to some of you?"

Then up spake stout Edward in a loud and angry voice: "Now I say nay! I am her father, and she shall marry Sir Stephen and none other."

Now all this time, whilst everything was in turmoil about him, Sir Stephen had been standing in proud and scornful silence. "Nay, fellow," said he, coldly, "thou mayst take thy daughter back again; I would not marry her after this day's doings could I gain all merry England thereby. I tell thee plainly, I loved thy daughter, old as I am, and would have taken her up like a jewel from the sty, yet, truly, I knew not that she did love this fellow, and was beloved by him. Maiden, if thou dost rather choose a beggarly minstrel than a high-born knight, take thy choice. I do feel it shame that I should thus stand talking amid this herd, and so I will leave you." Thus saying he turned, and, gathering his men about him, walked proudly down the aisle. Then all the yeomen were silenced by the scorn of his words, only Friar Tuck leaned over the edge of the choir loft, and called out to him ere he had gone, "Good den, Sir Knight. Thou wottest old bones must always make room for young blood." But Sir Stephen neither answered nor looked up, but passed out from the church as though he had heard naught, his men following him.

Then the Bishop of Hereford spoke hastily: "I, too, have no business here, and so will depart;" and he made as though he would go. But Robin Hood laid hold of his clothes and held him. "Stay, my Lord Bishop," said he, "I have yet somewhat to say to thee." The Bishop's face fell, but he stayed as Robin bade him for he saw he could not go.

Then Robin Hood turned to stout Edward of Deirwold, and said he: "Give thy blessing on thy daughter's marriage to this yeoman, and all will be well. Little John, give me the bags of gold. Look, farmer. Here are two hundred bright golden angels; give thy blessing, as I say, and I will count them out to thee as thy daughter's dower. Give not thy blessing, and she shall be married all the same, but not so much as a cracked farthing shall cross thy palm. Choose."

Then Edward looked upon the ground with bent brows, turning the matter over and over in his mind; but he was a shrewd man and one, withal, that made the best use of a cracked pipkin; so at last he looked up and said, but in no joyous tone, "If the wench will go her own gait, let her go. I had thought to make a lady of her; yet if she chooses to be what she is like to be, I have naught to do with her henceforth. Ne'ertheless I will give her my blessing when she is duly wedded."

"It may not be," spake up one of those of Emmet. "The banns have not been duly published, neither is there any priest here to marry them."

"How sayst thou?" roared Tuck from the choir loft. "No priest? Marry, here stands as holy a man as thou art, any day of the week, a clerk in orders, I would have thee know. As for the question of banns, stumble not over that straw, brother, for I will publish them." So saying, he called the banns; and, says the old ballad, lest three times should not be enough, he published them nine times o'er. Then straightway he came down from the loft, and forthwith performed the marriage service; and so Allan and Ellen were duly wedded.

And now Robin counted out two hundred golden angels to Edward of Deirwold, and he, upon his part, gave his blessing, yet not, I wot, as though he meant it with overmuch good will. Then the stout yeomen crowded around and grasped Allan's palm, and he, holding Ellen's hand within his own, looked about him all dizzy with his happiness.

Then at last jolly Robin turned to the Bishop of Hereford, who had been looking on at all that passed with a grim look. "My Lord Bishop," quoth he, "thou mayst bring to thy mind that thou didst promise me that did I play in such wise as to cause this fair lass to love her husband, thou wouldst give me whatsoever I asked in reason. I have played my play, and she loveth her husband, which she would not have done but for me; so now fulfil thy promise. Thou hast upon thou that which, methinks, thou wouldst be the better without, therefore, I prythee, give me that golden chain, that hangeth about thy neck as a wedding present for this fair bride."

Then the Bishop's cheeks grew red and his eyes flashed. He looked at Robin with a fell look, but saw that in the yeoman's face which bade him pause. Then slowly he took the chain from about his neck and handed it to Robin, who flung it over Ellen's head so that it hung glittering about her shoulders. Then said merry Robin, "I thank thee, on the bride's part, for thy handsome gift, and truly thou thyself art more seemly without it. Now, shouldst thou ever come nigh to Sherwood I much hope that I shall give thee there such a feast as thou hast ne'er had in all thy life before."

"May Heaven forfend!" cried the Bishop, earnestly; for he knew right well what manner of feast it was that Robin Hood gave his guests in Sherwood forest.

But now Robin Hood gathered his men together, and, with Allan and his young bride in their midst, they all turned their goodsteps towards the woodlands. On the way thither Friar Tuck came close and plucked him by the sleeve. "Thou dost lead a merry life, good master," quoth he, "but dost thou not think that it would be for the welfare of all your souls to have a good stout chaplain, such as I, to oversee holy matters? Truly, I do love this life mightily." At this merry Robin Hood laughed amain, and bade him stay and become one of their band if he wished.

That night there was such a feast held in the greenwood as Nottinghamshire never saw before. To that feast you and I were not bidden, and pity it is that we were not; so, lest we should both feel the matter the more keenly, I will say no more about it.

Thus ends the merry story of Allan a Dale, and how Robin Hood and Friar Tuck benefited him. And now we shall hear anon of other troubles than those that beset gentle lovers, and how Robin Hood helped a good stout knight that was in sore need of aid. So listen to what follows.

# Part Fifth

*In which it is told how that Robin Hood met a sorrowful knight, and brought him to Sherwood. Also, how the Bishop of Hereford was more generous than he desired to be. Likewise it is told how Sir Richard of the Lea paid his debts in due season, both to the Prior of Emmet and to Robin Hood.*

## Chapter One

# Robin Hood Aideth a Sorrowful Knight

So passed the gentle springtime away in budding beauty; its silver showers and sunshine, its green meadows and its flowers. So, likewise, passed the summer with its yellow sunlight, its quivering heat and deep, bosky foliage, its long twilights and its mellow nights, through which the frogs croaked and fairy folk were said to be out on the hillsides. All this had passed and the time of fall had come, bringing with it its own pleasures and joyousness; for now, when the harvest was gathered home, merry bands of gleaners roamed the country about, singing along the roads in the daytime, and sleeping beneath the hedgerows and the hay-ricks at night. Now the hips burned red in the tangled thickets and the haws waxed black in the hedgerows, the stubble lay all crisp and naked to the sky, and the green leaves were fast turning russet and brown. Also, at this merry season, good things of the year are gathered in in great store. Brown ale lies ripening in the cellar, hams and bacon hang in the smoke-shed, and crabs are stowed away in the straw for roasting in the winter time, when the north wind piles the snow in drifts around the gables and the fire crackles warm upon the hearth.

So passed the seasons then, so they pass now, and so they will pass in time to come, whilst we come and go like leaves of the tree that fall and are soon forgotten.

Quoth Robin Hood, snuffing the air, "Here is a fair day, Little John, and one that we can ill waste in idleness. Choose such men as thou dost need, and go thou east while I will wend to the west, and see that each of us bringeth back some goodly guest to dine this day beneath the greenwood tree."

"Marry," cried Little John, clapping his palms together for joy, "thy bidding fitteth my liking like haft to blade. I'll bring thee back a guest this day, or come not back mine own self."

Then they each chose such of the band as they wished, and so went forth by different paths from the forest.

Now, you and I cannot go two ways at the same time whilst we join in these merry doings; so we will e'en let Little John follow his own path while we tuck up our skirts and trudge after Robin Hood. And here is good company, too; Robin Hood, Will Scarlet, Allan a Dale, Will Scathelock, Midge, the Miller's son, and others. A score or more of stout fellows had abided in the forest, with Friar Tuck, to make ready for the home-coming, but all the rest were gone either with Robin Hood or Little John.

They travelled onward, Robin following his fancy and the others following Robin. Now they wended their way through an open dale with cottage and farm lying therein, and now again they entered woodlands once more. Passing by fair Mansfield Town, with its towers and battlements and spires all smiling in the sun, they came at last out of the forest lands. Onward they journeyed, through highway and byway, through villages where good wives and merry lasses peeped through the casements at the fine show of young men, until at last they came over beyond Alverton in Derbyshire. By this time high noontide had come, yet they had met no guest such as was worth their while to take back to Sherwood; so, coming at last to a certain spot where a shrine stood at the crossing of two roads, Robin called upon them to stop, for here on either side was shelter of high hedgerows, behind which was good hiding, whence they could watch the roads at their ease, whilst they ate their midday meal. Quoth merry Robin, "Here, methinks, is good lodging, where peaceful folk, such as we be, can eat in quietness; therefore we will rest here, and see what may, perhance, fall into our luck-pot." So they crossed a stile and came behind a hedgerow where the mellow sunlight was bright and warm, and where the grass was soft, and there sat them down. Then each man drew from the pouch that hung beside him that which he had brought to eat, for a merry walk such as this had been sharpens the appetite till it is as keen as a March wind. So no more words were spoken, but each man saved his teeth for better use – munching at brown crust and cold meat right lustily.

In front of them one of the high-roads crawled up the steep hill and then dipped suddenly over its crest, sharp-cut with hedgerow and shaggy grass against the sky. Over the top of the windy hill peeped the eaves of a few houses of the village that fell back into the valley behind; there, also, showed the top of a windmill, the sails slowly rising and dipping from behind the hill against the clear blue sky, as the light wind moved them with creaking and labored swing.

So the yeomen lay behind the hedge and finished their midday meal; but still the time slipped along, and no one came. At last, a man came slowly riding over the hill, and down the stony road toward the spot where Robin and his band lay hidden. He was a good stout knight, but sorrowful of face and downcast of mien. His clothes were plain and rich, but no chains of gold, such as folk of his stand in life wore at most times, hung around his neck, and no jewel was about him; yet no one could mistake him for aught but one of proud and noble blood. His head was bowed upon his breast and his hands drooped limp on either side; and so he came slowly riding, as though sunk in sad thoughts, whilst even his good horse, the reins loose upon his neck, walked with hanging head, as though he shared his master's grief.

Quoth Robin Hood, "Yon is verily a sorry-looking gallant, and doth seem to have donned ill-content with his jerkin this morning; nevertheless, I will out and talk with him, for there may be some pickings here for a hungry daw. Methinks his dress is rich, though he himself is so downcast. Bide ye here till I look into this matter." So saying, he arose and left them, crossed the road to the shrine, and there stood, waiting for the sorrowful Knight to come near him. So, presently, when the Knight came riding slowly along, jolly Robin stepped forward and laid his hand upon the bridle rein. "Hold, Sir Knight," quoth he. "I prythee tarry for a short time, for I have a few words to say to thee."

"What art thou, friend, who dost stop a traveller in this manner upon his most gracious Majesty's highway?" said the Knight.

"Marry," quoth Robin, "that is a question hard to answer. One man calleth me kind, another calleth me cruel; this one calleth me good, honest fellow, and that one vile thief. Truly, then world hath as many eyes to look upon a man withal as there are spots on a toad; so, with what pair of eyes thou regardest me lieth entirely with thine own self. My name is Robin Hood."

"Truly, good Robin," said the Knight, a smile twitching at the corners of his mouth, "thou has a quaint conceit. As for the pair of eyes with which I regard thee, I would say that they are as favorable as may be, for I hear much good of thee and little ill. What is thy will of me?"

"Now, I make my vow, Sir Knight," quoth Robin, "thou hast surely learned thy wisdom of good Gaffer Swanthold, for he sayeth, 'Fair words are as easy spoke as foul, and bring good will in the stead of blows.' Now I will show thee the truth of this saying; for, if thou wilt go with me this day to Sherwood Forest, I will give thee as merry a feast as ever thou hadst in all thy life."

"Thou art indeed kind," said the Knight, "but methinks thou wilt find me but an ill-seeming and sorrowful guest. Thou hadst best let me pass on my way in peace."

"Nay," quoth Robin, "thou mightst go thine own way but for one thing, and that I will tell thee. We keep an inn, as it were, in the very depths of Sherwood, but so far from high-roads and beaten paths that guests do not often come nigh us; so I and my friends set off merrily and seek them when we grow dull of ourselves. Thus the matter stands, Sir Knight; yet I will furthermore tell thee that we count upon our guests paying a reckoning."

"I take thy meaning, friend," said the Knight, gravely, "but I am not thy man, for I have no money by me."

"Is it sooth?" said Robin, looking at the Knight keenly. "I can scarce choose but believe thee; yet, Sir Knight, there be those of thy order whose word is not to be trusted as much as they would have others believe. Thou wilt think no ill if I look for myself in this matter." Then, still holding the horse by the bridle rein, he put his fingers to his lips and blew a shrill whistle, whereupon fourscore yeomen came leaping over the stile, and ran to where the Knight and Robin stood. "These," said Robin, looking upon them proudly, "are some of my merry men. They share and share alike with me all joys and troubles, gains and losses. Sir Knight, I prythee tell me what money thou hast about thee."

For a time the Knight said not a word, but a slow red arose into his cheeks; at last he looked Robin in the face and said: "I know not why I should be ashamed, for it should be no shame to me; but, friend, I tell thee the truth, when I say that in my purse are ten shillings, and that that is every groat that Sir Richard of the Lea hath in all the wide world."

When Sir Richard ended a silence fell, until at last Robin said: "And dost thou pledge me thy knightly word that this is all thou hast with thee?"

"Yea," answered Sir Richard, "I do pledge thee my most solemn word, as a true knight, that it is all the money I have in the world. Nay, here is my purse, ye may find for yourselves the truth of what I say." And he held his purse out to Robin.

"Put up thy purse, Sir Richard," quoth Robin. "Far be it from me to doubt the word of so gentle a knight. The proud I strive to bring low, but those that walk in sorrow I would aid if I could. Come, Sir Richard, cheer up thy heart and go with us into the greenwood. Even I may perchance aid thee, for thou surely knowest how the good Athelstane was saved by the little blind mole that digged a trench over which he that sought the king's life stumbled."

"Truly, friend," said Sir Richard, "methinks thou meanest kindness in thine own way; nevertheless my troubles are such that it is not likely that thou canst cure them. But I will go with thee this day into Sherwood." Hereupon he turned his horse's head, and they all wended their way to the woodlands, Robin walking on one side of the Knight and Will Scarlet on the other, whilst the rest of the band trudged behind.

After they had travelled thus for a time Robin Hood spake. "Sir Knight," said he, "I would not trouble thee with idle questions; but dost thou find it in thy heart to tell me thy sorrows?"

"Truly, Robin," quoth the Knight, "I see no reason why I should not so. Thus it is: my castle and my lands are in pawn for a debt that I owe. Three days hence the money must be paid or else all mine estate is lost forever, for then it falls into the hands of the Priory of Emmet, and what they swallow they never give forth again."

Quoth Robin, "I understand not why those of thy kind live in such a manner that all their wealth passeth from them like snow beneath the springtide sun."

"Thou wrongest me, Robin," said the Knight, "for listen: I have a son but twenty winters old, nevertheless he has won his spurs as knight. Last year, on a certain evil day, the jousts were held at Chester, and thither my son went, as did I and my lady wife. I wot it was a proud time for us, for he unhorsed each knight that he tilted against. At last he ran a course with a certain guest knight, Sir Walter of Lancaster, yet, though my son was so youthful, he kept his seat, albeit both spears were shivered to the haft; but it happened that a splinter of my boy's lance ran through the visor of Sir Walter's helmet, and pierced through his eye into his brain, so that he died ere his esquire could unlace his helm. Now, Robin, Sir Walter had great friends at court, therefore his kinsmen stirred up things against my son so that, to save him from prison I had to pay a ransom of six hundred pounds in gold. All might have gone well even yet, only that, by ins and outs and crookedness of laws, I was shorn like a sheep that is clipped to the quick. So it came that I had to pawn my lands to the Priory of Emmet for more money, and a hard bargain they drove with me in my hour of need. Yet I would have thee understand I grieve so for my lands only because of my dear lady wife."

"But where is thy son now?" asked Robin, who had listened closely to all the Knight had said.

"In Palestine," said Sir Richard, "battling like a brave Christian soldier for the cross and the holy sepulchre. Truly, England was an ill place for him because of Sir Walter's death, and the hate of the Lancastrian's kinsmen."

"Truly," said Robin, much moved, "thine is a hard lot. But tell me, what is owing to Emmet for thine estates?"

"Only four hundred pounds," said Sir Richard.

At this Robin smote his thigh in anger. "O the blood-suckers!" cried he. "A noble estate to be forfeit for four hundred pounds! But what will befall thee if thou dost lose thy lands, Sir Richard?"

"It is not mine own lot that doth trouble me in that case," said the Knight, "but my dear lady's; for should I lose my land she will have to betake herself to some kinsman and there abide in charity, which, methinks, would break her proud heart. As for me, I will over the salt sea, and so to Palestine to join my son in fight for the holy sepulchre."

Then up spake Will Scarlet. "But hast thou no friend that will help thee in thy dire need?"

"Never a man," said Sir Richard. "Whilst I was rich enow at home, and had friends, they blew great boasts of how they loved me. But when the oak falls in the forest the swine run from beneath it lest they should be smitten down also. So my friends have left me; for not only am I poor but I have great enemies."

Then Robin said, "Thou sayst thou hast no friends, Sir Richard. I make no boast, but many have found Robin Hood a friend in their troubles. Cheer up, Sir Knight, I may help thee yet."

The Knight shook his head with a faint smile, but for all that Robin's words made him more blithe of heart, for in truth hope, be it never so faint, bringeth a gleam into darkness, like a little rushlight that costeth but a groat.

The day was well-nigh gone when they came near to the greenwood tree. Even at a distance they saw by the number of men that Little John had come back with some guest, but when they came near enough, who should they find but the Lord Bishop of Hereford. The good Bishop was in a fine stew, I wot. Up and down he walked beneath the tree like a fox caught in a hencoop. Behind him were three black friars standing close together in a frightened group like three black sheep in a tempest. Hitched to the branches of the trees close at hand were six horses, one of them a barb with gay trappings upon which the Bishop was wont to ride, and the others laden with packs of divers shapes and kinds, one of which made Robin's eyes glisten, for it was a box not over large, but heavily bound with bands and ribs of iron.

When the Bishop saw Robin and those with him come into the open he made as though he would have run toward the yeoman, but the fellow that guarded the Bishop and the three friars thrust his quarterstaff in front, so that his lordship was fain to stand back, though with frowning brow and angry speech.

"Stay, my Lord Bishop," cried jolly Robin, in a loud voice, when he saw what had passed; "I will come to thee with all speed, for I would rather see thee than any man in merry England." So saying, he quickened his steps, and soon came to where the Bishop stood fuming.

"How now," quoth the Bishop in a loud and angry voice, when Robin had so come to him, "is this the way that thou and thy band treat one so high in the church as I am? I and these brethren were passing peacefully along the high-road with our packhorses, and a half score of men to guard them, when up comes a great strapping fellow full seven feet high, with fourscore or more men back of him, and calls upon me to stop – me, the Lord Bishop of Hereford, mark thou! Whereupon my armed guards – beshrew them for cowards! – straight ran away. But look ye; not only did this fellow stop me, but he threatened me, saying that Robin Hood would strip me as bare as a winter hedge. Then, beside all this, he called me such vile names as 'fat priest,' 'man-eating bishop,' 'money-gorging usurer,' and what not, as though I were no more than a strolling beggar or tinker. Moreover, when I came here I found a great fat man, a mock priest, that slapped me upon the shoulder as though I, God wot, were a pot-house fellow."

'Marry, come up with a wanion!" cried Friar Tuck bustling forward and thrusting himself in front of the Bishop; "Marry come up, I say!" and he snapped his fingers under the Bishop's nose, whereat the other started back as though the snap were a clap of thunder. "Mock priest! thou callest me, forsooth! Look ye now, Bishop, I wot I am as holy a man as thou art, and might have been a bishop mine own self, had I not been born under a hedge. I am as learned too, as thou art, albeit I could never master that vile Latin, my tongue being only shaped for good stout English; yet I tell thee, I can say my 'Paters' and 'Aves' with no more a slip o' the tongue than thou, thou fat man!"

At this the Bishop glared upon the stout Friar like an angry cat, whilst even Sir Richard laughed; only Robin kept a grave face. "Stand back, Tuck," said he, "thou shouldst not beard his lordship's reverence in this wise. Alas! my lord, that thou hast been so ill-treated by my band! I tell thee truly that we greatly reverence thy cloth. Little John, stand forth straightway."

At these words Little John came forward, twisting his face into a whimsical look, as though he would say, "Ha' mercy upon me, good master." Then Robin turned to the Bishop of Hereford and said: "Was this the man who spake so boldly to your lordship?"

"Ay, truly it was the same," said the Bishop; "a naughty fellow, I wot."

"And didst thou, Little John," said Robin, in a sad voice, "call his lordship a fat priest?"

"Ay," said Little John, sorrowfully.

"And a man-eating bishop?"

"Ay," said Little John, more sorrowfully than before.

"And a money-gorging usurer?"

"Ay," said Little John, in so sorrowful a voice that it might have drawn tears from the dragon of Wentley.

"Alas, that these things should be!" said jolly Robin, turning to the Bishop, "for I have ever found Little John a truthful man."

At this a roar of laughter went up, whereat the blood rushed into the Bishop's face till it was cherry red from crown to chin; but he said nothing, and only swallowed his words, though they well-nigh choked him.

"Nay, my Lord Bishop," said Robin, "we are rough fellows, but I trust not such ill men as thou thinkest, after all. There is not a man here that would harm a hair of thy reverence's head. I know thou art galled by our jesting, but we are all equal here in the greenwood, for there are no bishops nor barons nor earls among us, but only men, so thou must share our life with us whilst thou dost abide here. Come, busk ye, my merry men, and get the feast ready. Meantime we will show our guests our woodland sports."

So, whilst some went to kindle the fires for roasting meats, others ran leaping to get their cudgels and long bows. Then Robin brought forward Sir Richard o' the Lea. "My Lord Bishop," said he, "here is another guest that we have with us this day. I wish that thou mightest know him better, for I and all my men will strive to honor you both at this merrymaking."

"Sir Richard," said the Bishop, in a reproachful tone, "methinks thou and I are companions and fellow sufferers in this den of" – He was about to say "thieves," but he stopped suddenly and looked askance at Robin Hood.

"Speak out, Bishop," quoth Robin, laughing. "We of Sherwood check not an easy flow of words. 'Den of thieves' thou wast about to say."

Quoth the Bishop, "Mayhap that was what I meant to say, Sir Richard; but this I will say, that I saw thee just now laugh at the scurrilous jests of these fellows. It would have been more becoming of thee, methinks, to have checked them with frowns instead of spurring them on by laughter."

"I mean no harm to them"' said Sir Richard; "but a merry jest is a merry jest, and I may truly say would have laughed at it had it been against mine own self."

But now Robin Hood called upon certain ones of his band who spread soft moss upon the ground and laid deer skins thereon. Then Robin bade his guests be seated, and so they all three sat down, some of the chief men, such as Little John, Will Scarlet, Allan a Dale, and others, stretching themselves upon the ground near by. Then a garland was set up at the far end of the glade, and thereat the bowmen shot, and such shooting was done that day as it would have made one's heart leap to see. And all the while Robin talked so quaintly to the Bishop and the Knight that, the one forgetting his vexation and the other his troubles, they both laughed aloud again and again.

Ten men shot three rounds of arrows each, and although the garland was but three palms' breadth wide, and was full sevenscore yards distant, only two arrows went without the ring. "By Our Lady, good friend," said the Bishop to Robin, "never did I see such shooting in all my life as these men of thine do. But I have heard so oft of thy skill, canst thou not show us a touch of it?"

"Why," quoth Robin, "the light groweth somewhat dim, and things begin to glimmer, ne'ertheless I will try what I can do." So saying he arose from where he sat, then, drawing his dagger, he cut a hazel wand a little greater in girth than a man's thumb, and peeling the bark therefrom, he walked with measured steps fourscore yards distance. There he thrust the staff into the ground and came back to where the others sat, and Allan a Dale handed him his good stout yew bow, which Robin forthwith strung. Then emptying his quiver upon the ground, he searched among the arrows carefully till he had chosen one to his liking. Having so done, he nocked the arrow and stood in position, and all around was so hushed that you might have heard the falling of a leaf. Then he drew the string quickly to his ear, and straightened his bow arm, and ere you could draw a breath loosed the string with a twang. So swift flew the arrow that the eye could not follow it, but a great shout went up from the yeomen when it had sped, and Will Scathelock ran leaping and brought the wand, and lo, the arrow was sticking in the wood which it had cleft. Then all the yeomen shouted again till those about the fires came running, for they were proud of their master's skill, which none could hope to match.

But meantime Robin had set him down again between his guests; then, without giving them time for word of praise, he called upon those of his band who were the most deft at quarterstaff. So they sat and watched the game till the shades of evening fell, and there was no light in which to give stroke or parry.

Then Allan a Dale came forth and tuned his harp, and all was hushed around, and he sang in his wondrous voice songs of love, of war, of glory, and of sadness, and all listened without a movement or a sound. So Allan sang till the great round silver moon gleamed with its clear which light amid the upper tangle of the mazy branches of the trees.

At last two fellows came to say that the feast was ready spread, so Robin, leading his guests with either hand, brought them to where great smoking dishes, that sent savory smells far and near, stood along the white linen cloth spread on the grass. All around was a glare of torches that lit everything up with a red light. Then, straightway sitting down, all fell to with noise and hubbub, the rattling of platters blending with the sound of loud talking and laughter. A long time the feast lasted, but at last all was over, and the bright wine and humming ale passed briskly. Then Robin Hood called aloud for silence, and all was hushed till be spoke.

"I have a story to tell you all, so listen to what I have to say," quoth he; whereupon, without more ado, he told them all about Sir Richard, and how his lands were in pawn. But, as he went on, the Bishop's face, that had erst been smiling and ruddy with merriment, waxed serious, and he put aside the horn of wine he held in his hand, for he knew the story of Sir Richard, and his heart sank within him with grim forebodings. Then, when Robin Hood had done, he turned to the Bishop of Hereford. "Now, my Lord Bishop," said he, "dost thou not think this is ill done of any one, much more of a churchman, who should live in humbleness and charity?"

To this the Bishop answered not a word, but looked upon the ground with moody eyes.

Quoth Robin, "Now thou art the richest bishop in all England; canst thou not help this needy brother?" But still the Bishop answered not a word.

Then Robin turned to Little John, and quoth he, "Go thou and Will Stutely and bring forth five pack-horses yonder." Whereupon the two yeomen did as they were bidden, those about the cloth making room on the green, where the light was brightest, for the five horses which Little John and Will Stutely presently led forward.

"Who hath the score of the goods?' asked Robin Hood, looking at the Black friars.

Then up spake the smallest of all, in a trembling voice – an old man he was, with a gentle, wrinkled face. "That have I; but, I pray thee, harm me not."

"Nay," quoth Robin, "I have never harmed harmless man yet; but give it to me, good father." So the old man did as he was bidden, and handed Robin the tablet on which was marked down the account of the various packages upon the horses. This Robin handed to Will Scarlet, bidding him to read the same. So Will Scarlet, lifting his voice that all might hear, began:–

"Three bales of silk to Quentin, the mercer at Ancaster."

"That we touch not," quoth Robin, "for this Quentin is an honest fellow, who hath risen by his own thrift." So the bales of silk were laid aside without being opened.

"One bale of silk velvet for the Abbey of Beaumont."

"What do these priests want of silk velvet?" quoth Robin. "Nevertheless, though they need it not, I will not take all from them. Measure it off into three lots, one to be sold for charity, one for us, and one for the abbey." So this, too, was done as Robin Hood bade.

"Twoscore of great wax candles for the Chapel of Saint Thomas."

"That belongeth fairly to the chapel," quoth Robin, "so lay it to one side. Far be it from us to take from the blessed Saint Thomas that which belongeth to him." So this, also, was done according to Robin's bidding, and the candles were laid to one side, along with honest Quentin's unopened bales of silk. So the list was gone through with, and the goods adjudged according to what Robin thought most fit. Some things were laid aside untouched, and many were opened and divided into three equal parts, for charity, for themselves, and for the owners. And now all the ground in the torchlight was covered over with silks and velvets and cloths of gold and cases of rich wines, and so they came to the last line upon the tablet –

"A box belonging to the Lord Bishop of Hereford."

At these words the Bishop shook as with a chill, and the box was set upon the ground.

"My Lord Bishop, hast thou the key to this box?" asked Robin.

The Bishop shook his head.

"Go, Will scarlet," said Robin, "thou art the strongest man here – bring a sword straightway, and cut this box open, if thou canst." Then up rose Will Scarlet and left them, coming back in a short time, bearing a great two-handed sword. Thrice he smote that strong, iron-bound box, and at the third blow it burst open and a great heap of gold came rolling forth, gleaming red in the light of the torches. At this sight a murmur went all around among the band, like the sound of the wind in distant trees; but no man came forward nor touched the money.

Quoth Robin, "Thou, Will Scarlet, thou, Allan a Dale, and thou, Little John, count it over."

A long time it took to count all the money, and when it had been duly scored up, Will Scarlet called out that there were fifteen hundred golden pounds in all. But in among the gold they found a paper, and this Will Scarlet read in a loud voice, and all heard that this money was the rental and fines and forfeits from certain estates belonging to the Bishopric of Hereford.

"My Lord Bishop," said Robin Hood, "I will not strip thee, as Little John said, like a winter hedge, for thou shalt take back one third of thy money. One third of it thou canst well spare to us for thy entertainment and that of thy train, for thou art very rich; one third of it thou canst better spare for charity, for Bishop, I hear that thou art a hard master to those beneath thee and a close hoarder of gains that thou couldst better and with more credit to thyself give to charity than spend upon thy own likings."

At this the Bishop looked up, but he could say never a word; yet he was thankful to keep some of his wealth.

Then Robin turned to Sir Richard of the Lea, and quoth he, "Now, Sir Richard, the church seemed like to despoil thee, therefore some of the overplus of church gains may well be used in aiding thee. Thou shalt take that five hundred pounds laid aside for people more in need than the Bishop is, and shalt pay thy debts to Emmet therewith."

Sir Richard looked at Robin until something arose in his eyes that made all the lights and the faces blur together. At last he said, "I thank thee, friend, from my heart, for what thou doest for me; yet, think not ill if I cannot take thy gift freely. But this I will do: I will take the money and pay my debts, and in a year and a day hence will return it safe either to thee or to the Lord Bishop of Hereford. For this I pledge my most solemn knightly word. I feel free to borrow, for I know no man that should be more bound to aid me than one so high in that church that hath driven such a hard bargain with me."

"Truly, Sir Knight," quoth Robin, "I do not understand those fine scruples that weigh with those of thy kind; but, nevertheless, it shall all be as thou dost wish. But thou hadst best bring the money to me at the end of the year, for mayhap I may make better use of it than the Bishop." Thereupon, turning to those near him, he gave his orders, and five hundred pounds were counted out and tied up in a leathern bag for Sir Richard. The rest of the treasure was divided, and part taken to the treasure-house of the band, and part put by with the other things for the Bishop.

Then Sir Richard arose. "I cannot stay later, good friends," said he, "for my lady will wax anxious if I come not home; so I crave leave to depart."

Then Robin Hood and all his merry men arose, and Robin said, "We cannot let thee go hence unattended, Sir Richard."

Then up spake Little John: "Good master, let me choose a score of stout fellows from the band, and let us arm ourselves in a seemly manner, and so serve as retainers to Sir Richard till he can get others in our stead."

"Thou hast spoken well, Little John, and it shall be done," said Robin.

Then up spake Will Scarlet: "Let us give him a golden chain to hang about his neck, such as befits one of his blood, and also golden spurs to wear at his heels."

Then Robin Hood said, "Thou hast spoken well, Will Scarlet, and it shall be done."

Then up spake Will Stutely; "Let us give him yon bale of rich velvet and yon roll of cloth of gold to take home to his noble lady wife as a present from Robin Hood and his merry men all."

At this all clapped their hands for joy, and Robin said: "Thou hast well spoken, Will Stutely, and it shall be done."

Then Sir Richard o' the Lea looked all around and strove to speak, but could scarcely do so for the feelings that choked him; at last he said in a husky, trembling voice, "Ye shall all see, good friends, that Sir Richard o' the Lea will ever remember your kindness this day. And if ye be at any time in dire need or trouble, come to me and my lady, and the walls of Castle Lea shall be battered down ere harm shall befall you. I" – He could say nothing further, but turned hastily away.

But now Little John and nineteen stout fellows, whom he had chosen for his band, came forth all ready for the journey. Each man wore upon his breast a coat of linked mail, and on his head a cap of steel, and at his side a good stout sword. A gallant show they made as they stood all in a row. Then Robin came and threw a chain of gold about Sir Richard's neck, and Will Scarlet knelt and buckled the golden spurs upon his heel; and now Little John led forward Sir Richard's horse, and the Knight mounted. He looked down at Robin for a little time, then of a sudden stooped and kissed his cheek. All the forest glades rang with the shout that went up as the Knight and the yeomen marched off through the woodland with glare of torches and gleam of steel, and so were gone.

Then up spake the Bishop of Hereford in a mournful voice: "I, too, must be jogging, good fellow, for the night waxes late."

But Robin laid his hand upon the Bishop's arm and stayed him. "Be not so hasty, Lord Bishop," said he. "Three days hence Sir Richard must pay his debts to Emmet; until that time thou must be content to abide with me lest thou breed trouble for the Knight. I promise thee that thou shalt have great sport, for I know that thou art fond of hunting the dun deer. Lay by the mantle of melancholy, and strive to lead a joyous yeoman life for three stout days. I promise thee thou shalt be sorry to go when the time has come."

So the Bishop and his train abided with Robin for three days, and much sport his lordship had in that time, so that, as Robin had said, when the time had come for him to go he was sorry to leave the greenwood. At the end of three days Robin set him free, and sent him forth from the forest with a guard of yeomen to keep freebooters from taking what was left of the packs and bundles.

But, as the Bishop rode away, he vowed within himself that he would sometime make Robin rue the day that he stopped him in Sherwood.

But now we shall follow Sir Richard; so listen, and you shall hear what befell him, and how he paid his debts at Emmet Priory, and likewise in due season to Robin Hood.

## Chapter Two

# How Sir Richard of the Lea Paid His Debts to Emmet

The long highway stretched straight on, gray and dusty in the sun. On either side were dykes full of water bordered by osiers, and far away in the distance stood the towers of Emmet Priory with tall poplar trees around.

Along the causeway rode a knight with a score of stout men-at-arms behind him. The Knight was clad in a plain long robe of gray serge, gathered in at the waist with a broad leathern belt, from which hung a long dagger and a stout sword. But though he was so plainly dressed himself, the horse he rode was a noble barb, and its trappings were rich with silk and silver bells.

So thus the band journeyed along the causeway between the dykes, till at last they reached the great gate of Emmet Priory. There the Knight called to one of his men and bade him knock at the porter's lodge with the haft of his sword.

The porter was drowsing on his bench within the lodge, but at the knock he roused himself and, opening the wicket, came hobbling forth and greeted the Knight, whilst a tame starling that hung in a wicker cage within piped out, "*In cœlo quies! In cœlo quies!*" such being the words that the poor old lame porter had taught him to speak.

"Where is thy prior?" asked the Knight of the old porter.

"He is at meat, good knight, and he looketh for thy coming," quoth the porter, "for, if I mistake not, thou art Sir Richard o' the Lea.

"I am Sir Richard of the Lea; then I will go seek him forthwith," said the Knight.

"But shall I not send thy horse to stable?" said the porter. "By Our Lady, it is the noblest nag, and the best harnessed, that e'er I saw in all my life before." And he stroked the horse's flank with his palm.

"Nay," quoth Sir Richard, "the stables of this place are not for me, so make way, I prythee." So saying he pushed forward, and, the gates being opened, he entered the stony courtyard of the Priory, his men behind him. In they came with rattle of steel and clashing of swords, and ring of horses; feet on cobble-stones, whereat a flock of pigeons that strutted in the sun flew with flapping wings to the high eaves of the round towers.

Whilst the Knight was riding along the causeway to Emmet, a merry feast was toward in the refectory there. The afternoon sun streamed in through the great arched windows, and lay in broad squares of light upon the stone floor and across the board covered with a snowy linen cloth, whereon was spread a princely feast. At the head of the table sat Prior Vincent of Emmet all clad in soft robes of fine cloth and silk; on his head was a black velvet cap picked out with gold, and around his neck hung a heavy chain of gold, with a great locket pendant therefrom. Beside him, on the arm of his great chair, roosted his favorite falcon, for the Prior was fond of the gentle craft of hawking. On his right hand sat the Sheriff of Nottingham in rich robes of purple all trimmed about with fur, and on his left a famous doctor of law in dark and sober garb. Below these sat the high cellarer of Emmet, and others chief among the brethren.

Jest and laughter passed around, and all was as merry as merry could be. The weazened face of the man of law was twisted into a wrinkled smile, for in his pouch were fourscore golden angles that the Prior had paid him in fee for the case betwixt him and Sir Richard of the Lea. The learned doctor had been paid beforehand, for he had not overmuch trust in the holy Vincent of Emmet.

Quoth the Sheriff of Nottingham, "But art thou sure, Sir Prior, that thou hast the lands so safe?"

"Ay, marry," said Prior Vincent, smacking his lips after a deep draught of wine; "I have kept a close watch upon him, albeit he was unawares of the same, and I know right well that he hath no money to pay me withal."

"Ay, true," said the man of law in a dry, husky voice, "his land is surely forfeit if he cometh not to pay; but, Sir Prior, thou must get a release beneath his sign manual, or else thou canst not hope to hold the land without trouble from him."

"Yea," said the Prior, "so thou hast told me ere now, but I know that this knight is too poor that he will gladly sign away his lands for two hundred pounds of hard money."

Then up spake the high cellarer: "Methinks it is a shame to so drive a misfortunate knight to the ditch. I think it sorrow that the noblest estate in Derbyshire should so pass away from him for a paltry five hundred pounds. Truly I" –

"How now," broke in the Prior, in a quivering voice, his eyes glistening and his cheeks red with anger, "dost thou prate to my very beard, sirrah? By Saint Hubert, thou hadst best save thy breath to cool thy pottage, else it may scale thy mouth."

"Nay," said the man of law, smoothly, "I dare swear this same knight will never come to settlement this day, but will prove recreant. Nevertheless, we will seek some means to gain his lands from him, so never fear."

But even as the doctor spoke there came a sudden clatter of horses' hoofs and a jingle of iron mail in the courtyard below. Then up spake the Prior, and called upon one of the brethren that sat below the salt, and bade him look out of the window and see who was below, albeit he knew right well it could be none but Sir Richard.

So the brother arose and went and looked, and he said, "I see below a score of stout men-at-arms and a knight just dismounting from his horse. He is dressed in long robes of gray which, methinks, are of poor seeming; but the horse he rideth upon hath the richest coursing that ever I saw. The Knight dismounts and they come this way, and are even now below in the great hall."

"Lo, see ye there now," quoth Prior Vincent. "Here we have a knight with so lean a purse as scarce to buy him a crust of bread to much, yet he keeps a band of retainers, and puts rich trappings upon his horse's hide, whilst his own back goeth bare. Is it not well that such men should be brought low?"

"But art thou sure," said the little doctor, tremulously, "that this knight will do us no harm? Such as he are fierce when crossed, and he hath a band of naughty men at his heels. Mayhap thou hadst better give an extension of his debt." Thus he spake for he was afraid Sir Richard might do him a harm.

"Thou needst not fear," said the Prior, looking down at the little man beside him. "This knight is gentle, and would as soon think of harming an old woman as thee."

As the Prior finished, a door at the lower end of the refectory swung open, and in came Sir Richard, with folded hands and head bowed upon his breast. Thus humbly he walked slowly up the hall, whilst his men-at-arms stood about the door. When he had come to where the Prior sat, he knelt upon one knee. "Save and keep thee, Sir Prior," said he; "I am come to keep my day."

Then the first word that the Prior said to him was, "Hast thou brought my money?"

"Alas! I have not so much as one penny upon my body," said the Knight; whereat the Prior's eyes sparkled.

"Now, thou art a shrewd debtor, I wot," said he. Then, "Sir Sheriff, I drink to thee."

But still the Knight kneeled upon the hard stones, so the Prior turned to him again. "What wouldst thou have?" quoth he, sharply.

At these words, a slow red mounted into the Knight's cheeks; but still he knelt. "I would crave thy mercy," said he. "As thou hopest for Heaven's mercy, show mercy to me. Strip me not of my lands, and so reduce a true knight to poverty."

"Thy day is broken and thy lands forfeit," said the man of law, plucking up his spirits at the Knight's humble speech.

Quoth Sir Richard, "Thou man of law, wilt thou not befriend me in mine hour of need?"

"Nay," said the other, "I hold with this holy Prior, who hath paid me my fees in hard gold, so that I am bounden to him."

"Wilt thou not be my friend, Sir Sheriff?" said Sir, Richard.

"Nay, 'fore Heaven," quoth the Sheriff of Nottingham, "this is no business of mine, yet I will do what I may," and he nudged the Prior beneath the cloth with his knee. "Wilt thou not ease him of some of his debts, Sir Prior?"

At this the Prior smiled grimly. "Pay me three hundred pounds, Sir Richard," said he, "and I will give thee quittance of thy debt."

"Thou knowest, Sir Prior, that it is as easy for me to pay four hundred pounds as three hundred," said Sir Richard. "But wilt thou not give me another twelvemonth to pay my debt?"

"Not another day," said the Prior, sternly.'

"And is this all thou wilt do for me?" asked the Knight.

"Now, out upon thee, false Knight!" cried the Prior, bursting forth in anger. "Either pay thy debt as I have said or release thy land, and get thee gone from out my hall."

Then Sir Richard arose to his feet. "Thou false, lying priest!" said he, in so stern a voice that the man of law shrunk affrighted, "I am no false knight, as thou knowest full well, but have ever held my place in the press and the tourney. Hast thou so little courtesy that thou wouldst see a true knight kneel for all this time, or see him come into thy hall and never offer him eat or drink?"

Then quoth the man of law, in a trembling voice, "This is surely an ill way to talk of matters appertaining to business; let us be mild in speech. What wilt thou pay this knight, Sir Prior, to give thee release of his land?"

"I would have given him two hundred pounds," quoth the Prior, "but since he hath spoken so vilely to my teeth, not one groat over one hundred pounds will he get."

"Hadst thou offered me a thousand pounds, false Prior," said the Knight, "thou wouldst not have got an inch of my land." Then, turning to where his men-at-arms stood near the door, he called, "Come hither," and beckoned with his finger; whereupon the tallest of them all came forward and handed him a long leathern bag. Sir Richard took the bag and shot from it upon the table a glittering stream of golden money. "Bear in mind, Sir Prior," said he, "that thou hast promised me quittance for three hundred pounds. Not one farthing above that shalt thou get." So saying, he counted out three hundred pounds and pushed it toward the Prior.

But now the Prior's hands dropped at his sides and the Prior's head hung upon his shoulder, for not only had he lost all hopes of the land, but he had forgiven the Knight one hundred pounds of his debt and had needlessly paid the man of law fourscore angels. To him he turned, and quoth he, "Give me back my money, that thou hast."

"Nay," cried the other, shrilly, "it is but my fee that thou didst pay me, and thou gettest it not back again." And he hugged his gown about him.

"Now, Sir Prior," quoth Sir Richard, "I have held my day and paid all the dues demanded of me; so, as there is no more betwixt us, I leave this vile place straightway." So saying, he turned upon his heel and strode away.

All this time the Sheriff had been staring with wide-open eyes and mouth agape at the tall man-at-arms, who stood as though carved out of stone. At last he gasped out, "Reynold Greenleaf!"

At this, the tall man-at-arms, who was no other than Little John, turned, grinning, to the Sheriff. "I give thee good den, fair gossip," quoth he. "I would say, sweet Sheriff, that I have heard all thy pretty talk this day, and it shall be duly told unto Robin Hood. So, farewell for the nonce, till we meet again in Sherwood Forest." Then he, also, turned and followed Sir Richard down the hall, leaving the Sheriff, all pale and amazed, shrunk together upon his chair.

A merry feast it was to which Sir Richard came, but a sorry lot he left behind him, and little hunger had they for the princely food spread before them. Only the learned doctor was happy, for he had his fee.

But now a twelvemonth and a day has passed since Prior Vincent of Emmet sat at feast, as has just been told, and once more the mellow fall of another year has come. But the year had brought great change, I wot, to the lands of Sir Richard of the Lea; for, where before shaggy wild grasses grew upon the meadow lands, now all stretch away in golden stubble, betokening that a rich and plentiful crop had been gathered therefrom. A year had made a great change in the castle, also, for where were empty moats and the crumbling of neglect, all was now orderly and well kept.

Bright shone the sun on battlement and tower, and in the blue air overhead a flock of clattering jackdaws flew around the gilded weathervane and spire. Then, in the brightness of the morning, the drawbridge fell across the moat with a rattle and clank of chains, the gate of the castle slowly open, and a goodly array of steel-clad men-at-arms, with a knight all clothed in chain-mail, as white as frost on briar and thorn of a winter morning, came flashing out from the castle courtyard. In his hand the Knight held a great spear, from the point of which fluttered a blood-red pennant as broad as the palm of one's hand. So this troop came forth from the castle, and in the midst of them walked three packhorses laden with parcels of diver shapes and kinds.

Thus rode forth good Sir Richard of the Lea to pay his debt to Robin Hood this bright and merry morn. Along the highway they wended their way, with measured tramp of feet and rattle and jingle of sword and harness. Onward they marched till they came nigh to Denby, where, from the top of a hill they saw, over beyond the town, many gay flags and streamers floating in the bright air. Then Sir Richard turned to the man-at-arms nearest to him. "What is toward yonder at Denby to-day? quoth he.

"Please your worship," answered the man-at-arms, "a merry fair is held there to-day, and a great wrestling-match, to which many folk have come, for a prize hath been offered of a pipe of red wine, a fair golden ring, and a pair of gloves, all of which go to the best wrestler."

"Now, by my faith," quoth Sir Richard, who loved good sports right well, "this will be a goodly thing to see. Methinks we have time to stay a little while on our journey, and see this merry sport." So he turned his horse's head aside toward Denby and the fair and thither he and his men made their way.

There they found a great hubbub of merriment. Flags and streamers were floating, tumblers were tumbling on the green, bag-pipes were playing, and lads and lasses were dancing to the music. But the crowd were gathered most of all around a ring where the wrestling was going forward, and thither Sir Richard and his men turned their steps.

Now when the judges of the wrestling saw Sir Richard coming and knew who he was, the chief of them came down from the bench where he and the others sat, and went to the Knight and took him by the hand, beseeching him to come and sit with them and judge the sport. So Sir Richard got down from his horse, and went with the others to the bench raised beside the ring.

Now there had been great doings that morning, for a certain yeoman named Egbert, who came from Stoke over in Staffordshire, had thrown with ease all those that came against him; but a man of Denby, well known through all the countryside as William with the Scar, had been biding his time with the Stoke man; so, when Egbert had thrown every one else, stout William leaped into the ring. Then a tough bout followed, and at last he threw Egbert heavily, whereat there was a great shouting and shaking of hands, for all the Denby men were proud of their wrestler.

When Sir Richard came, he found stout William, puffed up by the shouts of his friends, walking up and down the ring, daring any one to come and try a throw with him. "Come one, come all!" quoth he. "Here stand I, William of the Scar, against any man. If there is none in Derbyshire to come against me, come all who will, from Nottingham, Stafford, or York, and if I do not make them one and all root the ground with their noses like swine in the forests, call me no more brave William the wrestler."

At this all laughed; but above all the laughter a loud voice was heard to cry out, "Sin' thou talkest so big, here cometh one from Nottinghamshire to try a fall with thee, fellow;" and straightway a tall youth with a tough quarterstaff in his hand came pushing his way through the crowd, and at last leaped lightly over the rope into the ring. He was not as heavy as stout William, but he was taller and broader in the shoulders, and all his joints were well knit. Sir Richard looked upon him keenly, then, turning to one of the judges, he said, "Knowest thou who this youth is? Methink I have seen him before."

"Nay," said the judge, "he is a stranger to me."

Meantime, without a word, the young man, laying aside his quarterstaff, began

*"Hold!" cried Little John, bursting from his cover*
*(Part III, Chapter 2)*

*"Nay, thou art in trouble!" (Part IV, Chapter 1)*

to take off his jerkin and body clothing until he presently stood with naked arms and body; and a comely sight he was when so bared to the view, for his muscles were cut round and smooth and sharp like swift-running water.

And now each man spat upon his hands, and, clapping them upon his knees, squatted down, watching the other keenly, so as to take the vantage of him in the grip. Then like a flash they leaped together, and a great shout went up, for William had gotten the better hold of the two. For a short time they strained and struggled and writhed, and then stout William gave his most cunning trip and throw, but the stranger met it with greater skill than his, and so the trip came to nought. Then of a sudden, with a twist and a wrench, the stranger loosed himself, and he of the scar found himself locked in a pair of arms that fairly made his ribs crack. So, with heavy, hot breathing, they stood for a while straining, their bodies all glistening with sweat, and great drops of sweat trickling down their faces. But the stranger's hug was so close that at last stout William's muscles softened under his grip, and he gave a sob. Then the youth put forth all his strength, and gave a sudden trip with his heel, and a cast over his right hip, and down stout William went, with a sickening thud, and lay as though he would never move hand nor foot again.

But now no shout went up for the stranger, but an angry murmur was heard among the crowd, so easily had he won the match. Then one of the judges, who was a kinsman to William of the Scar, rose with trembling lip and baleful look. Quoth he, "If thou hast slain that man it will go ill with thee, let me tell thee, fellow."

But the stranger answered boldly, "He took his chance with me as I took mine with him. No law can touch me to harm me, even if I slew him, so that it was fairly done in the wrestling ring."

"That we shall see," said the judge scowling upon the youth, whilst once more an angry murmur ran around the crowd; for, as I have said, the men of Denby were proud of stout William of the Scar.

Then up spoke Sir Richard, gently. "Nay, said he, "the youth is right; if the other dieth, he dieth in the wrestling ring, where he took his chance, and was cast fairly enow."

But in the mean time three men had come forward and lifted stout William from the ground, and found that he was not dead, though badly shaken by his heavy fall. Then the chief judge rose and said, "Young man, the prize is duly thine. Here is the red gold ring, and here the gloves, and yonder stands the pipe of wine to do with whatsoever thou dost list."

At this the youth, who had donned his clothes and taken up his staff again bowed, without a word, then, taking the gloves and the ring, and thrusting the one into his girdle and slipping the other upon his thumb, he turned and, leaping lightly over the ropes again, made his way through the crowd, and was gone.

"Now, I wonder who yon youth may be," said the judge, turning to Sir Richard; "he seemeth like a stout Saxon from his red cheeks and fair hair. This William of ours is a stout man, too, and never have I seen him cast in the ring before, albeit he hath not yet striven with such great wrestlers as Thomas of Cornwall, Diccon of York, and young David of Doncaster. Hath he not a firm foot in the ring, thinkest thou, Sir Richard?"

"Ay, truly; and yet this youth threw him fairly, and with wondrous ease. I much wonder who he can be." Thus said Sir Richard in a thoughtful voice.

For a time the Knight stood talking to those about him, but at last he arose and made ready to depart, so he called his men about him, and tightening the girths of his saddle, he mounted his horse once more.

Meanwhile the young stranger had made his way through the crowd, but, as he passed, he heard all around him such words muttered as, "Look at the cockeril!" "Behold how he plumeth himself!" "I dare swear he cast good William unfairly!" "Yea, truly, saw ye not bird-lime upon his hands?" "It would be well to cut his cock's comb!" To all this the stranger paid no heed, but strode proudly about as though he heard it not. So he walked slowly across the green to where the booth stood wherein was dancing, and standing at the door he looked in on the sport. As he stood thus a stone struck his arm of a sudden with a sharp jar, and, turning, he saw that an angry crowd of men had followed him from the wrestling ring. Then, when they saw him turn so, a great hooting and yelling arose from all, so that the folk came running out from the dancing booth to see what was to do. At last a tall, broad-shouldered, burly blacksmith strode forward from the crowd swinging a mighty blackthorn club in his hand.

"Wouldst thou come here to our fair town of Denby, thou Jack in the Box, to overcome a good honest lad with vile, juggling tricks?" growled he in a deep voice like the bellow of an angry bull. "Take that, then!" And of a sudden he struck a blow at the youth that might have felled an ox. But the other turned the blow deftly down with a groan, as though he had been smitten by lightning. When they saw their leader fall the crowd gave another angry shout; but the stranger placed his back against the tent near which he stood, swinging his terrible staff, and so fell had been the blow that he struck the stout smith, that none dared to come within the measure of his cudgel, so the press crowded back, like a pack of dogs from a bear at bay. But now some coward hand from behind threw a sharp jagged stone that smote the stranger on the crown, so that he staggered back, and the red blood gushed from the cut and ran down his face and over his jerkin. Then, seeing him dazed with this vile blow, the crowd rushed upon him, so that they overbore him and he fell beneath their feet.

Now it might have gone ill with the youth, even to the losing of his young lie, had not Sir Richard come to this fair; for of a sudden shouts were heard, and steel flashed in the air, and blows were given with the flat of swords, whilst through the midst of the crowd Sir Richard of the Lea came spurring on his white horse. Then the crowd, seeing the steel-clad knight and the armed men, melted away like snow on the warm hearth, leaving the young man all bloody and dusty upon the ground.

Finding himself free, the youth arose, and, wiping the blood from his face, looked up. Quoth he, "Sir Richard of the Lea, mayhap thou hast saved my life this day."

"Who art thou that knowest Sir Richard of the Lea so well?" quoth the Knight. "Methinks I have seen thy face before, young man."

"Yea, thou hast," said the youth, "for men call me David of Doncaster."

"Ha!" said Sir Richard; "I wonder that I knew thee not, David; but thy beard hath grown longer, and thou thyself art more set in manhood since this day twelvemonth. Come hither into the tent, David, and wash the blood from thy face. And thou, Ralph, bring him straightway a clean jerkin. Now I am sorry for thee, yet I am right glad that I have had a chance to pay a part of my debt of kindness to thy good master, Robin Hood, for it might have gone ill with thee had I not come, young man."

So saying, the Knight led David into the tent, and there the youth washed the blood from his face and put on the clean jerkin.

In the mean time a whisper had gone around from those that stood nearest that this was none other than the great David of Doncaster, the best wrestler in all the midcountry, who only last spring has cast stout Adam o' Lincoln in the ring at Selby, in Yorkshire, and now held the midcountry champion belt. Thus it happened that when young David came forth from the tent along with Sir Richard, the blood all washed from his face, and his soiled jerkin changed for a clean one, no sounds of anger were heard, but all pressed forward to see the young man, feeling proud that one of the great wrestlers of England should have entered the ring at Denby fair. For thus fickle is a mass of men.

Then Sir Richard called aloud, "Friends, this is David of Doncaster; so think it no shame that your Denby man was cast by such a wrestler. He beareth you no ill-will for what hath passed, but let it be a warning to you how ye treat strangers henceforth. Had ye slain him it would have been an ill day for you, for Robin Hood would have harried your town as the kestrel harries the dove-cote. I have bought the pipe of wine from him, and now I give it freely to you to drink as ye list. But never hereafterwards fall upon a man for being a stout yeoman."

At this all shouted amain; but in truth they thought more of the wine than of the Knight's words. Then Sir Richard, with David beside him and his men-at-arms around, turned about and left the fair.

But in after days, when the men that saw that wrestling bout were bent with age, they would shake their heads when they heard of any stalwart game, and say, "Ay, ay; but thou shouldst have seen the great David of Doncaster cast stout William with the Scar at Denby fair."

Robin Hood stood in the merry greenwood with Little John and most of his stout yeomen around him, awaiting Sir Richard's coming. At last a glint of steel was seen through the brown forest leaves, and forth from the covert into the open rode Sir Richard at the head of his men. He came straight forward to Robin Hood, and leaping from off his horse clasped the yeoman in his arms.

"Why, how now," said Robin, after a time, holding Sir Richard off and looking at him from top to toe; methinks thou art a gayer bird than when I saw thee last."

"Yea, thanks to thee, Robin," said the Knight, laying his hand upon the yeoman's shoulder. "But for thee I would have been wandering in misery in a far country by this time. But I have kept my word, Robin, and have brought back the money that thou didst lend me, and which I have doubled four times over again, and so become rich once more. Along with this money I have brought a little gift to thee and thy brave men from my dear lady and myself." Then, turning to his men, he called aloud, "Bring forth the packhorses."

But Robin stopped them. "Nay, Sir Richard," said he, "think it not bold of me to cross thy bidding, but we of Sherwood do no business till after we have eaten and drank; whereupon, taking Sir Richard by the hand, he led him to the seat beneath the greenwood tree, whilst others of the chief men of the band came and seated themselves around. Then, quoth Robin, "How cometh it that I saw young David of Doncaster with thee and thy men, Sir Knight?"

Then straightway the Knight told all about his stay at Denby and of the happening at the fair, and how it was like to go hard with young David; so he told his tale, and quoth he, "It was this, good Robin, that kept me so late on the way, otherwise I would have been here an hour agone."

Then, when he had done speaking, Robin stretched out his hand and grasped the Knight's palm. Quoth he in a trembling voice, "I owe thee a debt I can never hope to repay, Sir Richard, for let me tell thee, I would rather lose my right hand than have such ill befall young David of Doncaster as seemed like to come upon him at Denby."

So they talked until after a while one came forward to say that the feast was spread; whereupon all arose and went thereto. When at last it was done, the Knight called upon his men to bring the pack-horses forward, which they did according to his bidding. Then one of the men brought the Knight a strong box, which he opened and took from it a bag and counted out five hundred pounds, the sum of the money he had gotten from Robin.

"Sir Richard," quoth Robin, "thou wilt pleasure us all if thou wilt keep that money as a gift from us of Sherwood. Is it not so, my lads?"

Then all shouted "Ay" with a mighty voice.

"I thank you all deeply," said the Knight, earnestly, "but think it not ill of me if I cannot take it. Gladly have I borrowed it from you, but it may not be that I can take it as a gift."

Then Robin Hood said no more, but gave the money to Little John to put away in the treasury, for he had shrewdness enough to know that nought breeds ill-will and heart-bitterness like gifts forced upon one that cannot choose but take them.

Then Sir Richard had the packs laid upon the ground and opened, whereupon a great shout went up that made the forest ring again, for lo, there were tenscore bows of finest Spanish yew, all burnished till they shone again, and each bow inlaid with fanciful figures in silver, yet not inlaid so as to mar their strength. Beside these and in each quiver were a score of shafts with burnished heads that shone like silver; each shaft also was feathered with peacock's plumes and innocked with silver.

Sir Richard gave to each yeoman a bow and a quiver of arrows, but to Robin he gave a stout bow inlaid with the cunningest workmanship in gold, whilst each arrow in his quiver was innocked with gold.

Then all shouted again for joy of the fair gift, and all swore among themselves that they would die if need be for Sir Richard and his lady.

At last the time came when Sir Richard must go, whereupon Robin Hood called his band around him, and each man of the yeomen took a torch in his hand to light the way through the woodlands. So they came to the edge of Sherwood and there the Knight kissed Robin upon the cheeks and left him and was gone.

Thus Robin Hood helped a noble knight out of his dire misfortunes, that else would have smothered the happiness from his life.

Now listen, and you shall next hear of certain merry adventures that befell Robin Hood and Little John, and how one turned beggar and the other barefoot friar; likewise what each gained thereby.

# PART SIXTH

*In which it is told how that Robin Hood and Little John turned, the one a beggar and the other a strolling Friar, and went forth to seek adventures. Likewise it is told how Little John prayed to some purpose, and how Robin Hood drubbed four beggars and outwitted a corn engrosser.*

Chapter One

# Little John turns Barefoot Friar

Cold winter had passed and spring had come. No leafy thickness had yet clad the woodlands, but the budding leaves hung like a tender mist about the trees. In the open country the meadow lands lay a sheeny green, the cornfields a dark velvety color, for they were thick and soft with the growing blades. The plough-boy shouted in the sun, and in the purple new-turned furrows flocks of birds hunted for fat worms. All the broad moist earth smiled in the warm light, and each little green hill clapped its hands for joy.

On a deer's hide, stretched on the ground in the open in front of this greenwood tree, sat Robin Hood basking in the sun like an old dog fox. Leaning back with his hands clasped about his knees, he lazily watched Little John rolling a stout bowstring from long strands of hempen thread, wetting the palms of his hands ever and anon, and rolling the cord upon his thigh. Near by sat Allan a Dale fitting a new string to his harp.

Quoth Robin at last, "Methinks I would rather roam this forest in the gentle springtime that be king of all merry England. What palace in the broad world is as fair as this sweet woodland just now, and what king in all the world hath such appetite for plover's eggs and lampreys as I for juicy venison and sparkling ale? Gaffer Swanthold speaks truly when he saith, 'Better a crust with content than honey with a sour heart'."

"Yea," quoth Little John, as he rubbed his new-made bow-string with yellow beeswax, "the life we lead is the life for me. Thou speakest of the springtime, but methinks even the winter hath its own joys. Thou and I, good master, have had more than one merry day, this winter past, at the Blue Boar. Dost thou not remember that night thou and Will Stutely and Friar Tuck and I passed at that same hostelry with the two beggars and the strolling friar?"

"Yea," quoth merry Robin, laughing; "that was the night that Will Stutely must needs snatch a kiss from the stout hostess, and got a canakin of ale emptied over his head for his pains."

"Truly, it was the same," said Little John, laughing also. "Methinks that was a goodly song that the strolling friar sang. Friar Tuck, thou hast a quick ear for a tune, dost thou not remember it?"

"I did have the catch of it one time," said Tuck. "Let me see;" and he touched his forefinger to his forehead, humming to himself, and stopping ever and anon to fit what he had got to what he searched for in his mind. At last he found it all, and clearing his throat, sang merrily:-

*"In the blossoming hedge the robin cock sings,*
*For the sun it is merry and bright,*
*And he joyfully hops and he flutters his wings,*
*For his heart is all full of delight.*
*For the May bloometh fair,*
*And there's little of care,*
*And plenty to eat in the Maytime rare,*
*When the flowers all die,*
*Then off he will fly,*
*To keep himself warm*
*In some jolly old barn*
*Where the snow and the wind neither chill him nor harm.*

*"And such is the life of the strolling friar,*
*With a plenty to eat and to drink:*
*For the goodwife will keep him a seat by the fire,*
*And the pretty girls smile at his wink.*
*Then he lustily trolls,*
*As he onward strolls*
*A rollicking song for the saving of souls.*
*When the wind doth blow,*
*With the coming of snow,*
*There's a place by the fire*
*For the fatherly friar,*
*And a crab in the bowl for his heart's desire."*

Thus Friar Tuck sang in a rich and mellow voice, rolling his head from side to side in time with the music, and when he had done, all clapped their hands and shouted with laughter, for the song fitted him well.

"In very sooth," quoth Little John, "it is a goodly song, and, were I not a yeoman of Sherwood Forest, I had rather be a strolling friar than aught else in the world."

"Yea, it is a goodly song," said Robin Hood; "but methought those two burly beggars told the merrier tales and led the merrier life. Dost thou not remember what that great black-bearded fellow told of his begging at the fair in York?"

"Yea," said Little John, "but what told the friar of the Harvest-home in Kentshire? I hold that he led a merrier life than the other two."

"Truly, for the honor of the cloth," quoth Friar Tuck, "I hold with my good gossip, Little John."

"Now," quoth Robin, "I hold to mine own mind. But what sayst thou, Little John, to a merry adventure this fair day? Take thou a friar's gown from our chest of strange garments, and don the same, and I will stop the first beggar I meet and change clothes with him. Then let us wander the country about, this sweet day, and see what befalls each of us."

"That fitteth my mind," quoth Little John, "so let us forth, say I."

Thereupon Little John and Friar Tuck went to the storehouse of the band, and there chose for the yeoman the robe of a gray friar. Then they came forth again, and a mighty roar of laughter went up, for not only had the band never seen Little John in such guise before, but the robe was too short for him by a good palm's breadth. But Little John's hands were folded in his loose sleeve, and Little John's eyes were cast upon the ground, and at his girdle hung a great, long string of beads.

"Tut, tut!" quoth Friar Tuck, nudging him with his elbow, "look not down in that way; raise thine eyes boldly, or else all will know thee to be a cheat, and ne'er a lass will give thee a smile, and ne'er a goodwife a crust, in all the countryside." At this all laughed again, swearing that never was there so strapping a friar in all merry England as Little John made.

And now Little John took up his stout staff, at the end of which hung a chubby little leathern pottle, such as palmers carry at the tips of their staves; but in it was something, I wot, more like good Malmsey than cold spring water, such as godly pilgrims carry. Then up rose Robin and took his stout staff in his hand, likewise, and slipped ten golden angels into his pouch; for no beggar's garb was among the stores of the band, so he was fain to run his chance of meeting a beggar and buying his clothes of him.

So, all being made ready, the two yeomen set forth on their way, striding lustily along all in the misty morning. Thus they walked down the forest path until they came to the highway, and then along the highway till it split in twain, leading on one hand to Blyth and on the other to Gainsborough. Here the yeomen stopped.

Quoth Jolly Robin, "Take thou the road to Gainsborough, and I will take that to Blyth. So, fare thee well, holy father, and mayst thou not ha' cause to count thy beads in earnest ere we meet again."

"Good den, good beggar that is to be," quoth Little John, "and mayst thou have no cause to beg for money ere I see thee next."

So each stepped sturdily upon his way until a green hill rose between them, and the one was hid from the sight of the other.

Little John walked along, whistling, for no one was nigh upon all the road. In the budding hedges the little birds twittered merrily, and on either hand the green hills swept up to the sky, the great white clouds of springtime sailing slowly over their crowns in lazy flight. Up hill and down dale walked Little John, the fresh wind blowing in his face and his robes fluttering behind him, and so at last he came to a cross-road that led to Tuxford. Here he met three pretty lasses, each bearing a basket of eggs to market. Quoth he, "Whither away, fair maids?" And he stood in their path, with his legs apart, holding his staff in front of them, to stop them.

Then they huddled together and nudged one another, and one presently spake up and said, "We are going to the Tuxford market, holy Friar, to sell our eggs."

"Now out upon it!" quoth Little John, looking upon them with his head on one side. "Surely, it is a pity that such fair lasses should be forced to carry eggs to market. Let me tell you, an I had the shaping of things in this world, ye should all three have been clothed in the finest silks, and ride upon milk-white horses, with pages at your side, and feed upon nothing but whipped cream and strawberries; for such a life would surely befit your looks."

At this speech all three of the pretty maids looked down, blushing and simpering. One said, "La!" another, "Marry, a' maketh sport of us!" and the third, "Listen, now, to the holy man!" but at the same time they looked at Little John from out the corners of their eyes.

"Nay," quoth Little John, roundly, "holy man or no holy man, I know a fair lass when I see her, and if e'er a man hereabouts sayeth ye are not the fairest three in all Nottinghamshire, I'll knock his vile teeth down his lying throat with this stout staff. Hear ye that, now!"

Then all the lasses cried, "La!" again.

"Now, look you," said Little John, "I cannot see such dainty damsels as ye are carrying baskets a high-road. Let me take them mine own self, and one of you, if ye will, may carry my staff for me."

"Nay," said one of the lasses, "but thou canst not carry three baskets all at one time."

"Yea, but I can," said Little John, "and that I will show you presently. I thank the good Saint Wilfred that he hath given me a pretty wit. Look ye, now. Here I take this great basket, so; here I tie my rosary around the handle, thus; and here I slip the rosary over my head and sling the basket upon my back, in this wise." And Little John did according to his words, the basket hanging down behind him like a pedler's pack; then, giving his staff to one of the maids, and taking a basket upon either arm, he turned his face toward Tuxford Town, and stepped forth merrily, a laughing maid on either side, and one walking ahead, carrying the staff. In this wise they journeyed along, and every one they met stopped and looked after them, laughing, for never had anybody seen such a merry sight as this tall, strapping Gray Friar, with robes all too short for him, laden with eggs, and tramping the road with three pretty lasses. For this Little John cared not a whit, but when such folks gave jesting words to him he answered back as merrily, speech for speech.

So they stepped along toward Tuxford, chatting and laughing, until they came nigh to the town. Here Little John stopped and set down the baskets, for he did not care to go into the town lest he should, perchance, meet some of the Sheriff's men. "Alas! sweet chucks," quoth he, "here I must leave you. I had not thought to come this way, but I am glad that I did so. Now, ere we part, we must drink sweet friendship." So saying, he unslung the leathern pottle from the end of his staff, and, drawing the stopper therefrom, he handed it to the lass who had carried his staff, first wiping the mouth of the pottle upon his sleeve. Then each lass took a fair drink of what was within, and when it had passed all around, Little John finished what was left, so that not another drop could be squeezed from it. Then, kissing each lass sweetly, he wished them all good den, and left them. But the maids stood looking after him as he walked away whistling. "What a pity," quoth one, "that such a stout, lusty lad should be in holy orders."

"Marry," quoth Little John to himself, as he strode along, "yon was no such ill happening; Saint Dunstan send me more of the like."

After he had trudged along for a time he began to wax thirsty again in the warmth of the day. He shook his leathern pottle beside his ear, but not a sound came therefrom. Then he placed it to his lips and tilted it high aloft, but not a drop was there. "Little John! Little John!" said he sadly to himself, shaking his head the while, "woman will be thy ruin yet, if thou dost not take better care of thyself."

But at last he reached the crest of a certain hill, and saw below a sweet little thatched inn lying snugly in the dale beneath him, toward which the road dipped sharply. At the sight of this a voice within him cried aloud, "I give thee joy, good friend, for yonder is thy heart's delight, to wit, a sweet rest and a cup of brown beer." So he quickened his pace down the hill, and so came to the little inn, from which hung a sign with a stag's head painted upon it. In front of the door a clucking hen was scratching in the dust with a brood of chickens about her heels, and sparrows were chattering of household affairs under the eaves, and all was so sweet and peaceful that Little John's heart laughed within him. Beside the door stood two stout cobs with broad soft padded saddles, well fitted for easy travelling, and speaking of rich guests in the parlor. In front of the door three merry fellows, a tinker, a pedler, and a beggar, were seated on a bench in the sun quaffing stout ale.

"I give you good den, sweet friends," quoth Little John, striding up to where they sat.

"Give thee good den, holy father," quoth the merry Beggar with a grin. "But look thee, thy gown is too short. Thou hadst best cut a piece off the top and tack it to the bottom, so that it may be long enough. But come, sit beside us here and take a taste of ale, if thy vows forbid thee not."

"Nay," quoth Little John, also grinning, "the blessed Saint Dunstan hath given me a free dispensation for all indulgence in that line." And he thrust his hand into his pouch for money to pay his score.

"Truly," quoth the Tinker, "without thy looks belie thee, holy friar, the good Saint Dunstan was wise, for without such dispensation his votary is like to ha' many a penance to make. Nay, take thy hand from out thy pouch, brother, for thou shalt not pay this shot. Ho, landlord, a pot of ale!"

So the ale was brought and given to Little John. Then, blowing the froth a little away to make room for his lips, he tilted the bottom of the pot higher and higher, till it pointed to the sky, and he had to shut his eyes to keep the dazzle of the sunshine out of them. Then he took the pot away, for there was nothing in it, and heaved a full deep sigh, looking at the others with moist eyes and shaking his head solemnly.

"Ho, landlord!" cried the Pedler, "bring this good fellow another pot of ale, for truly it is a credit to us all to have one amongst us who can empty a canakin so lustily."

So they talked among themselves merrily, until after a while Little John, "Who rideth those two nags yonder?"

"Two holy men like thee, brother," quoth the Beggar. "They are now having a goodly feast within, for I smelt the steam of a boiled pullet just now. The landlady sayeth they come from Fountain Abbey, in Yorkshire, and go to Lincoln on matters of business."

"They are a merry couple," said the Tinker, "for one is as lean as an old wife's spindle, and the other as fat as a suet pudding."

"Talking of fatness," said the Pedler, "thou thyself lookest none too ill-fed, holy friar."

"Nay, truly," said Little John, "thou seest in me what the holy Saint Dunstan can do for them that serve him upon a handful of parched pease and a trickle of cold water."

At this a great shout of laughter went up. "Truly, it is a wondrous thing," quoth the Beggar; "I would have made my vow, to see the masterly manner in which thou didst tuck away your pot of ale, that thou hadst not tasted clear water for a brace of months. Has not this same holy Saint Dunstan taught thee a goodly song or two?"

"Why, as for that," quoth Little John, grinning, "mayhap he hath lent me aid to learn a ditty or so."

"Then, prythee, let us hear how he hath taught thee," quoth the Tinker.

At this Little John cleared his throat, and, after a word or two about a certain hoarseness that troubled him, sang thus:-

*"Ah, pretty, pretty maid, whither dost thou go?*
*I prythee, prythee, wait for thy lover also,*
*And we'll gather the rose*
*As it sweetly blows,*
*For the merry, merry winds are blo-o-o-wing."*

Now it seemed as though Little John's songs were never to get sung, for he had got no farther than this when the door of the inn opened and out came the two brothers of Fountain Abbey, the landlord following them, and, as the saying is, washing his hands with humble soap. But when the brothers of Fountain Abbey saw who it was that sang, and how he was clad in the robes of a gray friar, they stopped suddenly, the fat little Brother drawing his heavy eyebrows together in a mighty frown, and the thin Brother twisting up his face as though he had sour beer in his mouth. Then, as Little John gathered his breath for a new verse, "How, now," roared forth the fat Brother, his voice coming from him like loud thunder from a little cloud; "thou naughty fellow, is this a fit place for one in thy garb to tipple and sing profane songs?"

"Nay," quoth Little John, "sin' I cannot tipple and sing, like your worship's reverence, in such a goodly place as Fountain Abbey, I must e'en tipple and sing where I can."

"Now, out upon thee," cried the tall lean Brother in a harsh voice; "now, out upon thee, that thou shouldst so disgrace thy cloth by this talk and bearing."

"Marry, come up!" quoth Little John. "Disgrace, sayest thou? Methinks it is more disgrace for one of our garb to wring hard-earned farthings out of the gripe of poor lean peasants. Is it not so, brother?"

At this the Tinker and the Pedler and the Beggar nudged one another, and all grinned, and the friars scowled blackly at Little John; but they could think of nothing further to say, so they turned to their horses. Then Little John arose of a sudden from the bench where he sat, and ran to where the brothers of Fountain Abbey were mounting. Quoth he, "Let me hold your horses' bridles for you. Truly, your words have smitten my sinful heart, so that I will abide no longer in this den of evil, but will go forward with you. No vile temptation, I wot, will fall upon me in such holy company."

"Nay, fellow," said the lean Brother harshly, for he saw that Little John made sport of them, "we want none of thy company, so get thee gone."

"Alas," quoth Little John, "I am truly sorry that ye like me not nor my company, but as for leaving you it may not be for my heart is so moved, that, willy-nilly, I must go with you for the sake of your holy company."

Now at this talk all the good fellows on the bench grinned till their teeth glistened, and even the landlord could not forbear to smile. As for the friars, they looked at one another with a puzzled look, and knew not what to do in the matter. They were so proud that it made them feel sick with shame to think of riding along the high-road with a strolling friar, in robes all too short for him, running beside them, but yet could not make Little John stay against his will, for they knew he could crack the bones of both of them in a twinkling were he so minded. Then up spake the fat Brother more mildly than he had done before. "Nay, good brother," said he, "we will ride fast, and thou wilt tire to death at the pace."

"Truly, I am grateful to thee for the thought of me," quoth Little John; "but have no fear, brother; my limbs are stout, and I could run like a hare from here to Gainsborough."

At these words a sound of laughing came from the bench, whereat the lean Brother's wrath boiled over, like water into the fire, with great fuss and noise. "Now, out upon thee, thou naughty fellow!" he cried. "Art thou not ashamed to bring disgrace so upon our cloth? Bide thee here, thou sot, with these porkers. Thou art no fit company for us."

"La ye there now!" quoth Little John. "Thou hearest, landlord; thou art not fit company for these holy men; go back to thine ale-house. Nay, if these most holy brothers of mine do but give me the word, I'll beat thy head with this stout staff till it is as soft as whipped eggs."

At these words a great shout of laughter went up from those on the bench, and the landlord's face grew red as a cherry from smothering his laugh in his stomach; but he kept his merriment down, for he wished not to bring the ill-will of the brothers of Fountain Abbey upon him by unseemly mirth. So the two brethren, as they could do naught else, having mounted their nags, turned their noses toward Lincoln, and rode away.

"I cannot stay longer, sweet friends," quoth Little John, as he pushed in betwixt the two cobs, "therefore I wish you good den. Off we go, we three." So saying, he swung his stout staff over his shoulder and trudged off, measuring his pace with that of the two nags.

The two brothers glowered at Little John when he so pushed himself betwixt them, then they drew as far away from him as they could, so that the yeoman walked in the middle of the road, whilst they rode on the footpath on either side of the way. As they so went away, the Tinker, the Pedler, and the Beggar ran skipping out into the middle of the highway, each with a pot in his hand, and looked after them laughing.

Whilst they were in sight of those at the inn the two brothers walked their horses soberly, not caring to make ill matters worse by seeming to run away from Little John, for they could not but think how it would sound in folks' ears when they heard how the brethren of Fountain Abbey scampered away from a strolling friar, like the Ugly One, when the blessed Saint Dunstan loosed his nose from the red-hot tongs where he had held it fast; but when they had crossed the crest of the hill and the inn was lost to sight, quoth the fat Brother to the thin Brother, "Brother Ambrose, had we not better mend our pace?"

"Why truly, gossip," spoke up Little John, "methinks it would be well to boil our pot a little faster, for the day is passing on. So if it will not jolt thy fat too much, onward, say I."

At this the two friars said nothing, but they glared again on Little John with baleful looks; then, without another word, they clucked to their horses, and both broke into a canter. So they galloped for a mile and more, and Little John ran betwixt them as lightly as a stag, and never turned a hair with the running. At last the fat

Brother drew his horse's rein with a groan, for he could stand the shaking no longer. "Alas," said Little John, with not so much as a catch in his breath, "I did sadly fear that the roughness of this pace would shake thy poor old fat paunch."

To this the fat Friar said never a word, but he stared straight before him, and he gnawed his nether lip. And now they travelled forward more quietly, Little John in the middle of the road whistling merrily to himself, and the two friars in the footpath on either side saying never a word.

Then presently they met three merry minstrels all clad in red, who stared amain to see a Gray Friar with such short robes walking in the middle of the road, and two brothers, with heads bowed with shame, riding upon richly-caparisoned cobs on the foot-paths. When they had come near to the minstrels, Little John waved his staff like an usher clearing the way. "Make way!" he cried, in a loud voice, "Make way! make way! for here we go; we three!" Then how the minstrels stared, and how they laughed! But the fat Friar shook as with an ague, and the lean Friar bowed his head over his horse's neck.

Then next they met a stout burgher and his wife and their two fair daughters, all dressed in their Sunday best, riding from their cousin's house in the country back to Tuxford again. These Little John saluted gravely. Quoth he, "Good den, good folk. Here we go, we three." At this the women stared, for women do not take a joke so quickly as men; but the merry old burgher laughed till his fat side shook and his cheeks grew red and water stood in his eyes.

Then the third they met were two noble knights in rich array, with hawk on wrist, and likewise two fair ladies clad in silks and velvets, all a-riding on noble steeds. These all made room, staring, as Little John and the two friars came along the road. To them Little John bowed humbly. "Give you greeting, lords and ladies," said he. "But here we go, we three."

Then all laughed, and one of the fair ladies cried out, "What three meanest thou, merry friend?"

Little John looked over his shoulder, for they had now passed each other, and he called back, "Big Jack, lean Jack, and fat Jack-pudding."

At this the fat Friar gave a groan and seemed as if he were like to fall from his saddle for shame; the other brother said nothing, but he looked before him with a grim and stony look.

Just ahead of them the road took a sudden turn around a high hedge, and some twoscore paces beyond the bend another road crossed the one they were riding upon. When they had come to the cross-road and were well away from those they had left, the lean Friar drew rein suddenly. "Look ye, fellow," quoth he, in a voice quivering with rage, "we have had enough of thy vile company, and care no longer to be made sport of. Go thy way, and let us go ours in peace."

"La there, now!" quoth Little John. "Methought we were such a merry company, and here thou dost blaze up like fat in the pan. But truly, I ha' had enow of you to-day, though I can ill spare your company. I know ye will miss me, but gin ye want me again, whisper to Goodman Wind, and he will bring news thereof to me. But ye see I am a poor man and ye are rich. I pray you give me a penny or two to buy me bread and cheese at the next inn."

"We have no money, fellow," said the lean friar, harshly. "Come, Brother Thomas, let us forward."

But Little John caught the horses by the bridle-reins, one in either hand. "Ha' ye in truth no money about you whatsoever?" said he. "Now, I pray you, brothers, for charity's sake, give me somewhat to buy a crust of bread, e'en though it be only a penny."

"I tell thee, fellow, we have no money," thundered the fat little Friar with the great voice.

"Ha' ye, in holy truth, no money?" asked Little John.

"Not a groat," said the fat Friar, loudly.

"Nay," quoth Little John, "this must not be. Far be it from me to see such holy men as ye are depart from me with no money. Get both of you down straightway from off your horses, and we will kneel here in the middle of the cross-roads and pray to the blessed Saint Dunstan to send us some money to carry us on our journey."

"What sayeth thou, thou limb of evil!" cried the lean Friar, fairly gnashing his teeth with rage. "Dost thou bid me, the higher cellarer of Fountain Abbey, to get down from my horse and kneel in the dirty road to pray to some beggarly Saxon saint?"

"Now," quoth Little John, "I ha' a great part of a mind to crack thy head for thee for speaking thus of the good Saint Dunstan! But get down straightway, for my patience will not last much longer, and I may forget that ye are both in holy orders," So saying, he twirled his stout staff till it whistled again.

At this speech both friars grew as pale as dough. Down slipped the fat Brother from off his horse on one side, and down slipped the lean Brother on the other.

"Now, brothers, down on your knees and pray," said Little John; thereupon, putting his heavy hands upon the shoulder of each, he forced them to their knees, he kneeling also. Then Little John began to beseech Saint Dunstan for money, which he did in a great loud voice. After he had so besought the Saint for a time, he bade the friars feel in their pouches and see if the Saint had sent them anything; so each put his hand slowly in the pouch that hung beside him, but brought nothing thence.

"Ha!" quoth Little John, "have your prayers so little virtue? Then let us at it again."

Then straightway he began calling on Saint Dunstan again, somewhat in this wise: "O gracious Saint Dunstan! send some money straightway to these poor folk, lest the fat one waste away and grow as lean as the lean one, and the lean one waste away to nothing at all, ere they get to Lincoln Town; but send them only ten shillings apiece, lest they grow puffed up with pride. Any more than that that thou sendest, send to me."

"Now," quoth he, rising, "let us see what each man hath." Then he thrust his hands into his pouch, and drew thence four golden angels. "What have ye, brothers?" said he.

Then once again each friar slowly thrust his hand into his pouch, and once again brought it out with nothing in it.

"Have ye nothing?" quoth Little John. "Nay, I warrant there is somewhat that hath crept into the seams of your pouches, and so ye ha' missed it. Let me look."

So he went first to the lean Friar, and, thrusting his hand into the pouch, he drew forth a leathern bag, and counted therefrom one hundred and ten pounds of golden money. "I thought," quoth Little John, "that thou hadst missed, in some odd corner of thy pouch, the money that the blessed Saint had sent thee. And now let me see whether thou hast not some, also, brother." Thereupon he thrust his hand into the pouch of the fat Friar, and drew thence a bag like the other and counted out from it threescore and ten pounds. "Look, ye now," quoth he, "I knew the good Saint had sent thee some pittance that thou, also, hadst missed."

Then, giving them one pound between them, he slipped the rest of the money into his own pouch, saying. "Ye pledged me your holy word that ye had no money. Being holy men, I trust that ye would not belie your word so pledged, therefore I know the good Saint Dunstan hath sent this in answer to my prayers. But as I only prayed for ten shillings to be sent to each of you, all over and above that belongeth by rights to me, and so I take thee. I give you good den, brothers, and may ye have a pleasant journey henceforth." So saying, he turned and left them, striding away. The friars looked at one another with a woful look, and slowly and sadly they mounted their horses again and rode away with never a word.

But Little John turned his footsteps back again to Sherwood Forest, and merrily he whistled as he strode along.

And now we will see what befell Robin Hood in his venture as beggar.

## Chapter Two

# Robin Hood turns Beggar

After jolly Robin had left Little John at the forking of the roads, he walked merrily onward in the mellow sunshine that shone about him. Ever and anon he would skip and leap or sing a snatch of song, for pure joyousness of the day; for, because of the sweetness of the springtide, his heart was as lusty within him as that of a colt newly turned out to grass. Sometimes he would walk a long distance, gazing aloft at the great white swelling clouds that moved slowly across the deep blue sky; soon he would stop and drink in the fullness of life of all things, for the hedgerows were budding tenderly and the grass of the meadows was waxing long and green; again he would stand still and listen to the pretty song of the little birds in the thickets or hearken to the clear crow of the cock daring the sky to rain, whereat he would laugh, for it took but little to tickle Robin's heart into merriment. So he trudged manfully along, ever willing to stop for this reason or for that, and ever ready to chat with such merry lasses as he met now and then. So the morning slipped along, but yet he met no beggar with whom he could change clothes. Quoth he, "If I do not change my luck in haste, I am like to have an empty day of it, for it is well nigh half gone already, and, although I have had a merry walk through the countryside, I know nought of a beggar's life."

Then, after a while, he began to grow hungry, whereupon his mind turned from thoughts of springtime and flowers and birds and dwelt upon boiled capons, Malmsey, white bread, and the like, with great tenderness. Quoth he to himself, "I would I had Willie Wynkin's wishing coat; I know right well what I should wish for, and this it should be." Here he marked upon the fingers of his left hand with the forefinger of his right hand those things which he wished for. "Firstly, I would have a sweet brown pie of tender larks; mark ye, not dry cooked, but with a good sop of gravy to moisten it withal. Next, I would have a pretty pullet, fairly boiled, with tender pigeons' eggs, cunningly sliced, garnishing the platter around. With these I would have a long, slim loaf of wheaten bread that hath been baked upon the hearth; it should be warm from the fire, with glossy brown crust, the color of the hair of mine own maid, Marian, and this same crust should be as crisp and brittle as the thin white ice that lies across the furrows in the early winter's morning. These will do for the more solid things; but with these I must have three pottles, fat and round, one full of Malmsey, one of Canary, and one brimming full of mine own dear lusty sack." Thus spoke Robin to himself, his mouth growing moist at the corners with the thoughts of the good things he had raised in his own mind.

So, talking to himself, he came to where the dusty road turned sharply around the hedge, all tender with the green of the coming leaf, and there he saw before him a stout fellow sitting upon a stile, swinging his legs in idleness. All about this lusty rogue dangled divers pouches and bags of different sizes and kinds, a dozen or more, with great, wide, gaping mouths, like a brood of hungry daws. His coat was gathered in at his waist, and was patched with as many colors as there are stripes upon a Maypole in the springtide. On his head he wore a great tall leathern cap, and across his knees rested a stout quarterstaff of blackthorn, full as long and heavy as Robin's. As jolly a beggar was he as ever trod the lands and byways of Nottinghamshire, for his eyes were as gray as slate, and snapped and twinkled and danced with merriment, and his black hair curled close all over his head in little rings of kinkyness.

"Halloa, good fellow," quoth Robin, when he had come nigh to the other, "what art thou doing here this merry day, when the flowers are peeping and the buds are swelling?"

Then the other winked one eye, and straightway trolled forth in a merry voice:–

*"I sit upon the side,*
*And I sing a little while*
*As I wait for my own true dear, O,*
*For the sun is shining bright,*
*And the leaves are dancing light,*
*And the little fowl sings she is near, O.*

"And so it is with me, bully boy, saving that my doxy cometh not."

"Now that is a right sweet song," quoth Robin, "and, were I in the right mind to listen to thee, I could bear well to hear more; but I have two things of seriousness to ask of thee; so listen, I prythee."

At this the jolly Beggar cocked his head on one side, like a rogue of a magpie. Quoth he, "I am an ill jug to pour heavy things into, good friend, and, if I mistake not, thou hast few serious words to spare at any time."

"Nay," quoth jolly Robin, "what I would say first is the most serious of all thoughts to me, to wit, 'where shall I get somewhat to eat and drink?'"

"Sayst thou so?" quoth the Beggar. "Marry, I make no such serious thoughts upon the matter. I eat when I can get it, and munch my crust when I can get no crumb; likewise, when there is no ale to be had I wash the dust from out my throat with a trickle of cold water. I was sitting here, as thou camest upon me, bethinking myself whether I should break my fast or no. I do love to let my hunger grow keen ere I eat, for then a dry crust is as good to me as a venison pasty with suet and raisins is to stout King Harry. I have a sharp hunger upon me now, but methinks in a short while it will ripen to a right mellow appetite."

"Now, in good sooth," quoth merry Robin, laughing, "thou hast a quaint tongue betwixt thy teeth. But hast thou truly nought but a dry crust about thee? Methinks thy bags and pouches are fat and lusty for such thin fare."

"Why, mayhap there is some other cold fare therein" said the Beggar, slyly.

"And hast thou nought to drink but cold water?" said Robin.

"Never so much as a drop," quoth the Beggar. "Over beyond yon clump of trees is as sweet a little inn as ever thou hast lifted eyelid upon; but I go not thither, for they have a nasty way with me. Once, when the good Prior of Emmet was dining there, the landlady set a dear little tart of stewed crabs and barley-sugar upon the window-sill to cool, and seeing it there, and fearing it might be lost, I took it with me till that I could find the owner thereof. Ever since then they have acted very ill toward me, yet truth bids me say that they have the best ale there that ever rolled over my tongue."

At this Robin laughed aloud. "Marry," quoth he, "they did ill toward thee for thy kindness. But tell me truly, what hast thou in thy pouches?"

"Why," quoth the Beggar, peeping into the mouths of his bags, "I find here a goodly piece of pigeon pie, wrapped in a cabbage leaf to hold the gravy. Here I behold a dainty streaked piece of brawn, and here a fair lump of white bread. Here I find four oaten cakes and a cold knuckle of ham. Ha! in sooth 't is strange; but here I behold six eggs that must have come by accident from some poultry yard hereabouts. They are raw, but roasted upon the coals, and spread with a piece of butter that I see" -

"Peace, good friend!" cried Robin, holding up his hand. "Thou makest my poor stomach quake with joy for what thou tellest me so sweetly. If thou wilt give me to eat, I will straightway hie me to that little inn thou didst tell of but now, and will bring a skin of ale for thy drinking and mine."

"Friend, thou has said enough," said the beggar, getting down from the stile; "I will feast thee with the best that I have and bless Saint Cedric for thy company. But, sweet chuck, I prythee bring three quarts of ale at least, one for thy drinking and two for mine, for my thirst is such that methinks I can drink ale as the sands of the River Dee drink salt water."

So Robin straightway left the beggar, who, upon his part, went to a budding lime bush back of the hedge, and there spread his feast upon the grass and roasted his eggs upon a little fagot fire, with a deftness gained by long labor in that line. After a while back came Robin bearing a goodly skin of ale upon his shoulder, which he laid upon the grass. Then, looking upon the feast spread upon the ground, – and a fair sight it was to look upon, – he slowly rubbed his hand over his stomach, for to his hungry eyes it seemed the fairest sight that he had beheld in all his life.

"Friend," said the Beggar, "let me feel the weight of that skin."

"Yea, truly," quoth Robin, "help thyself, sweet chuck, and meantime let me see whether thy pigeon pie is fresh or no,"

So the one seized upon the ale and the other upon the pigeon pie, and nothing was heard for a while but the munching of food and the gurgle of ale as it left the skin.

At last, after a long time had passed thus, Robin pushed the food from him and heaved a great sigh of deep content, for he felt as though he had been made all over anew.

"And now, good friend," quoth he, leaning upon one elbow, "I would have at thee about that other matter of seriousness of which I spoke not long since."

"How!" said the Beggar, reproachfully; "thou wouldst surely not talk of things appertaining to serious affairs upon such ale as this!"

"Nay," quoth Robin, laughing. "I would not check thy thirst, sweet friend; drink whilst I talk to thee. Thus it is: I would have thee know that I have taken a liking to thy craft and would fain have a taste of a beggar's life mine own self."

Said the beggar: "I marvel not that thou hast taken a liking to my manner of life, good fellow, but 'to like' and 'to do' are two matters of different sorts. I tell thee, friend, one must serve a long apprenticeship ere one can learn to be even so much as a clapper-dudgeon, much less a crank or an Abraham-man.[1] I tell thee, lad, thou art too old to enter upon that which it may take thee years to catch the hang of."

"Mayhap that may be so" quoth Robin, "for I bring to mind that Gaffer Swanthold sayeth Jack Shoemaker maketh ill bread; Tom Baker maketh ill shoon. Nevertheless, I have a mind to taste a beggar's life, and need but the clothing to be as good as any."

"I tell thee, fellow," said the Beggar, "if you wert clad as sweetly as good Saint Wynten, the patron of our craft, thou wouldst never make a beggar. Marry, the first jolly traveller that thou wouldst meet would beat thee to a pudding for thrusting thy nose into a craft that belongeth not to thee."

"Nevertheless," quoth Robin, "I would have a try at it; and methinks I shall change clothes with thee, for thy garb seemeth to be pretty, not to say gay. So not

---

Classes of travelling mendicants that infested England as late as the middle of the seventeenth century. Vide Dakkar's English Villainies, etc.

only will I change clothes, but I will give thee two golden angels to boot. I have brought my stout staff with me, thinking that I might have to rap some one of the brethren of thy cloth over the head by way of argument in this matter, but I love thee so much for the feast thou hast given me that I would not lift even my little finger against thee, so thou needst not have a crumb of fear."

To this the Beggar listened with his knuckles resting against his hips, and when Robin had ended he cocked his head on one side and thrust his tongue into his cheek.

"Marry come up," quoth he at last. "Lift thy finger against me, forsooth! Art thou out of thy wits, man? My name is Riccon Hazel, and I come from Holywell, in Flintshire, over by the River Dee. I tell thee, knave, I have cracked the head of many a better man than thou art, and even now I would scald thy crown for thee but for the ale thou hast given me. Now thou shalt not have so much as one tag-rag of my coat, even could it save thee from hanging."

"Now, fellow," said Robin, "it would ill suit me to spoil thy pretty head for thee, but I tell thee plainly, that but for this feast I would do that to thee would stop thy travelling the country for many a day to come. Keep thy lips shut, lad, or thy luck will tumble out of thy mouth with thy speech!"

"Now out, and alas for thee, man, for thou hast bred thyself ill this day!" cried the Beggar, rising and taking up his staff. "Take up thy club and defend thyself, fellow, for I will not only beat thee but I will take from thee thy money and leave thee not so much as a clipped groat to buy thyself a lump of goosegrease to rub thy racked crown withal. So defend thyself, I say."

Then he leaped merry Robin and snatched up his staff also. "Take my money, if thou canst," quoth he. "I promise freely to give thee every farthing if thou dost touch me." And he twirled his staff in his fingers till it whistled again.

Then the Beggar swung his staff also, and struck a mighty blow at Robin, which the yeoman turned. Three blows the Beggar struck, yet never one touched so much as a hair of Robin's head. Then stout Robin saw his chance, and, ere you could count three, Riccon's staff was over the hedge, and Riccon himself lay upon the green grass with no more motion than you could find in an empty puddingbag.

"How now!" quoth merry Robin, laughing. "Wilt thou have my hide or my money, sweet chuck?" But to this the other answered never a word. Then Robin, seeing his plight, and that he was stunned with the blow, ran, still laughing, and brought the skin of ale and poured some of it on the Beggar's head and some down his throat, so that presently he opened his eyes and looked around as though wondering why he lay upon his back.

Then Robin, seeing that he had somewhat gathered the wits that had just been rapped out of his head, said: "Now, good fellow, wilt thou change clothes with me, or shall I have to tap thee again? Here are two golden angels if thou wilt give me all thy rags and bags and thy cap and things. If thou givest them not freely I much fear me I shall have to" – and he looked up and down his staff.

Then Riccon sat up and rubbed the bump on his crown. "Now, out upon it!"

quoth he. "I did think to drub thee sweetly, fellow. I know not how it is, but I seem, as it were, to have brought more beer than I can drink. If I must give up my clothes, I must, but first promise me, by thy word as a true yeoman, that thou wilt take nought from me but my clothes."

"I promise on the word of a true yeoman," quoth Robin, thinking that the fellow had a few pennies that he would save.

Thereupon the Beggar drew a little knife that hung at his side, and, ripping up the lining of his coat, drew thence ten bright golden pounds, which he laid upon the ground beside him with a cunning wink at Robin. "Now thou mayst have my clothes and welcome," said he, "and thou mightest have had them in exchange for thine without the coat of a single farthing, far less two golden angles."

"Marry," quoth Robin, laughing, "thou art a sly fellow, and I tell thee truly, had I known thou hadst so much money by thee maybe thou mightest not have carried it away, for I warrant thou didst not come honestly by it."

Then each stripped off his clothes and put on those of the other, and as lusty a beggar was Robin Hood as e'er you could find of a summer's day. But stout Riccon of Holywell skipped and leaped and danced for joy of the fir suit of Lincoln green that he had so gotten. Quoth he, "I am a gay feathered bird now. Truly, my dear Moll Peascod would never know me in this dress. Thou mayst keep the cold pieces of the feast, friend, for I mean to live well and lustily while my money lasts and my clothes are gay."

So he turned and left Robin and, crossing the stile, was gone, but Robin heard him singing from beyond the hedge as he strode away:-

*"For Polly is smiling and Molly is glad*
*When the beggar comes in at the door,*
*And Jack and Dick call him a fine lusty lad*
*And the hostess runs up a great score.*
*Then hey, Willy Waddykin,*
*Stay, Billy Waddykin,*
*And let the brown ale flow free, flow free,*
*The beggar's the man for me."*

Robin listened till the song ended in the distance, then he also crossed the stile into the road, but turned his toes away from where the Beggar had gone. The road led up a gentle hill and up the hill Robin walked, a half score or more of bags dangling about his legs. Onward he strolled for a long time, but other adventure he found not. The road was bare of all else but himself, as he went kicking up little clouds of dust at each footstep; for it was noontide, the most peaceful time of all the day, next to twilight. All the earth was silent in the restfulness of eating-time; the plough-horses stood in the furrow munching, with great bags over their noses holding sweet food, the ploughman sat under the hedge and the plough-boy also, and they, too, were munching, each one holding a great piece of bread in one fist and a great piece of cheese in the other.

So Robin, with all the empty road to himself, strode along whistling merrily, his bags and pouches bobbing and dangling at his thighs. At last he came to where a little grass-grown path left the road and, passing through a stile and down a hill, led into a little dell and on across a rill in the valley and up the hill on the other side, till it reached a windmill that stood on the cap of the rise where the wind bent the trees in swaying motion. Robin looked at the spot and liked it, and, for no reason but that his fancy led him, he took the little path and walked down the grassy sunny slope of the open meadow, and so came to the little dingle and, ere he knew it, upon four lusty fellows that sat with legs outstretched around a goodly feast spread upon the ground.

Four merry beggars were they, and each had slung about his neck a little board that rested upon his breast. One board had written upon it, "I am blind," another, "I am deaf," another, "I am dumb"' and the fourth, "Pity the lame one." But although all these troubles written upon the boards seemed so grievous, the four stout fellows sat around feasting as merrily as though Cain's wife had never opened the pottle that held misfortunes, and let them forth like a cloud of flies to pester us.

The deaf man was the first to hear Robin, for he said, "Hark, brothers, I hear some one coming." And the blind man was the first to see him, for he said, "He is an honest man, brothers, and one of like craft to ourselves." Then the dumb man called to him in a great voice and said, "Welcome, brother; come and sit whilst there is still some of the feast left and a little Malmsey in the pottle." At this the lame man, who had taken off his wooden leg and unstrapped his own leg, and was sitting with it stretched out upon the grass so as to rest it, made room for Robin among them. "We are glad to see thee, brother," said he, holding out the flask of Malmsey.

"Marry," quoth Robin, laughing, and weighing the flask in his hands ere he drank, "methinks" it is no more than seemly of you all to be glad to see me, seeing that I bring sight to the blind, speech to the dumb, hearing to the deaf, and such a lusty leg to a lame man. I drink to your happiness, brothers, as I may not drink to your health, seeing ye are already hale, wind and limb."

At this all grinned, and the Blind beggar, who was the chief man among them, and was the broadest shouldered and most lusty rascal of all, smote Robin upon the shoulder swearing he was a right merry wag.

"Whence cometh thou, lad?" asked the Dumb man.

"Why," quoth Robin. "I came this morning from sleeping overnight in Sherwood."

"Is it even so?" said the Deaf man. "I would not for all the money we four are carrying to Lincoln Town sleep one night in Sherwood. If Robin Hood caught one of our trade in his woodlands he would, methinks, clip his ears."

"Methinks he would, too," quoth Robin, laughing. "But what money is this that ye speak of?"

Then up spake the Lame man: "Our king, Peter of York," said he, "hath sent us to Lincoln with those moneys that" –

"Stay, brother Hodge," quoth the Blind man, breaking into the talk, "I would not doubt our brother here, but bear in mind we know him not. "What art thou, brother? Upright-man, Jurkman, Clapper-dudgeon, Dommerer, or Abram-man?"

At these words Robin looked from one man to the other with mouth agape. "Truly," quoth he, "I trust I am an upright man, at least, I strive to be; but I know not what thou meanest by such jargon, brother. It were much more seemly, methinks, if yon Dumb man, who hath a sweet voice, would give us a song."

At these words a silence fell on all, and after a while the Blind man spoke again. Quoth he, "Thou dost surely jest when thou sayest that thou dost not understand such words. Answer me this: Hast thou ever fibbed a chouse quarrons in the Rome pad for the loure in his bung?"[1]

"Now out upon it," quoth Robin Hood, testily; "an ye make sport of me by pattering such gibberish, it will be ill for you all, I tell you. I have the best part of a mind to crack the heads of all four of you, and would do so, too, but for the sweet Malmsey ye have given me. Brother, pass the pottle lest it grow cold."

"But all the four beggars leaped to their feet when Robin had done speaking, and the Blind man snatched up a heavy knotted cudgel that lay beside him on the grass, as did the others likewise. Then Robin, seeing that things were like to go ill with him, albeit he knew not what all the coil was about, leaped to his feet also, and, catching up his trusty staff, clapped his back against the tree and stood upon his guard against them. "How, now!" cried he, twirling his staff betwixt his fingers, "would you four stout fellows set upon one man? Stand back, ye rascals, or I will score your pates till they have as many marks upon them as a pot-house door! Are ye mad! I have done you no harm."

"Thou liest!" quoth the one who pretended to be blind, and who, being the lustiest villain, was the leader of the others; "thou liest! for thou hast come amongst us as a vile spy. But thine ears have heard too much for thy body's good, and thou goest not forth from this place unless thou goest feet foremost, for this day thou shalt die! Come, brothers, all together! Down with him!" Then, whirling up his cudgel, he rushed upon Robin as an angry bull rushes upon a red rag. But Robin was ready for any happening. "Crick! Crack!" he struck two blows as quick as wink, and down went the Blind man, rolling over and over upon the grass.

At this the others bore back and stood at a little distance scowling upon Robin. "Come on, ye scum!" cried he, merrily. "Here be cakes and ale for all. Now, who will be next served?"

To this speech the beggars answered never a word, but they looked at Robin as great Blunderbore looked upon stout Jack, the slayer of giants, as though they would fain eat him, body and bones; nevertheless, they did not care to come nigher to him and his terrible staff. Then, seeing them so hesitate, Robin of a sudden leaped upon them, striking even as he leaped. Down went the Dumb man, and away flew his cudgel from his hand as he fell. At this the others ducked to avoid another blow,

---

I.e., in old beggar's cant, "beaten a man or gallant upon the highway for the money in his purse." Dakkar's English Villainies.

then, taking to their heels, scampered, the one one way and the other the other, as though they had the west wind's boots upon their feet. Robin looked after them, laughing, and thought that never had he seen so fleet a runner as the Lame man; but neither of the beggars stopped nor turned around, for each felt in his mind the wind of Robin's cudgel about his ears.

Then Robin turned to the two stout knaves lying upon the ground. Quoth he, "These fellows spake somewhat about certain moneys they were taking to Lincoln; methinks I may find it upon this stout blind fellow, who hath as keen sight as e'er a trained woodsman in Nottingham or Yorkshire. It were a pity to let sound money stay in the pockets of such thieving knaves." So saying he stooped over the burly rascal and searched among his rags and tatters, till presently his fingers felt a leathern pouch slung around his body beneath his patched and tattered coat. This he stripped away, and, weighing it in his hands, bethought himself that it was mightily heavy. "It were a sweet thing," said he to himself, "if this were filled with gold instead of copper pence." Then, sitting down upon the grass, he opened the pocket and looked into it. There he found four round rolls wrapped up in dressed sheepskin; one of these rolls he opened; then his mouth gaped and his eyes stared, I wot, as though they would never close again, for what did he see but fifty pounds of bright golden money! He opened the other pockets and found in each one the same, fifty bright new-stamped golden pounds. Quoth Robin, "I have oft heard that the Beggars' Guild was over rich, but never did I think that they sent such sums as this to their treasury. I shall take it with me; for it will be better used for charity and the good of my merry band than in the enriching of such knaves as these." So saying he rolled up the money in the sheepskin again, and putting it back in the purse, he thrust the pouch into his own bosom. Then taking up the flask of Malmsey he held it toward the two fellows lying on the grass, and quoth he, "Sweet friends, I drink your health and thank you dearly for what ye have so kindly given me this day, and so I wish you good den." Then, taking up his staff, he left the spot and went merrily upon his way.

But when the two stout beggars that had been rapped upon the head roused themselves and sat up, and when the others had gotten over their fright and come back, they were as sad and woebegone as four frogs in dry weather, for two of them had cracked crowns, their Malmsey was all gone, and they had not so much as a farthing to cross their palms withal. As for the treasury of the Beggar's Guild at the Inn of the Beggar's Bush, near Lincoln Town, it was two hundred pounds poorer than it would have been had bold Robin not met the blind man, the deaf man, the dumb man and the lame man nigh to the highroad that led to Blyth.

But after Robin left the little dell he strode along merrily, singing as he went; and so blithe was he and such a stout beggar, and, withal, so fresh and clean, that every merry lass he met had a sweet word for him and felt no fear, whilst the very dogs, that most times hate the sight of a beggar, snuffed at his legs in friendly wise and wagged their tails pleasantly; for dogs know an honest man by his smell, and an honest man Robin was – in his own way.

Thus he went along till at last he had come to the wayside cross nigh Ollerton, and, being somewhat tired, he sat him down to rest upon the grassy bank in front of it. "It groweth nigh time," quoth he to himself, "that I were getting back again to Sherwood; yet it would please me well to have one more merry adventure ere I go back again to my jolly band." So he looked up and down the road to see who might come, until at last he saw some one drawing near, riding upon a horse. When the traveller came nigh enough for him to see him well, Robin laughed, for a strange enough figure he cut. He was a thin, weazened man, and, to look upon him, you could not tell whether he was thirty years old or sixty, so dried up was he even to skin and bone. As for the nag, it was as thin as the rider, and both looked as though they had been baked in Mother Huddle's Oven, where folk are dried up so that they live forever. The poor nag's neck bent down instead of up, as most horses' do, and his mane was as ragged as though the mice had made nests in it; his backbone stood up sharp and jagged, like a new-turned furrow when the plough first passes, and his ribs showed beneath his skin like the hoops on a barrel of five-year-old ale. Thus the horse came hobbling along, and at every step the rider popped up and down in his saddle, so that his head bobbed and wagged upon his lean neck all in time to the motion of the nag. At this sight merry Robin laughed till the tears stood on his cheeks, for, as though to make the sight still more droll, the rider wore great clogs upon his feet instead of shoon, the soles whereof were made of wood half a palm's breadth in thickness, and studded all over with great nails.

But although Robin laughed, he knew the wayfarer to be a certain rich corn engrosser of Worksop, who more than once had bought all the grain in the countryside and held it till it reached even famine prices, thus making much money from the needs of poor people, and for this he was hated far and near by every one that knew aught of him.

Quoth Robin to himself, when he saw who it was that came, "Oho, my thieving magpie! It is thou, is it? Now I would that I could pluck thee bare, even to the naked skin! But thou art so sly that I misdoubt finding aught of thy ill-gotten gains upon thee so nigh to Sherwood. Nevertheless, I will see what can be done; for, as Gaffer Swanthold says, 'If Ned never tries, Ned never does.'"

So, after a while, the Corn Engrosser came riding up to where Robin sat; whereupon merry Robin stepped straightway forth, in all his rags and tatters, his bags and pouches dangling about him, and laid his hand upon the horse's bridle-rein, calling upon the other to stop.

"Who art thou, fellow, that doth dare to stop me thus upon the King's highway?" said the lean man, in a dry, sour voice.

"Pity a poor beggar," quoth Robin. "Give me a farthing to buy me a piece of bread."

"Now, out upon thee!" snarled the other. "Such sturdy rogues as thou art are better safe in the prisons or dancing upon nothing, with a hempen collar about the neck, than strolling the highways so freely."

"Tut," quoth Robin, "how thou talkest! Thou and I are brothers, man. Do we not both take from the poor people that which they can ill spare? Do we not make our livings by doing nought of any good? Do we not both live without touching palm to honest work? Have we either of us ever rubbed thumbs over honestly-gained farthings? Go to! We are brothers, I say; only thou art rich and I am poor; wherefore, I prythee once more, give me a penny."

"Dost thou prate so to me, sirrah? cried the Corn Engrosser, in a rage. "Now I will have thee soundly whipped if ever I catch thee in any town where the law can lay hold of thee! As for giving thee a penny, I swear to thee that I have not so much as a single groat in my purse. Were Robin Hood himself to take me, he might search me from crown to heel without finding the smallest piece of money upon me. I trust I am too sly to travel so nigh to Sherwood with money in my pouch, and that thief at large in the woods."

Then merry Robin looked up and down, as if to see that there was no one nigh, and then, coming close to the Corn Engrosser, he stood on tiptoe and spake in his ear: "Thinkest thou in sooth that I am a beggar, as I seem to be? Look upon me. There is not a grain of dirt upon my hands or my face or my body; didst thou ever see a beggar so? I tell thee I am as honest a man as thou art. Look, friend." Here he took the purse of money from his breast, and showed to the dazzled eyes of the Corn Engrosser the bright golden pieces. "Friend, these rags serve but to hide an honest rich man from the eyes of Robin Hood."

"Put up thy money, lad," cried the other, quickly. "Art thou a fool, to trust to beggar's rags to shield thee from Robin Hood? If he caught thee he would strip thee to the skin, for he hates a lusty beggar as he doth a fat priest or those of my kind."

"Is it indeed so?" quoth Robin. "Had I known this, mayhap I had not come hereabouts in this garb. But I must go forward now, as much depends upon my journeying. Where goest thou, friend?"

"I go to Grantham," said the Corn Engrosser; "but I shall lodge to-night at Newark; if I can get so far upon my way."

"Why, I myself am on the way to Newark," quoth merry Robin; "so that, as two honest men are better than one in roads beset by such a fellow as this Robin Hood, I will jog along with thee, if thou hast no dislike to my company."

"Why, as thou art an honest fellow and a rich fellow," said the Corn Engrosser, "I mind not thy company; but, in sooth, I have no great fondness for beggars."

"Then forward," quoth Robin, "for the day wanes and it will be dark ere we reach Newark." So off the they went, the lean horse hobbling along as before, and Robin running beside, albeit he was so quaking not to laugh aloud, lest the Corn Engrosser should suspect something. So they travelled along till they reached a hill just on the outskirts of Sherwood. Here the lean man checked his lean horse into a walk, for the road was steep, and he wished to save his nag's strength, having far to go ere he reached Newark. Then he turned in his saddle and spake to Robin again, for the first time since they had left the cross. "Here is thy greatest danger, friend," said he, "for here we are nighest to that vile thief, Robin Hood, and the place where he dwells. Beyond this we come again to the open honest country, and so are more safe in our journeying."

"Alas!" quoth Robin, "I would that I had as little money by me as thou hast, for this day I fear that Robin Hood will get every groat of my wealth."

Then the other looked at Robin and winked cunningly. Quoth he, "I tell thee, friend, that I have nigh as much by me as thou hast, but it is hidden so that never a knave in Sherwood could find it."

"Thou dost surely jest," quoth Robin., "How could one hide so much as two hundred pounds upon his person?"

"Now, as thou art so honest a fellow, and, withal, so much younger than I am, I will tell thee that which I have told to no man in all the world before, and thus thou mayst learn never again to do such a foolish thing as to trust to beggar's garb to guard thee against Robin Hood. Seest thou these clogs upon my feet?"

"Yea," quoth Robin, laughing; "truly, they are large enough for any man to see, even were his sight as foggy as that of Peter Patter, who never could see when it was time to go to work."

"Peace, friend," said the Corn Engrosser, "for this is no matter for jesting. The soles of these clogs are not what they seem to be, for each one is a sweet little box; and by twisting the second nail from the toe, the upper of the shoe and part of the sole lifts up like a lid, and in the spaces within are fourscore and ten bright golden pounds in each shoe, all wrapped in hair, to keep them from clinking and so telling tales of themselves."

When the Corn Engrosser had told this, Robin broke into a roar of laughter, and, laying his hands upon the bridle-rein, stopped the sad-looking nag. "Stay, good friend," quoth he, between bursts of merriment' "thou art the slyest old fox that e'er I saw in all my life! – In the soles of his shoon, quotha! – If ever I trust a poor seeming man again, shave my head and paint it blue! A corn factor, a horse jockey, an estate agent, and a jackdaw for cunningness, say I!" And he laughed again till he shook in his shoes with mirth.

All this time the Corn Engrosser had been staring at Robin, his mouth agape with wonder. "Art thou mad," quoth he, "to talk in this way, so loud and in such a place? Let us forward, and save thy mirth till we are safe and sound at Newark."

"Nay," quoth Robin, the tears of merriment wet on his cheeks, "on second thoughts I go no farther than here, for I have good friends hereabouts. Thou mayst go forward if thou dost list, thou sweet pretty fellow, but thou must go forward barefoot, for I am afraid that thy shoon must be left behind. Off with them, friend, for I tell thee I have taken a great fancy to them."

At these words the corn factor grew pale as a linen napkin. "Who art thou that talkest so?" said he.

Then merry Robin laughed again, and quoth he, "Men hereabouts call me Robin Hood; so, sweet, friend, thou hadst best do my bidding and give me thy shoes, wherefore hasten, I prythee, or else thou wilt not get to fair Newark Town till after dark."

At the sound of the name of Robin Hood the corn factor quaked with fear, so that he had to seize his horse by the mane to save himself from falling off its back. Then straightway, and without more words, he stripped off his clogs and let them fall upon the road. Robin, still holding the bridle-rein, stooped and picked them up; then he said, "Sweet friend, I am used to ask those that I have dealings with to come and feast at Sherwood with me. I will not ask thee, because of our pleasant journey together; for I tell thee there be those in Sherwood that would not be so gentle with thee as I have been. The name of Corn Engrosser leaves a nasty taste upon the tongue of all honest men. Take a fool's advice of me and come no more so nigh to Sherwood, or mayhap some day thou mayst of a sudden find a clothyard shaft betwixt thy ribs. So, with this, I give thee good den." Hereupon he clapped his hand to the horse's flank and off went nag and rider. But the man's face was allbedewed with the sweat of fright, and never again, I wot, was he found so close to Sherwood Forest as he had been this day.

Robin stood and looked after him, and, when he was fairly gone, turned, laughing, and entered the forest carrying the shoes in his hand.

That night in sweet Sherwood the red fires glowed brightly in wavering light on tree and bush, and all around sat or lay the stout fellows of the band to hear Robin Hood and Little John tell their adventures. First Little John began and told about his meeting with the three lasses, amid great shouts of laughter, for he was quaint of speech, and told his doings merrily. Then Robin told of his meeting the stout beggar, and what befell behind the hedge under the lime tree. Then Little John told of meeting the good fellows at the inn, and Robin told of his adventure with the four beggars, and showed the money he had taken from them. Last of all, Little John told how he had prayed to Saint Dunstan with the gray Friars, and showed the gold that the Saint had sent him. This Robin matched with his story of meeting the Corn Engrosser at the cross near Ollerton, and held up the shoes that he had taken from the lean man. All listened closely, and again and again the woods rang with shouts of laughter.

When all was told, friar Tuck spoke up, "Good master," said he, "thou hast had a pretty time, but still I hold to my saying, that the life of the barefoot friar is the merrier of the two."

"Nay," quoth Will Stutely, "I hold with our master, that he hath had the pleasanter doings of the two, for he hath had two stout bouts at quarterstaff this day."

So some of the band held with Robin Hood and some with Little John. As for me, I think – But I leave it with you to say for yourselves which you hold with.

After you have settled the matter in your minds, we will see how merry Robin went to famous London Town, and how he shot with the long bow before Queen Eleanor; likewise we will hear of the adventures that befell him thereafter; so listen to what follows.

# Part Seventh

*In which it is told how Queen Eleanor sent for Robin Hood to come to the Court at famous London Town, and how Robin Hood came at her bidding. Likewise, it is told how King Henry chased Robin through the land, yet caught him not.*

## Chapter One

# Robin and Three of His Merry Men Shoot before Queen Eleanor

The high-road stretched white and dusty in the hot summer afternoon sun, and the trees stood motionless along the roadside. All across the meadow lands the hot air danced and quivered, and in the limpid waters of the lowland brook, spanned by a little stone bridge, the fish hung motionless above the yellow gravel, and the dragon-fly sat quite still, perched upon the sharp tip of a spike of the rushes, with its wings glistening in the sun.

Along the road a youth came riding upon a fair milk-white barb, and the folk that he passed stopped and turned and looked after him, for never had so lovely a lad or one to gayly clad been seen in Nottingham before. He could not have been more than sixteen years of age, and was as fair as any maiden. His long yellow hair flowed behind him as he rode along, all clad in silk and velvet, with jewels flashing and dagger jingling against the pommel of the saddle. Thus came the Queen's Page, young Richard Partington, from famous London Town down into Nottinghamshire, upon her majesty's bidding, to seek Robin Hood in Sherwood Forest.

The road was hot and dusty and his journey had been long, for that day he had come all the way from Leicester Town, a good twenty miles and more; wherefore young Partington was right glad when he saw before him a sweet little inn, all shady and cool beneath the trees, in front of the door of which a sign hung pendant bearing the picture of a Blue Boar. Here he drew rein and called loudly for a pottle of Rhenish wine to be brought him for stout country ale was too coarse a drink for this young gentleman. Five lusty fellows sat upon the bench beneath the pleasant shade of the wide-spreading oak in front of the inn door, drinking ale and beer, and all stared amain at this fair and gallant lad. Two of the stoutest of them were clothed in Lincoln green, and a great heavy oaken staff leaned against the gnarled oak tree trunk beside each fellow.

The landlord came and brought a pottle of wine and a long narrow glass upon a salver, which he held up to the Page as he sat upon his horse. Young Partington poured forth the bright yellow wine, and holding the glass aloft, cried, "Here is to the health and long happiness of my royal mistress the noble Queen Eleanor; and may my journey and her desirings soon have end, and I find a certain stout yeoman men call Robin Hood."

At these words all stared, but presently the two stout yeomen in Lincoln green began whispering together. Then one of the two, whom Partington thought to be the tallest and stoutest fellow he had ever beheld, spoke up and said, "What seeketh thou of Robin Hood, Sir Page? and what does our good Queen Eleanor wish of him? I ask this of thee, not foolishly, but with reason, for I know somewhat of this stout yeoman."

"An thou knowest aught of him, good fellow," said the young Partington, "thou wilt do great service to him and great pleasure to our royal Queen by aiding me to find him."

Then up spake the other yeoman, who was a handsome fellow with sunburnt face and nut-brown, curling hair, "Thou hast an honest look, Sir Page, and our Queen is kind and true to all stout yeomen. Methinks I and my friend here might safely guide thee to Robin Hood, for we know where he may be found. Yet I tell thee plainly, we would not for all merry England have aught of harm befall him."

"Set thy mind at ease; I bring nought of ill with me," quoth Richard Partington. "I bring a kind message to him from our Queen; therefore an ye know where he is to be found, I pray you to guide me thither."

Then the two yeomen looked at one another again, and the tall man said, "Surely it were safe to do this thing, Will;" whereat the other nodded. Thereupon both arose, and the tall yeoman said, "We think thou art true, Sir Page, and meanest no harm, therefore we will guide thee to Robin Hood as thou dost wish."

Then Partington paid his score, and the yeomen coming forward, they straightway departed upon their way.

Under the greenwood tree, in the cool shade that spread all around upon the sward, with flickering lights here and there, Robin Hood and many of his band lay upon the soft green grass, whilst Allan a Dale sang and played upon his sweetly-sounding harp. All listened in silence, for young Allan's singing was one of the greatest joys in all the world to them; but as they so listened there came of a sudden a sound of horse's feet, and presently Little John and Will Stutely came forth from the forest path into the open glade, young Richard Partington riding between them upon his milk-white horse. The three came toward where Robin Hood sat, all the band staring with might and main, for never had they seen so gay a sight as this young Page, nor one so richly clad in silks and velvets and gold and jewels. Then Robin Hood arose and stepped forth to meet him, and Partington leaped from his horse, and doffing his cap of crimson velvet, met Robin as he came.

"Now, welcome!" cried Robin. "Now, welcome, fair youth; and tell me, I prythee, what bringeth one of so fair a presence and clad in such noble garb to our poor forest of Sherwood?"

Then young Partington said: "If I err not, thou art the famous Robin Hood, and these thy stout band of outlawed yeomen. To thee I bring greeting from our noble Queen Eleanor. Oft hath she heard thee spoken of and thy merry doings hereabouts, and fain would she behold thy face; therefore she bids me tell thee that if thou wilt presently come to London Town, she will do all in her power to guard thee against harm, and will send thee back safe to Sherwood Forest again. Four days hence, in Finsbury Fields, our good King Henry, of great renown, holdeth a grand shooting match, and all the most famous archers of merry England will be thereat. Our Queen would fain see thee strive with these, knowing that if thou wilt come thou wilt, with little doubt, carry off the prize. Therefore she hath sent me with this greeting, and furthermore sends thee, as a sign of great good will, this golden ring from off her own fair thumb, which I give herewith into thy hands."

Then Robin Hood bowed his head, and taking the ring kissed it right loyally, and then slipped it upon his little finger. Quoth he, "Sooner would I lose my life than this ring; and ere it departs from me, my hand shall be cold in death or stricken off at the wrist. Fair Sir Page, I will do our Queen's bidding, and will presently hie with thee to London; but, ere we go, I will feast thee here in the woodlands with the very best we have."

"It may not be," said the Page; "we have no time to tarry, therefore get thyself ready straightway; and if there be any of thy band that thou wouldst take with thee, our Queen bids me say that she will make them right welcome likewise."

"Truly, thou art right," quoth Robin, "and we have but short time to stay; therefore I will get me ready presently. I will choose three of my men, only, to go with me, and these three shall be Little John, mine own true right-hand man, Will Scarlet, my cousin, and Allan a Dale, my minstrel. Go, lads, and get ye ready straightway, and we will presently off with all speed that we may. Thou, Will Stutely, shall be the chief of the band while I am gone."

Then Little John and Will Scarlet and Allan a Dale ran leaping, full of joy, to make themselves ready, whilst Robin also prepared himself for the journey. After a while they all four came forth, and a right fair sight they made, for Robin was clad in blue from head to foot, and Little John and Will Scarlet in good Lincoln green, and as for Allan a Dale, he was dressed in scarlet from the crown of his head to the toes of his pointed shoes. Each man wore beneath his cap a little head-covering of burnished-steel set with rivets of gold, and underneath his jerkin a coat of linked mail, as fine as carded wool, yet so tough that no arrow could pierce it. Then, seeing all were ready, young Partington mounted his horse again, and the yeomen having shaken hands all around, the five departed upon their way.

That night they took up their inn in Melton Mowbray, in Leicestershire; and the next night they lodged at Kettering, in Northamptonshire; and the next night they lodged at Bedford Town; and the next at St Albans, in Hertfordshire. This place they left not long after the middle of the night, and travelling fast through the tender dawning of the summer day, when the dews lay shining on the meadows and faint mists hung in the dales, when the birds sang their sweetest and the cobwebs beneath the hedges glimmered like fairy cloth of silver, they came at last to the towers and walls of famous London Town, whilst the morn was still young and all golden toward the east.

Queen Eleanor sat in her royal bower, through the open casements of which poured the sweet yellow sunshine in great floods of golden light. All about her stood her maids in waiting chatting in low voices, whilst she herself sat dreamily where the mild air came softly drifting into the room laden with the fresh perfumes of the sweet red roses that bloomed in the great garden beneath the wall. To her came one who said that her page, Richard Partington, and four stout yeomen waited her pleasure in the court below. Then Queen Eleanor arose joyously and bade them be straightway shown into her presence.

Thus Robin Hood and Little John and Will Scarlet and Allan a Dale came before the Queen into her own royal bower. Then Robin kneeled before the Queen with his hands folded upon his breast, saying, in simple phrase, "Here am I, Robin Hood. Thou didst bid me come, and lo, I do thy bidding. I give myself to thee as thy true servant, and will do thy commanding, even it if be to the shedding of the last drop of my life's blood."

But good Queen Eleanor smiled pleasantly upon him, bidding him to arise; then she made them all be seated to rest themselves after their long journey. Rich food was brought them and noble wines, and she had her own pages to wait upon the wants of the yeomen. At last, after they had eaten all they could, she began questioning them of their merry adventures. Then they told her all of the lusty doings herein spoken of, and among others that concerning the Bishop of Hereford and Sir Richard of the Lea, and how the Bishop had abided three days in Sherwood Forest. At this the Queen and the ladies about her laughed again and again, for they pictured to themselves the stout Bishop abiding in the forest and ranging the woods in lusty sport with Robin and his band. Then, when they had told all that they could bring to mind, the Queen asked Allan to sing to her, for his fame as a minstrel had reached even to the court at London Town. So straightway Allan took his harp in his hand, and, without more asking, touched the strings lightly till they all rang sweetly, then he sang thus:-

*"Gentle river, gentle river,*
*Bright thy crystal waters flow,*
*Sliding where the aspens shiver,*
*Gliding where the lilies blow."*

*"Singing over pebbled shallows,*
*Kissing blossoms bending low,*
*Breaking 'neath the dipping swallows,*
*Purpling where the breezes blow."*

*"Floating on thy breast forever*
*Down thy current I could glide;*
*Grief and pain should reach me never*
*On thy bright and gentle tide."*

*"So my aching heart seeks thine, love,*
*There to find its rest and peace,*
*For, though loving, bliss is mine, love,*
*And my many troubles cease."*

Thus Allan sang, and as he sang all eyes dwelt upon him and not a sound broke the stillness, and even after he had done the silence hung for a short space. So the time passed till the hour drew nigh for the holding of the great archery match in Finsbury Fields.

A gay sight were famous Finsbury Fields on that bright and sunny morning of lusty summer-time. Along the end of the meadow stood the booths for the different bands of archers, for the King's yeomen were divided into companies of fourscore men, and each company had a captain over it; so on the bright greensward stood ten booths of striped canvas, a booth for each band of the royal archers, and at the peak of each fluttered a flag in the mellow air, and the flag was the color that belonged to the captain of each band. From the centre booth hung the yellow flat of Tepus, the famous bow-bearer of the King; next to it, on one hand, was the blue flag of Gilbert of the White Hand, and on the other the blood-red pennant of stout young Clifton of Buckinghamshire. The seven other archer captains were also men of great renown; among them were Egbert of Kent and William of Southampton; but those first named were most famous of all. The noise of many voices in talk and laughter came from within the booths, and in and out ran the attendants like ants about an ant-hill. Some bore ale and beer, and some bundles of bowstrings or sheaves of arrows. On each side of the archery range were rows upon rows of seats reaching high aloft, and in the centre of the north side was a raised dais for the King and Queen, shaded by canvas of gay colors, and hung about with streaming silken pennants of red and blue and green and white. As yet the King and Queen had not come, but all the other benches were full of people, rising head above head high aloft till it made the eye dizzy to look upon them. Eightscore yards distant from the mark from which the archers were to shoot stood ten fair targets, each target marked by a flag of the color belonging to the band that was to shoot thereat. So all was ready and all waited for the coming of the King and Queen.

At last a great blast of bugles sounded, and into the meadow came riding six trumpeters with silver trumpets, from which hung velvet banners heavy with rich workings of silver and gold thread. Behind these came stout King Henry upon a dapple-gray stallion, with his Queen beside him upon a milk-white palfrey. On either side of them walked the yeomen of the guard, the bright sunlight flashing from the polished blades of the steel halberds they carried. Behind these came the Court in a great crowd, so that presently all the lawn was alive with bright colors, with silk and velvet, with waving plumes and gleaming gold, with flashing jewels and sword hilts; a gallant sight on that bright summer day.

Then all the people arose and shouted, so that their voices sounded like the storm upon the Cornish coast, when the dark waves run the shore and leap and break, surging amid the rocks; so, amid the roaring and the surging of the people, and the waving of scarfs and kerchiefs, the King and Queen came to their place, and, getting down from their horses, mounted the broad stairs that led to the raised platform, and there took their seats on two thrones bedecked with purple silks and cloths of silver and of gold.

When all was quiet a bugle sounded, and straightway the archers came marching in order from their tents. Fortyscore they were in all, as stalwart a band of yeomen as could be found in all the wide world. So they came in orderly fashion and stood in front of the dais where King Henry and his Queen sat. King Henry looked up and down their ranks right proudly, for his heart warmed within him at the sight of such a gallant band of yeomen. Then he bade his herald, Sir Hugh de Mowbray, stand forth and proclaim the rules governing the game. So Sir Hugh stepped to the edge of the platform and spoke in a loud clear voice, so that they could hear him even to the ends of the range, and thus he said:–

That each man should shoot seven arrows at the target that belonged to his band, and, of the fourscore yeomen of each band, the three that shot the best should be chosen. These three should shoot three arrows apiece, and the one that shot the best should again be chosen. Then each of these should again shoot three arrows apiece, and the one that shot the best should have the first prize, the one that shot the next best should have the second, and the one that shot the next best should have the third prize. Each of the others should have fourscore silver pennies for his shooting. The first prize was to be twoscore and ten golden pounds, a silver bugle horn inlaid with gold, and a quiver with ten white arrows tipped with gold and feathered with white swan's wing therein. The second prize was to be fivescore of the fattest bucks that run on Dallen Lea, to be shot when the yeoman that won them chose. The third prize was to be two tuns of good Rhenish wine.

So Sir Hugh spoke, and when he had done all the archers waved their bows aloft and shouted. Then each band turned and marched in order back to its place.

And now the shooting began, the captains first taking stand and speeding their shafts and then making room for the men who shot, each in turn after them. Two hundred and eightyscore shafts were shot in all, and so deftly were they sped that when the shooting was done each target looked like the back of a hedgehog when the farm dog snuffs at it. A long time was taken in this shooting, and when it was over the judges came forward, looked carefully at the targets, and proclaimed in a loud voice which three had shot the best from the separate bands. Then a great hubbub of voice arose, each man among the crowd that looked on calling for his favorite archer. Then ten fresh targets were brought forward, and every sound was hushed as the archers took their places once more.

This time the shooting was more speedily done, for only nine shafts were shot by each band. Not an arrow missed the targets, but in that of Gilbert of the White Hand five arrows were in the small white spot that marked the center; of these five three were sped by Gilbert. Then the judges came forward again, and looking at the targets, called aloud the names of the archer chosen as the best bowman of each band. Of these Gilbert of the White Hand led, for six of the ten arrows he had shot had lodged in the center; but stout Tepus and young Clifton trod close upon his heels; yet the others stood a fair chance for the second or third place.

And now, amid the roaring of the crowd, those ten stout fellows that were left went back to their tents to rest for a while and change their bowstrings, for nought must fail at this next round, and no hand must tremble or eye grow dim because of weariness.

Then whilst the deep buzz and hum of talking sounded all around like the noise of the wind in the leafy forest, Queen Eleanor turned to the King, and quoth she, "Thinkest thou that these yeomen so chosen are the very best archers in all merry England?"

"Yea, truly," said the King, smiling, for he was well pleased with the sport that he had seen; "and I tell thee, that not only are they the best archers in all merry England, but in all the wide world beside."

"But what wouldst thou say," quoth Queen Eleanor, "if I were to find three archers to match the best three yeomen of all thy guard?"

"I would say thou hast done what I could not do," said the King, laughing, "for I tell thee there lives not in all the world three archers to match Tepus and Gilbert and Clifton of Buckinghamshire."

"Now," said the Queen, "I know of three yeomen, and in truth I have seen them not long since, that I would not fear to match against any three that thou canst choose from among all thy fortyscore archers; and, moreover, I will match them with thy archers providing that thou wilt grant a free pardon to all that may come in my behalf."

At this the King laughed loud and long. "Truly," said he, "thou art taking up with strange matters for a queen. If thou wilt bring those three fellows that thou speakest of I will promise faithfully to give them free pardon for forty days, to come or to go wheresoever they please, nor will I harm a hair of their heads in all that time. Moreover, if these that thou bringest shoot better than my yeomen, man for man, they shall have the prizes for themselves according to their shooting. But as thou hast so taken up of a sudden with sports of this kind, hast thou a mind for a wager?"

"Why, in sooth," said Queen Eleanor, laughing, "I know nought of such matters, but if thou hast a mind to do somewhat in that way, I will strive to pleasure thee. What wilt thou wager upon thy men?"

Then the merry King laughed again, for he dearly loved a goodly jest; so he said, amidst his laughter, "I will wager thee ten tuns of Rhenish wine, ten tuns of the stoutest ale, and tenscore bows of tempered Spanish yew, with quivers and arrows to match."

All that stood around smiled at this, for it seemed a merry wager for a king to give to a queen; but Queen Eleanor bowed her head quietly. "I will take thy wager," said she, "for I know right well where to place those things that thou hast spoken of. Now, who will be on my side in this matter?" And she looked around upon them that stood about; but no one spake or cared to wager upon the Queen's side against such archers as Tepus and Gilbert and Clifton. Then the Queen spoke again: "Now, who will back me in this wager? Wilt thou, my Lord Bishop of Hereford?"

"Nay," quoth the Bishop, hastily. "it ill befits one of my cloth to deal in such matters. Moreover, there are no such archers as his majesty's in all the world; therefore I would but lose my money."

"Methinks the thought of thy gold weigheth more heavily with thee than the wrong to thy cloth," said the Queen, smiling; and at this a ripple of laughter went around, for every one knew how fond the Bishop was of his money. Then the Queen turned to a knight who stood near whose name was Sir Robert Lee. "Wilt thou back me in this matter?' said she. "Thou art surely rich enough to risk so much for the sake of a lady."

"To pleasure my Queen I will do it," said Sir Robert Lee, "but for the sake of no other in all the world would I wager a groat, for no man can stand against Tepus and Gilbert and Clifton."

Then turning to the King, Queen Eleanor said, "I want no such aid as Sir Robert giveth me; but against thy wine and beer and stout bows of yew I wager this girdle all set with jewels from around my waist; and surely that is worth more than thine."

"Now, I take thy wager," quoth the King. "Send for thy archers straightway. But here come forth the others; let them shoot, and then I will match those that win against all the world."

"So be it," said the Queen. Thereupon, beckoning to young Richard Partington, she whispered something in his ear, and straightway the Page bowed and left the place, crossing the meadow to the other side of the range, where he was presently lost in the crowd. At this all that stood around whispered to one another, wondering what it all meant, and what three men the Queen was about to set against those famous archers of the King's guard.

And now the ten archers of the King's guard took their stand again, and all the great crowd was hushed to the stillness of death. Slowly and carefully each man shot his shafts, and so deep was the silence that you could hear every arrow rap against the target as it struck it. Then, when the last shaft had sped, a great roar went up; and the shooting, I wot, was well worthy of the sound. Once again Gilbert had lodged three arrows in the white; Tepus came second with two in the white and one in the black ring next to it; but stout Clifton had gone down and Hubert of Suffolk had taken the third place, for, while both those two good yeomen had lodged two in the white, Clifton had lost one shot upon the fourth ring, and Hubert came in with one in the third.

All the archers around Gilbert's booth shouted for joy till their throats were hoarse, tossing their caps aloft, and shaking hands with one another.

In the midst of all this noise and hubbub five men came walking across the lawn towards the King's pavilion. The first was Richard Partington, and was known to most folk there, but the others were strange to everybody. Beside young Partington walked a yeoman clad in blue, and behind came three others, two in Lincoln green and one in scarlet. This last yeoman carried three stout bows of yew tree, two fancifully inlaid with silver and one with gold. Whilst these five men came walking across the meadow, a messenger came running from the King's booth, and summoned Gilbert and Tepus and Hubert to go with him. And now the shouting quickly ceased, for all saw that something unwonted was toward, so the folk stood up in their places and leaned forward to see what was the ado.

When Partington and the others came before the spot where the King and Queen sat, the four yeomen bent their knees and doffed their caps unto her. King Henry leaned far forward and stared at them closely, but the Bishop of Hereford, when he saw their faces, started as though stung by a wasp. He opened his mouth as though about to speak, but, looking up, he saw the Queen gazing at him with a smile upon her lips, so he said nothing, but bit his nether lip, whilst his face was as red as a cherry.

Then the Queen leaned forward and spake in a clear voice, "Locksley," said she, "I have laid a wager with the King that thou and two of thy men can outshoot any three that he can send against you. Wilt thou do thy best for my sake?"

"Yea," quoth Robin Hood, to whom she spake, "I will do my best for thy sake, and, if I fail, I make my vow never to finger bowstring more."

Now, although Little John had been somewhat abashed in the Queen's bower, he felt himself the sturdy fellow he was when the soles of his feet pressed green grass again; so he said boldly, "Now, blessings on thy sweet face, say I. An there lived a man that would not do his best for thee – I will say nought, only I would like to have the cracking of his knave's pate!"

"Peace, Little John!" said Robin Hood, hastily, in a low voice; but good Queen Eleanor laughed aloud, and a ripple of merriment sounded all over the booth.

The Bishop of Hereford did not laugh, neither did the King, but he turned to the Queen, and quoth he, "What are these men that thou hast brought before us?"

Then up spoke the Bishop, hastily, for he could hold his peace no longer: "Your Majesty," quoth he, "yon fellow in blue is a certain outlawed thief of the midcountry, named Robin Hood; yon tall strapping villain goeth by the name of Little John; the other fellow in green is a certain backsliding gentleman, known as Will Scarlet; the man in red is a rogue of a northern minstrel, named Allan a Dale."

At this speech the King's brows drew together blackly, and he turned to the Queen. "Is this true?" said he, sternly.

"Yea," said the Queen, smiling, "the Bishop hath told the truth; and truly he should know them well, for he and two of his friars spent three days in merry sport with Robin Hood in Sherwood Forest. I did little think that the good Bishop would so betray his friends. But bear in mind that thou hast pledged thy promise for the safety of these good yeomen for forty days."

"I will keep my promise," said the King, in a deep voice that showed the anger in his heart; "but when these forty days are gone let this outlaw look to himself, for mayhap things will not go so smoothly with him as he would like." Then he turned to his archers, who stood near the Sherwood yeomen, listening and wondering at all that passed. Quoth he, "Gilbert, and thou, Tepus, and thou, Hubert, I have pledged myself that ye shall shoot against these three fellows. If ye outshoot the knaves I will fill your caps with silver pennies; if ye fail ye shall lose your prizes that ye have won so fairly, and they go to them that shoot against you, man to man. Do your best, lads, and if ye win this bout ye shall be glad of it to the last days of your life. Go, now, and get you gone to the butts."

Then the three archers of the King turned and went back to their booths, and Robin and his men went to their places at the mark from which they were to shoot. Then they strung their bows and made themselves ready, looking over their quivers of arrows, and picking out the roundest and the best feathered.

But when the King's archers went to their tents, they told their friends all that had passed, and how that these four men were the famous Robin Hood and three of his band, to wit, Little John, Will Scarlet, and Allan a Dale. The news of this buzzed around among the archers in the booths, for there was not a man there that had not heard of these great midcountry yeomen. From the archers the news was taken up by the crowd that looked on at the shooting, so that at last everybody stood up, craning their necks to catch sight of the famous outlaws.

Six fresh targets were now set up, one for each man that was to shoot; whereupon Gilbert and Tepus and Hubert came straightway forth from the booths. Then Robin Hood and Gilbert of the White Hand tossed a farthing aloft to see who should lead in the shooting, and the lot fell to Gilbert's side; thereupon he called upon Hubert of Suffolk to lead.

Hubert took his place, planted his foot firmly, and fitted a fair, smooth arrow; then, breathing upon his finger-tips, he drew the string slowly and carefully. The arrow sped true, and lodged in the white; again he shot, and again he hit the clout; a third shaft he sped, but this time failed of the center, and but struck the black, yet not more than a finger's breadth from the white. At this a shout went up, for it was the best shooting that Hubert had yet done that day.

Merry Robin laughed, and quoth he, "Thou wilt have an ill time bettering that round, Will, for it is thy turn next. Brace thy thews, lad, and bring not shame upon Sherwood."

Then Will Scarlet took his place; but, because of over-caution, he spoiled his target with the very first arrow that he sped, for he hit the next ring to the black, the second from the center. At this Robin bit his lip. "Lad, lad," quoth he, "hold not the string so long! Have I not often told thee what Gaffer Swanthold sayeth, that 'over-caution spilleth the milk?'" To this Will Scarlet took heed, so the next arrow he shot lodged fairly in the center ring; again he shot, and again he smote the center; but, for all that, stout Hubert had outshot him, and showed the better target. Then all those that looked on clapped their hands for joy because that Hubert had overcome the stranger.

Quoth the King, grimly, to the Queen, "If the archers shoot no better than that, thou art like to lose thy wager, lady." But Queen Eleanor smiled, for she looked for better things from Robin Hood and Little John.

And now Tepus took his place to shoot. He, also, took over-heed to what he was about, and so he fell into Will Scarlet's error. The first arrow he struck into the center ring, but the second missed its mark, and smote the black; the last arrow was tipped with luck, for it smote the very center of the clout, upon the black spot that marked it. Quoth Robin Hood, "That is the sweetest shot that hath been sped this day; but, nevertheless, friend Tepus, thy cake is burned, methinks. Little John, it is thy turn next."

So Little John took his place as bidden, and shot his three arrows quickly. He never lowered his bow arm in all the shooting, but fitted each shaft with his long bow raised; yet all three of his arrows smote the center within easy distance of the black. At this no sound of shouting was heard, for, although it was the best shooting that had been done that day, the folk of London Town did not like to see the stout Tepus overcome by a fellow from the countryside, even were he as famous as Little John.

And now stout Gilbert of the White Hand took his place and shot with the greatest care; and again, for the third time in one day, he struck all three shafts into the clout.

"Well done, Gilbert!" quoth Robin Hood, smiting him upon the shoulder. "I make my vow, thou art one of the best archers that ever mine eyes beheld. Thou shouldst be a free and merry ranger like us, lad, for thou art better fitted for the greenwood than for the cobble-stones and gray walls of London Town." So saying, he took his place, and drew a fair, round arrow from his quiver, which he turned over and over ere he fitted it to his bowstring.

Then the King muttered in his beard, "Now, blessed Saint Hubert, if thou wilt but jog that rogue's elbow so as to make him smite even the second ring, I will give eightscore waxen candles three fingers' breadth in thickness to thy chapel nigh

Matching." But it may be Saint Hubert's ears were stuffed with tow, for he seemed not to hear the King's prayer this day.

Having gotten three shafts to his liking, merry Robin looked carefully to his bowstring ere he shot. "Yea," quoth he to Gilbert, who stood nigh him to watch his shooting, "thou shouldst pay us a visit at merry Sherwood." Here he drew the bowstring to his ear. "In London" – here he loosed his shaft – "thou canst find nought to shoot at but rooks and daws; there one can tickle the ribs of the noblest stags in England." So he shot even whilst he talked, yet the shaft lodged not more than half an inch from the very center.

"By my soul!" cried Gilbert. "Art thou the devil in blue, to shoot in that wise?"

"Nay," quoth Robin, laughing, "not quite so ill as that, I trust." And he took up another shaft and fitted it to the string. Again he shot, and again he smote his arrow close beside the center; a third time he loosed his bowstring, and dropped his arrow just betwixt the other two and into the very center, so that the feathers of all three were ruffled together, seeming from a distance to be one thick shaft.

And now a low murmur ran all among that great crowd, for never before had London seen such shooting as this; and never again would it see it after Robin Hood's day had gone. All saw that the King's archers were fairly beaten, and stout Gilbert slapped his palm to Robin's, owing that he could never hope to draw such a bowstring as Robin Hood or Little John. But the King, full of wrath, would not have it so, though he knew in his mind that his men could not stand against those fellows. "Nay!" cried he, clenching his hands upon the arms of his seat, "Gilbert is not yet beaten! Did he not strike the clout thrice? Although I have lost my wager, he hath not yet lost the first prize. They shall shoot again, and still again, till either he or that knave Robin Hood cometh off the best. Go thou, Sir Hugh, and bid them shoot another round, and another, until one or the other is overcome." Then Sir Hugh, seeing how wroth the King was, said never a word, but went straightway to do his bidding; so he came to where Robin Hood and the other stood, and told them what the King had said.

"With all my heart," quoth merry Robin, "I will shoot from this time till to-morrow day if it can pleasure my most gracious lord and king. Take thy place, Gilbert lad, and shoot."

So Gilbert took his place once more, but this time he failed, for, a sudden little wind arising, his shaft missed the center ring, but by not more than the breadth of a barley straw.

"Thy eggs are cracked, Gilbert," quoth Robin, laughing; and straightway he loosed a shaft, and once more smote the white circle of the center.

Then the King arose from his place, and not a word said he, but he looked around with a baleful look, and it would have been an ill day for any one that he saw with a joyous or a merry look upon his face. Then he and his Queen and all the court left the place, but the King's heart was brimming full of wrath within him.

After the King had gone, all the yeomen of the archer guard came crowding around Robin, and Little John, and Will, and Allan, to snatch a look at these famous fellows from the midcountry; and with them came many that had been onlookers at the sport, for the same purpose. Thus it happened presently that the yeomen, to whom Gilbert stood talking, were all surrounded by a crowd of people that formed a ring about them. "Marry," quoth Little John to Will Scarlet, "one would think that these poor fellows had never seen a stout yeoman ranger in all their lives before, or that we were some curious spectacle, like the Cumberland Giant, or the Welsh Dwarf, that we saw last month at the fair at Norwich."

After a while the three judges that had the giving away of the prizes came forward, and the chief of them all spake to Robin and said: "According to agreement, the first prize belongeth rightly to thee; so here I give thee the silver bugle, here the quiver of ten golden arrows, and here a purse of twoscore and ten golden pounds." And as he spake he handed those things to Robin, and then turned to Little John. "To thee," he said, "belongeth the second prize, to wit, fivescore of the finest harts that run on Dallen Lea. Thou mayest shoot them whensoever thou dost list." Last of all he turned to stout Hubert. "Thou," said he, "hast held thine own against the yeoman with whom thou didst shoot, and so thou hast kept the prize duly thine, to wit, two tuns of good Rhenish wine. These shall be delivered to thee whensoever thou dost list." Then he called upon the other seven of the King's archers who had last shot, and gave them each fourscore silver pennies.

Then up spake Robin, and quoth he, "This silver bugle I keep in honor of this shooting match; but thou, Gilbert, art the best archer of all the King's guard, and to thee I freely give this purse of gold. Take it, man, and would it were ten times as much, for thou art a right yeoman, good and true. Furthermore, to each of the ten that last shot I give one of these golden shafts apiece. Keep them always by you, so that ye may tell your grandchildren, an ye are ever blessed with them, that ye are the very stoutest yeomen in all the wide world."

At this all shouted aloud, for it pleased them to hear Robin speak so of them.

Then up spake Little John. "Good friend Tepus," said he, "I want not those harts of Dallen Lea that yon stout judge spoke of but now, for in truth we have enow and more than enow in our own country. Twoscore and ten I give to thee for thine own shooting, and five I give to each band for their pleasure."

At this another great shout went up, and many tossed their caps aloft, and swore among themselves that no better fellows ever walked the sod than Robin Hood and his stout yeomen.

Whilst they so shouted with loud voices, a tall burley yeoman of the King's guard came forward and plucked Robin by the sleeve. "Good master," quoth he, "I have somewhat to tell thee in thine ear; a silly thing. God wot, for one stout yeoman to tell another; but a young peacock of a page, one Richard Partington, was seeking thee without avail in the crowd, and, not being able to find thee, told me that he bore a message to thee from a certain lady that thou wottest of. This message he bade me tell thee privily, word for word, and thus it was. Let me see – I trust I have forgot it not – yea, thus it was: 'The lion growls. Beware thy head.'"

"Is it so?" quoth Robin, starting; for he knew right well that it was the Queen sent the message, and that she spake of the King's wrath. "Now, I thank thee, good fellow, for thou hast done me greater service than thou knowest of this day." Then he called his three yeomen together, and told them privately that they had best be jogging, as it was like to be ill for them so nigh merry London Town. So, without tarrying longer, they made their way through the crowd until they had come out from the press. Then, without stopping, they left London Town, and started away northward.

Thus ended the famous shooting match before Queen Eleanor. And now we will hear how ill King Harry kept his promise to his Queen that no harm should befall Robin Hood for forty days, in which time he might come and go as he wished.

## Chapter Two

# The Chase of Robin Hood

So Robin Hood and the others left the archery range at Finsbury Fields, and, tarrying not, set forth straightway upon their homeward journey. It was well for them that they did so, for they had not gone more than three or four miles upon their way when six of the yeomen of the King's guard came bustling amongst the crowd that still lingered, seeking for Robin and his men, to seize upon them and make them prisoners. Truly, it was an ill-done thing in the King to break his promise, but it all came about through the Bishop of Hereford's doing, for thus it happened:–

After the King left the archery ground, he went straightway to his cabinet, and with him went the Bishop of Hereford and Sir Robert Lee; but the King said never a word to these two, but sat gnawing his nether lip, for his heart was galled within him by what had happened. At last the Bishop of Hereford spoke. in a low, sorrowful voice: "It is a sad thing, your majesty," quoth he, "that this knavish outlaw should be let to escape in this wise; for, let him but get back to Sherwood Forest safe and sound, and he may snap his fingers at King and King's men."

At these words the King raised his eyes and looked grimly upon the Bishop. "Sayst thou so?" quoth he. "Now, I will show thee in good time, how much thou dost err, for, when the forty days are past and gone, I will seize upon this thieving outlaw, if I have to tear down all of Sherwood to find him. Thinkest thou that the laws of the King of England are to be so evaded by one poor knave without friends or money?"

Then the Bishop spoke again, in his soft, smooth voice: "Forgive my boldness, your majesty, and believe that I have naught but the good of England and your majesty's desirings at heart; but what would it boot though my gracious lord did root up every tree of Sherwood? Are there not other places for Robin Hood's hiding? Cannock Chase is not far from Sherwood, and the great Forest of Arden is not far from Cannock Chase. Beside these are many other woodlands in Nottingham and Derby, Lincoln and York, amid any of which your majesty might as well think to seize upon Robin Hood as to lay finger upon a rat among the dust and broken things of a garret. Nay, my gracious lord, if he doth once plant foot in the woodland, he is lost to the law forever."

At these words the King tapped his finger-tips upon the table beside him with vexation. "What wouldst thou have me do, Bishop?" quoth he. "Didst thou not hear me pledge my word to the Queen? Thy talk is as barren as the wind from the bellows upon dead coals."

"Far be it from me," said the cunning Bishop, "to point the way to one so clear-sighted as your majesty; but, were I King of England, I should look upon the matter in this wise: I have promised my Queen, let us say, that for forty days the cunningest rogue in all England shall have freedom to come and go; but lo! I find this outlaw in my grasp; shall I, then, foolishly cling to a promise so hastily given? Suppose that I had promised to do her majesty's bidding, whereupon she bade me to slay myself; should I, then, shut mine eyes and run blindly upon my sword? Thus would I argue within myself. Moreover, I would say unto myself, a woman knoweth nought of the great things appertaining to state government; and, likewise, I know a woman is ever prone to take up a fancy, even as she would pluck a daisy from the roadside, and then throw it away when the savor is gone; therefore, though she hath taken a fancy to this outlaw, it will soon wane away and be forgotten. As for me, I have the greatest villain in all England in my grasp; shall I, them, open my hand and let him slip betwixt my fingers? Thus, your majesty, would I say to myself, were I the King of England." So the Bishop talked, and the King lent his ear to his evil counsel, until, after a while, he turned to Sir Robert Lee, and bade him send six of the yeomen of the guard to take Robin Hood and his three men prisoners.

Now Sir Robert Lee was a gentle and noble knight, and he felt grieved to the heart to see the King so break his promise; nevertheless, he said nothing, for he saw how bitterly the King was set against Robin Hood; but he did not send the yeomen of the guard at once, but went first to the Queen, and told her all that had passed, and bade her send word to Robin of his danger. Thus he did not for the wellbeing of Robin Hood, but because he would save his lord's honor if he could. Thus it came about that when, after a while, the yeomen of the guard went to the archery field, they found not Robin and the others, and so got no cakes at that fair.

The afternoon was already well-nigh gone when Robin Hood, Little John, Will, and Allan set forth upon their homeward way, trudging along merrily through the yellow slanting light, which speedily changed to rosy red as the sun sank low in the heavens. The shadows grew long, and finally merged into the grayness of the mellow twilight. The dusty highway lay all white betwixt the dark hedgerows, and along it walked the four fellows like four shadows, the pat of their feet sounding loud, and their voices, as they talked, ringing clear upon the silence of the air. The great round moon was floating breathlessly up in the eastern sky when they saw before them the twinkling lights of Barnet Town, some ten or twelve miles from London. Down they walked through the stony streets and past the cosy houses with overhanging gables, before the doors of which sat the burghers and craftsmen in the mellow moonlight, with their families about them, and so came at last, on the other side of the hamlet, to a little inn, all shaded with roses and woodbines. Before this inn Robin Hood stopped, for the spot pleased him well. Quoth he, "Here will we take up our inn and rest for the night, for we are well away from London Town and our King's wrath. Moreover, if I mistake not, we will find sweet faring within. What say ye, lads?"

"In sooth, good master," quoth Little John, "thy bidding and my doing ever fit together like cakes and ale. Let us in, I say also."

Then up spake Will Scarlet: "I am ever ready to do what thou sayest, uncle, yet I could wish that we were farther upon our way ere we rest for the night. Nevertheless, if thou thinkest best, let us in for the night, say I also."

So in they went and called for the best that the place afforded. Then a right good feast was set before them, with two stout bottles of old sack to wash it down withal. These things were served by as plump and buxom a lass as you could find in all the land, so that Little John, who always had an eye for a fair lass, even when meat and drink were by, stuck his arms akimbo and fixed his eyes upon her, winking sweetly whenever he saw her looking toward him. Then you should have seen how the lass twittered with laughter, and how she looked at Little John out of the corners of her eyes, a dimple coming in either cheek; for the fellow had always a taking way with the women-folk.

"Come, come, Little John," quoth Robin, "leave the lass in peace, and fall to thy victuals, or thou wilt belike to with an empty stomach. Eat first and woo afterwards is as good a saying as one can open ears to."

"Nay," quoth Little John, boldly, "it is an ill saying for me, for who would turn to victuals and drink and let so fair a lass go, without paying heed to the sweet looks that the blessed saints have bestowed upon her? Come hither, thou dainty little duck and pour forth some wine for me, that I may drink to thy good health, and pray the good Saint Withold that he send thee what is meet, to wit, a lord or an earl for a husband. By my soul, I would rather drink water that thou hadst poured into my cup than rich Muscat after any other she in all England!"

At this speech the other yeomen roared with laughter, and the lass looked down, blushing, and thought that Little John was as nice a lad as she had seen in all her life.

So the feast passed merrily; and never had that inn seen such lusty feeders as these four stout fellows; but at last they were done their eating, though it seemed as though they never would have ended, and sat loitering over the sack. As they so sat, the landlord came in of a sudden, and said that there was one at the door, a certain young esquire, Richard Partington, of the Queen's household, who wished to see the lad in blue, and speak with him, without loss of time. So Robin arose quickly, and, bidding the landlord not to follow him, left the others gazing at one another, and wondering what was about to happen.

When Robin came out of the inn, he found young Richard Partington sitting upon his horse in the white moonlight, awaiting his coming.

"What news hearest thou, Sir Page?" said Robin. "I trust that it is not of an ill nature."

"Why," said young Partington, "for the matter of that, it is ill enow. The King hath been bitterly stirred up against thee by that vile Bishop of Hereford. He sent to arrest thee at the archery butts at Finsbury Fields, but not finding thee there, he hath gathered together his armed men, fiftyscore and more, and is sending them in haste along this very road to Sherwood, either to take thee on the way or to prevent thy getting back to the woodlands again. He hath given the Bishop of Hereford command over all these men, and thou knowest what thou hast to expect of the Bishop of Hereford – short shrift and a long rope. Two hands of horsemen are already upon the road, not far behind me, so thou hadst best get thee gone from this place straightway, for, if thou tarriest longer, thou art like to sleep this night in a cold dungeon. This word the Queen hath bidden me bring to thee."

"Now, Richard Partington," quoth Robin, "this is the second time that thou hast saved my life, and if the proper time ever cometh I will show thee that Robin Hood never forgets these things. As for that Bishop of Hereford, if I ever catch him nigh to Sherwood again, things will be like to go ill with him. Thou mayst tell the good Queen that I will leave this place without delay, and will let the landlord think that we are going to Saint Albans; but when we are upon the high road again, I will go one way through the country and will send my men the other, so that if one falleth into the King's hands the others may haply escape. We will go by devious ways, and so, I hope, will reach Sherwood in safety. And now, Sir Page, I wish thee farewell."

"Farewell, thou bold yeoman," said young Partington, "and mayst thou reach thy hiding in safety." So each shook the other's hand, and the lad, turning his horse's head, rode back towards London, whilst Robin entered the inn once more.

There he found his yeomen sitting in silence, waiting his coming; likewise the landlord was there, for he was curious to know what Master Partington had to do with the fellow in blue. "Up, my merry men!" quoth Robin, "this is no place for us, for those are after us with whom we will stand but an ill chance an we fall into their hands. So we will go forward once more, nor will we stop this night till we reach Saint Albans. Hereupon, taking out his purse, he paid the landlord his score, and so they left the inn.

When they had come to the high-road without the town, Robin stopped and told them all that had passed between young Partington and himself, and how that the King's men were after them with hot heels. Then he told them that here they should part company; they three going to the eastward and he to the westward, and so, skirting the main high-roads, would come by devious paths to Sherwood. "So, be ye wily," said Robin Hood, "and keep well away from the northward roads till ye have gotten well to the eastward. And thou, Will Scarlet, take the lead of the others, for thou hast a cunning turn to thy wits." Then Robin kissed the three upon the cheeks, and they kissed him, and so they parted company.

Not long after this, a score or more of the King's men came clattering up to the door of the inn at Barnet Town. Here they leaped from their horses and quickly surrounded the place, the leader of the band and four others entering the room where the yeomen had been. But they found that their birds had flown again, and that the King had been baulked a second time.

"Methought that they were naughty fellows," said the host, when he heard who the men-at-arms sought. "But I heard that blue-clad knave say that they would go straight forward to Saint Albans; so, an hurry forward, ye may, perchance, catch them on the high-road betwixt here and there." For this news the leader of the band thanked mine host right heartily, and, calling his men together, mounted and set forth again, galloping forward to Saint Albans upon a wild-goose chase.

After Little John and Will scarlet and Allan a Dale had left the highway near Barnet, they travelled toward the eastward, without stopping, as long as their legs could carry them, until they came to Chelmsford, in Essex. Thence they turned northward, and came through Cambridge and Lincolnshire, to the good town of Gainsborough. Then, striking to the westward and the south, they came at last to the northern borders of Sherwood Forest, without in all that time having met so much as a single band of the King's men. Eight days they journeyed thus ere they reached the woodlands in safety; but when they got to the greenwood glade, they found that Robin had not yet returned.

For Robin was not as lucky in getting back as his men had been, as you shall presently hear.

After having left the great northern road, he turned his face to the westward, and so came past Aylesbury, to fair Woodstock, in Oxfordshire. Thence he turned his footsteps northward, travelling for a great distance by way of Warwick Town, till he came to Dudley, in Staffordshire. Seven days it took him to journey thus far, and then he thought he had gotten far enough to the north, so, turning toward the eastward, shunning the main roads, and choosing byways and grassy lanes, he went, by way of Litchfield and Ashby de la Zouch, toward Sherwood, until he came to a place called Stanton. And now Robin's heart began to laugh aloud, for he thought that his dangers had gone by, and that his nostrils would soon snuff the spicy air of the woodlands once again. But there is many a slip betwixt the cup and the lip, and this Robin was to find. For thus it was:–

When the King's men found themselves foiled at Saint Albans, and that Robin and his men were not to be found high nor low, they knew not what to do. Presently another band of horsemen came, and another, until all the moonlit streets were full of armed men. Betwixt midnight and dawn another band came to the town, and with them came the Bishop of Hereford. When he heard that Robin Hood had once more slipped out of the trap, he stayed not a minute, but, gathering his bands together, he pushed forward to the northward with speed, leaving orders for all the troops that came to Saint Albans to follow after him without tarrying. On the evening of the fourth day he reached Nottingham Town, and there straightway divided his men into bands of six or seven, and sent them all through the countryside, blocking every highway and byway to the eastward and the southward and the westward of Sherwood. The Sheriff of Nottingham called forth all his men likewise, and joined with the Bishop, for he saw that this was the best chance that had ever befallen of paying back his score in full to Robin Hood. Will Scarlet and Little John and Allan a Dale had just missed the King's men to the eastward, for the very next day after they had passed the line and entered Sherwood the roads through which they had travelled were blocked, so that, had they tarried in their journeying, they would surely have fallen into the Bishop's hands.

But of all this Robin knew not a whit; so he whistled merrily as he trudged along the road beyond Stanton, with his heart as free from care as the yolk of an egg is from cobwebs. At last he came to where a little stream spread across the road in a shallow sheet, tinkling and sparkling as it fretted over its bed of golden gravel. Here Robin stopped, being athirst, and, kneeling down, he made a cup of the palms of his hands, and began to drink. On either side of the road, for a long distance, stood tangled thickets of bushes and young trees, and it pleased Robin's heart to hear the little birds singing therein, for it made him think of Sherwood, and it seemed as though it had been a lifetime since he had breathed the air of the woodlands. But of a sudden, as he thus stooped, drinking, something hissed past his ear, and struck with a splash into the gravel and water beside him. Quick as a wink Robin sprang to his feet, and, at one bound, crossed the stream and the roadside, and plunged headlong into the thicket, without looking around, for he knew right well that that which had hissed so venomously beside his ear was a gray goose shaft, and that to tarry so much as a moment meant death. Even as he leaped into the thicket six more arrows rattled among the branches after him, one of which pierced his doublet, and would have struck deeply into his side but for the tough coat of steel that he wore. Then up the road came riding some of the King's men at headlong speed. They leaped from their horses and plunged straightway into the thicket after Robin. But Robin knew the ground better than they did, so crawling here, stooping there, and, anon, running across some little open, he soon left them far behind, coming out, at last, upon another road about eight hundred paces distant from the one he had left. Here he stood for a moment, listening to the distant shouts of the seven men as they beat up and down in the thickets like hounds that had lost the scent of the quarry. Then, buckling his belt more tightly around his waist, he ran fleetly down the road toward the eastward and Sherwood.

But Robin had not gone more than three furlongs in that direction when he came suddenly to the brow of a hill, and saw beneath him another band of the King's men seated in the shade along the roadside in the valley beneath. Then he paused not a moment, but, seeing that they had not caught sight of him, he turned and ran back whence he had come, knowing that it was better to run the chance of escaping those fellows that were yet in the thickets than to rush into the arms of those in the valley. So back he ran with all speed, and had gotten safely past the thickets, when the seven men fame forth into the open road. They raised a great shout when they saw him, such as the hunter gives when the deer breaks cover, but Robin was then a quarter of a mile and more away from them, coursing over the ground like a greyhound. He never slackened his pace, but ran along, mile after mile, till he had come nigh to Mackworth, over beyond the Derwent River, nigh to Derby Town. Here, seeing that he was out of present danger, he slackened in his running, and at last sat him down beneath a hedge where the grass was the longest and the shade the coolest, there to rest and catch his wind.

"By my soul, Robin, quoth he to himself, "that was the narrowest miss that e'er thou hadst in all thy life. I do say most solemnly that the feather of that wicked shaft tickled mine ear as it whizzed past. This same running hath given me a most craving appetite for victuals and drink. Now I pray Saint Dunstan that he send me speedily some meat and beer."

It seemed as though Saint Dunstan was like to answer his prayer, for along the road came plodding a certain cobbler, one Quince, of Derby, who had been to take a pair of shoes to a farmer nigh Kirk Langley, and was now coming back home again, with a fair boiled capon in his pouch and a stout pottle of beer by his side, which same the farmer had given him for joy of such a stout pair of shoon. Good Quince was an honest fellow, but his wits were somewhat of the heavy sort, like unbaked dough, so that the only thing that was in his mind was, "Three shillings sixpence ha'penny for thy shoon, good Quince, – three shillings sixpence ha'penny for thy shoon," and this travelled round and round inside of his head, without another thought getting into his noddle, as a pea rolls round and round inside an empty quart pot.

"Halloa, good friend," quoth Robin, from beneath the hedge, when the other had gotten night enough, "whither away so merrily this bright day?"

Hearing himself so called upon, the Cobbler stopped, and, seeing a well-clad stranger in blue, he spoke to him in seemly wise. "Give ye good den, fair sir, and I would say that I come from Kirk Langly, where I ha' sold my shoon and got three shillings sixpence ha'penny for them in as sweet money as ever thou sawest, and honestly earned too, I would ha' thee know. But, an I may be so bold, thou pretty fellow, what dost thou there beneath the hedge?"

"Marry," quoth merry Robin, "I sit beneath the hedge here to drop salt on the tails of golden birds; but in sooth thou art the first chick of any worth I ha' seen this blessed day."

At these words the Cobbler's eyes opened big and wide, and his mouth grew round with wonder, like a know-hole in a board fence. "Alack-a-day," quoth he, "look ye, now! I ha' never seen those same golden birds. And dost thou in sooth find them in these hedges, good fellow? Prythee, tell me, are there many of them? I would fain find them mine ownself."

"Ay, truly," quoth Robin, "they are as thick here as fresh herring in Cannock Chase."

"Look ye, now!" said the Cobbler, all drowned in wonder. "And dost thou in sooth catch them by dropping salt on their pretty tails?"

"Yea," quoth Robin, "but this salt is of an odd kind, let me tell thee, for it can only be gotten by boiling down a quart of moonbeams in a wooden platter, and then one hath but a pinch. But tell me, now, thou witty man, what hast thou gotten there in that pouch by thy side and in that pottle?"

At these words the Cobbler looked down at those things of which merry Robin spoke, for the thoughts of the golden bird had driven them from his mind, and it took him some time to scrape the memory of them back again. "Why," said he at last, "in one is good March beer, and in the other is a fat capon. Truly, Quince the Cobbler will ha' a fine feast this day an I mistake not."

"But tell me, good Quince," said Robin, "hast thou a mind to sell those things to me? for the hearing of them sounds sweet in mine ears. I will give thee these gay clothes of blue and I have upon my body and ten shillings to boot for thy clothes and thy leather apron and thy beer and thy capon. What sayst thou, bully boy?"

"Nay, thou dost jest with me," said the Cobbler, "for my clothes are coarse and patched, and thine are of fine stuff and very pretty."

"Never a jest do I speak," quoth Robin. "Come, strip thy jacket off and I will show thee, for I tell thee I like thy clothes well. Moreover, I will be kind to thee, for I will feast straightway upon the good things thou hast with thee, and thou shalt be bidden to the eating." At these words he began slipping off his doublet, and the Cobbler, seeing him so in earnest, began peeling off his clothes also, for Robin Hood's garb tickled his eye. So each put on the other fellow's clothes, and Robin gave the honest Cobbler ten bright new shillings. Quoth merry Robin, "I ha' been a many things in my life before, but never have I been an honest cobbler. Come, friend, let us fall to and eat, for something within me cackles aloud for that good fat capon." So both sat down and began to feast right lustily, so that when they were done the bones of the capon were picked as bare as charity.

Then Robin stretched his legs out with a sweet feeling of comfort within him. Quoth he, "By the turn of thy voice, good Quince, I know that thou hast a fair song or two running loose in thy head like colts in a meadow. I prythee, turn one of them out for me."

"'A song or two I ha'," quoth the Cobbler; "poor things; poor things; but such as they are thou art welcome to one of them." So, moistening his throat with a swallow of beer, he began to sing thus:-

*"Of all the joys, the best I love,*
*Sing hey my frisking Nan, O,*
*And that which most my soul doth move,*
*It is the clinking can, O.*

*"All other bliss I'd thrown away,*
*Sing hey my frisking Nan, O,*
*But this" –*

The stout Cobbler got no further in his song, for of a sudden six horsemen burst upon them where they sat, and seized roughly upon the honest craftsman, hauling him to his feet, and nearly plucking the clothes from him as they did so. "Ha!" roared the leader of the band in a great big voice of joy, "have we then caught thee at last, thou blue-clad knave? Now, blessed be the name of Saint Hubert, for we are fourscore pounds richer this minute than we were before, for the good Bishop of Hereford hath promised that much to the band that shall bring thee to him. Oho! thou cunning rascal! thou wouldst look so innocent, forsooth! We know thee, thou old fox. But off thou goest with us to have thy brush clipped forthwith." At these words the poor Cobbler gazed all around him with his great blue eyes as round as those of a dead fish, while his mouth gaped as though he had swallowed all his words and so lost his speech.

Robin also gaped and stared in a wondering way, just as the Cobbler would have done in his place. "Alack-a-daisy, me," quoth he. "I know not whether I be sitting here or in no-man's land! What meaneth all this stir i' th' pot, dear good gentlemen? Surely this is a sweet, honest fellow."

"'Honest fellow,' sayst thou, clown?" quoth one of the men. "Why, I tell thee that this is that same rogue that men call Robin Hood."

At this speech the Cobbler stared and gaped more than ever, for there was such a threshing of thoughts going on within his poor head that his wits were all befogged with the dust and chaff thereof. Moreover, as he looked at Robin Hood, and saw the yeoman look so like what he knew himself to be, he began to doubt and to think that mayhap he was the great outlaw in real sooth. Said he in a slow, wondering voice, "Am I in very truth that fellow? – Now I had thought – but nay, Quince, thou art mistook – yet – am I? – Nay, I mist indeed be Robin Hood! Yet, truly, I had never thought to pass from an honest craftsman to such a great yeoman."

"Alas!" quoth Robin Hood, "look ye there, now! See how your ill-treatment hath curdled the wits of this poor lad and turned them all sour! I, myself, am Quince, the Cobbler of Derby Town."

"Is it so?" said Quince. "Then, indeed, I am somebody else, and can be none other than Robin Hood. Take me, fellows; but let me tell you that ye ha' laid hand upon the stoutest yeoman that ever trod the woodlands."

"Thou wilt play madman, wilt thou?" said the leader of the band. "Here, Giles, fetch a cord and bind the knave's hands behind him. I warrant we will bring his wits back to him again when we get him safe before our good Bishop at Tutbury Town." Thereupon they tied the Cobbler's hands behind him, and led him off with a rope, as the farmer leads off the calf he hath brought from the fair. Robin stood looking after them, and when they were gone he laughed till the tears rolled down his cheeks; for he knew that no harm would befall the honest fellow, and he pictured himself the Bishop's face when good Quince was brought before him as Robin Hood. Then, turning his steps once more to the eastward, he stepped out right foot foremost toward Nottinghamshire and Sherwood Forest.

But Robin Hood had gone through more than he wotted off. His journey from London had been hard and long, and in a se'ennight he had travelled sevenscore and more of miles. He thought now to travel on without stopping until he had come to Sherwood, but ere he had gone a half a score of miles he felt his strength giving way beneath him like a river bank which the waters have undermined. He sat him down and rested, but he knew within himself that he could go no farther that day, for his feet felt like lumps of lead, so heavy were they with weariness. Once more he arose and went forward, but after travelling a couple of miles he was fain to give the matter up, so, coming to an inn just then, he entered, and calling the landlord bade him show him to a room, although the sun was only then just sinking in the western sky. There were but three bedrooms in the place, and to the meanest of these the landlord showed Robin Hood, but little Robin cared not for the looks of the place, for he could have slept that night upon a bed of broken stones. So, stripping off his clothes without more ado, he rolled into the bed and was asleep almost ere his head touched the pillow.

Not long after Robin had so gone to his rest a great cloud peeped blackly over the hills to then westward. Higher and higher it arose until it piled up into the night like a mountain of darkness. All around beneath it came ever and anon a dull red flash, and presently a short grim mutter of the coming thunder was heard. Then up rode four stout burghers of Nottingham Town, for this was the only inn within five miles' distance, and they did not care to be caught in such a thunder-storm as this that was coming upon them. Leaving their nags to the stableman, they entered the best room of the inn, where fresh green rushes lay all spread upon the floor, and there called for the goodliest fare that the place afforded. After having eaten heartily they bade the landlord show them to their rooms, for they were aweary, having ridden all the way from Dronfield that day. So off they went, grumbling at having to sleep two in a bed, but their troubles on this score, as well as all others, were soon lost in the quietness of sleep.

And now came the first gust of wind, rushing past the place, clapping and banging the doors and shutters, smelling of the coming rain, and all wrapped in a cloud of dust and leaves. As though the wind had brought a guest along with it, the door opened of a sudden and in came a friar of Emmet Priory, and one in high degree, as was shown by the softness and sleekness of his robes and the richness of his rosary. He called to the landlord, and bade him first have his mule well fed and bedded in the stable, and then to bring him the very best there was in the house. So presently a savory stew of tripe and onions, with sweet little fat dumplings, was set before him, likewise a good stout pottle of Malmsey, and straightway the holy friar fell to with great courage and heartiness, so that in a short time nought was left but a little pool of gravy in the center of the platter, not large enow to keep the life in a starving mouse.

In the mean time the storm broke. Another gust of wind went rushing by, and with it fell a few heavy drops of rain, which presently came rattling down in showers, beating against the casements like a hundred little hands. Bright flashes of lightning lit up every raindrop, and with them came cracks of thunder that went away rumbling and bumping as though Saint Swithin were busy rolling great casks of water across rough ground overhead. The women-folks screamed, and the merry wags in the tap room put their arms around their waists to soothe them into quietness.

At last the holy friar bade the landlord show him to his room; but when he heard that he was to bed with a cobbler, he was as ill contented a fellow as you could find in all England, nevertheless there was nothing for it, and he must sleep there or nowhere; so, taking up his candle, he went off, grumbling like the now distant thunder. When he came to the room where he was to sleep he held the light over Robin and looked at him from top to toe; then he felt better pleased, for, instead of a rough, dirty-bearded fellow, he beheld as fresh and clean a lad as one could find in a week of Sundays; so, slipping off his clothes, he also huddled into the bed, where Robin, grunting and grumbling in his sleep, made room for him. Robin was more sound asleep, I wot, than he had been for many a day, else he would never have rested so quietly with one of the friar's sort so close behind him. As for the friar, had he known whom Robin Hood was, you may well believe he would almost as soon have slept with an adder as with the man he had for a bedfellow.

So the night passed comfortably enough, but at the first dawn of day Robin opened his eyes and turned his head upon the pillow. Then how he gaped and how he stared, for there beside him lay one all shaven and shorn, so that he knew it must be a fellow in holy orders. He pinched himself sharply, but, finding he was awake, sat up in bed, whilst the other slumbered as peacefully as though he were safe and sound at home in Emmet Priory. "Now," quoth Robin to himself, "I wonder how this thing hath dropped into my bed during the night." So saying he arose softly, so as not to waken the other, and looking about the room he espied the Friar's clothes lying upon a bench near the wall. First he looked at the clothes, with his head on one side, and then he looked at the Friar and slowly winked one eye. Quoth he, "Good brother, What-e'er-thy-name-may-be, as thou hast borrowed my bed so freely I'll e'en borrow thy clothes in return." So saying, he straightway donned the holy man's garb, but kindly left the cobbler's clothes in the place of it. Then he went forth into the freshness of the morning, and the stableman that was up and about the stables opened his eyes as though he saw a green mouse before him, for such men as the friar of Emmet were not wont to be early risers; but the man bottled his thoughts, and only asked Robin whether he wanted his mule brought from the stable.

"Yea, my son," quoth Robin, – albeit he knew nought of the mule, – "and bring it forth quickly, I prythee, for I am late and must be jogging." So presently the stableman brought forth the mule, and Robin mounted it and went on his way rejoicing.

As for the holy friar, when he arose he was in as pretty a stew as any man in all the world, for his rich, soft robes were gone, likewise his purse with ten golden pounds it it, and nought was left but patched clothes and a leathern apron. He raged and swore like any layman, but as his swearing mended nothing and the landlord could not aid him, and as, moreover, he was forced to be at Emmet Priory that very morning upon matters of business, he was fain either to don the cobbler's clothes or travel the road in nakedness. So he put on the clothes, and, still raging and swearing vengeance against all the cobblers in Derbyshire, he set forth upon his way afoot; but his ills had not yet done with him, for he had not gone far ere he fell into the hands of the King's men, who marched him off, willy nilly, to Tutbury Town and the Bishop of Hereford. In vain he swore he was a holy man, and showed his shaven crown; off he must go, for nothing would do but that he was none other than Robin Hood.

Meanwhile merry Robin rode along contentedly, passing safely by two bands of the King's men, until his heart began to dance within him because of the nearness of Sherwood; so he travelled ever on to the eastward, till, of a sudden, he met a noble knight in a shady lane. Then Robin checked his mule quickly and leaped from off its back. Now, well met, Sir Richard of the Lea," cried he, "for rather than any other man in England would I see thy good face this day!" Then he told Sir Richard all the happenings that had befallen him, and that now at last he felt himself safe, being so nigh to Sherwood again. But when Robin had done, Sir Richard shook his head sadly. "Thou art in greater danger now, Robin, than thou hast yet been," said he, "for before thee lie bands of the Sheriff's men blocking every road and letting none pass through the lines without examining them closely. I myself know this, having passed them but now. Before thee lie the Sheriff's men and behind thee the King's men, and thou canst not hope to pass either way, for by this time they will know of thy disguise, and will be in waiting to seize upon thee. My castle and everything within it are thine, but nought could be gained there, for I could not hope to hold it against such a force as is now in Nottingham of the King's and the Sheriff's men." Having so spoken, Sir Richard bent his head in thought, and Robin felt his heart sink within him like that of the fox that hears the hounds at his heels, and finds his den clocked with earth so that there is no hiding for him. But presently Sir Richard spoke again, saying, "One thing thou canst do, Robin, and one only. Go back to London and throw thyself upon the mercy of our good Queen Eleanor. Come with me straightway to my castle. Doff these clothes and put on such as my retainers wear. Then I will hie me to London Town with a troop of men behind me, and thou shalt mingle with them, and thus will I bring thee to where thou mayst see and speak with the Queen. Thy only hope is to get to Sherwood, for there none can reach thee, and thou wilt never get to Sherwood but in this way."

So Robin went with Sir, Richard of the Lea, and did as he said, for he saw the wisdom of that which the knight advised, and that this was his only chance of safety.

Queen Eleanor walked in her royal garden, amid the roses that bloomed sweetly, and with her walked six of her ladies-in-waiting, chattering blithely together. Of a sudden a man leaped up to the top of the wall from the other side, and then, hanging for a moment, dropped lightly upon the grass within. All the ladies-in-waiting shrieked at the suddenness of his coming, but the man ran to the Queen and kneeled at her feet, and she saw it was Robin Hood.

"Why, how now, Robin!" cried she, "dost thou dare to come into the very jaws of the raging lion? Alas, poor fellow! thou art lost indeed if the King finds thee here. Dost thou not know that he is seeking thee through all the land?"

"Yea," quoth Robin, "I do know right well that the King seeks me, and therefore I have come; for, surely, no ill can befall me when he hath pledged his royal word to your majesty for my safety. Moreover, I know your majesty's kindness and gentleness of heart, and so I lay my life freely in your gracious hands."

"I take thy meaning, Robin Hood," said the Queen, "and that thou dost convey reproach to me, as well thou mayst, for I know that I have not done by thee as I ought to have done. I know right well that thou must have been hard pressed by peril to leap so boldly into one danger to escape another. Once more I promise thee mine aid, and will do all I can to send thee back in safety to Sherwood Forest. Bide thou here till I return." So saying, she left Robin in the garden of roses, and was gone a long time.

When she came back Sir Robert Lee was with her, and the Queen's cheeks were hot and the Queen's eyes were bright, as though she had been talking with high words. Then Sir Robert came straight forward to where Robin Hood stood, and he spoke to the yeoman in a cold, stern voice. Quoth he, "Our gracious Sovereign the King hath mitigated his wrath toward thee, fellow, and hath once more promised that thou shalt depart in peace and safety. Not only hath he promised this, but in three days he will send one of his pages to go with thee and see that none arrest thy journey back again. Thou mayst thank thy patron saint that thou hast such a good friend in our noble Queen, for, but for her persuasion and arguments, thou hadst been a dead man, I can tell thee. Let this peril that thou hast passed through teach thee two lessons. First, be more honest. Second, be not so bold in thy comings and goings. A man that walketh in the darkness as thou dost may escape for a time, but in the end he will surely fall into the pit. Thou hast put thy head in the angry lion's mouth, and yet thou hast escaped by a miracle. Try it not again." So saying, he turned and left Robin and was gone.

For three days Robin abided in London in the Queen's household, and at the end of that time the King's head page, Edward Cunningham, came, and taking Robin with him, departed northward upon his way to Sherwood. Now and then they passed bands of the King's men coming back again to London, but none of those bands stopped them, and so, at last, they reached the sweet, leafy woodlands.

Thus end the merry adventures which befell Robin Hood when he went to the famous shooting-match at London Town. And now we will hear of how the Bishop of Hereford and the Sheriff of Nottingham sought once more to take him in a different way. Likewise we will hear how merry King Richard of the Lion's Heart visited Robin Hood in the depths of Sherwood Forest.

# Part Eighth

*In which it is told how Robin Hood met Guy of Gisbourne in Sherwood Forest, and of the famous fight betwixt them. Also, how Little John fell into the Sheriff's hands through saving the life of three men. Likewise, it is told how good King Richard of the Lion's Heart came to Nottinghamshire and visited Robin Hood in Sherwood Forest.*

CHAPTER ONE

# ROBIN HOOD AND GUY OF GISBOURNE

~

A long time passed after the great shooting-match, and during that time Robin followed one part of the advice of Sir Robert Lee, to wit, that of being less bold in his comings and his goings; for though mayhap he may not have been more honest (as most folks regard honesty), he took good care not to travel so far from Sherwood that he could not reach it again both easily and quickly.

Great changes had fallen in this time; for King Henry had died and King Richard had come to the crown that fitted him so well through many hard trials, and through adventures as stirring as any that ever befell Robin Hood. But though great changes came, they did not reach to Sherwood's shades, for there Robin Hood and his men dwelt as merrily as they had ever done, with hunting and feasting and singing and blithe woodland sports; for it was little the outside striving of the world troubled them.

The dawning of a summer's day was fresh and bright, and the birds sang sweetly in a great tumult of sound. So loud was their singing that it awakened Robin Hood where he lay sleeping, so that he stirred, and turned, and arose. Up rose Little John also, and all the merry men; then, after they had broken their fast, they set forth hither and thither upon the doings of the day.

Robin Hood and Little John walked down a forest path where all around the leaves danced and twinkled as the breeze trembled through them and the sunlight came flickering down. Quoth Robin Hood, "I make my vow, Little John, my blood tickles my veins as it flows through them this gay morn. What sayst thou to our seeking adventures, each one upon his own account?"

"With all my heart," said Little John. "We have had more than one pleasant doing in that way, good master. Here are two paths; take thou the one to the right hand, and I will take the one to the left, and then let us each walk straight ahead till he tumble into some merry doing or other."

"I like thy plan," quoth Robin, "therefore we will part here. But look thee, Little John, keep thyself out of mischief, for I would not have ill befall thee for all the world!"

"Marry come up," quoth Little John, "how thou talkest! Methinks thou art wont to get thyself into tighter coils than I am like to do."

At this Robin Hood laughed. "Why, in sooth, Little John," said he, "thou hast a blundering way that seemeth to bring thee right side uppermost in all thy troubles; but let us see who cometh out best this day." So saying, he clapped his palm to Little John's and each departed upon his way, the trees quickly shutting the one from the other's sight.

Robin Hood strolled onward till he came to where a broad woodland road stretched before him. Overhead the branches of the trees laced together in flickering foliage, all golden where it grew thin to the sunlight; beneath his feet the ground was soft and moist from the sheltering shade. Here in this pleasant spot the sharpest adventure that ever befell Robin Hood came upon him; for, as he walked down the woodland path thinking of nought but the songs of the birds, he came of a sudden to where a man was seated upon the mossy roots beneath the shade of a broad-spreading oak tree. Robin Hood saw that the stranger had not caught sight of him so he stopped and stood quite still, looking at the other a long time before he came forward. And the stranger, I wot, was well worth looking at, for never had Robin seen a figure like that sitting beneath the tree. From his head to his feet he was clad in a horse's hide, dressed with the hair upon it. Upon his head was a cowl that hid his face from sight, and which was made of the horse's skin, the ears whereof stuck up like those of a rabbit. His body was clad in a jacket made of the hide, and his legs were covered with the hairy skin likewise. By his side was a heavy broadsword and a sharp, double-edged dagger. A quiver of smooth round arrows hung across his shoulders, and his stout bow of yew leaned against the tree beside him.

"Halloa, friend," cried Robin, coming forward at last, "who art thou that sittest there? And what is that thou that thou hast upon thy body? I make my vow I ha' never seen such a sight in all my life before. Had I done an evil thing, or did my conscience trouble me, I would be afraid of thee, thinking that thou wast some one from down below bringing a message bidding me come straightway to King Nicholas."

To this speech the other answered not a word, but he pushed the cowl back from

*"Why, how now! What have we here?... lilies in the cheeks, and not rose such as befit a bonny bride" (Part IV, Chapter 3)*

*"Nay, my Lord Bishop," said Robin... "we are all equal here in the greenwood." (Part V, Chapter 1)*

his head and showed a knit brow, a hooked nose, and a pair of fierce, restless, black eyes, which altogether made Robin think of a hawk as he looked on his face. But beside this there was something about the lines on the stranger's face, and his thin cruel mouth, and the hard glare of his eyes, that made one's flesh creep to look upon.

"Who art thou, rascal?" said he at last, in a loud, harsh voice.

"Tut, tut," quoth Robin, "speak not so sourly, brother. Has thou fed upon vinegar and nettles this morning that thy speech is so stinging?"

"An thou likest not my words," said the other, fiercely, "thou hadst best be jogging, for I tell thee plainly, my deeds match them."

"Nay, but I do like thy words, thou sweet, pretty thing," quoth Robin, squatting down upon the grass in front of the other; "moreover, I tell thee thy speech is witty and gameson as any I ever heard in all my life."

The other said not a word, but he glared upon Robin with a wicked and baleful look, such as a fierce dog bestows upon a man ere it springs at his throat. Robin returned the gaze with one of wide-eyed innocence, not a shadow of a smile twinkling in his eyes or twitching at the corners of his mouth. So they sat staring at one another for a long time, until the stranger broke the silence suddenly. "What is thy name, fellow?" said he.

"Now," quoth Robin, "I am right glad to hear thee speak, for I began to fear the sight of me had stricken thee dumb. As for my name, it may be this or it may be that; but methinks it is more meet for thee to tell me thine, seeing that thou art the greater stranger in these parts. Prythee, tell me, sweet chuck, why wearest thou that dainty garb upon thy pretty body?"

"At these words the other broke into a short, harsh roar of laughter. "By the bones of the Dæmon Odin," said he, "thou art the boldest spoken man that ever I have seen in all my life. I know not why I do not smite thee down where thou sittest, for only two days ago I skewered a man over back of Nottingham Town for saying not half so much to me as thou hast done. I wear this garb, thou fool, to keep my body warm; likewise it is near as good as a coat of steel against a common swordthrust. As for my name, I care not who knoweth it. It is Guy of Gisbourne, and thou mayst have heard it before. I come from the woodlands over in Herefordshire, upon the lands of the Bishop of that ilk. I am an outlaw, and get my living by hook and by crook in a manner it boots not now to tell of. Not long since the Bishop sent for me, and said that if I would do a certain thing that the Sheriff of Nottingham would ask of me, he would get me a free pardon, and give me tenscore pounds to boot. So straightway I came to Nottingham Town and found my sweet Sheriff; and what thinkest thou he wanted of me? Why, forsooth, to come here to Sherwood to hunt up one Robin Hood, also an outlaw, and to take him alive or dead. It seemeth that they have no one here to face that bold fellow, and so sent all the way to Herefordshire, and to me, for thou knowest the old saying, 'Set a thief to catch a thief.' As for the slaying of this fellow, it galleth me not a whit, for I would shed the blood of my own brother for the half of two hundred pounds."

To all this Robin listened, and as he listened his gorge rose. Well he knew of this Guy of Gisbourne, and of all the bloody and murderous deeds that he had done in Herefordshire, for his doings were famous throughout all the land. Yet, although he loathed the very presence of the man, he held his peace, for he had an end to serve. "Truly," quoth he, "I have heard of thy gentle doings. Methinks there is no one in all the wide world that Robin Hood would rather meet than thee."

At this Guy of Gisbourne gave another harsh laugh. "Why," quoth he, "it is a merry thing to think of one stout outlaw like Robin Hood meeting another stout outlaw like Guy of Gisbourne. Only in this case it will be an ill happening for Robin Hood, for the day he meets Guy of Gisbourne he shall die."

"But thou gentle, merry spirit," quoth Robin, "dost thou not think that mayhap this same Robin Hood may be the better man of the two? I know him right well, and many think that he is one of the stoutest men hereabouts."

"He may be the stoutest of men hereabouts," quoth Guy of Gisbourne, "yet, I tell thee, fellow, this sty of yours is not the wide world. I lay my life upon it I am the better man of the two. He an outlaw, forsooth! why I hear that he hath never let blood in all his life, saving when he first came to the forest. Some call him a great archer; marry, I would not be afraid to stand against him all the days of the year with a bow in my hand."

"Why, truly, some folk do call him a great archer," said Robin Hood; "but we of Nottinghamshire are famous hands with the long bow. Even I, though but a simple hand at the craft, would not fear to try a bout with thee."

At these words Guy of Gisbourne looked upon Robin with wondering eyes, and then gave another roar of laughter till the woods rang. "Now," quoth he, "thou art a bold fellow to talk to me in this way. I like they spirit in so speaking up to me, for few men have dared to do so. Put up a garland, lad, and I will try a bout with thee."

"Tut, tut," quoth Robin, "only babes shoot at garlands hereabouts. I will put up a good Nottingham mark for thee." So saying he arose, and going to a hazel thicket not far off, he cut a wand about twice the thickness of a man's thumb. From this he peeled the bark, and, sharpening the point, stuck it up in the ground in front of a great oak tree. Thence he measured off fourscore paces, which brought him beside the tree where the other sat. "There," quoth he, "is the kind of mark that Nottingham yeomen shoot at. Now let me see thee split that wand if thou art an archer."

Then Guy of Gisbourne arose. "Now out upon it!" cried he. "The Devil himself could not hit such a mark as that."

"Mayhap he could and mayhap he could not," quoth merry Robin, "but that we shall never know till thou hast shot thereat."

At these words Guy of Gisbourne looked upon Robin with knit brows, but, as the yeoman still looked innocent of any ill meaning, he bottled his words and strung his bow in silence. Twice he shot, but neither time did he hit the wand, missing it the first time by a span and the second time by a good palm's breadth. Robin laughed and laughed. "I see now," quoth he, "that the Devil himself could not hit that mark. Good fellow, if thou art no better with the broadsword than thou art with the bow and arrow, thou wilt never overcome Robin Hood."

At these words Guy of Gisbourne glared savagely upon Robin. Quoth he, "thou hast a merry tongue, thou villain; but take care that thou makest not too free with it, or I may cut it out from thy throat for thee."

Robin Hood strung his bow and took his place with never a word, albeit his heartstrings quivered with anger and loathing. Twice he shot, the first time hitting within an inch of the wand, the second time splitting it fairly in the middle. Then, without giving the other a chance for speech, he flung his bow upon the ground. "There, thou bloody villain!" cried he, fiercely, "let that show thee how little thou knowest of manly sports. And now look the last upon the daylight, for the good earth hath been befouled long enough by thee, thou vile beast! This day, Our Lady willing, thou diest – I am Robin Hood." So saying, he flashed forth his bright sword in the sunlight.

For a time Guy of Gisbourne stared upon Robin as though bereft of wits; but his wonder quickly passed to a wild rage. "Art thou indeed Robin Hood?" cried he. "Now I am glad to meet thee, thou poor wretch! Shrive thyself, for thou wilt have no time for shriving when I am done with thee." So saying, he also drew his sword.

And now came the fiercest fight that ever Sherwood saw; for each man knew that either he or the other must die, and that no mercy was to be had in this battle. Up and down they fought, till all the sweet green grass was crushed and ground beneath the trampling of their heels. More than once the point of Robin Hood's sword felt the softness of flesh, and presently the ground began to be sprinkled with bright red drops, albeit not one of them came from Robin's veins. At last Guy of Gisbourne made a fierce and deadly thrust at Robin Hood, from which he leaped back lightly, but in so leaping he caught his heel in a root, and fell heavily upon his back. "Now, Holy Mary aid me!" muttered he, as the other leaped at him with a grin of rage upon his face. Fiercely Guy of Gisbourne stabbed at the other with his great sword; but Robin caught the blade in his naked hand, and, though it cut his palm, he turned the point away so that it plunged deep into the ground close beside him; then, ere a blow could be struck again, he leaped to his feet, with his good sword in his hand. And now despair fell upon Guy of Gisbourne's heart in a black cloud, and he looked around him wildly, like a wounded hawk. Seeing that his strength was going from him, Robin leaped forward, and, quick as a flash, struck a back-handed blow beneath the sword arm. Down fell the sword from Guy of Gisbourne's grasp, and back he staggered at the stroke, and, ere he could regain himself, Robin's sword passed through and through his body. Round he spun on his heel, and, flinging his hands aloft with a shrill, wild cry, fell prone upon his face upon the green sod.

Then Robin Hood wiped his sword and thrust it back into the scabbard, and, coming to where Guy of Gisbourne lay, he stood over him with folded arms, talking to himself the while. "This is the first man I have slain since I shot the King's forester in the hot days of my youth. I ofttimes think bitterly, even yet, of that first life I took, but of this I am as glad as though I had slain a wild boar that lay waste a fair country. Since the Sheriff of Nottingham hath sent such a one as this against me, I will put on the fellow's garb and go forth to see whether I may not find his worship, and perchance pay him back some of the debt I own him upon this score."

So saying, Robin Hood stripped the hairy garments from off the dead man, and put them on himself, all bloody as they were. Then, strapping the other's sword and dagger around his body and carrying his own in his hand, together with the two bows of yew, he drew the cowl of horse's hide over his face, so that none could tell who he was, and set forth from the forest, turning his steps toward the eastward and Nottingham Town. As he strode along the country roads, men, women, and children hid away from him, for the terror of Guy of Gisbourne's name and of his doings had spread far and near.

And now let us see what befell Little John while these things were happening.

Little John walked on his way through the forest paths until he had come to the outskirts of the woodlands, where, here and there, fields of barley, corn, or green meadow lands lay smiling in the sun. So he came to the high-road and to where a little thatched cottage stood back of a cluster of twisted crab-trees, with flowers in front of it. Here he stopped of a sudden, for he thought that he heard the sound of some one in sorrow. He listened, and found that it came from the cottage; so, turning his footsteps thither, he pushed open the wicket and entered the place. There he saw a gray-haired dame sitting beside a cold hearthstone, rocking herself to and fro and weeping bitterly.

Now Little John had a tender heart for the sorrows of other folk, so, coming to the old woman and patting her kindly upon the shoulder, he spoke comforting words to her, bidding her cheer up and tell him her troubles, for that mayhap he might do something to ease them. At all this the good dame shook her head; but all the same his kind words did soothe her somewhat, so after a while she told him all that bore upon her mind. That that morning she had three as fair, tall sons beside her as one could find in all Nottinghamshire, but that they were now taken from her, and were like to be hanged straightway; that, want having come upon them, her eldest boy had gone out, the night before, into the forest, and had slain a hind in the moonlight; that the King's rangers had followed the blood upon the grass until they had come to her cottage, and had there found the deer's meat in the cupboard; that, as neither of the younger sons would betray their brother, the foresters had taken all three away, in spite of the oldest saying that he alone had slain the deer; that, as they went, she had heard the rangers talking among themselves, saying that the Sheriff had sworn that he would put a check upon the great slaughter of deer that had been going on of late by hanging the very first rogue caught thereat upon the nearest tree, and that they would take the three youths to the King's Head Inn, near Nottingham Town, where the Sheriff was abiding that day, there to await the return of a certain fellow he had sent into Sherwood to seek for Robin Hood.

To all this Little John listened, shaking his head sadly now and then. "Alas," quoth he, when the good dame had finished her speech, "this is indeed an ill case. But who is this that goeth into Sherwood after Robin Hood, and why doth he go to seek him? But no matter for that now; only that I would that Robin Hood were here to advise us. Nevertheless, no time may be lost in sending for him at this hour, if we would save the lives of thy three sons. Tell me, hast thou any clothes hereabouts that I may put on in place of these of Lincoln green? Marry, if our stout Sheriff catcheth me without disguise, I am like to be run up more quickly than thy sons, let me tell thee, dame."

Then the old woman told him that she had in the house some of the clothes of her good husband, who had died only two years before. These she brought to Little John, who, doffing his garb of Lincoln green, put them on in its stead. Then, making a wig and false beard of uncarded wool, he covered his own brown hair and beard, and, putting on a great, tall hat that had belonged to the old peasant, he took his staff in one hand and his bow in the other, and set forth with all speed to where the Sheriff had taken up his inn.

A mile or more from Nottingham Town, and not far from the southern borders of Sherwood Forest, stood the cosy inn bearing the sign of the King's Head. Here was a great bustle and stir on this bright morning, for the Sheriff and a score of his men had come to stop there and await Guy of Gisbourne's return from the forest. Great hiss and fuss of cooking was going on in the kitchen, and great rapping and tanning of wine kegs and beer barrels was going on in the cellar. The Sheriff sat within, feasting merrily of the best the place afforded, and the Sheriff's men sat upon the bench before the door, quaffing ale, or lay beneath the shade of the broad-spreading oak trees, talking and jesting and laughing. All around stood the horses of the band, with a great noise of stamping feet and a great switching of tails. To this inn came the King's rangers, driving the widow's three sons before them. The hands of the three youths were tied tightly behind their backs, and a cord from neck to neck fastened them all together. So they were marched to the room where the Sheriff sat at meat, and stood trembling before him as he scowled sternly upon them. "So," quoth he, in a great, loud, angry voice, "ye have been poaching upon the King's deer, have you? Now I will make short work of you this day, for I will hang up all three of you as a farmer would hang up three crows to scare others of the kind from the field. Our fair county of Nottingham hath been too long a breeding-place for such naughty knaves as ye are. I have put up with these things for many years, but now I will stamp them out once for all, and with you I will begin."

Then one of the poor fellows opened his mouth to speak, but the Sheriff roared at him in a loud voice to be silent, and bade the rangers to take them away till he had done his eating and could attend to the matters concerning them. So the three poor youths were marched outside, where they stood with bowed heads and despairing hearts, till after a while the Sheriff came forth. Then he called his men about him, and quoth he, "These three villains shall be hanged straightway, but not here, lest they breed ill-luck to this goodly inn. We will take them over yonder to that belt of woodlands, for I would fain hang them upon the very trees of Sherwood itself, to show those vile outlaws therein what they may expect of me if I ever have the good luck to lay hands upon them." So saying he mounted his horse, as did his men-at-arms likewise, and altogether they set forth for the belt of woodlands he had spoken of, the poor youths walking in their midst guarded by the rangers. Soon they came at last to the spot, and here nooses were fastened around the necks of the three, and the ends of the cords flung over the branch of a great oak tree that stood there. Then the three youths fell upon their knees and loudly besought mercy of the Sheriff; but the Sheriff of Nottingham laughed scornfully. "Now," quoth he, "I would that I had a priest here to shrive you; but, as none is nigh, you must e'en travel your road with all your sins packed upon your backs, and trust to Saint Peter to let you in through the gates of Paradise like three pedlers into the town."

In the mean time, whilst all this had been going forward, an old man had drawn near and stood leaning on his staff, looking on. His hair and beard were all curly and white, and across his back was a bow of yew that looked much too strong for him to draw. As the Sheriff looked around ere he ordered his men to string the three youths up to the oak tree, his eyes fell upon this strange old man. Then his worship beckoned to him, saying. "Come hither, father, I have a few words to say to thee." So Little John, for it was none other than he, came forward, and the Sheriff looked upon him thinking that there was something strangely familiar in the face before him. "How, now," said he, "methinks I have seen thee before. What may thy name be, father?"

"Please your worship," said Little John, in a cracked voice like that of an old man, "my name is Giles Hobble, at your worship's service."

"Giles Hobble; Giles Hobble;" muttered the Sheriff to himself, turning over the names that he had in his mind to try to find one to fit to this. "I remember not thy name," said he at last, "but it matters not. Hast thou a mind to earn sixpence this bright morn?"

"Ay, marry," quoth Little John, "for money is not so plenty with me that I should cast sixpence away an I could earn it by an honest turn. What is it your worship would have me do?"

"Why, this," said the Sheriff. Here are three men that need hanging as badly as any e'er I saw. If thou wilt string them up I will pay three twopence apiece for them. I like not that my men-at-arms should turn hangmen. Wilt thou try thy hand?"

"In sooth," said Little John, still in the old man's voice, "I ha' never done such a thing before; but an a sixpence is to be earned so easily I might as well ha' it as anybody. But, your worship, are these naughty fellows shrived?"

"Nay," said the Sheriff, laughing, "never a whit; but thou mayst turn thy hand to that also if thou art so minded. But hasten, I prythee, for I would get back to mine inn betimes."

So Little John came to where the three youths stood trembling, and, putting his face to the first fellow's cheek as though he were listening to him, he whispered softly into his ear, "Stand still, brother, when thou feelst thy bonds cut; but when thou seest ne throw my woollen wig and beard from my head and face, cast the noose from thy neck and run for the woodlands." Then he slyly cut the cord that bound the youth's hands; who, upon his part, stood still as though he were yet bound. Then he went to the second fellow, and spoke to him in the same way, and also cut his bonds. This he did to the third likewise, but all so slyly that the Sheriff, who sat upon his horse laughing, wotted not what was being done, nor his men either.

Then Little John turned to the Sheriff. "Please your worship," said he, "will you give me leave to string my bow? for I would fain help these fellows along the way, when they are swinging, with an arrow beneath the ribs."

"With all my heart," said the Sheriff, "only, as I said before, make thou haste in thy doings."

Little John put the tip of his bow to his instep, and strung the weapon so deftly that all wondered to see an old man so strong. Next he drew a good smooth arrow from his quiver and fitted it to the string; then, looking all around to see that the way was clear behind him, he suddenly cast away the wool from his head and face, shouting in a mighty voice, "Run!" Quick as a flash the three youths flung the nooses from their necks and sped across the open to the woodlands as the arrow speeds from the bow. Little John also flew toward the covert like a greyhound, while the Sheriff and his men gazed after him all bewildered with the sudden doing. But ere the yeoman had gone far the Sheriff roused himself. "After him!" he roared in a mighty voice; for he knew now who it was with whom he had been talking, and wondered that he had not known him before.

Little John heard the Sheriff's words, and seeing that he could not hope to reach the woodlands before they would be upon him, he stopped and turned suddenly, holding his bow as though he were about to shoot. "Stand back!" cried he, fiercely. "The first man that cometh a foot forward, or toucheth finger to bowstring, dieth!"

At these words the Sheriff's men stood as still as stocks, for they knew right well that Little John would be as good as his word, and that to disobey him meant death. In vain the Sheriff roared at them, calling them cowards, and urging them forward in a body; they would not budge an inch, but stood and watched Little John as he moved slowly away toward the forest, keeping his gaze fixed upon them. But when the Sheriff saw his enemy thus slipping betwixt his fingers he grew mad with his rage, so that his head swam and he knew not what he did. Then of a sudden he turned his horse's head, and plunging his spurs into its sides he gave a great shout, and, rising in his stirrups, came down upon Little John like the wind. Then Little John raised his deadly bow and draw the gray goose feather to his cheek. But alas for him! for, ere he could loose the shaft, the good bow that had served him so long, split in his hands, and the arrow fell harmless at his feet. Seeing what had happened, the Sheriff's men raised a shout, and, following their master, came rushing down upon Little John. But the Sheriff was ahead of the others, and so caught up with the yeoman before he reached the shelter of the woodlands, then leaning forward he struck a mighty blow. Little John ducked and the Sheriff's sword turned in his hand, but the flat of the blade struck the other upon the head and smote him down, stunned and senseless.

"Now, I am right glad," said the Sheriff, when the men came up and found that Little John was not dead, "that I have not slain this man in my haste! I would rather lose five hundred pounds than have him die thus instead of hanging, as such a vile thief should do. Go, get some water from yonder fountain, William, and pour it over his head."

The man did as he was bidden, and presently Little John opened his eyes and looked around him, all dazed and bewildered with the stun of the blow. Then they tied his hands behind him, and lifting him up set him upon the back of one of the horses, with his face to its tail and his feet strapped beneath its belly. So they took him back to the King's Head Inn, laughing and rejoicing as they went along. But in the mean time the widow's three sons had gotten safely away, and were hidden in the woodlands.

Once more the Sheriff of Nottingham sat within the King's Head Inn. His heart rejoiced within him, for he had at last done that which he had sought to do for years, taken Little John prisoner. Quoth he to himself, "This time to-morrow the rogue shall hang upon the gallows tree in front of the great gate of Nottingham Town, and thus shall I make my long score with him even." So saying he took a deep draught of Canary. But it seemed as if the Sheriff had swallowed a thought with his wine, for he shook his head and put the cup down hastily. "Now," he muttered to himself, "I would not for a thousand pounds have this fellow slip through my fingers; yet, should his master escape that foul Guy of Gisbourne, there is no knowing what he may do, for he is the cunningest knave in all the world, – this same Robin Hood. Belike I had better not wait until to-morrow to hang the fellow." So saying, he pushed his chair back hastily, and going forth from the inn called his men together. Quoth he, "I will wait no longer for the hanging of this rogue, but it shall be done forthwith, and that from the very tree whence he saved those three young villains by stepping so boldly betwixt them and the law. So get ye ready straightway."

Then once more they sat Little John upon the horse, with his face to the tail, and so, one leading the horse whereon he sat and the others riding around him, they went forward to that tree from the branches of which they had thought to hang the poachers. On they went, rattling and jingling along the road till they came to the tree. Here one of the men spake to the Sheriff of a sudden. "Your worship," cried he, "is not yon fellow coming along toward us that same Guy of Gisbourne whom thou didst send into the forest to seek the outlaw, Robin Hood?"

At these words the Sheriff shaded his eyes and looked eagerly. "Why, certes," quoth he, "yon fellow is the same. Now, Heaven send that he hath slain the master thief, as we will presently slay the man!"

When Little John heard this speech he looked up, and straightway his heart crumbled away within him, for not only were the man's garments all covered with blood, but he wore Robin Hood's bugle horn and carried his bow and broadsword in his hand.

"How now!" cried the Sheriff, when Robin Hood, in Guy of Gisbourne's clothes, had come nigh to them. "What luck hath befallen thee in the forest? Why, man, thy clothes are all over blood!"

"An thou likest not my clothes," said Robin, in a harsh voice like that of Guy of Gisbourne, "thou mayst shut thine eyes. Marry, the blood upon me is that of the vilest outlaw that ever trod the woodlands, and one whom I have slain this day, albeit not without wound to myself."

Then out spake Little John, for the first time since he had fallen into the Sheriff's hands. "O thou vile, bloody wretch! I know thee Guy of Gisbourne, for who is there that hath not heard of thee and cursed thee for thy vile deeds of blood and rapine? Is it by such a hand as thine that the gentlest heart that ever beat is stilled in death? Truly, thou art a fit tool for this coward Sheriff of Nottingham. Now I die joyfully, nor do I care how I die, for life is nought to me!" So spake Little John, the salt tears rolling down his brown cheeks.

But the Sheriff of Nottingham clapped his hands for joy. "Now, Guy of Gisbourne," cried he, "if what thou tellest me is true, it will be the best day's doings for thee that ever thou hast done in all thy life."

"What I have told thee is sooth, and I lie not," said Robin, still in Guy of Gisbourne's voice. "Look, is not this Robin Hood's sword, and is not this his good bow of yew, and is not this his bugle horn? Thinkest thou he would hath given them to Guy of Gisbourne of his own free will?"

Then the Sheriff laughed aloud for joy. "This is a good day!" cried he. "The great outlaw dead and his right-hand man in my hands! Ask what thou wilt of me, Guy of Gisbourne, and it is thine!"

"Then this I ask of thee," said Robin. "As I have slain the master I would not kill the man. Give this fellow's life into my hands, Sir Sheriff."

"Now thou art a fool!" cried the Sheriff. "Thou mightst have had money enough for a knight's ransom if thou hadst asked for it. I like ill to let this fellow pass from my hands, but as I have promised, thou shalt have him."

"I thank thee right heartily for thy gift," cried Robin. "Take the rogue down from the horse, men, and lean him against yonder tree, whilst I show you how we stick a porker whence I come!"

At these words some of the Sheriff's men shook their heads; for, though they cared not a whit whether Little John were hanged or not, they hated to see him butchered in cold blood. But the Sheriff called to them in a loud voice, ordering them to take the yeoman down from the horse and lean him against the tree, as the other bade.

Whilst they were doing this Robin Hood strung both his bow and that of Guy of Gisbourne, albeit none of them took notice of his doing so. Then, when Little John stood against the tree, he drew Guy of Gisbourne's sharp, double-edged dagger. "Fall back! fall back!" cried he. "Would ye crowd so on my pleasure, ye unmannerly knaves? Back, I say! Farther yet!" So they crowded back, as he ordered, many of them turning their faces away, that they might not see what was about to happen.

"Come!" cried Little John. "Here is my breast. It is meet that the same hand that slew my dear master should butcher me also! I know thee, Guy of Gisbourne!"

"Peace, Little John!" said Robin, in a low voice. "Twice thou hast said thou knowest me, and yet thou knowest me not at all. Couldst thou not tell me beneath this wild beast's hide? Yonder, just in front of thee, lie my bow and arrows, likewise my broadsword. Take them when I cut thy bonds. Now! Get them quickly!" So saying, he cut the bonds, and Little John, quick as a wink, leaped forward and caught up the bow and arrows and the broadsword. At the same time Robin Hood threw back the cowl of horse's hide from his face and bent Guy of Gisbourne's bow, with a keen, barbed arrow fitted to the string. "Stand back!" cried he, sternly. "The first man that toucheth finger to bowstring dieth! I have slain thy man, Sheriff; take heed that it is not thy turn next." Then, seeing that Little John had armed himself, he clapped his bugle horn to his lips and blew three blasts both loud and shrill.

Now when the Sheriff of Nottingham saw whose face it was beneath Guy Gisbourne's hood, and when he heard those bugle notes ring in his ear, he felt as if his hour had come. "Robin Hood!" roared he, and without another word he wheeled his horse in the road and went off in a cloud of dust. The Sheriff's men, seeing their master thus fleeing for his life, thought that it was not their business to tarry longer, so, clapping spurs to their horses, they also dashed away after him. But though the Sheriff of Nottingham went fast, he could not outstrip a clothyard arrow. Little John twanged his bowstring with a shout, and when the Sheriff dashed in through the gates of Nottingham Town at full speed, a gray goose shaft stuck out behind him like a moulting sparrow with one feather in its tail. For a month afterwards the poor Sheriff could sit upon nought but the softest cushions that could be gotten for him.

Thus the Sheriff and a score of men ran away from Robin Hood and Little John; so that when Will Stutely and a dozen or more of stout yeomen burst from out the covert, they saw nought of their master's enemies, for the Sheriff and his men were scouring away in the distance, hidden within a cloud of dust like a little thunder-storm.

Then they all went back into the forest once more, where they found the window's three sons, who ran to Little John and kissed his hands. But it would not do for them to roam the forest at large any more; so they promised that, after they had gone and told their mother of their escape, they would come that night to the greenwood tree, and thenceforth become men of the band.

Thus end the bravest adventures that ever befell Robin Hood and Little John. So next we shall hear how stout King Richard of the Lion's Heart visited Robin in Sherwood Forest.

## CHAPTER TWO

# KING RICHARD COMETH TO SHERWOOD FOREST

~

Not more than two months had passed and gone since these stirring adventures that have just been told of befell Robin Hood and Little John , when all Nottinghamshire was in a mighty stir and tumult, for King Richard of the Lion's Heart was making a royal progress through merry England, and every one expected him to come to Nottingham Town in his journeying. Messengers went riding back and forth between the Sheriff and the King, until at last the time was fixed upon when his majesty was to stop in Nottingham, as the guest of his worship.

And now came more bustle than ever; a great running hither and thither, a rapping of hammers and a babble of voices sounded everywhere through the place, for the folk were building great arches across the streets, beneath which the King was to pass, and were draping these arches with silken banners and streamers of many colors. Great hubbub was going on in the Guild Hall of the town, also, for here a grand banquet was to be given to the King and the nobles of his train, and the best master carpenters were busy building a throne where the King and the Sheriff were to sit at the head of the table side by side.

It seemed to many of the good folk of the place as if the day that should bring the King into the town would never come; but all the same it did come in its own season, and bright shone the sun down into the stony streets, which were all alive with a restless sea of people. On either side of the way great crowds of town and country folk stood packed as close together as dried herring in a box, so that the Sheriff's men, halberds in hands, could hardly press them back to leave space for the King's riding.

"Take care whom thou pushest against!" cried a great, burly friar to one of these men. "Wouldst thou dig thine elbows into me, sirrah? By'r Lady of the Fountain, an thou dost not treat me with more deference I will crack thy knave's pate for thee, even though thou be one of the mighty Sheriff's men."

At this a great shout of laughter arose from a number of tall yeomen in Lincoln green that were scattered through the crowd thereabouts; but one that seemed of more authority than the others nudged the holy man with his elbow. "Peace, Tuck," said he; didst thou not promise me, ere thou camest here that thou wouldst put a check upon thy tongue?"

"Ay, marry," grumbled the other, "but a did not think to have a hard-footed knave trample all over my poor toes as though they were no more than so many acorns in the forest."

But of a sudden all this bickering ceased, for a clear sound of many bugle horns came winding down the street. Then all the people craned their necks and gazed in the direction whence the sound came, and the crowding and the pushing and the swaying grew greater than ever. And now a gallant array of men came gleaming into sight, and the cheering of the people ran down the crowd as the fire runs in dry grass.

Eight and twenty heralds in velvet and cloth of gold came riding forwards. Over their heads fluttered a cloud of snow-white feathers, and each herald bore in his hand a long silver trumpet, which he blew musically. From each trumpet hung a heavy banner of velvet and cloth of gold, with the royal arms of England emblazoned thereon. After these came riding fivescore noble knights, two by two, all fully armed, saving that their heads were uncovered. In their hands they bore tall lances, from the tops of which fluttered pennons of many colors and devices. By the side of each knight walked a page clad in rich clothes of silk and velvet, and each page bore in his hands his master's helmet, from which waved long, floating plumes of feathers. Never had Nottingham seen a fairer sight than those fivescore noble knights, from whose armor the sun blazed in dazzling light as they came riding on their great warhorses, with clashing of arms and jingling of chains. Behind the knights came the barons and the nobles of the midcountry, in robes of silk and cloth of gold, with golden chains about their necks and jewels at their girdles. Behind these again came a great array of men-at-arms, with spears and halberds in their hands, and, in the midst of these, two riders side by side. The other, who was a head taller than the Sheriff, was clad in a rich but simple garb, with a broad, heavy chain about his neck. His hair and beard were like threads of gold, and his eyes were as blue as the summer sky. As he rode along he bowed to the right hand and the left, and a mighty roar of voices followed him as he passed; for this was King Richard.

Then, above all the tumult and the shouting a great voice was heard roaring. "Heaven, its saints bless thee, our gracious King Richard! and likewise Our Lady of the Fountain, bless thee!" Then King Richard, looking toward the spot whence the sound came, saw a tall, burly, strapping priest standing in front of all the crowd with his legs wide apart as he backed against those behind.

"By my soul, Sheriff," said the King, laughing, "ye have the tallest priests in Nottinghamshire that e'er I saw in all my life. If Heaven never answered prayers because of deafness, methinks I would nevertheless have blessings bestowed upon me, for that man yonder would make the great stone image of Saint Peter rub its ears and hearken unto him. I would that I had an army of such as he."

To this the Sheriff answered never a word, but all the blood left his cheeks, and he caught at the pommel of his saddle to keep himself from falling; for he also saw the fellow that so shouted, and knew him to be Friar Tuck; and, moreover, behind Friar Tuck he saw the faces, of Robin Hood and Little John and Will Scarlet and Will Stutely and Allan a Dale and others of the band.

"Now now," said the King hastily, "art thou ill, Sheriff, that thou growest so white?"

"Nay, your majesty," said the Sheriff, "it was nought but a sudden pain that will soon pass by." Thus he spake, for he was ashamed that the King should know that Robin Hood feared him so little that he thus dared to come within the very gates of Nottingham Town.

Thus rode the King into Nottingham Town on that bright afternoon in the early fall season; and none rejoiced more than Robin Hood and his merry men to see him come so royally unto his own.

Eventide had come; the great feast in the Guild Hall at Nottingham Town was done, and the wine passed freely. A thousand waxen lights gleamed along the board, at which sat lord and noble and knight and squire in goodly array. At the head of the table, upon a throne all hung with cloth of gold, sat King Richard with the Sheriff of Nottingham beside him.

Quoth the King to the Sheriff, laughing as he spoke, "I have heard much spoken concerning the doings of certain fellows hereabouts, one Robin Hood and his band, who are outlaws and abide in Sherwood Forest. Canst thou not tell me somewhat of them, Sir Sheriff? for I hear that thou hast had dealings with them more than once."

At these words the Sheriff of Nottingham looked down gloomily, and the Bishop of Hereford, who was present, gnawed his nether lip. Quoth the Sheriff, "I can tell your majesty but little concerning the doings of those naughty fellows, saving that they are the boldest law-breakers in all the land."

Then up spake young Sir Henry of the Lea, a great favorite with the King, under whom he had fought in Palestine. "May it please your majesty," said he, "when I was away in Palestine I heard ofttimes from my father, and in most cases I heard of this very fellow, Robin Hood. If your majesty would like I will tell you a certain adventure of this outlaw."

Then the King laughingly bade him tell his tale, whereupon he told how Robin Hood had aided Sir Richard of the Lea with money that he had borrowed from the

Bishop of Hereford. Again and again the King and those present roared with laughter, whilst the poor Bishop waxed cherry red in the face with vexation, for the matter was a sore thing with him. When Sir Henry of the Lea was done, others of those present, seeing how the King enjoyed this merry tale, told other tales concerning Robin and his merry men.

"By the hilt of my sword," said stout King Richard, "this is as bold and merry a knave as ever I heard tell of. Marry, I must take this matter in hand and do what thou couldst not do, Sheriff, to wit, clear the forest of him and his band."

That night the King sat in the place that was set apart for his lodging whilst in Nottingham Town. With him were young Sir Henry of the Lea and two other knights and three barons of Nottinghamshire; but the King's mind still dwelt upon Robin Hood. "Now," quoth he, "I would freely give a hundred pounds to meet this roguish fellow, Robin Hood, and to see somewhat of his doings in Sherwood Forest."

Then up spake Sir Hubert of Bingham, laughing: "If your majesty hath such a desire upon you it is not so hard to satisfy. If your majesty is willing to lose one hundred pounds, I will engage to cause you not only to meet this fellow, but to feast with him in Sherwood."

"Marry, Sir Hubert," quoth the King, "this pleaseth me well. But how wilt thou cause me to meet Robin Hood?"

"Why, thus," said Sir Hubert; "let your majesty and us here present put on the robes of seven of the Order of Black Friars, and let your majesty hang a purse of one hundred pounds beneath your gown; then let us undertake to ride from here to Mansfield Town to-morrow, and, without I am much mistaken, we will both meet with Robin Hood and dine with him before the day be passed."

"I like thy plan, Sir Hubert," quoth the King merrily, "and to-morrow we will try it and see whether there be virtue in it."

So it happened that when early the next morning the Sheriff came to where his liege lord was abiding, to pay his duty to him, the King told him what they had talked of the night before, and what merry adventure they were set upon undertaking that morning. But when the Sheriff heard this he smote his forehead with his fist. "Alas!" said he, "what evil counsel is this that hath been given thee! O my gracious lord and king, you know not what you do! This villain that you thus go to seek hath no reverence either for king or king's laws."

"But did I not hear aright when I was told that this Robin Hood hath shed no blood since he was outlawed, saving only that of that vile Guy of Gisbourne, for whose death all honest men should thank him?"

"Yea, your majesty," said the Sheriff, "you have heard aright. Nevertheless" -

"Then," quoth the King, breaking in on the Sheriff's speech, "what have I to fear in meeting him, having done him no harm? Truly, there is no danger in this. But mayhap thou wilt go with us, Sir Sheriff."

"Nay," quoth the Sheriff hastily, "Heaven forbid!"

But now seven habits such as black friars wear were brought, and the King and those about him having clad themselves therein, and his majesty having hung a purse with a hundred golden pounds in it beneath his robes, they all went forth and mounted the mules that had been brought to the door for them. Then the King bade the Sheriff be silent as to their doings, and so they set forth upon their way.

Onward they travelled, laughing and jesting, until they passed, through the open country; between bare harvest fields whence the harvest had been gathered home; through scattered glades that began to thicken as they went farther along, till they came within the heavy shade of the forest itself. They travelled in the forest for several miles without meeting any one such as they sought, until they had come to that part of the road that lay nearest to Newstead Abbey.

"By the holy Saint Martin," quoth the King, "I would that I had a better head for remembering things of great need. Here have we come away and brought never so much as a drop of anything to drink with us. Now I would give half a hundred pounds for somewhat to quench my thirst withal."

No sooner had the King so spoken, than out from the covert at the roadside stepped a tall fellow with yellow beard and hair and a pair of merry blue eyes. "Truly, holy brother," said he, laying his hand upon the King's bridle rein, "it were an unchristian thing to not give fitting answer to so fair a bargain. We keep an inn hereabouts, and for fifty pounds we will not only give thee a good draught of wine, but will give thee as noble a feast as ever thou didst tickle thy gullet withal." So saying he put his fingers to his lips and blew a shrill whistle. Then straightway the bushes and branches on either side of the road swayed and crackled, and threescore broad-shouldered yeomen in Lincoln green burst out of the covert.

"How now, fellow," quoth the King, "who art thou, thou naughty rogue? Hast thou no regard for such holy men as we are?"

"Not a whit," quoth merry Robin Hood, for the fellow was he; "for in sooth all the holiness belonging to rich friars, such as ye are, one could drop into a thimble and the good wife would never feel it with the tip of her finger. As for my name, it is Robin Hood, and thou mayst have heard it before."

"Now out upon thee!" quoth King Richard. "Thou art a bold and naughty fellow and a lawless one withal, as I have often heard tell. Now, prythee, let me, and these brethren of mine, travel forward in peace and quietness."

"It may not be," said Robin, "for it would look but ill of us to let such holy men travel onward with empty stomachs. But I doubt not that thou hast a fat purse to pay thy score at our inn since thou offerest freely so much for a poor draught of wine. Show me thy purse, reverend brother, or I may perchance have to strip thy robes from thee to search for it myself."

"Nay, use no force," said the King sternly. "Here is my purse, but lay not thy lawless hands upon our person."

"Hut, tut," quoth merry Robin, "what proud words are these? Art thou the King of England, to talk so to me? Here, Will, take this purse and see what there is within."

Will Scarlet took the purse and counted out the money. Then Robin bade him keep fifty pounds for themselves, and put fifty back into the purse. This he handed to the King. "Here, brother,"quoth he, "take this half of thy money, and thank Saint Martin, on whom thou didst call before, that thou hast fallen into the hands of such gentle rogues that they will not strip thee bare, as they might do. But wilt thou not put back thy cowl? for I would fain see thy face."

"Nay," said the King, drawing back, "I may not put back my cowl, for we seven have vowed that we will not show our faces for four and twenty hours."

"Then keep them covered in peace," said Robin, "and far be it from me to make you break your vows."

So he called seven of his yeomen and bade them each one take a mule by the bridle; then, turning their faces toward the depths of the woodlands, they journeyed onward until they came to the open glade and the greenwood tree.

Little John, with threescore yeomen at his heels, had also gone forth that morning to wait along the roads and bring a rich guest to Sherwood glade, if such might be his luck, for many with fat purses must travel the roads at this time, when such great doings were going on in Nottinghamshire; but though Little John and so many others were gone, Friar Tuck and twoscore or more stout yeomen were seated or lying around beneath the great tree, and when Robin and the others came they leaped to their feet to meet him.

"By my soul," quoth merry King Richard, when he had gotten down from his mule and stood looking about him, "thou hast in very truth a fine lot of young men about thee, Robin. Methinks King Richard himself would be glad of such a body guard."

"These are not all of my fellows," said Robin, proudly, "for threescore more of them are away on business with my good right-hand man, Little John. But, as for King Richard, I tell thee, brother, there is not a man of us all but would pour out our blood like water for him. Ye churchmen cannot rightly understand our King; but we yeomen love him right loyally for the sake of his brave doings which are so like our own."

But now Friar Tuck came bustling up. 'Gi' ye good den, brothers,"' said he. "I am right glad to welcome some of my cloth in this naughty place. Truly, methinks these rogues of outlaws would stand but an ill chance were it not for the prayers of Holy Tuck, who laboreth so hard for their well being." Here he winked one eye slyly and stuck his tongue into his cheek.

"Who art thou, mad priest?" said the King in a serious voice, albeit he smiled beneath his cowl.

At this Friar Tuck looked all around with a slow gaze. "Look you now," quoth he, "never let me hear you say again that I am no patient man. Here is a knave of a friar calleth me a mad priest, and yet I smite him not. My name is Friar Tuck, fellow, – the holy Friar Tuck."

"There, Tuck," said Robin, "thou hast said enow. Prythee, cease thy talk and bring some wine. These reverend men are athirst, and sin' they have paid so richly for their score they must e'en have the best."

Friar Tuck bridled at being so checked in his speech, nevertheless he went straightway to do Robin's bidding; so presently a great crock was brought, and wine was poured out for all the guests and for Robin Hood. Then Robin held his cup aloft. "Stay!" cried he. "Tarry in your drinking till I give you a pledge. Here is to good King Richard of great renown, and may all enemies to him be confounded."

Then all drank the King's health, even the King himself. "Methinks, good fellow," said he, "thou hast drunk to thine own confusion."

"Never a whit," quoth merry Robin, "for I tell thee that we of Sherwood are more loyal to our lord the King than those of thine order. We would give up our very lives for his benefiting, whilst ye are content to lie snug in your abbeys and priories, let reign who will."

To this the King laughed. Quoth he, "Perhaps King Richard's welfare is more to me than thou wottest of, fellow. But enough of that matter. We have paid well for our fare, so canst thou not show us merry entertainment? I have oft heard that ye are wondrous archers; wilt thou not show us somewhat of your skill?"

"With all my heart," said Robin; 'we are always pleased to show our guests all the sport that is to be seen. As Gaffer Swanthold sayeth, "'T is a hard heart that will not give a caged starling of the best;' and caged starlings ye are with us. Ho, lads! set up a garland at the end of the glade."

Then, as the yeomen ran to do their master's bidding, Tuck turned to one of the mock friars. "Hearest thou our master?" quoth he, with a sly wink. "Whenever he cometh across some poor piece of wit he straightway layeth it on the shoulders of this Gaffer Swanthold, – whoever he may be, – so that the poor good man goeth travelling about with all the odds and ends and tags and rags of our master's brain packed on his back." Thus spake Friar Tuck, but in a low voice so that Robin could not hear him, for he felt somewhat nettled at Robin's cutting his talk so short.

In the mean time the mark at which they were to shoot was set up at sixscore paces distance. It was a garland of leaves and flowers two spans in width, which same was hung upon a stake in front of a broad tree-trunk. "There," quoth Robin, "yon is a fair mark, lads. Each of you shoot three arrows thereat; and if any fellow misseth by so much as one arrow, he shall have a buffet of Will Scarlet's fist."

"Hearken to him!" quoth Friar Tuck. "Why, master, thou dost bestow buffets from thy strapping nephew as though they were love taps from some bouncing lass. I warrant thou art safe to hit the garland thyself, or thou wouldst not be so free of his cuffing."

First David of Doncaster shot, and lodged all three of his arrows within the garland. "Well done, David!" cried Robin, "thou hast saved thine ears from a warming this day." Next Midge, the Miller, shot, and he, also, lodged his arrows in the garland. Then followed Wat, the Tinker, but alas for him! for one of his shafts missed the mark by the breadth of two fingers.

"Come hither, fellow," said Will Scarlet, in his soft, gentle voice; "I owe thee somewhat that I would pay forthwith." Then Wat, the Tinker, came forward and stood in front of Will Scarlet, screwing up his face and shutting his eyes tightly, as though he already felt his ears ringing with the buffet. Will Scarlet rolled up his sleeve, and, standing on tiptoe to give the greater swing to his arm, he struck with might and main. "*Whoof!*" came his palm against the Tinker's head, and down went stout Wat to the grass, heels over head, as the wooden image at the fair goes down when the skillful player throws a cudgel at it. Then, as the Tinker sat upon the grass, rubbing his ear and winking and blinking at the bright stars that danced before his eyes, the yeomen roared with mirth till the forest rang. As for King Richard, he laughed till the tears ran down the his cheeks. Thus the band shot, each in turn, some getting off scot free, and some winning a buffet that always sent them to the grass. And now, last of all, Robin took his place, and all was hushed as he shot. The first shaft he shot split a piece from the stake on which the garland was hung; the second shaft lodged within an inch of the other. "By my halidorm," said King Richard to himself, "I would give a thousand pounds for this fellow to be one of my guard!" And now, for the third time Robin shot; but, alas for him! the arrow was ill-feathered, and, wavering to one side, it smote an inch outside the garland.

At this a great roar went up, those of the yeomen who sat upon the grass rolling over and over and shouting with laughter, for never before had they seen their master so miss his mark; but Robin flung his bow upon the ground with vexation. "Now, out upon it!" cried he. "That shaft had an ill feather to it, for I felt it as it left my fingers. Give me a clean arrow, and I will engage to split the wand with it."

At these words the yeomen laughed louder than ever. "Nay, good uncle," said Will Scarlet, in his soft, sweet voice, "thou hast had thy fair chance and hast missed thine aim out and out. I swear the arrow was as good as any that hath been loosed this day. Come hither; I owe thee somewhat, and would fain pay it."

"Go, good master," roared Friar Tuck, "and may my blessing go with thee. Thou hast bestowed these love-taps of Will Scarlet's with great freedom. It were pity an thou gottest not thine own share."

"It may not be," said merry Robin. "I am king here, and no subject may raise hand against the king. But even our great King Richard may yield to the holy Pope without shame, and even take a tap from him by way of penance; therefore I will yield myself to this holy friar, who seemeth to be one in authority, and will take my punishment from him." Thus saying, he turned to the King, "I prythee, brother, wilt thou take my punishing into thy holy hands?"

"With all my heart," quoth merry King Richard, rising from where he was sitting. "I owe thee somewhat for having lifted a heavy weight of fifty pounds from my purse. So make room for him on the green, lads."

"An thou makest me tumble," quoth Robin, "I will freely give thee back thy fifty pounds; but I tell thee brother, if thou makest me not feel grass all along my back, I will take away every farthing thou hast for thy boastful speech."

"So be it," said the King, "I am willing to venture it." Thereupon he rolled up his sleeve and showed an arm that made the yeomen stare. But Robin, with his feet wide apart, stood firmly planted, waiting the other, smiling. Then the King swung back his arm, and, balancing himself a moment, he delivered a buffet at Robin that fell like a thunderbolt. Down went Robin headlong upon the grass, for the stroke would have felled a stone wall. Then how the yeomen shouted with laughter till their sides ached, for never had they seen such a buffet given in all their lives. As for Robin, he presently sat up and looked all around him, as though he had dropped from a cloud and had lit in a place he had never seen before. After a while, still gazing about him at his laughing yeomen, he put his finger-tips softly to his ear and felt all around it tenderly. "Will Scarlet," said he, "count this fellow out his fifty pounds; I want nothing more either of his money or of him. A murrain seize him and his buffeting! I would that I had taken my dues from thee, for I verily believe he hath deafened mine ear from ever hearing again."

Then, while gusts of laughter still broke from the band, Will Scarlet counted out the fifty pounds, and the King dropped it back into his purse again. "I give thee thanks, fellow,' said he, "and if ever thou shouldst wish for another box of the ear to match the one thou hast, come to me and I will fit thee with it for nought."

So spake the merry King; but, even as he ended, there came suddenly the sound of many voices, and out from the covert burst Little John and threescore men, with Sir Richard of the Lea in the midst. Across the glade they came running, and, as they came, Sir Richard shouted to Robin: "Make haste, dear friend, gather thy band together and come with me! King Richard left Nottingham Town this very morning, and cometh to seek thee in the woodlands. I know not how he cometh, for it was but a rumor of this that reached me; nevertheless, I know that it is the truth. Therefore hasten with all thy men, and come to Castle Lea, for there thou mayst lie hidden till thy present danger passeth. Who are these strangers that thou hast with thee?"

"Why," quoth merry Robin, rising from the grass, "these are certain gentle guests that came with us from the high-road over by Newstead Abbey. I know not their names, but I have become right well acquaint with this lusty rogue's palm this morning. Marry, the pleasure of this acquaintance hath cost me a deaf ear and fifty pounds to boot!"

Sir Richard looked keenly at the tall friar, who, drawing himself up to his full height, looked fixedly back at the knight. Then of a sudden Sir Richard's cheeks grew pale, for he knew who it was that he looked upon. Quickly he leaped from off his horse's back and flung himself upon his knees before the other. At this, the King, seeing that Sir Richard knew him, threw back his cowl, and all the yeomen saw his face and knew him also, for there was not one of them but had been in the crowd in the good town of Nottingham, and had seen him riding side by side with the Sheriff. Down they fell upon their knees, nor could they say a word. Then the King looked all around right grimly, and, last of all, his glance came back and rested again upon Sir Richard of the Lea.

"How is this, Sir Richard?" said he, sternly. "How darest thou step between me and these fellows?" and how darest thou offer thy knightly Castle of the Lea for a refuge to them? Wilt thou make it a hiding-place for the most renowned outlaws in England?"

Then Sir Richard of he Lea raised his eyes to the King's face. "Far be it from me," said he, "to do aught that could bring your majesty's anger upon me. Yet, sooner, would I face your majesty's wrath than suffer aught of harm that I could stay to fall upon Robin Hood and his band; for to them I owe life, honor, everything. Should I, then, desert him in his hour of need?"

Ere the Knight had done speaking, one of the mock friars that stood near the King came forward and knelt beside Sir Richard, and throwing back his cowl showed the face of young Sir Henry of the Lea. Then Sir Henry grasped his father's hand and said, "Here kneels one who hath served thee well, King Richard, and, as thou knowest, hath stepped between thee and death in Palestine; yet do I abide by my dear father, and here I say also, that I would freely give shelter to this noble outlaw, Robin Hood, even though it brought thy wrath upon me, for my father's honor and my father's welfare are as dear to me as mine own."

King Richard looked from one to the other of the kneeling knights, and at last the frown faded from his brow and a smile twitched at the corners of his lips. "Marry, Sir Richard," quoth the King, "thou art a bold-spoken knight, and thy freedom of speech weigheth not heavily against thee with me. This young son of thine taketh after his sire both in boldness of speech and of deed, for, as he sayeth, he stepped one time betwixt me and death; wherefore I would pardon thee for his sake even if thou hadst done more than thou hast. Rise all of you, for ye shall suffer no harm through me this day, for it were pity that a merry time should end in such a manner as to mar its joyousness."

Then all arose and the King beckoned Robin Hood to come to him. "How now," quoth he, "is thine ear still too deaf to hear me speak?"

"Mine ears would be deafened in death ere they would cease to hear your majesty's voice," said Robin. "As for the blow that your majesty struck me, I would say that though my sins are haply many, methinks they have been paid up in full thereby."

"Thinkest thou so?" said the King with somewhat of sternness in his voice. "Now I tell thee that but for three things, to wit, my mercifulness, my love for a stout woodsman, and the loyalty thou hast avowed for me, thine ears, mayhap, might have been more tightly closed than ever a buffet from me could have shut them. Talk not lightly of thy sins, good Robin. But come, look up. Thy danger is past, for hereby I give thee and all thy band free pardon. But, in sooth, I cannot let you roam the forest as ye have done in the past; therefore I will take thee at thy word, when thou didst say thou wouldst give thy service to me, and thou shalt go back to London with me. We will take that bold knave Little John also, and likewise thy cousin, Will Scarlet, and thy minstrel, Allan a Dale. As for the rest of thy band, we will take their names and have them duly recorded as royal rangers; for methinks it were wiser to have them changed to law-abiding caretakers of our deer in Sherwood than to leave them to run at large as outlawed slayers thereof. But now get a feast ready, for I would fain see how ye live here in the leafy woodlands."

So Robin bade his men make ready a grand feast; and straightway great fires were kindled and burned brightly, at which fires savory things roasted sweetly. While this was going forward, the King bade Robin Hood call Allan a Dale for he would hear him sing. So word was passed for Allan, and presently he came, bringing his harp.

"Marry," said King Richard, "if thy singing match thy looks it is fair enough. Prythee strike up a ditty and let us have a taste of thy skill."

Then Allan touched his harp lightly, and all words were hushed while he sang thus:-

*"'Oh where has thou been, my daughter?*
*Oh where hast thou been this day,*
*Daughter, my daughter?'*
*'Oh, I have been to the river's side,*
*Where the waters lie all gray and wide,*
*And the gray sky broods o'er the leaden tide,*
*And the shrill wind sights a straining.'*

*'What sawest thou there, my daughter?*
*What sawest thou there this day,*
*Daughter, my daughter?'*
*'Oh, I saw a boat come drifting nigh,*
*Where the quivering rushes hiss and sigh.*
*And the water soughs as it gurgles by,*
*And the shrill wind sighs a straining.'*

*'What sailed in the boat, my daughter?*
*What sailed in the boat this day,*
*Daughter, my daughter?'*
*'Oh, there was one all clad in white,*
*And about his face hung a pallid light,*
*And his eyes gleamed sharp like the stars at night,*
*And the shrill wind sighed a straining.'*

*'And what said he, my daughter?*
*What said he to thee this day,*
*Daughter, my daughter?'*
*'Oh, said he nought, but did he this:*
*Thrice on my lips did he press a kiss,*
*And my heartstrings shrunk with an awful bliss,*
*And the shrill wind sighed a straining.'*

*'Why growest thou so cold, my daughter?*
*Why growest thou so cold and white,*
*Daughter, my daughter?'*
*Oh never a word the daughter said,*
*But she sat all straight with a drooping head,*
*For her heart was stilled and her face was dead:*
*And the shrill wind sighed a straining."*

All listened in silence: and when Allan a Dale had done King Richard heaved a sigh. "By the breath of my body, Allan," quoth he, "thou hast such a wondrous sweet voice that it strangely moves my heart. But what doleful ditty is this for the lips of a stout yeoman? I would rather hear thee sing a song of love and battle than a sad thing like that. Moreover, I understand it not; what meanest thou by the words?"

"I know not, your majesty," said Allan, shaking his head, "for ofttimes I sing that which I do not clearly understand mine own self."

"Well, well," quoth the King, "let it pass; only I tell thee this, Allan, thou shouldst turn thy songs to such matters as I spoke of, to wit, love or war; for in sooth thou hast a sweeter voice than Blondell, and methought he was the best minstrel that ever I heard."

But now one came forward and said that the feast was ready; so Robin Hood brought King Richard and those with him to where it lay all spread out on fair white linen cloths which lay upon the soft green grass. Then King Richard sat him down and feasted and drank, and when he was done he swore roundly that he had never sat at such a lusty repast in all his life before.

That night he lay in Sherwood Forest upon a bed of sweet green leaves, and early the next morning he set forth from the woodlands for Nottingham Town, Robin Hood and all of his band going with him. You may guess what a stir there was in the good town when all these famous outlaws came marching into the streets. As for the Sheriff, he knew not what to say nor where to look when he saw Robin Hood in such high favor with the King, whilst all his heart was filled with gall because of the vexation that lay upon him.

The next day the King took leave of Nottingham Town; so Robin Hood and Little John and Will Scarlet and Allan a Dale shook hands with all the rest of the band, kissing the cheeks of each man, and swearing that they would often come to Sherwood and see them. Then each mounted his horse and rode away in the train of the King.

*Thus end the merry adventures of Robin Hood; for, in spite of his promise, it was many a year ere he saw Sherwood again. After a year or two at court Little John came back to Nottinghamshire, where he lived in an orderly way, though within sight of Sherwood, and where he achieved great fame as the champion of all England with the quarterstaff. Will Scarlet after a time came back to his own home, whence he had been driven by his unlucky killing of his father's steward. The rest of the band did their duty as royal rangers right well. But Robin Hood and Allan a Dale did not come again to Sherwood so quickly, for thus it was:-*

*Robin, through his great fame as an archer, became a favorite with the King, so that he speedily arose in rank to be the chief of all the yeomen. At last the King, seeing how faithful and how loyal he was, created him Earl of Huntingdon; so Robin followed the King to the wars, and found his time so full that he had no chance to come back to Sherwood for even so much as a day. As for Allan a Dale and his wife, the fair Ellen, they followed Robin Hood and shared in all his ups and downs of life.*

*Thus all things have an end, but not such a lucky ending as befell Robin Hood and his band of stout yeomen in famous Sherwood Forest.*

# How Robin Hood Died by the Treachery of His Cousin, the Prioress of the Nunnery of Kirklees

And now, dear friend, – you who have journeyed with me in all these merry doings, – I will not bid you follow me further, but will drop your hand here with a "good den," if you wish it; for that which cometh hereafter speaks of the breaking up of things, and shows how joys and pleasures that are dead and gone can never be set upon their feet to walk again. I will not dwell upon the matter over long, but will tell as speedily as may be of how that stout fellow, Robin Hood, died as he had lived, not at court as Earl of Huntingdon, but with bow in hand, his heart in the greenwood, and he himself a right yeoman.

King Richard died upon the battlefield, in such a way as properly became a lion-hearted king, as you yourself, no doubt, know; so, after a time, the Earl of Huntingdon – or Robin Hood, as we will still call him as of old – finding nothing for his doing abroad, came back to merry England again. With him came Allan a Dale and his wife, the fair Ellen, for these two had been chief of Robin's household ever since he had left Sherwood Forest.

It was in the spring-time when they landed once more on the shores of England. The leaves were green and the small birds sang blithely, just as they used to do in fair Sherwood when Robin Hood roamed the woodland shades with a free heart and a light heel. All the sweetness of the time and the joyousness of everything brought back to Robin's mind his forest life, so that a great longing came upon him to behold the woodlands once more. So he went straightway to King John and besought leave of him to visit Nottingham for a short season. The King gave him leave to come and to go, but bade him not stay longer than three days at Sherwood. So Robin Hood and Allan a Dale set forth without delay to Nottinghamshire and Sherwood Forest.

The first night they took up their inn at Nottingham Town, yet they did not go too pay their duty to the Sheriff, for his worship bore many a bitter grudge against Robin Hood, which grudges had not been lessened by Robin's rise in the world. The next day at an early hour they mounted their horses and set forth for the woodlands. As they passed along the road it seemed to Robin that he knew every stick and stone that his eyes looked upon. Yonder was a path that he had ofttimes trod of a mellow evening, with Little John beside him; here was one, now nigh choked with brambles, along which he and a little band had walked when they went forth to seek a certain curtal friar.

"Look, Allan!" cried Robin. "Dost thou not see the scar on yonder beechen tree? That was made when thine arrow stripped away a piece of the bark the day thy shaft missed the noble hart so sadly. That was the same day that we were caught by the storm, and had to lodge over night at the old farmer's house – he who had the three buxom daughters."

Thus they rode slowly onward, talking about these old, familiar things; old and yet new, for they found more in them than they had ever thought of before. Thus at last they came to the open glade, and the broad, wide-spreading greenwood tree which was their home for so many years. Neither of the two spoke when they stood beneath that tree. Robin looked all about him at the well known things, so like what they used to be and yet so different; for, where once was the bustle of many busy fellows was now the quietness of solitude; and, as he looked, the woodlands, the greensward, and the sky all blurred together in his sight through salt tears, for such a great yearning came upon him as he looked on these things (as well known to him as the fingers of his right hand) that he could not keep back the water from his eyes.

That morning he had slung his good old bugle horn over his shoulder, and now, with the yearning, came a great longing to sound this bugle once more. He raised it to his lips, he blew a blast. "Tirila, lirila," the sweet, clear notes went winding down the forest paths, coming back again from the more distant bosky shades in faint echoes of sound. – "Tirila, lirila, tirila, lirila," until it faded away and was lost.

Now it chanced that on that very morn Little John was walking through a spur of the forest upon certain matters of business, and as he paced along, sunk in meditation, the faint, clear notes of a distant bugle horn came to his ear. As leaps the stag when it feels the arrow at its heart, so leaped Little John when that distant sound met his ear. All the blood in his body seemed to rush like a flame into his cheeks as he bent his head and listened. Again came the bugle note, thin and clear, and yet again it sounded. Then Little John gave a great, wild cry of yearning, of joy, and yet of grief, and, putting down his head, he dashed into the thicket. Onward he plunged, crackling and rending, as the wild boar rushes through the underbrush. Little recked he of thorns and briars that scratched his flesh and tore his clothing, for all he thought of was to get, by the shortest way, to the greenwood glade whence he knew the sound of the bugle horn came. Out he burst from the covert, at last, a shower of little broken twigs falling about him, and, without pausing a moment, rushed forward and flung himself at Robin's feet. Then he clasped his arms around the master's knees, and all his body was shaken with great sobs; neither could Robin nor Allan a Dale speak, but stood looking down at Little John, the tears rolling down their cheeks.

Whilst they thus stood, seven royal rangers rushed into the open glade and raised a great shout of joy at the sight of Robin; and at their head was Will Stutely. Then, after a while, came four more, panting with their running, and two of these four were Will Scathelock and Midge, the Miller; for all of these had heard the sound of Robin Hood's horn. All these ran to Robin and kissed his hands and his clothing, with great sound of weeping.

After a while Robin looked around him with tear-dimmed eyes, and said, in a husky voice, "Now, I swear that never again will I leave these dear woodlands. I have been away from them and from you too long. Now do I lay by the name of Robert, Earl of Huntingdon, and take upon me once again that nobler title, Robin Hood, the Yeoman." At this a great shout went up, and all the yeomen shook one another's hands for joy.

The news that Robin Hood had come back again to dwell in Sherwood as of old spread like wildfire all over the countryside, so that ere a se'ennight had passed nearly all of his old yeomen had gathered about him again. But when the news of all this reached the ears of King John, he swore both loud and deep, and took a solemn view that he would not rest until he had Robin Hood in his power, dead or alive. Now there was present at court a certain knight, Sir William Dale, as gallant a soldier as ever donned harness. Sir William was well acquainted with Sherwood Forest, for he was head keeper over that part of it that lay nigh to good Mansfield Town; so to him the King turned, and bade him take an army of men and go straightway to seek Robin Hood. Likewise the King, gave Sir William his signet ring to show to the Sheriff, that he might raise all his armed men to aid the others in their chase of Robin. So Sir William and the Sheriff set forth to do the King's bidding and to search for Robin Hood; and for seven days they hunted up and down, yet found him not.

Now, had Robin Hood been as peaceful as of old, everything might have ended in smoke, as other such ventures had always done before, but he had fought for years under King Richard, and was changed from what he used to be. It galled his pride to thus flee away before those sent against him, like a chased fox flees from the hounds; so thus it came about, at last, that Robin Hood and his yeomen met Sir William and the Sheriff and their men in the forest, and a bloody fight followed. The first man slain in that fight was the Sheriff of Nottingham, for he fell from his horse with an arrow in his brain ere half a score of shafts had been sped. Many a better man than the Sheriff kissed the sod that day, but at last, Sir William Dale being wounded and most of his men slain, he withdrew, beaten, and left the forest. But scores of good fellows were left behind him, stretched out all stiff beneath the sweet green boughs.

But though Robin Hood had beaten off his enemies in fair fight, all this lay heavily upon his mind, so that he brooded over it until a fever seized upon him. For three days it held him, and though he strove to fight it off, he was forced to yield at last. Thus it came that, on the morning of the fourth day, he called Little John to him, and told him that he could not shake the fever from him, and that he would go to his cousin, the Prioress of the nunnery near Kirklees, in Yorkshire, who was a skilful leech, and he would have her open a vein in his arm and take a little blood from him, for the bettering of his health. Then he bade Little John make ready to go also, for he might perchance need aid in his journeying. So Little John and he took their leave of the others, and Robin Hood bade Will Stutely be the captain of the band until they should come back. Thus they came by easy stages and slow journeying until they reached the nunnery of Kirklees.

Now Robin had done much to aid this cousin of his; for it was through King Richard's love of him that she had been made prioress of the place. But there is nought in the world so easily forgot as gratitude; so when the Prioress of Kirklers heard how her cousin, the Earl of Huntingdon, had thrown away his earldom and gone back again to Sherwood, she was vexed to the soul, and feared lest her cousinship with him should bring the King's wrath upon her also. Thus it happened that when Robin came to her and told her how he wished her services as leech, she began plotting ill against him in her mind, thinking that by doing evil to him she might find favor with his enemies. Nevertheless, she kept this well to herself, and received Robin with seeming kindness. She led him up the winding stone stair to a room which was just beneath the eaves of a high, round tower; but she would not let Little John come with him.

So the poor yeoman turned his feet away from the door of the nunnery, and left his master in the hands of the women. But, though he did not come in, neither did he go far away; for he laid him down in a little glade near by, where he could watch the place that Robin abided, like some great, faithful dog turned away from the door where his master has entered.

After the women had gotten Robin Hood to the room beneath the eaves, the Prioress sent all of the others away; then, taking a little cord, she tied it tightly about Robin's arm, as though she were about to bleed him. And so she did bleed him, but the vein she opened was not one of those that lie close and blue beneath the skin; deeper she cut than that, for she opened one of those veins through which the bright red blood runs leaping from the heart. Of this Robin knew not; for, though he saw the blood flow, it did not come fast enough to make him think that there was anything ill in it.

Having done this vile deed, the Prioress turned and left her cousin, locking the door behind her. All that livelong day the blood ran from Robin Hood's arm, nor could he check it, though he strove in every way to do so. Again and again he called for help, but no help came, for his cousin had betrayed him, and Little John was too far away to hear his voice. So he bled and bled until he felt his strength slipping away from him. Then he arose, tottering, and bearing himself up by the palms of his hands against the wall, he reached his bugle horn at last. Thrice he sounded it, but weakly and faintly, for his breath was fluttering through sickness and loss of strength; nevertheless, Little John heard it where he lay in the glade, and, with a heart all sick with dread, he came running and leaping toward the nunnery. Loudly he knocked at the door, and in a loud voice shouted for them to let him in; but the door was of massive oak, strongly barred, and studded with spikes, so they within felt safe, and bade Little John begone.

Then Little John's heart was mad with grief and fear for his master's life. Wildly he looked about him, and his sight fell upon a heavy stone mortar, such as three men could not lift now-a-days. Little John took three steps forward, and, bending his back, heaved the stone mortar up from where it stood, deeply rooted. Staggering under its weight, he came forward and hurled it crashing against the door. In burst the door, and away fled the frightened nuns, shrieking, at his coming. Then Little John strode in, and never a word said he, but up the winding stone steps he ran till he reached the room wherein his master was. Here he found the door locked also, but, putting his shoulder against it, he burst the locks as though they were made of brittle ice.

There he saw his own dear master leaning against the gray stone wall, his face all white and drawn, and his head swaying to and fro with weakness. Then, with a great, wild cry of love and grief and pity, Little John leaped forward and caught Robin Hood in his arms. Up he lifted him as a mother lifts her child, and carrying him to the bed, laid him tenderly thereon.

And now the Prioress came in hastily, for she was frightened at what she had done, and dreaded the vengeance of Little John and the others of the band; then she stanched the blood by cunning bandages; so that it flowed no more. All the while Little John stood grimly by and after she had done he sternly bade her to begone, and she obeyed, pale and trembling. Then, after she had departed, Little John spake cheering words, laughing loudly, and saying that all this was a child's fright, and that no stout yeoman would die at the loss of a few drops of blood. "Why," quoth he, "give thee a se'ennight and thou wilt be roaming the woodlands as boldly as ever."

But Robin shook his head and smiled faintly where he lay. "Mine own dear Little John," whispered he, "Heaven bless thy kind, rough heart. But, dear friend, we will never roam the woodlands together again."

"Ay, but we will!" quoth Little John, loudly. "I say again, Ay – out upon it – who dares say that any more harm shall come upon thee? Am I not by? Let me see who dares touch" – Here he stopped of a sudden, for his words choked him. At last he said, in a deep husky voice, "Now, if aught of harm befalls thee because of this day's doings, I swear by Saint George that the red cock shall crow over the roof-tree of this house, for the hot flames shall lick every crack and cranny thereof. As for these women," – here he ground his teeth, – "it will be an ill day for them!"

But Robin Hood took Little John's rough, brown fist in his white hands, and chid him softly, in his low, weak voice, asking him since what time Little John had thought of doing harm to women, even in vengeance. Thus he talked till, at last, the other promised, in a choking voice, that no ill should fall upon the place, no matter what happened. Then a silence fell, and Little John sat with Robin Hood's hand in his, gazing out of the open window, ever and anon swallowing a great lump that came in his throat. Meantime the sun dropped slowly to the west, till all the sky was ablaze with a red glory. Then Robin Hood, in a weak, faltering voice, bade Little John raise him, that he might look out once more upon the woodlands; so the yeoman lifted him in his arms, as he bade, and Robin Hood's head lay on his friend's shoulder. Long he gazed, with a wide, lingering look, whilst the other sat with bowed head, the hot tears rolling one after another from his eyes, and dripping upon his bosom, for he felt that the time of parting was near at hand. Then, presently, Robin Hood bade him string his stout bow for him, and choose a smooth fair arrow from his quiver. This Little John did, though without disturbing his master or rising from where he sat. Robin Hood's fingers wrapped lovingly around his good bow, and he smiled faintly when he felt it in his grasp; then he nocked the arrow on that part of the string that the tips of his fingers knew so well. "Little John," said he, "Little John, mine own dear friend, and him I love better than all others in the world, mark, I prythee, where this arrow lodges, and there let my grave be digged. Lay me with thy face toward the east, Little John, and see that my resting-place be kept green, and that my weary bones be not disturbed."

As he finished speaking, he raised himself of a sudden and sat upright. His old strength seemed to come back to him, and, drawing the bowstring to his ear, he sped the arrow out of the open casement. As the shaft flew, his hand sank slowly with the bow till it lay across his knees, and his body likewise sank back again into Little John's loving arms; but something had sped from that body, even as the winged arrow sped from the bow.

For some minutes Little John sat motionless, but presently he laid that which he held gently down, then, folding the hands upon the breast and covering up the face, he turned upon his heel and left the room without a word or a sound.

Upon the steep stairway he met the Prioress and some of the chief among the sisters. To them he spoke in a deep, quivering voice, and said he, "An ye go within a score of feet of yonder room, I will tear down your rookery over your heads so that not one stone shall be left upon another. Bear my words well in mind, for I mean them." So saying, he turned and left them, and they presently saw him running rapidly across the open, through the falling of the dusk, until he was swallowed up by the forest.

The early gray of the coming morn was just beginning to lighten the black sky toward the eastward when Little John and six more of the band came rapidly across the open toward the nunnery. They saw no one, for the sisters were all hidden away from sight, having been frightened by Little John's words. Up the stone stair they ran, and a great sound of weeping was presently heard. After a while this ceased, and then came the scuffling and shuffling of men's feet as they carried a heavy weight down the steep and winding stairs. So they went forth from the nunnery, and, as they passed through the doors thereof, a great, loud sound of wailing arose from the glade that lay all dark in the dawning, as though many men, hidden in the shadows, had lifted up their voices in sorrow.

Thus died Robin Hood, at Kirklees Nunnery, in fair Yorkshire, with mercy in his heart toward those that had been his undoing; for thus he showed mercy for the erring and pity for the weak through all the time of his living.

His yeomen were scattered henceforth, but no great ill befell them thereafter, for a more merciful sheriff and one who knew them not so well succeeded the one that had gone, and they being separated here and there throughout the countryside, they abided in peace and quietness, so that many lived to hand down these tales to their children and their children's children.

A certain one sayeth that upon a stone at Kirklees is an old inscription. This I give in the ancient English in which it was written, and thus it runs:-

Dear undernead dis latitl stean
lais robert earl of huntingtun
nea arcir ver as hie sae geud
an pipl kauld im Robin Heud
sick utlaws as hi an is men
vil England nidir si agen.
ohiit 24 hal. dehembris 1247.

And now, dear friend, we also must part, for our merry journeyings have ended, and here, at the grave of Robin Hood, we turn, each going his own way.

# Classic Library Titles

**Jane Eyre**
*by Charlotte Brontë*
*Illustrated by Monro S. Orr and Edmund H. Garrett*
**Wuthering Heights**
*by Emily Brontë*
*Illustrated by Percy Tarrant*

**Treasure Island**
**Kidnapped**
*by R. L. Stevenson*
*Illustrated by Eleanor Plaisted Abbott, Wal Paget and David Price*

**Anne of Green Gables**
**Anne of Avonlea**
*by L. M. Montgomery*
*Illustrated by Kim Palmer*

**The Call of the Wild**
**White Fang**
*by Jack London*
*Illustrated by Philip R. Goodwin and Charles Livingstone Bull*

**Robinson Crusoe**
*by Daniel Defoe*
*Illustrated by J. Ayton Symington*
**Swiss Family Robinson**
*by M. Wiss*
*Illustrated by Bob Ellis*

**Pride and Prejudice**
**Sense and Sensibility**
*by Jane Austen*
*Illustrated*

**The Story of King Arthur and his Knights**
**The Merry Adventures of Robin Hood**
*by Howard Pyle*
*Illustrated by Roland Wheelwright and Howard Pyle*

**Norse Myths**
*by Dorothy Belgrave and Hilda Hart*
*Illustrated by Harry G. Theaker*
**Classical Myths**
*by Nathaniel Hawthorne and Blanche Winder*
*Illustrated by Milo Winter*